A Comprehensive Biography of Composer Gustav Holst

with Correspondence and Diary Excerpts

Front Cover: Gustav Holst in America, Spring 1923
Courtesy of Cheltenham Art Gallery & Museums Service, Cheltenham, U.K.

A Comprehensive Biography of Composer Gustav Holst
with Correspondence and Diary Excerpts
Including His American Years

Jon C. Mitchell

Studies in the History and Interpretation of Music
Volume 73

The Edwin Mellen Press
Lewiston•Queenston•Lampeter

Library of Congress Cataloging-in-Publication Data

Mitchell, Jon C.
A comprehensive biography of composer Gustav Holst, with correspondence and diary excerpts : including his American years / Jon C. Mitchell.
p. cm. -- (Studies in history and interpretation of music ; v. 73)
Includes chronological listing of composer's works.
Includes bibliographical references (p.) and index.
ISBN 0-7734-7522-2
1. Holst, Gustav, 1874-1934. 2. Composers--England--Biography. I. Title. II. Studies in the history and interpretation of music ; v. 73)

ML410.H748 M57 2001
780'.92--dc21
[B] 00-051144

This is volume 73 in the continuing series
Studies in History & Interpretation of Music
Volume 73 ISBN 0-7734-7522-2
SHIM Series ISBN 0-88946-426-X

A CIP catalog record for this book is available from the British Library.

The Edwin Mellen Press
Box 450
Lewiston, New York
USA 14092-0450

The Edwin Mellen Press
Box 67
Queenston, Ontario
CANADA L0S 1L0

The Edwin Mellen Press, Ltd.
Lampeter, Ceredigion, Wales
UNITED KINGDOM SA48 8LT

Printed in the United States of America

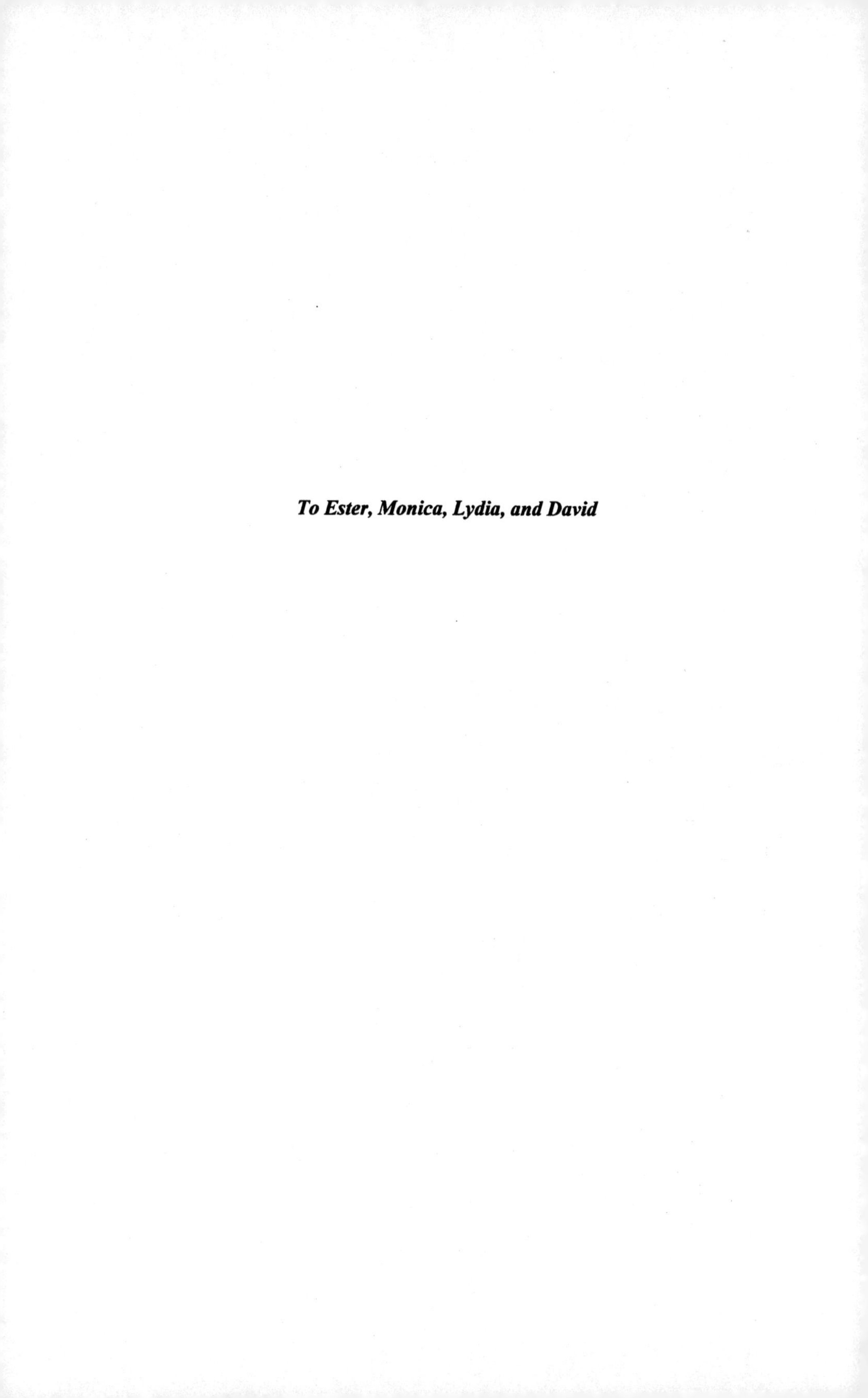

To Ester, Monica, Lydia, and David

TABLE OF CONTENTS

Appendices:

PREFACE

Gustav Holst has been largely ignored by traditional musicology. With the exception of the outstanding work performed on his behalf by his daughter Imogen and by Michael Short, Holst (along with a number of other composers of his generation) has been relegated to a cursory mention in most music history textbooks. The reason for this neglect is, quite simply, an accident of birth. Holst had the misfortune to reach compositional maturity during the first decades of the twentieth century--a time when music was experiencing perhaps the greatest crisis of its existence, and when the important "isms" (impressionism, serialism, primitivism, futurism, neo-classicism, etc.) were being born. Musicologists have, with considerable justification, focused their attention on these influential developments, and since Holst's music does not fully participate in any of them, he and his creations have been pushed to the fringes of musicological inquiry.

This, however, is not to say that Holst has ever been neglected by performers or listeners. His works form a significant part of the core repertoire of orchestras, choirs, and bands, receiving numerous performances before enthusiastic audiences. In a real sense, his music illustrates one of the paradoxes of music in the past century. Many of the composers considered most significant in academic circles were (and are) rarely heard in the concert hall, while other figures deemed undeserving of comprehensive study continue to dominate the programmes of performing musicians. Among academics, Holst's music is seen as largely inconsequential and too dependent on the past, despite the fact that works like "The Planets", "Hammersmith" and "Egdon Heath" contain passages as innovative as anything written at the time. While these remarkable passages may be acknowledged, music historians note that after creating them Holst withdrew to more comfortable territory, and this retreat is considered a lack of courage or imagination on his part.

Now, however, we know better! Jon C. Mitchell's richly detailed book, *Gustav Holst: An American Perspective*, presents Holst as composer, musician, family man, friend and, most important, as teacher. Holst was deeply committed to teaching throughout his life, and when he retreated from musical experimentation, it was often to create works for his students. As Dr. Mitchell makes clear, Holst did not consider such works to be any less worthy of his best efforts than those written for professionals--he simply did not categorize music according to a scale of value. Holst was a practical musician who enjoyed writing "music for use", was always willing to consider difficulty levels, and was pleased when his music was successful in its intended venue, whether that be amateur or professional. For him, music was human communication and writing "music for the future", as Schoenberg might have done, was unthinkable. Two items quoted by Dr. Mitchell make his approach easily understandable. In a letter to Vaughan Williams written in April, 1932, while Holst was a visiting professor at Harvard, he claims "My idea of composition is to spoil as much manuscript paper as possible", and expresses his amazement at how his students at Harvard were more interested in talking about music than in actually writing it. A month earlier he had responded to a journalist's question about his theories of teaching with: "O, you Americans, how you love to analyze everything!"

As can be gleaned from the title, this new book vastly expands our knowledge about Holst's American connections. It is perhaps not surprising that in Short's biography the three visits to the United States are passed over rather quickly. Since they represent a rather small part of Holst's life, Short probably considered them to be of limited importance. Dr. Mitchell obviously thought otherwise. Using a very wide range of published and unpublished documents, he presents a fascinating picture of not only Holst in America, but of North American musical life in the 1920s and 30s. These chapters make captivating reading.

With this publication we have a new and much broader context against which to measure Holst's accomplishments, both personal and professional. Twenty years ago, Imogen Holst called for a re-evaluation of her father's music, and there can be little question that such a re-consideration has been occurring in the two decades since her book appeared. Dr. Mitchell has moved the discussion forward by providing a framework within which we are invited to take a fresh look at not just the music but at the man as well. This is a huge step toward countering the neglect inflicted on Holst for so long, and toward assigning him the place in music history that he so richly deserves.

Keith Kinder
McMaster University
Hamilton, Ontario, Canada
August, 2000

FOREWORD

In March, 1938 eminent English composer Ralph Vaughan Williams wrote the following about his closest friend Gustav Holst, who had passed away four years earlier:

> Gustav Holst was a great composer, a great teacher, and a great friend. These are really different aspects of the same thing; his pupils were his friends, his friends were always learning from him, his music made friends for him all over the world, even among those who had never seen him, and will continue to make more friends for him in the years to come.[1]

Vaughan Williams' profetic words ring true more than a half century later. Holst's stature as a composer has continued to grow and his music is performed with increasing frequency throughout the world. On the personal level, Holst was many things to many people. To the three roles in Vaughan Williams' description--composer, teacher, and friend-- may be added several others: devoted husband and father, performer, lecturer, conductor, international traveller, hiker, morale booster, birthday enthusiast, humorist (to the extent that Vaughan Williams suggested that Holst would have done well as a night club comedian)--and prolific correspondent.

Few composers wrote as many letters as Holst. Casual conversation aside, letter writing was his primary form of communication and, some would say, recreation. Notebook listings containing the names of a dozen or more people to whom he needed to write in a single day are not uncommon. Conversely, Holst was also the recipient of a great quantity of written correspondence--as many as nineteen letters on any given day. It is indeed fortunate for posterity that Holst generally eschewed the telephone in favor of the written word. Many of the composer's innermost thoughts have been preserved in more than 500 extant pieces of written correspondence. It is also fortunate that he lived in an era before computers--and disposable e-mail--had arrived.

The genesis of the present book stems from searches made of several collections of letters to and from Holst appearing in various libraries throughout the United States. Most of these letters deal with various aspects of Holst's three visits to this country (in 1923, 1929, and 1932). At first the author attempted to confine the subject matter of the present text to Holst's American visits and related topics, but there is so much in Holst's correspondence that both relates and refers to other aspects of his life that to deal only with isolated time vignettes would not have done the composer justice. Besides, some of the "American" letters deal with non-American topics, such as the commissioning of *Egdon Heath* or the setting up of appointments with English portrait artist William Rothenstein. On the other hand, some of the letters found in British libraries shed light on American topics, such as the projected Hollywood pageant for which *The Song of Solomon* was composed. Still other letters, such as Holst's correspondence with Percy Grainger, have nothing to do with American topics at all, yet they enhance what we already know of Holst's work ethic and friendships with other composers. Thus it was not long after starting the research for the present text that the author realized the book had to be centered here yet also be inclusive, hence the title *Gustav Holst: An American Perspective*.

The letters penned by Holst fall into four overlapping categories. The first category contains the business letters, with the intended receiver addressed formally as "Miss," "Mrs," or "Mr" (with the abbreviations almost never followed by periods) and signed by the author either in full or (after 1918) as "G T Holst." These are generally hand-written, although some are typed. The second category is made up of letters to people who may have started out as business acquaintances but who eventually became friends. Holst's use of just the surname of the addressee and the sentence "Do let us drop the Mr" often signaled an advancement to this level. Edwin Evans, Harold Bauer and Frederick Stock were among those at this level of correspondence.

The third and fourth categories were tougher for correspondents to enter. William Rothenstein never quite made it; William Gillies Whittaker did. The third category of letter recipients were Holst's personal friends, colleagues, and relatives who were not of the immediate family. Holst generally referred to them by their first names and signed his letters "Gustav." The fourth category includes immediate family and Holst's closest personal friends. Headings usually feature some abbreviated form of the person's name: "Dear Iso," "Dear R," or, occasionally, a minimalistic "D V." These are also signed with single letters: "G v H" (before 1918), "Y G" ("Yours, Gustav"), "B L G" ("Best Love, Gustav") to his wife and daughter, or the simplest: "G."

In addition to the letters, Holst left a plethora of other primary sources of information. Extant *Diaries* begin in 1912. At first Holst used these simply as appointment books but, beginning with his eight-month stint with the British YMCA at the end of World War I, they become true diaries which give us details about daily events in the composer's life. Closely related to the *Diaries* are Holst's surviving Notebooks, which begin in 1913. These contain Holst's "laundry lists," often referring to plans for international travel, but sometimes containing some of the composer's innermost thoughts. Not to be ignored are the sketchbooks and manuscript scores of Holst's musical compositions; in addition to the musical content, there are often notes written in the the margins, sometimes about unrelated topics. Other forms of paraphernalia in Holst's hand include telegrams, bills, invitations, prescriptions, and receipts. Manuscript letters to Holst and correspondence between other people that contain references to Holst round out the incredible array of primary source material.

Secondary source materials are also used in the present text. These are not in short supply. There is so much material here that the author was often faced with the decision about what to exclude rather than what to incorporate into the text. These sources include letters in published books, published speeches by Holst (often paraphrased by the press), published articles about Holst, concert reviews, newspaper accounts, and other miscellaneous odds and ends.

Gustav Holst died some fifteen years before I was born, yet he lives on through his music and written word. Writing this book has been a real adventure, and a joyous one at that. In many instances there was a true sense of discovery as many stones were unturned. Yet for all of the documentation available, the written word alone is certainly no substitute for Gustav Holst's music. Perhaps Edmund Rubbra said it best in 1932:

> ....for a real understanding of Holst one must go to the actual music, There will be found one of the finest and clearest musical minds of this age....when most of the would-be music of this age has passed into oblivion his music will survive as an inspiration to all who endeavor to write from the core of their being.[2]

Enjoy.

Jon Ceander Mitchell
Natick, Massachusetts, USA
August, 2000

---

[1]Ralph Vaughan Williams, "A Note on Gustav Holst," in Imogen Holst, *Gustav Holst: A Biography, 2nd ed.* (Oxford: Oxford University Press, 1969), vii.

[2]Edmund Rubbra, "Holst: Some Technical Characteristics," in *Monthly Musical Record,* LXII (October, 1932), 173.

ACKNOWLEDGEMENTS

First and foremost, the author wishes to express his sincerest thanks to Rosamund Strode of The Holst Foundation, Aldeburgh, Suffolk, England, without whose remarkable help and kindness this book could not have been written. The assistance and generosity of Mrs. Helen Lilley, Assistant Secretary to The Holst Foundation, greatly facilitated the progress of this volume.

Scores of library personnel on both sides of the Atlantic lent valuable assistance to the author. Those in the United Kingdom include Jenny Doctor, Keiron Cook, Judith LeGrove, Paul Banks, Philip Reed, and Helen Risdon of the Britten-Pears Library in Aldeburgh, as well as Lowinger Maddison of The Holst Birthplace Museum and Mary Greensted of the Cheltenham Art Gallery and Museums. Also included here are Major Roger Swift and Major Gordon Turner (ret.) of the Royal Military School of Music at Kneller Hall, Twickenham, and personnel at The British Library, City of Westminster Central Public Library, and the Royal College of Music Library. Holst taught at many different places. The author wishes to thank Anna Bracht of Morley College, Frances Miller of The University of Reading, Cynthia Pullin and Barbara K. Kley of James Allen's Girls' School, and Mrs. Alison Heath of Wycombe Abbey School as well as personnel at St. Paul's Girls' School for valuable information and assistance.

A special note of thanks to library personnell in the United States is extended to Gillian B. Anderson of The Library of Congress, Kristine Krueger of the Margaret Herrick Center of Motion Picture Study, Suzanne Eggleston of the Yale University Music Library, Bonnie Jo Dopp of the University of Maryland Performing Arts Library, Sion M. Honea of the Sibley Music Library at the Eastman School of Music, Virgina Dajami of the American Academy of Arts and Letters, Bridget Carr of the Boston Symphony Orchestra Archives, and Theresa McDermott of St. Thomas the Apostle Roman Catholic Church in Chicago, as well as Mary Jo Pugh, Nancy Bartlett, and Christine Dykgraf of the Bentley Historical Library at the University of Michigan. The author would also like to acknowledge the assistance of personnel at the following American libraries: Boston Public Library, Pierpont-Morgan Library, Houghton Library and University Archives at Harvard University, Healey Library at University of Massachusetts Boston, and Beinecke Rare Book and Manuscript Library at Yale University.

The author also wishes to express his thanks to Stanley Brasgold of the Bibliothèque de Montréal in Canada and to Rosie Florimell of The Grainger Museum at The University of Melbourne in Australia.

Finally, the author wishes to thank fellow researchers, musicians, and friends who have assisted him at one point or another during the past six years. Among them, listed in no particular order, are Colin Matthews, Michael Short, Patricia M. Rogers, Hugh Cobbe, Alan Gibbs, Ursula Vaughan Williams, Sally Hain, Helen Gaskell, Frank Battisti, Nicholas Tawa, Keith Kinder, and Timothy McFarland.

CHAPTER I

CHELTENHAM THROUGH STUDENT DAYS AT THE THE ROYAL COLLEGE OF MUSIC

The Gloucestershire borough of Cheltenham, on the River Chelt, is no ordinary place. Situated ninety-seven miles west of London, it lies on the western edge of the Cotswold Hills, a range of limestone hills which in itself is an enchanting rural area of picturesque villages, sleepy pubs, beauteous landscapes and medieval churches. Once a center of England's wool trade, the Cotswolds area today enjoys its reputation as an outdoor tourist center, with a plethora of hiking and bicycling trails cutting through its largely unspoiled countryside. Cheltenham correctly advertises itself as the "Centre for the Cotswolds" since, as the area's largest population base, it serves as a convenient point of departure for trips into the hills. This in itself would make the town a desirable place to live and to visit, but the discovery of spring waters around 1716 and the construction of the Pittville Pump Room in 1738 on the north end of town caused it to gain distinction as an inland spa resort. In 1788 King George III visited; this and a later visit by the Duke of Wellington[1] confirmed the town's reputation as a spa and a place for leisure for Britain's middle and upper classes.

Much of Cheltenham was built in the 1830's; due to careful planning, the town became famous for its architecture, parks and gardens. Regency buildings dominate much of the town, from Montpellier Gardens on the south end, through The Promenade. "Cheltenham Spa," as it was now known, also became a center for education. Cheltenham College (1841) was the second-largest public school in England by the end of the nineteenth century and Cheltenham Ladies' College (1853) grew to become the largest girls' boarding school in Europe.

Music also had a rather prominent place in Cheltenham. By 1783 music was being provided for the balls held during the summer season. By the1830's a band was playing regularly at the Old Well and the Montpellier Rotunda and by 1846 a band of twenty musicians played every morning and three evenings per week for the Musical Promenades. There was also a series known as "Mr. Woodward's Grand Concerts," attracting the finest musicians in Europe, including Franz Liszt in 1840.[2] When the chamber orchestra concerts at the Montpellier Rotunda, the Three Choirs Festival, and countless other society and church functions are added to this, it is evident that music was thriving in Cheltenham. Thus it was that by the middle of the Victorian era Cheltenham, with a population of about 40,000, had established itself as a a major cultural center.

It was just north of the center of Cheltenham, at 4, Pittville Terrace (now Clarence Road) that Gustavus Theodore von Holst was born on September 21, 1874. He was the first-born child of Adolph and Clara Lediard von Holst. The Holst side of the family, of mixed Swedish, Latvian, and German descent, was very musical; there had been a musician in every generation of the family for at least four generations.

Matthias Holst, Gustav's great grandfather, was born in Riga. A minor classical period composer, his reputation had become sufficiently well-known that he became keyboard and harp teacher to the Imperial Russian Court in St. Petersburg. He married a Russian woman, Katharina Rogge. Their first son, Gustavus Valentin , was born in Riga in1799. Around 1802 the family was forced to flee, presumably for political reasons, and Matthias restablished himself as a composer of light operas and as a music teacher in the Fitzroy Square area of London. Their second son, Theodore, a well-known romantic painter, was born in London in 1810.

Gustavus Valentin, also a composer and music teacher, was Gustav's grandfather. It was Gustavus Valentin who added the "von" prefix to the family name. During the early 1800's the myth of "unmusical England" was firmly established and he wanted to take advantage of his foreign birth and foreign sounding name to attract students. Gustavus Valentin married an English woman, Honaria Goodrich and together they had five children: Gustavus Matthias, Catherine, Lorenz, Adolph (Gustav's father), and Benigna (Nina). Gustavus Matthias became a composer and organist, enjoying considerable success in Scotland. Attribution of his music and that of his father is sometimes confused with his nephew's (Gustav's) due to the similarity in names. The family settled in Cheltenham in 1849,[3] where Gustavus Valentin catered to the culturally elite. On at least one "musical afternoon" he conducted twenty-four young women seated at twelve pianos in performance of his own arrangements of overtures and other selections before a select audience. In reality this may not have actually been as exotic as it sounds for Gustavus Valentin taught piano at Cheltenham Ladies' College from 1854 to 1860 and regularly had his students perform together.

Adolph von Holst, Gustav's father, was born in London in 1846. He was a brilliant pianist and frequently gave concerts throughout his career at the Assembly Rooms on High Street and at the Montpellier Rotunda on the Promenade. As time passed, he became involved with chamber music and was organizer and pianist of the Cheltenham Quartet Society and the "Popular Classical Concerts" held at the Corn Exchange. These concerts usually featured a string quartet plus piano and one or two woodwinds. In 1878, Adolph conducted forty musicians in a "Grand Orchestral Concert"[4] and this led to his being conductor of the chamber orchestra stationed at the Montpellier Rotunda. A sought-after teacher, Adolph was also organist at All Saints' Church, in the Pittville section of Cheltenham, from 1868 to 1895. By the time of his sons' births in the mid-1870's, it is safe to say that Adolph von Holst was the best known and most highly respected professional musician in Cheltenham.

On July 11, 1871 Adolph married one of his students, Clara Cox Lediard, the daughter of a respected Cirencester solicitor. She was five years his senior. The von Holsts set up residence in a townhouse owned by Clara's father, at 4 Pittville Terrace, located about a half-mile northwest of All Saint's Church. It was there that the couple's two sons, Gustavus Theodore and Emil Gottfried were born in 1874 and 1876, respectively. From all accounts it was a happy marriage, although Clara's nerves forced Adolph into buying a silent keyboard for his constant practicing.[5]

Tragedy struck the family on February 12, 1882, when Clara, weakened by a still birth a few months earlier, died of heart disease and dropsy. Adolph was beside himself and moved the family to 1 Victoria Walk. Adolph's young sons were only seven and five years old, respectively, and his younger sister Nina was brought in to help raise the boys. Gustav in particular recognized Nina's devotion to the family and dedicated a number of his earlier compositions to her. In August, 1885 Adolph remarried. His bride this time was Mary Thorley Stone, the daughter of Reverend Edward Stone, Rector of Queenhill at Upton-upon-Severn. Mary presented Adolph with two more sons: Matthias Ralph Bromley (known as "Max"), born in 1886 and Evelyn "Thorley," born in 1889. For Adolph, Gustav's half brothers almost constituted a second generation of children; at the inside, Max was a full decade younger than Emil while at the outside, Gustav was fifteen years older than Thorley. The family moved once again in 1891, to 46 Lansdown Crescent.

Mary has been described as a theosophist. She was not the domestic type, and her passion in philosophical and religious matters often pushed the family's well-being aside. This benign neglect was detrimental to all four boys, but it was Gustav who may have suffered the most. From the very beginning he had a rather fragile constitution and his bouts with athsma and his near-sightedness were allowed to continue uncorrected for too long a time. On the positive side of things, Gustav was exposed to the many theosophical conversations that went on in the drawing room between Mary and her friends. Such intellectual discussions had an impact on his thinking and soon he was discussing the possibilities of reincarnation with his friends at school.[6]

Gustav (the -us suffix disappeared early from common usage) first attended Pate's Grammar School, where Adolph was music master. From 1886 to 1891 he attended Cheltenham Grammar School, which was then going through a period of reconstruction. He did well in his studies, although his physical weakness contributed to his being constantly bullied by fellow classmates.[7] He was described as "very quiet and retiring."[8] As in the case of so many others in that same situation, Gustav sought and found solace within, primarily through music.

Music had always been a way of life in the von Holst household. Music was, after all, central to Adolph's being and he was more than willing to pass it on to his first-born son. Choir rehearsals at All Saints' Church, chamber orchestra concerts at the Montpellier Rotunda and, at home, a steady stream of Adolph's piano students practicing the early romantics were things that were unavoidable. Gustav himself studied piano from a very early age, often practicing Chopin, Liszt, and (against his father's wishes), Grieg. It wasn't long before Gustav's musical scope expanded through the study of three additional and very different instruments: violin, organ, and trombone. Still, at this point the keyboard instruments dominated and both Gustav and his father had dreams of his becoming a concert pianist. As time passed Gustav became interested in composition as well. One of his first attempts was *Horatius* [App. II, 1]. It was almost his last. Years later he wrote the following on the first page of the manuscript:

> This was written before I knew any harmony or counterpoint--probably in 1887. The only book on the theory of music that I knew was Berlioz' Instrumentation which I knew practically by heart. I wrote this (the words being part of my homework at Cheltenham Grammar School) in secret bit by bit until one day--the family being out--I tried to play it on the piano. The result on my nerves was that I never wrote another note of it.[9]

The setback, however, was only temporary. Holst's compositional interest was piqued again by the appearance of the following advertisement in *The Boys'*

Own Paper:

> We once more offer, as during several previous years, two prizes of two guineas and one guinea respectively, for the best musical setting with organ or pianoforte accompaniment, of any of the verses appearing in our last volume (Volume 11) or in the Extra Summer and Christmas parts of 1889. There will be two classes only (not including the "over the age" class), the Junior embracing all ages up to eighteen; and the Senior, from 18 to 24.[10]

Holst won the contest for three years running, 1890-92. Encouraged by these results, the budding composer completed no fewer than twenty-eight musical works over the next few years. During this time a family friend, Frank Forty, saw to it that Holst's works received the attention that they deserved. The works from this "Cheltenham" period are, as one might expect, reflective of Holst's musical environment and owe a lot to Mendelssohn, Chopin, Grieg, and Gilbert & Sullivan, whose operettas were then sweeping the country. More than half of this output consists of vocal pieces with keyboard accompaniment, although there are some more ambitious attempts as well. Not surprisingly, there is little of the later Holst in these pieces, although indicators of at least three personal attributes associated with his musical maturity had already begun to surface: 1) acoustical staging, 2) a flexibility in performance practice, and 3) a personal apology in his notes of dedication.

The first two of these appear in one of his earliest compositions, *The Listening Angels* [App I, 5], an "Anthem for Solo Contralto and Hidden Choir with Organ Accompaniment." Holst later employed hidden choruses in three substantial works: *Sita,* Op. 23 [H89] (1899-1906), *Savitri*, Op. 25 [H96] (1908), and in "Neptune" of *The Planets*, Op. 32 [H125] (1916). The following indication to his singers in *The Listening Angels* indicates a flexibility of performance on the composer's part: "Sing the notes in the brackets if possible; if not, sing the others." Optional levels of difficulty in parts and flexibility in instrumentation would become a Holst trademark throughout his compositional career, particularly in works intended for amateurs. Part of this was from his own personal experiences with working with such groups; part was due to an unofficial apprenticeship of cuing in missing orchestral winds for his father's orchestra.

The third indicator, that of personal apology, appears in at least two of the four organ voluntaries from 1891. The first, *March in C Major* [App I, 8], contains the following dedication: "Most respectfully Dedicated without any permission whatsoever to Miss Nina von Holst." The fourth voluntary, *Funeral*

March in G Minor [App I, 11] has the following ending note, probably intended for Nina von Holst:

> Thank Miss Scott tremendously from me for Ivanhoe. I know this is atrociously written out but I am so sick of it that I cannot copy it any more. The stops are meant for large organ[11], and will not do for yours. I am thinking of writing a piano duet for you and Miss Scott. It will be very difficult! and therefore will just suit you.[12]

Such notes are not uncommon in original works and arrangements that Holst wrote for close friends and relatives. Vally Lasker, Nora Day, Adrian Boult and others would be beneficiaries of such characteristic selflessness.

Although Holst's name must have appeared in the press at an earlier date[13], his earliest public performance documented in the Holst scrapbooks[14] is from November 11,1891. The opening piece on the 3:30 Wednesday afternoon concert, the "5th Musical Afternnoon" held at the Montpellier Rotunda, was Brahms' "Duo Pianoforte 'Hungarian Dances'" performed by Messrs. Adolph von Holst and Gustav von Holst.

The earliest documentation in the scrapbooks of Holst as a composer is the program from the "10th and Last Musical Afternoon" of the series. His *Scherzo* [App I, 13] for chamber orchestra was performed "by request" on December 16, 1891.[15] His *Intermezzo* [App I, 12] was performed three days later, at a "Saturday Afternoon popular concert." This event was covered in *The Cheltenham Looker-On:*

> The instrumental numbers included a polka by the conductor[16], which was bright and tuneful, and an Intermezzo by Mr. Gustav von Holst, the opening movement with muted first violin with pizzicato accompaniment and a tuneful melody in the second part for clarionet and flute. The work was well-received and the youthful composer bowed his acknowledgments.[17]

One can get a sense of the orchestral forces available at the Montpellier Rotunda from Holst's orchestration. For the *Intermezzo*, he used flute, clarinet and strings (the same instrumentation employed by him in 1910 for his two sets of *Morris Dance Tunes*). For the *Scherzo* he added a cornet to the same combination. He added a bassoon to this combination for the "Country Dance" in Act II of the operetta *Lansdown Castle* [App I, 21], composed in the following year, and added another cornet and timpani in his *Bolero* [App I, 24] (1893).

Greatly encouraged by the 1891 events, Holst decided to write a much larger work. The forty-two page *Symphony in C Minor* [App I, 14] (1892) employs late Schubertian forces. In contrast to Holst's normal working habits, it was composed very quickly. The title page of the four-movement work proudly states: "Begun Jan: 11th Finished: Feb: 5th."[18] There are no indications of whether or not the symphony was actually performed. Years later Holst considered *The Cotswolds: Symphony in F*, Op. 8 [H47] (1899-1900), and not the *Symphony in C Minor*, to be his first work in that form.

Adolph still wanted his son to become a concert pianist but by this time Gustav's main interest had shifted to composition. Turned down for a scholarship at Trinity College, Gustav was allowed to go to Oxford for a semester to study counterpoint with George Frederick Sims, organist at Merton College. Upon his return Holst obtained his first real job in the music world, that of organist and choir director at Wyck Rissington, a small Cotswolds village of two hundred people. The position paid only £4 annually, but attached to this was a real opportunity: the conductorship of the Bourton-on-the-Water Choral Society. Here Holst was able to develop some conducting skills while inspiring his singers to tackle some rather substantial works. Among the performances that Holst conducted there was a "Grand Sacred Concert" given by the society on Wednesday, April 12, 1893 featuring John Farmer's oratorio *Christ and His Soldiers*.[19] Bourton-on-the-Water was then serviced by passenger railway lines, but Wyck Rissington, located about one and one-half miles to the northeast, was not. Holst regularly walked between the two; he had already been accustomed to walking in the Cotswolds and this was just the start of what would turn out to be a life-long penchant for the experience.

In late 1892, Holst completed his most ambitious work to that point. *Lansdown Castle, or the Sorcerer of Tewksbury* [App 1, 21] was a two act operetta with six featured singing roles. The libretto, involving magic and mirrors, was supplied by Major A. C. Cunningham. The sizeable Lansdown area of Cheltenham is located southwest of the town's center; there are a half dozen streets bearing the Lansdown name. At that time the von Holst family lived at 46 Lansdown Crescent, actually quite a distance from Lansdown Castle Road. Still, the connections are obvious and the young composer's familiarity with the Lansdown environs coupled with Cunnigham's fanciful yet melodramatic story line aroused Holst's imagination. Two selections from the work, "The Lovelorn Maid" and "When a Charming Young Bachelor,"[20] were presented at a "Grand Orchestral Concert" held at Cheltenham's Assembly Rooms on December 22, 1892. The *Gloucester Chronicle* had the following commentary:

> We are glad to welcome Mr. Gustav von Holst as a clever and original composer, from whom we may reasonably expect some sterling compositions in the future.[21]

The entire work was premiered on Tuesday, February 7, 1893 at the Corn Exchange in Cheltenham. Again the composer received accolades from the press:

> The remarkable musical treatment treatment of Major Cunningham's Libretto more than justified the production of the operetta, and Mr. Gustav von Holst gives evidence in his work not only of genius, but of careful laborious study.[22]

The success of *Lansdown Castle* may have been the determining factor that convinced Adolph that his son stood a chance to make it as a composer. Gustav applied for a scholarship to the Royal College of Music in London but, submitting *Lansdown Castle* as an example of his work, he was turned down (the libretto could not have helped). Samuel Coleridge-Taylor won the composition scholarship that year. Adolph was still sufficiently impressed with Gustav's work to borrow £100 from a relative, enough to get his son started at the Royal College of Music. Gustav did not let his father down; he took the entrance examinations and passed. In late May, 1893 the young composer entered the Royal College of Music at the start of its summer term.

Financially, things were very tight for Holst during his first two years at the college. He took up lodgings in the nearby Borough of Hammersmith; rent in the South Kensington area, where the college is located, was far too expensive. In addition to being a non-smoker, Holst became a vegetarian and a teetotaler, partly due to frugality and partly because he felt that it suited him. During breaks, he often walked at least part of the way from London to Cheltenham in order to save money. Symphonist Edmund Rubbra, who was a student of Holst in the 1920's, comments:

> Holst knew the country well, being always a good walker, and often as a student he would walk the 100-odd miles to Cheltenham, which lies on the borders of the Cotswolds, with his trombone slung on his back! Indeed there is a story that an irate farmer, hearing him practice his trombone during a rest on one such walk, turned him out of his land, fearing the effects of such sounds on sheep about to lamb.[23]

Holst's applied teachers at the Royal College of Music included Frederick

Sharpe (piano), William Stephenson Hoyte (organ) and George Case (trombone). Neuritis in his right arm had bothered him since his childhood and he did not fare well with either of the keyboard instruments. This was worsened by the fact that he did not hit it off well with Hoyte. His father took him to task for this:

> Dear Gustav,
>
> I am sorry that you have not prepossessed Hoyte in your favour. Do you know that when I have been giving you a lesson I have often been struck by the way in which you kept to your own method, not doing what was required. What is it that keeps you back in organ playing? For goodness sake try and extort eulogium from Hoyte; if you are not clever at present, make yourself so.
>
> Do you go to Sunday Organ Recitals at the Albert Hall? For 3d you get a very good seat.
>
> Enclosed you will find a postal order for a pound. Do you require so much every week?
>
> Affectionately yours,
>
> Adolph von Holst[24]

As his neuritis continued, Holst soon had to abandon any hopes of becoming a concert pianist. His concentration was now on trombone. Holst comments from a 1921 perspective:

> But when I was twenty-one a misfortune overtook me. I began to have trouble with my right arm, due to overwork. Eventually I had to abandon the piano and organ, and had to earn my livelihood as a trombone player....[25]

Holst also studied with Georg Jacobi (instrumentation) and with the college's director Charles Hubert Hastings Parry (history), of whom he later said, "At last I had met a great man who did not terrify me."[26] Holst had wanted to study theory with Charles Villiers Stanford, but Stanford insisted that he first take some preparatory courses with W. S. Rockstro and John Frederick Bridge.

It was undoubtedly for Bridge's class that Holst composed the *Penitential Fugue*, a four-part fugue in four different clefs for unaccompanied SATB voices. This uncatalogued work not only displays Holst's wit, but also his ability to make the best of a bad situation--something he would do extremely well in some of his future teaching positions. The text of the fugue is certainly Holst's own:

> Oh!
> Doctor Bridge
> I have lost the proper subject and I am very sorry very sorry indeed
> and I hope I hope that you will forgive me for I am very sorry very sorry indeed
> [Resoluto] And I will never do it again
> [Adagio] Until the next time![27]

It was no wonder that when Holst finally did enter Stanford's composition class that Stanford described him as "enthusiatic, and happily not devoid of humour."[28]

Holst composed quite a number of works while studying with Stanford. His earliest effort was the *Theme and Variations for String Quartet* [App I, 29] (1893). This was followed by additional works for various combinations of chamber music, including an *Air and Variations for Piano and String Quartet* [App. I, 32] and *Short Trio in E Major* for violin, cello, and piano [App I, 33]. There were also some vocal ensemble settings of the words of W. M. Harding and Walter Scott done during this first year of study.

Holst's spirits were kept afloat by an ever-increasing circle of friends. He had met Fritz Bennicke Hart at the entrance examinations in the spring of 1893. Hart extolled the virtues of Wagner to Holst, but may have been "preaching to the choir." Holst had already been taken in by Wagner's influence by 1892 when, after attending a Covent Garden performance of *Die Gotterdammerung* conducted by Gustav Mahler, he composed his own *Song of the Valkyrs* [App I, 22] for two sopranos and alto accompanied by a double string orchestra and trumpet (with harp ad lib.). Holst's passion for Wagner continued for about a decade. It was fueled not only by fellow students such as Hart, but also by his music history teacher Charles Hubert Parry who, in his text *The Art of Music* (1893), deemed Wagner's music dramas "the high-water mark of music to the present."[29]

While a student, Holst collaborated with Hart on no fewer than eight projects, including the operettas *Ianthe* [App I, 42] (1894?), for children, *The Revoke*, Op. 1 [H7] (1895), under Stanford's guidance, and *The Idea* [H21] (1896), another operetta for children that met with a degree of success; portions of it were included in the Novello catalogue for half a century. In each instance, Holst set music to Hart's words.

Other close friends included Thomas Dunhill, Samuel Coleridge-Taylor, John Ireland, and Evlyn Howard-Jones. Together with Holst and Hart, this group of student composers frequented Wilkin's Tea Shop in Kensington, discussing the hot topics of the day. Coincidentally, a parallel occurrence was happening at the Hoch Conservatory in Frankfurt am Main, Germany where another handful of English student composers--Henry Balfour Gardiner, Norman O'Neill, Roger Quilter, Cyril Scott and the teen-aged Percy Grainger--had been studying. Not surprisingly composers from these two groups, Kensington and particularly Frankfurt, would dominate the Balfour Gardiner Concerts of 1912 and 1913.

The Wilkin's Tea Shop group was not the only social outlet that Holst had. Early on he had joined the Hammersmith Socialist Society, which held its meetings and forums at Kelmscott House, the home of William Morris. Today Morris is remembered as an artist, a craftsman, a poet, and a social leader. Preaching against the dehumanizing effects of the Industrial Revolution--he detested machine-made products--Morris advocated a return to a utopian medievalism, one in which the public could enjoy craftsmanship and a simplicity of expression. He championed an egalitarianism that would allow people to earn enough money so that they could have enough leisure time to appreciate the arts. His conviction that "art cannot have real life and growth under the present system of commercialism and profit-mongering"[30] naturally led into socialism. In 1886 Morris founded the Socialist League and in 1890 the Kelmscott Press, which featured hand-printed books.

The appeal of Morris's socialism to students of the arts in the 1890's is not difficult to see and Holst as well as a number of his friends became involved in the Hammersmith Socialist Society. Ralph Vaughan Williams comments:

> In early days he was strongly attracted by the ideals of William Morris, and though in later years he discarded Morris's medievalism, the "Kelmscott Club" ideal of comradeship remained with him throughout his life. He wanted to work with and teach and have the companionship of his fellow beings. The word "comrade" has nowadays lost its savor through misuse, but it is the right word to use of Holst's relations to his fellow men. To him, unselfconsciously and without any sense of propaganda, all men were brothers.[31]

For the more radical students Morris's socialism was a form of rebellion, but for Holst it was a natural exfoliation from his liberal Cheltenham upbringing. Perhaps too much has been made of Morris' influence on Holst. The philosophies of his step-mother Mary Thorley Stone von Holst and the Promenade statue of William IV celebrating the Reform Act of 1833 that he passed by nearly every time that he went to the Montpellier Rotunda had already been ingrained into his sense of being long before any contact with Morris. Still, the lectures of Morris and others who addressed the society on occasion, such as George Bernard Shaw, left their mark on Holst's own approach to teaching. Morris died in 1896 and Holst's interest in the society appears to have waned somewhat thereafter.

Holst had had financials difficulties all along and by the end of 1894, after he had been at the Royal College of Music for a year and a half, his funds began to dry up; the hundred pounds that Adolph had borrowed were just about gone. Things looked very bad and Holst referred to his repeated attempts to secure a scholarship from the Royal College of Music as "a meloncholic hobby."[32] Finally, on his eighth attempt and just before reaching the age limit, Holst secured a composition scholarship. This was no easy task. There were a total of only twelve Open Free Scholarships available and, according to the Royal College of Music examination report dated February 23, 1895, a total of 456 candidates from the United Kingdom had applied to attend the preliminary examinations. Of these, 136 were chosen to take the final examinations; seven withdrew. This left 129 candidates spread out over nine categories. The largest category, singing, had forty-seven candidates; pianoforte was second with thirty-seven. Only four candidates were selected to take the final composition examination. Holst won out over the other three, including Alfred L. Hirst of Batley, who was one of the twenty-one candidates to achieve the rating of *proxime accesserunt*.[33]

The Open Free Scholarship in Composition wasn't much--free tuition and a maintennance grant of £30 per annum--but it was a welcomed relief. As a means of celebration Adolph, who had just retired from his All Saints' Church position at the ripe old age of forty-nine, arranged for a performance of Holst's *Duet for Organ and Trombone* [App I, 31] (1894) on Wednesday, May 8, 1895 as part of an organ recital held at the Highbury Congregational Church in Cheltenham. The two-movement C minor work is substantial, lasting nearly twenty minutes and, while in a heavy Wagnerian mode, it is representative of Holst's developing skills as a composer.[34] For this performance Adolph played the organ and J. Boyce the trombone. Three hundred people were in attendence and the local press covered the event:

> ....interesting duet for trombone and organ composed by Gustav von Holst. The association of the two instruments is highly effective, as the strident tones of the trombone are not overwhelmed by the accompanying mass of organ sound, and an epic character is preserved throughout, which is thoroughly impressive.[35]

When Holst returned to the Royal College of Music in the autumn of 1895, he started to take himself more seriously[36] and began to list his important compositions in a small black book. He would make entries into this "List of Compositions"[37] for the remainder of his life. In addition to this, Holst started to assign opus numbers to works that he considered particularly worthy, beginning with *The Revoke*, Op. 1 [H7]. He also met the person who would have more influence on his composing than anybody else: Ralph Vaughan Williams. Two years his senior, Vaughan Williams was raised at Leith Hill, Surrey. He had an entirely different background from Holst. For one thing, he was from a family of eminent lawyers; both sides enjoyed financial independence. For another, Vaughan Williams grew up fatherless; his father had passed away when he was only three. Also not to be discounted is that, unlike Holst, Vaughan Williams was discouraged by family members from becoming a musician. Yet Vaughan Williams shared with Holst the humanistic and socialistic attitude that music was for the people--all classes of people. This was Vaughan Williams' second go at the Royal College of Music. He had entered there in 1890 and stayed two years before going to Trinity College in Cambridge to study with Charles Wood for the next three. By the time of his return to the Royal College of Music in 1895 he already had attained his Music Baccalaureate and Bachelor of Arts degrees. Day comments:

> It was during this second period of study at the Royal College that he [Ralph Vaughan Williams] met and became friendly with the man whose relationship with him has only one parallel in the whole field of art and literature--that between Goethe and Schiller. Gustav Holst was twenty-one, having won a scholarship to the Royal College in 1895,...his intimate knowledge of orchestral problems partly gained during this period, was of invaluable aid to Vaughan Williams when, soon afterward, they began their celebrated "field days," on which they would together spend a whole day or part of it, at least once a week, studying and criticizing each other's latest work with a frankness that would have caused offense to acquaintances of less mutual sympathy. Though they were both reserved by nature, they took to each other at once....[38]

Thus, from the very beginning of their friendship, Vaughan Williams replaced Fritz Hart as Holst's primary peer mentor.[39] Holst and Vaughan Williams were at the Royal Conservatory together for only one year, yet amazingly that year proved to be long enough to provide the foundation for a continuous mutual life-long professional development.

In the meantime, Holst continued his involvement with the Hammersmith

Socialist League. When Holst agreed to organize and conduct the Hammersmith Socialist Choir, it was probably more for the enjoyment of leading others in making music than for any other reason; he had already had a taste of this experience with the Bourton-on-Water Choral Society. One of the members new to the Hammersmith Socialist Choir in 1896 was a blond soprano named Emily Isobel Harrison. "Iso," as she was called, and Holst were immediately attracted to each other and, before long, they became engaged. Since neither had any money, the engagement turned out to be a lengthy one. Iso reformed Holst and took care of him. His strict personal austerity, which had resulted in a weakened condiction, was quickly corrected through a diet of home-cooked meals at the Harrison home. His appearance was also improved; a beard that he had grown for the sake of appearing to be older at job interviews was shaved off at Iso's insistence. Two of Holst's songs for voice and piano, "Song to the Sleeping Lady" [H17] (1897) and "Not a Sound but Echoing in Me" [H32] (1897) were dedicated to Iso and the first performance of a third, "Two Brown Eyes" [H39] (1898?), was sung by her.

Holst continued to study with Stanford. His technique continued to develop and smoothen. His chamber music now had a chromatic Wagnerian flow to it, as displayed in the *Quintet in A Minor*, Op. 3 [H11] (1896) for piano, oboe, clarinet, horn and bassoon, the *Scherzo* [H23] for string sextet, and the beautiful but unfinished *Wind Septet* [App II, 9]. One such work, the *Fantasiestucke*, Op. 2 [H8] (1896) for oboe and string quartet was uncharacteristically revised by the composer in 1910, first titled *Suite* and then *Three Pieces for Oboe and String Quartet*, Op. 2 [H8A][40]; it has recently been published by Thames. He also produced one substantial but unperformed orchestral work, *A Winter Idyll* [H31] (1897). At this time Holst was still struggling to find his own place as a composer and seemed bent on imposing a foreign stamp onto his work. The title page for the woodwind quintet mentioned above, for example, is entirely in German.

It was with two choral works that Holst enjoyed his greatest success as a student composer. *Clear and Cool: Song of the River*, Op. 5 [H30] (1897), with words by Charles Kingsley, was originally composed for five-part mixed chorus and full orchestra. The Hammersmith Socialist Choir performed it under the composer's direction with piano accompaniment at the Athenaeum in Shepherd's Bush on March 26, 1897. A less ambitious composition from the previous year, *Light Leaves Whisper* [H20], a six-part F major setting of words by Fritz Hart, gained him four things: 1) the prize in a contest for composition students of the Royal College of Music offered by the Magpie Madrigal Society, 2) a second performance by the same society at St. James Hall, Piccadilly, 3) a favorable review of that performance in *The Times*, and 4) publication by Laudy & Co., making it the first of his works to be published.[41] Dedicated to his aunt, Nina von Holst, *Light Leaves Whisper* displays a characteristic sensitivity to text; Holst changes meter where appropriate in order to create the most suitable fit to Hart's words:

Andante con moto
4/4 Light leaves whisper
Touched by the evening breeze
Pale moonbeams glimmer
A-falling thro' the trees
6/8 Sweet are the sights to weary hearts
Sweet are these sights to me
Tho' I can understand them ne'er unless
Unless I am with thee
4/4 The nightingale may melt his soul in song
Shed all the thoughts which his small bosom throng
But Oh my love, my gentle love
I ne'er can understand
The hidden meaning of these things
Unless thou art at hand.

At the end of his music, Holst wrote the following motto: "Only the Strong can Love; only Love can fathom Beauty; only Beauty can fashion Art."[42]

Holst soon realized that he had to supplement his maintenance grant in order to survive. £30 annually was not much money; he had spent more than that in his first year and a half at the college. He did occasional tutoring and served as a substitute organist for various churches, but found that playing the trombone during holidays and breaks between terms was more lucrative. Although he found some work playing for the pantomimes in London, most of his engagements were at seaside resorts. He was often employed as a member of an ensemble that billed itself as the White Viennese Band. The conductor of this group was the rather flambouyant Stanislaus Würm. Holst often referred to him as "The Worm" and to the act of playing in seaside bands for Würm and others like him as "worming." In a 1932 interview, Holst commented about his experiences with this band:

> In the nineties, I was one of a little band that used to look for seaside jobs in the summer. One summer we had an English conductor and one-third foreign musicians. We got paid £2 a week, no travelling

> expenses. The next summer we had a foreign conductor, were dressed up in uniforms with gold braid, and were billed as a foreign orchestra. Two-thirds of the players were still English but the difference was this: we got paid three guineas a week and all expenses found.[43]

To give credence to their foreign status, band members were ordered to speak in fake foreign accents whenever the possibility existed of them being overheard in public. Here Holst was thrust into the same "nonmusical England" myth that had plagued his grandfather Gustavus Valentin sixty years earlier. Such experiences would provide fodder for Holst's future lectures, particularly his one on "England and Her Music." Likewise the experience of playing the same medleys and potboilers again and again would alert Holst to the need for improving the repertoire of bands and non-professional groups. He would assume a leading role in bettering this situation in the decades that lie ahead.

Amidst the pathos there was a lighter side to Holst's seaside adventures. Vaughan Williams comments:

> At the end of our summer holidays some of us students would get together to tell each other how we spent our vacation. One of us had been at Bayreuth and gave, I am sure, a highly critical appraisement of the proceedings. Often, perhaps, one had been to the Dolomites or to Brittany and were doubtless very poetical about it. In all this we listeners were mildly interested, but what remained in the memory of those who heard him was Holst's enthralling account of his experiences as a member of a seaside band, enthralling because of his great human sympathy, his unique humour, his strong sense of values.[44]

Ralph Vaughan Williams left the Royal College of Music in 1896, although he continued to study composition. For two years he had been organist and choir director at St. Barnabas' Church in South Lambeth, a job for which he had an extreme dislike. When he decided to wed Adeline Fisher in 1897, Vaughan Williams made plans to leave his St. Barnabas post; time and peace of mind were more important than to him than any amount of financial remuneration. He let Holst know that the position would be open:

[July, 1897]

Dear von Holst

Excuse this paper but I have no other.

I am leaving this damned place in October and going abroad.

Suppose you were offered it would you consider the matter? The screw is fifty pound and the minimum duties:

Monday:	boys any time after 6.0
Wed.	boys 7.0 service 8.0-9.0
Thurs.	full practice 8.30 or 8.15 till 10 past if you can get them to stop.
Sunday:	11.0 with choral communion once a month
	7.0 and children's service at 3.0 once a month

Besides this you are supposed to run the choral society whenever it intermittently exists, and give occasional organ recitals.

Mind I am not offering it you *only* if you would like it. I will do my best to back you.

Will you any way take my practice and service Wed: Aug 4th at 7.0 Practice Aug. 5 at 8.15 and the services Aug. 8th (Sunday) at 11.0 & 7.0 for the usual fee whatever that is? Then the Vicar could have an opportunity to find out your merits; he is already rather struck by the way you took that choir practice.

Please answer *at once*

R. Vaughan Williams
2 St. Barnabas Villas
S. Lambeth Rd.
S.W.[45]

Holst must have agreed to do this, for in a follow-up letter Vaughan Williams gave a detailed description of the duties. Holst was also being considered for a position at a Presbyterian church and Vaughan Williams makes reference to this in his closing remarks:

I don't know what to do about the permanent job. I shall see the Vicar tomorrow or possibly tonight; all I can say is keep the Presbyters waiting as long as you can without endangering your position there; since if you fall between two stools I shall feel morally bound to give you £30 a year out of my salary for the rest of your life which I do not want to do.

Try also and get hold of your testimonials--hire a burglar.

Yours always
R. Vaughan Williams[46]

Fortunately or unfortunately, Holst was not offered the St. Barnabas position; it was given to John Ireland.

In the meantime, Holst was getting some solid professional trombone playing experience. On December 7th of the same year, he played in the Queen's Hall Orchestra under the direction of Richard Strauss, who was making his British conducting debut. Another engagement entailed performing under the eminent German conductor Hans Richter, then guest conducting at Covent Garden. Richter was conductor of the Manchester's Halle Orchestra (1897-1911) and later would become the regular "Wagnerian" conductor at Covent Garden (1903-10) as well as conductor of the London Symphony Orchestra (1904-11). Richter told the budding professional that he (Holst) was one of the people that he (Richter) would have liked to taken back with him to Germany.[47] This meant a great deal to Holst. Such experiences gave him the encouragement he needed to consider becoming a career trombonist. In the summer of 1898 Holst applied for a position with the Carl Rosa Opera Company.

---

[1]*Cheltenham Spa: Centre for the Cotswolds* (Cheltenham: Architext Publications, 1993), 2.
[2]Kenneth Young, *Music's Great Days in the Spas and Watering Places* (London: Macmillan & Co., 1968), 190.
[3]Information for this family history section is extracted largely from exhibits at the Holst Birthplace Museum in Cheltenham. The 1849 date is somewhat suspect as highly respected Holst scholar Michael Short, whose research is very thorough, states on page 10 of his *Gustav Holst: The Man and His Music* (Oxford: Oxford University Press, 1990) that Gustavus Valentin was established in Cheltenham by 1832. Another possiblity is that Gustavus Valentin may have established his teaching studio in Cheltenham many years before bringing his family to live there. Before the advent of the railway Cheltenham was a rather long commute from London, although spending weekends or even two or three weekdays in succession there may have been a possibility.
[4]Programmes and Press Cuttings, Vol. I at the Holst Birthplace Museum, Cheltenham.
[5]Michael Short, *op. cit.*, 10-11.
[6]Imogen Holst, *Gustav Holst: A Biography, 2nd ed.* (Oxford: Oxford University Press, 1969), 7.
[7]For a contrite acknowledgment of guilt over this, see the personal correspondence from Harold Bauer to Holst in the New York chapter of this book.
[8]*The Gloucester Echo* (n.d.) [May, 1934].
[9]Gustav Holst, *Horatius*, British Library Add MS 47804.
[10]Response of G. J. H. Northcroft, Editor of *The Boys' Own Paper*, in *The Musical Times*, September 1, 1934. Holst won in1892 for his *New Year Chorus* [App. I, 16], for satb and piano.
[11]The organ at All Saints Church.
[12]These works are a part of the Holst collection at the Britten-Pears Library, Aldeburgh.

[13]As a result of *The Boys' Own Paper* contests.
[14]Holst and his family kept scrapbooks of press coverage and programs almost from the beginning. This huge collection exists in a series of twenty volumes. Most of the entries are well-preserved, although many have become partially illegible due to either chemical deterioration or glue-and-newspaper print interaction. The entire collection is on microfilm.
[15]The *Scherzo* had actually been performed for the first time on the November 4, 1891 concert.
[16]P. Jones.
[17]*The Cheltenham Looker-On*, December 26, 1891.
[18]British Library Add MS 57865.
[19]Programme, Bourton-on-the-Water Choral Society, Wednesday, April 12, 1893.
[20]These two selections may have been the only two that were scored for orchestra. The surviving British Library manuscript (Add MS 47805) of *Lansdown Castle* is for voices and piano.
[21]*The Gloucester Chronicle*, December 24, 1892.
[22]*The Gloucester Echo*, February 9, 1893.
[23]Edmund Rubbra, *Gustav Holst* (Monaco: The Lyrebird Press, 1947), 10.
[24]Personal correspondence, Adolph von Holst to Gustav Holst [1893 or 1894], quoted in Imogen Holst, *op.cit.*, 13.
[25]*Daily News* (London), June 29, 1921.
[26]*The Music Student*, November, 1918.
[27]Gustav Holst, *Penitential Fugue*, RCM MS 5360a.
[28]Imogen Holst, *op.cit.*, 13.
[29]Charles Hubert Hastings Parry, *Evolution of the Art of Music* (London: D. Appleton-Century, 1935), 463. The final chapter of this edition was added by H. C. Colles. Parry's original tome was titled *The Art of Music* (London: Kegan Paul, 1893).
[30]William Morris, quoted in Gillian Naylor, "Design and Industry," in *The Cambridge Guide to the Arts in Britain, VIII: The Edwardian Age and the Interwar Years* (Cambridge, England: Press Syndicate of the University of Cambridge, 1989), 255.
[31]Ralph Vaughan Williams, "Gustav Holst: Man and Musician" in *The R.C.M. Magazine*, XXX, No. 3 (December, 1934), 79.
[32]*The Gloucester Echo* (n.d.) [May, 1934].
[33]The Royal College of Music, Open Free Scholarship Examination Report submitted by George Watson, Secretary and Registrar, February 23, 1895.
[34]For additional information about this work, see the author's article, "Gustav Holst's *Duet for Organ and Trombone*," in *International Trombone Association Journal*, XVIII, 1 (Spring, 1990), 22-25.
[35]"Musical Gossip," [n.d.], newspaper clipping from Vol. 2 of the Holst Scrapbooks at the Holst Birthplace Museum.
[36]Imogen Holst recognized this when she catalogued her father's compositions in the early 1970's. Works written before 1895 are assigned "App. I" numbers. Original works from 1895 onwards are assigned "H" numbers.
[37]British Library Add MS 57863.
[38]James Day, *Vaughan Williams*, 2nd rev. ed. (London: J. M. Dent & Sons Ltd., 1975), 13.
[39]Holst and Hart did remain close friends, however, and in 1907 Hart was asked to be Imogen Holst's godfather.
[40]Gustav Holst, *Three Pieces for Oboe and String Quartet*, Op. 2 [H8A] (1896), Britten-Pears Library MS. The three movements are "March," "Minuet," and "Scherzo."
[41]Not counting the publication of his winning entries in the 1890-92 contests sponsored by *The*

Boys' Own Paper. "Slumber-Song" and "Margrete's Cradle-Song," the first two of Holst's *Four Songs*, Op. 4 [H14] for voice and piano were published by Laudy in 1897, probably in the wake of the success of *Light Leaves Whisper*. Both of the songs were dedicated to Holst's aunt, Anna E. Newman, who ran St. Mary's School in Barnes.

[42]Gustav Holst, *Light Leaves Whisper* [H20], Britten-Pears Library MS.

[43]Gustav Holst, quoted by Quaintence Eaton in "Gustav Holst on American Visit, Approves Our Ways," in *Musical America*, LII, No. 3 (February 10, 1932), 6.

[44]Ralph Vaughan Williams, *op. cit.*, 80.

[45]Personal correspondence, Ralph Vaughan Williams to Gustav Holst, n.d. [July, 1897], quoted in Ursula Vaughan Williams (ed.) and Imogen Holst (ed.), *Heirs and Rebels: Letters to Each Other and Occasional Writings by Gustav Holst and Ralph Vaughan Williams* (Oxford: Oxford University Press, 1959), 3.

[46]Personal correspondence, Ralph Vaughan Williams to Gustav Holst, n.d. [late July, 1897], quoted in Ursula Vaughan Williams (ed.) and Imogen Holst (ed.), *op. cit.*, 4-5.

[47]Imogen Holst, *op. cit.*, 20.

CHAPTER II

THE PROFESSIONAL TROMBONIST

Carl Rosa (real name Karl August Nikolaus Rose) was born in Hamburg, Germany in 1842. He was a violinist and conductor who, with his wife the singer Euphrosyne Parepa, organized an English opera company that toured America. After her death in 1874, Rosa continued to produce operas in English in various London locales; this lead to the eventual formation of the Carl Rosa Opera Company in 1875. From 1883 the company's home was the Theatre Royal at Drury Lane, near Covent Garden. Rosa died in 1889 yet the company continued, endearing itself to England through its tours. Unfortunately it began to founder musically and became infamous for its second rate musicianship and shoddy productions. This didn't seem to matter to Queen Victoria, who granted the company the title of Royal Carl Rosa Opera Company in 1893.[1]

Gustav Holst was offered the position of trombonist and repetiteur by the Royal Carl Rosa Opera Company in the summer of 1898. Holst had spent the previous five years at the Royal College of Music and was feeling the urge to leave its protection. His composition scholarship had expired, but he was offered a year's extension. Additional study no longer had the appeal that it once had, however, and he ultimately rejected the offer. Holst was starting to enjoy some success with his compositions and his trombone playing, having improved dramatically through George Case's teaching, was now very proficient. There were other factors that contributed to his decision to leave the Royal College of Music. Holst was nearing his twenty-fourth birthday and he had been engaged for two years; it was time for him to set off on his own. Being the repetiteur for the Carl Rosa while performing under Henry Wood's direction offered Holst an excellent opportunity to get his feet wet in the world of professional music-making. He gladly accepted the offer.

Holst wrote to Hubert Parry, Director of the Royal College of Music, about his decision. He did not want to offend the people who had assisted him in his musical development. He needn't have worried. Parry sent the following reply:

Highnam Court
Gloucester
Sept. 10. [18]98

My dear Von Holst

You are not at all likely to 'give offense' to any authorities at the R.C.M.; they have much too good an opinion of you. I am very sorry we shall not have the benefit of your presence at the R.C.M. this next term, but you are quite right to take an opportunity of the kind you tell me of....[2]

At first the position with the Carl Rosa was extremely challenging. As repetiteur, Holst had to coach and accompany singers on operatic selections with which he himself was unfamiliar. As time went on, however, Holst's own musicianship took hold and the tasks became much easier. Since the Carl Rosa did not pay very well, Holst continued to play trombone for the Pantomime in London during the season and for the seaside bands during the summer. He still had not given up the keyboard entirely and, in addition to the supplementary trombone jobs, served for a number of seasons as organist at the Royal Opera House at Covent Garden.[3] He also continued to play piano on some of his own concerts, as evidenced by a program of his songs and piano works from April 22, 1902 that featured both his aunt Nina and himself as performers.

An unfortunate result of being so busy was that in 1898 Holst composed only one large work, *Ornulf's Drapa*, Op. 6 [H34], a "scena for baritone and orchestra" which he may have started while still a student at the Royal College of Music. He rescored the work in January, 1900. The text of *Ornulf's Drapa* is taken from William Archer's translation of Henrik Ibsen's *Vikings at Helgenland.* The Wagnerian influence is clearly in evidence, although this work may be considered an intermediate step between his borrowing of the Norse gods of Wagner's *Ring* (as in his 1892 *Song of the Valkyrs*) and his next exploration beyond the borders of his deep-rooted yet liberal Anglican upbringing: Hindu deities.

It was in the following year (1899) that Holst began studying Sanskrit, the classical sacred and literary language of India. He may have started to read some of the Hindu literature while still a student, but his interest appears to have been piqued by reading some borrowed material while he was on tour with the Carl Rosa. Before long Holst found himself mesmerized by the hymns from the religious *Vedas* as well as by the epics found in the *Mahabarata* and *Ramayana*. He yearned to set some of the verses to music but was frustrated with the available English translations, which were either paraphrases or did not convey the true meaning of the texts. Ralph T. H. Griffith had finished a workable translation of the *Rig Veda* by 1889. It is not known if Holst had read Griffith's work, or, if he had, what he thought about it. Whatever the case, Holst decided to make his own translations but, unable to read the original Sanskrit volumes in the British Library, he realised that he needed to acquire some sort of working knowledge of the language. As a result, Holst enrolled at the London School of Oriental Languages and took Sanskrit lessons there during breaks in his Carl Rosa schedule. His teacher was Mabel "Patsy" Bode, an Irish woman reported to have a great sense of humor. He was her very first student. She set Holst straight on the mechanics of the language and gave him enough information so that he could make serviceable translations of the verses in which he was interested. He soon started on the libretto for *Sita*, Op. 23 [H89] (1906), an opera founded on the *Ramayana*. He sought additional help from Ramesh Date, who wrote:

> I rejoice to learn that you are writing an opera on the *Ramayana* story. I sincerely hope it will be a success.
>
> If your scenario is type-written, I shall be very happy to look over it and to let you have any hints and suggestions that I can. But I should mention that I can only be of help in reference to the wording of the story, etc.--for I have no knowledge of music, either European or Indian.[4]

Just exactly how long it took Holst to complete the translation for *Sita* is unknown, but he would take over six years to complete the opera itself. At least two instrumental works influenced by Sanskrit literature preceded its completion: *Maya* [H55] (1903?), a romance for violin and piano, and the orchestral symphonic poem *Indra*, Op. 13 [H66] (1903). Musically, these works are in Holst's developing style, which at this time could be classified as late romantic; neither these nor those that followed were influenced by Indian music. In spite of their titles, Holst was writing western works for western instruments. He never went to India, although it is likely that he heard Indian music at soirees and festivals.

Perhaps it was Sanskrit that served as a catalyst for Holst's creativity for, in spite of all that he had to do in order to stay afloat financially, 1899 was a good year for composition. He completed the *Walt Whitman Overture*, Op. 7 [H42], written in deference to the American poet whose works he had been reading during his involvement with the socialist movement. Of more importance than the overture is the *Suite de Ballet in E Flat*, Op. 10 [H43], the earliest of Holst's orchestral works to have attained a permanent (yet tenuous) place in the orchestral repertoire. Its four movements are "Dance rustique," "Valse," "Scene de Nuit," and "Carnival" (which, as a separate movement, is programmed far more often than the suite). Bandsmen are often surprised to discover that the more mature *First Suite in E Flat for Military Band*, Op. 28 No. 1 [H105] (1909) was neither Holst's first suite nor his first suite in that particular key.

Holst also started work at this time on *The Cotwolds: Symphony in F*, Op. 8 [H47] in 1899, finishing it while on the following year on July 24 at Skegness. This was the first symphony that Holst claimed as his own; he more or less disowned his very early *Symphony in C Minor* [App I, 14], wrapping it up in the bundle of works from his Cheltenham and Royal College of Music student periods that he labelled "Early Horrors."

The Cotswolds: Symphony in F is in the four traditional movements: "Allegro con brio," "Molto Adagio (Elegy In Memoriam William Morris)," "Presto (Scherzo)," and "Allegro moderato."[5] The 19-page "Allegro con brio," perhaps the weakest of the four, features the severely classical orchestration of woodwinds, horns, trumpets, and timpani in pairs, in addition to the customary strings. The "Adagio" that follows is perhaps the most impressive movement of the piece; it bears the dedication "In Memoriam William Morris." In mood, at least, it foreshadows the shorter but more mature *A Dirge for Two Veterans* [H121] (1914). For this movement (and the remainder of the symphony) Holst adds two additional horns, a third trumpet (*ad lib.*), three trombones, a tuba, and enhances the percussion. The "Scherzo" is quite substantial and adventurous, featuring a ten-bar segment in six sharps concert. The "Allegro moderato," not intended to be a rousing finish, is in a lilting 6/4. An unusual thing about this symphony is that there are no repeat signs in any of the movements. Neither the *Walt Whitman Overture* nor this symphony would be published during Holst's lifetime and the *Suite de Ballet in E flat* was not published until 1914, long after a drastic change had taken place in Holst's compositional style.

It is important for the author to take a bit of a digression at this point. Neither contempory critics nor those up to the present era have been kind regarding Holst's work prior to 1906. It is important to realize two things: 1) that Holst was a "late bloomer," so to speak, and his own particular compositional style, which began to surface with *Two Songs without Words* [H88] (1906), would not firmly establish itself until about the last decade of his life and 2) that Holst would naturally write in a late romantic style at the turn of the century and that there was nothing wrong with this. A look at Holst's contemporaries shows that Arnold Schoenberg (1874-1951), born in the same year as Holst, still had not bent totally toward atonality at this time and Serge Rachmaninoff (1873-1943), born one year earlier, would remain a romantic throughout his entire life. Even Igor Stravinsky, eight years younger, produced his Rimsky-Korsakov inspired *Symphony No. 1 in E flat*, Op. 1 as late as 1907. Although not masterpieces, works such as *The Cotswolds: Symphony in F* and the *Walt Whitman Overture* do deserve occasional hearings.

Although *The Cotswolds: Symphony in F* was much larger in scope, Holst's most significant work of 1900 may have been his *Ave Maria*, Op. 9[B] [H49] for unaccompanied eight-part women's chorus. The earliest of Holst's choruses for women's voices to enter the repertoire, it was first performed May 23, 1901 at St. James' Hall by the Magpie Madrigal Society under the direction of Lionel Benson. This was the same organization and conductor that had premiered *Light Leaves Whisper* some four years earlier. Vaughan Williams commented about *Ave Maria* and *Sita*:

> My Dear V.
>
> I am ashamed at not having written to you before. I will first thank you for the 'Ave Maria' which I still think beautiful as I always did. I have [been] playing it over and pointing out its beauties to a cousin of mine who sings in the Magpies and have persuaded her to take an interst in it.
>
> I admire Sita very much--I had some criticisms to make but I can't remember what they are--and to tell you the truth I feel too lazy tonight to find the drawer where I have put it away.
>
> I think the chief criticism was levelled against the dressing up device--which seems to me rather mechanical and not quite 'rein menschlich' enough. Also it is not quite 'inevitable' to fit in with the fantastic nature of the rest of the plot....
>
> Y
>
> R.V.W.[6]

Concerned about his own use of counterpoint and possible publication, Holst sent a copy of *Ave Maria* to Ebenezer Prout, theorist, author and editor of the infamous "Victorian edition" of Handel's *Messiah*. Prout, who was on the faculty at the Royal Academy of Music at that time, wrote to Holst:

246 Richmond Road
Hackney, N.E.
4 March 1901.

Dear Sir,

Accepting thanks for your 'Ave Maria', which I found awaiting me at the R.A.M.[7] this morning. It is very ingeniuosly written, and I do not think the counterpoint too free. Nobody would expect such a piece to be written in Strict Counterpoint. I am afraid that the fact of it being written for 8 part female chorus will prevent it having a large sale; there are very few female choirs good enough to divide into eight parts without coming to grief.

I am sorry I shall not be able to do anything for it myself, as I have no connection with any choir at all.

Thanking you for your kind expression with regard to my books,

I am dear Sir,
Yours very faithfully,

Ebenezer Prout[8]

Ironically, publication of *Ave Maria* by Laudy actually preceded its premiere. It was a very welcome event, for about the only other works that Holst was able to get published during these years were pot boilers (usually for violin and piano, voice and piano, or piano solo) which did nothing for his status as a composer.

While things remained frustrating for Holst on the publications front (and they would continue to be so for a number of years), his employment picture improved drastically in 1900 when he was offered the position of second trombonist with the Scottish Orchestra. The orchestra, which performed at the Paterson Concerts at McEwen Hall in Glasgow, was conducted by Frederick H. Cowan, who was new to the organization that year. Cowen was well in demand; in that same year he had also assumed the conductorship of the Liverpool Philharmonic and had just resumed conducting the Philharmonic Society of London after an eight year hiatus.

Musically, the decision to accept the position was not a difficult one for Holst to make. The Scottish Orchestra was a much more disciplined group than the Carl Rosa Opera Company; it also performed at a much higher level. There were some drawbacks, however. One was the fact that the Scottish Orchestra was based in Glasgow, and Holst had to live away from Isobel during the season. The salary that he drew from the Scottish probably would have been sufficient for two people to live on in Glasgow, and one would imagine that naturally Holst and Isobel would relocate to Scotland once they were married. Holst, however, did not see himself as only a performer; composing was his passion and for that he felt it necessary to maintain a London base. Therefore a good portion of what he earned with the Scottish was spent on travel between Glasgow and London. Another drawback to the position was that the Scottish Orchestra's season was more intense than that of the Carl Rosa. There were as many as four concerts per week and such a heavy rehearsal and peformance schedule left Holst little time for composing. This is evidenced by the fact that the 1901 page of Holst's "List of Compositions" is the only page in the entire book that is blank!

There were additional reasons for that blank page. One was the continued bout with neuritis. A letter from Parry confirms this:

Prince Consort Road
South Kensington
Royal College of Music London. SW.

April 2, 1901

My dear von Holst

I am very sorry to hear you are so sadly handicapped by writer's cramp. Of course I shall be delighted to be of any help I can in recommending you for a theatre band or for teaching theory, if any chance turns up. I hope I shall hear your Agnus[9] next term. I heard that it came out very well, and thought it would when I looked at it. Unfortunately I have had to be away for some time--quite bowled over through overwork, so I missed hearing the Choral Class singing it this term.

Better luck another time.

Very sincerely yours

C. Hubert H. Parry[10]

Another reason for the blank page is that Holst was side-tracked by a major event in his life. On June 22, 1901 he and Isobel were married in a civil ceremony at the Fulham Registrar's Office. Their first place of residence was a small two-room apartment at 162 Shepherd's Bush Road, just north of Hammersmith. They were in only the eighth week of wedded bliss when news arrived that Holst's father Adolph had died suddenly on August 17 at the age of fifty-five. Holst's ties with Cheltenham were loosening fast--his brother Emil had long since run away from home, his father had now passed away and soon his step-mother and Thorley would emigrate to California. Holst was slated to receive a small inheritance from Adolph's estate but this was tied up for the next year and a half due to the slowness of the courts.

Holst's compositional activity was operating at a slow grind. 1901 (during which time he made some progress on *Sita* and other works) had been blank and 1902 was not a great year for composition either. He completed two of the *Five Part-Songs*, Op. 12 [H61] and, more prophetically, the first of his Sanskrit-inspired vocal works: "Invocation to the Dawn," No. 1 of *Six Songs*, Op. 15 for baritone and piano. His major work that year was *The Youth's Choice*, Op. 11 [H60], described as "A Musical Idyll in one act," for four vocal soloists and orchestra. Holst supplied his own libretto and had some solicited advice from Ralph Vaughan Williams who wrote, "You'll think me a very 'destructive' critic--as I have scratched out most of your lines. I think the whole scheme of the verses is bad."[11] He followed this up with a detailed criticsm of various parts. Holst revised the work and had the libretto translated into Italian by Linetta Palamidessi da Castelvecchio in Cheltenham, since the work was intended for a contest sponsored by Sonzogno, a Milan publisher.[12] Signorina Palamidessi da Castelvecchio was a great great niece of Napoleon I and was later Professor of Italian at the University of Birmingham. Although having a proper translation was an absolute necessity, it made no difference in the long run; *The Youth's Choice* did not win the contest.

Even if 1902 was disappointing in terms of composing, all was not lost, for the highlight of the year for Holst was that for the first time ever he was able to hear a work of his performed by a professional orchestra. Dan Godfrey, youngest member of the Godfrey military band dynasty, was conductor of the Bouremouth Orchestra, on England's south coast. Godfrey was a champion of English music and was always searching for formidable works by living English composers. On April 24, 1902 Godfrey's orchestra premiered *The Cotswolds: Symphony in F* at the Bournemouth Winter Gardens. It was the collaboration of the second generation; Adolph von Holst had performed as piano soloist with the Grenadier Guards Band under the direction of Daniel Godfrey (Godfrey's father) on December 14, 1878, during the band's visit to Cheltenham.[13]

Holst and Isobel left London at four o'clock in the morning in order to be there for the rehearsal, which in itself did not go smoothly. Imogen Holst comments:

> That rehearsal was an appalling experience for Gustav. To begin with, there were the inevitable mistakes in the parts. But what he found so unnerving was the way that Dan Godfrey kept calling out: "Do you mean G or G flat there in the violas? when he was feeling too over-wrought to remember what he had meant. And to make matters even more difficult, in the middle of the rehearsal several members of the orchestra had to go out and play selections on the pier. When things were at their very worst, Vaughan Williams walked in and sat behind Gustav; he listened to a few bars, and then leaned over and said, 'I like this.'
>
> After that it was all right.[14]

The performance was reasonably well-received. Godfrey appears to have forgotten about it altogether, for he made no mention of it in his 1924 autobiography *Memories and Music.* He did remember Holst for his later appearances and conveyed the following story that is so Holstian that it deserves mentioning here:

> Of the younger British composers, there is none for whom I have greater regard than Gustav Holst, whose acquaintence I first made when he came to Bournemouth to conduct his "Somerset Rhapsody" in November, 1911....Now [1924] he is worthily famous, not only for his genius as a composer but for his work at Morley College. He assisted at our 1922 Festival and for that purpose cycled from town. On the Sunday morning he arrived at my house in a somewhat disshevelled condition and rang the bell. My wife leaned out the window--we lived in an upper flat--and, seeing someone with a dirty haversack on his back, concluded that he was the newspaper man and told him to leave the papers in the service lift. Then he called out, "I am Gustav Holst; I want to see Mr. Godfrey." My wife quickly admitted him, and as I was resting in bed after a heavy week's work he was shown into my bedroom. As he entered he cried out, "I have brought the papers." It was not until he had gone that I saw the joke.[15]

The estate of Adolph von Holst was finally settled by early 1903. The inheritance awarded Holst was not large, but it was sufficient enough to allow him and his wife to take a long-postponed honeymoon to Germany during the Scottish

Orchestra's winter hiatus. Holst, who had not been out of the country previously, approached the trip as a combined honeymoon and working holiday. The early Sansrit works seemed to have benefitted the most; he had time to chip away at *Sita* and to complete his symphonic poem *Indra*. In addition to this, Holst and Isobel did some copying for Vaughan Williams.

This extended holiday also gave him plenty of time to contemplate the future. Holst was at a the most important crossroads of his career. He enjoyed playing with the Scottish Orchestra, but was it and the other necessary income-producing activities that came along with it getting in the way of his development as a composer? The Berlin holiday allowed Holst to clear his head. The twenty-eight year old composer shared many of his deepest concerns in a telling series of letters to Ralph Vaughan Williams. Some of the correspondence is lost; the first four pages of this first surviving letter are missing:

> In the evening we went to some friend of Gertrude Peppercorn. There was an artist there who told my wife that he learnt English from some sailors and some gold diggers from Australia and was slightly surprised when on his first speaking English at a Dinner party all the ladies got up and left the room!!![16] Yesterday (Sunday) I went ticket buying in the biggest gale (with snow) I ever remember. 'Was ihr wollt' in the afternoon was 'Twelfth Night' and was a failure somehow or another. Today we had lunch with Matthias[17] and his family. Alas! I am learning to swill beer and wine like a native. Afterwards we had an hour in the National Gallery. Do you know the Arnold Boecklin room? Gorgeous. Nearly all the pictures were added after your Baedeker came out.
>
> Jesus sent me a postcard this morning--I am going to see him at 9:30 tomorrow.
>
> Great news--I have written three postcards and two letters in German! The recipients talk of having them framed!! Rather a doubtful compliment I fear.
>
> I have been trying to think where we (you and I) are and where we come in and what we ought to do.
>
> (Being together so much I think we work along in much the same way but I may be wrong).
>
> To begin with I think we crawl along too slowly--of course it is something to get along at all and I do not think our progress is very genuine--but there ought to be more.
>
> The 'getting on' theory is damned rot. Howard[18] and Harford[19] both spoil themselves by it. It seems to give them a sort of hardness and I feel

sorry for them both when I compare them to Gertrude Peppercorn and Mac. Don't tell this to anyone because it sounds so beastly. Of course you understand that I am really deeply sorry especially for Howard. I don't know whether Bell has it because honestly Bell is a mystery to me. I like him immensely but I cannot get into sympathy with his music.

I now think the MCC a magnificant idea and I hope it will grow but as regards our two selves I feel we ought to do a lot more but cannot think what!

Seeing foreigners is a mistake as a rule. Don't you think we ought to victimize Elgar[20]? Write to him first and then bicycle to Worcester and see him a lot? I wish we could do that together. Or else make a list of musicians in London whom we think worthy of the honour of being bothered by us and who have time and inclination to be bothered and then bother them. For instance those two fellows that Robin Legge[21] raves about. They ought to listen to all our stuff and we to all theirs. It would be dreadful while it lasted but I think the effect would be good.

Somehow we seem too comfortable--we don't strain every nerve. Anyhow I don't. And composing is a fairly impossible affair as things go even at the best of times. While I think of it, is Henry J[22] open to victimizing? We ought never to send anything to him by post if it can be avoided but always to see him.

I don't know whether you are in the same box but I feel I want to know a lot of poets and painters and other fearful wild fowl.

As for opera I am bewildered. 'Die Feuersnot'[23] is in reality quite simple and unoriginal as opera. Charpentier's 'Louise' is idiotic as opera. And I do feel sometimes inclined to chuck Sita in case it is only bad Richard I.[24] Unless one ought to follow the latter until he leads you to fresh things. What I feel is that there is nothing else but Wagner excepting Italian one act horrors.

As for conducting (which we ought to learn) it is impossible to attain in England and I fear we must give up all hopes of it. As an orchestral player I really do feel sorry, as England is crying out (unconsciously) for real conductors. Henry J. is the nearest approach...And it is not all a question of unlimited rehearsals.

Your last letter was the result of thinking matters over--this is a poor return as it is the result of waking up too early in the morning and trying to go to sleep unsuccessfully! So you must excuse if I write more than my usual allowance of rot.

Of course the matter is made rather worse for me owing to lack of cash and I feel more and more that my mode of living is very unsatisfactory. It is not so bad in London say during the 'French Milliner' when I did a fair amount of writing every day but the Worm[25] is a wicked and loathesome waste of time. Yet the only alternative I know is stick wagging for one of George Edwarde's touring companies. People who are victims of the 'getting on' theory always advise this but if one does it at all one must do it properly and then good bye to music!

There is the theory that one should get rich first and then compose.

When I was a child my father told me that Sterndale Bennett worked out a theory during his life very satisfactory. When I was older I heard Sterndale Bennett's music....

Getting rich requires a 'teshneek' of its own that some people learn slowly and others never. I don't know which class I belong to and don't care. There is no time to learn that <u>and</u> composition. Not that I believe one should cram theory from childhood. But that once having started (after school etc is over) an Englishman may think himself lucky if, after hard work, he writes anything decent before he is fifty. For now [that] I have been abroad I see what a terrible lot we have to contend against in England.

And I also feel that there is no time for pot-boiling. As tromboning is so damnably uncertain I must do it but it is really bad for one I am sure. I almost feel I can now trace its evil effect in Tchaikowsky[26] but it is a very insidious disease.

Stiil I think it would be a great thing for me if I could always live in London and say goodbye to the Worm (bye the bye I must try and get a summer engagement from him for my return in July and August!) and all seaside bands. I should be sorry to leave the Scottish for some things but it really would be better on the whole. But this is all off the main point.

If money matters were quite satisfactory with me I still should be just as puzzled as to what you and I ought to do--money matters only make things worse.

I think we are 'all right' in a mild sort of way. But then mildness is the very devil. So something must happen and we must make it happen.

While I remember--the voice parts of your opera[27] are impossible. You must not do this sort of thing. Don't show them to a singer but get <u>singers to sing them</u>. Then recollect that singing in an opera house means twice as much exertion. I think you will be convinced.

I hope that our letters will not cross any more--send me one soon. Our time is up next Monday but my wife wants to stop on while this jolly blizzard lasts as we are more or less at home in Berlin. I will let you know when we have decided and everything will be forwarded from here.

Yours Ever

G v H[28]

In a follow-up letter Holst wrote about composing. Vaughan Williams had slipped into a temporary creative rut and Holst offered some advice:

Berlin. [1903]
Monday

Dear RVW

I went to Jesus[29] but I didn't drink. He was awfully nice and kept me an hour and a half. But he said that the tune at the end of the Drapa[30] and the 'Invocation'[31] were written too much in the 'popular English style' to be of any use in Germany. In fact he seemed to think that I had written both things in order to suit Messrs Chappell & Co. If I time I would tell you about an awful German-American professor that he took me to but that must wait as I have so much to say that is more important, for the professor turned out to be an utter fraud....

In one of Parry's lectures he played all the sketches Beethoven made for the 'Eroica' Funeral March (first theme). Sketch No 1 was not all bad. No 3 was beautiful. No 6 was stupid. No 9 was bloody. The final one was a return to no 3. The moral of which is that if you spoil good stuff by working at it you must spoil the spoilation by more work. Of course waiting plays a small part but I think you are wrong in thinking that working at a theme or idea will ruin it. Even suppose the working out is not so good as the original you can always go back and then you will have the result of your experience into the bargain.[32]

I know there is a good deal to be said for the other side but I think that the only true waiting for ideas is the waiting or resting after a long spell of hard work.

Then again when you spoil good ideas is not that because you write too much--that is you go ahead too fast--instead of grinding away bar by bar which is the only true hard work?

Would it be good, do you think, for you to rewrite as a matter of course <u>everything</u> you write about six months after it is finished? (<u>Really</u> finished, not merely sketched). Whenever I have re-copied or re-scored anything, I have improved it very much. Anyhow I would never score at once--wait until your mud pie is hardened and until you can compare it in cold blood to others.

Another idea of mine is madder and perhaps even more harmful but anyhow you shall have it. Cannot invention be developed like other things? And would not it be developed by your trying to write so many themes every day? Three decent themes a day for instance (probably in trying, you would get a few more that were verging on indecency). Then at the end of the week you could see how many were worth anything.

I am sure I am right about us being too comfortable. When you work hard you merely cover a lot of ground instead of making sure of your ground as you go on. (This is not absolutely true but I think you have a tendency in that way....

As for me I think I have got careless owing to Worming[33] and pot-boiling. For I am certain that Worming is very bad for one--it makes me so sick of everything so that I cannot settle down to work properly. And pot-boiling as I have done it is bad because I got into the way of thinking that anything would do. Whereas we must write now chiefly so that we may write better in the future. So that every detail of everything we do must be as perfect as possible. For the next few years not only ought we to write more carefully than we have ever done before but more carefully than we ever need ever write again.

My wife has had another idea which I think I shall adopt. That is when when we return I shall not take any Worming job or go out of London until the Scottish begins. If I can get a theatre well and good, if not I will even accept your offer of lending me some money rather than play two or three times a day. (You see our living in London is pretty cheap). Then I should like to try to work systematically from August to November both at writing and studying music. I rather think you know music than I do, anyhow I am sure I don't know enough about Beethoven's sonatas or Schubert's songs and heaps of other things. I wonder if it would be possible to lock oneself up for so many hours every day. If so it would be far easier for me than for you as you have so many friends. I feel it would be so splendid to 'go into training' as it were, in order to make one's music as beautiful as possible. And I am sure that after a few months' steady grind we should have made the beginning of our own 'atmospheres' and so should not feel the need of going abroad so much.

For it is all that makes up an 'atmosphere' that we lack in England. I am sorry I have to make such a commonplace remark. Here people actually seem anxious to hear new music, still more wonderful, they even seem anxious to find out all about a new composer! That in itself would work a revolution in England.

Bye the bye I am certainly going to rewrite the words to Sita as you suggest. They are disgraceful and that was largely due to Worming, etc. I used to write them at odd moments.

Which reminds me--one may get hold of a decent theme on top of a bus etc but I deny utterly that one can do 'splendid work' there--especially the work we most need. I used to be proud of writing things at odd times. It was great fun but it was damned rot and it helped on my present carelessness. I should like to keep ,up this sort of correspondence all the time I am away. Don't you think it might do us good? Only you must tell me more about yourself.

One problem puzzles me. Is it really bad to write at the piano?[34] I try one or the other as it suits me best. If it is bad, wherein does the badness lie and what bad results accrue from it?....

Poste Restante, Dresden

Yours Ever

G v H[35]

He continues his advice in the next letter, possibly written at Dresden:

Tuesday

Dear RVW

....I hope you bear in mind that all the rot I write is merely a collection of stray thoughts. Well to begin with what the Hell do you mean by talking about premature decay and getting fat?

I meant 'getting old' in the sense of 'becoming mature'--that is when progress either stops or becomes slower. We must not get old over the next forty years because we have such a stiff job and

(1) you sometimes have said that you feel that 'it is time you did

something' after all these years--I forget your exact words but I have felt the same myself often but it is rot. We are not old enough and we have not had enough training of the right sort (I am coming to that).
(2) Sometimes when anything turns out an awful failure it may teach us more than a thundering success--it does not follow that it will but it may--which would be of little use if one was growing old.

So for these two reasons and for the further one that we have so much to learn and it is so difficult to find out how to learn it, we must regard ourselves as very 'E flat' chickens.

As I told you once before, Richard II[36] seems to me to be the most 'Beethovenish' composer since Beethoven. Perhaps I am wrong but anyhow you will agree that whatever his faults, he is a real life composer.

As far as I can make out his training seems to have been

(1)
Bach, Mozart, Beethoven
(2)
Schumann and Brahms
(3)
Wagner

Mine has been:

(1)
Mendelssohn
(2)
Grieg
(3)
Wagner

This alone speaks volumes.

Richard II had such a such terrific classical training that Brahms and Wagner never lifted him off his feet.[37]

Whereas I (as you say of yourself) 'don't seem to fit on to their music at all.' (Mozart and Beethoven). And I believe, as you once said about Richard II himself, that one ought to be able to feel that every composer is the result of those who have gone before him. So we must begin by feeling it about ourselves.

Now if you can prove to me that all of this is nonsense I shall be only too delighted as it is a serious thing to discover and if true it means years and years of extra study with the usual lot thrown in.

If it is true there is no one in England to teach us as far as I know. Twelve years ago Parry would have been the man. As far as I can tell, McCunn[38] has a lot to learn from you. If you really must have lessons in London I sometimes think that Stanford is the only man now that he has learnt the elements of good manners towards you. <u>But I don't want you to go to him</u>.

Could not you go to H.J.W.[39] once every two months or so and get his opinion on all you have written? (Paying him of course.)

But I believe the only good that will last will be done by struggling away on your own. Stanford is all crotchets and fads and moods although the latter have improved. And that healthy vigorous beefsteak optimism of Parry is a delusion that blinds one to the real difficulties in the way. When under a master I instinctively try to please him whereas our business is to learn to please ourselves which is far more difficult as it is so hard to find out what we want.

I thought that perhaps trying to write so many themes every day might possibly develop one's invention but I expect that is all nonsense. Anyhow I can think of no other way.

I have been trying to make up my mind as to what is the best way of settling down to compose. On the whole I think its chief ingredients are:

(1) Hard work. (But not this alone as I have always thought until now--as you say, one cannot be always composing.)
(2) Having just the very best art of all kinds.
(3) Complete change from music. To be divided into
    (a) other work or exercise, and (this is most important)
    (b) *Absolute laziness.*

All this sounds cheap and obvious but unless you can assure me that it is false there are one or two conclusions to be drawn from it. To begin with, 'Worming' is absolutely criminal. One gets wearied by false art--becomes saturated by it in fact. It is bad enough when I get sick of it but it is worse when I enter into the spirit of it and enjoy it in a beastly sort of way. Maybe one ought to do something besides composition, but it ought to be something <u>outside</u> music I think....

Are you quite sure that analysing a Beethoven sonata and then writing one in the same form would not be good? Wagner did it (see 'Grove'[40]) and he was the greatest master of form and also one of the most original of all composers. Besides is it not what all painters and poets do? It seems much more sensible to me than counterpoint....We go to Munich on Friday.

Yours

G v H[41]

Holst had more to say about the details of compositional technique in his next letter:

Munich
Saturday [1903]

We remain here until next Saturday when we bicycle away into the Tyrol for a week only and then come home to England. Do you think that is sensible? It will leave me enough money to do without a Worms job so that I can stick at home and write. Munich is lovely and so very un-English. We thought of biking to one of the lakes but not too far away though. Do you know any of them? If so just send me a post card with any bit of advice you can give. We should like boating and bathing above everything else....

Now as regards details of technique I fear I have never given them sufficient thought. And as it is always good to know one's weak points this is where you are again ahead of me. In fact this question of climaxes rather bewilders me and I shall have to leave it alone until I return. As to how to study I feel rather floored again. But what I personally should like would be to have all of Beethoven's chamber music at my fingers' ends as Wagner apparently had: to be able to wallow in it--to soak it in and make it part of one's being. That is my idea. I wish we were better players for then the Cowley Str Wobblers[42] would be of great use.

I know that awful kind of laziness you speak of. It is the very devil. But when it is very strong I almost think that it is best to give way to it.

One little dodge I sometimes try in order to cure it is to play a lot of my old stuff for ten minutes or so, so as to settle my mind on composition.

As to writing at the boiling point. this is the only real thing I feel fairly certain about. Writing at boiling point is THE very worst way of composing. Whenever I have done it, it has always turned out badly and the only good that ever came of it was when I was able to work the stuff up afresh the next day into something fairly presentable. It may be different with you but anyway I wouldn't worry about it.

Before I left Dresden I really managed to see the beauty of Veronese and I think a Rubens crowd is terrific. I always understood that Titian and Raphael were a kind of painters' Bach and Beethoven. But barring the Sistine I cannot see it all. I like Francia etc much better. By the bye is it my fault or is it a fact that in all creation there is nothing so absolutely and appallingly BLOODY as the average modern German picture. The New Pinakothek is an exaggerated nightmare to me.

Yours

G v H[43]

The Holsts returned to England with barely enough money in their pockets to make it through the summer. Still, they were able to move out of their Shepherd's Bush apartment and into new quarters south of the Thames at 31 Grena Road in the Sheen Park neighborhood of Richmond. Within walking distance of Deer Park and the Kew Gardens, the new place was in a setting much more conducive to Holst's walking habits. They were in dire need, since Holst did not take any "worming" jobs. To make up the lost income from these jobs, he wrote a couple of potboilers which brought in a little bit of money and Isobel helped supplement that feable income through some dressmaking. The largest serious work composed by Holst at that time was *King Estmere*, Op. 17 [H70], for mixed chorus and orchestra, but arguably a better work was the *Quintet in A Flat*, Op. 14 [H67][44] for woodwind quintet. Perhaps he did find time to study some of Beethoven's chamber music after all.

Holst returned to the Scottish Orchestra in November, 1903, but only for the first four concerts of the season[45]; his life was about to change forever.

---

[1]Nicholas Slonimsky (ed.), *The Concise Edition of Baker's Biographical Dictionary of Musicians*, 8th rev. ed. (New York: Schirmer Books, 1994), 840.

[2]Personal correspondence, Hubert Parry to Gustav Holst, Sept[ember] 10, [18]98, The Holst

Foundation.
[3]Michael Short, *Gustav Holst: The Man and His Music* (Oxford: Oxford University Press, 1990), 39.
[4]Personal correspondence, Ramesh Date to Gustav Holst, Dec. 17. 1901, The Holst Foundation.
[5]British Library Add MS 47814.
[6]Personal correspondence, Ralph Vaughan Williams to Gustav Holst, n.d., quoted in Ursula Vaughan Williams (ed.) and Imogen Holst (ed.), *Heirs and Rebels: Letters to Each Other and Occasional Writings by Ralph Vaughan Williams and Gustav Holst* (Oxford: Oxford University Press, 1959), 8.
[7]Royal Academy of Music.
[8]Personal correspondence, Ebenezer Prout to Gustav Holst, March 4, 1901, The Holst Foundation.
[9]Parry probably meant the *Ave Maria.* Holst did edit an "Agnus Dei" from a William Byrd mass, but that was later, in 1916.
[10]Personal correspondence, Hubert H. Parry to Gustav Holst, April 2, 1901, The Holst Foundation.
[11]*Ibid.*, 6.
[12]Michael Short, *op. cit.*, 45.
[13]*Programme*, Band of the Grenadier Guards, Daniel Godfrey, conductor, December 14, 1878.
[14]Imogen Holst, *Gustav Holst: A Biography*, 2nd ed. (Oxford: Oxford university Press, 1969), 23-24.
[15]Sir Dan Godfrey, *Memories and Music: Thirty-five Years of Conducting* (London: Hutchinson, 1924), 195.
[16]This was not the only time Holst would provide humorous commentary about the misuse of English. See his January 26, 1932 letter to his daughter Imogen quoted in the New York chapter.
[17]Holst's distant German cousin Matthias Johann von Holst, not to be confused with Holst's English half brother, Matthias ("Max") Ralph Bromley von Holst.
[18]Possibly Evlyn Howard-Jones.
[19]Probably Francis Harford, singer and composer.
[20]Edward Elgar.
[21]Critic with *The Times.*
[22]Henry Joseph Wood (1869-1944), eminent British conductor who, at the time of Holst's letter, was best known for "The Proms," series of concerts held in Queen's Hall.
[23]Richard Strauss' 1901 one-act opera.
[24]Richard Wagner.
[25]Stanislaus Würm, conductor of the White Viennese Band.
[26]Holst held this opinion of Tchaikovsky's music throughout his life. The arranger Henry Geehl recalls a disagreement that he and Holst had over Tchaikovsky's work in his article "The Unrecognized Arranger," published in *The Conductor*, April, 1960, 8.
[27]This may have referred to the vocal parts on Vaughan Williams *'A Sea Symphony'* or to a discarded work. His first opera, *Hugh the Drover*, dates from 1911-14.
[28]Personal correspondence, Gustav Holst to Ralph Vaughan Williams, n.d. [1903], British Library Add MS 57853.
[29]This is an unidentified musician, possibly of Spanish birth.
[30]*Ornulf's Drapa*, Op. 6 [H34].
[31]"Invocation to the Dawn," from *Six Songs*, Op. 15 [H68].
[32]Holst held this opinion throughout his life. He left extensive sketches for some of his compositions, particularly *Hammersmith.* He also insisted that his students spoil a lot of paper as well and had a difficult time accepting the esoteric and argumentative approaches in vogue at Harvard University when he was lecturing there in 1932.

[33]Playing with Stanislaus Würm and the White Viennese Band.
[34]During his student years at the Royal College of Music, Holst did not have a piano in his apartment.
[35]Personal correspondence, Gustav Holst to Ralph Vaughan Williams, Berlin. [1903], British Library Add MS 57853.
[36]Richard Strauss.
[37]Many readers will vehemently disagree with this, but then Holst's letter was written in 1903, before Strauss's composed many of his operatic masterpieces, including *Salome* and *Elektra.*
[38]Scottish composer Hamish McCunn (1868-1916).
[39]Henry Joseph Wood.
[40]The primary work of Sir George Grove (1820-1900) was the *Dictionary of Music and Musicians*, completed in 1889. The most recent edition edition at the time of this writing is the sixth, which still bears his name. At the time of Holst's letter a second edition, under the editorship of J. A. Fuller Maitland, was in its early stages.
[41]Personal correspondence, Gustav Holst to Ralph Vaughan Williams, Tuesday [1903, Dresden?], British library Add MS 57853.
[42]An amateur string quartet in which Vaughan Williams played viola and his wife Adeline played cello.
[43]Personal correspondence, Gustav Holst to Ralph Vaughan Williams, Munich, Saturday [1903], British Library Add MS 57853
[44]In 1914 Holst sent the manuscript of the work to flautist Albert Fransella. What Fransella did with it is uncertain and the manscript was considered to be lost until 1952, when it was purchased by a London flautist from a private owner.
[45]*The Scotsman*, May [26], 1934.

CHAPTER III

GIRLS' SCHOOLS AND FOLK TUNES

Holst entered the teaching profession through the back door. He was still playing with the Scottish Orchestra in the autumn of 1903 when Ralph Vaughan Williams asked him to substitute for him on a number of occasions at James Allen's Girls' School (known as JAGS), East Dulwich Grove, in Southeast London. The school was founded in 1741 as the Reading School; it was later known as the Free School, the Dulwich Girls' School, and finally, on its present site, as James Allen's Girls' School. It had a fine reputation. When Vaughan Williams tired of the position and decided to leave it the following year, Holst was asked if he wanted to replace him. The offer had its merits. Teaching there meant having a permanent part-time day job in London, one which would practically eliminate travel expenses, allow him to spend more time with Isobel, and give him additional time for composing. It also meant having to give up the Scottish Orchestra, but Holst saw the orchestra as part of a package that included playing a lot of dreaded outside engagements. He decided to take the risk and on April 20, 1904 accepted the position in Class Singing on probation at JAGS; on September 16th the position was made permanent.[1]

Barbara Kley, Head of the JAGS Music Department from 1960 to 1980, offers the following commentary about Holst's work at the school:

> With the advent of Gustav Holst in 1903...things changed and soon the Friday singing classes became something approaching a highlight of the week. Holst would arrive early in the morning in order to play for the hymn at Prayers and he introduced many of the fine tunes in the English Hymnal in the preparation of which he had a large share. He also

> inaugurated the singing of carols by the whole school in the Hall of the last Friday of the Christmas term, again introducing many less well-known carols, and it seems that this practice continued for some years after he gave up teaching at JAGS. Apart from singing classes, Holst also formed a small orchestra which was described in the school magazine of Spring 1925: 'Although [it] was very small, so great was its conductor's energy and compelling power, that to its great surprise it got through the "Water Music" of Handel at the first Prize Giving after its inauguration.'[2]

Holst's initial salary, £50 per annum, was eventually raised to £75 and, due to a Special War Grant, increased by another £3 starting in September,1916.[3] £50 was a reasonable sum in 1904 for an appointment that involved teaching only on Fridays.

Some members of the music profession would have viewed (and some unenlightened souls would still view) this step--going from a professional performance position to that of a music teacher--as a step in the wrong direction. This was not the case for Holst, for teaching came to him as naturally as composing did. Accepting the JAGS post was, in fact, only the first step toward a personal fulfillment which would come to him only through teaching. Over time he would establish many real friendships through teaching. One of his pupils at the school was Dorothy Callard, who continued her studies with Holst at Morley College and become instrumental in many of his future efforts. Several of the school's alumnae (referred to as the JAGS Old Girls) have written reminiscences about Holst:

> The first thing I remember about Mr. Von Holst is that he insisted willy-nilly on dispensing with a "chaperone," a mistress seated near him on the platform keeping watch over us and quite obviously unnecessary. He had been preceded by a shy and shaggy young man, his friend, who had deputised for him until he was available and who taught us some difficult and rather dull songs. He should have known better since he was a folk song specialist. His name was Ralph Vaughan Williams. We should never have guessed how famous he would become though I think we recognised quite early Gustav Holst's genius. It was he who gave us the folk songs we loved.... [Violet Kelsey-Smith, left JAGS in 1907]
>
> Gustav Holst came one day a week for senior singing and choir. One day he brought [his daughter] Imogen, aged eighteen months; she sat on the Hall table and conducted. [Nora Edmed, JAGS 1906-1915]

What glorious times we had singing with him! I shall never forget one day in the hall when we were left to do just that whilst all the mistresses went to a meeting. We were singing the Marseillaise when a tremendous thunderstorm [began] and the world became quite dark and we all went on singing to the thunder and the flashes although we couldn't see him at all up on the platform. [Margaret Jepps (1969)]

On the afternoon of one Founder's Day we celebrated by dancing on the grass some of the old country and morris dances. Mr. Holst produced his fiddle and, from the shade of an old oak, came the haunting strains of music so familiar to those who love the old country airs. [Evelyn Hile, JAGS 1896-1907][4]

I could not help recalling my school days, now 53 years ago, at which time Gustav von Holst was music master at the school. Fortunately for me he chose his choir when I was at the school. I remember standing at the piano while he played and asked me to sing. Afterwards my name was called, I had been chosen as a member of the Choir--the only one out of a form[5] of nineteen pupils. How beautifully he taught us to sing--such care and such patience. I do not think that any member of the Choir could forget his interpretation of "Knowest thou the Lord?" We did not fail him on speech day. [Elizabeth E. Curtis (nee Ward)][6]

Everybody loved him and did her utmost to make a pleasant noise for him. He liked brisk, vivid songs and maintained in his gentle, cajoling voice that 'we could sing loudly, without shouting.' [Alma Digby (nee Buley)][7]

Barbara Kley offers an additional commentary from a JAGS Old Girl:

One of Holst's pupils, Olive Cooper, remembers having her piano lessons with him on an upright piano in the gym. Girls were not allowed to play on the grand in the Hall. He was, she says, very kindly and patient. He wore his half-rimmed spectacles well down his nose and apparently carried no wrist or pocket watch, which might have accounted for his frequent late arrival--and sometimes early departure. Olive Cooper recalls that her lessons always included some theory and some aural work and that Holst maintained that scales are more necessary than the pupil ever imagines. She also has a vivid recollection of the Friday afternoon singing

> classes when, at a certain point, Holst would call upon any individuals to sing a solo. The girls would often anticipate him by asking to leave the room, but he soon got wise to this and dealt with it accordingly![8]

1904 also saw Holst conduct an orchestra in public for the first time. The Royal College of Music Patron's Fund for the encouragement of young composers, had been established during the previous year through a £20,000 gift by S. Ernest Palmer. The Patron's Fund's purpose was to provide the opportunity for open rehearsals with professional orchestras in the hands of experienced conductors, charging them with the important task of bringing young British composers and performers to the public ear.[9] At the Patron's Fund concert of May 20, 1904, six composers' works were performed. Holst conducted his own *Suite de Ballet in E Flat*. According to *The Times*, the work went over quite well:

> Mr. [William] Hurlstone's superb, even masterly "Fantasie-variations on a Swedish air and Mr. von Holst's orchestral suite in E flat, which have health and happiness written all over them, towered to our thinking. over the rest of the programme.[10]

The reviewer from the *Daily Graphic* was just as encouraging, saying "Mr. von Holst will have no reason to be ashamed of his early work in years to come."[11]

In terms of composition, Holst was feeling more comfortable than he had for some time. In 1904 he was able to finish his *Six Songs*, Op. 16 [H69] for soprano and piano and the underrated *The Mystic Trumpeter*, Op. 18 [H71], a scena for soprano and orchestra set to Walt Whitman's "From Noon to Starry Night" from *Leaves of Grass*. Whitman's writings generally assert the worth of the individual and the universality of all humanity. For Holst, they were complementary to William Morris' socialism and medievalism. It is not difficult to see why Holst was inspired by this American poet. Holst would revisit Whitman more than once.

The Mystic Trumpeter is of considerable interest in that it anticipates the open fifths trumpet calls later used by Holst in a more aleatoric fashion in the *Incidental Music for The Pageant of London* [H114] (1910), the brass calls in "Mars" of *The Planets* as well as the more subtle usage of the rising fifth in the "Scherzo" from *A Moorside Suite*. It was premiered on June 29, 1905 at another Royal College of Music Patron's concert at Queen's Hall featuring Cicely Gleeson-White as soprano soloist and Holst as conductor of the London Symphony and Royal College of Music orchestras. One critic's comment about the work being a "magnificent failure"[12] seems to have been overemphasised; the overall reaction of the press was more positive than negative and, in the opinions of at least two critics, the composer of the work showed promise:

> Mr. Gustav von Holst's "The Mystic trumpeter" for voice and orchestra, proved very modern, and at times wild, but the composer has talent.[13]

> The most ambitious work of the evening was Mr. von Holst's 'The Mystic Trumpeter' for voice and orchestra....Mr. von Holst possesses ideas--simple, strong, and interesting--and he has the fire and temperament of a true-born musician-poet. The treatment of his orchestra was entirely modern, and he gained his efforts by intelligent and happy combinations, not by mere multiplication of sound. The middle parts were based to a great extent on thematic material, and that was the post-Wagnerian polyphonic treatment present that we look for in modern orchestral work. Altogether we place high hopes in Mr. von Holst's career, and trust to see him become more and more individual and clarified, when he has emerged out of his "Sturm und Drang" period.[14]

As the result of this performance, *The Mystic Trumpeter* was performed the following season by the Philharmonic Society. Still, if one had to identify a single work of Holst from 1904-05 that has best survived the temporal element, it would have to be his four-part strophic setting of Christina Rossetti's 1872 poem, "In the Bleak Mid-winter" [H73]. This peaceful Christmas hymn was the first of three that Holst was requested to write for *The English Hymnal*, then being compiled for use in the Anglican Church. Ironically, Ralph Vaughan Williams, an avowed atheist with occasional leanings towards agnosticism, was the hymnal's musical editor.

In the fall of 1904 Holst took on another teaching position. The Passmore Edwards Settlement[15], located not far from Euston Station in Bloomsbury, offered evening instruction to adults. Once again it was Ralph Vaughan Williams who was a factor in Holst's being hired. Vaughan Williams was already known at the Settlement, for he and his wife Adeline had played in a string quartet there during the tenure of Holst's predecessor, Richard Walthew. It may have been through Vaughan Williams' suggestion that Holst was hired to fill the vacancy created by Walthew's departure. Yet is wasn't just Vaughan Williams who was willing to speak up for Holst. After being in London on and off for the past eleven years, the composer had acquired a number of rather distinguished supporters. Among them was Hubert Parry, who supplied the following general letter of recommendation, full of the "healthy vigorous beefsteak optimism" to which

Holst had referred during the previous year:

> Royal College of Music
> Prince Consort Road
> South Kensington
> London. S. W.
> July 19, 1904
>
> I have the honour to state that Mr. Gustav von Holst was a pupil of the Royal College of Music for sixteen terms between May 1893 and July 1898 taking composition, organ, pianoforte, trombone, harmony and counterpoint as his studies. He attained to a distinguished position in the highest grades for composition, organ, trombone, harmony and counterpoint, and was an Open Scholarship for Composition in 1895. He proved himself a musician of exceptionally varied and ample equipment, of high intelligence and artistic insights; and his formal record during his whole time at the College was as good as possible.
>
> He has since had considerable experience as a teacher and has made considerable marks as a composer. It would be difficult to speak too well of him whether as a Musician or as an individual.
>
> C. Hubert H. Parry
> Director R.C.M.[16]

Parry himself had been the beneficiary of increased political credentials since Holst's departure from the Royal College of Music. He was knighted in 1898 and made a baronet in 1903.

Holst's hiring at The Passmore Edwards Settlement established the teaching pattern that he would adhere to for the next two decades--youth during the day, adults in the evening. He did whatever it took to make both of his teaching programs successful and this "leg work" set the stage for his even more successful ventures at St. Paul's Girls' School and Morley College. Friends were often brought in to help out. In addition to singing, Isobel played cello and bass and the Vaughan Williams's sang or played whatever was needed. Others were brought in as featured soloists. Francis Harford, for example, performed (and possibly premiered) "The Sergeant's Song" from *Six Songs*, Op. 15 [H68] at the Settlement.

Repertoire was often difficult to find, especially for James Allen's Girls' School. Holst did what classics he could there; Lasso's *Adoremus Te*, Vittoria's *Duo Seraphim* and Brahms' *Four Part Songs*, Op. 17 were all a part of the JAGS repertoire.[17] At that time publishers did not offer much quality literature appropriate for school choirs, especially choirs in girls' schools. Sometime after he started his teaching at St. Paul's Girls' School in 1905, Holst wrote to a friend:

> I find the question of getting music for girls' schools perfectly hopeless. I get reams of twaddle sent me periodically, and that is all the publishers seem to think is suitable for girls. So I have had some di Lasso and Palestrina lithographed for St. Paul's.[18]

Thus out of sheer desperation Holst often found himself arranging and even composing in order to fill this void. Within his first full year at James Allen's Girls' School, Holst had already written a piece for his students there. Alfred Lord Tennyson's 1847 blank verse poem about a royal feminist, "The Princess" provided the source material for *Songs from "The Princess,"* Op. 20[A] [H80] (1905). Two of the five songs, "Sweet and low" and "The splendour falls," contain the Holstian trait of an echo chorus. In the latter, the echo chorus fades, anticipating its usage in "Neptune" of *The Planets*. Holst also composed a sixth song for this group, "Home they brought her warrior dead" [H81], which was catalogued separately. Evelyn Hile comments:

> The school was most fortunate in having for a number of years such a celebrity as Mr. Holst as a visiting singing master. During his tenure at J.A.G.S., Miss Lloyd and Miss Jones produced Tableaux from Tennyson's "The Princess" and Mr. Holst composed the well-known music for the songs that occurred in the poems--a great honour for the school.
>
> I shall never forget the wonderful echo effect he produced by making the choir walk backwards down the stone corridor. It was a masterly device and the memory of those lovely songs so beautifully rendered made a lasting impression which even today after so many years remains vividly with me.[19]

Holst dedicated *Songs from "The Princess"* to James Allen's Girls' School.

The dirth of suitable published repertoire for girls' school chorus was eventually relieved somewhat with the publication Donald Tovey's edition of *Laudate...Pueri...Sacred Music of the XVIth Century for high voices being the first Part of the Northlands Singing Book* in 1910. The volume contained thirty-four selections altogether: thirty-one pieces from sixteenth centruy composers (di Lasso, Victoria, Palestrina, Gabrieli, Croce, Constantini, and Agostini), and three from Mozart ("Two Rounds" and a "Kyrie for Five

Sopranos"). Intended for ecclesiatical boys choruses, the book served Holst's purposes extremely well.

Sometimes Holst's search for suitable repertoire from other composers yielded some very positive results and even at this early stage of his teaching career his students were doing English premieres of important works. The first complete performance of J. S. Bach's *Peasant Cantata*, (*Mer hahn en neue Oberkeet*) [No. 212] (1742) in England, for example, was given by the Passmore Edwards Settlement Choral Society on November 5, 1905. One month later *The Musical Standard* carried an article about their December 10th concert, when two more Bach cantatas, *Schmuecke dich, o liebe Seele* [No. 180] (1724) and *Es ist nichts Gesundes an meinem Leibe* [No. 25] (1723) were performed for the first time in England. The hall's size could not accommodate the crowd and the concert had to be repeated.[20] *The Morning Leader* cited, "The work done at Passmore Edwards Settlement deserves more publicity than is accorded to it."[21]

About this same time there was a growing awareness of the aesthetic import of folk music not only throughout England, but in other countries as well. Nationalistic use of folk melodies by composers was nothing new of course, but the systematic collecting of these songs offered a different way of dealing with them. Composers and music educators found in them new sources of inspiration. In Hungary, Bela Bartok and Zoltan Kodaly were collecting folk songs and employing them in musical compositions. Kodaly would later use them as one of his bases for developing his system of music education, incorporating ideas from many lands, including those used much earlier by John Curwen at the Tonic Sol-fa College in London.

In England modern interest in endemic folk songs and folk dances actually started long before the turn of the century. In 1843 the Reverend John Broadwood published a small collection of Sussex folk songs.[22] This spurred interest on the part of others, particularly his niece Lucy who became one of the most prolific collectors of folk songs of her time. In 1898 Lucy Broadwood, Frank Kidson, and J. A. Fuller Maitland founded the English Folk-Song Society. The society remained relatively inactive for the first few years of its existence until Cecil Sharp joined the committee in 1904. Sharp was an Englishman who, after a brief turn as a lawyer in Australia, returned to his native land in 1892 and became a music teacher. More than any other person Sharp provided the impetus for what eventually became known as "First English Folk-Song Revival," publishing more than forty editions of folk songs. He also collected more folk songs than anybody else; from about 1903 onwards he collected nearly 5,000 English folk songs and songs of English origin from the Appalachian Mountains in the United States. Holst, with his wry sense of humor, frequently used "C#" to stand for any written references to or about Cecil Sharp.

One of the first collectors of folk songs in the twentieth century was Percy Grainger. Grainger not only travelled the countryside but also searched the workhouses for folk songs. What made Grainger's contribution unique is that he carried around with him an early phonograph with wax cylinders, making him the first person in the British Isles to actually record folk music as a part of his field work.[23] Vaughan Williams also did his fair share of collecting--actually considerably more than his fair share. He collected more than 800 songs. It was through Vaughan Williams that Holst became interested in the English folk song. Although it is doubtful that Holst collected any folk songs himself, it was his settings of folk songs and dances as well as his use of their inherent qualities in his own original compositions that forever tied his name to the First English Folk-Song Revival.

The folk song influence began to enter Holst's music writing around 1906 and a change in his own personal style had begun to emerge. There has long been a tendency for musicologists and others to define three compositional periods in the lives of composers; the works of some composers fall into defined periods more easily than others, the classic example being Beethoven. For Beethoven, as for most composers, there is a large grey area between periods; there will always be arguments about whether the *Symphony No. in 2 in D*, Op. 36 (1802) and the *Piano Concerto No. 3 in c, Op. 37* (1803) belong to the first or second periods or whether the *Namensfeier Overture*, Op. 115 (1814-15) belongs to the second or third. For Holst, this grey area between his first two periods, if it had yet existed, was interrupted by his <u>deliberate</u> adoption of the English folk song. The unlikely Wagner-Gilbert & Sullivan pairing of styles that had so heavily permeated his writing at the turn of the century had now either been joined by or, upon occasion, superseded by an even more unlikely pairing of influences: Sanskrit and the English folk song. Blatant chromaticism had now taken a back seat to modal harmonies. While the earlier Sanskrit works (including all of those cited up to this point) still sound much like latter-day Wagner, those that followed generally display a leaner, more direct approach. In her 1937 biography of her father's life, Imogen Holst wrote "folk-songs finally banished the traces of Wagner from his work."[24] This is not entirely accurate. Some of the most beautiful passages in *Savitri*, Op. 25 [H96] (1908-09), and the collapse of the London Bridge in the "Second Battle Music" of the *Incidental Music for The Pageant of London* [H114] (1910) are only two examples in which the more romantic Holst comes to the fore. These are neither aberrations nor excesses, for in these temporary diversions from modal economy the composer has pooled his resources most effectively.

Holst's first attempts at dealing with the English folk song came in the form of arranging a large group of these songs for voice and piano. The sixteen *Folk Songs from Hampshire* [H83] (1906) were published in 1909 as Book III of *Folk-Songs of England*, a project edited by Cecil Sharp. These folksongs were collected by Dr. G. B. Gardiner, with the help of Charles Gamblin, H. Balfour Gardiner, and J. F. Guyer. Holst's concern for his inexperience in harmonizing folk songs is displayed in a letter to Cecil Sharp:

> I send you two arrangements from Dr. Gardiner's folksongs in order for you to decide whether I am to arrange his Hampshire tunes for your Novello series or not. I have no wish to do this unless you are quite sure that you have not got anyone better. Personal feelings should not enter into these matters at all and I shall most cheerfully bow to your decision whatever it may be. I have added F sharp to the signature of 'The Seeds of Love'. As it does not affect the tune I thought I was justified in following my own inclinations. Would it be 'mixing drinks' too much to have alternate verses of the tunes in Dorian and Aeolian?[25]

Two other unpublished sets followed: the names of the collectors and dates of arrangements of the nine *Folk Songs* [H84] are unknown, and the seven *Folk Songs* [H85], arranged for unison voices and small orchestra, make use of six of the songs from the previous sets.

An original choral work from this time, obviously inspired by the folk song, was the *Four Old English Carols*, Op. 20B [H82] (1907), composed for mixed chorus (satb) and piano. Holst also provided an alternative setting for female chorus (ssaa) and piano. This grouping, taken from anonymous fifteenth century texts, includes "A Babe is Born," "Now Let Us Sing," "Jesu, Thou the Virgin-born" (unaccompanied) and "The Savior of the world is born." For unknown reasons this work was first published by an American publisher, Arthur P. Schmidt of New York, in 1908, before being picked up by the British firm of Bayley and Ferguson in 1913.

Holst's first instrumental work from this time period heavily displays the folk song influence. The *Two Songs without Words*, Op. 22 [H88] (1906), bearing a Mendelssohnian title, forges a new path in terms of economy. The work lasts about eight minutes and small orchestral forces are employed. The melodies, mostly employing folk song modalities (aeolian, mixolydian, and dorian) are Holst's own. The two movements, "Country Song" and "Marching Song," although often programmed separately, were meant to be performed together; there are unifying thematic fragments that in this case make the whole greater than the sum of its parts. Holst himself conducted the first performance of this work on July 19, 1906 at the Royal College of Music. He dedicated it to Ralph Vaughan Williams which, while surprising the dedicatee, was certainly appropriate; a substitute church job, the positions at James Allen's Girls' School and Passmore Edwards Settlement, Holst's contributions to *The English Hymnal*, and many more intangible items had been gained through his friend's connections.

It is amazing for one to realize that at the same time he was successfully grappling with his new-found economy in *Two Songs without Words*, Holst was putting the finishing touches on his last late romantic opera, *Sita*. His style had changed considerably by the time he had finished *Sita*, but it would have been a grave mistake to rewrite its 142 pages. A glance at the title page indicates that *Sita* was conceived on a grand scale:

Sita
Opera in 3 Acts
Founded on the ancient Hindu Epic
"The Ramayana"
Gustav von Holst

10 The Terrace
Barnes SW

Prologue	The Jungle
Act I	A ravine in the forest of Dandaka
Act II	The Vale of Panchavati
Act III	Scene 1: On the banks of the torrent before Lanka
	Scene 2: In Lanka

Characters

Rama (Incarnation of Vishnu)	Baritone	The Earth	Mezzo-soprano
Lakohman (His brother)	Tenor	Surpanakha (Sister of Ravana)	Mezzo-soprano
Ravana (King of the Rakshas, Lord of Lanka)	Bass	Sita (daughter of The Earth)	Soprano
Maritcha, a Raksha Chief	Baritone		

Chorus of Rakshas	SAT and B	
Chorus of Mortals	T and B	
Hidden Chorus of Voices of the Earth	Sop and Alto	
Duration of Performance	Prologue and Act I	45 min.
	Act II	60 "
	Act III	55 "
		160 min.

The orchestra that Holst used for *Sita* was very large, almost rivaling that of *The Planets*: three flutes, two oboes, cor anglais, two clarinets, bass clarinet, two bassoons, contrabassoon, four horns, two trumpets, two cornets, two tenor trombones, bass trombone, contrabass trombone, timpani, harp, percussion, and strings.[26]

Sita took nearly seven years to complete. It was entered into a contest sponsored by Ricordi. It failed to win the £500 prize, but it did share second place.[27] The committee's decision, finally announced in January, 1908, was quite a blow to Holst, although he eventually dismissed *Sita* as "good old Wagnerian bawling."[28] It is possible that Holst said this as a way of covering up his pain rather than as a denunciation of the work. In its entirety, the opera has remained unpublished and unperformed. Latter-day audiences have thus been deprived of seeing a production of *Sita* or of even hearing a recording of it in its entirety. *Sita* deserves a better fate. Although a "first-period" work, it is not an early work.

Vaughan Williams tried to console Holst:

> My Dear V.
>
> Do you really think that because your work has been crowned with the disfavor of Joseph Bennet, that my &other people's labours, in scratching out your mistakes is made any the more or less worthwhile?--The point is that it's a big work & naturally anything one does to help on that is not wasted.
>
> I'm sorry (a) that you haven't got £500,
> (b) that you are not promised a performance.
>
> Perhaps these are rather more important side issues but they *are* side issues--the real, important thing is that you have not been put in the awful position when 'all men speak well of you'--Think, the awful stigma to have gone through life with a prize on your back--almost as damning as a mus: doc:[29]

I'm glad on the whole that you are 'highly commended'--because it probably that one judge (perhaps Stanford?[30]--or Percy Pitt?) did really know a good thing when they saw it--and it may be practically useful as far as performance goes....

I don't know that my faith in you wd have been quite strong enough to have stood the shock of approval by J. Bennet.

So after all, at the expense of worldly advantages, you've saved your honour.

Perhaps you think it is too serious a matter to joke about--well, I know it is--but then after all the *most* important thing is that you've written a big work and that you aren't in the awful position of being continually praised by those whose opinions & methods you despise in every way.

Y

RVW[31]

In 1905-06 Vaughan Williams composed his first *Norfolk Rhapsody*[32] for orchestra and this inspired Holst to compose two somewhat similar pieces. *Songs of the West*, Op. 21 [No. 1] [H86] (1906) was his first try at writing a one-movement rhapsodic piece. Comprised originally of fourteen folk songs, it was a difficult undertaking and although he revised it extensively the following year, cutting out half of the songs in the process, it was not particularly successful. *Songs of the West* remained unpublished throughout his lifetime. The second work, *A Somerset Rhapsody*, Op. 21 [No. 2] [H87] (1906) met with a greater degree of success. Holst revised this work as well and for the first time combined two folk songs simultaneously ("Sheep Shearing Song" and "High Germany"). He would successfully do this again in *Christmas Day* [H109] (1910) ("Come ye lofty, come ye lowly" and "The First Noel") and still more successfully in "Fantasia on the Dargason" (the "Dargason" and "Greensleaves"), the last movement of the *Second Suite in F for Military Band*, Op. 28, No. 2 [H106] (1911-22), which he tranposed, rescored, and enlarged with five additional variations for the *St. Paul's Suite*, Op. 29, No. 2 [H118] (1913). The revised version of *A Somerset Rhapsody* was premiered at Queen's Hall on April 6, 1910 by the New Symphony Orchestra conducted by Edward Mason. Well-received by both audiences and critics, it was Holst's first real success.

Holst's interest in the English folk song may have indirectly had something to do with his being hired for his next teaching position--the only one that he would retain for his entire life--in the autumn of 1905. The St. Paul's School, a public school for boys, was founded by John Colet, Dean of St. Paul's Cathedral, in 1509. In 1903, nearly four hundred years later, the St. Paul's Girls' School was established at Brook Green, Hammersmith. The school officially opened in January, 1904, with a staff of twelve and a student body of fifty-three.[33] The first music teacher hired by Francis Ralph Gray, the school's Head Mistress (later High Mistress) until 1926, was Adine O'Neill, wife of composer Norman O'Neill. A celebrated pianist who had studied with Clara Schumann, she was given the title of Chief Music Mistress. Within two years the school's enrollment had swelled to 157 students and the search was on to find an additional music teacher. Adine O'Neill preferred to concentrate on teaching piano and so it was determined that the new position should be that of "Singing Mistress."[34]

Candidates were interviewed for the position; some were more suitable than others. Francis Ralph Gray commented about one, "She had no enthusiasm for the folk song, she had never turned over a book of Irish or Scottish songs and presented blank looks to *Annie Laurie and the Hundred Pipers.*"[35] Actually none of the candidates who interviewed were chosen for the position and Adine O'Neill was consulted about seeking additional candidates. She recommended Holst, whom she known through her husband. Holst was already respected for his work at James Allen's Girls' School and was comfortable with using folk songs and national airs in his teaching. Although there were no other male teachers at that time at St. Paul's, Holst was happily married and considered a "safe" prospect. Miss Gray contacted Holst, who interviewed the next day and was immediately offered the position. Initially, Holst was to teach at the school two days per week, which pleased him since that allowed him to retain his post at James Allen's Girls' School. He thus became St. Paul's Girls' School's first "Singing Master."

At first Holst's duties were limited to teaching singing, but he assumed additional duties with with the passing of time. He was not a vocalist--his major instruments were the keyboards and trombone--yet he knew the principles of the correct ways of singing and knew what it took to produce a beautiful vocal tone. Irene Bonnett, who was a student of Holst at St. Paul's Girls' School from 1909 to 1916, comments:

> It was during my first week at school that I was sent to a singing class and so met Mr. Holst. It was quite a new experience to come into contact with such a vital personality. His looks did not suggest his power. He was thin and looked shy; he was rather short-sighted, and his voice was so exceedingly quiet in class that his laughter came as a surprise. It was the most robust thing about him, and how infectious it was! We always felt we were having a good time and that singing was the most worth-while

thing to be doing; that was why he could always get the best out of us, His insistence on good breathing, strict rhythm and clear words set a standard which was perhaps less general than it is to-day [1934]; and I think that many teachers and choir trainers owe something to him for this pioneer work.

We progressed gradually until at about the age of sixteen we were singing motets by Palestrina and Lasso almost at sight. "Laudate Pueri," our book of these motets, was our Bible, and our enthusiasm was great. Mr. Holst also introduced us to the madrigals just then being brought out by Dr. Fellowes,[36] and at the same time gave us a lot of national and folk songs. We sang some of his [Holst's] earlier part-songs, beside arrangements of folk songs, some by himself and some by his pupils, for he had begun to teach us to do this for ourselves.[37]

Holst's ways of teaching were considered unorthodox for their time. He disliked using standardized textbooks and he abhorred tests. Holst believed strongly in learning by doing and he did whatever was necessary in order to reach his students. If this involved conducting while standing on a chair, putting on a costume, eating lunch with the students, telling jokes, or whatever else, then he was prepared to do it. Yet Holst was neither a buffoon nor a buddy to the students. Oboist Helen Gaskell, a student at St. Paul's Girls' School in the early 1920's, commented, "It's a funny thing, but the mere mention of Gussie and I'm inclined to have a broad smile. Awfully comforting. He was very nice but kept you away, at a distance. It was his nature."[38] Holst could also be a disciplinarian and occasionally sent students who misbehaved down to the office, but he did not demean them. Nancy Gotch, who attended the school from 1913 to 1917, wrote, "He always said what he thought, and was firm, but never, never unkind."[39]

Holst was very clear about how he felt about teaching. He took particular offense to George Bernard Shaw's platitude "Those who can, do. Those who can't teach." Holst offered an alternative view in his Henry Elias Howland Lecture, "The Teaching of Art," given at Yale University in 1929:

That remark of Shaw is not *essentially* true.
Teaching is not an alternative to doing.
Teaching *is* doing; teaching is an art.
'Those who can, do.' Those who teach also do'....

The teaching of art is itself an art....

We who are teachers should hold up our heads more proudly. We are among the lucky ones of the earth.

If we are real artists in teaching we have the greatest joy this world can give--that of creative work.

We also have what I have called the world's greatest honour, the companionship of honourable men and women.

There is more in that same lecture that reveals much about Holst's philosophy of teaching. Some of the words he had written to Vaughan Williams from Berlin in 1903 had since metamorphosized into teaching tenets. He speaks here on "Heirs and Rebels":

> In the teaching of art we aim at the production of artists, of exceptional people, of aristocrats, in whatever department of life they happen to be, whether builders of cathedrals or or good cooks in village inns.
>
> The best definition of what I call an aristocrat is Gilbert Murray's: 'Every man who counts is a child of tradition and a rebel from it.'
>
> The production of such a man is the aim of the teaching of art. If we are teachers our first duty is to make our pupil a child of tradition.
>
> We can only do that if we are ourselves its children. Not merely students but children, steeped in the love of our tradition--that unconscious love that children possess and which is the most contagious emotion in the world.
>
> Our influence on our pupil is assured if we have this.
>
> This influence will be first directed towards developing technical power in the pupil.
>
> By technique I mean the means by which you express yourself.
>
> And the method of acquiring technique is, for nearly all of us, Hard Work.
>
> People like Mozart, in whom all necessary technique seems to have been born, are too rare to form the basis of an argument....
>
> I have said that the first aim of the teacher should be to make the pupil a child of tradition.
>
> It must be a living tradition--one of great art and great men.
>
> Such things as standard textbooks and technical exercises must never usurp the place of a living tradition.
>
> But they must not be ignored even if their place be a lower one....
>
> If we, as teachers, force the character of our pupils into a mould or allow them them to drift there, we are not artists but experts in

> standardized mass-production.
>
> I have been told that standardized mass-production is excellent for motor-cars; it is sometimes fairly effective for detective-stories. But it is iniquitous for human beings and impossible for art....
>
> This is being the creative artist--the creator of men and women who live their own lives.
>
> And this should be the ideal of the teacher of art. It will be so if he is an artist in teaching.
>
> A moment will come when he realizes that he has done his share in the work of creating a 'rebel' who will 'count.' The man who spent his life always retouching one picture instead of leaving it for another would not be a real artist but a more or less interesting study in morbid psychology.
>
> The last and hardest duty of a teacher is to make himself unnecessary.[40]

This was in certain ways a follow-up (or a refinement) of a lecture he had given in 1922 at Connaught Hall, Newcastle to the Newcastle branch of the British Music Society. That lecture was covered in the *North Star* :

Mr. Gustav Holst and the "Place of Joy"

> ....Art, he [Holst] said, is one of the few great sources of joy: and if it is not creative it is of no use. The teaching of music should be on such lines as would show to the child mind what joy could be gained from music. The piano was the key that opened the door to music, but not the only key; the singing class was another potent key.
>
> He objected strongly to the piano as a social convention. It was to requisite to foster in children alone of the beautiful in music, and to encourage them to express themselves in music. To train a nation of listeners and teach appreciation was advisable up to a certain point, but art entailed activity.
>
> The test of a teacher, he added, was what do your pupils do without you? The ideal of a teacher should be to make oneself unnecessary.[41]

By "make himself (or oneself) unnessary," Holst meant that the teacher should inspire the students to eventually arrive at a point where they can work things out for themselves. In an interview for the *Christian Science Monitor* in 1924 he spoke about such an occurrence at St. Paul's Girls' School:

> It was one of the great moments of my career when I came in early one morning on a dark winter day to fetch my letters before school hours. I found several of the girls had come earlier still, without saying a word to me and were sitting round the classroom fire singing 'Palestrina' for sheer love of music.[42]

Holst had an infectious enthusiasm for his art as well as for his students. He loved being a music teacher and commented about the advantange that music teachers had:

> Music teachers have a great advantage over teachers of other subjects. Suppose, for instance, they went into a village or soldiers' camp and invited support for lectures on Latin. The response would not be very great. Let them offer music teaching and the response would be very different. That shows where the music teacher scores.[43]

Holst had excellent support from the Head Mistress. Sometimes student schedules were changed to accommodate the music program. Francis Ralph Gray comments:

> Some of the girls who were very happy in their musical studies were working on a lightened time-table because the claim of their music was recognised. Others managed to secure odd bits of time when they were entitled to do as they pleased.[44]

She continues:

> Shortly after the [Music] Wing was opened Mr. Holst remarked to one of the Form Mistresses[45], "If things go on like this much longer, we shall be pitching into the girls for practising the piano when they ought to be on the playground." The Form Mistress opened her eyes very wide and said in a sad tone of voice, "Don't you know that happens every week?"[46]

Just as he was doing at James Allen's Girls' School, Holst continued to supplement the meager amount of girls' school chorus repertoire then suitable for academic purposes with his own compositions and arrangements. His original compositions of this type that were composed during his first years at St. Paul's Girls' School include *Pastoral* [H93] (1907?), *A Song of Fairies* [H104] (1908?) and the *Four Part Songs* [H110] (1910), set to the words of John Greenleaf

Whittier. He also edited a number of pieces for three part women's chorus (ssa), primarily for use in his singing classes. These include "How Merrily We Live" [App. III, 7] a madrigal by Michael East, "Benedictus" [App. III, 8] by William Byrd, "Help me, O Lord" [App. III, 9] by Thomas Augustine Arne, "Adoramus Te, Christe" [App. III, 10] by Orlando di Lasso, three sets (each containing four selections) of *Sacred Rounds and Canons* [App. III, 13] (1911-16), and *Old Airs and Glees* [App. III, 16] (1913-16), featuring words by Clifford Bax.

In certain classes Holst taught his students how to compose rounds. Often students would spend half the period composing them and the other half performing them. Some of these student compositions were programmed on concerts. Learning by doing--some would say "active learning, not passive learning"--was a trademark of Holst's teachings. Even when working on a one-to-one basis, as he would later do at the Royal College of Music, University College at Reading, or Harvard University, he encouraged his students to maintain an alertness not through theorizing or pontificating, but through writing and then more writing.

In the autumn of 1906 the Holsts discovered that they were "in the family way." Once again Holst was faced with the necessity of augmenting the family income. The question was "How?" By this time he had absolutely no desire to return to "Worming." He was by now incurably a teacher. The pantomime and the pier were things of the distant past, a past that he did not want to revisit. But Holst wouldn't have to return to trombone playing for, once again, it was his close friend Ralph Vaughan Williams who opened the door of opportunity.

---

[1]*Staff Register*, James Allen's Girls' School.

[2]Barbara Kley, "A Brief History of Music at JAGS" in *Programme, James Allen's Girls' School 250th Anniversary Celebration Concert*, 13.

[3]*Staff Register*, James Allen's Girls' School.

[4]Reminiscences of Violet Kelsey-Smith, Nora Edmed, Margaret Jepps, and Evelyn Hile are from letters in the James Allen's Girls' School Archives.

[5]Class.

[6]*James Allen's Girls' School Magazine*, 1957, 40.

[7]Alma Digby quoted in *Programme, James Allen's Girls' School 250th Anniversary*, 17.

[8]Barbara Kley, "Gustav Holst," in *Ibid.*, 17.

[9]Donald Mitchell, ed., *Letters from Life: The Selected Letters and Diaries of Benjamin Britten, 1913-76* (London: Faber & Faber, 1991), 182.

[10]*The Times*, May 21, 1904.

[11]*The Daily Graphic*, May 21, 1904.

[12]Imogen Holst, *Gustav Holst: A Biography*, 2nd ed. (Oxford: Oxford University Press, 1969), 26.

[13]*Lady's Pictorial*, July 22, 1905.

[14]*Music Trade Journal*, July 15, 1905.

[15]Now called the Mary Ward Settlement.
[16]C. Hubert H. Parry, Recommendation letter for Gustav Holst, July 19, 1904, The Holst Foundation..
[17]Imogen Holst, *op. cit.*, 37.
[18]Gustav Holst, quoted in Imogen Holst, *Gustav Holst: A Biography*, 2nd ed., 27.
[19]James Allen's Girls' School Archives.
[20]*The Musical Standard*, December 16, 1905.
[21]*The Morning Leader*, December 19, 1905.
[22]John Bird, *Percy Grainger* (South Melbourne, Australia: Sun Books, 1976), 102-103.
[23]*Ibid.*, 107. Grainger entered the folk songs into his compositions exactly as the singers had sung them to him, including any irregular meters. Grainger's best-known compilation of recorded folk songs is his concert band masterpiece Lincolnshire Posy (1937).
[24]Imogen Holst, *Gustav Holst: A Biography* (Oxford: Oxford University Press, 1938), 28.
[25]Personal correspondence, Gustav Holst to Cecil Sharp [n.d.], quoted in Imogen Holst, *A Thematic Catalogue of Gustav Holst's Music* (London: Faber Music Ltd., 1974), 68.
[26]British Library Add MS 47821.
[27]On page 72 of his *Gustav Holst: The Man and His Music* (Oxford: Oxford University Press, 1990), Michael Short has presented the case that the decisions may have been a political compromise. This is based upon Fritz Hart's 1943 article, "Early Memories of Gustav Holst," in the *Royal College of Music Magazine*, XXXIX, No. 2, in which Hart says that Charles Villiers Stanford, one of the four judges of the competition hated *Sita* and sabotaged the outcome. Compare this with Vaughan Williams' take presented in his following letter.
[28]Imogen Holst, *Gustav Holst*, 31.
[29]This was meant to be humorous; Vaughan Williams took his Mus. Doc. at Cambridge in 1901.
[30]Charles Villiers Stanford.
[31]Personal correspondence, Ralph Vaughan Williams to Gustav Holst [n.d., early 1908], British Library Add MS 57953.
[32]Vaughan Williams actually composed a total of three Norfolk Rhapsodies, but withdrew the second and third.
[33]*The Schoolmistress*, September 22, 1927.
[34]Francis Ralph Gray, *And Gladly Wolde He Lerne and Gladly Teche* (London: Sampson, Low, Marsteon & Co., 1931), 129.
[35]*Ibid.*, 131.
[36]English musicologist Edmund Horace Fellowes (1870-1951) edited thirty-six volumes of *The English Madrigal School* from 1913 to 1924.
[37]Irene Bonnett, "Mr. Holst in School," in *R.C.M. Magazine*, XXX, No. 3 (December, 1934), 86-87.
[38]Personal correspondence, Sally Hain (Helen Gaskell's niece) to the author, August 9, 1999. Ms. Hain interviewed Ms. Gaskell.
[39]Nancy Strode [nee Gotch], "Across the Years: a Personal Recollection of Gustav Holst," in *Conductors Guild Bulletin*, Summer, 1974.
[40]Holst lectured from notes; his lectures were not necessarily written out in their entirety. "The Teaching of Art" was printed in Ursula Vaughan Williams (ed.) and Imogen Holst (ed.), *Heirs and Rebels: Letters to Each Other and Occasional Writings by Gustav Holst and Ralph Vaughan Williams* (Oxford: Oxford University Press, 1959), 66-73. It is possible that parts of it were reconstructed, although the thoughts presented are consistent with those expressed by Holst elsewhere. Holst's use of language, considered sexist for our time, was the norm for his time and has not been retouched by the author. Holst was asked to extend his notes for this speech into a

journal article, but did not feel inclined to do so. This is dealt with in more detail in the Second American Visit chapter.

[41]*The North Star*, February 6, 1922.

[42]Gustav Holst, quoted in the *Christian Science Monitor*, n. d. [1924].

[43]Gustav Holst, quoted in "Music Education: What It Is and What It Is Not," in *The Westminster Gazette*, n.d., [1921].

[44]Francis Ralph Gray, *op. cit.*, 140.

[45]Classroom teacher.

[46]*Ibid.*.

CHAPTER IV

MORLEY COLLEGE

Morley College for Working Men and Women was opened in September, 1889. Its mission was "to promote the advanced study by working men and women of subjects not directly connected to any handicraft, trade, or business."[1] As such it eventually became and still remains one of the largest centers of adult education in Great Britain. It was coeducational from the very start. Named for Samuel Morley, an eminent textile manufacturer and anthropologist, it was located next door to the Royal Victoria Hall (known affectionately as "The Old Vic") on Waterloo Road. Today this area is rather nondescript workaday London, although in the middle Victorian era it held a rather unfavorable reputation, being in close proximity to the Dickensian Lambeth slums and Bedlam Insane Asylum.

Ralph Vaughan Williams became connected with Morley College in 1906, serving as University Extension Lecturer in music history and music appreciation. Early in the following year the choir director H. J. B. Dart passed away, and there was an immediate search to find his successor. Vaughan Williams was approached about the taking the position but, instead of applying for it himself, he recommended Holst. This was the third time that Vaughan Williams had been instrumental, in securing a teaching position for Holst. After some negotiating about fees and payment Holst was hired on April 8, 1907.[2] The timing was impeccable for Imogen Clare Holst came into the world on April 12th. Holst started teaching at Morley College at the beginning of the summer term.

Holst's hiring was carried in the *Morley College Report, 1906-7*. After mentioning Dart's death, the report continued, "In his place the Council has been fortunate enough to secure the services of Mr. Gustav von Holst, who is already well-known in the musical world as a composer and teacher."[3] The report also contained information about the claim for the Board of Education Grant for 1906. The low amounts that were notated reflected not only the paltry amounts the Board was willing to subsidize, but also the fact that the clientele were on the lower end of the economic scale. For "Singing" classes some 1320 hours of instruction were recognized. 2s. 6d. was the Rate of Grant per twenty hours. The total amount of this grant was a mere eight pounds and five schillings.[4]

The claim for the Board of Education Grant was reported by statistics that give a clear profile of the students that Holst would teach:

Age of Students	Number of Students who have attended at any time during the year		
	Men	Women	Total
17	33	13	46
18	26	18	44
19	29	8	37
20	29	15	44
21+	347	241	588
Total	464	295	759[5]

Morley College was clearly an adult college. The 759 students were taught by a faculty of nineteen men and twelve women. The students were of various occupations, the most common being that of clerk (196), followed by dressmaker (34).[6] Not surprisingly, nearly all of the the class sessions at Morley College were held at night.

Morley College was fourth teaching job held by Holst simultaneously. Just as he alternated days between St. Paul's and James Allen's, he now alternated evenings between Passmore Edwards Settlement and Morley College. Such a heavy schedule was burdening. It didn't matter; Holst jumped into his new position at Morley with a passion, for he knew no other way. It was only two months later, in June, 1907--partly through the necessity of having more time to compose and partly as a result of increased activities elsewhere--that he was able to give up his Passmore Edwards Settlement position.[7] Holst taught a number of courses at Morley College, including theory, sightsinging, the choral society and the orchestra. The 1917 music department schedule shows what classes were offered one decade after Holst's arrival:

List of Classes and Teachers

Sight Singing and Voice Production	Gustav von Holst	T	8:30
Choral Society	"	M	8:30
Orchestra	"	W	8:30
Harmony and Counterpoint (Elementary)	"	T	7:30
Harmony and Counterpoint (Advanced)	James Brown, Mus. Bac.	M	7:30
Violin (Elementary)	"	T	7:15
(Intermediate)	"	Th	7:55
(Advanced)	"	Th	8:35
Orchestral Class	"	Th	9:15[8]

Holst inherited a tenuous situation as far as performing groups were concerned. The Morley College Choral Society was actually quite new, having been founded earlier in the decade. In a school such as Morley, where students were in attendence one semester and out the next, the organization had not yet had enough time to develop a substantial core. Even later, after Holst had been around many years, he was always searching for musical balance in his mixed chorus. That meant finding enough men, and particularly tenors. The conditions of membership were entirely non-musical: regular attendence. The orchestra situation, particularly at the beginning of his tenure, was in even worse shape. It had existed sinced 1892 but again, owing to Morley's existence as a working class commuter college, it had not yet blossomed into a viable ensemble. The instrumentation of Holst's first Morley College Orchestra consisted of only eight players: two violins, one flute, three sharp-pitched clarinets[9], one cornet and a piano.[10] It may have been directly for this nascient ensemble that Holst composed his *Seven Scottish Airs* [H93] (1907). The work was published in 1908 for piano and strings. The string parts are neither very difficult nor overly idiomatic, and Holst may have had the other instruments join in where appropriate. Whatever the case, Holst did not think very highly of *Seven Scottish Airs*. In 1925 Edwin Evans, who was writing articles for *Cobbett's Encyclopedia of Chamber Music*, asked Holst what works should be included. The composer replied, "'The Seven Scottish Airs' was written for school purposes and published because I was hard up--I would neither it or ops 2 [*Three Pieces for Oboe and String Quartet* [H8A]], 3 [*Quintet in A Minor* for Woodwinds and Piano[H11]], and 11 [*Woodwind Quintet in A Flat* [H67]] went into Cobbett's Encyclopedia."[11]

Holst had a rocky start at Morley College. As in the case of many new teachers with new ideas, some of the "old guard" of students quit. Yet this didn't matter, for these students were replaced with better ones. Within a year, Holst's hard work had begun to pay off. The orchestra would always have its musical troubles, yet the ensemble was starting to develop into some sort of a cohesive unit. The following review is from *Morley College Magazine*:

> Students' Concert
>
> On Saturday, December 19 the students, under the direction of Mr. Gustav von Holst, gave one of the most enjoyable and interesting concerts ever credited to Morley College....We have to consider the materials which he has at his disposal in forming an opinion as to the level which the performance reached on this occasion. Excepting one or two, the players were purely amateur. Yet, the ensemble, especially at the climaxes, were magnificent. The attack left a little to be desired; there seemed a want of confidence on the part of the section of the "strings." At the same time, there is no doubt that such an ambitious effort would be responsible for a certain amount of nervousness. Faulty intonation was especially noticeable in the slow introduction of the Haydn. But the finishes, especially that of Lorelei were truly superb. Climax upon climax followed with such startling dramatic effect that we were amazed at the stupendous results which von Holst was able to obtain from his orchestral forces.[12]

Also performed on this concert were the first three ("On the Banks of the Nile," "The Willow Tree" and "Our ship she lies in the harbour") of Holst's *Seven Folk Songs* [H85] for unison chorus and orchestra.

This concert was just the beginning. Over time the membership of both the choral society and the orchestra increased and the performances greatly improved. Holst himself would probably say it was a result of "hard work," but there was more. Arnold Foster, Holst's second successor at Morley College, comments:

> No one enjoyed music more keenly than he did and he passed on this capacity for enjoyment on to his students. Herein lies one of the secrets of his success as a teacher. Another was that he never relaxed his high professional standard when dealing with amateurs. He expected everyone to give of their best and by his own untiring hard work, leadership, and enthusiasm, he led his students to astonishing achievement. Yet, so great was his practical knowledge that he always knew where he could drive his students to achieving perfection and where (owing to their technical

> limitations) to attempt to do so would lead to discouragement and disaster. Many an enthusiastic professional comes to grief in his dealings with amateurs in forgetting to take this subtle point into account.[13]

Holst believed that all people were capable of having their musical instincts developed and that naturally it followed that there was really no kind of music which could not be appreciated and practiced by anyone. There was no better proof of this than Holst's work at Morley College:

> Mr. von Holst is doing yeoman work at Morley College. He has an ideal position , for he has access to the best kind of material in the unsophisticated working men and women of the vast southeast district of London. The only way to create a sincere love of the finest works of musical art is to get the people themselves to perform, and this is what Mr. von Holst is doing. He also has the unique opportunity of sowing the seeds of staid admiration for British music, and this is a special feature of Mr. von Holst's activities.[14]

Hubert H. Parry, Director of the Royal College of Music, attended one of Holst's concerts during his third year at Morley College and wrote the following:

> Royal College of Music
> Prince Consort Road
> South Kensington
> London S.W.
> Feb. 2. 1910
>
> My dear von Holst
>
> These seem to be grand doings! What a pioneer you are. I am very glad to see that your most invaluable work is prospering so well. Music amongst these sort of folks is just after my own heart.
>
> I gaze at your Choir and Orchestra with most comfortable feelings, on your account as well as theirs: for it must be a joy to you to get these people into touch with our dear J. S. B.[15]. And such a jolly lot of them!
>
> Good luck to you and my blessings upon your doings....
>
> Yours very sincerely,

C. Hubert H. Parry[16]

In Holst's later years at Morley College, when the fame and reputation of the music department had become well-known, concerts became a big draw, not just to friends and relatives of the students, but to all of Greater London. He commented, "Morley College is a place where poor people give concerts to the discerning rich."[17] Class never made any difference to Holst.

Byron Adams has suggested that Holst's approach to teaching stemmed directly from William Morris' educational and aesthetic theories. He comments from a 1992 perspective:

> Examining Holst's career in light of his relationship to William Morris provides at least a partial answer to one of the central questions concerning this enigmatic composer: why did such a supreme technician choose to compose so much music for amateurs? The answer is to be found not solely in the accidents of his life, but in his aesthetic view. For Holst, like Morris, there was no dichotomy between the beautiful and the useful. Holst became the William Morris of music, a craftsman par excellence who applied the highest standards of technical accomplishment to bear on each task at hand, no matter how humble.[18]

Adams is correct; Holst did indeed become "the William Morris of music," at Morley College and elsewhere. He did take composing for amateurs very seriously. Yet Adams' assumption about there being no dichotomy between the beautiful and the useful in Holst's mind is negated by Holst's letter to Evans, quoted earlier in this chapter, asking Evans to exclude certain of his works from Cobbett's *Encyclopaedia*. Yet Holst's frequently quoted comment about a piece of music he didn't particularly care for-- "Was it necessary?"--does unveil a perspective developed through familiarity with Morris' teachings. Still Morris' idealistic socialism merely reinforced what had already been established in Holst's mind during his Cheltenham years and Morris, who died in 1896, probably would not have approved of Holst's mass distribution of his own musical product through manufactured recordings or radio broadcasts.

A *Morley College Magazine* article by an anonymous former student had the following to say about the matching of Holst to Morley College.

> Holst was the ideal musical director for Morley (and I do not mean by that to disparage the work of his present very worthy successor) while Morley afforded him the right medium for the expression of that very definite

> outlook on life and music which seems to me the most valuable part of his teaching. Holst often talked of "the Morley Spirit," that sense of self-obliterating co-operation which always enabled unexpected difficulties to be surmounted. For a long time I suspected that in the sense in which he spoke of it, the Morley spirit was nothing but his own faculty for inspiring everyone to work happily together for the common end. I later discovered that the Morley spirit was real enough, but Holst's delight in it was typical. His reluctance to abandon the College when considerations of health made that course imperative, and his loyalty to it when fame might have taken him into the limelight elsewhere, showed that the Morley spirit and Holst were one.[19]

Whatever "the Morley Spirit" was, it firmly took hold, and it wasn't confined to Morley College; certainly there was a "James Allen's Girls' School Spirit," a "Passmore Edwards Settlement Spirit" and a "St. Paul's Girls' School Spirit" as well. As was the case at St. Paul's, it was a situation of learning by doing and Holst's students composed rounds in class. He edited a dozen of these and arranged for their publication; two sets of *Morley Rounds* [App. III, 23] were published by Oxford University Press in 1924. Holst strongly believed that the practice of music as an art form should be spread as widely as possible and that most people, once given music of the highest possible standard, would respond to it. He commented, "Good taste in music is like good taste in food--a sign of refined insight and knowledge well used."[20] He advocated every amateur (as well as every professional) participating in some sort of communal music. Holst offered no apologies, saying, "We are training amateurs in our ordinary school work. Budding professionals are rare and will be none the worse for a little amateur training."[21] One of the mottos he used with all his students was from Johann Sebastian Bach: "The aim of music is the glory of God and pleasant recreation therin." When doing Bach, at least, they lived it.

Friends, from his Sanskrit teacher Mabel Bode to folk song collector extraordinaire Cecil Sharp, were brought in to lecture. Extra-curricular events were planned; the "Music Students' Tea and Social" became an annual function at Morley College as did combined musical efforts with St. Paul's Girls' School. Ringers were brought in regularly to fill in weak or non-existent sections of the Morley College chorus and orchestra. Holst brought in students from St. Paul's, parents, and professionals--no one was immune from being invited to help out. Holst even wrote to Adrian Boult, before he knew him very well:

St. Paul's Girls' School

W6
Feb 5 [1918]

Dear Boult

....We are singing Madrigals at Morley on March 2nd at 7:30. Will you come and bring

1) your voice
2) Weelkes vols X, XI, XII, XIII
3) any tenor who can read
4) any singer who can "
5) and body who wants to listen?

On Feb 23rd at 7 we are performing a new work 'English Opera as she is wrote' in six acts and five languages (one of them being tonic solfa).[22]

If you'd like to write a notice of it for the Mag[23] we'd be grateful.

If you'd like to act in the chorus (Italian brigands disguised as foot inspectors) you must come to rehearsal on the 22nd

Yr

GH[24]

Holst tried to include one student work on each concert. In the adult education world of Morley College, there was such a motley assortment of students that nearly every one of them was some sort of an exception. Charles Burke, an Irishman who attended Morley while in his sixties, was Holst's oldest student and yet was an exemplar of the forementioned "Morley Spirit." On June 13, 1914 his work, *Fantasia on Two Irish Hymn Tunes: St. Patrick's Prayer*, was premiered at a Morley concert. The following program note may have been written by Holst or by the composer himself:

> The first tune is played by the strings against repeated notes on the trumpets and drums. It is played again by the wind instruments, then by full orchestra, and a third time with a counter melody above it, by the bass instruments. The second tune is first sung by a solo voice, and later by the choir. The two tunes then alternate with one another in a series of variations ending in a powerful climax. From this point to the end the first tune is sung against repeated notes on the brass as at the beginning.[25]

Holst was so proud of his student that he invited Percy Grainger, whom he knew was interested in Irish music, to attend the concert:

10, The Terrace,
Barnes. S. W.
May 30[, 1914]

Dear Grainger

I teach at a working man's college and my pupils are giving a concert on Saturday week 8 at which we are doing a work by one of the students--a choral fantasia on two old Irish hymns. The composer is 64 and this is his op 1!

That may not sound very promising but the work is really fine and Vaughan Williams suggested to me that perhaps you would care to come and hear it. We should be very proud if you would.

Yrs sincerely

Gustav von Holst[26]

Grainger was unable to attend and Holst acknowledged:

10, The Terrace,
Barnes, S.W.
June 3d[, 1914]

Dear Grainger

Thanks very much for your kind letter. I also hope that we may meet soon. After this week I shall have no night work until September and so I hope we can fix something up.

I'm very sorry you cannot come on Sat--the work is really wonderful.

Forgive me for this hurried scrawl--there is much I want to say but--

Yr Sincerely

GvH[27]

Charles Kennedy Scott, conductor of the Oriana Madrigal Society, wrote an extensive review of the concert, ending it with the following remarks:

> Young men dream dreams at Morley College;--that is to be expected; but old men see visions too. It is a place of queer happenings, this Morley College. Where it is placed you would not expect to find music at all, certainly not such music as we got last night. But the bravest thing of all was to see an old man--his first fruits (I believe) as a composer. We sometimes hear of an old head on young shoulders; but here was the reverse, and touching it was. In "St. Patrick's Prayer" Mr. Charles Burke has taken two magnificent old Irish hymns and joined them skillfully and well in the construction of his composition. There is but little development or original thematic development, but the harmonies he uses are invariably good, befitting the dignity of the tunes; and the counterpoints have a touch of primitive uncouthness about them that well agrees with the subject matter. Mr. Burke has not learned yet the airs and graces of polite composition, and it is almost to be hoped he never will.
>
> Such musical work as is being done at Morley College is a tribute not only to the healthy striving of the students, but to the fine spirit of their leader. In Mr. von Holst and Dr. Vaughan Williams, who, I understand, often associates himself with Morley College activities, we have two remarkable English musicians and I do not doubt that it is through such sympathies that they show for their less fortunate brethern, through their democratic tendencies (in the best sense), in short, that they have arrived at such an esteemed position in the art of our country. The artist may view life and its wrongs merely as so much material for the creation of his works of art. There is always this danger unless an artist has strong social sympathies: the danger of humanity being offered up to art, instead of art to humanity. With Mr. von Holst and Dr. Vaughan Williams it is far otherwise, and they will forgive me if I make bold to honour them publically for it.[28]

Three years later Charles Burke passed away at the age of sixty-seven and his work was performed *in memoriam* on the June 9, 1917 Students' Concert.[29]

A personal perspective on Holst's work at Morley College was provided by Katharine E. Eggar, who spent the greater part of a workday evening with Holst. A graduate of the Royal Academy of Music, she was a composer and pianist who had strong journalistic tendencies; at about the same time she was writing on Holst, she also was writing articles about Arnold Bax and on Adrian Boult's conducting classes. Later, she would write about her speculations on the true identity of the author of Shakespeare's plays. She was a feminist and eventually served as Vice President of the Society of Women Musicians. Perhaps it was her identity as a real musician that helped her get a good interview from Holst--something very rarely achieved by regular reporters. Her imaginative article, "How They Make Music at Morley College: A Chat with Mr. Holst and a Sight of His Work There," appeared in *The Music Student* (later renamed *The Music Teacher*) and is far too long to include in its entirety. A substantial article, it provides not only a first-hand view of Holst at work, but also captures the essence of the music department at the college. Here are some excerpts:

> Of course you know where Morley College is? Next door to the "Old Vic" in the Waterloo Road, Lambeth. And that being so, my journey to it from Campden Hill, is only to be understood by unmasking the dark designs of Mr. Holst when he consented to be "interviewed" on the subject of his Morley College work. If you were to ask him, he would say briskly, "Always bribe your interviewer. So of course I bribed her--with an egg for tea."
>
> So our interview started (would that all interviews had such a pleasant background!) over a--well, to be brief, a scrumptious tea at Hammersmith, was continued under difficulties in Stations, Lifts and Tubes[30], and reached its final stages at the College itself.
>
> ....When I asked him whether any special circumstances had led to his being appointed to what has been such a remarkable piece of work, he said characteristically, "Oh! somebody died, and so I went there."
>
> ....The first piece of line from Hammersmith runs in the open, and is comparatively quiet, so we were able to continue our conversation without much difficulty to begin with, and I learnt that Morley College has a Choir of about sixty, a Sight-singing class of about forty, and an Orchestra of about fifty.
>
> "In the orchestra," said Mr. Holst, "we have everything but Bassoons and Trombones. The Bassoons, however, I'm glad to say, are coming along. Oh yes, they're learning. And the Trombones we don't want. So we get along very nicely, though we want more 'Cellos and Basses. Then we have twenty-five students in the Elementary Harmony Class under Mr. P. J. Collis[31], and seven in the Advanced Harmony Class. There are elementary, intermediate and advanced Violin Classes working with Miss Bodkin, which take about forty students, besides individual lessons. For Singing, we have about thirty students taking private lessons with

Miss Twiselton[32], and then about six taking private lessons in Piano....We turn from twenty to twenty-five [piano] students away every year. And the old ones don't want to leave off."

By this time, we were getting into the Piccadilly regions, and the noise of the train was becoming frantic....He shouted, "I think I ought to tell you THE WORST about Morley College; before we get any further." The roar and rattle rose to a climax, and above it he yelled in a whisper, "WE WANT A NEW BUILDING, AND THREE NEW PIANOS."

The train rushed into Piccadilly Circus Station, and in the comparative quiet of thrusting our way into another platform, he went on, "You know, it's perfectly dreadful we have to put some of the audience in an adjoining room at concerts, and we have to give our lessons in rooms just before they are wanted for classes--and as to the pianos, well, you'll hear them this evening."

Before we reached the Waterloo Road, I had gleaned what was being prepared for the next concert.

"With the Choir, we're doing Beethoven's *Choral Fantasia*. And we're using a new translation and new chorus parts, both done by Morley-ites. Then we're doing three choruses from the Bach *B minor Mass* (and we shall be doing more from that later on), Brahms' *Song of Destiny*, two Madrigals and an arrangement of "Green grow the rushes," by one Gandy[33] of the Advanced Harmony Class. We always do something by a Student at the public concerts. The orchestra is doing two movements of the *Seventh Symphony* (Beethoven) and there will be four songs--two Elizabethan, and two of Brahms, by two of our students."

"Oh! and this is interesting. After next concert, we're going to do the Incidental Music to Purcell's *Dioclesian.* Not the Masque--The Incidental Music, which has never been done. So we're having a tremendous task of copying--all being done by students."

Once there, Katharine Eggar got more than a first-hand view of learning-by-doing at an informal session twenty minutes before the first class was due to begin. She was "set up" on the spot by Holst:

> [Holst to a student composer] "Brought a song? All right. Brought your wife to sing it? She couldn't come. How are we to manage? Well, here's a singer" (the copyist was hailed)--"You come and have a try. But your'e not very good at reading, *are* you? Oh! Miss Eggar--*you'll* come and help, won't you?"

> "But I'm not a singer."
>
> "But then you can read. Come along--I do so want to see what this song's like. Now then, quite slowly. Ah--we'd better read the words through first."
>
> So we found that it was Bridges' *Love on my heart from heaven fell*, and having all got our bearings, we slowly piped through the first verse of the beautifully clear, but by no means ordinary manuscript.

Toward the end of the choral and orchestral rehearsal that followed, Holst approached the interviewer:

> "What would you like as you've got to leave at 9 o'clock?" The Interviewer thought it would be interesting to hear the Brahms. "Certainly." He turned to the performers--"We'll take the *Song of Destiny* next..." There was a fluttering of music as the Brahms was sought. The conductor wheeled around again to the visitor. "Did you see that? Their faces fell! Some of them don't like Brahms--they'd like to go singing Bach all night!...And to tell you the truth..." [*Here he told me the truth*] "Ha ha! But I always do learn from my pupils."
>
> He mounted the desk again, and all too soon the clock pointed to the fatal hour of nine. I crept towards an inconspicuous exit just as the wind were being exhorted not to hurry. But this advice was not enough to save them from disaster. A stop was necessary, and they were condoled with for the lack of a trombone which would have made their passage clearer.
>
> "We'll go back to...You have no letters? Oh...Yes, what did you say? Yes, "free from care." *Free from care*. That's it. Start at 'Free from care.'" And with those happy words ringing in my head I made my way to Waterloo Station.[34]

---

[1]Imogen Holst, *Holst* (London: Faber & Faber, 1974), 30.

[2]Michael Short, *Gustav Holst: The Man and His Music* (Oxford: Oxford University Press, 1990), 68.

[3]*Morley College Report for 1906-7*, 5.

[4]*Ibid.*, 2.

[5]*Ibid.*, 9.

[6]*Ibid.*.

[7]James Allen's Girls' School Staff Register.

[8]*Morley College Magazine*, XXVI, No. 7 (June, 1917), 18.

[9]These were military band instruments which, having been made before 1929, were tuned to the

Ancient Philharmonic Pitch of A=452.5 cps.

[10]Imogen Holst, *loc. cit.*.

[11]Personal correspondence, Gustav Holst to Edwin Evans, April 15[, 1925], Central Public Library, Westminster.

[12]*Morley College Magazine*, XVII, No. 2 (January, 1908), 57.

[13]Arnold Foster, "Holst and the Amateur," in *R.C.M. Magazine*, XXX, No. 3 (December, 1934), 89.

[14]*Musical Standard*, January, 1918.

[15]Johann Sebastian Bach.

[16]Personal correspondence, C. Hubert H. Parry to Gustav Holst, Feb[ruary] 2, 1910, The Holst Foundation.

[17]*Liverpool Daily Courier*, July 5, 1921.

[18]Byron Adams, "Book Review: *Gustav Holst: The Man and His Music* by Michael Short," in *Musical Quarterly*, LXXVI, No. 4 (Winter, 1992), 586.

[19]"C.," "An Appreciation of Gustav Holst by an old pupil of Morley College," *Morley College Magazine*, XX, No. 2 (November, 1934), 27-28.

[20]Gustav Holst quoted in *The Halifax Courier*, December, 2, 1922.

[21]Gustav Holst quoted in *"School Music: The Vacation Conference Official Report," in The Music Student*, February, 1916.

[22]*Opera as She Is Wrote* [App. II, 15] (1917-18) was a parody written as a release during World War I. The libretto was written by Morley College students. Rehearsed in underground air raid shelters among other places, it was first performed March 9, 1918.

[23]*Morley College Magazine.*

[24]Personal correspondence, Gustav Holst to Adrian Boult, Feb[ruary] 5[, 1918], British Library Add MS 60498.

[25]Programme: Students' Concert [Morley College], Saturday June 9th, 1917, 7:30 p.m.

[26]Personal correspondence, Gustav Holst to Percy Grainger, May 30[, 1914], Grainger Museum, University of Melbourne, Melbourne, Australia..

[27]Personal correspondence, Gustav Holst to Percy Grainger, June 3d[, 1914], Grainger Museum, The University of Melbourne, Melbourne, Australia.

[28]Charles Kennedy Scott, "Morley College Students' Concert, Saturday, June 13th, 1914," in *Morley College Magazine*, XXIV, No. 1 (September/October, 1914), 11-12.

[29]Programme: Students' Concert [Morley College], Saturday, June 9th, 1917, 7:30 p.m..

[30]For Americans, elevators and subways.

[31]Philip Collis.

[32]Lillian Twiselton, herself a former student at Morley College.

[33]Walter Gandy.

[34]Katharine E. Eggar, "How They Make Music at Morley College: A Chat with Mr. Holst and a Sight of His Work There," in *The Music Student*, XIII, No. 6 (March, 1921), 359-361.

CHAPTER V

10 THE TERRACE, BARNES

1908 began inauspiciously with the announcement that Edward Naylor's opera *The Angelus* had been declared the winner of the Riccordi competition. Second place, in order of merit, was given to two operas: *Helen* and *Sita*. To share second place in such a competition was an honor, yet Holst found it depressing not to win. This event turned out to be the start of a winter of discontent. The neuritis in his right arm was acting up and he had to keep it near a heat source to relieve the pain. The myriad responsibilities from his three part-time jobs were taking their toll and he badly needed a break. That break came just at the right moment from Ralph Vaughan Williams, who was in Paris, studying with Maurice Ravel:

Hotel de L'Universe et du
Portugal
Paris

Dear V.

What do you say to £50 at Easter (or when you want it) & £25 more in September--It might be £50 in September--but I can't be sure yet--so we mustn't count on it. Now is this enough to do you any good? If not, say so & we will try & devise something else--because if we do this job at all we must do it properly.

It is most important--to my mind--that this should be a real holiday to make up for all your past years of strain. If you compose during it all the better--but if you have an idea all the time that you must have something to show for it--then you will spoil your holiday and effectually prevent yourself composing. If--even--you only come back teaching very well it wd mean that it came easier & left you more energy for other work.

I think abroad sounds good--but I don't know why it should be very long abroad--enough to give you a change and a filip--but we can discuss all this when I get back....

Yr
R.V.W.[1]

Holst seized the opportunity. Travel abroad to a warm place might be just the thing to cure what was ailing him. He and Isobel decided that bicycling in the dry heat of Algeria, then a French colony, was an excellent idea for him, although there was not enough money for both of them to go. There were also concerns for Imogen, then only a year old. With that in mind it was decided that Holst should go alone. He secured a leave of absence from his schools and by Good Friday, which was in mid-April that year, he was in Algiers. He wrote to Isobel:

Hotel de la Poste.
Algiers.
Good Friday. [1908]

Dearest Isobel,

Je suis arrive et j'ai l'honneur a vous saluer de l'Afrique!

After which I think English would be a welcome relief to both of us.

I am in the busiest part of the city, quite close to the bay, and the view is just perfect but the noise is terrific.

Beyond Mustapha the country seems lovely and the *village* Arabs delightful, but I shall know more when I have cycled out some distance.

There is something so soft and gentle in the air here and at Marseilles--I suppose it comes from the Mediterranian. Anyhow it is a great contrast to Paris, and I think it affects the people:--they seem kinder that the Parisians and not in such a hurry.

But Algiers is a weird mixture of East and West. This morning I saw Arab women coming from a mosque, and then I caught sight of an advertisement of an American Cinematograph which gave 'Grands Representations de la Passion de N. S. Jesus Christ' with a footnote that you could get in for half price with coupons of somebody's chocolate!

Easter Monday

I am quite at home now and have visited a Mosque, 3 churches, a synagogue and a Casbah and a few other things of the sort.

But the chief glory of Algiers is the native quarter. The streets are really flights of steps with dirty shops or houses *and* the 'Smell of the East'!

Nothing can give you any idea of the sights to be seen at any street corner, even in the European quarter. The native dresses are so varied, and so are the natives themselves. The real Arab is a blooming aristocrat who hardly deigns to notice you. He is comparatively clean and sometimes handsome--always dignified. But there are others who are wild, dirty-looking blackguards with the faces of fiends.

In the mosque, instead of taking my boots off the guide brought me a pair of slippers to go over them like galoshes and then told me to 'glisser'. You know the size of my boots!

By the bye, last Saturday I heard a baby in one of the dirtiest of the native streets howl exactly like Imogen! It made me feel at home immediately.

I do wish I could speak French. I am trying very hard and am reading a mild French novel by way of practice.

Gruss mir das kind und unsere Freunde,

Immer,

G.[2]

Later he wrote the following:

Michelet. Kabylie.
Thursday. [1908]

Dear Isobel,

....Yesterday I took The Supremely Slow train of the world to Tizi Ouzou. It rained like the deuce all day and I thought the only thing was to go back and take the night train to Biskra and then if it rained to go to Tunis and then if it rained to go home and then if it rained to go to bed and stop there! Also there was an incapable military band practising near the hotel--it would have been amusing, but I had six hours of it--during the rain!

To make amends, today has been my greatest day in Africa so far. Although the roads were awful I started early on the bike, and it has been a glorious day and the roads dried quickly and never, never have I seen such mountains.

I hope to reach Biskra next week.

Best love,

G.[3]

The holiday was a success; it soothed Holst's physical pain and cleared his head. Holst did no actual composing in Algeria, but did jot down some melodies. Holst's oldest surviving sketch-book[4], begun during this trip contains, among other items, a two-bar phrase 'Arabe' (girl singing to two birds--they reply), 'Chanson des femmes Arabes--not like it!', a 'Beduin Nomad--fairly correct' and 'oboe tune in procession 5 am (they had been at it all night!)'. Some of these would surface either literally or germinally in future compositions.

When Holst returned from Algeria he thrust himself into composing his chamber opera *Savitri*, Op. 25 [H96] (1908-09). Just as his *Two Songs without Words* had announced a new compactness in Holst's approach to instrumental composition two years earlier, so did *Savitri* do the same for his operas, except even moreso. *Savitri* provided a break from all operas composed in the century that preceded it, and not just Holst's. About the only thing that *Savitri* and Holst's previous opera *Sita* have in common is the fact that each comes from a later Sanskrit source. Only about four months' time--containing Holst's trip to Algeria--separated the Riccordi Competitions' announcement of *Sita*'s non-victory and the start of *Savitri*. That *Savitri* was an intentional reaction either to the Riccordi judgment or to the huge wasted effort on *Sita*, or both, needs hardly to be stated. Taken from the *Mahabharata*, *Savitri* was conceived as a chamber opera from the beginning. It is in one act and lasts only about one-half hour. The entire musical component consists of three soloists, a hidden wordless female (originally mixed) chorus, and an orchestra consisting of nine strings, two flutes and a *cor anglais*. Very little, if any, staging is required. Holst wrote the libretto himself. The title page of the work, front and back, contains the following information:

<u>Savitri</u>

Characters

Satvayan (a woodman)	Tenor
Savitri (his wife)	Soprano
Death	Bass

Scene: A wood at evening

Time of performance: 30 minutes

NOTE. This piece is intended for performance in the open air or else in a small building.

No curtain is required.

The orchestra consists of two string quartets, a contrabass, two flutes and an English Horn.

There is also a hidden chorus of female voices in four parts. They are to sing throughout to the sound of 'u' in 'sun'.

Conductor, chorus and orchestra are to be invisible to the audience.

When performed out of doors, there should be a long avenue or path through a wood in the center of the scene.

Death (who first appears at the further end of this path) is to be represented as a tall vigorous man with shaven head, dressed in a long robe.

He may be surrounded by a dull red glow whenever it can be arranged quietly and unostentatiously but this is by no means essential.[5]

The 62-page full score was completed April 27, 1909.

Holst's "minimalism," if it can be called that, doesn't stop with the production requirements. In the *Mahabharata*, the story of Savitri is more complex. Satvayan is a noble prince; Holst turned him into a woodsman. In the original story, to save the life of her husband, Satvayan, Savitri manipulates Death into granting her three chances. In order to pare his opera down to the bone, Holst incorporates only one and it works perfectly. To incorporate all three would have at least doubled the length of the opera.

The music in *Savitri* is a microcosm of Holst's styles--new and old--up to that point. Most of the music is linear and somewhat modal. The impression given by the intense duet between Savitri and Death at the beginning, although written out note-for-note, is almost aleatoric. At the very least, it comes off as alternating or successive bitonality. Holstian characteristics--frequent meter changes (including liberal amounts of 7/4), gliding harmonies (especially in the flutes), stepwise bass patterns--combine with late romantic harmonies to achieve the desired musical effect. Everything is planned; there are no extra notes here. This was a composer in complete control of his material and as a result, *Savitri* is considered by many to be Holst's first masterpiece. Recognition of the work would take some time, however: *Savitri* would have to sit on the shelf for nearly eight years before its first performance and nearly thirteen years--in the wake of the first performances of *The Planets*--before a professional company would perform it.

During the summer of 1908, Holst moved his family from Richmond to a house situated on the south bank of the Thames, at 10 The Terrace, Barnes. Here he had a music room on the second floor overlooking the river all to himself. Financial circumstances had improved somewhat (several of his smaller works were published), and he and Isobel were also able to rent a summer cottage on the Isle of Sheppey, to the northeast of London, where they could escape the city on weekends. These two things--better writing conditions and better finances--combined to make composing much easier for Holst and during the next five years a number of distinctive and multifarious works flowed from his pen.

Savitri was the first of his second period Sanskrit works. While he was completing the chamber opera, he began a series of four groups of *Choral Hymns from the Rig Veda*, Op. 26. The *Rig Veda* is the older, more religious component of Sanskrit literature. As in the case of *Savitri*, Holst provided his own translations. The four groups of *Choral Hymns from the Rig Veda* were not meant to be performed together and were premiered separately.[6] The First Group [H97] (1908-1910), consisting of "Battle Hymn," "To the Unknown God," and "Funeral Hymn," is scored for mixed chorus and orchestra. "Battle Hymn" is particularly noteworthy in that one can sense hints of "Mars" within its 5/4 bars. The Second Group [H98] (1909), comprised of "To Varuna (God of the Waters)," "To Agni (God of Fire)" and "Funeral Hymn," is scored for female chorus (ssa *divisi*) and orchestra. The Third Group [H99] (1910), consisting of "Hymn to the Dawn," "Hymn to the Waters," "Hymn to Vena," and "Hymn of the Travellers," is scored for female chorus (ssaa) plus harp. Holst indicated that the "Hymn of the Travellers" could be used as a prelude to *Savitri*. The Fourth Group [H100] (1912), comprised of "Hymn to Agni (the sacrificial fire)," "Hymn to Soma," "Hymn to Manas," and "Hymn to Indra," is scored for male chorus (ttbb) plus strings with optional brass. All four groups were published by Stainer & Bell; Holst put up the expense.

All four groups of the *Choral Hymns from the Rig Veda* are written in Holst's second period style. Although sometimes quite contrapuntal, they are very direct and contain no attempts at pseudo-eastern effects. Richard Capell, who spoke highly of Holst throughout his career, commented about this shortly after the composer's death:

> ....So far as the spirit of the music went, the hymns might almost as well have belonged to prehistoric Gloucestershire as to the vally of the Indus. It was a misapprehension of twenty-five years ago to put the strangeness of the musical style down to Oriental influences....[7]

1909 was an eventful year for Holst. Major events took place at Morley College and at St. Paul's Girls' School in June and July, respectively, yet it was an earlier event that shows Holst at his selfless best. The Stepney Children's Pageant was held at the Whitechapel Art Gallery in East London from May 4th to the 20th. In terms of distance and culture, East London was a long way from Brook Green (or even from Waterloo Road). Holst was associated with the event simply because he wanted to be. *The Globe* covered the event:

> A two-fold purpose is served by the Stepney Children's Pageant....Not only will it brighten the lives of a large number of East End children, but it will also prove of great educational value as far as the history of London is concerned....The children participating are all members of Stepney schools, while the weapons and other properties have been constructed at the Stepney Jewish School and the Sir John Cass Institute, so that the whole production is essentially an East London one....[8]

The program featured the following:

Overture by Gustav von Holst
Opening Chorus by G. K. Menzies

I.	AD 61	Death of Boadicea
II.	AD 1066	William the Conqueror's Charter
III.	AD 1141	The Rejection of the Empress Maud including a Morris Dance
IV.	AD 1191	Granting of the Commune

Interlude: The Blind Beggar's Daughter of Bethnel Green

V.	AD 1381	The King's Meeting with Rebels at Mile End
VI.	AD 1588	Departure of the Stepney Men to Fight in the Armada

"The chief characters form a group round Queen Elizabeth during the singing of the Choral Ode (by Dempsey St. School) at the close of which, with the audience, they sing the National Anthem."[9]

The script was largely the work of W. Pett Ridge. All of the incidental music was, of course, supplied by Holst, although not necessarily composed or even collected by him. A sufficient number of folk songs and dances were used. A program note states: "Certain songs and dances are founded on English traditional melodies. Permission to use the latter has been kindly granted by Dr. G. B. Gardiner, Mr. Fuller Maitland, Messrs. Novello & Co., and Mr. Cecil Sharp."[10] Undoubtedly one of the dances used was "The Blind Beggar from Bethnel Green," which was one of the morris dances later set by Holst for chamber orchestra. Holst had help in copying out parts for the pageant from Isidore Schwiller, a violinist whom Holst had known from his trombone playing days in the Carl Rosa Opera. This wasn't their last collaboration; Schwiller is listed as "leader" on a Morley College concert program from the following year and again in the 1911 revival of Purcell's *Fairy Queen.*

Only two of Holst's compositions for the *Incidental Music to The Stepney Children's Pageant*, Op. 27B [H102] survive. "A Song of London" [H102A], for unison voices and piano set to the words of G. K. Menzies, served as the "Opening Chorus" for the pageant; it was privately printed by Novello. The other composition, "O England My Country" [H103] also set to Menzies' words, survives in three different versions: as a unison chorus with piano accompaniment (originally published by Novello in 1909, by Stainer & Bell in *The Motherland Song Book*, and in 1925 as No. 325 in the Church of England's *Songs of Praise*), unison chorus with orchestral accompaniment (published in full score by Stainer & Bell, 1924), and in a non-autograph military band version (which may respresent Holst's first work in that medium).[11]

On Saturday, June 5th, Holst's Morley College students performed Purcell's 1691 opera (or operatic cantata) *King Arthur, or The British Worthy*. According to Holst, this was only the second performance of the work in modern times. The Morley College performance was quite an ambitious undertaking, for Holst had only been there two years. *The London Press* commented on the quality of performance:

> The Morley College Choir is a small one, but so admirably has Mr.

> Gustav von Holst trained the members, and so excellent is the material that the volume of tone was equal to that of a chorus twice as large....an orchestra of thirty did well.[12]

The following month saw an undertaking that was even larger at St. Paul's Girls' School. The school's parent foundation, St. Paul's School, was celebrating its 400th anniversary. It was decided to do a special performance in commemoration of the event. *Masque: The Vision of Dame Christian*, Op. 27A [H101] was first performed on July 22, 1909 and has been performed at the school and only at the school every ten years hence. Francis Ralph Gray wrote the script and Holst, of course, composed the music. As St. Paul's Girls' School had no orchestra at that time, an orchestra from the outside (with a sizeable Morley College contingent) was brought in for the occasion. The masque's setting is detailed in Holst's copy of the programme, which is signed "Gustav von Holst, Master of the Masque":

> Christian, the wife of Sir Henry Colet, was a daughter of the house of Knyvett, a family which, for generations, had produced able and useful men. Her mother was a woman of exceptional courage and resolution. Dame Christian survived her husband and all of her children, many of these died in infancy, and none grew up except her son John, who became Dean of St. Paul's and Founder of St. Paul's School. She lived to a vigorous old age, in cheerful tranquility, showing, as Erasmus says, but little trace of sorrow or suffering, yet her son's letters afford us proof that she was of a tender and sympathetic spirit.[13]

Holst's incidental music, for four-part women's chorus (ssaa) and chamber orchestra, is in five sections: Prelude, First Chorus ("Knowest Thou not the Warning?"), A Hymn of Praise to God ("Oh let us render thanks to God above"), Choral Dance ("How shall we tell of him?"), and Last Chorus ("Now let the word go forth!"). Of particular interest is the prelude, which features a solo oboe playing a theme, the first four tones (also appearing in "Oh let us render") of which are reiterated in the main theme of the "Intermezzo" of the *St. Paul's Suite*, Op. 29, No. 2 [H118} composed three years later. *The Times* described the music as "charming music of a more or less austere quality, finely felt and most cleverly devised by Mr. Gustav von Holst."[14] Years later, Frances Ralph Gray wrote to Adine O'Neill, "There has always seemed to me something of Mr. Holst in the masque music that did not show itself elsewhere."[15]

It was during the rehearsals for the masque that Holst met Vally Lasker. She had been teaching at St. Paul's Girls' School for two years, but on the days of the week when Holst was not there.[16] As time went by, Vally Lasker, with pianist Helen Bidder and Paulinas Nora Day and Jane Joseph, formed the nucleus of a group of performers and amanuenses who willingly served Holst during the various stages of development of his musical compositions. This involved a variety of tasks, from trying out Holst's works in two-piano versions to copying scores and writing out parts. Holst's neuritis was always with him; sometimes it was so painful that it prevented him from writing anything at all. On these occasions, Holst's "scribes" would write from his verbal instructions, sometimes providing the only complete extant manuscript scores to certain works.

In addition to the completion of *Savitri* and two of the sets of *Choral Hymns from the Rig Veda*, there was one other major work that came from his pen in 1909, although, like *Savitri*, it was one that took many years to become known to the general public. Little is known about the circumstances surrounding the composition of the *First Suite in E Flat for Military Band*, Op. 28 No. 1 [H105], other than the year in which it was composed.[17] Some sketches for the second theme of its third movement appear at the opposite end of the sketchbook begun in Algeria and Holst himself entered the work into his "List of Compositions"[18] on the 1909 page. The work may have been intended for a military band composition contest sponsored by The Worshipful Company of Musicians in that year. A First prize of fifty guineas was offered. Holst was kean to enter contests; a number of his compositions, including the operas *The Youth's Choice* and *Sita*, had been entered into such competitions. Holst's name, however, is not listed among The Worshipful Company of Musicians' list of four prize recipients, and it is difficult to conceive this suite losing out to the contest winner, Percy Fletcher's *Back to the Land*, although stranger things have happened. Holst's suite could also have been composed for use at the Royal Military School of Music at Kneller Hall, Whitton, although the strongest evidence for this to date is in a periodical article written twenty years after the work's composition: "In response to an appeal from Kneller Hall for works specifically written for Military Band, Gustav Holst produced two suites."[19] Without further evidence but taking into account that the first documented performance of the suite (then in manuscript) took place at Kneller Hall, it appears more likely that Holst wrote the work for Kneller Hall than for The Worshipful Company of Musicians.

The *First Suite in E Flat for Military Band* is in three movements, all of which are built on the same rising motif of a major second followed by a major fifth. The "Chaconne," solidly in E flat major, not only provides a textbook example of continuous theme and variations, but also displays Holst's acute sense of timbre--a sense developed through his years of professional trombone playing, while simultaneously reveling in the Scottish Orchestra and suffering at the hands of Stanislaus Würm in the White Viennese Band. In choosing the passacaglia/chaconne form for his first movement, Holst satisfied two needs: 1) his natural inclination toward the music of the baroque era and 2) finding a form that would work as an opening movement, both in regard to the medium for which he was composing and in regard to his compact second period style. The lyrical "Country Song" from *Two Songs without Words* had worked well as the first of a one-two punch, but for this suite Holst needed something of a more germinal nature.

The "Intermezzo" is a more theoretically complex movement, displaying folk tune modality and Holst's natural inclinations toward a non-abrasive polytonality. The influence of music he heard in Algeria is felt here, be it ever so subtle. The "March" movement concluding this work is one of the most successful march movements ever written. A totaly new theme of rigid martial quality is stated by the brass and percussion. After bringing the first theme to its conclusion, Holst introduces his "motivic" theme in the low woodwinds and horns. After a developmental section featuring a modern-day "Mannheim crescendo," Holst skillfully combines the two themes in a stirring climax that defies description. Most of Holst's compositions end softly; this one ends with one of the most stentorian climaxes he would ever write.

Much information can be gleaned from the original manuscript title page:

Suite in E Flat
for Military Band
Gustav von Holst
Chaconne
Intermezzo
March

Time of performance: 11 minutes

As each movement is founded on the same phrase it is requested that the Suite shall be played straight through without a break.

It is requested that in the absence of a string bass the ad lib part for that instrument in the intermezzo shall not be played on any brass instrument but omitted excepting where the notes are cued in other parts. Also in the absence of Timpani the ad lib part for the latter is to be omitted entirely.

> The introduction of extra flutes, piccolos, and side drums at the end of the march is only advised when there are sufficient brass instruments to make the countermelody that they play, stand out.

By the time of publication, in 1921, Holst had composed a second military band suite and had removed the "von" part of his name. He also had second thoughts about suggesting the length of performance and the addition of extra instruments at the end of the march. The published title page reflects these changes.

A glance at the first page of the actual composition indicates that Holst was writing for a medium that was in a state of flux. Saxophones, relative newcomers to the military band, were gradually replacing the alto and bass clarinets; likewise, B flat trumpets were replacing those in E flat. It was partially in response to these changes, but also the result of years of offering optional instrumentation--a practice that had started as far back as the 1880's with the cuing in of missing instruments for his father's orchestra at the Montpellier Rotunda--that Holst's manuscript full score offers several options in the instrumentation of this work. Of the thirty-eight instrumental parts listed, some sixteen--over 40% of the total--are listed as "ad lib."

Opinions about the *First Suite in E Flat for Military Band* have varied widely among band conductors, from the late John Paynter, who maintained in clinic sessions that the work was "never a great piece for Holst" to Frederick Fennell's calling it a cornerstone for the repertoire and "an investment in the band and its literature."[20] Perhaps Richard Frank Goldman best put things into perspective:

> Grainger's *Hill-Songs*, the march, *Lads of Wamphray*, and parts of his *Lincolnshire Posy* had...been sketched or completed by 1905....These works were not published until much later and the credit for being the first available and universally recognized original band work of the [20th] century must unquestionably go to Holst's suite. This credit belongs to the work for reasons other than simply a priority of time. For this work of Holst, together with his *Second Suite*, in F major, of 1911, established an altogether new style of idiomatic band writing and, one might say with all justice, a new conception of band sound and the kind of forthright music most suited to the performing medium...no more effective pieces have been written for band.[21]

Whatever the case, one thing is clear: with this work Holst established the suite as *his* primary form of instrumental composition for the next decade. No fewer than five additional suites-- *Beni Mora,* Op. 29 No. 1 [H107] (1909-1910), *Second*

Military Suite in F Minor, Op. 28, No. 2 [H106] (1911, rev. 1922), *St. Paul's Suite*, Op. 29, No. 2 [H118] (1912-13), *Japanese Suite*, Op. 33 [H126] (1915) and *The Planets*, Op. 32 [H125] (1914-1917) flowed from his pen during this period of time. To this total one could easily add nine more: the *Incidental Music for The Pageant of London* [H114] (1910), the withdrawn *Phantastes Suite* [H108] (1911), the suite movement known as "Three Folk Tunes" [H106A] (1913?), two sets of *Morris Dance Tunes* [App. III, 12] (1911), and Holst's 1916-18 arrangements of Purcell's music into four suites for an orchestra of elastic instrumentation: two suites from *The Gordian Knot Untied* [App. III, 18], and one each from *The Virtuous Wife* [App. III, 19] and *The Married Beau* [App. III, 20].

In late 1909 Holst was contacted about writing music for a ballet project. Holst completed one orchestral movement, "Eastern Dance," before the project fell through. He retained his score and in the following year created a suite by adding two additional movements. The suite remained in manuscript for over a decade and was performed under various titles until it was finally published as *Beni Mora*, Op. 29, No. 1 [H107]. While the *First Suite in E Flat for Military Band* hints at Holst's Algerian experience in its second movement, *Beni Mora* bases its entire third movement, "Finale: In the street of Ouled Nails," on one of tunes he wrote into his sketchbook. Holst used the tune as an ostinato. Edwin Evans supplied the following information:

> The "Ouled Nails" are Bedouin dancing girls; and in Biskra a street is set aside for them in which nearly every house is a dancing hall or cafe. The opening (Adagio) suggests a desert at night. The lower strings have a melody...which continues till a few flute figures bring us to the second section, *Allegro moderato*. We are to imagine a traveller drawing nearer to the village, and hearing the flute paly a monotonous little tune which continues throughout the whole movement. On entering the village, fragments of other tunes are heard....These gradually grow clearer. In the street of "Ouled Nails" the ear is bewildered by the variety of strains that pour from the dancing halls, and the mind instinctively grasps the connection between this scene and the greater chaos of the Sahara that lies beyond. But, on turning the corner, the noise quickly subsides, and soon all fades away in the silence of the night.[22]

There were a variety of compositions to come from Holst's pen in 1910. *Christmas Day* [H109], a "Choral Fantasy" on old carols, was composed for his students at Morley College. The carols used are "Good Christian men rejoice," "God rest ye merry gentlemen," "Come ye lofty, come ye lowly," and "The first

Nowell." The accompaniment, for small orchestra or piano, shows Holst at his most accommodating; nearly everything is optional. Holst thought almost as little of this work as of the *Seven Scottish Airs*. In 1918 he wrote to his friend William Gillies Whittaker, then Conductor of the Newcastle Bach Choir and Assistant Conductor of the Newcastle and Gateshead Choral Union, "Xmas Day can be done pf and str or any combination but it's poor stuff anyhow and not worth doing."[23]

The Cloud Messenger, Op. 30 [H111] was composed in 1910 and revised two years later. Over forty minutes in length, it is his largest Sanskrit choral work. Taking into account the amount of time involved in doing his own translation, the work took Holst some seven years to bring to fruition. The manuscript title page contains the following:

The Cloud Messenger
Ode for Chorus and Orchestra
on a Sanscrit poem of Kalidasa
Words and Music by
Gustav von Holst Op. 30

The work is scored for mixed chorus and a huge orchestra which includes two harps and organ, although on the title page Holst characteristically notes that some of the instruments listed "can be dispensed with."[24]

Holst's translated text is taken from *Meghaduta*, a lyric poem of Kalidasa, perhaps the most important writer of Indian drama. Kalidasa, who flourished during the second period of Sanskrit literature, probably lived in the fourth century, although some sources place him as much as five hundred years earlier. The story of *The Cloud Messenger* is that of a poet who asks a cloud moving toward the Himalayas to take a message of love to his wife, from whom he is separated. The cloud travels over the Ganges, by the holy temple at Kailasa, where the ruling deity is he who holds the three worlds in his grasp: Shiva, the great God, the Lord of the Dance.

The Cloud Messenger looks both to Holst's past and his future as a composer. In certain ways the work is a return to *Sita*, with its gargantuan proportions and Wagnerian tendencies. Yet it is not old-style Holst and in many other ways, particularly with the initial entrance of the chorus, it anticipates *The Hymn of Jesus*, Op. 37 [H140](1917). As such, *The Cloud Messenger* is a neglected work, often unjustifiably dismissed as another rung on the ladder that Holst had to climb in order to find his way to his own unique style of composition.

Wagnerian harmonies once again surface occasionally in the *Incidental Music for The Pageant of London* [H114], but this time when they are used they fit perfectly into the scheme of things. The Pageant of London was the centerpiece of the Festival of Empire, the largest event ever held on the grounds of the Crystal Palace in southeast London. The festival was a great exposition in which all of the overseas Dominions of the British Commonwealth of Nations took part. Originally scheduled for 1910, the event was postponed a year due to the death of Edward VII, the reigning monarch. The Festival of Empire was eventually held from May 12th through October 27, 1911, in conjunction with the coronation of George V.

The Pageant of London itself was an immense undertaking; some 15,000 performers from all walks of life were involved. A natural amphitheatre designed by Aston Webb and seating 12,000 was constructed for the event. Among its many unique physical features were a stream representing the Thames, an ancient bridge, and a "cloud curtain" used during and between many of the scenes. An impressive *Book of the Pageant* was published. Sophie Crawford Lomas, editor of the book, explained the purpose of the pageant:

> The aim of the Pageant of London is to show the gradual growth and development of the English nation as seen in the history of this Empire City, and to set forth some of the most striking scenes in the life of its inhabitants, from the time of the primitive stronghold with its dwellings on the banks of the Fleet River to modern days....[25]

The pageant was divided into four epochs; each epoch was in turn divided into eight scenes. The production was somewhat of a poor man's *Ring Cycle*; the epochs were rotated, with one being performed each day (two on Sunday). After July 21st the pageant was shortened considerably and the entire sequence was performed each day.

Among those serving on the Pageant Music Advisory Committee were Hubert Parry and Frederick Cowen. Frank Lascelles was the Master of the Pageant and William Henry [W.H.] Bell, Professor of Harmony at the Royal Academy of Music, served as the Director of the Pageant Music. Twenty of the finest British composers of the day wrote music for the pageant. In addition to Holst and Bell (who also contributed) were Frederick Austin, Hubert Bath, Frank Bridge, Frederick Corder, Percy Fletcher, Cecil Forsyth, H. Balfour Gardiner, Edward German, John Mackenzie-Rogan, Ralph Vaughan Williams and Haydn Wood. Since the arena was outdoors, a military band of fifty players and a chorus of five hundred voices were assembled for the occasion.[26]

Holst composed the incidental music for Scene IV of the first epoch. This dealt with London in the wake of the Danish invasion of 1013. King Ethelred the Unready, through the assistance of Norway's King Olaf Haraldssen, recovers his kingdom. Integral to the plot is the destruction of the London Bridge by the combined English and Norse forces, forcing the Danes to retreat. The text of this scene was complied by Albany F. Major, Sigrid E. Magnussen, and Prof. Collingwood. A synopsis of the event was provided in the huge program book compiled for the festival by Sophie Lomas:

> According to Icelandic Sagas its [Ethelred's Kingdom] recovery by King Ethelred after the first submission to the Danes was signalised by a remarkable victory, and by a striking incident, the breaking of London Bridge, which has perhaps come down in tradition to us in the children's game, "London Bridge is broken down." It is this incident, unrecorded in the English chronicles, which has been chosen for illustration in this scene.[27]

Holst's music is in six parts:

A. Trumpet Calls
B. First Battle Music
C. The Raven Song
D. Biarkamal
E. Second Battle Music
F. The Praise of King Olaf

The "Trumpet Calls" feature four different trumpet calls played by four different groups of instruments (first cornets; second and third cornets; horns or baritone; euphonium or trombone). Holst wrote the following note in the score for the conductor:

> These four calls are to come from the distance if possible. They can be heard singly if required but are written so as to mingle together regardless of rhythm. In fact they will sound better if they do not all start together and if they do not keep the same tempo.[28]

Here Holst takes trumpet call motifs first introduced in *The Mystic Trumpeter* into aleatoric experimentation and to great effect.

The "First Battle Music," marked *Allegro agitato* is in D dorian. In this movement and elsewhere late romantic harmonies surface, but do not fully take over; Holst was well beyond that stage in his own stylistic development and most of the incidental music is linear and modal.

The remaining four movements feature a unison chorus. The text of the "Raven Song" refers to the legend concerning the ravens in the Tower of London--that when they leave the tower will fall. After an initial trumpet call, Holst has the chorus singing a capella for much of the "Biarkamal" movement. Lomas comments:

> "Biarkamal" is a very ancient and famous song, which was actually sung on the field before the battle of Stiklestad in Norway, where King Olaf was killed in 1030. It was probably the custom of that time for "Biarkamal" to be sung before battle. That song has not come down to us complete.[29]

"Second Battle Music," the longest of the six movements, features the fall of the London Bridge. This is the climax of Holst's incidental music. He prepares the listener for it with six measures of woodwind trills, trumpet calls, and percussion rolls to which he indicates "repeat these bars until cue." The climax, marked "The Bridge Falls" is *ffff* before subsiding into a very suitable 14-measure Wagnerian decrescendo leading to a feeling of remorse. This leads to the now-familiar trumpet calls and the sounds of victory.

The final movement, "The Praise of King Olaf," a unison strophic song in D dorian, sounds somewhat anticlimactic when the work is performed as a suite, although in its original context, as the closing piece of the pageant scene, it undoubtedly served its purpose very well.

The *Incidental Music for the Pageant of London* is occasionally performed by college and university wind bands and choruses. With the exception of a private printing of the vocal parts done for the Pageant of London, the work has never been published and remains one of Holst's most obscure compositions. This is ironic, for this music was heard live by over 2,000,000 people, probably more people than heard any other single work of Holst during the composer's lifetime.

There was at least one additional 1910 work of Holst, albeit an arrangement, not an original composition, that was performed at the 1911 Festival of Empire. Following the successful use of folk song material in the Stepney Children's Pageant (and possibly after the successful premiere of the revised version of *A Somerset Rhapsody* in April, 1910), Holst was asked by Cecil Sharp to arrange two sets of *Morris Dance Tunes* [App. III, 12] for chamber orchestra. The sets were to be released in connection with *The Morris Book* (London: Novello, 1907-1913), edited by Sharp, Herbert C. Macilwaine, and George Butterworth.

Holst's task was not a difficult one, since Sharp had already completed a pianoforte harmonization of the tunes. It was made even simpler by the fact that each dance has a plethora of repeats and *dal segnos*, thereby saving Holst's arm. The orchestration was kept simple: flute, clarinet, and string quartet. These arrangements--although they stand well as purely instrumental pieces--were intended to accompany dancers. There are no tempo or dynamic markings. At the beginning of each tune there are up to four introductory measures marked "Once to Yourself." These measures were probably meant to be played before the dancers began. The two sets orchestrated by Holst contain the following dances:

SET I	SET II
1. Bean setting (Stick Dance)	1. Rigs o'Marlow (Stick Dance)
2. Laudnum Bunches (Corner Dance)	2. Bluff King Hal (Handkerchief Dance)
3. Country Gardens (Handkerchief Dance)	3. How d'ye do? (Corner Dance)
4. Constant Billy (Stick Dance)	4. Shepherd's Hey (Stick, or Hand-clapping Dance)
5. Trunkles (Corner Dance)	5. The Blue-eyed Stranger (Handkerchief Dance)
6. Morris Off	6. Morris Off

Published parts for the above sets are readily available, although there are no scores. It is possible that Holst did not write any.

Sometime after the publication of these two orchestral sets, there was a reorganization of the piano sets either by Sharp or by someone at Novello, so that each new set contained eight tunes instead of six. As such, a total of ten "new edition" piano sets were released. To avoid confusion, in its advertisements Novello specified exactly which dances were available in Holst's orchestral arrangements.

During the following year, 1911, Sharp founded the English Folk Dance Society and was heavily involved with music at the Festival of Empire. The Festival of Empire Military Band and others were performing regularly on the grounds of the Crystal Palace and Holst was asked to score six sets of Morris Dances for military band. The sets that Holst arranged corresponded with Sets I and II of the "old edition" orchestral sets plus Sets III through VI of the "new edition" piano sets. Apparently there were no orchestral or military band arrangements made for Sets VII through X, perhaps due to the fact that these four sets contain many dances already found in the previous sets. All six sets of Holst's military band arrangements were placed on hire. They have been missing for a very long time.

---

[1]Personal correspondence, Ralph Vaughan Williams to Gustav Holst, n.d. [1908], quoted in Ursula Vaughan Williams (ed.) and Imogen Holst (ed.), *Heirs and Rebels: Letters to Each Other and Occasional Writings by Gustav Holst and Ralph Vaughan Williams* (Oxford: Oxford University Press, 1959), 42.

[2]Personal correspondence, Gustav Holst to Isobel Holst, Good Friday[, 1908], quoted in Imogen Holst, *Gustav Holst: A Biography*, 2nd ed. (Oxford: Oxford University Press, 1969), 32-33.

[3]Personal correspondence, Gustav Holst to Isobel Holst, Thursday, n.d. [1908], quoted in I. Holst, *Gustav Holst: A Biography*, 34.

[4]Gustav Holst, *Sketch-book* [App. IV, 1], Britten-Pears Library.

[5]Gustav Holst, *Savitri*, Op. 25, Bodleian Library MS Don.c.3.

[6]According to Imogen Holst in *A Thematic Catalogue of Gustav Holst's Music* (London: Faber Music, 1974), pp. 87-92, The First Group [H97] was premiered on December 6, 1911 by the Newcastle-upon-Tyne Musical Union conducted by Edgar Bainton, the Second Group [H98] on March 22, 1911 by the Edward Mason Choir conducted by Edward Mason, the Third Group [H99] on March 16, 1911 by the Blackburn Ladies' Choir and Howard Jarvis, harp conducted by Frank Duckworth, and the Fourth Group [H100] on March 18, 1914 by the Edward Mason Choir and the New Symphony Orchestra conducted by Edward Mason.

[7]Richard Capell, *Radio Times*, XLIX (October 18, 1935), 629.

[8]*The Globe* (London), May 5, 1909.

[9]*Stepney Programme*, Holst Birthplace Museum.

[10]*Ibid.*

[11]No full score has yet been located. The following unused incomplete set of parts, possibly in Schwiller's hand, were found at the publishing house of Stainer & Bell: flute/piccolo in D flat, oboes, E flat clarinet, B flat tenor saxophone, B flat cornets, E flat solo saxhorn, tenor trombone, bass trombone, 1st and 2nd B flat baritone, euphonium, bombardons, percussion. From a score assembled by Colin Matthews, the piece was premiered by the Hanover College Wind Ensemble, Hanover Indiana, on December 6, 1984, the author conducting. At the very least the scoring sounds like Holst's.

[12]*The London Press*, June 11, 1909.

[13]*Programme: The Vision of Dame Christian*, Holst Birthplace Museum.

[14]*The Times*, July 23, 1909.

[15]Personal correspondence, Frances R. Gray to Adine O'Neill, June 20, 1934, The Holst Foundation.

[16]Michael Short, *Gustav Holst: The Man and His Music* (Oxford: Oxford University Press, 1990), 82.

[17]In a 1980 telephone conversation, Imogen Holst told the author that she had been unable to determine for what purpose the work had been composed.

[18]British Library Add. MS 57863.

[19]*Musical Mirror*, October, 1929.

[20]Frederick Fennell, *Time and the Winds* (Kenosha, WI: LeBlanc, 1954), 35.
[21]Richard Franko Goldman, *The Wind Band: Its Literature and Technique* (Boston: Allyn & Bacon, 1961), 225.
[22]*Programme*, Royal Philharmonic Society, May 21, 1935.
[23]Personal Correspondence, Gustav Holst to William Gillies Whittaker, quoted in Michael Short, *Gustav Holst: Letters to W. G. Whittaker* (Glasgow: University of Glasgow Press, 1974), 41.
[24]Gustav Holst, *The Cloud Messenger*, Op. 30, Yale University Beinecke Library MS 500.
[25]*The Times*, July 11, 1911.
[26]Sophie Crawford Lomas, ed., *Festival of Empire Imperial Exhibition and Pageant of London* (London: Festival of Empire, 1911), ix, 162.
[27]*Ibid.*, 11.
[28]Gustav Holst, *Scene IV, Part I [Incidental Music for the Pageant of London]*, British Library Add MS 57876.
[29]Sophie Crawford Lomas, *op.cit.*, 11.

CHAPTER VI

MORE SUITES AND THE CLOUD MESSENGER

In early 1911 music critic Edwin Evans was preparing an article, "Music and Sanskrit Literature: Gustav Holst's compositions," for publication in the *Blackburn Times*. As part of his preparation for the article, Evans had asked Holst to supply him with a list of his musical compositions. Holst responded:

10 The Terrace,
Barnes, S. W.
January 29th [1911]

Dear Evans,

I find it very difficult to select a list of things of mine as I cannot decide what standpoint to take up. If your imaginary millionaire came along I'd make him print rather more than you need!

I have something within me that prompts me to write quite light music every now and then. For instance my Suite in E flat written in 1899 and performed in 1904 by the Patron's Fund: Two songs without words for small orchestra done at the R.C.M. in 1906 and published by Novello: A Suite in E flat for military band: and 'King Estmere' written in 1903 and done twice in London (Edward Mason's choir 1908 and Handel Society in 1910). All these are as genuinely a part of me as the Veda hymns. The question of their ultimate value lies with the critic--with you. But they are not pot-boilers and I shall probably continue to do this sort of thing.

Perhaps the 'Somerset Rhapsody' belongs to this type together with its companion 'Songs of the West'. Both are founded on Folksongs--as you know, I consider the English tunes magnificent but their words often unworthy of them. The Rhapsody was written in 1907 and had fearfully bad luck at first. Then Mason did it last April and I had my biggest success with it. Landon Ronald heard it and did it again at Queen's Hall in June and in Birmingham in October. I conducted it in Bath in November and I believe it is to be done in town this spring.

Perhaps the Oriental Suite[1] and its companion the Fantastic Suite[2] (latter not yet completed) belong to the lighter style--you can decide for yourself re the former.

There is another series of compositions you may think unnecessary to mention and that is my works for female voices. It has been a natural predeliction fostered by having to teach 600 girls per week for some years. In spite of obvious drawbacks I consider that I have learnt as much through my school teaching as I did previously as trombone player in the Carl Rosa and Scottish Orchestra. Of course I give the elder girls fairly exciting stuff--motets of Vittoria and Lasso, etc.

The chief things for female voices are 'Ave Maria' in 8 parts (Laudy) written in 1900, performed first by the 'Magpies' and subsequently throughout England. 'Songs from the "Princess"' (Novello) written in 1905--in 4, 5, and 8 parts. Novellos seems to be doing well out of these. Four old Carols (Schmidt, Boston, U.S.A.) written in 1907. Incidental music to the Stepney Children's Pageant 1909. And above all, the incidental music to the Masque[3] of St. Paul's Girl's School Hammersmith (1909). This is to be done every ten years and the music is not to be done outside the school. Personally I value this very highly--all the performers were my own pupils (choir and orchestra of about 120) and the music is quite elaborate--not a bit of the ordinary school girl stuff. Finally it contains my best tune--a solemn dance.

All this may be pure waste of time but, again, you are the judge and if it <u>is</u> a waste of time just comfort yourself by remembering that it has taken me longer to write it than it has for you to read it!

There remains The Mystic Trumpeter written in 1904, done in 1905 (Patron's Fund) and 1906 (Phil:) and 'A Song of the Night' for violin and orchestra. Invocation (1911) for cello and orchestra. May Mukle is doing the latter at Queen's Hall in May.

Forgive lengthy scrawl.

Yrs

Gustav von Holst[4]

There a number of things to be gained from reading this letter. First of all, it gives one a clear picture of what Holst himself thought of many of the works that he had written up to this point in his career.[5] Quite noticeable is the fact that some of the earlier "heavy" instrumental pieces, such as the *The Cotswolds: Symphony in F*, Op. 8 [H47], *Indra*, Op. 13 [H66] and all of the operas are left out. It could be that Evans provided Holst with a list of "serious" works and asked the composer to add to it. Secondly, this letter provides us with Holst's thoughts on his own perceived dichotomy (or trichotomy) in his compositions. He wasn't certain about how to classify his folk rhapsodies or his recent orchestral suites. Thirdly, the letter reveals Holst's pride in his teaching. That he considered the *Incidental Music to the Masque: The Vision of Dame Christian*, a work that would never be heard by the general public, to contain his best tune and that he even mentions the production in this letter speaks mountains about the value he placed upon his educational work at St. Paul's Girls' School.

Holst now felt that he had established a path for himself, one that was far removed from both his student days and current happenings at the Royal College of Music, including social activities. He comments in a letter to his college friend Marion Scott:

10 The Terrace Barnes
Barnes, S.W.
Feb[ruary] 13th[, 1911?]

Dear Miss Scott

During the last few days I have had extra lessons shifted on to Monday nights and I should like this to form the <u>public</u> reason why I shall not be able to come on February 21st....

As regards the RCM I have tried for years to maintain a sense of loyalty but find it very difficult.

I would rather not remain a member of the Union but I do not much mind either way....In any case please do not have anything of mine done at a Union meeting. It is practically impossible for me to ever come.

Moreover I hope I shall be able to keep in touch with you and Miss Hunter by other means.

Yrs sincerely

Gustav von Holst

P.S. I am so sorry to hear about the cramp. After twelve years experience the only way I know to keep it in check is:

a) over-eating!
b) over-drinking!
and
c) over-sleeping!!!

I invented this for myself on finding that electricity and massage are almost useless.
Since then I have been told that on the continent this sort of thing is the recognised cure![6]

At this stage in Holst's career, the vast majority of his works remained unpublished. As expected, publishers were more than happy to take a chance on the smaller works, but not the larger ones. According to his daughter Imogen, Holst had resolved at the start of 1911 (perhaps at New Year's) to get this corrected. If the reality of publication for many of his larger works still lie years ahead, at the very least he was starting to win votes in the court of public opinion. In March, 1911 Edgar Bainton, composer and conductor of the Newcastle-upon-Tyne Choral Union, wrote a very supportive article in *Musical Opinion and Music Trade Review*:

> Mr. von Holst has published a good deal; but, like most of his contemporaries, his published work gives a very inadequate idea of the music as a whole, though much of it is both beautiful and valuable....
>
> Some years ago a vocal scena, "The Mystic trumpeter," was produced at a Patron's Fund concert, where it had an instantaneous success, the critics being unanimous in its favour. After some considerable time had elapsed, the work received a second performance under the dignified auspices of the Philharmonic Society, where its success was even greater than before. Since that time, as far as I know, it has lain idle on the shelves of the composer's study. What can be the the reason for this strange neglect of a work to which the audiences on both occasions of its performance gave their warmest approval and upon which the most

> discerning critics in the country besetowed their highest encomiums? The immediate success of theis scena is all the more remarkable when we take into consideration the fact that the music has a very marked quality of austerity, a quality which generally prejudices the appeal of a work at its first hearing. A foreign composition , obtaining but a tithe of the praise accorded to the work would have been instantly added to the repertoire of most if not all great orchestras. For Mr. von Holst, despite his name, is an Englishman and still awaits his "hour"...."The Mystic Trumpeter" is a glory to British music; and the fact that the public has no opportunity of becoming familiar with a composition of such originality, strength, and beauty is a sad testimony to the prejudice against native art on the part of our conductors, singers, and entrepreneurs in general which seems to be nigh insuperable....
>
> Austerity would seem to be the predominating quality in Mr. von Holst's music, but there is never any suggestion of harshness. On the contrary, there is a strong vein of tender delicate feeling; and at times even a leaning towards purely sensuous beauty. Yet the austere mood soon returns, which suggests that Puritanism is an insistent trait of the composer's character....[7]

Bainton's article also contains substantial commentary on the *Songs from "The Princess"* and the Rig Veda hymns, some of his most individualistic compositions up to that time. It is interesting to note Bainton's focus on austerity, a trait which would surface even moreso in Holst's later style compositions that lie some fifteen or so years in the future.

If publication of his larger works still eluded Holst, then at least premieres and subsequent performances of his works were becoming more commonplace during the first part of 1911. On January 28th, the out-of-season premiere of *Christmas Day* took place on a concert at Morley College. The work was so successful that it was repeated there three weeks later.[8] In March, there were two important premieres of *Choral Hymns from the Rig Veda*. On March 16th the Blackburn Ladies' Choir performed the Third Group under Frank Duckworth's direction at the Blackburn Town Hall and on March 22nd the Edward Mason Choir, Edward Mason, conductor, premiered the Second Group at Queen's Hall, accompanied by a full orchestra. Both groups of hymns were dedicated to the performing personnel and their conductors.

On April 6th, the premiere of *Three Pieces for Oboe and String Quartet*, Op. 2 [H8A], a 1910 revision of Holst's 1896 *Fantasiestucke*, was given at the Oxford and Cambridge Musical Club in London. Although performed again a few weeks later, the work did not gain a foothold. At least part of the reason for this was that was an amalgamation of two styles. Holst's compositional style and technique were now lightyears beyond what they had been during his student days and his modal austerity did not patch well onto his late romantic beginnings. The work received little notice and remained unpublished throughout Holst's lifetime.

As he had done for the past three years, Holst continued to compose at what for him was a torrid pace. The beginning of 1911 found him at work on a piece for solo violoncello and orchestra. Originally titled *A Song of the Evening* in order to be considered as a tandem piece to his earlier solo violin and orchestra composition *A Song of the Night*, op. 19 No. 1 [H74], he changed its title to *Invocation*, Op. 19, No. 2 [H75] before its first performance. This was wise for two reasons: (1) the two works represent two different stylistic periods and (2) although both works are scored for string soloist with the accompaniment of a small orchestra, the demands placed by each upon the orchestra are entirely different. *A Song of the Night* could be performed by a college or community orchestra--possibly Morley College, but the orchestral part of *Invocation* is much more difficult. Unexpectedly, it is *Invocation* that contains the following note:

> This piece can be played by a small orchestra having only 'single wind.' If the harp part is played on the piano all glissando passages are to be omitted.[9]

Uncharacteristically, the easier work, *A Song of the Night*, has no instrumentation options. One reason for this apparent disparity is that Holst composed *A Song of the Night* in 1905, two years before he had to come to grasps with the instrumentation problems of the orchestra at Morley College. As he continued with his teaching endeavors, Holst wrote more and more pieces with optional instrumentation. Still, as displayed in his two remaining works for solo members of the string quartet, there was no rule. The *Double Concerto*, Op. 49 [H175] (1929) for two violins, premiered by the Royal Philharmonic no less, features optional instrumentation while the *Lyric Movement* [H191] (1933), for viola soloist accompanied by an orchestra of strings and single woodwinds, does not.

Invocation was premiered by cellist May Mukle on May 2, 1911 at Queen's Hall. She was accompanied by the New Symphony Orchestra under the direction of Landon Ronald. Ronald, then conductor of the New Symphony Orchestra of London and eventually editor of the 1935 *Who's Who in Music*, was an early supporter of Holst. He commented about his relationship with Holst following the composer's death:

> Mr. Holst was a very old friend of mine. I knew him just after he had been a trombone in the Scottish Orchestra. Many, many years ago he wrote the "Somerset Rhapsody" which I produced for him....
>
> He was very keen on conducting his own works and believed in being taught how to conduct. Once he brought his famous *Hymn of Jesus* and begged me, as an old friend, to take him through the work from a conducting point of view. My association with him and memories of him are most delightful. He was a nervous and shy man.[10]

Two Eastern Pictures [H112], for four-part female chorus (ssaa) and harp or piano was composed for Frank Duckworth and the Blackburn Ladies Choir, the same ensemble that had recently premiered the Third Group of the *Choral Hymns from the Rig Veda*. Duckworth and the choir early were also early supporters of Holst. He later wrote to Duckworth, "You were the first people to take any serious trouble over my stuff in days gone by, which means that you were the only people who gave me real encouragement when I most needed it."[11] The texts of *Two Eastern Pictures*, "Spring" and "Summer," were translated by Holst from Kalidasa's Sanskrit poem *Ritsusamhara*.

Holst was also busy with the orchestral suite *Phantastes,* Op. 29, No. 2 [H108]. Originally titled *Fantastic Suite*, the work is in four movements, "Prelude." "March," "Sleep," and "Dance." Each movement is preceded by a literary quotation. The suite's instrumentation is huge, uncharacteristically quirky, and features an abundance of special effects. Holst conducted the more than auspicious premiere of *Phantastes* on July 23, 1912 at Queen's Hall on a Royal College of Music Patron's Fund concert; The King and Queen were in attendence. Although the work was warmly received by the audience, the critics, as usual, were divided in their opinions:

> In Mr. Holst's suite its dainty orchestration is not less than notable than the wit and grace of the work as a whole.[12]

> Phantastes revealed the composer in a humorous mood. Unfortunately, the joking did not quite "come off"; the march illustrative of Carroll's Jabberwock was heavy and the dance of Pickninnies, joblillies, garyulies, and the Great Panjandrum himself was inconclusive--one expected a final whirl and excitement, a point the composer missed.[13]

After considering the work further, Holst decided it was not among his efforts and not a worthy companion suite to *Beni Mora.* He withdrew *Phantastes* and eventually assigned its opus number to the *St. Paul's Suite*.

The late spring of 1911 saw Holst involved in his most ambitious undertaking yet at Morley College. Two years earlier, his students had performed only the second production in modern times of Purcell's *King Arthur*. Now it was time for another Purcell stage work, *The Fairy Queen*, to receive its due. This time, however, Holst and his students were giving the first performance of the work since Purcell's death. The text of Purcell's 1691-92 work is an anonymous "barbarous 17th-century perversion"[14] of William Shakespeare's comedy *A Midsummer Night's Dream*. Purcell's full score for the five-act work disappeared shortly after his death and for two centuries was thought to be irretrievably lost. In 1901 it was rediscovered and subsequently published in a limited edition by The Purcell Society. No parts were published, however, and this meant that, in pre-photocopying days, if the work was to be performed then all of the parts for two hours' worth of music had to be written out by hand--a daunting task! What made matters worse was that some vocal parts had to be transposed into more comforable registers. Perhaps to aid the copyists, some adjustments were made; Act V was eliminated, although four of its pieces were interpolated elsewhere. Holst recognized the time and effort involved and had the following note printed on the first page of the program:

> The full score of this work was lost shortly after Henry Purcell's death in 1695. It was recently discovered and the Purcell Society published it. By their permission, the Students of Morley College copied the entire Vocal and Orchestral Parts (1,500 pages).

Below this note were, for all to see, the names of the twenty-eight copyists involved. Vally Lasker was among them. Vaughan Williams commented, "All worked like slaves--when Holst drives, he spares neither himself nor others."[15] Still, those involved saw it as a labor of love.

The revival of *The Fairy Queen* was given on June 10, 1911 at the Royal Victoria Hall, which had been rented specially for the occasion. Ralph Vaughan Williams was on hand to give a pre-concert lecture to the audience. It was truly an event and one which influenced other revivals. *The Musical News* commented:

> The occasion was not one that calls for detailed criticism. Indeed, bearing in mind that the performers and orchestra were almost wholly composed of students, the rendering of the music deserves praise. The orchestra was efficient; the chorus sang extremely well, while the soloists,

> though not to speak, "acclimated" to Purcell's style, yet acquitted themselves with much credit. Mr. Gustav von Holst was the conductor, and may justly be congratulated on the success of the performance.[16]

The Fairy Queen was the capstone of six of the most active months that Holst had known. The next six provided a palette that was just as full. The activities associated with The Festival of Empire at London's Crystal Palace, postponed from the previous year, had begun as early as April, with rehearsals for the Pageant of London. Holst had completed his *Incidental Music for The Pageant of London* during the previous year but the extent of Holst's further involvement with the actual production of the pageant is not known. Still there was at least one other festival activity that involved Holst. At Cecil Sharp's bidding Holst transcribed six sets of *Morris Dance Tunes* for the military bands that were continously performing there.

A major military band work that may have been composed with The Festival of Empire in mind was the *2nd Military Suite in F Minor*, Op. 28 [H106]. As in the case of the *First Suite in E Flat for Military Band*, nothing is known about the conditions (musical and otherwise) surrounding the composition of this work other than the fact that it was first composed in 1911[17] and that is was altered significantly by the composer on at least two occasions, becoming the *Second Suite in F for Military Band*, Op. 28, No. 2 in the process. There is only one extant sketch for the suite and it involves phrasing, not actual composition. Unlike the *First Suite in E Flat*, this suite is made up of actual folk tunes, most of which were collected in Hampshire by George B. Gardiner. The uniqueness of this composition lies not with the tunes themselves, but in how they are used and how they are scored. The use of mixed meters (often adding up to Holst's characteristic seven beats) in the "Song of the Blacksmith," the use of an anvil in the same, and the skillful juxtaposition of "Green Sleaves" with the "Dargason" in the Finale are only some examples of Holst's deft skills at orchestration and arranging that occur in this suite.

The *2nd Military Suite in F Minor* was scored for the small regimental band of the British Army of 1911, leaving out many of the instruments included in the *First Suite in E Flat* of two years earlier. Internal evidence[18] indicates that the work originally probably contained only three movements, each containing one or more English folk songs:

I. March: "Young Reilly," "Swansea Town," "Claudy Banks"
II. "I'll Love My Love"
III. Fantasia on "The Dargason" (also containing "Green Sleaves")

Sometime after 1912, after he had stopped writing his time signatures as fractions, Holst scrapped "Young Reilly" as the first tune used in the first movement. For its replacement, he reached into an untitled military march movement, known today as *Three Folk Tunes* [H106A] and extracted the Bampton "Glorishears," a morris handkerchief dance. Holst's first contact with this tune may have been when he scored it as part of Set V of the morris dance tunes military band transcriptions done for Cecil Sharp. The other two tunes found in *Three Folk Tunes*, "He-back, She-back" and "The Sons of Levy," were not utilized. At about the same time he made use of "Glorishears," Holst interpolated another folk song, "Song of the Blacksmith," into the suite, fashioning it into a separate third movement. Thus at least the layout of the four movements of the present suite was established, although Holst would extensively revise the work again in 1922.

Holst was able to get away for a short while during the summer of 1911. The money that he had been paid by Cecil Sharp for the morris dance tunes projects enabled him to travel to Switzerland. Holst was accompanied by Cecil Coles, a young composer and conductor who had substituted for him at Morley College during his Algerian trip in 1908. Coles had been in Stuttgart, Germany for the past three years, studying at the conservatory there. He would remain for another two years, serving as assistant conductor at the Stuttgart Royal Opera House. Holst wrote to Isobel:

> I'm having the biggest rest of my life. And Cecil *ist ein ausgezeichnet practvoll Fuehrer*![19] The only drawback is that I'm not as young and vigorous as I was. I don't get over the ground as I did once, and like Hamlet I am fat and scant of breath. However, I now know the joys of hob-nailed boots and alpenstock; also I have bought a rucksack.[20]

Holst returned from Switzerland ready to face the autumn terms. As always, Morley College resumed earlier than St. Paul's Girls' School, but in this year it was a particular blessing, for his duties at St. Paul's had increased. The school's High Mistress Frances Ralph Gray wrote about this:

> ....I asked Mr. Holst to form and train an orchestra....Flute, oboe, and clarinet were supplied by the organ. Later (when flute, oboe, and clarinet were real), a harmonium was added to cover bassoon.[21]

Holst, however, was not the one who founded the orchestra at St. Paul's Girls' School; the school's violin mistress, Dorothea Walenn, had actually started the ensemble[22]. Descriptions of her group indicate that there were some strings and some toy instruments; it was not a serious venture. Holst's success with the orchestra at Morley College undoubtedly caught the attention of Frances Ralph Gray, who saw the desirability of a change in approach. Irene Bonnett Swann, who played oboe during the early days of the orchestra, commented:

> The school orchestra was taken over by Mr. Holst in 1911, and grew from a small body of strings to a strong force, complete with woodwind, timpani and percussion. Here again I think of him as a pioneer, for his introduction of the wind opened this branch of music music to women, of whom a number have now made their mark as players of wind instruments. The music we played in the school orchestra included Haydn symphonies, a lot of Purcell and Bach--and a strong dose of Strauss Waltzes! Later on more ambitious schemes were undertaken, including a complete performance of Bach's cantata *Sleepers wake!* [No. 140] with duets arranged for girl's voices. Parts of the *Christmas Oratorio* were also given.[23]

Helen Gaskell, who played oboe in the orchestra in the early 1920's remembers Holst's approach to the orchestra to have been "school masterly." She continues about Holst's choice of repertoire: "I was always looking forward to something to play. I dare say there would be some...symphonies and small, good music. Never played any rubbish at all. Just once in a while we had something jolly nice."[24] Her orchestral experience at St. Paul's Girls' School served her well; from 1932 until 1966 she was an oboist with the BBC Symphony Orchestra. As such she was the first female member of that orchestra.

Holst operated his orchestra at St. Paul's in much the same manner as he did at Morley College, enlisting everybody that he could--including the music faculty. Nora Day played oboe; Helen Bidder played violin. Vally Lasker, who had learned to play viola in four days for the Morley College revival of Purcell's *Fairy Queen*, became the mainstay of that section and Isobel was recruited to play bass. Nancy Gotch Strode, who studied at St. Paul's from 1913 to 1917, commented:

> I was told when I arrived into the Music Wing that as I had played the violin I would from now be a viola and sit with Miss Vally Lasker. So I got hold of an instrument from my sister and set about to learn the clef as best I could. My older sister really <u>was</u> a violinist and later became a professional viola player. I was neither, by a very long chalk, but I did enjoy the school orchestra as Vally lasker and I sawed away happily

> together. Our Director of Music was referred to affactionately as "Gussie", and what an inspiring conductor he was. We could have played anything if he had willed it so. His fair-haired wife played the double bass and she sometimes argued with him; we listened in silent awe when this happened. It never lasted long.[25]

The orchestra program at St. Paul's Girls' School flourished, so much so that eventually a second orchestra--a junior orchestra--was added. Holst remained conductor of the original "senior" orchestra and Vally Lasker headed the "junior" orchestra. It wasn't just the orchestra program that grew. By 1929 St. Paul's Girls' School had a music staff of about twenty and a flourishing music society. Holst commented about the orchestra in that year:

> Here an orchestra exists of varying constituents. At present its "wind" included three flutes, two clarinets, and two horns (all played by girls), but no oboes; at one time it had six oboes and no clarinets and at another time six flutes. Whatever instruments there may happen to be have been worked into the scheme, and the orchestra boasts of having performed more of Purcell's orchestra music than any orchestra in the world.[26]

At the beginning of the 1911 fall term at Morley College, Holst reduced his teaching load there so that he could spend more time composing. The result was that he was able to write *Hecuba's Lament*, Op. 31, No. 1 [H115], a setting for contralto solo, three-part female chorus (ssa) and orchestra of a passage from the *Trojan Women* of Euripides. This was the first of three works that Holst set to Gilbert Murray's English translations from the ancient Greek. Knowing first-hand the difficulties of getting his larger works performed, Holst made an alternate setting of the work for voices, strings and piano. Even so, the twelve-minute work had to wait over a decade for its first performance. It remains one of Holst's most neglected and obscure works.

The extraordinarily busy year of 1911 ended with the premiere performance of the First Group of the *Choral Hymns from the Rig Veda*, Op. 26, No. 1 [H97] on December 6th at the Newcastle Town Hall. The Newcastle-upon-Tyne Musical Union was conducted by Edgar Bainton, who had written the very supportive article about Holst for *Musical Opinion and Trade Review* nine months earlier. Thus is was that all three of Holst's then-existing groups of the *Choral Hymns from the Rig Veda* received their premieres in the same calendar year.

1912 began with Holst taking on yet another girls' school music teaching position. Perhaps it was instigated by Holst feeling the financial pinch from reducing his work load at Morley College or perhaps the success of his program at St. Paul's Girls' School had attracted the attention of a sister school's administration. Whatever the case, Holst taught singing each Wednesday for the next five years at the Wycombe Abbey School. Founded in 1896, the school is located on the outskirts of High Wycombe, Buckinghamshire, about twenty miles northwest of London. The school was not difficult for Holst to reach--only a thirty-minute train ride from Paddington Station, followed by a seven minute walk. During the time that Holst was there, the school had about 200 students, ages thirteen to nineteen, and was entirely residential.

Singing classes were classified among the "Voluntary Subjects" and a fee of three pounds three schillings was charged per term.[27] Nonetheless, the singing classes were very popular and Holst's met in the 120 foot-long hall known as Big School. In such a hall and with large enrollments there was little chance of true teacher-pupil interaction. From three accounts written by seniors many years afterwards, the boarding school was far from Holst's favorite place:

> Gustav Holst visited Wycombe Abbey in order to teach singing. I can only imagine he did so for financial reasons, as he had not in the years of the 1914-1918 war become a celebrity. And how he must have hated it, because we did not want to sing and behaved atrociously. He himself was not interested in traditional English folk songs and wished us to sing a ballad entitled "Sir Eglamore." It had a refrain 'Ri fol Ril fol, tiddle iddle I doh' and ended with 'Lanky down lanky down tiddle diddle day'--we thought it utter nonsense--poor Mr. Holst.
>
> He complained of our behavior to the Headmistress and we were duly ticked off for our discourtesy. She did, however, say that possibly "the song was unsuitable". Also, very sensibly, she suggested that tests should be carried out at house level to eliminate the tone deaf or otherwise handicapped so that they were excused from singing classes....
>
> And then one never-to-be-forgotten singing period Gustav Holst himself abandoned Sir Eglamore and sat at the grand piano on the platform of Big School and <u>played</u> to us. We sat, as still as mice, utterly entranced, and when the bell went and he stopped playing we implored him to go on."[28]

> On Wednesday mornings a rather gnomelike little man would stride across that platform to the piano and thunder out 'For all the saints' to Vaughan Williams' fine setting. I never remember him playing any other hymn though no doubt he sometimes did, but his accompaniment to this

one I shall never forget--its splendor has sounded now through seventy years....He brought the vision of 'that glorious day' into Big School each Wednesday.

He remained all that day to teach various classes. My impression is, alas, that we were largely unresponsive yet I have also never forgotten those classes. He would stride up and down the platform and try his hardest to galvanize us into life. I remember once how he shook his foot at us after a feeble attempt at 'Scots wha hae we' Wallace bled'. 'It's your gory bed' he shouted at us, 'not a cushioned couch. Now feel it, feel it."

'Welcome to your gory bed,
Or to victory'

I think he did manage to evoke some response from us but I fear he did not like us so much as his pupils at St. Paul's. But I like to feel that I was conscious of some special quality about him and I am fond of boasting to my musical friends that I was once taught singing by Gustav Holst.[29]

There was even a mild student rebellion:

I was at Wycombe Abbey from May, 1913 to July, 1916. I have a very vivid memory of this 'little man,' as we thought. To start with he was known as 'Von Slosh'. We saw him once a week. Our music consisted of a red bound linen edition of the National Song book, and we sang nothing else than the eternal John Peel, Annie Laurie, Scot wa'hae, the Ash Grove etc. until we were heartily sick of them. Finally one day--I think it must have been August, 1914--we struck! I can't remember the circumstances, but I was in the thick of it.

'Well, what do you want?' said Von Slosh, looking over his round metal spectacles at us.

I replied, 'Well, can't we have some English folk songs?'
I, at that time was very enthusiastic about the E.F.D.S. summer schools and the tremendous pleasure we got at them, with Cecil Sharp himself at the piano. My memory is dim now and I can't remember what we then sang. But I do know that we were all a bit peeved that (1) we never did any part songs with him; (2) we were never conducted--von Slosh always played the accompaniments, and (3) we knew St. Paul's School, Hammersmith, was his favourite. But we felt we, with 300 girls, could easily compete with St. Paul's if we had been given the chance....[30]

Holst was not the central figure in the music department at Wycombe Abbey.

That honor went to one Miss Reynell, a Royal College of Music graduate and a fine accompanist who served as head of the music department from 1913 to 1948. Holst left the school in 1917, perhaps due to an improved financial situation. He was not forgotten. Holst returned four years later (by which time he had become famous) to adjudicate the school's annual Singing Competition between the school's houses. Today the music program still flourishes at Wycombe Abbey and there is a room named after Holst in the new music school.[31]

By the time he began his position at Wycombe Abbey, Holst's works were being performed with reasonable frequency. *A Somerset Rhapsody* in particular was gaining a real foothold. It was performed in November, 1911 at Bournemouth and repeated there on January 11, 1912 with the composer conducting. One week later it appeared on a program of the Halle Concert Society.[32] On March 21st *Two Eastern Pictures* were premiered by it dedicatees, Frank Duckworth and the Blackburn Ladies Choir, at Blackburn Town Hall and four days later the First Group of the *Choral Hymns from the Rig Veda* was given its first London performance at Queen's Hall by the Edward Mason Choir and New Symphony Orchestra.

In addition to performances that were the result of self-promotion or reputation, there were at least two other opportunities open to younger British composers in 1912. The Royal College of Music Patrons Fund concerts, long established by now, was one of them; Holst's conducting of *Phantastes* on their July 23rd concert has already been mentioned. The other was a brand new series of concerts sponsored by the independently wealthy musical philanthropist Henry Balfour Gardiner. The objective of this series was to promote the music of younger British composers.

Balfour Gardiner, as he was known, was many things to many people. A member of the Frankfurt am Main Hoch Conservatory group of the 1890's, Gardiner was a composer, conductor, amateur architect, and pioneer forester. The single role for which he is best remembered, however, is that of champion and patron of British music. Percy Grainger wrote of Gardiner in 1947:

> His knowledge of music is vast, his personality generous and constructive. In many ways he has been the good angel of British music--the comforter of Delius, the supporter of Holst, the financier of the London Philharmonic and the personal "good fairy" of all good composers in need of a holiday or help.[33]

There were four Balfour Gardiner concerts in 1912. Many young British composers were represented in this series; among them were Arnold Bax, Percy

Grainger, Norman O'Neill, Charles Kennedy Scott, and Cyril Scott. Holst conducted the New Symphony Orchestra in the premiere of *Beni Mora* on the fourth program, held at Queen's Hall on May 1st.

Holst completed two major works during the early months of 1912. The Fourth Group of *Choral Hymns from the Rig Veda*, Op. 26 (No. 3) [H100], for male chorus (ttbb), string orchestra and optional brass, was published by Stainer and Bell (at Holst's expense) shortly after it was written. It was the last of his Sanskrit works to be composed. The fourth hymn in the set, the comparatively bombastic "Hymn to Indra," gave Holst considerable trouble and he wrote in a 1923 notebook "scrap 4th hymn in Veda IV."[34] He may have been haunted somewhat by his other "Indra," the unperformed symphonic poem *Indra*, Op. 13 [H66], of 1903. *Two Psalms* [H117], a slighter composition, was composed for mixed chorus (satb) accompanied by strings and organ or brass. The melody of the first movement, "Psalm 86" ("To My Humble Supplication"), was taken from the 1543 *Geneva Psalter*; it contains a tenor solo. The melody of the second, "Psalm 148" ("Lord, Who Hast Made Us for Thine Own"), is taken from the *Geistliche Kirchengesaenge* of 1623, and is known to Protestants in the English-speaking world as "Ye Watchers and Ye Holy Ones." The translation of "Psalm 148" was written by Frances Ralph Gray for the inauguration of the organ at St. Paul's Girls' School in 1910. The mixed chorus version of the second psalm was a further development of the version for female chorus (ssaa) composed for the inauguration.

Following the completion of these two works, Holst took a short time off from original composition and revised three earlier works--*Suite de Ballet in E Flat*, *The Mystic Trumpeter*, and *The Cloud Messenger*--for future performance. In all three cases, his revisions bore fruit. *The Cloud Messenger* was published later in the year by Stainer and Bell and the *Suite de Ballet* would be published within two years for the Royal College of Music Patron's Fund. *The Mystic Trumpeter* and *The Cloud Messenger* would be performed on Balfour Gardiner Concerts during the following year.

In was probably during August, 1912 in his music room overlooking the Thames at 10 The Terrace, Barnes that Holst did the bulk of the work on one of his most endearing compositions, the *St. Paul's Suite*, Op. 29, No. 2 [H118]. Holst appears to have been at ease while writing it; there were no other works in progress at this time to worry about and the original score displays few revisions. Holst wrote the following note on the cover sheet that he supplied a decade later:

St Paul's Suite
for string orchestra

Original Score Not to be used for performance.
This Suite was written for St Paul's Girls' School orchestra in 1912.
By the time it was finished and copied the orchestra possessed wood wind instruments. Parts for the latter were added.
The Suite was published in 1922 by Messrs Goodwin Tabb for strings only. The MS wind parts are the property of the School.

Gustav Holst
July 1922[35]

This score was probably not the one used by the publishers Goodwin & Tabb when the work was prepared in 1922 for publication. As such it raises several questions. First of all, there are many extra measures in the manuscript that did not find their way to publication. The first movement, "Jig," is more or less as Holst left it; the composer himself eliminated eight measures just before the C sharp major passage in the manuscript score. The second movement, "Ostinato," contains four extraneous bars (mm. 131-132 and mm.135-136) that the composer probably removed before publication. The removal of these measures tightened the thematic material and eliminated phrasal monotony. Also there is a fifty-two bar ending for this movement that was crossed out by Holst and replaced with superior material.

It is the third movement, labeled "Dance" on the manuscript score ("Intermezzo" in the published version) that is the most problematical. On the manuscript score there are a total of sixty-five measures right in the center of the movement that do not exist in the published score. These beautifully sculpted measures, mostly but not entirely in E major, give the movement a perfect sonata-rondo form (ABACABA). They were not crossed out by the composer on the manuscript score; in fact there are even wind parts cued in, as they are throughout the remainder of the suite. It is the author's opinion that the elimination of these measures was probably done by the publisher (in order to conserve space) and not by Holst.

The fourth movement, "Finale (The Dargason)," is a transcription of the "Fantasia on 'The Dargason'" of the *Second Suite in F for Military Band*, with five additional variations. The manuscript score contains two redundant measures that were mistakenly put in at a page turn and crossed out by Holst. The last two measures were also rewritten by the composer. The printed score reflects these corrections.

Another question has to do with the optional wind parts. These were not published. Holst's other original suite for St. Paul's Girls' School, *Brook Green Suite* [H190], published in 1934, has its optional wind parts included in the set of parts. An entry from his July, 1922 notebook reads:

order SP str Goodwin
ask for fl ob " "

This implies that it was Goodwin & Tabb's decision, not Holst's, to exclude the optional wind parts from publication.[36]

Birthday greetings were an important part of Holst's life. When he was not giving them, either in the form of letter writing or gift-giving that often took the form of short compositions, he was receiving them. His Sanskrit teacher, Mabel "Patsy" Bode wrote to him:

Sept. 20th [19]12.
52, Fordwych Road
West Hampstead, N.W.

My dear Gustav,

You are such a very unsentimental sort of person but all the year round one does not dare to tell you nice things to your face....the only thing one can do is to say nice things behind your back. But there is one day in the year, on which one may be as demonstrative (on paper) & as gushing as one likes and that day dawns for you tomorrow. Well, I wish you all the good things of this earth, chiefly the extermination of girls' schools from your life. I wish you a few publishers who know a good thing when they see it, a few Balfour Gardiners with rich fathers & a German or English Opera-manager who will do Sita or Savitri. Before your next birthday comes round again, I wish to see Trojan Women[37] & Cloud Messenger performed, The Mystic Trumpeter, Beni Mora & Phantastes published, the successor to Trojan Women[38] finished and a few more trifles like that. I also, from my heart, wish you & Isobel & Imogen & myself many happy returns of this day & may we spend it together often. If I were not so grasping & wanted to give you a real treat I ought not to come tomorrow & give you a holiday...for once--but I am grasping & selfish & so 10 The Terrace will see me, as usual. I am very sorry to hear that you have a cold, you did the very same clever thing last year at this time!

We did have some music last night, Ernst Wolff & I. 2 Symphonies of

Mozart,...Brahms Liebeslieder Waltzes, 2 overtures by Weber, some Bach Cantatas, some Schumann duets, & in the middle of the evenings the Vedas which he graciously approved of....

Until to-morrow then,
in the best love,

[Mabel Bode][39]

During the first part of 1913 Holst was at work on the *Hymn to Dionysus*, Op. 31, No. 2 [H116] for female chorus and large orchestra. For this companion piece to *Hecuba's Lament* Holst again used Gilbert Murray's English translations, this time from *The Bacchae* of Euripides. Once again Holst wrote a version of the accompaniment for reduced instrumentation--strings and piano. The work is dedicated to H. Balfour Gardiner.

Holst also saw a number of his works performed on important concerts. The first of these was on January 3rd, when Holst himself conducted *Beni Mora* in Birmingham Town Hall before the joint conference of the Musical League and Incorporated Society of Musicians. On February 27th at Queen's Hall, the Edward Mason Choir gave the first London performance of the Third Group of *Choral Hymns from the Rig Veda* and on March 10th the Blackburn Ladies' Choir presented a program with Frank Duckworth and Holst sharing the conducting duties.

In addition to these performances, Holst's works appeared on three separate Balfour Gardiner Concerts at Queen's Hall. This, the second year of the concert series, was also its last. Gardiner had become frustrated not only with the amount of effort needed to produced the concerts, but also with the attitudes of many of the orchestra members. Undoubtedly the series would have stopped the following year anyhow due to the inception of World War I. On Tuesday, February 11th *Two Eastern Pictures* were given their London premiere by Charles Kennedy Scott and the Oriana Madrigal Society. Two weeks later, on February 25th, Holst conducted the New Symphony Orchestra in the revised version of *The Mystic Trumpeter*. Cicely Gleeson-White, who had sung the soprano solo in the 1905 premiere of the original, reprised her role. One week later, on Thursday, March 4th, Holst's most ambitious Sanskrit choral work, *The Cloud Messenger*, was premiered, featuring Holst conducting the London Choral Society and the New Symphony Orchestra. The work caused a great deal of difficulty to the choir in the two Saturday rehearsals, in fact so much difficulty that the program had to be changed in order to accommodate it. In a letter to his girlfriend Karen Holten,

Percy Grainger commented about the situation:

31A King's Road
Sloane Square

To Karen Holten
Monday 3.3.13

....My "At Twilight"[40] will not be performed tomorrow. Fagge's Choir can do so little of von Holst's work that Gard asked me to put Irish[41] instead of it, so they could take time for von Holst's work....[42]

Grainger was not offended by this; his own *Father and Daughter*, for thirty mandolins, had upstaged all of the other composers--including Holst--on the fourth Balfour Gardiner Concert of the preceding year. As it happened, Arthur Fagge and the London Choral Society were able to give a performance of *At Twilight* on a concert in Queen's Hall on December 3rd of that same year.

For whatever reason, *The Cloud Messenger* did not go well in performance and reviews were mixed. Perhaps the problem lie in the inherent difficulties of the work, perhaps in it's forty-minute length. Whatever the case, Holst was distraught after the performance and wrote to Frank Duckworth, "The 'Cloud' did not go well, and the whole thing has been a blow to me. I'm 'fed up' with music, especially my own."[43] Although the vocal score was published almost immediately, the work fell into a state of semi-oblivion. Holst's friend William Gillies Whittaker was about the only person to program the work again during the composer's lifetime.

Holst's depression over *The Cloud Messenger* was alleviated somewhat when Balfour Gardiner invited the composer to accompany him, fellow composer Arnold Bax, and his brother, playwright Clifford Bax, on an all-expenses paid holiday to Spain. Specifically, the destinations were Gerona and Barcelona in Catalonia, and Mallorca, largest of the Balearic Islands off Spain's southeast coast. Language was not much of a problem. Arnold Bax knew some Spanish; he picked up some of the language from his wife, Elisita Luisa Sobrino, who was a Spanish concert pianist. Gardiner had also studied some of the language. The dates of the holiday did not correspond with Holst's school breaks, but he was able to arrange for substitutes to take his place. He was now free to spend a guiltless holiday; his *Diary* entry for Thursday, March 27th reads simply "Off to Spain."[44]

At Victoria Station, the point of departure for the foursome, Holst met Clifford Bax for the first time. The two of them hit it off very well. Holst, worn out from fourteen years of Sanskrit translations, was looking for other areas of interest. Bax comments:

> We met for the first time at Victoria Station on a day of March in 1913, that halcyon year; and together with Balfour Gardiner and my brother (Arnold Bax) we set out on a holiday in Spain which was happy and at peace. I think Miss [Imogen] Holst is wrong when she says Gustav had already studied the old and despised art of astrology. Having already heard his Rig-Veda Hymns I guessed that here was a kindred spirit, an artist who, even in the middle of the Shaw-Wells-Bennett age, had recognized the depth of old Indian philosophy; and it was, I believe, during that long journey that I introduced him to the elements of astrology--much to the disapproval of our more orthodox friend Balfour Gardiner. All the musical world knows to what fine purpose Gustav subsequently put his study of "the stars", and it was characteristic in him that once he had transmuted the subject into music he almost entirely lost interest in it....[45]

The two of them would collaborate on no fewer than five future projects, including *The Sneezing Charm* [H143] and *Tale of The Wandering Scholar*, Op. 51 [H176].

This three and one-half week trip to Spain is discussed in great detail in Clifford Bax's 1925 book *Inland Far*. It is much more than a simple account. Conversations are recalled and Bax brings the personalities of his three composer companions to life:

> ....In Spain I discovered at least what it is that composers talk about. They can discuss orchestration for hours and hours, for days and days. Before we came to Dover, my three composers touched lightly upon the subject, as fencers will ceremoniously salute one another. At Calais they began to skirmish, vigorously differing from one another concerning the emotional value of the trombone. Halfway across France their rapiers were making merry play, and the sparks began to fly. With irreproachable courtesy they demonstrated misjudgments of orchestration by quoting from each other's works...by Gerona they were brandishing the most tremendous generalizations....[said] Holst, "There are only three men who have understood the orchestra: Bach, Mozart, and Wagner. Bach had colour, Mozart had balance, Wagner had both."[46]

Yet Holst was not always so quick to enter discussions:

> During most of the pyrotechnical discussions with which we enlivened our month in Spain he resolutely stuck to his position as audience. "Now Gustav," I would say at the end of a dinner in Barcelona, "let us hear what you think about---" And he would say, "No, No! Don't ask me. Ask Balfour."[47]

The first stop was in Gerona (Girona, in Catalonian), just northeast of Barcelona.

> It was now late afternoon and we agreed that we would explore the city before dinner. By the time, however, that the others were ready, Holst could nowhere be found, and leaving him to the protection of the gods, we walked through the narrow streets to the river....At the farther end of the bridge there was now a sedate crowd of peasants, artisans, and their womenfolk. The most conspicuous figures were several old men who wore red cotton nightcaps. In the centre stood three women, three bundles of bright clothes. One was thrumming a guitar. Another, blind and very ancient, lustily sang a ballad to an emphatic and reiterated tune. The third came among us, into the crowd, offering copies of a broadsheet.
>
> "I wonder what's happened to Gustav," mused Gardiner,--he'd love this."
>
> "He does," said a voice at our elbows."
>
> "Why," asked someone, "what on earth have you been doing?"
>
> "Losing myself," replied Holst. "If you want to know a city, you must manage to lose yourself."[48]

From Gerona, the foursome travelled to Barcelona.

> ....a brief journey peppered by a variance of opinion about Wagner's use of the piccolo, and agreeably peppered by a discussion between Holst and myself. Clifford Bax: "The words 'an olive-tree by a well' give us more delight than the well and the olive tree could give"....Holst, however, championed actualities. In vain did I point out triumphantly to the acknowledged fact that memory lends enchantment to experience, obliterating the tiresome qualities of matter and leaving only a residium of delight. Holst rejoined that he would rather hear Parsifal than remember it; nor would he assent to the notion that heaven will be a sublime memory

of earth....[49]

After spending several days in Barcelona, where they saw the sights, including a bullfight, the foursome decided to visit the Benedictine monastery of Montserrat and spend a night there. They took the train northward from Barcelona to Monistrol, which lies at the foot of the mountain on which Montserrat sits. Bax comments:

> You can get there either by a mountain-railway or on foot by a carriage road. "The road for me," said Holst....he resisted the seduction of the light railway and set off, alone on foot.[50]

Holst caught up with the others early that evening at the monastery. The following day they returned to Barcelona and set off for Mallorca. On this voyage Holst spoke from the very essence of his soul:

> The following night we took the steamer to Mallorca. No sooner had we come aboard than Gardiner and my brother sought refuge in their berths. Holst, who was in high spirits throughout the holiday, had no intentions of squandering it; for his need of a holiday was too great; and accordingly he promenaded the deck with me while the lamps of Barcelona were dwindling behind us....
>
> "Some day," replied Holst, "I expect you'll agree with me that it's a great thing to be a failure."
>
> "How do you make that out?"
>
> "Well," he continued, "if nobody likes your work, you have to go on just for the sake of the work. And you're in no danger of letting the public make you repeat yourself. Every artist ought to pray that he not be 'a success.' If he's a failure he stands a good chance of concentrating upon the best work of which he's capable."[51]

In Palma, there was a local liquer called *verdad*. Holst had a particular penchant for it:

> ....Rarely have I seen a man look more blessed than Gustav Holst as he fondled his evening glass....
>
> At lunch I suggested that, as their stay in palma was nearing its end, they should crown not only their dinners but their lunches with *verdad*.
>
> "No," answered Holst, "not at least for me."

"You've turned ascetic, Gustav?"

"My dear boy," he replied, "your true sybarite is always ascetic. The sensation of drinking *verdad* is worth saving up."[52]

On at least one occasion the discussion centered on women. In 1913 attitudes were quite different from what they are at the present. Even so, in the following discussion Holst comes off as being somewhat of a feminist for his time:

> Remarked someone, "Consciously or unconsciously, women are always thinking of the next generation. That's why an abstract idea is never real to them ,--merely an amusing toy. It doesn't help to keep life going, and women only feel ardently to that end."
>
> "What's that?" cried Holst, awaking from contemplation of his *verdad*. "Well, I've taught girls all my life--Sorry! I mean, of course, ever since I bicycled round the provinces from theatre to theatre, with a trombone on my back. And I don't think there's much difference women and men."
>
> "Well, Balfour," said I [Clifford Bax]. "and what's your opinion?"
>
> "You must leave me out of it," answered Gardiner, shaking his head respectfully. "They're incomprehensible to me. I should feel more at home with an Eskimo."
>
> "That's just it. What makes them so foreign?"
>
> "I don't know. I never shall. And such an extraordinary shape."
>
> "They can't be impersonal," said my brother [Arnold Bax]. "They don't consider an idea that's put forward, but the person who advances it."
>
> "I can only say," commented Holst, "that my experience provides more exceptions to your rule than illustrations of it."
>
> "Anyway," broke in my brother impatiently, "we all hate intellectual women."
>
> Holst's eyebrows rose markedly. His lower lip fell. He pinched the tip of his nose.[53]

Holst returned from Spain on April 21st[54], refreshed and ready to resume his work. Yet, due to one particularly fortuitous event that summer, his approach to composition, teaching, and lifestyle would change forever.

---

[1]*Beni Mora Suite*, Op. 29, No. 1 [H107] (1909-10).

[2]Renamed *Phantastes,* originally Op, 29, No. 2 [H108]; it was withdrawn by the composer after its

1912 premiere.

[3]*Masque: The Vision of Dame Christian*, Op. 27A.

[4]Personal correspondence, Gustav Holst to Edwin Evans, January 29[, 1911], The Holst Foundation.

[5]On the one hand, this moment of reflection could be called a mid-point in Holst's career. He had completed 111 of the 192 works listed as "H" by Imogen Holst. On the other hand, nearly all of his greatest works lie ahead.

[6]Personal correspondence, Gustav Holst to Marion Scott, Feb[ruary] 13[, 1911?].

[7]Edgar Bainton, "Some British Composers: IV.--Gustav von Holst" in *Musical Opinion and Music Trade Review*, XXXIV, No. 402 (March, 1911), 397.

[8]Michael Short, *Gustav Holst: The Man and His Music* (Oxford: Oxford University Press, 1990), 90.

[9]Gustav Holst: *Invocation*, Op. 19, No. 2, British Library Add. MS 47819.

[10]Landon Ronald, quoted in *The Yorkshire Post*, May 25, 1934.

[11]Gustav Holst, quoted in Imogen Holst, *Gustav Holst: A Biography*, 2nd ed. (Oxford: Oxford University Press, 1969), 37.

[12]*Westminster Gazette*, July 24, 1912.

[13]*Pall Mall Gazette*, July 24, 1912.

[14]*Birmingham Daily Post*, June 12, 1911.

[15]Ralph Vaughan Williams, "Gustav Holst" in *Music and Letters*, I, No. 3 (July, 1920), 188.

[16]*The Musical Press*, June 17, 1911.

[17]Gustav Holst, *List of Compositions*, British Library Add. MS 57863.

[18]Gustav Holst, *Second Suite in F for Military Band*, Op. 28, No. 2, British Library Add. MS 47825.

[19]Approximately, an "excellent gorgeous leader."

[20]Personal correspondence, Gustav Holst to Isobel Holst, n.d. [1911], quoted in Imogen Holst, *op. cit.*, 40.

[21]Frances Ralph Gray, *And Gladly Wolde He Lerne and Gladly Teche* (London: Sampson, Low, Marston & Co., Ltd., 1931), 132.

[22]Michael Short, *op. cit.*, 104.

[23]Irene Bonnett, "Mr. Holst in School," in *Royal College of Music Magazine*, XXX, No. 3 (December, 1934), 87.

[24]Personal correspondence, Sally Hain (Helen Gaskell's niece) to the author, August 9, 1999. Ms. Hain interviewed Ms. Gaskell.

[25]Nancy Strode, "Across the Years: A Personal Recollection of Gustav Holst," *The Conductors' Guild Bulletin*, Summer, 1974.

[26]Gustav Holst, quoted in T*he Observer*, November 21, 1929.

[27]*Wycombe Abbey School [Prospectus]* (The Girls' Education Co., Ltd., 1914).

[28]Ella Monckton, Wycombe Abbey School, n.d..

[29]U. K. Moore, Wycombe Abbey School, n.d..

[30]Dorothy Phybus, Wycombe Abbey School, 1973.

[31]Personal correspondence, Alison Heath, Wycombe Abbey School Archivist, to the author June 21, 1999.

[32]*Programme, Halle Concert Society*, January 18, 1912. This is very elaborate and includes incipits from *A Somerset Rhapsody*.

[33]Personal correspondence, Percy Grainger to Bernard Heinze, December 3, 1947, quoted in Malcolm Gillies (ed.) and Daid Pear (ed.), *The All-Round Man: Selected Letters of Percy Grainger, 1914-1961* (Oxford: Clarendon Press, 1994), 218.

[34]Gustav Holst, Notebook, n.d. (1923), the Holst Foundation.

[35]Gustav Holst, *St. Paul's Suite*, MS, St. Paul's Girls' School. Although Holst cites the date of composition as 1912 on this score, the work itself is included on the 1913 page of his own "List of Compositions," British Library Add. Ms 57863.

[36]Gustav Holst, Notebook [July, 1922], The Holst Foundation.

[37]*Hecuba's Lament*, Op. 31, No. 1 [H115].

[38]*Hymn to Dionysus*, Op. 31, No. 2 [H116].

[39]Personal correspondence, Mabel "Patsy" Bode to Gustav Holst, September 20, 1912, The Holst Foundation.

[40]Percy Grainger's 1900-1909 work for tenor solo and unaccompanied chorus.

[41]*Irish Tune from County Derry.*

[42]Personal correspondence [original in Danish], Percy Grainger to Karen Holten, Monday, March 3, 1913, quoted in Kay Dreyfuss, ed., *The Farthest North of Humanness: Letters of Percy Grainger, 1901-1914* (St. Louis: MMB Inc., 1985), 489.

[43]Personal correspondence, Gustav Holst to Frank Duckworth, quoted in Imogen Holst, *op. cit.,* 41.

[44]Gustav Holst, *Diary*, Thursday, March 27, 1913, The Holst Foundation.

[45]Clifford Bax, "Recollections of Gustav Holst" in *Music and Letters*, XX, No. 1 (January, 1939), 1-2.

[46]Clifford Bax, *Inland Far: A Book of Thoughts and Impressions* (London: William Heinemann Ltd., 1925).

[47]*Ibid.*, 208.

[48]*Ibid.*, 212.

[49]*Ibid.*, 215.

[50]*Ibid.*, 221-222.

[51]*Ibid.*, 225.

[52]*Ibid.*, 236.

[53]*Ibid.*, 228.

[54]Gustav Holst, *Diary*, Monday, April 21, 1913, The Holst Foundation.

CHAPTER VII

NEW MUSIC WING, DIRGE, AND THE PLANETS

The summer of 1913 witnessed the completion of the Music Wing at St. Paul's Girls' School. The school and its music department had grown considerably in the ten years since the school's founding and through the work of Adine O'Neill, Holst and others, music had long since become integral to the very essence of the school. Gerald Horsley, architect uncle of Nancy Gotch (who would enter the school as a student that autumn), had designed the wing. There was a sizeable singing hall that could accommodate 300 and round the top of it were twelve sound-proofed practice rooms. There were two other sound-proofed rooms, one for chamber music and the other one to be known forever as "Mr. Holst's Room." Imogen Holst comments about it:

> It had double windows, and two pianos, and a writing-desk that was wide enough for the widest full score, and a system of central heating that sent the thermometer shooting up to heights rivalling the deserts of Algeria.
>
> On week-days he would be teaching in it, and there would be people to interview. But on Sundays, when the school was locked up, it would be all his own. And every August there would be thirty-one days of absolute quietness, and he would be able to write and write.[1]

From this time forward, Holst did most of his composing in this room. He would also do the vast majority of his correspondence from there. It was not entirely coincidental that Holst and his family moved their lodgings during that same summer. His music room on the first floor at "10 the Terrace, Barnes" had served him exceedingly well over the past five years, from *Savitri* through revisions of *The Cloud Messenger*, but now there was no longer the absolute necessity of maintaining such a large townhouse. True, the housed offered picturesque views, but that fact that it was on the banks of the Thames meant that it was frequently engulfed in fog and mist and this caused problems for Holst's throat So, Holst and his family moved to 10 Luxemburg Gardens, just around the corner from St. Paul's Girls' School. Thus it was that the school literally became the center of Holst's life, both in physical and cerebral terms.

The Music Wing was dedicated on July 1, 1913 and many consider the first work written by Holst in his new room there to have been the *St. Paul's Suite*, Op. 29, No. 2 [H118] (originally known as *Suite in C*). This is not quite true, for the work had essentially been composed in the previous year. In structure and content it is more assocated with with the Barnes years than with the years that followed. A. E. F. Dickinson has even referred to the suite as "gay but retrogressive[2]." Completion of the score, however, almost certainly took place in Holst's new room during the summer of 1913. The key to this room was considered by Holst to be one of his two most valuable worldly possessions; the other was Beethoven's tuning fork, given to him by an aficionado in the early1920's.

In addition to this physical shift, there was a numinous one. In terms of composition, Holst was looking for answers. He perceived that there was something wrong with his latest large-scale work, *The Cloud Messenger*, that it--and possibly Sanskrit when taken as a whole--had failed him. *The Cloud Messenger* had received far less critical acclaim than *Phantastes*, which he himself had withdrawn for musical reasons. Fourteen years of Sanskrit study and thirty translations of verses had contributed to about ten musical works, but in his opinion, these had not produced the expected results. The four groups of *Choral Hymns from the Rig Veda*, among the most individualistic works he or any other British composer had written at the time, met with modest success, but his larger Sanskrit works either met with indifference or were entirely igmored; his two Sanskrit operas, *Sita* and *Savitri*, remained unperformed. Holst had had enough; he would compose no more musical works based on Sanskrit. It is not that he would feel badly in the future about having composed these works; he simply needed a new paths to explore. Thus Holst's perception of failure in *The Cloud Messenger* was at least partially responsible for the shifting of interests that resulted in *The Planets*.

He found a new path in astrology. Discussions with Clifford Bax in Spain had motivated him to pursue the subject. Soon after his return to London he was reading Alan Leo's *What Is a Horoscope?* (London, 1913) and casting horoscopes for his friends. Although his interest in astrology would wane soon after completion of *The Planets*, he enjoyed working out horoscopes for his friends throughout his life. Christopher Palmer comments about Holst doing just that for the children of Herbert and Dorothy Howells in the 1930's:

> Ursula tells me that Holst did a horoscope for both her and Michael. Her parents saw hers (it has not survived) and it made some mention of the theatre. Michael's however, Holst could never be persuaded to part with; instead he kept asking his parents to confirm that such-and-such had indeed been the correct time of birth, couldn't it have been a few minutes before or after? Whether we should read any introspective significance into this is hard to say. Did Holst see something which he felt it would be better for Herbert and Dorothy not to know?[3]

Another path presented itself to Holst in the form of attending rehearsals or performances of modern music during that summer and the following winter. Sergei Diaghilev's Ballet Russe of Paris had been coming to London on a regular basis and in 1913 the company was there for two month-long stays. During the first stay (in February and March) they introduced London to Stravinsky's *Petrushka*; during the second, on July 11th, they gave the London premiere of *Le Sacre du Printemps* (*The Rite of Spring*). Six months later, on January 17, 1914, Arnold Schoenberg was in town to conduct his *5 Orkesterstuecke*, Op. 16 *(Five Pieces for Orchestra)*, which had received its world premiere in London two years earlier under the baton of Henry Wood. Holst attended the performance conducted by Schoenberg; in fact he owned a score to the work. Holst had not composed a purely orchestra work on large scale for over a dozen years. His suites *Phantastes* and *Beni Mora* were quite recent, but his last symphonic poem was *Indra* and his latest symphony was *The Cotswolds: Symphony in F.* The latter two had been composed during Holst's first stylistic period.

The musical manifestation of these two paths--astrology and hearing large modern orchestral works-- lie some months ahead, however, as Holst had plenty of other things to keep himself busy --at least during the second half of 1913.

The year ended with the now customary bevy of performances of Holst works. In Newcastle William Gillies Whittaker conducted *The Cloud Messenger* in a version for voices, piano,and strings[4] and Holst himself conducted *Beni Mora* twice, at Queen's Hall and in Birmingham. He also conducted the third ("Jesu, Thou Virgin-born") and fourth ("The Saviour of the world is born") of his *Four Old English Carols*, Op. 20B [H82] at Westminster Cathedral.

Holst celebrated the end of his very busy term with a five-day walk in Essex. He started in one of the oldest cities in England--Colcester, located about sixty miles northeast of London, and hiked in a northwesterly direction, eventually ending up at the village of Thaxted. Located a few miles south of Saffron Walden, Thaxted boasts a unique timber-framed guildhall, large medieval church, and an operating windmill, not to mention scores of beautiful fifteenth-century houses and cobblestone streets. Holst was so attracted by what Thaxted had to offer, that he had thoughts about bringing his family to live there. A few months later, these thoughts became reality when he received word that a three hundred year-old thatched-roof cottage had become available for rent on Monk Street. Located at Dunmow Road on top of a hill, the cottage was located about two miles south of town and provided an extremely rural setting. Thaxted itself was out of the way; the closest rail link was from Liverpool Street Station via Elsenham. From Elsenham one could travel the remaining six miles on a light railway. Once in Thaxted, getting from the town to the cottage involved a forty-minute uphill walk. The cottage itself had few if any of the modern conveniences, which didn't seem to bother Holst, even though this meant having to do chores that one otherwise wouldn't have to even think about in the city. The isolation and quiet meant that he could have a second place to compose without interruption. Holst and Isobel went to see the cottage, liked it, and rented it. Luxemburg Gardens soon became history, as the family made this cottage their home. Although they moved into town from the Monk Street cottage at the end of their three-year lease in 1917, the Holsts remained in the Thaxted-Great Easton-Great Dunmow area until 1933.

1914 began with two lectures at St. Paul's Girl's School. Holst was clearly thinking about expanding the instrumentation of his orchestra there. On Thursday, January 29th there was a lecture on brass instruments and on the following Thursday, February 5th, a lecture on woodwinds[5]. The lectures bore fruit; the orchestra soon included woodwinds and horns. In March there were two premieres of Holst works. On the 10th, the *Hymn to Dionysis* was performed by the Oriana Society and Queen's Hall Orchestra at Queen's Hall under Holst's direction, fully eight years before its earlier companion piece, *Hecuba's Lament,* and on the 18th, the last premiere of a Holst Sanskrit work to be given during the composer's lifetime, that of the Fourth Group of the *Choral Hymns from the Rig Veda*, Op. 26 [No. 4] [H100], was performed by the Edward Mason Choir and New Symphony Orchestra at Queen's Hall.

The storm clouds of war were forming during the early months of 1914; war with Germany was imminent. The prospect of war drew forth various works from the pens of many of England's best composers. Most of these works were written along strictly patriotic lines and rightfully cast aside immediately after the war. Holst's answer to the impending war, however, was not one of patriotism, but one of grief. For his source Holst turned to an American poet whose works he knew very well: Walt Whitman. Holst's *A Dirge for Two Veterans* [H121] is a musical setting of Whitman's poem of the same name. One of many poems about the American Civil War, "A Dirge for Two Verterans" was published in 1865 as part of a volume titled *Drum Taps*. This volume was later included in Whitman's best-known collection, *Leaves of Grass*. There were at least two other settings of Whitman's poem done in the same era. One was a 1911 setting by Ralph Vaughan Williams; the other was done by his composition teacher Charles Wood. Michael Kennedy comments:

> Cyril Rootham conducted the C.U.M.S. [Cambridge University Musical Society] in Wood's *Dirge for Two Veterans* and Vaughan Williams' *A London Symphony*. Did Wood know that his pupil had set the same words in 1911--a setting which was to lie in a drawer until it was incorporated into *Dona Nobis Pacem*[6] in 1936?....It is likely, although he would never have admitted it, that Vaughan Williams suppressed his own setting to Wood and Holst.[7]

Holst's scoring for *A Dirge for Two Veterans* is unique: male chorus (TTBB), three cornets, two bombardons, side (snare) drum and bass drum. Holst included the following note on his manuscript score:

> Three cornets in B flat, two bombardons, side drum and bass drum are required. If preferred a trombone may be substituted for one bombardon or (in a concert room) cellos and string basses may be used instead of the two bombardons. In either case a few notes towards the end must be omitted by the trombones or cellos where the part goes below their compass.[8]

Thus, even in a work calling for only five wind instruments, flexibility in instrumentation is maintained. Holst undoubtedly envisioned this work being performed at some sort of military concert, but did not want to confine performances of it to that particular situation. The bombardons provide a drone for Whitman's "sad procession" while the cornets, used sparingly, seem to ask why. It is extremely doubtful that Holst would have known Charles Ives' *Unanswered Question*, although *A Dirge for Two Veterans*, in an entirely different musical setting, harnesses a futility of a not dissimilar nature. Holst's work was published immediately by Curwen and, although there is no record of a premiere performance, it is not unreasonable to assume that the work was performed on a number of occasions during wartime. Holst, however, would not hear a performance of it until 1923, during his first American visit, and then under his own direction.

Following the composition of *A Dirge for Two Veterans*, Holst began work *The Planets*, Op. 32 [H125], by far his most famous composition[9]. The idea for the work had been taking shape for some time. Astrology had been the beginning, but only the beginning. Holst commented to the press:

> As a rule I only study things that suggest music to me. That's why I worried at Sanskrit. Then recently the character of each planet suggested lots to me, and I have been studying astrology fairly closely.
>
> It's a pity we make such a fuss about these things. On the one side there is nothing but abuse and ridicule, with the natural result that when one is brought face to face with overwhelming proofs there is danger of going to the other extreme.
>
> Whereas, of course, everything in this world--writing a letter for instance--is just one big miracle. Or rather, the universe itself is one.[10]

Holst began work on *The Planets* during the spring of 1914. "Mars" was the first to be composed. Some critics tried to claim that it had been written directly as a musical response to World War I; it was not. Others claimed that the tension and arms race had something to do with its composition; this also was untrue. Although "Mars'" subtitle, "The Bringer of War," seems to make it a candidate as a harbinger for the war, Holst maintained that it's timing was purely coincidental. In actuality, Holst finished the vast majority of "Mars" before the conflict began. The title of the second movement composed, "Venus: The Bringer of Peace," didn't bear up to any more political significance than "Mars" had; it was finished nearly four years before the Treaty of Versailles.

At the time of the composition of *The Planets*, there were eight known planets; Pluto would not be discovered until 1930. Holst reduced this number to seven by eliminating Earth. In composing the work, Holst considered the astrological character of each planet and what this character suggested to him musically. The result was a suite of seven individual tone poems, each self-contained. None of them borrows music from nor even influences musical events in any of the others. Holst determined the order of the suite in accordance with what made sense musically. According to his own "List of Compositions[11]," Holst composed "Mars," "Venus," and "Jupiter" in 1914, "Saturn," "Uranus," and "Neptune" in 1915, and "Mercury" in 1916. All are in the order of the suite, except "Mercury," which fits in after "Venus." Why Holst composed it last is not known, other than that it may have taken longer to formulate in his mind than the others.

Once composed, it took a while for Holst to sanction *The Planets, Op. 32: Suite for Large Orchestra* as the work's title. The inside title page of the original 1917 manuscript full score has a Schoenbergian feel:

Seven Pieces for Large Orchestra

Gustav von Holst
Op 32

I The Bringer of War
II The Bringer of Peace
III The Winged Messenger
IV The Bringer of Jollity
V The Bringer of Old Age
VI The Magician
VII The Mystic[12]

Of interest is the fact that there are no planet names written either on this page or on the flip-side which lists the instrumentation. The first page of each movement does contain the name of its planet, although written in a haphazard manner. Holst originally wrote in the astrological symbols, then erased and replaced them. Holst was into symbols; his diary and notebook entries are full of them. In addition to offering a sense of sophistication, writing astrological symbols and Sanskrit titles for appropriate works was a way of saving his hand.

Holst required an enormous orchestra for *The Planets*; in fact it was the largest that he ever used, surpassing *Beni Mora, Indra* and *Phantastes*, which required the large post-romantic orchestras of the time. He indicated the instrumentation on the outer title page:

Four Flutes (3rd to combine 1st Piccolo, 4th to combine 2nd Piccolo and Bass Flute[13].)
Three Oboes (3rd to combine bass oboe[14])
Corno Inglesi
Three clarinets
Bass Clarinet
Three Bassoons
Double Bassoon
Six Horns in F

Two Tenor Trombones
One Bass Trombone
One tenor tuba in B flat[15]
One bass tuba
Six timpani (two players)[16]
Big Drum[17]
Side[18] "
Cymbals
Bells
triangle
tambourine
Glockenspiel
Gong
Celesta
Xylophone
Two Harps
Organ
Strings
In the Seventh Piece only A Hidden Choir of female voices in six parts.[19]

Not all instruments are used in all of the movements, of course, but the score is incredibly large--198 pages in all. Keeping with the individuality of each planet, each movement has its own numbering system. The task of writing out the score alone would in itself appear to be daunting. When on considers the neuritis in Holst's right arm it appears to be an impossibility and would have were it not for three ananuenses. Vally Lasker wrote out some of "Venus," "Jupiter," and "Uranus" while Nora Day wrote out some of "Mars," "Jupiter," and "Saturn." Both were St. Paul's Girls' School music faculty member. Jane Joseph, a recent graduate of the school then studying composition with Holst, wrote out part of "Neptune"[20]. All three worked from a number of sources: (1) The parts of the full score entirely written by Holst, (2) two-piano drafts on which Holst indicated instrumentation, and (3) Holst's verbal instructions. According to Imogen Holst, nearly all of the full score to "Mercury" and a great deal of "Mars," "Venus," and "Saturn" are in Holst's hand. The skill of the three amanuenses in imitating Holst's writing and each others' sometimes makes it difficult to determine which section was written by whom.

Two-piano drafts had by now become a regular feature of Holst's compositional process. Vally Lasker and Nora Day, and/or Helen Bidder would play these drafts to Holst so that he could hear the harmonies over an extended period of time. It was generally in these two-piano versions that Holst and Ralph Vaughan Williams would "try out" their music on celebrated "field days."

In 1949 and 1951, some fifteen and seventeen years after Holst's death, his two-piano arrangements of the movements of *The Planets* were published. The question that arises from this is whether or not these piano versions were meant for publication. If these simply represent a stage in *The Planets'* composition, then Holst probably would not have wanted them in print. On the other hand, he did sanction the 1923 F & B Goodwin publication of a piano duet arrangement of the entire work done by Vally Lasker and Nora Day.

Holst also wrote an organ duet version of "Neptune." Vally Lasker commented, "Holst first made us play Neptune on the organ, thinking it too nebulous for a percussion instrument like the piano."[21] Fifteen years later Holst harbored similar feelings about the "Lento" portion of *Hammersmith*, Op. 52 [H178] and likewise arranged that section for organ duet.

In addition to his colleagues, Holst occasionally solicated help from his students. Nancy Gotch comments:

> ....one of the greatest experiences of my school life came when a friend and I peered through the double windows of Mr. Holst's room (as it is still called) and he, catching sight of us, called us in and said, "What about not doing any harmony today--I've just finished a new piece, and shall we play it?" It was Saturn, and it has always remained my favourite of all the Planets. The three of us sat in a row at the grand piano, and we were allotted lines of the huge pencil score. Was it the first-ever performance? I like to think so. The composer sat between us and talked about it now and again; he never spoke of it as his Creation but more as if it were something that he had happened to write down. Later, I sat near him in the Queen's Hall when Adrian Boult conducted all the Planets. Holst might have been anyone up from the country, staring at the orchestra with a hand on each knee--completely absorbed, but with a "this is none of me" expression. The applause and the singling of him out at the end to acknowledge it seemed to mystify and embarrass him. Our school-girl lack of comment but interested acceptance of Saturn as his "new piece" may have been more to his own mood.[22]

The Planets occupied the majority of Holst's compositional thought over the next two years, and there were other significant works to come from his pen during this time, but actual full-scale performances of his larger works were far fewer due to the outbreak of war. What had started out as a regional conflict on

July 28, 1914, when Austria-Hungary declared war on Serbia, had escalated into a European war within a week. By August 4th, eight nations had become involved and the United Kingdom had declared war on Germany. Many of Holst's composer friends, including George Butterworth, Cecil Coles, and even forty-two-year-old Ralph Vaughan Williams, enlisted in the military. Holst, too, wanted to enlist but was disqualified due to poor eyesight and neuritis. He therefore remained in England for the time being, continuing in his roles as teacher and composer the best he could.

Anti-German sentiment was extremely high during the war. Not only were the works of modern German composers banned from the concert hall, but entire music literature books appeared without any references to German composers. Perhaps worst of all was that anybody with a German-sounding name (even if it were Swedish by way of Latvia) was in for a difficult time. People in Thaxted distrusted him to the point of reporting him to the police and nearly every time a work of Holst's was presented in public, there was some sort of written "apology" made to explain his name. Still, Holst managed to take things in stride and continued composing.

The war meant a curtailment in the programming of many large works. Still there were occasional performances and the performance of smaller works was not as affected. Sometimes solo works composed with an orchestral accompaniment were performed with piano instead. Holst's concert piece *Invocation*, for example, showed up on a violoncello recital in October, 1914.

Aside from his continued work on *The Planets*, the first work Holst composed during the war was *Philip the King* [H122], some incidental music written for a play of that name by John Masefield. The play was given a matinee performance on November 5th at the Royal Opera House, Covent Garden in aid of "The Arts Fund for the relief of members of the artistic professions in distress owing to the war." Granville-Barker was the producer. Politically speaking, the work was on target and Holst was seen by the public as making a contribution to the war effort. *The Referee*'s music critic offered accolades: "I must congratulate Mr. Gustav von Holst on the appropriateness of his incidental music, which was discreetly played under his direction."[23] Unfortunately, the music itself has vanished although stage directions in the libretto contain some information about the music:

1) Bells ring for the supposed Spanish victory while 'monks are singing'
2) Recalde's men, who are survivors of the Armada, are heard 'singing off':

   Out of the deep, out of the deep we come
   Preserved from death at sea to die at home.

3) 'A muffled march of the drums' at the end of the play.[24]

Whatever the music may have been, it probably did not amount to very much since Holst did not include it in his "List of Compositions." Thirteen years later Holst would write far more substantial incidental music for another Masefield play, *The Coming of Christ* [H170].

The first work completed by Holst in 1915 was *Nunc Dimittis* [H127], for unaccompanied eight-part mixed chorus (satb/satb). It may have been written at the request of Richard Terry, choir director at the Westminster Cathedral[25]. The text is from the Roman Catholic Liturgy, then in Latin. Holst's fine sense of counterpoint is felt throughout and the beginning, featuring melodic chord construction, underscores the fact that he had just finished composing "Jupiter." *Nunc Dimittis* was first performed under Terry's direction as part of the Easter Sunday mass at Westminster Cathedral on April 4th.

Most of the remainder of 1915 was spent on *The Planets*. The solitude of his rooms at St. Paul's Girls' School and Monk Street Cottage had given him the impetus he needed and by summer's end he had composed six of the seven movements. Before working on "Mercury," however, Holst turned his thoughts to a commissioned project. The Japanese Dancer Michio Ito, then appearing at London's Coliseum Theatre, had asked Holst to write a dance suite based on Japanese themes that he (Ito) would supply. The resultant work was the *Japanese Suite*, Op. 33 [H126], for large orchestra. It consists of the following movements:

Prelude: Song of the Fisheries
1. Ceremonial Dance
2. Dance of the Marionette
Interlude: Song of the Fisherman
3. Dance under the Cherry Tree
4. Finale: Dance of the Wolves

Holst supplied his own theme for "Dance of the Marionette."

The first performance of *Japanese Suite* may have occurred for as part of a performance by Ito in late 1915 or 1916, although there are no records of this. The work was given a concert performance by Henry J. Wood and the New Queen's Hall Orchestra on October 19, 1919. Although published in 1925, *Japanese Suite* has never really found its audience. Some have looked upon the eleven-minute work as a mere offshoot of *The Planets*; others have confused it with *Beni Mora: Oriental Suite*, which is not "oriental" in the least. Aside from its title, the *Japanese Suite* isn't oriental either; it is representative of the composer's work from that time.

As the war dragged on, Holst's work at Morley College became difficult as more and more of his students enlisted. Tenors, which had always been in short supply, were practically non-existant and now basses were also in great demand. Holst's work at his girls' schools, however, was not as affected. Occasionally there were reminders, such as the appearance of soldiers at St. Paul's Girls' School on December 4, 1915[26] and December 16th of the following year. More important to Holst at the moment, however, were the reminders of the continuation of normal professional life. Holst wrote to his friend W.G. Whittaker of an upcoming event:

> I had hoped that you might be coming up for the music conference here in Jan. I'm down to speak on school orchestras and I wish I wasn't. It will probably do me good but I'm doubtful about the audience. Besides which I object to things doing me good in the Xmas holidays.[27]

The music conference to which Holst referred in this letter was the Vacation Conference on Music Education, held at St. Paul's Girls' School January 3-8, 1916. The conference was given under the auspices of the Music Teachers' Association, the Home Music Study Union, the Girls' School Music Union and the Union of Directors of Music in Secondary Schools. This important conference featured a number of composers in vice presidential roles: Frederick Bridge, Granville Bantock, Landon Ronald, and Charles Villiers Stanford. Among the members of the executive committee were Kathryn Eggar, who would later write on his work at Morley College, and Percy Scholes, who would soon have a major impact on Holst's "military" life.

Holst's speech, "Certain Possibilities of the School Orchestra (with Illustrations)" was given at 11:45 a.m. on January 8th. Thomas F. Dunhill, Holst's old-time friend from his student days at the Royal College of Music, chaired the session.[28] Although the entire text of Holst's speech is lost (if, in fact, it ever really existed), highlights were reported in *The Music Student*:

> We are training amateurs in our ordinary school work. Budding professionals are rare and will be none the worse for a little amateur training.
>
> An amateur orchestra isn't meant to be listened to. Over the door of every amateur concert a notice should be written: 'Audience only admitted at owner's risk; the company does not hold itself responsible for any damage incurred.'

> Never do anything because someone else does; also beware of giving music to an orchestra because it will do them good (like medicine).
>
> Your are there to make them love music, and the first and obvious thing to do is to give them music you like yourself.
>
> Then as to arranging (or perhaps one should say rearranging) music for the orchestra. Don't be afraid of altering notes--music is sound, and it is this that matters, not the printed notes.[29]

In addition to his speech, Holst was an active participant. He wrote to Whittaker, "I'm going to every meeting of this conference and feel ill in consequence!"[30]

After the conference had ended most of Holst's free time during early months of 1916 were taken up by work on "Mercury" and the establishment of a music festival at Whitsuntide (Pentecost) in the town that he lived. Perhaps it was his attendence at this music education conference (in addition to listening to his own words) that served as an incentive for him to pursue such a concept.

---

[1]Imogen Holst, *Gustav Holst: A Biography*, 2nd ed. (Oxford: Oxford University Press, 1969), 42.

[2]A. E. F. Dickinson, ed. Alan Gibbs, *Holst's Music: A Guide* (London: Thames Publishing, 1995), 167.

[3]Christopher Palmer, *Herbert Howells: A Centenary Celebration* (London: Thames Publishing, 1992), 275.

[4]Michael Short (ed.), *Gustav Holst: Letters to W. G. Whittaker* (Glasgow: University of Glasgow Press, 1971), 127.

[5]Gustav Holst, *Diary*, Thursday, January 29 and Thursday, February 5, 1914, the Holst Foundation..

[6]Ralph Vaughan Williams, *Dona Nobis Pacem* (1936), a cantata for soprano and baritone soloists, mixed chorus, and orchestra. "A Dirge for Two Veterans" is the fourth of six movements.

[7]Michael Kennedy, *The Works of Ralph Vaughan Williams*, 2nd ed. (London: Oxford University Press, 1980), 163.

[8]Gustav Holst, *A Dirge for Two Veterans*, British Library Add MS 57880.

[9]Alan Gibbs mentions forty-three complete recordings of *The Planets* on page v in his edition of A.E.F. Dickinson's *Holst's Music: A Guide.*

[10]Imogen Holst, *Gustav Holst*, 43.

[11]"List of Compositions," British Library Add. MS 57863.

[12]Gustav von Holst, *Seven Pieces for Large Orchestra*, inner title page in *Imogen Holst (ed.) and Colin Matthews (ed.), Gustav Holst: Collected Facsimile Edition of Manuscripts of the Published Works, Volume III: The Planets, Op. 32* (London: Faber Music Ltd. in association with G & I Holst Ltd., 1979), 15.

[13]Actually an Alto Flute in G.

[14]Heckelphone.

[15]Not only constructed in B flat, but also pitched in B flat, as the "B Flat Baritone" part in his *First Suite in E Flat for Military Band*, Op. 28, No. 1 [H105].

[16]Holst indicated six percussionists: two on timpani, one covering celesta and xylophone, and three to cover the remaining instruments.
[17]Bass Drum.
[18]Snare Drum.
[19]Gustav von Holst, *Seven Pieces for Large Orchestra* in Imogen Holst (ed.) and Colin Matthews (ed.), *op. cit.*, 15.
[20]*Ibid.*, 10.
[21]*Ibid.*
[22]Nancy Gotch Strode, "Across the Years: A Personal Recollection of Gustav Holst" in *The Conductors' Guild Bulletin*, Summer, 1974.
[23]*The Referee*, November 8, 1914.
[24]Imogen Holst (ed.), *A Thematic Catalogue of Gustav Holst's Music* (London: Faber Music Ltd., 1974), 117.
[25]Not to be confused with Westminster Abbey, Westminster Cathedral is London's Roman Catholic cathedral. It is located in the vicinity of Victoria Station.
[26]Gustav Holst, *Diary*, Saturday, December 4, 1915, The Holst Foundation.
[27]Personal correspondence, Gustav Holst to William Gillies Whittaker, Dec[ember] 13[, 1915], quoted in Michael Short (ed.), *op.cit.*, 3.
[28]*Programme, Vacation Conference on Musical Education at St. Paul's Girls' School, Brook green, Hammersmith, London, W., January 3rd-8th, 1916.*
[29]Gustav Holst, quoted in *The Music Student*, February, 1916.
[30]Personal correspondence, Gustav Holst to W. G. Whittaker [January 6, 1916], quoted in Michael Short (ed.), *loc. cit.*.

CHAPTER VIII

THAXTED AND THE HYMN OF JESUS

It was probably during his walk through northwest Essex in late December of 1913 that Holst first met Conrad Noel, the famous radical Anglo-Catholic vicar of Thaxted. Noel was many things to many people. He was a medievalist and a socialist; some would call him a Christian communist. He was author of a number of books, including *Socialism in Church History* (1910). His appointment to the Thaxted pulpit in 1910 by the Countess of Warwick had been met with bitter opposition, especially from the upper classes. Ironically Noel himself was from a well-to-do family. His cousin Noel Buxton (eventually Lord Noel-Buxton of Aylsham) was active in politics, first in the Liberal Party and later, in the 1920's as Labour's Minister for Agriculture.

Conrad Noel preached a fire and brimstone social Gospel, one which extended a long arm toward the working classes--with an overtly radical approach. To remind his congregation of his sentiments, he had the Sinn Fein flag placed on display in the church from 1916. It was soon joined by the Red Flag, which was placed in the church even before the Russian revolution had started and remained there long after the communists had achieved control.[1] Noel also supported the 1921 miners' strike, which created much political difficulty for him. Noel's Gospel was a Gospel of change--not only in socialist doctrine but in ceremonial doctrine as well--in banners, hymnals, and in a renewal of folk song and folk dancing traditions that had long since disappeared from the mass and from other services. Noel was not alone; he had many clerical followers throughout England. Noel's huge ego did not prevent him from unabashedly labelling this the Thaxted Movement. He later he spearheaded the Catholic Crusade (1919-31).

Most of Noel's reforms initially set well with Holst. After the composer's family relocated there in 1914, the two of them became good friends. Holst more than willingly assisted with the church's choir and often assumed organist duties on the weekends that he was home. Dinners were often shared between the Holsts and the Noels. As a teen-ager Imogen Holst capriciously yet truthfully referred to Noel as "our revolutionary vicar!"[2].

In researching church history, Noel had come across a medieval Cornish poem in William Sandy's 1833 collection *Christmas Carols, Ancient and Modern* that supported his views about dancing and religion. He copied out the words and put them on display on the churches' bulletin board:

> Tomorrow shall be my dancing day,
> I would that my true love did so chance
> To see the legend of my play,
> To call my true love to the dance,
> Sing oh my love,
> Oh my love, my love, my love,
> This have I done for my true love....

The poem made quite an impression on Holst, who created his own setting of these words for mixed (satb) chorus. Although officially titled *This Have I Done for My True Love*, Op. 34 (No. 1) [H128](1916), Holst himself referred to the piece by its first line. The music is entirely his, one which displays the "musical idiom of the English language" he had so often sought. The work is dedicated to Conrad Noel.

For some time Holst had been thinking about putting together a music festival at the Thaxted church during Whitsuntide. Holst's concept was based at least partially on the universality of music education; the festival would involve the Thaxted church choir, Holst's own students from Morley College and St. Paul's Girls' School, and townspeople. The choir would be accompanied by an orchestra and all the performances would take place within the church's services. Holst presented his idea to Noel, who readily approved. The first Thaxted festival was held on June 10-12, 1916. The following account appeared in the *Morley College Magazine*:

> Mr. von Holst's choir and orchestra, consisting of Morleyites and Paulinas, arrived on the Saturday and were joined by the Thaxted singers for a rehearsal in the church. Whit Sunday was grey and showery: by 9:45 a.m. the singers and players were in their places in the Becket Chapel, almost hidden from the congregation by a carved screen.

> The church made an impression which will never be forgotten; at intervals bars of light struck down through the great windows and lit up the pillars and hangings in golden patches; here and there on the stone floor stood great earthenware jars filled with larkspurs, peonies, and beech boughs; and, high, up among the vaulting swallows darted in and out. It was one of the most beautiful services we shall ever take part in.
> Both choir and orchestra felt satisfied when they saw their conductor's face.
>
> Whit Monday made no pretences, but rained steadily all day. On both afternoons Mrs. von Holst entertained the musicians at Monk Street Cottage for tea; driven indoors by the rain they resorted at once to music--Elisabethan love songs, rounds and part-songs. On Monday evening we were invited by Mr. Noel to a Garden Party at the vicarage; owing to the downpour it was held in the dining room--a varied and festive evening, beginning with folk-songs and morris dances by the Thaxted singers, which they vainly tried to teach us till the house shook to its foundations--then a melodrama in the barn--and finally more dancing.[3]

The last of the musicians had left town by Tuesday morning but, according to one observer, the music may not have stopped even then:

> I remember coming out of a train at a country junction one day at the end of Whitsuntide when Gustav Holst was living at Thaxted, where, I believe, he helped to organize the musical side of certain of the big open-air processions that created so much attention. Some of his Morley College students had come down to assist and were returning to town [London] together.
>
> There was a half hour wait before the London train came in so the students sang on the platform under Holst's directions. Staid farmers on their way to market stared in amazement, a few of the old country women seemed to be quite alarmed, but the singers were in no way troubled, and Holst himself was quite unconcerned that he had an audience.[4]

Holst wrote about the festival to his friend William Gillies Whittaker:

June 18 [1916]

Dear Whittaker,

Thanks again for all your good deeds. I would have written before but I was so tied up with our music festival (or rather feast) at Thaxted last week.

It was a feast--an orgy. Four whole days of perpetual singing and playing either properly or arranged in the church or impromptu in various houses or still more impromptu in ploughed fields during thunderstorms or in the trains. It has been a revelation to me. And what it has revealed to me and what I shall never be able to persuade you is that quantity is more important than quality. We don't get enough. We practice stuff for a concert at which we do athing once and get excited over it and then go off and something else. Whereas on this occasion things were different. Take the Missa Brevis[5] for instance. The Morleyites had practised it since January. On June 3rd they did it twice through at their concert. On June 10th they rehearsed it and other things for three hours in Thaxted Church. On Whitsunday we did it during service in the morning, again in the evening, again on Monday morning. And some enthusiasts went through it again on Tuesday morning with violin and piano. This applies to the other things we did. Some of the motets were learnt a year ago.

In the intervals between the services people drifted into the church and sang more motets or played violin or cello etc. And between all this others caught bad colds through going on long walks in the pouring rain singing folksongs and round the whole time. The effect on us was indescribable. We weren't merely excited--we were quite normal only rather more alive than usual.

Most people are overcome by mountain air at first. In the same way others are excited by certain big music. The remedy in both cases is to have more and more and More! What a mercy it is that we cannot meet otherwise I'd jaw your head off. I enclose the program. There were about 15 Morleyites, 10 St. Paul's girls, 10 outsiders and 10 Thaxted singers. The latter did grandly. Most of them work at a factory here and I have been asked to give them quicker music next year. It seems that they sang all day at their work for months and the slow notes of the Bach chorals seriously affected their output!

Yrs Ever,

GVH[6]

By this time Holst and Whittaker had become quite close. Whittaker had performed a number of Holst's works with his Newcastle groups, including the Third Group of *Choral Hymns from the Rig Veda* and *The Cloud Messenger*. Holst had sent him a copy of *This Have I Done for My True Love* and followed it in April with an unaccompanied mixed chorus (satb) setting of the folk song "I sowed the seeds of love," which Holst had used earlier in *Nine Folk Songs* [H84] for voice and piano. Over the remainder of the spring and summer of 1916, Holst wrote five more. The next two, "There was a tree," and "Matthew, Mark, Luke and John" were dedicated, along with the first, "To W. G. Whittaker and his singers." For the remaining three of the *Six Choral Folksongs*, Op. 36 [B][H136], Holst chose folksongs he had already used in his *Second Suite in F for Military Band*: "The Song of the Blacksmith," "I love my love," and "Claudy Banks." These three were dedicated to Charles Kennedy Scott and the Oriana Madrigal Society.

Holst also wrote to Ralph Vaughan Williams about the Whitsuntide festival and received the following encouraging response:

> Your letter about Thaxted was splendid--I sometimes feel that the future of musical England rests with you--because every Paulina who goes out, & for the matter of that every Morleyites, will infect 10 others & they in their turn will infect 10 others--I will leave you to make the necessary calculation....[7]

Holst's first Thaxted festival was an unqualified success and a number of compositions were directly inspired by it. The stimulus for *Four Songs*, Op. 35 [H132] (1916-17) for voice and violin occurred during the festival in the church at dusk, during one of the breaks. There Holst saw one of the female violinists playing very softly while improvising a wordless song. He had the idea to write a piece for a violinist to play and sing simultaneously. This turned out to be impractical, for the violinist could not open up her mouth sufficiently to enunciate clearly or to project. The result was that the work needed to be performed by two people. For his texts, Holst turned to *A Medieval Anthology*, a collection of fifteenth-century writings edited by Mary Segar. The four songs that he chose are "Jesu Sweet, now will I sing," "My soul had nought but fire and ice," "I sing of a maiden," and "My Lemon is so true." The first, second, and fourth of these were performed for the first time at the second Thaxted festival by Morleyites Christine Ratcliffe (violin) and Dulcie Nutting (voice) on May 24, 1917.

Holst found additional inspiration from Mary Segar's collection and produced three unaccompanied carols with the Thaxted singers in mind: "Lullay My Liking" [H129], "Of One that Is So Fair and Bright" [H130], and "Bring Us in Good Ale"

[H131]. Holst included the first and third of these along with *This Have I Done for My Own True Love*, composed before the festival, as Op. 34 in his "List of Compositions."[8] Also included by Holst in Op. 34 is "Terly Terlow" for mixed chorus, with the accompaniment of oboe and cello. Due to its instrumentation, Imogen Holst catalogued "Terly Terlow" as the second of *Two Carols* [H91]. The first is "A Welcome Song," composed before1909. With seven years separating the two, it is doubtful that Holst would have perceived them as a pair. "Lullay My Liking" and "Terly Terlow" were first performed by Charles Kennedy Scott and the Oriana Madrigal Society on December 19, 1916.

Holst was also planning for a second Thaxted festival and in doing so composed what he originally called "3 Hymns for Thaxted"[9]. These three *Festival Choruses*, Op. 36 [A] [H134] were scored for mixed chorus (satb) and full orchestra, including organ. They include "Let all mortal flesh keep silence" (words: Liturgy of St. James translated by G. Moultrie; melody: traditional French), "Turn back O Man" (words: Clifford Bax; melody: Old 124th from the *Genevan Psalter*), and "A Festival Chime" (words: Clifford Bax; melody: traditional Welsh tune "St. Denio"). The first line of the latter, which reads "Our church bells in Thaxted at Whitsuntide say," was modified upon publication to be less exclusive. It should also be mentioned that there was one additional "production" chorus to come from Holst's pen at about this same time. "All People that on Earth Do Dwell" [App. III, 17] (words: *Day's Psalter*, 1561; melody: "Old 100th" from the *Genevan Psalter*) is not included in Holst's "List of Compositions" but is definitely a part of this series. All four choruses were written with amateur voices in mind and an orchestra of "elastic" instrumentation.

In this very productive year Holst also composed a string quartet. The *Phanstasy Quartet on British Folk Songs*, Op. 36 [H135], in one movement, was actually performed in 1917, but Holst was not satisfied with it and withdrew it. Either he or his publishers assigned its opus number to the [*Three*] *Festival Choruses* [Op. 36A] and *Six Choral Folk Songs* [Op. 36B].

By the autumn of 1916 the war was really starting to take its toll. England had run out of volunteers and was now drafting all unmarried men between the ages of eighteen and forty-one. The impact of this essentially dismantled any plans involving men at Morley College. Holst was still able to keep his sense of humor in writing to Whittaker:

> ....don't ask me for tenors--Morley choir started last month with 50 women and 2 men and 50 percent of the men could not sing! Max[10] was up on leave yesterday--he is a Bombardier now. Fine title isn't it?[11]

Yet Holst worked around the situation the best he could. Adrian Boult comments:

> His [Holst's] corresponding delight in the humblest effort, if he sensed the right thrust behind it, made him an inspiration to everyone who came near him. At Morley College in the later years of the War he used to give staggering choral and orchestral performances with the help of a remarkable voice called the 'war tenor.' The sparcity of double basses was, I believe, the cause of Mrs. Holst's doing such useful work on that unwieldy instrument.[12]

Still, a far sadder aspect of the war was felt by Holst. At least three composer friends were killed in action: George Butterworth, Edward Mason (whose choir had performed so much of Holst's music), and Cecil Coles (who had accompanied Holst in Switzerland in 1911). Vaughan Williams commented:

> I sometimes dred coming back to normal life with so many gaps--especially of course George Butterworth--he left most of his MS to me--& now I hear that [F. B.] Ellis is killed--out of those 7 who joined up together in August 1914 only 3 are left--I sometimes think now that it is wrong to have made friends with people much younger than oneself--because soon there will only be the middle aged left--& I have got out of touch with most of my contemporary friends--but then there is always you & thank Heaven we have never got out of touch & I don't see why we ever should.[13]

Sometime late in October Holst received an unusual request through Whittaker. James Causley Windram, Bandmaster of the First Battalion of the Royal Northumberland Fusiliers, stationed near Newcastle, had spoken to Whittaker about his wanting to write a military band transcription of Holst's "Hymn of the Travellers," from the Third Group of *Choral Hymns from the Rig Veda*. Holst responded: "Yr bandmaster certainly may score the Travellers in--of course if he wants to publish it we must come to some arrangement."[14] Windram did score "Hymn of the Travellers" for military band, but never published it. It did, however, become the third movement of a make-shift suite, featuring Windram's military band transcriptions of Holst's "Battle Hymn" from the First Group and "Hymn to Vena" from the Third Group as its first and second movements, respectively.[15]

1916 ended with the premiere of *Savitri*, which had been collecting dust for eight years. Holst's chamber opera was performed on December 5th in Wellington Hall by the London School of Opera at St. John's Wood. The principals were Mabel Corran (Savitri), George Pawlo (Satvyan), and Harrison Cook (Death). Henry Grunebaum conducted. It was Grunebaum who suggested the substitution of a female chorus for the original mixed chorus that Holst had originally indicated; male singers were at a premium during the war. Whatever the case, the female chorus works perfectly and Holst was eternally grateful to Grunebaum for the suggested change. On this occasion *Savitri* was paired with another short opera, *Pierrot and Pierrette*, with music by Josef Holbrooke, words by Walter E. Grogan. Reviews were mixed, as might be expected. The critic from *The Globe* said, "It is extremely unlikely that Mr. Gustav von Holst's *Savitri* will ever attain a wide popularity. It is too austere, too declamatory and too destitute of stage trimmings to be accepted by the general public."[16] The critic from *The Referee*, however, found Holst's treatment to be "refreshingly new."[17]

The early months of 1917 saw the completion of the full score to *The Planets* by Holst and his amanuenses. The two-piano version was also being fine-tuned and it was through that version that a number of Holst's friends became familiar with the work; the possibility of a performance of the work in its orchestral setting during wartime was almost nil, yet this did not stop Holst from starting his next large-scale work. Although by his own disclosure an English nationalist, Holst had always been looking for literary influences that stretched beyond the reaches of his native land. Sanskrit had provided him with more than enough literature for ten works, and his disallowance of it after the 1913 premiere of *The Cloud Messenger* had left a void that needed to be filled. Astrology had filled this void temporarily, yet Holst continued to seek other avenues. He found one in the literature of ancient Greece. Gilbert Murray's translations of Euripides inspired Holst to compose *Hecuba's Lament*, *Hymn to Dionysus*, and, later, the *Seven Choruses from the Alcestis of Euripides* [H146] (1919-20). The literature of Ancient Greece may have been only a partial replacement for the Sanskrit of India, but it was one of two particulars that pointed Holst toward *The Hymn of Jesus*, Op. 37 [H140] (1917). The other particular--the more important of the two--was his increasing interest in the connection of dance and Christian religious ceremony, an interest sparked by Conrad Noel and *This Have I Done for My True Love*.

Holst's search for scriptural passages involving dance and religion led him not to the canon of scripture, but to the *Apocryphal Acts of St. John*. F. F. Bruce comments:

> The Acts of John is ascribed to an author named Leucius....It contains

> a number of curious anecdotes about the apostle John, who is presented as a gnostic teacher. It includes an interesting gnostic hymn in which Jesus accompanies his disciples, performing a solemn dance at the same time. The hymn has been set to music by Gustav Holst.[18]

Dissatisfied with the English translations then available, Holst decided to translate the text from the Greek original on his own. Jane Joseph, who had a reasonable command of Greek, taught him enough to get him started. He also had help in shaping his text from Clifford Bax and G. R. S. Mead. Just as he had done with Sanskrit, Holst translated the text word by word and then tied the words together. In doing so, he achieved a text well-suited to his musical needs. What had been the quatrain

> I am a lamp to you who see me,
> I am a mirror to you who know me,
> I am a door to you who knock on me,
> I am a way to you the traveller.[19]

became more poetic in Holst's words:

> To you who gaze, a lamp am I; To you that know, a mirror.
> To you who knock, a door am I; To you who fare, the way.[20]

For *The Hymn of Jesus* Holst again chose forces of epic proportions: two mixed choruses (satb), a semi-chorus (ssa) and an orchestra consisting of the following: 3 flutes (alternating piccolo), 2 oboes, *Cor Anglais*, 2 clarinets, 2 bassoons, 4 horns, 2 trumpets, 3 trombones, timpani, bass drum, snare drum, cymbals, tambourine, celesta, piano, organ, and strings. The work itself is in two parts. The first is a "Prelude" founded on the Gregorian chants "Pange lingua" and "Vexilla regis." The second is "The Hymn of Jesus" itself, in Holst's English translation.

The Hymn of Jesus is filled with elements not to be found in the traditional English-language oratorio: a prelude in Latin sung by a semi-chorus (ssa) and introduced by unison tenor trombones, free-time vs. ostinato, parallel triads on "Amen," a 5/4 allegro dance meter, experiments in voiced consonants, timbrel touches including tambourine and celesta. Imogen Holst comments:

> When the Hymn of Jesus was first performed the music came as a shock to those of the listeners who were not prepared to accept such

> astoundingly unfamiliar religious music. Holst had no use whatsoever for conventionality; he was utterly free from any routine piety, his memories of the B minor Mass were of ecstacy, his Sanskrit studies had taught him to think beyond the boundaries of Europe, and his idea of Christ included the terrifying unexpectedness of the Byzantine mosaics. It was only natural that he should disregard the nineteenth-century oratorio as if it had never existed.[21]

While her comments may strike one as being overly judgmental, one thing is clear: this music is something quite new. The unison C to 2nd inversion E major triad choral entry with descending step-wise bass on "Glory to Thee, Father" is one of the most awe-inspiring passages that Holst ever wrote. Yet, is the work an oratorio? Is it an ode? Is it neither? Holst left categorization of the work to the beholder. Regardless of the type, it is one of Holst's greatest works. Michael Short has called it "one of the most important Christian choral works of the twentieth century."[22] Holst chipped away at the work through most of 1917. Dulcie Nutting assisted him in preparing the full score.[23]

Meanwhile, Holst was more than busy with trying to stay financially solvent. Teaching at four different places simultaneously was difficult even in times of peace, but in wartime, when supplies and personnal were in short supply, it could be very demoralizing. Occasionally, however, Holst did receive accolades from his employers. Frances Ralph Gray, High Mistress at St. Paul's Girls' School, wrote the following:

> St. Paul's Girls' School
> Brook Green Hammersmith,
> W.
> 16th Feb. '17
>
> My Dear Mr. von Holst,
>
> At their meeting here today the Governors expressed much gratitude to you for the highly satisfactory results of your teaching and for the thoroughly disinterested and generous contributions which you make to the musical life of the school. I am adopting the words which appear in the minutes.
>
> The Governors think that in the future the fee for the orchestra should be fifteen guineas and the fee for each of the seven singing divisions should be seven guineas a term.[24]

I need not say--need I? how heartily I add my thanks to those of the Governors.

Yours very sincerely,

F. R. Gray[25]

Holst avoided hero worshipers like the plague, but to be appreciated on the job by someone who had witnessed his struggles on an almost daily basis for the past dozen years must have meant a great deal to him.

Also valued by Holst was the fact that one of his military band suites was at least being considered for performance. James Causley Windram had requested it through Whittaker and Holst complied, sending the parts to Newcastle on March 30.[26] Later, in July, Holst asked, "Does W want the full score of the military suite?"[27] There is no real way of telling which of the two suites was being discussed, but since Windram would be instrumental in helping Holst get the *First Suite in E Flat for Military Band* published in the not-too-distant future, it seems that it is the likely choice.

Meanwhile, other Holst works continued to be performed. In March there were three important events. On Monday, the12th in Newcastle, Holst visited W. G. Whittaker and conducted the Armstrong College choir in a concert[28] featuring the Second Group of the *Choral Hymns from the Rig Veda*, the unaccompanied three-part *Pastoral* [H92], "Tears, Idle Tears" from *Songs from "The Princess"*, and *Ave Maria*.[29] The following evening Holst's 1911 violoncello piece, *Invocation*, turned up again, this time at an important Wigmore Hall recital given by Thelma Bentwich and Myra Hess. Reviews were mixed, from *The Globe*'s "pleasing"[30] to *The Observer's* "Invocation by Mr. Gustav von Holst did not reveal this clever composer at his best."[31] On the 24th, Holst had his Sanskrit teacher Mabel "Patsy" Bode out to Morley College to lecture to his students on Sanskrit as a prelude to a performance of the Second Group of *Choral Hymns from the Rig Veda* at the annual Music Students' Social.[32]

Whitsun occurred on the last Sunday of May, two weeks earlier than it had in 1916, and by early spring Holst's thoughts had turned to the second Thaxted festival. He planned for the form of the 1917 festival to be essentially a repeat of the previous year's, with the performances being an integral part of the church's services on Sunday morning and evening, as well as on Monday morning. Fortunately, the new music for the festival had already been composed. Holst's *Three Festival Choruses*, Op. 36A were given their first performances at this festival and it was here that violinst Christine Ratcliffe and soprano Dulcie

Nutting premiered three of the *Four Songs*, Op. 35 for voice and violin. There was, of course, the "orgy" of singing and socializing that had guaranteed the success of the first festival. There was also a new banner in the church, adorned with Holst's favorite Bach quotation: "The aim of music is the glorification of God and pleasant recreation."

Sometime during 1917 Holst moved his family from the isolated Monk Street cottage to a townhouse known as The Steps, located in the center of Thaxted. It is likely that they were already in their new abode at the time of the second Whitsun festival. Here they would reside for the next eight years. The Holsts moved around a lot; the longest they had previously stayed in any one place had been five years, at 10, the Terrace, Barnes. It could be that Holst simply wanted to be closer to the center of things, or possibly that his landlord had other ideas in mind for the Monk Street cottage after the normal three-year lease had expired. Whatever the case, The Steps suited the family's needs, and Holst was able to do some composing there, although he continued to do most of it in his sound-proof room at St. Paul's Girls' School.

The autumn of 1917 was a difficult one for London. Air raids had become commonplace. Many of London's Underground stations as well as structurally sound basements all over the city were turned into make-shift shelters. St. Paul's and James Allen's Girls' Schools were each located far enough away from the center of London so as not to be imminently threatened, but Morley College was located too close to Waterloo Station for comfort. To make matters worse, the building that it occupied with the Old Vic was box-shaped and could easily have been mistaken for some sort of military factory by enemy aircraft. Thus Morley College's basement gymnasium was turned into the air raid shelter for the local area. After descending the stairways to the shelter, local citizens were often astonished to discover themselves in the midst of a Morley College rehearsal. In one particularly bad week, Holst's classes were interrupted three times:

> September 24 Monday Morley classes (raid)
> September 25 Tuesday (raid) no class
> October 1 Monday raid--harmony class[33]

After a few months of this, he wrote to Whittaker, "I am fed up with raids--in the day time the children are worn out and nervy and at night the cellar concerts are a great success but they last hours without any interval and leave one limp for tomorrow's work."[34]

January of 1918 found Whittaker coming to London at Holst's invitation for the purpose of conducting and lecturing. Holst the scheduler was busy at work and arranged his friend's week for him. The following not only gives a clear view of Whittaker's schedule, and but sheds light on Holst's as well:

> ....I cannot meet you at the station on Friday the 11th--at least not at 2. (I could do so any time after 4.)
>
> So will you please take the Inner circle to Notting Hill Gate station. Hillsleigh Rd is a 5 min walk from there. Could you arrange to have an early meal so that I could call you at 7:30?
>
> Shall we go and see Terry[35] on Sunday morning--it is his free time for visitors after Mass. Our programme will be
>
> Friday Morley 8.30 to 10
>
> Saturday morning we'll have Whinnies and Carols and other North Country fare--
>
> I'll come to Hillsleigh Rd.
>
> Saturday afternoon?
>
> More Whinnies?
>
> or resting?
>
> or talking?
>
> or--best of all--you shall escape from me for a bit!
>
> Saturday evening Morley 7:30 (no evening dress in Waterloo Rd!)
>
> Sunday morning Westminster Cathedral
>
> The rest of Sunday? Another escape? (of course there's still the Gnostic Hymn![36])
>
> Monday all day publishers etc. (another escape!)
>
> Monday evening more escape as I shall be at Morley
>
> Tuesday morning at St. Paul's School. We want to inflict all the Planets on you.
>
> Tuesday afternoon rehearsal for Wed afternoon lecture.
>
> Tuesday evening 'Old Vic' lecture
>
> Wednesday morning escape or Whinnies or Gnostic Hymn or what you will
>
> Wednesday afternoon St. Paul's lecture
>
> Wed evening escape--I'm at Morley
>
> I haven't a spare moment after that until Saturday so we will have a farewell tea together after the lecture.[37]

The lecture given at the Old Vic and repeated at St. Paul's Girl's School was Whittaker's; its title was "The Work of Gustav Holst." In it Whittaker focused on Holst's *Ave Maria* and his mastery of the English folk tune. The following humorous anecdote appeared in a 1934 article. It most likely was furnished by Whittaker himself in remembrance of this occasion:

> One of Holst's intimate friends and fellow workers sends in the following story.
>
> 'I was lecturing on Holst's works to the girls of St. Paul's Girls' School. The janitor, one of Holst's warm admirers, expressed his regrets to someone that he could not attend my lecture. This came to Holst's ears, and he offered to take the janitor's place. So the janitor went to the lecture, while the subject of it sat in the lodge, attending to errand boys, callers, phone calls, etc.'[38]

By early 1918 conductor Adrian Boult had established himself as a force on the London musical landscape. He and Holst had known each other in writing for about four years at that time. Boult comments:

> Gustav and I had corresponded before we met. I was concerned with some concerts in Liverpool in the early days of the 1914 War, and I wrote to ask him what he could suggest for small orchestra. He told me about the Somerset Rhapsody and the Country and Marching Songs which I much enjoyed doing.[39]

The two of them met personally in 1916 and became good friends.

Boult got his big break when he was invited to conduct the London Symphony Orchestra (cut back to fifty players during wartime) in a series of four concerts set for February and March, 1918 in Queen's Hall. Boult programmed Holst's "Country Song" from *Two Songs without Words* on the first of these concerts, held February 4th. It was a rousing success. Holst wrote to the conductor:

> Everybody is wild with enthusiasm over your beautiful rendering of the Country Song. Please accept my (a) thanks (b) blessing (c) congratulations. I hope you were satisfied. It's a splendidly plucky enterprise of yours and I do hope you'll get adequate support.[40]

Boult conducted Ralph Vaughan Williams' *A London Symphony* two weeks later on the second concert of the series. Vaughan Williams commented:

> May I say how much I admired your conducting--it is real conducting--you get just what you want and know what you want & your

> players trust you because they know it also--I heard many expressions of admiration from both audience and performers (von Holst & A. Hobday among others)--of course you are an experienced conductor by now....[41]

Boult was not a flambouyant conductor, nor was he a dictator. He did not set the world on fire with his mannerisms or his temper. He was conservative in his movements on the podium, allowing the tip of the baton to serve as his means of communication with the orchestra. His supreme knowledge of the score and profound musical sensitivity placed him in the top rank of British conductors. Yet it was not below Boult's dignity to dine with and socialize with his players. It is no wonder then, that when the opportunity arose, Holst chose Boult to conduct the first performance of *The Planets*.

The war continued to take its toll. The April 6, 1917 entry of the Americans on the side of the Allies was expected to bring things to a quick end, but, although the tide of the war had changed, the end was still not in sight. Partially as a means of breaking the monotony, Holst and a group of Morley College students "composed" *Opera As She Is Wrote* [App. II, 15], a burlesque parody in "six acts and five languages (including tonic sol-fa)."[42] The choice of title was probably influenced by Frederic Cowen's 1915 humorous glossary of musical terms, *Music as She Is Wrote*. It was not the first time for Holst's involvement in such musical mockery. Five years earlier Holst put together a *Futuristic Tone-Poem in H*, spoofing Schoenberg. Italian brigands disguised as foot inspectors, a mermaids' chorus over a cello *ppp* pedalpoint on low C, and a French scene featuring parallel chords on the piano played *una corda*, were only some of the clever devices employed in *Opera As She Is Wrote*.[43] It is doubtful that a full score ever existed, although on one of the fragments Holst indicated an orchestra of woodwind quintet plus strings. The "work" was rehearsed in Morley College's basement gymnasium during air raids. Holst invited Boult to participate in the February 23rd performance. Whether or on Boult actually participated is anyone's guess although the following implies that he certainly was in attendence:

> [Holst] could...be the source of endless fun, as all Morleyites will remember. In particular I think a mock opera in five acts culminating in Debussy and Wagner was a masterpiece--produced it was with the simplest means imaginable.[44]

Opera As She Is Wrote was performed many times that spring.

In the midst of all this frivolity, Holst found time to compose *The Sneezing Charm* [H143], some incidental music to a play of the same name by Clifford

Bax. The play, described by its author as "An Arabian Night's Phantasy in Rhyme," is about a djinni imposing her will on a princess. Presented by The Plough Society, it opened on June 9, 1918 at the Royal Court Theatre.[45] Rosabel Watson, who had conducted Holst's music nine years earlier at the Stepney Children's Pageant, served as musical director.

Holst composed three movements: "Prelude," "Song," and "Ballet." The first and third utilize a "trombone" motif originally used in *Opera as She Is Wrote*. This same motif later found its way into the beginning of the "Ballet Music" from *The Perfect Fool*, Op. 39 [H150]. Much of the music in the latter, in fact, is based upon *The Sneezing Charm*. Still, the incidental music from *The Sneezing Charm* had a life of its own; it was used for various events over the next five years and could have even been the mysterious "Jack in the Green" music used to accompany Russian Ballerina Tamara Karsavina during the 1921 summer season. It was not uncommon for Holst to do some self-borrowing--certainly the finale of the *St. Paul's Suite* and the first movement of the final form of the *Second Suite in F for Military Band* benefitted from that--but it was unusual for Holst to allow any of his music to be so blatantly recycled. In this case there is a ready explanation: Holst would soon be involved in the war effort outside of the country and, due largely to the success of *The Planets*, he would find a very high demand for his music upon his return.

There were occasional performances of other Holst works that spring. Three of Holst's *Vedic Hymns*, Op. 24 were performed at Wigmore Hall on March 18th by George Pawlo, who had earlier sung the role of Satyavan in the first performance of *Savitri*, and on April 16th Charles Kennedy Scott and the Oriana Madrigal Society premiered the last three of *Six Choral Folk Songs* at the Old Vic Theatre.

Spring also meant another Thaxted festival at Whitsuntide. It was on that occasion that *This Have I Done for My True Love* and *Diverus and Lazarus* [H137] were given their first performances. There was the usual extra-curricular singing and merrymaking, but the overall atmosphere had changed. In the wake of the Bolshevik revolution Conrad Noel had embraced communism and expected all parishioners, including guests, to become involved in the Thaxted Movement. When he cited Holst's students--who sang their hearts out--to be part of the problem, it offended some of them and they refused to return. Noel wrote to Holst:

Thaxted
May 23, 1918

Dear Gustav,

I have been thinking sentimentallyof the issues that I raised in my message last Saturday and from talk that night. And now the very issues are raised again in an acute form by the Feast of the Blessed Trinity....We shall be singing the praises on the Blessed Trinity in the same spirit as a sharp instigation to rebellion against present-day Imperialism. The Feast of Corpus Cristi was introduced to fire people with a passion of hatred and of the denial of this doctrine which had arisen at that time. We shall be singing His praises to stir a like passion of devotion and of hatred. We started the Festival of Faith in adoration of the Whole Faith and especially of those sterner parts of it which have been dropped out by the modern world. It is therefore principally year by year and inspiration to rebellion. We maintain and believe that Gospel on a set of misguided cranks is not the immediate question. The point is that the Thaxted movement means this at bottom end and that music, dancing, ceremonial, and ethics can go to hell unless they are expressions of this.

It was because I believed that you and others that you so kindly brought to help here from time to time were coming to believe these things as fundamentals without which life was so quite meaningless that I welcomed your help in building up the Faith in this place. The movement is becoming too intense to allow of the easier-going experiments of earlier years....

....When I listened to the wonderful music of the General Dance, I thought that your true self was not expressed in the conversation of Saturday but the music of Monday. I hope from the bottom of my heart that your ultimate choice will be made in favor of those things which we have here come to believe are the things to live by and if this proves so, I can hardly overstate how infinitely I should value your cooperation in this Movement. But whatever your decision--we can never thank you enough for the outpouring of yourself...in helping our people in their music and for the wonderful help you have been able to provide--and I only hope from the bottom of my heart that it will still be possible to have a real cooperation.

Ever yours in sincerity,

Conrad Noel[46]

Holst personally took Noel's rantings with a grain of salt, referring to them as "Conrad's comic Gospel of hate."[47] He continued to help out with the choir and play organ from time to time but, as a teacher, Holst remained non-political and did not allow his students to become pawns in Noel's radical schemes. It was Conrad Noel who killed the Whitsun Festivals in Thaxted--at least for the time being. Holst held other Whitsun festivals in later years, but never again in Noel's church. Today there is a Thaxted Festival held over a four-week period in June and July; although it acknowledges its existence to the three festivals held by Holst there, it is more secular in nature and not quite the same thing.

---

[1]Maurice Bennington Rickitt, *For Christ and the People: Studies of Four Socialist Priests and Prophets of the Church of England between 1870 and 1930* (London: SPCK, 1968), 147.

[2]Personal correspondence, Imogen Holst to Helen Asquith, July 26, 1923, The Holst Foundation.

[3]*Morley College Magazine*, September-October, 1916.

[4]*The Daily Dispatch*, May 29, [1923?]. This article may have been applicable to any of three Whitsuntide festivals held at Thaxted from 1916 to 1918.

[5]Johann Sebastian Bach's *Missa Brevis in A*, BWV 234.

[6]Personal correspondence, Gustav Holst to William Gillies Whittaker, June 18 [, 1916], quoted in Michael Short (ed.), *Gustav Holst: Letters to W. G. Whittaker* (Glasgow: University of Glasgow Press, 1974), 9-10.

[7]Personal correspondence, Ralph Vaughan Williams to Gustav Holst, n.d. [June, 1916], quoted in Ursula Vaughan Williams (ed.) and Imogen Holst (ed.), *Heirs and Rebels: Letters to One Another and Occasional Writings by Gustav Holst and Ralph Vaughan Williams* (Oxford, Oxford University Press, 1959), 45.

[8]Gustav Holst, "List of Compositions," British Library Add. MS 57863.

[9]*Ibid.*

[10]Holst's half brother, cellist Matthias von Holst.

[11]Personal correspondence, Gustav Holst to W. G. Whittaker, Oct[ober] 23[, 1916], quoted in Michael Short (ed.), *op.cit.*, 11.

[12]Adrian Boult, "Gustav Holst: The Man and His Work" in *The Radio Times*, XLIII, No. 559 (June 15, 1934), 819. It is unclear from Boult's commentary what a "war tenor" actually was. Two of the many possibilities are (1) a female tenor, as used in many small church choirs, and (2) Isobel Holst playing the tenor part on the harmonics of the string bass.

[13]Personal correspondence, Ralph Vaughan Williams to Gustav Holst, n.d. [August, 1916?], quoted in Ursula Vaughan Williams (ed.) and Imogen Holst (ed.), *op. cit.*, 45-46.

[14]Personal correspondence, Gustav Holst to W. G. Whittaker, Nov[ember] 1[, 1916], quoted in Michael Short (ed.), *op.cit.*, 12.

[15]Parts for Windram's transcriptions were discovered in the library of the Band of the Coldstream Guards by the author in 1986. Windram's full score, if indeed it ever existed, is missing; it has been reconstructed by the author. The American premiere of the suite was given in Athens, Georgia by the University of Georgia Symphonic Band on May 14, 1992, the author guest conducting.

[16]*The Globe*, December 6, 1916.

[17]*The Referee*, December 10, 1916.

[18]F. F. Bruce, *The Canon of Scripture* (Downers Grove, IL: Intervarsity Press, 1988), 202.
[19]*Ibid.*
[20]Gustav Holst, *The Hymn of Jesus, Op. 37* (Stainer and Bell, 1919).
[21]Imogen Holst, *The Music of Gustav Holst and Holst's Music Reconsidered*, 3rd rev. ed. (Oxford: Oxford University Press, 1986), 47.
[22]Michael Short, *Gustav Holst: The Man and His Music* (Oxford: Oxford University Press, 1990), 153.
[23]*Ibid.*
[24]This apparent increase in fees may have been the determining factor that allowed Holst to resign from his Wycombe Abbey post at about this same time.
[25]Personal correspondence, Frances Ralph Gray to Gustav Holst, February 16, 1917, The Holst Foundation.
[26]Personal correspondence, Gustav Holst to W. G. Whittaker, [March 30, 1917], quoted in Michael Short (ed.), *op. cit.*, 20.
[27]Personal correspondence, Gustav Holst to W. G. Whittaker, July 9[, 1917], quoted in Michael Short (ed.), *op. cit.*, 27.
[28]Gustav Holst, *Diary,* Monday, March 12, 1917.
[29]Personal correspondence, Gustav Holst to W. G. Whittaker, March 13[, 1917], quoted in Michael Short (ed.), *op.cit.*, 19.
[30]*The Globe*, March 15, 1917.
[31]*The Observer*, March 18, 1917.
[32]Michael Short, *op.cit.*, 148.
[33]Gustav Holst, *Diary,* Monday, September 24, Tuesday, September 25, and Monday, October 1, 1917.
[34]Personal correspondence, Gustav Holst to W. G. Whittaker [February, 1918], quoted in Michael Short (ed.), *op. cit.*, 38.
[35]Richard Terry, organist and choir director at Westminster Cathedral.
[36]*The Hymn of Jesus*, Op. 37.
[37]Personal correspondence, Gustav Holst to W.G. Whittaker, Dec[ember] 31[, 1917], quoted in Michael Short (ed.), *op. cit.*, 36.
[38]"Holstiana" in *The Musical Times*, September, 1934.
[39]Adrian Boult, *"Gustav Holst" in* The Royal College of Music Magazine, LXX, No. 2 *(Summer, 1974), 52.*
[40]Personal correspondence, Gustav Holst to Adrian Boult, Feb[ruary] 5[, 1918], British Library Add MS 60498.
[41]Personal correspondence, Ralph Vaughan Williams to Adrian Boult, Feb[ruary] 25[, 1918], quoted in Jerold Northrop Moore (ed.), *Music and Friends* (London: Hamish Hamilton, 1979), 27.
[42]Personal correspondence, Gustav Holst to Adrian Boult, Feb[ruary] 5[, 1918], British Library Add MS 60498.
[43]Gustav Holst, *Opera As She Is Wrote*, MS fragment, Britten-Pears Library.
[44]Adrian Boult, "Gustav Holst: The Man and His Work," *loc. cit.*.
[45]*Programme, The Sneezing Charm*, Royal College of Music MS 4555.
[46]Personal correspondence, Conrad Noel to Gustav Holst, May 23, 1918, The Holst Foundation.
[47]Personal correspondence, Gustav Holst to Vally Lasker, Dec[ember] 18[, 1918], The Holst Foundation.

CHAPTER IX

WARTIME SERVICES WITH THE YMCA

Throughout the First World War, Holst had offered his services to various entities throughout the country, only to be turned down for reasons of health (chiefly poor eyesight) or, in the latter stages of the war, age. Isobel had been doing some work for the Green Cross and Holst, too, wanted to do something that would help the war effort. The opportunity finally came through the YMCA Universities Committee Music Section, which had been founded to establish musical activities throughout hospitals and training camps in neutral and enemy countries. Musicians who had previously been turned down for active military duty had now become sought-after commodities. Holst immediately volunteered and, after passing a physical on June 14, 1918, was accepted. Still, Holst would not be going anywhere without approval by the Military Intelligence and formal clearance would take a while. Thus Holst continued his regular civilian work until the end of the summer term, with a couple of variances. At 4:30 p.m. on Saturday, June 15th, there was a Soldiers' Concert at Morley College[1] which may have involved Holst and on Tuesday, July 23rd *Masque:The Vision of Dame Christian* was performed at St. Paul's Girls' School[2]--one year before its tenth anniversary, perhaps in anticipation of Holst's absence during the following school year.

Holst finally received word about his formal clearance in late August. Music critic Percy Scholes, who was then editor of *The Music Student*, served as the Organizing Secretary of the YMCA Universities Committee Music Section. He wrote to Holst:

National Council of

Young Men's Christian Associations
Universities Committee
Music Section

Universities House
25 Bloomsbury Square
London WC1
16th August 1918

G. T. Von Holst, Esq.
St. Paul's Girls' School
Brook Green, Hammersmith
SW

My Dear Von Holst,

I have just got a reply to an enquiry that we put to the Millitary Intelligence Department. Your papers have been examined on behalf of the Imperial General Staff, and you have been approved for Auxilliary work overseas. There is, therefore, no reason why we should not employ your so kindly offered service (Elsewhere than in Holland[3] and some other countries where special conditions exist).

As you know I am most anxious to have your help in the big Musical task we have undertaken. Will you, therefore, let me know whether you would be prepared to go to one of the field of war if required?

I think it quite possible that I could find you a splendid sphere of work in Salonica[4] or in Mesopotamia.[5] I know it is a big thing to suggest to a man with a wife and child, but there is no harm in asking your views. I have had a man here to-day from Salonica and the need there is very great. I have also had a suggestion this week that I should go to Mesopotamia myself, which is, unfortunately, impossible. Please think this over and let me know your mind.

In closing this letter I just want to say how much I appreciate the fact that your wife is evidently willing to make the sacrifice of letting you take up work of this character.

Percy Scholes[6]

Holst evidently gave positive responses to Scholes' questions. Scholes wrote back to him:

Universities House
25, Bloomsbury Square
London WC1
August 21st 1918

Dear von Holst,

I want to thank you for the fine spirit you show in your letter. I want to make you this offer which I have taken special pains to secure--the Y.M.C.A. will definitely engage you as Musical Organizer for a year certain, on the terms agreed upon in our last interview, the engagement to start within a few weeks from the present.

You are very much needed in Salonica, and from special enquiries I have made I believe the climate would suit you, but I cannot say yet whether the military authorities there would accept you though I have ascertained that the military authorities here would let you go. If we could not send you to Salonica, we might send you to Mesopotamia or France or Italy or use you in this country. All that I can say is that I am empowered to make you a firm offer and to leave the question of where you would work for further enquiry. It might be that for a time we would use you at headquarters here, or we might send you to some camp in this country. I can promise this--that we would find you an opportunity of real service to the boys.

Does this suggestion enable you to make arrangements such as will obviate the useless excitement amongst your various educational authorities in which we involved you last time?[7]

I do not know what the law is of change of name. I think it might be worth asking a solicitor to find out for you.

All the music you so kindly promised will be very welcome.

I am going away after next Monday for a fortnight. If you can come and see me before then, please do.

Kindest regards, and again admiration for the way in which your wife and yourself look at this opportunity of service.

Yours sincerely,

Percy Scholes

Ring me up if possible.[8]

Holst now had to take care of two major issues. The first was to clear things with his employers and arrange for substitutes. At St. Paul's Girls' School Norman O'Neill took over the orchestra and at Morley College, where he was initially guaranteed only a semester's leave, Richard Terry filled in. The second issue involved getting rid of the "von" portion of his name, which in the eyes and ears of many people, made his entire name sound unmistakably and unforgivingly German. This was accomplished by deed poll in mid-September. Imogen Holst commented:

> ....when he had gone through the lengthy proceedings and had paid what he considered to be an exorbitant amount of money, he discovered that his particular branch of the family never had any claim to the title. A second cousin in the eighteenth century had been honoured by the German Emperor for a neat piece of work in international diplomacy, and the unscrupulous Matthias[9] had calmly borrowed the 'von' in the hopes that it it might bring in a few more piano pupils. So all the fuss had been about nothing.[10]

Both items having been taken care of, Holst attended a preliminary training course at Welbeck Camp in Nottinghamshire, which featured some very wet weather. It was here that Holst got his first taste of military protocol. He wrote to Frances Ralph Gray:

> I am writing this in the driest part of the camp--the YMCA cookhouse, of which only 3/4 of the ground is flooded so far....
>
> Would you object if I come home a raging Bolshevik? If I had a clear way with the lads here I could do some good work. But their superiors! Especially those in charge of their minds!![11]

Following this course Holst returned to London. The only thing for him to do now was to sit and wait. He knew that he would be leaving soon, but the precise date was not known. Just as the anticipation was getting to him, his friend Balfour Gardiner gave him the greatest going-away present imaginable: a private all-expenses-paid performance of *The Planets* at Queen's Hall. For Holst, this was a dream. He knew when he wrote the suite that it would have to wait many years before its first performance; the immense orchestral forces required for it would not be available during wartime. Yet here it was, only a year following the completion of the full score, that the work was being performed professionally--and for an audience of Holst's choosing. The only hitch was that a professional chorus was unavailable, so the female chorus at the end of "Neptune" consisted of his own students from Morley College and St. Paul's Girls' School.

On at least three separate occasions Adrian Boult wrote of how this first private performance of *The Planets* came into being. All three are consistent. The following is from his autobiography *My Own Trumpet*. Although stationed in England, Boult had been doing government jobs during the war:

> Just before the Armistice, Gustav Holst burst into my office. 'Adrian, the YMCA are sending me to Salonica quite soon and Balfour Gardiner, bless his heart, has given me a parting present consisting of Queen's Hall, full of the Queen's Hall orchestra for the whole of a Sunday morning. So we're going to do *The Planets* and you've got to conduct.' Then followed feverish activity: I think the whole of St. Paul's Girls' School helped to copy the parts. Somebody trained the choir. Scores were sent me as they were released from the copyists...[12]

Boult made several visits to St. Paul's Gilrs' School to hear Vally Lasker and Nora Day play through the two-piano versions of each of the movements. He continues in another source:

> I'm not sure how much work was done at St. Paul's Girls' School that term--anyhow all the Parts were copied by somebody, and as each Movement was finished the Score came to me for study, right up to the great day, which was September 29th, 1918.[13]

Boult didn't have much time to learn the score. After some in-depth score study, he wrote some comments to Holst on a postcard:

> G. T. Holst, Esq.
> Thaxted
> Essex
>
> 1. The great unison tune at the end of Saturn is muted surely? The 'Con Sord' is written where 2 harps only are playing, & should be repeated at the Tutti, surely?
> 2. Am I right, when the D Basses play Bassoon cues, to make it arco? (In

Mercury I mean). I have repeated the pizz.after the cues wherever necessary.

3. If you have a score, will you compare the scoring and expression marks (particularly the 1st, 2d violin) on p. 80 bar 2. p. 102 bar 4. It is not important.

4. I am all for musical esperanto, and therefore disapprove of 'Dbn' & 'Doublebass' & which can mean nothing to a player off this island, just F.G. says this has been 'discussed' by you & H.B.G.[14], or it is not in a proof. Needs to express opinions!!

I hope to return the study parts tomorrow....[15]

In the meantime Holst was making plans for the social end of things. He had a free hand to invite anybody he wanted to the event; family, friends, and students came first. He wrote to Edwin Evans:

St. Paul's Girls' School
W6
Sep 22 [1918]

Dear Evans

My 'Planet' pieces are to be done at Queen's Hall next Sunday morning 10:30 to 1:30. From 12:15 to 1:30 will be the best time. Boult is conducting. It will be a purely private affair but please tell anyone who you think would care to come. Entrance at orch door.

I am going to Salonica for the YMCA and in order to be of more help to them I am dropping my 'von.'

Yr faithfully

G T Holst[16]

At 7:30 p.m. on the evening preceding the performance there was a dinner at Saville's on Piccadilly.[17] Boult comments about that evening and about the following day's performance:

The day before the performance the full score and I were spending the evening with some friends. Geoffrey Toye, who was one of them, put his finger on one of those very mysterious brass chords in the middle of

'Neptune'[18] and said: 'I am awfully sorry, Gustav, but surely that chord is going to sound frightful.' Gustav opened his eyes wider than ever and said: "Yes I know it will, but what are you to do when they come like that'?

Queen's Hall was 'full of the Queen's Hall Orchestra' whose Leader was then Maurice Sons, a distinguished RCM Professor. Sir Henry Wood came as a keen listener, also several generations of Paulinas, and, in the grand circle, nearly all the musicians of London. The Choir was, of course, made up of Pauline volunteers; they sat in the stalls, and slowly walked out when the 'Neptune' diminuendo came, and this has, I think, been done ever since; it certainly enhances the effect of 'the door which is slowed and silently closed', according to the Score. We rehearsed until about 11:40 , and at 12 began the performance, which made a deep impression, and some of the Philharmonic Directors promptly planned a second performance for their next season.[19]

Holst wrote to Boult immediately following the performance:

Monday [September 30,
1919]

Dear Adrian

I have discovered that there is no need for me to thank you or to congratulate you. It would be as ridiculous as for you to tell the Queen's Hall orchestra that you didn't know the scores!

You've covered yourself with glory and the players are tremendously impressed so is Henry J[20] and your success is so certain that anything I could say or write would be impertinent.

Bless you!
Y

Gustav[21]

Conducting *The Planets* was a remarkable achievement for the twenty-nine year old Boult, who was asked by board members of the Royal Philharmonic Society to include it in a concert during the regular season. Although news of this came in a timely fashion, it took a while for it to catch up to Holst. On Tuesday,

October 29th[22], after a six-weeks wait, Holst received notice to sail; he had only thirty-six hours to get his things in order. Much of the following day was spent at the permit office and at the French and Italian consulates, before Imogen came to see him off.[23] On the 31st, Holst left from Waterloo Station and dealt with his "1st muddle"--having to pay his own ticket to Southampton. From there he sailed to Le Harve, a quiet overnight crossing except for the fact that his luggage was lost on the boat. After spending the day in the officer's club (Holst had officer's privileges, although he was not a part of the regular army) and the YMCA and RTO, Holst finally found his luggage on the docks at 8:30 p.m..[24]

It took the entire next month for Holst to get to Salonica. Wartime security plus red tape slowed things down. On November 2nd Holst took the train to Paris and on the next day he attended a requiem at Notre Dame and, courtesy of a Frenchman and his son, heard a Horse Guards band.[25] That night he began a forty-hour train ride to Rome, which included a two and one-half hour stop in Modane, an electric train ride through the Savoy Alps, and a two-hour victory celebration in Turin. Holst arrived in Rome at 11:00 a.m. on November 5th and stayed there for the next two days. Despite the bureaucracy, Holst did manage to see some sights. His diary entry for Wednesday, November 6th reads "Rome all day. S Pietro in morning[,] officials in afternoon" and, for the next day, "more officials. Pantheon, Camalidoglio Forum etc."[26] Another long and aggravating train ride followed, complete with a washed-out bridge, and two-hour delay in arrival. This time the ride was to Brindisi, a town with its own set of problems. Holst wrote: "all registered luggage lost yesterday. Football match and caves. Hotel horrible. At the station an old man made us come to a house in the old town--both he and his sister unintelligible" and "after service naval lieutenant takes us to the house and interprets. He also takes us to Convent. Row at Hotel--we go to the house."[27] He wrote to Isobel:

> We have left Rome and have almost left civization. I believe I must not mention the town I am in, but Algeria was Bond St. compared to this. The fun is beginning.[28]

The following day, November 11th, was Armistace Day, which marked the end of hostilities. Holst's official wartime experience amounted to only twelve days. The demobilization of forces would take many months, however, and Holst's services were still desperately needed to keep up the morale of the troops. He wrote Isobel about the festivities:

Nov[ember] 11[, 1918]

Dear Isobel,

To-day we had the news of peace almost before you, as a wireless message was sent by Foch to 'All Ships', and this place went mad on the spot. The only sane people are the English sailors here--bless them. Even they had a wild sing-song--all mixed up with native children.

But the natives got a lot of flags and a thing they call a band--at least I suppose they do--and paraded the town and nearly embraced every Englishman they met. I have been told that the band played 'God Save the King' amongst other things, but I did not notice the fact myself.

I wonder how many times I have shaken hands with strangers to-day.

It has been wonderful beyond words, but all along I have felt that there will be deep disappointment for most of us if we expect the mere signing of peace to reform the world.

I haven't any news, but I felt I must write to you on this day.

B.L.G.[29]

Holst attended a mass in the Brindisi's Cathedral that morning and the celebrations in the afternoon. Although Holst had been spared from having to experience the harshness of the war first-hand, the results of it were all around him. On the 13th some 300 Serbian refugees arrived at nearby Gallipoli and there was not enough food for them. The next day Holst spent a "long day" playing the piano at the local Canteen. A Serbian musician gave him some tunes to play that evening (including the Serbian national anthem) and perhaps this was what prompted Holst to visit a Serbian refugee camp on the following day.[30]

In the meantime Holst received word that on January 30, 1919 Adrian Boult was slated to conduct the Royal Philharmonic Orchestra in a public performance of *The Planets*. He wrote to Boult:

Y.M.C.A.
On active service with the
British Expeditionary Force

Nov[ember] 14[, 1918]

Dear Adrian

We are stranded here waiting for a boat. 'Here' being an out-of-the-way little port in South Italy where we get English papers 10 days old. I believe the censorship still holds good so I won't mention its name.

I want to try and collect all my ideas for Jan 30 into this letter Probably you will get postcards containing all the things I forget now.
1) Mars. You made it wonderfully clear--in fact everything came out clearly that wonderful morning.

Now could you make more row? And work up more sense of climax? Perhaps hurry certain bits? Anyhow it must sound more unpleasant and more terrifying.

In the middle of 5/2 make a lot of [crescendo, decrescendo]. In the last 5/2 in the 2nd bar the brass have to shorten the last note of the firstphrase (F in treble and bass) in order to take breath. The organ chord should also have been shortened--it was careless of me to make it a minim. Would you make it a crotchet followed by a crotchet rest so that the organ and brass finish the phrase more or less together?

Whenever there are semiquavers it might be well to pull back a little so that they come out clearly and heavily but I leave this to you to decide. The end must be louder and heavier and much more *rall*.
2) Mercury. The part I want to alter is when the strings have [triplets] or something of the sort. I have arranged it very clumsily between the instruments. It sounds quite well later on the wind and my first idea was to put it on the latter every time. But I am now wishing that I could rearrange the string parts better. Would you? Or you and Norman.[31] The cellos in particular were out of the picture. I forget if they are muted each time it occurs. I hope they are. (If this is too much bother leave it as it is). Otherwise Mercury might be all right. Keep him soft and quick.
3) Saturn. In the opening some instruments are quite dead. Others have [crescendo, decrescendo]. Make the latter as emotional as possible. You got the quicker time just right--all that part goes all right.

The 4 flute tune (Tempo I) was soft enough but try and get the timp, harps, and basses also down to nothing. This part must begin from another world and gradually overwhelm this one. That is the nearest verbal suggestion I can give you. Of course there is nothing in any of the planets (my planets I mean) that can be expressed in words.

Make the climax as big and overwhelming as possible. Then the soft ending will play itself as long as there is no suggestion of crescendo.

The organ must be softer. It dominated all instead of merely adding

depth. Use fewer and softer stops--perhaps 32 ft alone or 16 ft alone instead of both. Let it be too soft rather than too loud.
4) Jupiter. As long as he gets the wonderful joyousness you gave he'll do. I wish you had Gyp as 1st trumpet!

At the recapitulation this part (tutti in unison) [16ths] did not come out clearly. Perhaps it should be broadened out. Do as you like.

And accept my blessing and thanks.

I have been writing this while serving at the canteen with intervals to play for the men. We have about 60 British sailors here also this place has been inundated with 300 Serbian refugees. They are dear people, far nicer than these natives but there is not enough food for us all in the town. Also they--like us--are taking the first boat to Salonica. It will be certainly overcrowded and probably filthy and there is a gale blowing! However I presume that there will be more than one first boat.

This evening was most interesting. One of the Serbians was a musician. He got a piece of YMCA paper like this one and ruled some lines and wrote out the Serbian national anthem and two dances for me and I played them and they all sang.

Letters will be very welcome

Address G. T. Holst
c/o C W Bates
YMCA
Piccadilly Circus
Salonica.

Yrs ever

Gustav[32]

On Saturday, November 16th the long-awaited boat had come. There were problems, however, as there had been for the entire trip. Holst's diary entry reflects the humorous style usually reserved by him for letters:

Visit officials and buy food for boat in morning. Get on board 2PM via small boat
Boat supposed to start at 5 PM
Passage " " last 15 hours.
Boat does not start at all. Hung up all night.[33]

The boat, crowded with Serbs, finally left at 1PM the next day and arrived on the Greek island of Corfu at 9:30 a.m. the following day. While Holst was crossing the Adriatic, Boult was having some second thoughts about programming all seven of *The Planets* and wrote to Vally Lasker:

> Gustav told me he would like to have all 7 planets done at the first performance, & of course there is no question that it would be best for musicians, but the general public is a different matter, & I do most strongly feel that when they are being given a totally new language like that, 30 minutes of it is as much as they can take in, & I am quite sure that 90% if not 95% of people only listen to one moment after another, & never think of music as a whole at all. I will certainly speak to O'Neill again about it--& I need not tell you where my own personal inclinations are in the matter, but I am very much afraid that the practical side of it that I have dwelt on in this letter (in fact, the same point of view that made me cut the Vaughan Williams[34] the second time I did it) is the right one. I will let you know if O'Neill thinks any other arrangement might be made in the program....[35]

Holst was on Corfu, awaiting yet another boat, when word reached him about Boult's intentions. He always preferred that all seven movements be performed and particularly didn't like the idea of conductors making a "symphony" out of the first four movements. He responded:

> Nov[ember] 21[, 1918]
>
> Dear Adrian
>
> In the 'Phil' program I should like it to be clearly stated that the four planets belong to a Suite of seven pieces. Also I think the sources of origin and names of all seven should appear but I leave this to you....
>
> If any of the Planets are not copied well enough would you have them recopied and let me know the cost?
>
> Yr Ever
>
> Gustav

> [P.S.] I am stuck on a rather jolly island waiting for a boat. I met my first earthquake the other day![36]

Indeed, after Brindisi, Corfu was a "jolly island" for Holst; he was treated almost like royalty. He wrote to Isobel:

> The island contains British, American, French, Italian, Greek, and Serbian soldiers, and I am getting hardened to being saluted. It makes me feel like a fraud, but on the other hand the cordial welcome a Y.M.C.A. worker gets everywhere is very touching. For instance, yesterday as I was going through the citadel an English soldier came round the corner and started saluting, but on seeing my badge he converted it into a long handshake and we were pals at once. He took me over the citadel and from the top I got a wonderful view of blue sea, blue mountains, and black thunder-clouds. But imagine my feelings when, on leaving the citadel, a huge Sengalese sentry PRESENTED ARMS to me!....[37]

Holst remained on Corfu another week. In addition to sight-seeing, he found time to repair and tune the YMCA piano, putting to use some piano tuning lessons he had taken just before leaving London. He also found time to do some solo playing as well as playing with a Greek violinist and a flautist.[38]

On the 27th in the rain Holst and 1,000 Yugoslavs boarded the *Timgad*, which he described as "Fine boat but dirty."[39] The boat arrived at Itea the next morning and from there Holst had a "wonderful drive in motor lorry" to Bralo. From there where he began an adventurous train ride that left seven hours late and lasted two days. The trip had its pleasures--passing near Vale of Tempi and Mt. Olympus--and irritations--a crash into a Greek troop train that delayed the trip an additional seven and one-half hours--before finally arriving near Salonica on Sunday, December 1st.[40]

Once at Summer Hill Camp, Salonica, Holst, who had expected to be teaching right away, found himself doing all sorts of administrative odds and ends. Even before he had departed England there had been some speculation that, once back in England, he might move on to administrative positions and not return to his teaching. Holst put that to rest in a letter to Vally Lasker:

> ....My first twenty-four hours in Salonica was a nightmare of organisation, co-ordination, schemes, army forms, etc.
>
> I don't see why I am expected not to come come back to my old jobs which I love so much.

> The only alternative I can see is that I should be put on some committee or such tomfoolery--in short become an 'expert'.
>
> Do you really suppose I would forsake Morley, J.A.G.S. and S.P.G.S. for co-ordination and Co?
>
> ....I'm not going to waste time with that game. I'm going round in a friendly way, helping people when they want me and clearing out when they don't. I've done so for three days already with complete and most surprising success. And when I've had enough of them or they've had enough of me I am coming back to my old work, partly because I want to, and partly because I know of no alternative that does not make me blaspheme vigorously.[41]

He waxed on more philosophically in a later letter to Isobel:

> ....About going back to my old work, or getting 'something better':--I am skeptical about the latter. You see, my old work was very jolly. There was a fearful lot of it, but it was the real thing:--real people to teach, and real music to give them....Now the only 'better' thing I can conceive is something to do with committees, education schemes, and coordination. In other words, talking about a thing instead of doing it. It may be necessary--I fear it is--but I don't feel it's my job, whereas teaching a kindergarten or the Thaxted choir is. I believe you thought I was going to get away from the teaching atmosphere. I've been in it worse than ever from the day we left! My only consideration is a slum school headmaster for 30 years and who therefore knows that at the moment one ceases to think of human beings and dwells mentally amid schemes and systems one is just damned as a teacher.
>
> This is a bit mixed, but all I mean is that I'm not so keen on a big education job, and I don't see that I should be offered any sort of 'something better'.[42]

Holst offered a willing hand to any musical activity in Salonica. He played more keyboard than he had in some time--harmonium for British masses, organ at San Sofia, and supplying piano accompaniments for the silent movies held at the General Headquarters on Saturday evenings. Holst also gave and hosted a number of lectures at various locations. On his second day in Salonica, Holst overheard Captain William Vowles practicing selections from Bach's *Well Tempered Clavier* on the YMCA's upright piano and insisted on acting as chairman to Vowles' lecture that evening. Apparently, the lecture had been too much for Holst to handle. Vowles comments:

> A few days later we met again. He had a bandage round his head and various pieces of plaster on his face and nose. 'This is your fault,' he said. 'I was so excited after your talk, that on my way back I was gazing up at the stars and humming the themes of the pieces you played and did not see a big hole in the road!'[43]

The two became good friends and within a week Holst had "pressed him to do musical work."[44]

At first the bulk of Holst's teaching at Salonica consisted of giving private lessons at the General Headquarters. Attendence was somewhat sporadic, so Holst ended up sorting music a great deal of the time. With the passage of time, however, things improved. He discussed plans with some of the YMCA personnel for starting a choir and orchestra and in time was able to do these things. In one way it was fortunate that Holst started his work there in December. He would be able to instill enthusiasm for singing through directing Christmas Carols in practices and in performance. One of the people to whom Holst submitted his proposals was Joseph J. Findlay, Dean of Education at the University of Manchester, and Civilian Advisor on Education for the British Salonica forces. Holst and Findlay got to know each other quite well and shared a number of walks and visits to various schools.

Holst wrote to Isobel about his early activities at Summerhill Camp:

> Salonica
> Xmas Day
>
> Dear Isobel,
>
> ....The thing promises to be a great success, and I am overwhelmed both by the quantity and the quality of the men who want music here. Occasionally, but not often, I am overwhelmed--or partly so--by the difficulties.
>
> Every morning I am on view at the Education Office where we get officers and men and nurses, and sometimes we have staff meetings which I dread because I so rarely see the points raised.
>
> The leader at the GHQ hut is a dear:--a Scottish Presbyterian minister whose pawky humour hides his deep sympathy and very wide learning and wisdom from all superficial people. Behind the hut is a den which he has

given me as a music room. I have been there every afternoon to arrange teaching wounded French and Serbians, (fancy teaching tonic solfa to Serbians!) and men come for lessons whenever they can. It is a free and easy arrangement that appeals to them greatly. They also appreciate the only strict rules I have made for them so far--

1) Any pupil finding me having tea with an officer is to disturb me without fail!

2) Every man entering my room will half turn to the right and help himself to the cigarette tin. The Y. M. C. A. presents me with 100 free cigarettes per week, so I was forced to make this second rule.

The work has been fascinating. Sometimes a man comes for a long lesson, sometimes he drops in for five minutes taken out of his tea time, sometimes we drift into a general talk about music. They are usually theory pupils. The first pianist I had had let his hands become as stiff as pokers so I gave him some easy technical exercizes, and during his first practise he had things flung at him. So the leader got the key-board out of a smashed-up piano, and now all exercizes are done in silence. It works very well, and two of the men are getting quite flexible. As I have told them, it is not really piano playing, but it will make the latter easier when they get home.

This way of getting to work has made an excellent start for me, as I have met men, officers, and nurses individually and have made friends. Besides actual pupils I have interviewed scores of people from various parts of the area.

But it would never do to keep on like this as I should not get in touch with even one per cent of the men.

The first development happened in my second week--lecturing and choral training outside the city. It means getting there by motor--either a Tin Lizzie or a Ford touring. I didn't like the night driving much at first, but I'm getting used to it now. The British drivers are amazing (everything British is!). The French ones are dare-devils--they either take a delight in running unnecessary risks or else they are (or seem to be) members of a suicide club. I'll tell you about the Greek drivers when the censorship is lifted! But my driver is British--and an artist.

I want to get the GHQ work organized and then go further afield. I have had some pathetic appeals from up country. Also about 365 unofficial invitations to Serbia, but I shall not be allowed there yet, I expect. Although the Serbs love music, transport is required for more material things.

Best love,

Gustav[45]

1919 started with Holst having severe throat problems. This did not stop him from teaching or from taking steps to get the orchestra going. After spending days on end copying out parts, there was a problem with the GHQ instruments, leading to a row between Holst and Colonel Banks.[46] The situation was quickly corrected and Holst began holding weekly orchestra classes at the GHQ at 2:30 on Tuesday afternoons, followed by choir rehearsals at 8:30. He also continued to visit and lecture at various camps, and performaned all sorts of instructional duties, including the teaching of "I saw three ships" to a group of Serbs at the Scottish Women's Hospital.[47] Sometimes his lectures were improvised. He commented to Katherine Eggar:

> The best bit of inventing I ever did was an impromtu History of Music one night during the war in Salonica. It was dark; we were waiting for the lorries. Nothing to do while we waited, so I started talking a History of Music. I couldn't <u>see</u> anybody, you know--only the ends of lighted cigarettes. I just went on talking to the cigarette ends. I don't know whether anybody listened...[48]

Conditions at Holst's camp were actually very good. He wrote to Vally Lasker:

> ....We live sumptuously--food overwhelming in quantity and quite good in quality, wine cheap, and the average YM worker here is a really fine fellow. When I go up into Bulgaria I shall probably have a rough time for a night or two but in Salonica I have a warm bed and lately we can have as much charcoal for braziers as we like....[49]

What Holst left out is that he occasionally got breakfast in bed![50]

The Salonica area, though revaged by war was still scenic. He wrote to Isobel:

> There is no tide on the Aegean sea, and it comes right up to the roadside along the quay. The Greek sailing boats are beautiful:--lovely broad bows, often brilliantly painted.
>
> And across the bay is the one supreme thing of beauty--Mount Olympus. No wonder the gods lived there. Its base is usually covered

with mist from the marshes, so that it appears lifted off the earth. It is the only Grecian thing here:--it is calm and classic and not rugged and Gothic. This is probably nonsense, but that is how it appeals to me.[51]

In late January Holst took a side trip to Bulgaria. While there he wrote to his Morley College students:

To the Morley Music Students
8:30 p.m., January 25th, 1919
In a tent near the ruins of a shelled city on the borders of Bulgaria

Dear Friends,

I have just been lecturing and playing to some soldiers for an hour and a half, and am now sitting in my tent wondering how the concert is going on and trying to imagine the sound of your voices and instruments. In time I hope I shall get heaps of letters from you letting me know how it all goes, and whether Dr. Terry is pleased with you.

On the whole I am having a very good time. But the army is scattered over an enormous area, and even when you reach a place very often you find the camp breaking up and very few men left. Of course one is very glad that things like that are happening, bit it is sometimes a little disconcerting. I am nearly a hundred miles north of Salonica, and have come all the way by motor car along with a sleeping bag, two blankets, lots to eat and drink, and about a dozen parcels of music. I had to cross the Struma Valley, where so much fighting took place. Also I have had a long walk through the ruined city out on to the hills beyond, jumping over trenches, avoiding--or not avoiding--barbed wire, exploring dug outs and gun emplacements, finally visiting an ancient Acropolis the ruins of which were cleverly used by the Bulgars in a manner as horrible as it was clever. But the greatest sight I saw was also the greatest sight I have ever seen; indeed I felt was witnessing the greatest scene on earth. I saw Greek peasants and their oxen ploughing the battlefield for the first time since the fighting ceased!

Good luck to them and to you.

Yours sincerely,

G. T. Holst

> P.S.--Jan. 27th. I returned to Salonica last night, and have been out all day motoring in a "Tin Lizzie" with the Pardar wind blowing--a really cold job. After making arrangements to form a choir in one camp, ditto plus a harmony class in a second, settling final arrangements for a lectures at a third, discussing the possibility of forming a sing-song during a cinema show by throwing the words of a song on the screen (owing to the non-arrival of song books) at a fourth, and finally conducting the Unfinished Symphony and the Mendelssohn violin concerto with the splendid Artillery School orchestra founded by Captain [H. C.] Colles, the musical critic of the *Times*, who is now in England. The orchestra was lead by a Morleyite--Gunner Keyes, who sends his greetings to you all.[52]

He wrote in more detail about the Artillery School orchestra experience in a letter to Isobel:

> I am conducting the remains of the Artillery School orchestra founded by Colles of the Times. I had a delightful experience with them on Saturday. We were rehearsing in their theatre which has no windows--we had to take out panels in the wall to let in the light, but it also let in a violent snow storm right onto their backs. I gave them as good a time as I could under the conditions (we had one small brazier which we passed round from one to another) and when it was over, instead of grousing, a man told me it had been his happiest morning in Salonica.[53]

Colles, who had departed Salonica in November, left the conductorship of the orchestra to his assistant, who in turn had left it to Holst. The "remains" of the Artillery School orchestra, even after demobilization had begun, still featured an more-or-less intact instrumentation of winds in pairs plus about fifteen strings. This was the Royal Philharmonic compared with the normal amorphous complement with which Holst had to work.

Time was running out in Salonica. Holst sensed in early February that if there were to be any large musical event programmed, then it had to happen soon. He proposed a concert of British music, received approval, and set the date for Tuesday, February 24th. There were a sufficient number of rehearsals, but the reality of demobilization had set in. He wrote to Jane Joseph:

> We have been having an exciting time over our big concert of British works. One rehearsal began with the demobilisation of the 1st horn and

> only double bass, and ended with that of the 1st trombone and 2nd clarinet. We got deputies from other units and they got demobolised. We got deputy-deputies and they got demobilised or malaria.
>
> And each little group had to be fetched and returned at each rehearsal by lorry or car:--what price staff work?[54]

To garner interest in the "big" concert, Holst gave a lecture and "sneak preview" rehearsal on Wednesday, February 19th at Summerhill. He defined it as a "great success."[55] It was, and with an audience of over 500. For the next five days, the concert preoccupied his thoughts. Even though William Vowles was there to assist him with various matters, such as arranging for a platform as well as taking over some of the conducting duties, Holst was sleeping badly during this time.[56] Final rehearsals on the evening of Sunday, the 23rd, and at 3:00 p.m. on the day of the concert attracted hundreds of uninvited guests, prompting Holst to wonder if the concert itself would be anticlimactic. He needn't have worried; over 3,000 attended the concert. Vowles commented:

> There could not be much stability at all in Holst's work among the troops in Salonica. Everybody was hoping to be demobilised without delay, and many were being sent further East. Eventually he was moved to Constantinople, but before this temporary separation, we had been able to organize a choral and orchestral concert (under canvas). The programme included [Samuel Coleridge-Taylor's] 'Hiawatha,' [Edward Elgar's] 'Pomp and Circumstance,' and [Percy Grainger's] 'Mock Morris.' This concert delighted Holst; he referred to it again and again when I met him in later years in the United States and in London. He never forgot his amusement at seeing three senior staff officers and a dog sitting on the doublebass case. At this time Holst appeared to be entirely happy and well, his complete devotion to the work he had undertaken was unmistakable....[57]

Holst commented about the concert to Isobel:

> The choir was on stage and the band in the orchestra pit, and for purely instrumental items I found it better to turn round and face the audience and the conductor's stand was close up by the footlights. Also as the only baton was heavy I did without one.
>
> And now I am disgusted at finding myself famous as a freak conductor!!
>
> The climax was when Prof. Findlay told me that it was a wonderful

example of Eurhythmics. And he wasn't trying to be funny![58]

Holst sent program copies to many of his friends. Among them was Percy Grainger, who had emigrated to the United States in 1914 to avoid conscription. Ironically, Grainger joined the United States Army as a saxophonist in the latter years of the war.

On Active Service
Young men's Christian Association
with the
Salonica Forces

YMCA
British post Office
Constantinople
March 3[, 1919]

Dear Grainger

I am asking Balfour to forward this and the enclosed programme in the hope it may interest you. It was not meant as representative of British music but merely as a performance of what British music we could do out here. I was sent out by the YMCA as Musical Organiser to Salonica and this was my farewell venture before leaving for the above address.

The audience was the biggest I have ever seen. About 300 were standing inside besides a big crowd outside and those who got seats spread into the orchestra and round the back of the choir. We had to repeat it the next day and we also gave it the week before at another camp. Also we had big audiences at the rehearsals. So that the Mock Morris has been applauded, cheered, and encored by at least 3000 people here.

Good luck to it and its composer!

Yr Sincerely

G T Holst[59]

After the concert had ended, a mishap occurred. Holst commented to Isobel:

After every concert at night I always get someone to guide me to my car

> because I can never see the ditches, and on Monday night the oboe player took me by the arm until we got on to the main road and then let me go saying 'there you are' and before I could say 'thanks' I had disappeared into a three foot gulley and sprained my ankle....[60]

With his bad ankle Holst stayed in bed until 4:00 p.m. the next day. He then made his way over to the 43rd General hospital. That evening he felt well enough to conduct the repeat of the previous evening's concert, but afterwards returned to the hospital where he spent the next two days. X-rays revealed no fracture and he felt fine. Then, uncharacteristically, he took advantage of the situation. He continued in his letter to Isobel:

> Early yesterday morning the Y.M.C.A. Secretary for Salonica came into my bedroom and told me that the concert had been the most delightful and successful evening he had ever spent in Macedonia. So by way of a suitable reply I told him I wanted a holiday in Athens.
>
> He was not quite prepared for that, but after gazing thoughtfully at the poor suffering invalid lying there haggard and wan he said he would apply for a permit! It will cost a small fortune but it is a chance not to be missed.[61]

The next week was spent recuperating as well as packing instruments and music for the inevitable journey to Constantinople. He was also preparing for his week-long stay in Athens. Holst was a long way from London, yet it was there during that week that one particular event took place that would change the way critics, audiences, and history would treat the composer. The first public performance of five movements of *The Planets*, originally scheduled for January 30th, ultimately took place on Thursday, February 27th, when Holst was in the hospital. Adrian Boult conducted the Royal Philharmonic Society Orchestra in a performance of "Mars," "Mercury," "Saturn," "Uranus," and "Jupiter"--in that order--at Queen's Hall. It triggered a series of events that included more partial performances of *The Planets*, and the premieres of *Japanese Suite, The Hymn of Jesus*, *Two Psalms*, and the *First Suite in E Flat for Military Band.* This culminated in the complete performance of *The Planets*, which in turn lead to the first professional performance of *Savitri*, and premiere of the *Second Suite in F for Military Band.* Within a half dozen years all of Holst's major pre-war works, save *Sita*, were premiered and published.

Boult immediately sent the composer a congratulatory cable and Isobel sent press cuttings. Unfortunately, due to Holst's trip to Athens and the demobilization process that followed, neither the cable nor the press cuttings caught up with him for another four weeks.

On Saturday, March 8th Holst boarded a train bound for Athens. He spent the next week in the capitol city, getting entirely lost among its wonders. Time seemed to stand still for him; he showed up at the Acropolis one day two hours before its opening and that same evening got locked in the Dionysus Theatre after its closing.[62] Yet these things didn't matter, for he was totally enamored of the city. He commented to Vaughan Williams:

> In order to avoid extatic drivel I will just tell you three impressions I got.
>
> First, the modern buildings--library, museum, university, etc--are really beautiful. I mean beautiful in the sense that no other building of the last hundred years that I have seen is.
>
> Second, Rome simply is not it. Athens is beautiful, and Rome is handsome or something that does not include joy. For instance, there is a Roman theatre at the foot of the Acropolis which looks like a well-built jail!
>
> Lastly, I've learnt what 'classical' means. It means something that sings and dances through sheer joy of existence. And if the Parthenon is the only building in the world that does so, then there is only one classical building in the world.
>
> All the old talk of classical v romantic used to irritate me but it is only now I realise what twaddle it is.
>
> And the uncanny thing is that two-thirds of the Parthenon isn't there. The thing is a ruin and ruins are expected to look pathetic. Which is a farcical idea when you've seen the Parthenon.
>
> To recall it is like recalling the Sanctus of the b minor--one blushes all over. Anyhow I do. And the first glimpse of it after going through the Propylea was like love at first sight....[63]

Holst returned to Salonica on the 15th. There he found that the song books sent from England the previous October had finally arrived and he had his "first proper singsong" at Salonica on Monday the 17th.[64] It turned out to be the only one, since a singsong scheduled for the following day at a concentration camp had to be cancelled. Holst himself was demobilzed two days later and he boarded a train bound for Constantinople. During the two-day rail journey Holst kept a close eye on his baggage--his valese, containing music, sketchbooks, and addresses, had been stolen right out of his car on the way to the station.

Holst spent his first few days in Constantinople getting organized and oriented to his new surroundings. In 1919 the Ottoman Empire was in a state of ruin. Turkey had lost one quarter of its population either through the Turks' genocide of the Armenian population there or through the Turks' own casualties of war. The British and the Turks had been enemies during the war and the British and French forces occupying Constantinople were bitter pills for the Turks to swallow. The Ottoman caliph, though defeated, was still present and the reforms of Ataturk, including the Latinization of the Turkish alphabet and the founding of the Turkish republic were still years away.

Things were slow at first, as they had been at the start in Salonica. Holst once again spent time working on his keyboard skills, putting them to use by playing for Sunday evening services at the base and eventually playing organ for Sunday morning services at the Crimean church. At first he had plenty of time for sight-seeing. On Sunday, March 23rd, his first full day in Constantinople, Holst attended an Armenian concert.[65] The following day he went to see St. Sophia (known by Islamics as the Aya Sofia or Hagia Sofia). He commented about his impressions of the city to Isobel:

> The great joy of Constantinople is the view from the Bosphorus and the Sea of Marmara. All round the coasts of the Golden Horn there are gardens, woods, field, hills and flowers for miles....
>
> St. Sophia is quite painful and almost grotesque. I understand that it was originally built to face Jerusalem and that the Turks have turned the carpets and everything else in the direction of Mecca. The first effect is not unlike being light-headed.
>
> Whenever people have told me how beautiful Gothic churches must have been when the walls were covered with paintings, I have always felt doubtful. But there is no doubt about St. Sophia--it just cries out for ornament. In fact it screams--huge walls with niches and places for mosaics right up to the dome all bare and hungry and waiting to be filled.
>
> Like everyone else, I've got my own ideas about the future of the building, and as they are hardly 'practical politics' perhaps the censor will pass them. They are:
>
> 1) Keep all priests and politicians off the premises for 20 years unless they agree on a working plan before then.
>
> 2) Deliver St. Sophia and 200,000 pounds sterling (I think that would be enough) to you and Balfour, giving you absolute freedom.

The building itself is as near perfection as it can be. Although it is enormous it gives a wonderful feeling of lightness and grace.

The other mosques leave me very cold. Probably because they are cold. I feel they have taken over the St. Sophia style without realising it does not suit them. The little mosques in Algeria were much more to the point--severe puritanical spotlessly white praying houses. Probably what Mohamet intended.

The Stamboul market is good. It is a maze of underground passages all leading the wrong way, and filled with noisy shops and stalls selling the wrong goods.

My favorite place is Anatolia, where I have to go teach twice a week. There are few signs of war, and spring is in full swing and the whole countryside is well-cultivated, (you don't know how the absence of this affects one's soul unless you've been in Salonica), and there are flowers everywhere....[66]

The cable from Adrian Boult about the success of *The Planets* on February 27th and Iosbel's collection of press cuttings finally reached Holst in Constantinople. He wrote to Boult immediately:

YMCA British Post Office
Constantinople
March 25[, 1919]

Dear Adrian

It was very

a) nice of you

b) like you to send that cable.

Many many thanks for it. Unfortunately I only arrived here three days ago and nobody troubled to send the wire on to me.

And now a mail is in and I have learnt details. And the chief detail I have learnt--if one could call it a detail--is your triumphant success. You saw the papers long before I did so I won't quote them. But you seem to have won the hearts of my young lady pupils very thoroughly also those of others who are neither young or ladies. 'I must tell you how beautifully Mr. Boult conducted. One hardly noticed him at all but from the way things went one realised how masterly he was.' That is real deep praise from a discerning musician. 'Boult was absolutely glorious'. 'The performance was beautiful, Boult took immense trouble and conducted finely.' Etc. etc.

So it is good to know that you have reaped your reward and that other people have expressed the gratitude that I can only feel.

I had all my kit stolen the other day so do not know your address. I shall therefore enclose it in the next letter I write to my wife or Miss Lasker.

Yr Ever
Wishing you much more of
the same and myself also

Gustav[67]

Boult returned the complement:

The Abby Manor
West Kirby,
Cheshire

or

25/4/19
6 Chelsea Court
SW3

Dear Gustav,

Thank you very much for your very jolly letter, but don't you see that none of the nice hings you & your friends have said would have been possible if you hadn't made them so?

It was sickening that you weren't there to see the enthusiasm and to be the butt of it! I hear that it may be possible for the R.P.S. to repeat the Planets next season. I don't know who will conduct--but it would be splendid to hear it and splendid to do it again.

It was gorgeous the way it did come off, & the way the orchestra loved it, & how well people spoke of it afterwards.

By the by--we shortened the organ glissando--starting at [C3] because otherwise the notes had hardly time to speak. As it was I only know the last note, but this with the feel of it came through to the audience. All blessings and hoping we'll have them all again soon.

Yr ever

Adrian[68]

Never one to take credit for what he perceived to be the work of others, Holst wrote to Isobel, "I'm returning the press-cuttings about the Planets. I'm so glad Boult gets his due. It's all quite nice, except that people seem to dislike Saturn, which is my favourite."[69]

Within weeks, Holst's teaching and lecturing routines at Constantinople were established. Most of his time was spent at the army camp located at Feneraki, within the walls of the old city on the south shore of the Golden Horn. He also spent considerable time at Haydarpasa (Haidar), on the Asian side southeast of the Bosphorus. He commented enthusiastically to Vally Lasker:

> Yesterday between the hours of 10AM and 4PM I started two orchestras in two different continents.
>
> In fact yesterday was a great day. My only objection to it being that it contained rather too much work--I might as well be in London if this goes on.

9AM to 10	violin class (1 violin with four strings, two with 3, one with 2)
10-11	orchestral class
11-11:45	special interviews with special pupils
11.45-12.15	walk to station with toothbrush, razor, etc. a violin, a flute, a coat and a book
12.15-12.30	in train
12.30-12.50	in steamer across Bosphorus--lovely!
12.50-1.30	instead of landing something or somebody went wrong and we drifted away into midstream amidst a heap of craft of all sizes. The number of boats that we did not sink and which did not sink us was wonderful. It was quite a pleasant change but it made me late....
2	my first pupil (harmony and piano) besides letters from Nora, Jane, and Elgar
2.50-3.10	This was a wild time. The room had to be prepared for the orchestra--there were no music stands and

> no E strings. Six people wanted to see me on six different points, most of them confidential. And I had a cable from Scholes. There were other disturbances but I forget what they were, except two demands for music, one from the Black Sea and the other from Smyrna.
>
> | | |
> |---|---|
> | 3.10-4.30 | Orchestra. 4 violins, 1 sharp pitch clarinet, one rather sharp pitch oboe, one piano just over a tone flat.[70] |
> | 4.30 | Two interviews about organizing |
> | 5 | Tea |
> | 5.30 | A lesson on the prologue to 'Pagliacci'. |
> | 7 | dinner |
> | 7.30-9.30 | sightsinging and choir |
> | 9.30-10.30 | a philosophical talk with Prof. Findlay! |
>
> And to think that when I first arrived at Constantinople things were so slack that in despair I started practising the piano....[71]

At an education conference held at General Headquarters on April 14th, it was suggested to Holst that an international musical competition be held that would include representative choral and instrumental ensembles from all bases of the Army of the Black Sea. Announced on April 25th,[72] the competition was slated for Saturday, June 7th. The location was to be the Theatre Petits-Champs. On the Monday following the competition [Whit Monday] there was to be a massed choral and orchestral concert, to be repeated every evening of the following week, climaxed by an awards ceremony on the 14th. For Holst it would be a grand displacement of the 1916-1918 Thaxted festivals. Holst was in charge of setting everything up, of course, and he threw himself into things as only he knew how. Only British music was to be featured and for the competition Holst was able to persuade the YMCA to sponsor publication of an English language edition of the Communion Service of William Byrd's *Three-part Mass* that he and Jane Joseph had originally prepared for the Thaxted choir. The publishers included the following note:

> The Music Section of the Y.M.C.A. have asked Messrs. Stainer and Bell to publish this edition with English words in the belief that our soldiers will learn to love singing and listening to this masterpiece of English music....[73]

Holst considered this act of convincing the YMCA authorities to publish this work to be one of the greatest accomplishments of his lifetime.

Holst's efforts were duly noted and the YMCA considered asking him to remain beyond the terms of his initial contractual agreement. With this a very real possibility, Holst found himself torn between staying and leaving. He wrote to Frances Ralph Gray:

> YMCA
> British Base Post Office
> Constantinople
> May 5[, 1919]
>
> Dear Miss Gray
>
> I have been told that the YMCA may ask me to stay on either until Xmas or until spring 1920.
>
> I feel that the work at home is the more important of the two as it is the more permanent and certain in the results. The work here is that of a pioneer and it <u>might</u> be that at the end of a year I <u>might</u> lay the foundations for someone else to carry on with.
>
> So I have decided to stay on if asked on condition that you are satisfied that the music will not suffer at school. Otherwise I shall come back as soon as possible after next month. I have asked my wife to speak or write to you about it.
>
> Things are really moving now and I am tremendously busy. And the work is very jolly and very promising.
>
> Yr Sincerely
>
> G T Holst
>
> What I hope to achieve if I stay on is to get so much musical work going that the army or YMCA would feel compelled to keep it going after I left. It is all chance but it would be worth trying as long as I felt sure the work at home was going on well.[74]

Holst's ultimate decision not to stay on may have been determined by his needs as a composer. Reminders of his rising status, through press releases sent to him about *The Planets* and news of *The Hymn of Jesus* receiving the Carnegie United Kingdom Trust Award (and subsequent publication by Stainer & Bell), served as incentives. Yet in Constantinople, as in Salonica, there was no sound-proof room of his own in which to compose.

As the June 7th competition approached, Holst was involved in a flurrish of activity: the piano was repaired, parts were copied, and extra choir rehearsals took place. Holst at least tried to acquire a set of bells for "A Chime for Homecoming" (new words to "A Festival Chime" from the *Three Festival Choruses*) and may have sought the services of an Egyptian princess who, it turned out, did not sing.[75] He also sought and obtained the services of Captain William Vowles, whom he had not seen since departing Salonica. Vowles had no idea what was in store for him, just that he had been ordered to report to General Headquarters in Constantinople for temporary duty. Due to problems in transit, Vowles arrived late on June 6th, the date he was supposed to report. His description of what followed is a classic:

> ....I reported to G.H.Q., where I was told to go immediately to see Holst. I found him in a state of great agitation and he said, "I was in despair! Tomorrow morning we have Musical Competions for the whole of the Army of the Black Sea. Some of the competitors are coming a thousand miles. We have bands, choirs, composers, violinists, pianists, and singers, coming from as far away as Batoum and Baku, and *you* are the judge!"
>
> The Competitions were followed by a week's Musical Festival in the principal theatre in Pera. It was practically the same 'all British' concert given each evening, to which free invitations were sent to all ranks of the army and navy and to the civilian population. At the first of these concerts, the Commander-in-Chief sent for Holst and thanked and congratulated him. I was not expecting to take any share in these concerts, but at the last moment he said to me, 'Take charge of the "invisible' choir" which will start singing "Sumer is Icumen In" a long way off and will approach the main chorus gradually. Then lead them away, so as to make an opposite effect at the end.' When this was over he said, 'Now hurry down to the orchestra, where there is a spare viola waiting for you!' When the orchestral piece was finished he turned to me and said, 'Go up to the choir and sing second tenor in the Byrd *Three-Part Mass* .' No sooner was that done than he told me to accompany a singer who was going to sing the song which had won the prize in the composition class. I was unprepared for this role of quick-change artist. It was typical of

> Holst. He liked people to *do* things, no matter how imperfect or how inexperienced they might be. And he had not finished with me yet. During the interval he thrust a programme into my hand, saying 'Go and talk about it!' "But I haven't prepared anything to say!' Then, very emphatically, 'Go and talk about it.' Before I could reply a second time, he had taken me by the shoulders and pushed me through the wings and onto the stage. Holst knew I had very decided views on English music; these I began to express with a great deal of fervor. He was pleased, telling me later that I had opened up a new line of thought to many of those taking part in the concerts.[76]

The week's events were successful, although some things did not measure up to Holst's expectations. The concert set for Whit Monday featured a massed choir of only thirty and an orchestra of twenty; it was somewhat anticlimactic. Holst wrote "Concert rather dull in Evening."[77] Over the ensuing week the quality of the nightly performances and audience size varied greatly from one evening to the next. On Saturday, the last day of the festival, there was a tension-releasing comic song competition followed by the prize giving. He commented to Isobel, "On the whole our musical competiton has been a success, although not a brilliant one. But it has left a deep impression on many, especially the choir, and that is the main point."[78]

The week's activities summed up Holst's work in Constantinople. The next day, Sunday, June 15th, Holst relaxed in his room and at the Bomonti Gardens, a place that he frequented during his stay in Constantinople. He also packed, and had a final get together with Vowles and other friends that evening at the Petits-Champs.[79] The following evening he began the long journey back home. He had been away nearly eight months and, though now officially "on leave," he would never return. His work in Constantinople, however, did make quite an impression with the military. His replacement was not another YMCA volunteer, but one of the army's own: Captain William Vowles.

The good news about Holst's return journey was that it lasted two weeks, only half as long as his journey to Salonica. The bad news was that it proved to be just as arduous and irritating as the first one. Holst's ship left Constantinople at 7:30 p.m. on Monday, June 16th. Prior to his 3:00 p.m. boarding, he had time to buy some embroidery for Isobel at the Co-op stores.[80] After an uneventful overnight passage, the ship stopped at Chanuk (Canakkale) for a day to load more troops. Possibly to break the boredom, Holst engaged in a lengthy discussion about the occult with one of his fellow passengers. From Chanuk, it was a three-day journey across calm seas to Taranto, in southern Italy, where Holst had to bear terrific heat and a "rowdy hut at night."[81]

From Taranto, Holst had three hot and horrible train rides through Italy. The first, from Taranto to Castelmaria, was in a car so filthy that it featured a "bug hunt;" the second, from Castelmaria to Faenza, featured a journey in a 3rd class carriage that Holst described as "uncomfortable, but clean," and the third, from Faenza to Turin--still in 3rd class--featured lengthy waits at Bologna, Voghera, and Allesandria. Holst took advantage wherever he could to get off the train and see the sights. On Wednesday, the 25th, when the train stopped near Turin, Holst learned that the Germans had signed the Treaty of Versailles.[82]

The overnight rail journey across the Savoy Alps that followed was just as uncomfortable; this time the weather was cold and wet. Holst's car had a roof that leaked. The next day there was a noontime stop in France at St. Germaine, near Lyons. The next day Holst was let off at Joigny, about 120 kilometers south of Paris, where he had a long wait at the station. The train that picked him up, "crawling round Paris all night," was even slower than the Italian ones had been. What followed was a comedy of errors. After several short stops, the train arrived at Boulogne at 2 p.m. on Saturday, the 28th. Holst was promised a passage across the Channel, and then ordered to an army camp. Once there he was told that he should have gone to the YMCA. He telephoned from the camp and was advised to try for a boat, which he did. At 5 p.m. he sailed across the Channel, arriving at Folkestone at 7:30. More than anxious to end the journey, he took the next available train to Victoria Station. He arrived there at 10:30 and by 11:00 was at Vally Lasker's flat at 103 Talgarth Road, where he usually stayed during the week.[83]

The following morning, at least partially recovered from the trip, Holst visited with his aunt Nina and half-brother Max. In the afternoon he visited twelve year-old Imogen at Eothen School in Caterham (where she had been attending the past two years) and that evening visited with Frances Ralph Gray. The next morning Holst played for the prayer service at St. Paul's Girls' School before calling at the Royal College of Music and the YMCA. Finally, that afternnoon, he returned to Thaxted and to Isobel, who eagerly awaited him.[84]

---

[1]Gustav Holst, *Diary*, Saturday, June 15, 1918, The Holst Foundation.

[2]Gustav Holst, *Diary*, Tuesday, July 23, 1918, The Holst Foundation.

[3]In a letter, quoted on p. 43 in Michael Short (ed.) *Gustav Holst: Letters to W.G. Whittaker* (Glasgow: University of Glasgow Press, 1974), to William Gillies Whittaker dated July 25, 1918, Holst wrote directly, "Not allowed to go to Holland because of my name."

[4]Thessaloniki, Greece.

[5]Iraq.

[6]Business correspondence, Percy Scholes to Gustav Holst, August 16, 1918, The Holst Foundation.
[7]This may refer to the June 15, 1918 Soldiers' Concert at Morley College.
[8]Business correspondence, Percy Scholes to Gustav Holst, August 21, 1918, The Holst Foundation.
[9]Holst's great-grandfather.
[10]Imogen Holst, *Gustav Holst: A Biography, 2nd ed.* (Oxford: Oxford University Press, 1969), 52.
[11]Personal correspondence, Gustav Holst to Frances Ralph Gray, Sept[ember] 17, 1918, The Holst Foundation.
[12]Adrian Boult, *My Own Trumpet* (London: Hamish Hamilton, 1973), 35.
[13]Adrian Boult, "Gustav Holst," in *The Royal College of Music Magazine*, LXX, No. 2 (Summer, 1974), 52.
[14]Henry Balfour Gardiner.
[15]Personal correspondence, Adrian Boult to Gustav Holst, n.d. [September, 1918], British Library Add. MS 60498.
[16]Personal correspondence, Gustav Holst to Edwin Evans, Sep[tember] 22[, 1918], Central Public Library, Westminster.
[17]Gustav Holst, *Diary*, Saturday, September 28, 1918, The Holst Foundation.
[18]Figure III in 'Neptune,' where the brass are playing *pp* chords of e minor and g sharp minor simultaneously.
[19]Adrian Boult, "Gustav Holst," *loc. cit.*.
[20]Henry J. Wood.
[21]Personal correspondence, Gustav Holst to Adrian Boult, Monday[, September 30, 1918], British Library Add MS 60498.
[22]Gustav Holst, *Diary,* Tuesday, October 29, 1918, The Holst Foundation. From this point forward, Holst's diaries, which had been used more-or-less as appointment books, now document his activities. By this time a well-seasoned traveller, Holst approached his wartime travel as just that, travel.
[23]Gustav Holst, *Diary*, Wednesday, October 30, 1918, The Holst Foundation.
[24]Gustav Holst, *Diary*, Friday, November 1, 1918, The Holst Foundation.
[25]Gustav Holst, *Diary*, Sunday, November 3, 1918, The Holst Foundation.
[26]Gustav Holst, *Diary*, Wednesday, November 6 and Thursday, November 7, 1918, The Holst Foundation.
[27]Gustav Holst, *Diary*, Saturday, November 9 and Sunday, November 10, 1918, The Holst Foundation.
[28]Personal correspondence, Gustav Holst to Isobel Holst, November 10, 1918, quoted in Imogen Holst, *Gustav Holst: A Biography, 2nd ed.* (Oxford: Oxford University Press, 1969), 54.
[29]Personal correspondence, Gustav Holst to Isobel Holst, November 11, 1918, quoted in Imogen Holst, *op.cit.*, 54-55. Holst frequently signed his correspondence to Isobel and Imogen "B.L.G."--Best Love, Gustav.
[30]Gustav Holst, *Diary,* Wednesday, November 13 through Friday, November 15, 1918, The Holst Foundation.
[31]Norman O'Neill.
[32]Personal correspondence, Gustav Holst to Adrian Boult, Nov[ember] 14[, 1918], British Library Add MS 60498.
[33]Gustav Holst, *Diary*, Saturday, November 16, 1918, The Holst Foundation.
[34]Ralph Vaughan Williams' *London Symphony*.
[35]Personal correspondence, Adrian Boult to Valley Lasker, November 17, 1918, quoted in Jerrold Northrup Moore (ed.), *Music and Friends* (London: Hamish Hamilton, 1979), 33-34.
[36]Personal correspondence, Gustav Holst to Adrian Boult, Nov[ember] 21[, 1918], British Library

Add. MS 60498.

[37]Personal correspondence, Gustav Holst to Isobel Holst, Nov[ember] 19[, 1918], quoted in Imogen Holst, *op. cit.*, 55-56.

[38]Gustav Holst, *Diary*, Saturday, November 23 through Tuesday, November 26, 1918, The Holst Foundation.

[39]Gustav Holst, *Diary*, Wednesday, November 27, 1918, The Holst Foundation.

[40]Gustav Holst, *Diary*, Friday, November 29 through Sunday, December 1, 1918, The Holst Foundation.

[41]Personal correspondence, Gustav Holst to Vally Lasker, Dec[ember] 5[, 1918], quoted in Imogen Holst, *op. cit.*, 56-57.

[42]Personal correspondence, Gustav Holst to Isobel Holst, Dec[ember] 29[, 1918], quoted in Imogen Holst, *op. cit.*, 60-61.

[43]William Vowles, "Gustav Holst in the Army: Salonica and Constantinople, 1919," in *The Musical Times*, LXXV, No. 1099 (September, 1934), 794.

[44]Gustav Holst, *Diary*, Saturday, December 7, 1918, The Holst Foundation.

[45]Personal correspondence, Gustav Holst to Isobel Holst, Xmas Day, 1918, quoted in Imogen Holst, *op.cit.*, 57-59.

[46]Gustav Holst, *Diary*, Monday, January 6, 1919, The Holst Foundation.

[47]*Ibid.*

[48]Gustav Holst, quoted in Katherine Eggar, "How They Make Music at Morley College," in *The Music Student*, XIII, No. 6 (March, 1921), 359.

[49]Personal correspondence, Gustav Holst to Vally Lasker, Jan[uary] 13[, 1919], The Holst Foundation.

[50]Gustav Holst, *Diary*, Friday, January 17 and Sunday, January 19, 1919, The Holst Foundation.

[51]Personal correspondence, Gustav Holst to Isobel Holst, Feb[ruary] 10[, 1919], quoted in Imogen Holst, *op.cit.*, 65.

[52]Personal correspondence, Gustav Holst to the Morley College Music Students, quoted in *Morley College Magazine*, XXVIII, No. 6 (April, 1919), 79-80.

[53]Personal correspondence, Gustav Holst to Isobel Holst, February 10, 1918, quoted in Imogen Holst, *op.cit.*, 64.

[54]Personal correspondence, Gustav Holst to Jane Joseph, Feb[ruary, 1919], quoted in Imogen Holst, *op. cit.*, 65.

[55]Gustav Holst, *Diary*, Wednesday, February 19, 1919, The Holst Foundation.

[56]Gustav Holst, *Diary*, Saturday, February 22, 1919, The Holst Foundation.

[57]William Vowles, *op. cit.*, 794-795.

[58]Personal correspondence, Gustav Holst to Isobel Holst, Feb[ruary] 25[, 1919], quoted in Imogen Holst, *op. cit.*, 66.

[59]Personal correspondence, Gustav Holst to Percy Grainger, March 3[, 1919], Grainger Museum, University of Melbourne, Melbourne, Australia.

[60]Personal correspondence, Gustav Holst to Isobel Holst, Feb[ruary] 25[, 1919], quoted in Imogen Holst, *op. cit.*, 66-67.

[61]*Ibid.*

[62]Gustav Holst, *Diary*, Thursday, March 13, 1919, The Holst Foundation.

[63]Personal correspondence, Gustav Holst to Ralph Vaughan Williams, March [1919], quoted in Imogen Holst, *op. cit.*, 70.

[64]Gustav Holst, *Diary*, Monday, March 17, 1919, The Holst Foundation.

[65]Gustav Holst, *Diary*, Sunday, March 23, 1919, The Holst Foundation.

[66]Personal correspondence, Gustav Holst to Isobel Holst, April 18[, 1919], quoted in Imogen Holst,

op. cit., 73-75.

[67]Personal correspondence, Gustav Holst to Adrian Boult, March 25[, 1919], British Library Add. MS 60498.

[68]Personal correspondence, Adrian Boult to Gustav Holst, April 25, 1919, British Library Add. MS 60498.

[69]Personal correspondence, Gustav Holst to Isobel Holst, April 18[, 1919], quoted in Imogen Holst, *op.cit.*, 76.

[70]In his article "Music in the British Salonica Force," in *Musical Opinion*, XLIII, No. 505 (October, 1919), Holst described a similar 3:00 p.m. rehearsal as having "Three violins, one viola, two flat pitch flutes, one oboe (has not touched an instrument since 1914), one sharp pitch clarinet, one double bass (who has learned a fortnight, but means business and is a real musician) and a piano approximately half a tone below the flat pitch flute." Prior to 1929, the British military bands used instruments tuned to the "Ancient Philharmonic" pitch of A=452.5, hence "sharp-pitched." "Flat pitch" instruments were tuned to the international A=440.

[71]Personal correspondence, Gustav Holst to Vally Lasker [April 25, 1919], quoted in Imogen Holst, *op cit.*, 72-73.

[72]Gustav Holst, *Diary,* Monday, April 14, 1919 and Friday, April 25, 1919, The Holst Foundation.

[73]William Byrd, *Short Communion Service*, ed. Jane M. Joseph and Gustav Holst (London: Stainer & Bell, 1919).

[74]Personal correspondence, Gustav Holst to Frances Ralph Gray, May 5[, 1919], The Holst Foundation.

[75]Gustav Holst, *Diary*, Sunday, June 1 and Friday, June 6, 1919, The Holst Foundation.

[76]William Vowles, *op. cit.*, 795.

[77]Gustav Holst, *Diary*, Monday, June 9, 1919, The Holst Foundation.

[78]Personal correspondence, Gustav Holst to Isobel Holst, June [1919], quoted in Imogen Holst, *op. cit.*, 77.

[79]Gustav Holst, *Diary*, Sunday, June 15, 1919, The Holst Foundation.

[80]Gustav Holst, *Diary*, Monday, June 16, 1919, The Holst Foundation.

[81]Gustav Holst, *Diary*, Saturday, June 21, 1919, The Holst Foundation.

[82]Gustav Holst, *Diary*, Sunday, June 22 through Wednesday, June 25, 1919, The Holst Foundation.

[83]Gustav Holst, *Diary*, Wednesday, June 25 through Saturday, June 28, 1919, The Holst Foundation.

[84]Gustav Holst, *Diary*, Sunday, June 29 and Monday, June 30, 1919, The Holst Foundation.

CHAPTER X

THE EDUCATION OF COMPOSERS

Holst rested at Thaxted only for a few days before returning to public life. The occasion that stirred him from his brief respite was a concert held at the Royal College of Music, attended by the Prince of Wales, in which Holst conducted his *Two Songs without Words* and "Carnival" from *Suite de Ballet.*[1] At his places of employment summer term was in full swing and Holst had a difficult time staying away. His reception at James Allen's Girls' School was a harbinger of the celebrity status that was just around the corner. He wrote to Whittaker, "I'm having a wild time. My clothes were almost torn off by 350 small people at my Dulwich school yesterday."[2] Still, Holst was to have a relatively restful July, having arranged to be in London only three days per week, from Monday through Wednesday, with the remainder of the time spent at Thaxted. He wanted to take it easy and when Whittaker suggested a rather strenuous walking tour, Holst responded, "What the YMCA do you mean by suggesting such physical torture?"[3] However, Holst did celebrate the end of the school term with a walking tour. This time it was in his beloved Cotswolds and surrounding areas. He wrote to Mrs. Boult about a rather embarrassing incident:

Grosvenor Hotel
Stockbridge
Tuesday [August, 1919]

Dear Mrs. Boult

Our otherwise excellent Fuji has forgotten my pyjamas!!

It came on to rain just before I got here and as I was wet I went to bed so that my clothes should be dried and there you are! I mean, there I was!

Could they be sent to me

c/o Balfour Gardiner
Ashampstead
Pangbourne Berks

Many many thanks for all your kindness. Thanks to it I'm another man.

The walk today has been splendid and the Teste Valley is beautiful.

Yr Sincerely

Gustav Holst

My love to the Hound![4]

After this walking tour, Holst returned to Thaxted, where he did the bulk of his composing that summer. Two very dissimilar works flowed from his pen. The *Ode to Death*, Op. 38 [H144], for mixed chorus (satb) and orchestra serves as Holst's musical commentary on World War I. For the fourth and final time Holst turned to Walt Whitman's *Leaves of Grass* for the right words; he found them in "When lilacs last in the dooryard bloom'd," one of the "Memories of President Lincoln." Here Whitman speaks of the "pure deliberate notes" of the solitary thrush, serving as an introduction to "Come, lovely and soothing death." England had lost a number of composers whose lives had been taken in the line of duty, among them Cecil Coles and George Butterworth. In its eerie serenity Holst's work reaches for and achieves a peaceful acceptance of death. Perhaps due partially to its subject matter, *Ode to Death* remains one of the composer's most neglected and underrated works.

Ode to Death was performed for the first time in Boston on February 10, 1928. It was only the second time that one of Holst's compositions had been performed in that city.[5] Philip Hale, music critic of the *Boston Herald* and writer of program notes for the Boston Symphony Orchestra, reviewed the concert. Conrad Beck's *Symphony No. 3* for strings, which Hale absolutely hated, preceded the work and unfortunately established the mood for his column:

> That an "Ode to Death" immediately followed the symphony was peculiarly fitting...
>
> Gustav Holst was a brave man when he set out to add music to the

> famous excerpt from Walt Whitman's "When Lilac's Last in Dooryard Bloom'd" or "President Lincoln's Burial Hymn," a title perhaps more familiar. There are poems that mock the efforts of composers; yet [Granville] Bantock presumed to write music for the choruses in "Atalanta in Calydon" and neither Shelley nor Keats has escaped the ambitious endeavors of British composers. No one will deny that there are poetic and impressive passages in Holst's music--as when he came to "the huge and thoughtful night." The music for the lines beginning "Dark Mother always gliding near" is poetically imagined; there are impressive climaxes of a quiet nature: there is a largeness to "The night in silence," but on the whole, in spite of certain pianissimos emphasizing Whitman's thought, the Ode is of uneven merit. One turns to Whitman's rapt song and finds it the more imaginative, the more musical....[6]

The *Short Festival Te Deum* [H145] is the polar opposite *Ode to Death*. This celebratory work was written by Holst for his students at Morley College with Whitsunday festivities in mind. Beginning with a powerful descending dorian fortissimo choral unison on "We praise thee, O God!" over sixteenth note string sextuplets, the work does not let up in intensity over its compact four-minute length. Indeed it is one of Holst's most exhilarating works. It is scored for mixed chorus (satb) and orchestra featuring optional (elastic) instrumentation. Its words are taken from the *Book of Common Prayer*.

Another work which occupied Holst's thoughts during the summer of 1919 was his comic opera *The Perfect Fool*, Op. 39 [H150]. Holst began sketching the ballet in 1918, using materials from *The Sneezing Charm*, and may have continued work on the project while in Salonica and Constantinople. Certain diary entries from December, 1918 make reference to "PF," although it is possible that Holst was referring to playing the piano during idle moments rather than working on his opera. At any rate, Holst was working on the libretto of *The Perfect Fool* by the summer of 1919. After approaching Jane Joseph (who may or may not have begun work on a libretto) and Clifford Bax, who "did not feel that the story was so amusing as he [Holst] thought it to be,"[7] Holst decided to write his own.

By the fall of 1919, the two performances of *The Planets* conducted by Adrian Boult to that point in time (the private affair of September 29, 1918 and the five-movement public performance of February 27, 1919) were just beginning to cast their spell over the British musical populace and Holst began to realize greater opportunities to conduct his own works. On September 1st he conducted the New Queen's Hall Orchestra in the London premiere of his *Japanese Suite* at a Queen's Hall Promenade concert; the work would be repeated on October 19th, by the same orchestra under the direction of Henry Wood. On November 22nd, Holst conducted the New Queen's Hall Orchestra in a performance of "Venus," "Mercury," and "Jupiter;" this was the first time "Venus" was heard by the public. Holst repeated these three movements on December 14th, once again at Queen's Hall, on a Sunday Musical Union concert. The final London premiere of a Holst work in 1919 was on December 23rd, when Charles Kennedy Scott conducted the Oriana Madrigal Society at Aeolian Hall in *This Have I Done for My True Love.*

Some of Holst's works were just starting to gain international attention, either through performances or references made in articles by Edgar Bainton, Edwin Evans, Sydney Grew, and others. American organist Philip James, who had just become conductor of the Victor Opera Company in New York, wrote directly to Holst for information on obtaining works. Holst responded:

St. Paul's Girls' School
Brook Green, Hammersmith,
W. 6
Oct. 28th, 1919

Dear Mr. James,

Thank you for your kind letter. I have great pleasure in sending a copy of my "Cloud Messenger" and am sorry you have had so much trouble about getting a copy. I should be glad to know if the American agents are able to supply copies. With regard to my opera "Savitri", it is still in manuscript but the Carnegie Trust are bringing out a limited number of copies and I shall be delighted to send you one when they are ready. Please let me know if I can send you copies of any other compositions.

Yours faithfully,

G T Holst[8]

Two prestigious teaching opportunities opened up for Holst over the few months. The first was from his *alma mater*. Charles Hubert Hastings Parry, Director of the Royal College of Music, had passed away during the previous year. His successor was Hugh P. Allen, who had been Director of Music at University College in Reading. In an effort to strengthen the Royal College of Music faculty, Allen invited Adrian Boult, Ralph Vaughan Williams, and Holst to serve as part-time instructors. An undated notebook from about 1919 contains some notes by Holst that could have been meant for his interview with Allen:

> Allen
> amateur v. prof.
> " basis "
> emotion--love of m--hard work--but no critical power
> all training makes it sham science
> worship of hard work
> Butler 'never learn anything' etc.[9]
> writing not quickly but well
> harmony: cut everything beyond [?]
> counterpoint: Weelkes, Byrd or [?]
> sing it first
> only use beautiful tunes
> beauty and style from the first
> each student should sing in choir
> exams=drugs[10]

Many of these ideas would carry over into his lectures.

The *Daily Telegraph* carried the news of Holst's and Vaughan Williams' hirings:

> It seems to me that most of the younger generation of British musicians will welcome the announcement of the appointment to the teaching staff of the Royal College of Music of Dr. Ralph Vaughan Williams (composition) and Mr. Gustav Holst (theory). Both are past-pupils of Sir Charles Stanford, so that the "royal line" of continuity so long established should remain unbroken. Clearly there is an abundance of really vital life in the Royal College of Music![11]

Actually, Holst taught composition in addition to theory.

The second of the two teaching opportunities was offered to Holst in early 1920. University College in Reading was located about forty miles west of London. When Hugh Allen, who had been Director of the Music Department for ten years, left there in 1918 to become Director of the Royal School of Music, he recommended Adrian Boult to take over as conductor of the choral society and college orchestra. Boult's tenure at University College, however, lasted only one year. Fueled partially by his performances of *The Planets*, Boult's conducting career was at the beginning of a meteoric rise and he found himself swamped with opportunities. Boult had just become conductor of Diaghilev's *Ballets Russes* in London, conductor of the British Symphony Orchestra (comprised largely of returning war veterans), and had just accepted the position of teacher of conducting at the Royal College of Music. With Boult's resignation, the Music Committee at University College decided to combine the conducting position with theory and composition. For Holst this meant a substantial teaching load: theory classes to music majors, private composition lessons, chorus and orchestra. He received the following letter in regard to scheduling, months before he actually began:

University College,
Reading.
February 25, 1920.

Dear Sir,

I have just heard from the Principal that you have accepted our invitation to join the staff of this College as Conductor of the College Choral Society and Orchestra, and Teacher of Composition and Harmony. It is now, I fear, too late to arrange practices of the Choral Society and Orchestra during this term, but I shall be glad to know your proposals for next term. Mr. Walter Ford[12] tells me that the only evening likely to be suitable for practices in the near future is Thursday as Tuesday (our ordinary evening) is, I believe, not possible for you, and other evenings mentioned by you would not suit us. Thursday is not a very good evening, owing to the large number of Church Choir practices in Reading on that evening, but it will perhaps be best to start on Thursdays with a view to a possible reconsideration of the evening later on. The Choral practice begins at 8:15, and I shall be obliged if you will kindly let me know whether it will be convenient for you to come for the first practice on Thursday, April 29. Before Mr. Boult resigned he had arranged for the Chorus to practise J. S. Bach's "Come, Jesu, Come," and R. T. Woodman's "Falmouth," and several members of the Chorus have bought copies of these works so that it will be best, I think, if you can arrange to take these works (with possibly one or two others) for practice during the Summer Term. Kindly let me know what you think about this. Arrangement fo Orchestral practices are made by Mrs. Duffield,...who is Secretary of your section of the Orchestra. I am asking her to communicate with you.

There will be the possibilitiy of one or two students in the Department of Music who will be glad to have the opportunity of studying Composition with you during the Summer Term, and if you can find time to take such students I shall be obliged if you will let me know what you suggest as your fee for individual lessons in Composition and Theory. I enclose a copy of the College Music prospectus, on pages 9 and 10 of which you will find the fees charged by other teachers. You will see that the usual fee charged by leading teachers is 5£. 5s. or 6£. 6s. for ten lessons of half an hour each. You will, I think, have learned from the Principal that one-eighth of the fees for individual lessons is retained by the College. The remaining seven-eighths is paid to the teacher. The Summer Term begins on Thursday, April 22, but it would probably be sufficient if you gave individual lessons for the first time on April 29 if you are starting the Choral practices on that date. I shall be exceedingly glad to give as much as much assistance as I can in making arrangements for your work here, and I hope to have the pleasure of meeting you soon.

Yours faithfully,

H. K.
Tutorial Secretary[13]

Holst responded:

St. Paul's Girls' School,
Brook Green,
Hammersmith,
W.6

Feb[ruary] 29[, 1920]

Dear Sir

I thank you for your letter and shall have much pleasure in coming to University College for the first time on April 29. I presume that the orchestra will meet before the Choir.

I think I should be able to give a few composition lessons on Thursday afternoons but could not do much of this work before the autumn. My terms would be 6£. 6 per term. For actual composition as apart from harmony etc it might be better for each student to have one hour per fortnight and to attend another student's lesson in the intervening week. This could be arranged later. We will start the choir with the music you mention.

I understand that I am to supervise the theory teaching generally. Would it be possible to meet the Principal earlier in the day and, after having seen him and you, to meet the other theory of music teachers? I could come any time after midday on the 29th. Or if you prefer I could come after midday on the 27th.

Would you let me know as soon as possible about next autumn. I could keep the whole of Friday clear for Reading if I know in good time and this arrangement would suit me far better than any other.

Yr faithfully

Gustav Holst[14]

Over the next two weeks things began to clarify for Holst:

St. Paul's Girls School
Brook Green
W6
March 13[, 1920]

Dear Mr. Knapman

I have definitely arranged to give up Tuesdays for Reading College from April 27. Next term I will come some time in the afternoon. Next autumn I can arrange to come all day if necessary.

We will begin the Choral practices at 8:15 on April 27 and I hope to meet Mrs. Duffield soon in order to arrange about the orchestra. Until the latter is settled I cannot make definite arrangements about private pupils but I shall certainly be able to take Miss Gates the lady you mention and one or two others. Possibly I shall not be able to take more than three until the autumn. The Principal mentioned in his letter to me that I was to receive 10£ per term for supervising the whole teaching of theory of music (I am writing in the country and have not his letter by me but this was the gist of the matter).

My first idea is was to ask the theory teachers to meet me but perhaps that would be a little difficult. In any case I should be glad of some advice from you and if it should afterwards prove that this work is unnecessary I should be quite ready to be relieved of it. It was chiefly because of this that I wished to see the Principal. I particularly wish to be sure of my ground before entering into this part of the work. Perhaps however there is no immediate hurry about it.

I will not write to Mr. Boseley or Miss Vincent until I hear from you.

Yr Sincerely

G T Holst

I <u>may</u> be able to come in the morning of April 27--I will let you know later. It would enable me to see people....[15]

Acceptance of the Royal College of Music and University College, Reading positions meant additional encumbrances on Holst's time. As a result, Holst relinquished his post at James Allen's Girls' School. While the decision to leave there may have been the obvious one, the act of leaving was not easy. James Allen's was Holst's first teaching job; he had been teaching there for sixteen years and while it was not quite the "home base" that St. Paul's Girls' School was, but it was still "home"; he had taken great pride in his work there. Even after he officially left there in July, 1920, he still returned to give lectures and lead carol singing. He also donated a number of published scores of his works to the school in July, 1923. Holst's departure from the James Allen's Girls' School still left him with four teaching positions: St. Paul's Girls' School, Morley College, Royal College of Music, and University College, Reading.

During his three years as conductor at Reading, Holst felt at home. One of his friends from his Royal College of Music student days, Evlyn Howard-Jones, was on the faculty there. Holst immediatley placed his mark on the ensembles entrusted to him, feeding them the same basic diet of Bach cantatas, Haydn symphonies, and a peppering of English madrigals that his students had come to know and love in the other places he taught. Upon occasion he would also feature works by his composition students. One would suspect that the performance level at University College, Reading would have been somewhat higher than at Morley College, but many of the same problems persisted. For the College Choral Society it was the lack of male voices, as attested to in an issue of the *Tamesis* from 1923:

....one would like to say how sad it seems that there are not more College

> men in the Choral Society. Out of a College membership of some eight or nine hundred only six or seven College men sing in their Choral Society! If only the remainder could realise what they miss--!![16]

The orchestra seems to have fared somewhat better. One of the more ambitious works that Holst programmed was Beethoven's *Second Symphony*:

> I was pleased to hear the orchestra attempting such a work as the great Symphony in D No. 2 (Beethoven). I agreed generally with the conductor's reading. There were places, particularly in the Allegro con Brio, where the strings showed indecision. The Larghetto and Allegro Molto were admirably played. The rendering of the Scherzo appealed to me the most. The rhythm was brought out adequately yet always with discretion. The orchestra seemed to be somewhat under-rehearsed for a clear-cut performance.[17]

Over the next four years, Holst taught a number of composition students who would became famous in their own right. Organists W. Probert-Jones and Douglas W. Clarke studied with Holst at Reading. Clarke eventually became Dean of the Music Faculty at McGill University, Montreal, Canada and conductor of The Montreal Orchestra. Violist Anthony Collins studied with Holst at the Royal College of Music; Gordon Jacob, who later taught composition to Imogen Holst, also received occasional lessons from him there. Edmund Rubbra studied with Holst at both places and was named to the University College faculty in 1924. In addition to being a prolific composer (eleven symphonies), Rubbra wrote more about his mentor than any of Holst's other pupils. His writings include a short book, *Gustav Holst: A Monograph* (Monaco: Lyrebird Press, 1947), and at least fifteen articles, most of which were republished as *Gustav Holst: Collected Essays* (London: Triad, 1974). Rubbra comments about Holst as a composition teacher:

> His period of teaching at the Royal College, all too short as it was, exercised a remarkable influence. His own vision was so wide-eyed, and his own sincerity so unequivocal, that to have been in contact with him was an experience one would not willingly have missed, and it is a tribute to his teaching to say that none of his composition pupils have turned out works that might have been "chips from the master's workshop"....
>
> Being aware of the irregular occurrence of seemingly barren periods in any creator's life, Holst never insisted that the pupil should bring fresh

work at each lesson. The pupil was therefore freed from the strain and anxiety of forcing out unfelt ideas. If no original work was forthcoming, then the lesson could be spent in any number of delightful and profitable ways, for Holst was never at a loss to show how surprise and delight could be mingled in a single lesson. There might be a score to read through, either a Beethoven symphony (how he enjoyed uttering his unorthodox opinions about the scoring of Beethoven!), a Brahms orchestral work (he used to say that the scoring of the Brahms-Haydn Variations was perfect in aptness), or a modern work. He might on the other hand arrange for the performance of a pupil's work, and this he would set about doing with as much genuine enthusiasm as if the work were his own. Holst had the rare gift of identifying himself completely with another's work: his insight was at times clairvoyant. His interest in his pupils' work would not cease when the lesson was over: he has been known to brood over a pupil's difficulties to the extent of initiating a correspondence upon the matter....

I must mention here Holst's spontaneous and rather elfish humour. A setting of some Whitman words for two tenors and piano that I once took to him elicited the query "But are there two tenors?"[18]

W. Probert-Jones, on the University College faculty from 1923, was Holst's student and, eventually, his assistant there. He also became Holst's personal friend. In the months Holst's death, Probert-Jones wrote an extensive obituary for *Tamesis*; a significant portion of it describes Holst's work at Reading:

He was a curious blend of the visionary and the practical--a rare combination indeed. He had a sincere and unbounded love and enthusiasm for all beautiful music and perhaps the secret of his success with his pupils came as much from the joy which he got from music and with which he infected them, as from anything else that he did. He simply radiated a love for music and it was bound to be refected by those with whom he came into contact. I have referred...to his enthusiasm for folk music and for the madrigalists, but it must not be thought that he had no love left for anything else. Those who played in the orchestra or sang in the choral society will remember the joy with which he produced a Haydn Symphony, a Bach cantata, the Brahms Gypsy Songs, or a simple old Latin carol which he made the choir sing in unison with an orchestral accompaniment which he had arranged.

But in addition to this immense enthusiasm he possessed a very practical and commonsense outlook. One has only to look at the beginning of a Holst score to see a list of instruments which can be dispensed with in order to make performances by smaller bodies practical, to realize that he had a good grasp of practical politics. In his conducting too this sound common sense was invaluable. Few people realized better than he what was possible for an amateur body of musicians, and by this very realization of the difficulties and limitations of the singers or players he was able to do things which before seemed to verge on the impossible. His composition pupils too were brought up to keep this practical point of view ever before them and were encouraged to write down their ideas in such a way as rendered them easy in performance. I well remember taking the score of a short orchestral work to him, in which I had written a trumpet part which might have been played by Solomon, but hardly by anyone of lesser calibre. Holst very gently said, "You will never get this played, you know. Now if you write this trumpet part like this--and this--and just give him a high A here so that it gives him a chance of showing us what he can do."

His nature was essentially simple and kindly, with an unlimited store of sympathy for the deserving. He had a genius for getting straight to the root of the matter--a characteristic which showed itself in his works. "Padding" or "talking for the sake of talking" was anathema to him; one's ideas had to be expressed succinctly and must be germane to the subject in hand. This of course implies the possession of ideas; almost his first words to me were to this effect:--"If you have no ideas, I can't do anything for you; I can only try to bring out what is already inside, I cannot put music into you." But to those who had music within them and were prepared to work hard his kindliness, patience, sympathy and encouragement were invaluable. In criticism he was rarely harsh but always pointed and the only thing which ever really roused his ire was unworthy work. Then he could be severe!!![19]

Arthur Bliss studied with him independently and had the following to say:

By great fortune I got the assent of Holst. I had heard movements from his gigantic suite The Planets and to have a lesson from a man who could make an orchestra sound so magnificently vivid as he could was a wonderful opportunity. I took my Studies along to his room in Brook Green.

....I was with him only a few times, but each is indelibly engraved on my memory by some short pithy statement that he made. He had the utter

> honesty of opinion that riveted attention: there was no possibility of misunderstanding what he thought or what he felt.
>
> On this first occasion at Brook Green he pounced on a tune that I had rather weakly given to the cellos. "But that is a trombone tune," Holst said, "it can't be anything else!" How right he was when I heard it![20]

Ralph Vaughan Williams commented about Holst's work in two oft-quoted articles:

> Holst has no use for half measures; all the little vanities, insincerities, and compromises which go to make up one's daily life are entirely outside his ken; they leave him dumb and puzzled. But with all his mysticism Holst has never allowed himself to become a mere dreamer. He is a visionary, but he never allows dreams to inhibit action. He also has a strong saving sense of humour--indeed he might if he had chosen, have made a name for himself as a comedy actor.[21]

> .... Like all great teachers Holst not only gives but expects to receive, and he will have no half-measures; he is sympathetic to ignorance, over-exuberance or even stupidity--but half heartedness, insincerity or laziness have no chance with him; for that reason he will never become a 'fashionable' teacher whose metier is to impart useless accomplishments to rich people who do not want to learn them....[22]

Holst himself had plenty to say about the subject. On July 10, 1920 he read a paper titled "The Education of Composers" before a conference sponsored by the Society of Women Musicians:

> The most successful education (of a composer) would be that which would leave the composer the true amateur, like Oliver Twist, always asking for more, of like the Japanese painter whose epitaph ran "Here lies an old man who was fond of painting." The ideal method of training is comradeship with a master and imitation the best training of the technique of an art.
>
> I myself have come into contact with three native traditions of teaching:
>
> > 1) The Victorian, which was academic and blunted the listening capacity. It made the study of the theory of music an affair of the

eye, reduced the art of counterpoint, originally a method of making beautiful sounds, to a method of arbitrary rules, and side-tracked the pupils' natural desire for expression.

2) the great reaction, which might roughly be reckoned as occurring about 1895. This was generally in the direction of freedom, not the freedom of today, which is really the direction of the new convention (a Cubist would have been impossible in 1895), but a freedom founded like the preceding academic tradition, on the fallacy that because a small quantity of something is good, therefore 100% of it is better.

3) the teaching which since about 1915 has been founded on the discovery that the chief function of the teacher is to watch the pupil; to be like the gardener who does the necessary preparation of the soil and keeps vermin and weeds away, but leaves the growing to the plant.

Predilections and Principles:

The teacher, however, is bound to do one of two things: either he will work from a strong personal predilection; in favour it may be of Palestrina, or it may be of Skryabin, or he will work from abstract principles. If from these, they must be defined. The question arises, are there such things as abstract principles in art? It would seem that for the composer in any art, clearness of outline, fineness of texture, and beauty of form in relation to content were essentials. The greatest problem in the training a composer of music was how to induce what was perhaps best expressed by the word "Clarity" in the Greek sense, by which the speaker would imply the inclusion of balance and unity.

Clarity, not Sentimentality:

Composers and periods in which Clarity predominate should be studied. The XVIII Century was a period of clear thinking and precise work, and its music was accordingly valuable to study. Clarity was usually wanting in the latter half of the XIX Century in all its doings, in spite of its wonderful achievements. It was an age of sentimentality and sentimentality is a muddy emotion. Ruskin,[23] who strove to clarify the thinking of his period, had said that the mind of the artist is not excited, but still and clear like the reflecting surface of a lake. Art, in fact, is clear feeling, clear thinking, clear seeing.

Emotion: the Deciding Factor:

Emotion, though it was always the deciding factor in the artist's work, must be left to develop itself. There was a great deal in teaching that we know nothing about--we bring the horse to water, but we can't make him drink--but we can give our pupils one infallible instruction--"What you do, you've got to do clearly." To fix a mould in the pupil's idea and then bid him merely pour emotion into it, is bad teaching. The usual bother is that a pupil is urged to express not what he or she wants to express, but what Palestrina wanted to express. The XIX Century mistook excitement for artistic emotion--the more exciting the music, the better the music. Silly people in the XX Century confuse artistic expression with stunts.

Art, however, is always with us; no one period is really more artistic than another. But though Art does not develop and does not decay, it is always taking fresh forms, often unrecognisable. It cannot be found by seeking; it must be given. Three lines of Gordon Bottomley's expressed very finely the significance of the artist's work:

Where line and sound, colour and phrase
Rebuild in clear essential ways
The powers behind the veil of sense.[24]

He commented further:

A composer is one who records in music what all men feel. The problem of educating a composer is twofold:

1). craftmanship (easier)
2). fostering an emotion or love.

The question of music education is one of natural growth. Music is universal.[25]

Yet Holst wasn't always serious about composition. When asked by a reporter from The *Christian Science Monitor* what text he used for teaching composition at St. Paul's Girls' School, he responded, "The best book for composers is the textbook in composition we use in this school--Walter de la Mare's *Peacock Pie*"[26]--a children's fantasy book!

---

[1]Michael Short, *Gustav Holst: The Man and His Music* (Oxford: Oxford University Press, 1990), 176.

[2]Personal Correspondence, Gustav Holst to William Gillies Whittaker, July 12 [, 1919], quoted in Michael Short (ed.), *Gustav Holst: Letters to W. G. Whittaker* (Glasgow: University of Glasgow Press, 1974), 49.

[3]*Ibid.*.

[4]Personal Correspondence, Gustav Holst to Mrs. Boult, Tuesday [either August 5 or August 12, 1919], British Library Add. MS 60498.

[5]*The Planets* had been performed by the Boston Symphony Orchestra on January 26, 1923.

[6]*The Boston Herald*, February 11, 1928.

[7]Clifford Bax, "Recollections of Gustav Holst" in *Music and Letters*, XX, No. 1 (January, 1939), 3.

[8]Personal Correspondence, Gustav Holst to Philip James, October 28, 1919, Library of Congress.

[9]"Never learn anything until the not knowing of it has come to be a nuissance to you." Samuel Butler, Notebooks.

[10]Gustav Holst, Notebook [1919], The Holst Foundation.

[11]*The Daily Telegraph*, December 9, 1919.

[12]Singing tutor at University College, Reading.

[13]Business correspondence, H. K. [?, initials not entirely legible], Tutorial Secretary, to Gustav Holst, February 25, 1920, The Library, The University of Reading.

[14]Business correspondence, Gustav Holst to H. K. [?, addressed simply as "Dear Sir"], Feb[ruary] 29[, 1920], The Library, The University of Reading.

[15]Business correspondence, Gustav Holst to Mr. Knapman, March 13[, 1920], The Library, The University of Reading.

[16]*Tamesis*, XXII, No. 2 (Lent, 1923), 65.

[17]*Tamesis*, XX, No. 3 (Summer Term, 1921), 88.

[18]Edmund Rubbra, "Holst the Teacher" in *Gustav Holst: Collected Essays* (London: Triad Press, 1974), 42-43.

[19]W. Probert-Jones, "Gustav Holst" in *Tamesis*, XXXIII, No. 2 (Lent, 1935), 59-60.

[20]Arthur Bliss, *As I Remember* (London: Faber & Faber, 1970), 65.

[21]Ralph Vaughan Williams, quoted in *The Reading Mercury*, July [1920].

[22]Ralph Vaughan Williams, "Gustav Holst" in *Music and Letters*, I, No. 3 (July, 1920), 187.

[23]John Ruskin (1819-1900), English writer, art critic, and reformer.

[24]Gustav Holst, "The Education of Composers," paper presented Saturday, July 10, 1920 before the Society of Women Musicians, quoted in *The Music Student*, XII, No. 12 (September, 1920). The article is a report on Holst's speech, but nearly all of it is Holst verbatum. The author has taken the liberty of placing a couple of sentences from the report into [Holst's] first person.

[25]*The Scotsman*, May 19, 1921.

[26]*The Christian Science Monitor* [1921].

CHAPTER XI

IN THE WAKE OF THE PLANETS

At the same time Holst was starting with his teaching at University College, Reading and the Royal College of Music, the School of Conductorship at the latter institution was in its infancy. Adrian Boult had been set in charge of it by Hugh Allen in February, 1919 and it quickly succeeded. A typical 5-class day consisted of the following:

AM conducting
being conducted (singing)
PM scoring-playing (two pianos--one taking strings, the other taking winds)
criticism regarding the morning's conducting
a study of a particular concerto or symphony in theory[1]

The object of the course was not to produce a tribe of virtuoso conductors, but to prepare students to make the best of those opportunities for conducting which previously often occurred only after leaving college. Boult's course had "an atmosphere of keenness, friendliness, and frankness."[2]

Boult's efforts did not go unnoticed. In a letter to Frances Ralph Gray, High Mistress at St. Paul's Girls' School, Holst mentions Boult's class and asks about the possibility of a similar happening at St. Paul's. Holst also brings up other things in this letter. It appears that even after having been back for a semester, he was still thinking of the possibility of returning to Constantinople to continue his YMCA work, only this time as a member of the regular army:

Thaxted
Dunmow
Jan[uary] 26[, 1920]

Dear Miss Gray

Thanks for programme. The only addition I can suggest is a small 's to Jane's name to show whose pupil she is.
1) If you haven't found a male caretaker for your house who will stay for the whole of the holidays would you accept one who would greatly appreciate the privilege of spending half each week there?

Meaning me.

2) May I bring a friend to Speech Day? Even if the friend is Joan Wadge's brother? (I believe Joan knows nothing about it--he and I are old pals).
3) Would you have any objection to Mr. Adrian Boult having a class for conducting at school for certain of my old pupils--Nora, Vally, Jane, Irene[3] etc. on Saturday mornings? I have not asked him yet but I am very keen on something being done. Frankly, I know <u>no</u> woman who can conduct. And he has started such a class at the R.C.M. and I have attended it and he is by far the best man we could have. It would be glorious if the SPGS turned out the only woman conductors in the world!

I am sending these three questions by post so as to avoid taking up your time on Monday. Perhaps Miss Chawner would kindly give me answers to all three.

I should like to add that before leaving Constantinople I went very fully into the question of army versus YMCA educational work in music.

Quite apart from the question of salary and of getting out of the army when one is once in, I came to two definite conclusions:

1) If the YMCA did not wish to employ me I would decline the offer because the chances for effective work under it did not seem to me to justify my leaving my work at home.

2) Considering what happened during my last two months in Constantinople and the conditions that await me if I return and considering how splendidly everyone has carried on in my absence at school I do feel justified in asking leave to go back for another ten months as long as I go back to the same conditions of work.

I decided on the YMCA and not the army for the sake of the army itself as much as for other reasons!

Yr Sincerely

G T Holst[4]

Holst never did return to Constantinople; there was too much going on at home.

In March, 1920 Holst's commentary on the function of the artist in society, "The Mystic, the Philistine and the Artist" was published in *Quest*. This rather lengthy essay serves as a philosophical foil to his earlier post-war article, "Music in the British Salonica Force,"[5] which is more anecdotal in nature. In "The Mystic, the Philistine and the Artist," Holst defines the title terms:

> The real view of the matter is that we are all Mystics, Artists and Philistines. These names stand for three attributes of every human being. The difference between a Mystic who communicates with God and a man who feels a power not himself making for good is obviously one of degree. Moreover, we are all Mystics in childhood.
>
> In Art the difference between Mozart and an ordinary British soldier during the war was one of degree only. Both made music because they could not help doing so. Again all children are creative Artists. As for the Philistine spirit, surely none of us is entirely free from it. I accept the ordinary definition of Philistine--'inaccessible to and impatient of ideas'. I suggest another--'one governed by common sense', using 'common' as meaning 'communal'; in other words, one whose mind is a storehouse of other people's prejudices. The Philistine is strong in all of us....But the biggest and wildest Philistines I know are those who are either Modernist or Classical.
>
> In music the Modernist Philistine is he for whom music began with Beethoven's *Ninth Symphony*, or Wagner's *Tristan*, or Strauss' *Don Juan*, or Debussy's *Nocturnes*. It is quite immaterial which; the point is that he looks at music as something that began at some definite date. The Classical Philistine on the other hand is he for whom music ended with the death of Handel, or the death of Beethoven, or the death of Brahms, or the death of any other composer--in short, one for whom music ended at a definite date. I see absolutely nothing to choose between these two types....
>
> How do we define a Mystic? I suggest that all mystical experiences (like all artistic ones) are either illusions or *direct and intimate realizations*....

> All mystical experiences seem to be forms of union....The highest Mystic is, I suppose, one who experiences union with God. Is he alone a Mystic? Or is Whitman[6] a Mystic in his intense feeling of unity with all men, all life?

Holst then discusses the interrelationship among the three.:

> I know no Philistine definition of a Mystic. But we all know the Philistine one of a Metaphysician. 'A Metaphysician is a blind man looking in a dark cellar for a needle that is not there.'...If the Philistine is tender-hearted--he is occasionally--one can imagine him looking gently and sadly at the poor Metaphysician groping his way out of that cellar after his weary search....
>
> But what does he say when the Mystic rushes out? For the Mystic is he who leaves that cellar proclaiming that he has seen the needle. In former days the Philistine either knocked the Mystic down or made him a saint, according to which was more in fashion. Now-a-days the Philistine tries mildness. He reasons with the Mystic, which shows a lack of sense of humour....He explains that the Mystic could not have seen the needle, because (a) the cellar was dark; (b) the seeker was blind; (c) the needle was not there. The Mystic replies: 'The cellar may not have been dark, in fact I am not sure the cellar existed. I am not sure that you exist. I know of only one thing: I have seen the needle!' Situation impossible! The situation between the Mystic and Philistine in each of us is impossible. We get through life by ignoring it.
>
> Meanwhile the Artist comes out of the cellar. Unlike the Mystic he is silent; but he brings the needle in his hand....what the Philistine says or does is not of much consequence. He has played his part in helping us to see the Mystic and Artist more clearly; let him go....[7]

"The Mystic, the Philistine and the Artist" tells us nearly as much about Holst as he tells us. For one thing, Holst was a well-read and well-educated composer. Clive Bell's *Significant Form* surfaces about half-way through the article and provides a discourse on true inspiration leading to true form versus imitation or, in Holst's words, "cold storage." His "was it necessary?" comment on works that he judged to be bad art stem from this.[8] Holst was also an adaptor, stretching the Samuel Butler quote "Never learn anything until the not learning of it becomes an utter nuisance to you" to apply to his own comparison between Mozart and British soldiers making music ("one of degree only"), a somewhat controversial comparison on which he does not elaborate. Holst adapted Butler's quote once again two years later when pressed for advice on careers:

> I am not impertinent enough to choose other people's careers. If you come to me for advice because you cannot decide whether to choose art or any other career, I shall probably advise you to choose the latter.
>
> But if you come to me for advice because you cannot help choosing art, I shall probably advise you to do what you cannot help doing; but I shall make one condition--that you never look for any recompense or reward beyond art itself.[9]

A few years later Edwin Evans, Holst's personal friend and one of his staunchest supporters, commented about the composer's supposed mysticism:

> [Holst] has been credited with mysticism. To me he appears to be more of an idealist without ideals--far too practical to encumber his philosophy with imagined ideals, but at the same time so keyed as to be an idealist without them, serving a high purpose but always less conscious of its height than of the demands of its service. I find it difficult to imagine his being carried away by any elation other than that of the artist content with his work....[10]

March, 1920 also witnessed double premiere performances of *The Hymn of Jesus*. The first performance of any type occurred on the 10th at the Royal College of Music. Holst himself conducted the choral class; a piano accompaniment was used for this occasion. The first professional performance occurred on the 25th, at Queen's Hall, when Holst conducted the Royal Philharmonic Society Orchestra and Chorus. This performance was quite possibly the most successful that Holst ever had. Nobody in the audience was prepared for such a refreshing blend of unfamiliar apocryphal verses, dance emphasis, the semi-choruses' gliding chords, and imaginative orchestration. An immediate encore was demanded, although one was not given. Ralph Vaughan Williams, the work's dedicatee, wanted "to get up & embrace everyone & then get drunk."[11] Donald Tovey, a person of keen insight, wrote rather profetically to Holst about the work:

> I have been reading The Hymn of Jesus. It completely bowls me over. Your presentation of it is the poem, the whole poem, and nothing but the poem....I am thoroughly familiar with that kind of enjoyment of a poem

> where one feels "ah--that's a clever way to set this verse,--not a way that would have occurred to me --perhaps better, perhaps not quite so good as my idea of how to set it;--aha, I like this---etc., etc."
>
> Well, your Hymn of Jesus doesn't occupy me in that way at all. It is there, just as if neither you nor I had any say in the matter. It couldn't have been done before (I have not a very adequate knowledge of your works--but it makes no difference what step or approximations you may have made before it)--and it can't be done again (i.e. the next equally real thing will be very different). It's a blessed abiding fact; and not a matter of taste at all. If anybody doesn't like it, he doesn't like life....[12]

Tovey was correct. Holst had not written anything like *The Hymn of Jesus* before and the masterful choral works that followed, namely the *First Choral Symphony*, Op. 41 [H155] and *A Choral Fantasia*, Op. 51 [H177] were of an entirely different nature.

Alfred Kalisch of *The Musical Times* wrote about the first performance:

> By far the most important new orchestral work produced in London since my last article appeared has been Mr. Gustav Holst's 'Hymn of Jesus', which was heard at the Philharmonic Concert on March 25 and is a setting of an ancient Gnostic hymn from the Apocryphal Acts of St. John, elaborately laid out for two choruses, semi-chorus, orchestra, pianoforte and organ.
>
> It is a very remarkable work, the full importance of which it is difficult to estimate on first acquaintence, the more so as the composer has sedulously striven to invent a new idiom, in which primitive simplicity and modern complexity go hand in hand. At one hearing, it can only be said that the whole result is impressive, and that it shows as clearly as does any other work by the same composer his easy mastery in handling large masses of sound. In some places he resorts to realism, as in the beginning, 'Divine Grace is Dancing,' and in the section where we have a picturesque representation--the general outlook of which may be considered as analagous to that of Holbein or Duerer--of the conflict of the human soul with evil. It is a daring but convincing interpretation of the spiritual meaning of the hymn, 'Vexilla Regis prodeunt'.
>
> It would be interesting to compare the former in detail with the similar section of the dance of Superman in Strauss' 'Zarathrustra'.
>
> The Amens, intoned by the semi-chorus in the organ-loft, which punctuate the end of each section--slightly varied each time--play an

> important part in producing the total other-worldly effect. In the climaxes the composer reaches a high level of massive power....[13]

The Hymn of Jesus was performed with great frequency and in many locations over the next few years. By 1923, the 1919 Carnegie United Kingdom Trust-Stainer & Bell publication had gone through several editions and had sold more than 8500 copies. The immense popularity of this work was baffling to Holst. Imogen Holst commented, "He knew that this was the best thing he had written, but this was the first time that his opinion and public opinion had coincided."[14]

Since 1916, Holst had been involved in festivals at Whitsuntide. The first three had been at Thaxted, of course, and the 1919 festival had taken the form of a competition and a week's worth of nightly concerts given by the troops at Constantinople. Under normal circumstances, the logical thing to do for the 1920 festival would have been to return to Thaxted, but Conrad Noel's extremist views and demands of allegiance to "The Thaxted Movement" by all participants had effectively blocked that. Thus, the festival was held Saturday, May 22nd through Monday, May 24th in a new location, Dulwich College Chapel at Old College Garden, near James Allen's Girls' School.. As usual, Holst's students from Morley College were involved in the choir and orchestra. The music included the premieres of Holst's *Short Festival Te Deum*, the "Kyrie" from Vaughan Williams' *Mass in G Minor*, and "the delightful dancing of Mr. Holst's gifted little daughter and her troop of nymphs and swains, the orchestral music for which was composed by the little dancer herself."[15] This may have been the first time that any piece of music by Imogen Holst was heard in public.

The following month saw another premiere performance--or was it? Holst had composed his *First Suite in E Flat for Military Band*, Op. 28, No. 1 in 1909 and for the past eleven years the work had been floating around in manuscript. Non-autograph manuscript parts with the composer's name indicated as "Gustav von Holst" prove that the work was at least rehearsed before September, 1918. It is very likely that it (or, less likely, the *Second Suite in F*) was performed in 1917 by the band of the 5th Royal Northumberland Fusiliers under the direction of James Causley Windram. Holst's correspondence with William Gillies Whittaker indicates that he sent the condensed score and parts to Windram via Whittaker on March 30th of that year.[16] Whether or not Windram's performance took place doesn't really matter, for there may have been previous performances of the suite by other bands in other places. Whatever the case, the work's entry into the standard repertoire dates from 1920.

At 11:00 a.m. on Monday, June 7, 1920, Col. John A. C. Somerville,

Commandant of the Royal Military School of Music, visited Holst at St. Paul's Girls' School.[17] It is not known which one of the two men instigated the meeting. The result was that on Wednesday, June 23rd, Holst took the #27 bus to Twickenham and, after being treated to dinner at 6:15, attended the 7:00 p.m. concert of the 165-piece Royal Military School of Music Band held on the grounds of Kneller Hall.[18] The work, then labelled *Suite in E Flat*, was the sixth of seven programmed works, placed after selections from Bizet's *Carmen*. Holst's suite was conducted by D.W. Jones, a member of the Student Bandmasters' Course.[19] Jones was no novice; he had already conducted the band on four separate concerts that spring.[20] Nevertheless, it does seem strange that if this truly were the premiere, that it would been trusted to a student conductor rather than to the Director of Music or to Holst himself. It was probably the first time the work was performed at Kneller Hall and definitely the first time there since 1914, from which date all Royal Military School of Music programs have been documented. Nevertheless, it was from this performance that the suite became known; the work was performed several times that summer. *The Times* dared to critique separate performances of the suite and Brahms' *Symphony No. 3 in F*, Op. 90 in the same review:

> There were two things of interest to be heard yesterday--Holst's Suite for Military Band at Kneller Hall and Brahms' Third Symphony at Queen's Hall.
> ....Holst's Suite is one of the first compositions for a military band by a composer of standing. (It is a healthy, cleanly written, diatonic, and generally ourspoken and single-eyed composition)....[21]

Another reviewer called the work "a little masterpiece of its own kind, but, then, it is the work of Gustav Holst, who has a master mind, which invests the military band with as much interest and individuality as the orchestra."[22]

The summer of 1920 also witnessed the first performance of *Two Psalms* [H117], completed by Holst eight years earlier. W. G. Whittaker had arranged for its glorious (or inglorious) premiere to be part of the half-time festivities at a soccer match held on July 18th at St. James's Football Park in Newcastle. Since this was to be held outdoors, Holst transcribed the original organ part for brass. The performers included the Newcastle and District Festival Choir and Orchestra, supported by the St. Hilda Brass band. The choir numbered 800, the orchestra 100, the band 30--and the crowd some 20,000.[23]

Holst celebrated the end of the summer term in his usual manner, by leaving town. This time he went south to Quarr Abbey, a Benedictine Monastery located near Ryde on the northeast edge of the Isle of Wight. He intended to finish his libretto to *The Perfect Fool* while there, but found it an unsuitable place in which to work. Upon his return in August, Holst was able to make some significant musical progress on the entire work. In addition to this he completed the final three of his *Seven Choruses from the Alcestis of Euripides* [H146] for voices in unison, three flutes, and harp. The text is taken from Gilbert Murray's translation; this was the third and final time that Holst would write music to fit Murray's words. Holst had started the piece before enlisting for his YMCA work, for the original title page is signed "G von Holst". Originally there were to have been only five choruses, beginning with what is now II ("Daughter of Pelias"). Nos. I ("O Paian wise!") and VI ("I have sojourned in the Muses' land") were the two that were added later.[24] Holst's intent was that each of the choruses would function as incidental music to Euripedes' play and that there would be no breaks between speaking and singing. The work is dedicated to Frances Ralph Gray, High Mistress of St. Paul's Girls' School. The music has an exotic feel to it. The vocal parts are mid-range, lying well within the capabilities of non-professional singers. The flutes generally have a liquid dorian diatonicism over block chords supplied by the harp. In at least one performance at St. Paul's Girls' School, pizzicato strings were used to cover the harp part and in a later performance at Morley College, Holst rescored the harp part for an orchestra of elastic instrumentation. Neither of these arrangements has been located.

While Holst was fine tuning the *Seven Choruses*, his friend Edwin Evans was writing a series of articles about Holst for *The Musical Times*. Holst supplied much of the material to Evans himself. After giving a brief perusal to Evan's articles, he responded:

St. Paul's Girls' School
Brook Green, Hammersmith
W. 6
Oct. 30, 1920

Dear Evans,

Thanks for your letter. I will read your articles carefully and will write later. For the present I should like to offer a little criticism but I do not know that it is of much importance because naturally the articles strike me in a different way from what they do the general public. For instance your articles are more appreciative than critical, unlike that of Vaughan Williams in 'Music and Letters'[25]. I much value the criticism in the latter.

> Then I suggest you write less about the old things and more about the new things, such as 'The Planets' and 'The Hymn of Jesus.' I have only two works of any importance. One is a setting of Walt Whitman's 'Ode to Death.' This is practically finished. The other is a comic opera 'The Perfect Fool' which I sketch[ed] very roughly in the summer.
>
> I could show them both to you if you care to come here some Saturday morning when I was in town. The opera only exists in pencil and would be unintelligible as there are gaps every now and then. It is the merest and roughest sketch.
>
> Yours sincerely,
>
> Gustav Holst[26]

The autumn of 1920 was different from any that had preceded it. For one thing, Holst's schedule now included his college and university teaching; for another, he was busier than ever as a conductor. On September 19th he conducted the City of Birmingham Symphony Orchestra at the Theatre Royal in performances of his *Japanese Suite*, "Jig" from *St. Paul's Suite*, and "Dance--The Djinn" from *The Sneezing Charm*. Music from *The Sneezing Charm* also was conducted by Holst at Royal Victoria Hall on October 5th as accompaniment to "The Magic Hour," a ballet performed at the Morley College Distribution of Prizes and Certificates. Five days later Holst returned to Birmingham to conduct "a band mostly composed of Cinema players"[27] in five movements of *The Planets*: "Mars," "Venus," "Mercury," "Saturn," and "Jupiter." This performance drew a very positive response from the media, but it was nothing like the frenzy that would be stirred up one month later.

On Monday, November 15, 1920 *The Planets* was performed in its entirety for the very first time. This Queen's Hall performance featured the London Symphony Orchestra and Chorus performing under the direction of thirty-eight year old Albert Coates. It was the first time that "Neptune" had been included in a public performance. Audience response was positive and immediate. They had never heard anything like "Neptune." All of a sudden the suite made sense. L. Dunston Green, reviewer for the *Arts Gazette*, commented about Adrian Boult's earlier partial performance, "It was an injustice to the composer to rob his planetary system of the two stars [Venus and Neptune] whose soft light would have relieved the fierce glare of the five others."[28]

Albert Coates, the conductor of the first complete performance, was born in St. Petersburg of an English father and Russian mother. He was educated in

England before he studied conducting at the Leipzig Conservatory with Artur Nikisch. Coates had already made a name for himself through operatic conductorships he held at Dresden, Mannheim, and the Imperial Opera of St. Petersburg. Since 1913 he had been conducting in England, specializing in the music of Wagner and the Russian romantics.

It not known to this author why Coates conducted this performance instead of Adrian Boult; it more than likely had to do with scheduling. Boult and Holst remained close throughout Holst's lifetime, so the selection of conductor does not appear to have been entirely in Holst's hands. Although there is no extant correspondence between them, it appears that Holst and Coates had, at the very least, a good professional relationship, for Coates conducted *The Planets* in its entirety on a number of other occasions.[29]

Richard Greene, who has written an entire book on *The Planets*, did a detailed study of press reviews of early performances of the suite. He comments:

> Part of the success of the suite must be attributed to the variety of language from one movement to the next. Yet a study of the reviews of various performances suggests that it was not until the suite was heard in its entirety that it was so widely acclaimed. Also to be considered is the reception of *The Hymn of Jesus*, which was certainly as enthusiastic and as wide ranging as that of the suite. Perhaps the most important point is that, unlike most compositions, *The Planets* was introduced over a two-year period, and by 1920 many of the movements were like "old friends," as claimed by L. Dunton Green in the *Arts Gazette* (29 November, 1919). [30]

In this aspect, Adrian Boult's decision not to program the entire work at the February, 1919 public premiere appears to have been correct. After hearing partial performances, the audience was now ready to absorb the entire suite. And absorb they did. No fewer than seventy-five performances of *The Planets* were given in the United Kingdom alone during the next half dozen years! For the moment, the suite was seen as England's answer to both German romanticism and Stravinsky's primitivism. England had discovered a new composer-hero and his name was Gustav Holst. The craving of the masses for multitudinous performances of this universally appealing work is not difficult to understand. The public's appetite was further whettened by frequent broadcasts of its movements over the newfangled radio. Such a happening would not have been possible before the war.

Following the first complete performance, Holst heard from all sorts of fans and admirers. Most of this correspondence he dismissed as hero-worship, although letters from musicians and friends were always welcomed. One such letter was from a young Arthus Bliss:

21 Holland Park
W.

Thursday [November 25, 1920]

Dear Holst,

I have been meaning ever since last Monday evening to write you and say how greatly I was affected and moved by the beauty of your great work. I can only remember the first performance of V. W.'s Symphony[31] as producing in me the same pride that here at last we have 2 peaks rivaling Purcell after hundreds of years of dreary waste. I think that Saturn and Neptune are of the magical stuff that lives immortal and has been passed down like the old Grecian torch from hand to hand ever since Palestrina and I feel again pride that it is an Englishman who has grasped it firmly now.

This is a mere phantasy of the imagination, I know, but looking last night at the darkened sky, and being reminded that Saturn is nearer the earth this next month than it has been for many years, I liked [connecting?] that fact with your music...

Do not think of answering this, but I was inspired by a [spurious aspriration?] to tell you how much I felt the greatness of its conception.

Arthur Bliss[32]

Holst joked about the reception given to *The Planets*, writing to W. G. Whittaker, "It was a real vulgar success!"[33] He was pleased but puzzled by the public's response--pleased that his suite was recognized for its greatness, yet puzzled by the celebrity status suddenly granted him. He hadn't a clue about what the public expected of him, not did he try to find out. And the media attention was something that he had not expected; he summarily dismissed most reporters, photographers, and portrait artists. Yet fame did not go to his head; he saw no reason whatsoever to sever his work with amateurs; it was too much a part of him. So he continued to do what he had always done: teach, compose, and occasionally conduct. On November 21st the first London performance of *Two Psalms* was given at the Temple Church and on December 9th Holst conducted the Strolling Players Amateur Orchestral Concert Society in *Two Songs without Words* in a concert at Queen's Hall.

In the meantime Albert Coates, who had been doing a sufficient amount of guest conducting with Walter Damrosch's New York Symphony Society, arranged to present the American premiere of *The Planets* with that orchestra in that city. The only problem with this was that Frederick Stock, conductor of the Chicago Symphony Orchestra, who had heard the two-piano version of the work, had also asked to do it. Eventually things were worked out so that both orchestras would give the American premiere at the same time on the same evening, although New York, being in the Eastern time zone (one hour ahead of Chicago, which is in the Central zone) technically won out. This was of little or no consequence to Stock, who wrote to Holst:

5477 Hyde Park Boulevard
Chicago--Jan. 10th/1921

Dear Mr. Holst:

Just a few lines to say that "The Planets" had a most successful performance at our concerts Dec. 31st and Jan. 1st, so much indeed that I shall play them again before the close of this season, some time in March, perhaps. I am sending program-book and some newspaper reviews under separate cover, and it might please you to know that all the members of the Orchestra were most enthusiastic about your work and gave their best at both performances. I wish indeed that it might have been possible for you to hear your splendid work, knowing that you would have been very happy with it all.

With all good wishes for you and yours, and heartiest congratulations upon the fine success of your inspired and inspiring work, I am

Most sincerely yours

Frederick A. Stock[34]

---

[1]Katherine Eggar, "The Career of Mr. Adrian Boult" in *The Music Student*, XIII, No. 4 (January, 1921), 221.

[2]*Ibid.*, 223.

[3]Nora Day, Vally Lasker, Jane Joseph, and Irene Bonnett.

[4]Personal correspondence, Gustav Holst to Frances Ralph Gray, Jan[uary] 26[, 1920], The Holst

Foundation.

[5]Gustav Holst, "Music in the British Salonica Force," *Musical Opinion*, XLIII, No. 505 (October, 1919).

[6]America poet Walt Whitman (1819-1892).

[7]Gustav Holst, "The Mystic, the Philistine, and the Artist," *in Quest*, XI, No. 3 (April, 1920), 366-372.

[8]See Holst's tongue-in-cheek letter to Austin Lidbury, June 19, 1923, quoted in the First American Visit chapter.

[9]Gustav Holst, quoted in *Musical News and Herald*, March 4[, 1922].

[10]*The Dominant*, I, No. 6 (April, 1928), 24.

[11]Personal Correspondence, Ralph Vaughan Williams to Gustav Holst, n.d. [1925], quoted in Ursula Vaughan Williams (ed.) and Imogen Holst (ed.), *Heir and Rebels: Letters Written to Each Other and Occasional Writings on Music by Gustav Holst and Ralph Vaughan Williams* (Oxford: Oxford University Press, 1959), 61.

[12]Donald Tovey, quoted in Imogen Holst, *Gustav Holst: A Biography*, 2nd ed. (Oxford: Oxford University Press, 1969), 80.

[13]*The Musical Times*, LXI, 927 (May 1, 1920), 313-314.

[14]Imogen Holst, *op. cit.*, 80-81.

[15]*Morley College Magazine*, XXIX , No. 9 (June, 1920).

[16]Personal correspondence, Gustav Holst to W. G. Whittaker, March 30, 1917 and July 9, 1917, quoted in Michael Short (ed.), *Gustav Holst: Letters to W. G. Whittaker* (Glasgow: Universirty of Glasgow Press, 1974), 20 and 27. Holst also offered to send the full score.

[17]Gustav Holst, *Diary*, Monday, June 7, 1920, The Holst Foundation.

[18]Gustav Holst, *Diary*, Wednesday, June 23, 1920, The Holst Foundation.

[19]Programme of the Royal Military School of Music, Kneller Hall, Whitton, Wednesday, June 23, 1920.

[20]Other dates (all Wednesdays) for D. W. Jones' conducting included May 19th (Sullivan's *Overture to MacBeth*), June 2nd (Selections from Gounod's *Romeo e Giuletta*), June 9th (Wagner's *March from Tannhauser*) and June 16th (his own march, *Cuirassier*). Jones may have returned to Kneller Hall nine years later to guest conduct; a "Bandmaster W. Jones" conducted the *First Suite in E Flat for Military Band* on May 22, 1929. All information is taken from the Royal Military School of Music's *Concerts at Kneller Hall, 1914-1954*.

[21]*The Times*, September 16, 1920.

[22]*The Morning Post*, September 30, 1921.

[23]Michael Short, *Gustav Holst: The Man and His Music* (Oxford: Oxford University Press, 1990), 188.

[24]Gustav Holst, *Seven Choruses from the Alcestis of Euripedes*, British Library Add. MS 57889.

[25]Ralph Vaughan Williams, "Gustav Holst," in *Music and Letters*, I, No. 3 (July, 1920), 181-190 and I, No. 4 (October, 1920), 305-17.

[26]Personal Correspondence, Gustav Holst to Edwin Evans, October 30, 1920, Central Public Library, Westminster.

[27]Personal correspondence, Gustav Holst to William Gillies Whittaker, Oct[ober] 5[, 1920], quoted in Michael Short (ed.), 61.

[28]*The Arts Gazette*, March 8, 1919.

[29]According to p. 321 of Norman Lebrecht's *The Maestro Myth* (New York: Birch Lane Press, 1991), Coates' normal London Symphony Orchestra conducting fee in 1921 was £63. This was modest when compared with Nikisch's usual LSO £105 fee.

[30]Richard Greene, *Holst: The Planets* (Cambridge: Cambridge University Press, 1995), 30.

Greene's findings of the press' reaction to the November 15, 1920 premiere of the entire suite, given in tabular format on pp. 34 and 35, include five extremely positive reviews (*Daily Mail*, *Daily Telegraph*, *Monthly Musical Record*, *The Outlook*, and *The Sunday Times*),
five positive reviews (*Athenaeum*, *Daily News* ((*and Leader*)), *Queen*, *The Saturday Review*, and *The Observer*--neutral preview, but positive review), one neutral review (*Evening Standard* ((and *St. James Gazette*))), one mixed review (*The Times*), one negative review (*The Globe*) and two extremely negative reviews (*Sackbut* and *Truth*).

[31]Probably Ralph Vaughan Williams' *A London Symphony* (*Symphony No. 2*).

[32]Personal correspondence, Arthur Bliss to Gustav Holst, Thursday [November 25, 1920], The Holst Foundation.

[33]Personal correspondence, Gustav Holst to William Gillies Whittaker, Nov[ember] 24[, 1920], quoted in Michael Short (ed.), 63.

[34]Personal correspondence, Frederick A. Stock to Gustav Holst, January 10, 1921, The Holst Foundation.

CHAPTER XII

COPING WITH FAME

During the next few years *The Planets* was premiered in various cities throughout the United States. The work was greeted favorably, though not with the English chauvinism that was displayed in so many British press reviews. Richard Greene accurately described the situation by saying, "...in England, more was at stake. This is a clear distnction between the worlds of Europe and the United States, for in America the European scene was imported and, as in a museum, put on display."[1] In Boston *The Planets* was premiered on January 26, 1923, on a program that also featured Edward MacDowell's *Indian Suite*. Sixty-nine year old Philip Hale, music critic for *The Boston Herald*, wrote a rather bizarre introduction to what turned out to be a generally positive review:

> ....Some, reading the announcement of this concert, may have thought that the composer of "the Planets" purposed to give his hearers a fair idea of the music of the spheres. This music, by the way, has never been heard by mortal man, except by Pythagoras. We do not hear it, he said, because we are accustomed to it from our birth and cannot distinguish any sound wave by the silence opposed to it. Accoprding to the great philosopher, so cruelly mocked by Lusian, Saturn sounds the lowest tone; the moon the highest. Those who wish to inquire curiously into this celestial music should read the treatise by the learned Professor Piper, "Von der Harmonie der Sphaeren," published in 1849.
>
> Holst, an Englishman of Swedish descent, born in 1874, and now reckoned as a leader in the more advanced body of British musicians, was not so ambitious. He contented himself by composing in 1915 and

1916 seven tone-poems which should illustrate musically the astrological significance of Mars, the Bringer of War; Venus, the Bringer of Peace; Mercury, the Winged Messenger; Jupiter, the Bringer of Jollity; Saturn, the Bringer of Old Age; Uranus, the Magician and Neptune, the Mystic.

The composer has said that these tone-poems are without a program; they have no connection with the deities bearing the same names; the subtitles are a sufficient guide.

It will astonish some to find Venus described as the Bringer of Peace. The common opinion is that she has stirred up foreign and domestic strife, invaded households; a goddess smiling on battle, murder, and sudden death. A famous but unquotable line of Horace tells how she brought on the Trojan War. In astrology Uranus is a transformer, hence a magician, while Neptune represents the state of union with the infinite, the seeking after the ideal. We fear that those now consulting the astrologers are more concerned with fortunate days for doing business or marrying than the sublime attributes of the planets.

Holst has certainly written uncommon music. He has fancy, if not imagination, and the two are not always easily distinguished in spite of Coleridge's long-winded definitions. He has learned thoroughly harmonic and orchestration technique, and, as his invention is fertile and he has a pronounced sense of color, this cycle contains in turn ravishing, impressive, surprising pages. Take "Mars" for example. There is the suggestion of iron and brass; defiant inexorable militarism. And here the tremendous effect is gained by comparatively simple means. In "Venus," charming as much of the music is, Holst is more sophisticated, more audacious in his harmonic scheme. "Mercury" is, appropriately, a nimble Scherzo, lightly scored, for the most part. The "jollity" in Jupiter is inspired by ale rather than wine; it is heavy-footed and the tunes are not free from vulgarity. The composer's imagination is at its height in "Saturn" and in "Neptune." The former is music that should not accompany old age as Walt Whitman knew it: "Old Age superbly rising! Ineffable grace of dying days." Here is sullen, complaining, dismal old age, but how graphic the expression! "Neptune," on the contrary, is, indeed, mystic, beautifully so, not vaguely, not gropingly.

There are drawbacks to the full enjoyment of this cycle. There is the besetting sin of many modern English composers--prolixity. Endless repetitions of unimportant themes or fragments of themes fret the nerves, no matter how ingeniously they are tossed from one group of instruments to the another or proclaimed by the full orchestra. Mr.

> Carpenter of Chicago puts his trust in the xylophone; Mr. Holst puts his in the celesta, which is worked overtime. Mr. Holst once told a friend that he loved to write a tune. Unfortunately, some of his tunes, such as those in "Jupiter" are common. Strange to say in this cycle there are few, if any, truly sensuous strains. "Mercury" in myth was the god of thieves as well as the heavenly messenger. Mr. Holst did not take advantage of this fact in his "Mercury," but when the bassoons began their business early in "Uranus" we thought for a moment that Mr. Monteux was interpolating "The Sorcerer's Apprentice" by one Paul Dukas.
>
> "The Planets" is in many ways a remarkable work, one that should be heard again, and soon. The performance was brilliant...[2]

With the exception of his diversion into the discussion of Venus' personality and, possibly, Mercury's thievery, Hale resisted the temptation to put too much of the mythological end of things into his review. Yet it may have been this very review that came under attack by Greek music critic Michael Dmitri Calvocaressi in the June 1, 1923 edition of the *Musical Times*:

> On the other day, I read in a foreign periodical that Holst in his *Planets* expresses his conception of the planets' astrological properties. Such statements encourage readers to seek symbols rather than music, prejudice those who have no use for symbols, and help to propogate the notion that it is the symbols that matter.
>
> This notion is especially dangerous. So long as people are content with accepting the fact that music has a symbolic meaning for themselves and none for others, and do not judge it from the point of view of its symbolism, real or alleged, all goes well. But imagine a music-lover concerned with symbolism, and trying to achieve estimates of Scriabin's *Prometheus* and of Holst's *Planets*: if from his point of view Prometheus is more interesting than *The Planets*, he may see no need to proceed further, and be unable to conceive that people judging from the point of view of music may think otherwise.[3]

Hale made reference to the similarities between the opening bassoon passage in "Uranus" and the Dukas' "The Sorcerer's Apprentice." He was not alone among critics in his search for borrowings. Another critic went way over the edge, as evinced by this rebuttal in the *Shields Daily News*:

Holst and Respighi

> It is difficult to remove certain fixed ideas that England has no musical originality. One amusing result occurred recently from this attitude of mind. In Gustav Holst's "The Planets" one critic discovered an influence if not an imitation of Respighi's "The Fountains of Rome." When it was pointed out to him that not only was Holst the older composer, but that "The Planets" was written and produced before the Italian's work, the critic replied that this might be true but that it was evident that Holst had been influenced by Respighi. It did not occur to him, nor would he admit that it was possible, that Respighi might at a time when he was definitely seeking for foreign influences, have been influenced by an Englishman a few years older than himself, whose orchestral methods are based on his experience as a player.[4]

The 1920 performances of *The Hymn of Jesus* and *The Planets* had delivered a one-two punch that catapulted Holst into fame. Over the next five years, from 1921 to 1926, there were no fewer than seventy-five separate performances of *The Planets* in England alone[5], not to mention those in other countries. The public's appetite for *The Planets* was in no small way whetted by the newfangled radio, which brought Holst's music into everybody's living rooms. Such a wide dissemination of musical performance would not have been possible before broadcasting had begun.

Holst wanted absolutely nothing to do with being a "really popular composer." Curtain calls made him extremely uncomfortable. Autograph seekers were given type-written slips of paper saying that Holst never gave his autograph to strangers. He disliked publicity of all kinds and felt that his music should entirely speak for itself. He shunned all honorary awards and degrees. He dodged the press; whenever they caught up with him he froze, having little to say. Often reporters would have to fill up their columns with descriptions of his physical apperance. Photograpers were treated no better; they found him fidgeting around as he watched the clock tick. There were few exceptions, such as Herbert Lambert, a friend and musician, but by and large Holst fought for and maintained his privacy.[6]

One person who had difficulty getting through to see Holst was the English portrait artist William Rothenstein--and he had solid credentials. He was Principal of the Royal College of Art in South Kensington and Professor of Civic Art at Sheffield University. Rothenstein saw his place in life to be one pursuing the Whistler tradition, drawing and/or painting portraits of his contemporaries. It is not surprising that in the post-war years Rothenstein targeted both Holst and

Ralph Vaughan Williams as suitable subjects for the canvass. In July and October,1920 Vaughan Williams' two-part article "Gustav Holst" appeared in *Music and Letters*. Accompanying the article was a drawing of Holst by Rothenstein, probably taken from a photograph. That same year, Rothenstein's *Twenty-four Portraits* (London: Chatto & Windus) was published, but Rothenstein's work was not done. He was already working on his *Twenty-four Portraits: Second Series*, which would features sketches of Holst and Vaughan Williams.

According to dates on extant letters, it is safe to assume that Rothenstein first contacted Vaughan Williams about sitting for him. Vaughan Williams responded in a friendly but not-too-accommodating manner:

Northern Lights
Sheringham
Norfolk
22 August, 1919

Dear Rothenstein,

Very many thanks for your kind letter. My plans are so vague that I don't want to make any promises to be at any particular place at any particular time.

All I can suggest is that when you happen to be in London you should let me know of any times that are convenient to you--But I feel that it would be a most awkward arrangement for you and that you w'd prefer to drop it altogether.

Ys sincerely

R Vaughan Williams[7]

Rothenstein did not "drop it altogether" and eventually was able to draw Vaughan Williams. When the second series of portraits was published, the artist sent Vaughan Williams a copy. Vaughan Williams responded:

13 Cheyne Walk
SW3

21/10/23

Dear Rothenstein,

Thank you very much for your most interesting series of portraits. One advantage the artist has over the musician is that he is obliged to study human nature and get into contact with other interesting minds.

I feel proud, though slightly embarrassed, at being in such a distinguished company.

Yrs sincerely

R Vaughan Williams[8]

Holst was another matter; it appears that he was more difficult to reach. The following was probably not Holst's first letter to Rothenstein. He generally did not sign his name with just his initials nor did he address people by just their surnames until there was some acquaintence established. It is the only one of a group of eight that is fully dated; it is also uncharacteristically typed:

St. Paul's Girls' School
Brook Green, Hammersmith
W6
October 5th, 1922

Dear Rothenstein,

I regret that I am terribly and cannot spare a moment this term.

Yours sincerely,

GH[9]

Holst truly was busy. On at least one instance he tried to accommodate Rothenstein while composing:

St. Paul's Girls' School
Brook Green, Hammersmith

W6

Sep 26

Dear Rothenstein,

I am up to my ears in work and cannot spare a moment.

Forgive the suggestion but could you come here and draw me while I am writing? I have a good north light and shall be writing Tuesday, Thursday, and Friday mornings 10-1.

Yrs in haste

GH[10]

There was even one time when Holst forgot an appointment with the artist:

St. Paul's Girls' School
Brook Green, Hammersmith
W6
Nov. 13

Dear Rothenstein

I am ashamed to think of how badly I treated you.

On the 4th I suddenly decided to throw up everything and go home for the weekend to Thaxted and forgot about everything and everybody. I did the latter so successfully that I have only just realized that I should have come to you last Sunday!

Please forgive me and give me another chance.

How about next Sunday morning?

Y Sincerely

GH[11]

On at least one occasion Rothenstein had invited Holst out to be his daughter Rachel, who was a singer of English folk songs. It is unknown whether they actually met:

May 4

Dear Mr. Rothenstein

Thanks very much but I am full up just now and cannot go anywhere.

I have sent word to Rachel via Howells[12] to look me up at the RCM as I hope to make her acquaintence that way.

After the next six weeks life will be less hectic and I hope we can all meet then.

Y Sincerely

G T Holst[13]

Yet there was at least one instance when Holst was able to accept an invitation from Rothenstein It was scrawled in pencil on a postcard:

W. Rothenstein
18 Sheffield Terrace
Campden Hill
W

Please excuse pencil and accept my best thanks both for the portrait and for the invitation. May I come late (about 9) and will you forgive me if I am very tired and dirty?

I look forward to meeting and hearing Tagore with great joy.

Y

GH[14]

The above letter probably dates from 1922. The eminent Indian poet and philosopher Rabindranath Tagore (1861-1941) had at least three extensive visits to London--in 1912, 1922, and 1930. During the second visit, the Hungarian-born violinist Jelly d'Aranyi (who, with her sister Adila Fachiri, would be the featured soloists in the 1930 premiere of Holst's *Double Concerto*, Op. 49 [H175]) was introduced to Tagore at Rothenstein's studio. This may have been the event to which Holst was invited. Although his Sanskrit works were now behind him, Holst maintained a strong interested in Hindu culture. Tagore's self-congratulatory nature and boorish self-serving cotery were well-known throughout London. This apparently was not enough to dissuade Holst from meeting the 1913 Nobel Prize recipient.

So there were advantages to being famous, and Holst could not deny them. In the early 1920's, there were a plethora of performances of Holst's works. Some of these involved forgotten compositions that were more than two decades old. In addition to performance, publication had also become a sure thing for Holst. In 1921 alone no fewer than six large-scale compositions were published: *Beni Mora* (Goodwin & Tabb), *First Suite in E Flat for Military Band* (Boosey & Hawkes), *Hecuba's Lament* (Stainer & Bell), *Short Festival Te Deum* (Stainer & Bell), *Seven Choruses from the Alcestis of Euripides* (Augener), and, of course, *The Planets* (Goodwin & Tabb). The first three listed had been in manuscript for at least a decade; among these the suddenly red-hot *Hecuba's Lament* was published a year *before* its first performance![15] Three more followed in 1922: *Ode to Death* (Novello), *St. Paul's Suite* (Goodwin & Tabb), and the *Second Suite in F for Military Band* (Boosey & Hawkes). *Savitri* (Goodwin) was published in 1923. Thus nearly all of Holst's major works (save *Sita*) were published by the time that Holst's fame had reached its peak and many of these works were published only after *The Planets* had found its audience.

In spite of all that was happening around him, Holst managed to hang onto his not-so-mundane existence of teaching, lecturing, and composing pretty much as he had done before. He had family, students, and friends there when he needed them to help fend off hero-worshippers and the media. There were a number of events during the spring of 1921 that took his mind off the fame frenzy. One such event was an April 20th Queen's Hall concert conducted by his Reading student Douglas Clarke.[16] Another April event was the first Southeast London Music Festival, held at Manor Place Baths. In the competitions there Holst's students from Morley College made a clean sweep of the prizes.[17] There were also a number of "Field Days" with Ralph Vaughan Williams, who was now working on such compositions as the *Mass in G minor* and the *Pastoral Symphony*. Holst was also lecturing. On May 20th he gave his "Education of a Composer" lecture at Goold Hall, Edinburgh, under the auspices of The Incorporated Society of Musicians. It was repeated many times since. He remarked to Whittaker, "Ed of composer is quite fit for a general audience."[18] Holst wrote a follow-up speech, "The Teaching of Composition," which evolved into "The Teaching of Art," given at Yale University in 1929. He continued lecturing in the fall. On October 14th at the Forum Club Holst gave a lecture on "Modern Tendencies" in which he was quoted as having said "To go into a concert hall where modern music was being played was like being invited into a gymnasium for five minutes with the gloves."[19]

One of the things Holst looked forward to the most was putting together each year's Whitsun Festival. The 1920 festival held at Dulwich was extremely successful but, perhaps feeling a tinge of guilt for having left James Allen's Girls' School, he decided to hold the 1921 festival elsewhere. Two sites were chosen: Isleworth Church, located not far from the Royal Military School of Music in Middlesex, and Bute House, the boarding house of St. Paul's Girls' School in Hammersmith. It was largely through Jane Joseph's efforts that at Bute House on May 16th, Holst's Morley College and St. Paul's Girls' School students gave the first performance since 1784 of Henry Purcell's 1690 semi-opera *The Profetess, or the History of Dioclesian.*[20] The performance was so successful that it was repeated at Morley College on June 4th and October 4th as well as at Hyde Park on July 2nd.

On June 23rd the first professional performance of *Savitri* was given. It was paired with the ballet-pantomine *A Doll's House*, by Komisarjewsky and Liadov. Clive Carey, who sang the part of Death, produced the event. Arthur Bliss, who conducted the performance, comments:

> I was able to repay a little of [Holst's] kindness by giving three performances of his one-act opera Savitri at the Lyric Theatre, Hammersmith, in late June, 1921. As *The Times* wrote, "it is a perfect little masterpiece of its kind." The three singers in these performances were Dorothy Silk, Clive Carey and Steuart Wilson. Before the opera, I gave three of Holst's Hymns from the Rig Veda, sung by women's voices and harp accompaniment.[21]

Holst was very pleased with the performance and presented Bliss with a signed copy of the full score to *The Hymn of Jesus* as a token of his appreciation.

W. McNaught wrote of the perfomance in *The Musical Times*:

> Mr. Gustav Holst's 'Savitri' comes near to the idea of intimate opera. One scene, three characters, no 'supers,' emotional restraint, subtlety in the music--all these place it definitely in a *genre* to which few works belong, and into which few, if any, can be forced by cutting down....
>
> The music was everything. It was a new flavour in modernism--delicate, only half earthy, recalling nothing else, and mixed with no bitter spices. Perhaps it suggested vegetarian diet; but that was better than bad meat. Mr. Holst can be seen as daring as any experimentalist, but his effects are certain, and they make music. In 'Savitri,' as in other things, he is one of the artist-craftsmen (mostly British, it seems) who are building future music....

> Miss Dorothy Silk as Savitri, the woman, showed unsuspected gifts for the stage, and her singing was excellent. Mr. Steuart Wilson as the Woodman and Mr. Carey as Death were capable in their smaller parts.[22]

All three singers became good friends of the composer and from this time forward, Dorothy Silk was Holst's soprano of choice. *Savitri* had not been easy for her. She described the part as "rather a brute, with so little accompaniment!"[23]

The professional premiere of *Savitri* was given the same evening that Eugene Goosens conducted a performance of *The Planets* at Queen's Hall. Such conflicts had become increasingly common and Holst often had difficulty deciding on which to attend. The *Savitri-Planets* situation was not impossible. The same company presented *Savitri* on three different evenings and notes in his diaries indicate that Holst attended at least three of Goosens' rehearsals.[24] Holst himself conducted movements from *The Planets* at Queen's Hall thrice in 1921, on August 17th, September 18th, and October 8th.[25]

On June 30th, one week after the professional premiere of *Savitri*, there was another important musical happening involving Holst's music. His "Ballet Music" from *The Perfect Fool* had its first informal run-through at a Patron's Fund Rehearsal at the Royal College of Music. Holst was originally slated to conduct it, but after having trouble with the 7/8 in "The Spirits of Fire" due to neuritis in his right arm, he turned the baton over to Adrian Boult, who was in attendence. After hearing the piece, Alfred Kalisch commented in *The Musical Times*, "This should certainly find its way into the concert repertoire."[26] Two years later a grateful Holst gave Boult a copy of the full score with the inscription "To its 1st Conductor from his Inefficient but Grateful Pupil. G.H. 9th July 1923."[27]

1921 was not a particularly bountiful year for Holst in regard to composition. The maelstrom of activity in which he was involved had taken its toll. The musical setting to Cecil Spring-Rice's *I Vow to Thee, My Country* [H148] may never have been composed had Holst not discovered that the words fit the middle section of "Jupiter" perfectly.[28] Still, he did make significant progress on his opera *The Perfect Fool* and he had time to fulfill a minor commission. *The Lure, or the Moth and the Flame* [H149] was written for a ballet to be produced in Chicago. The scenario was supplied by Alice Burney:

> The Flame of a candle is shining brilliantly in the room.
> He... looks disdainfully at the poor little moths who flutter round him in adoration, [and] as they come too near him he scorches them. 'Folia' appears--the most beautiful of moths. The Flame awaits her homage but she ignores him at first. Filled with desire for her beauty, and anger at her

> indifference, he puts forth all his powers and she is irresistably drawn towards him only to be crushed and burnt in his embrace...He flings her aside...But there are greater powers than he. As the grey dawn appears a large snuffer slowly descends and covers him.[29]

Holst's rather short work (thirty-two pages) is scored for a large late-romantic orchestra with a large percussion section. In early autumn he was searching for themes for the work when a two-volume set, *North Countrie Ballads, Songs & Pipe-Tunes*, edited by W. G. Whittaker, was delivered to him. He wrote to Whittaker:

> St. Paul's Girls' School
> Brook Green, Hammersmith,
> W. 6
> Oct[ober] 2[, 1921]
>
> Dear W,
>
> The books of songs make a feast indeed. Thanks 1000 times. I have not heard the piano parts yet and have not even looked at them much yet because the tunes have fascinated me.
>
> Would you allow me to murder two or three of them in a ballet for Chicago? It sounds mixed but I got the books and a little commission from the USA about the same time and your tunes ran through my head when I thought of the ballet. But I shall ill-treat them disgracefully.
>
> Don't trouble to acknowledge this. I know how busy you are.
>
> Yrs,
>
> G[30]

The longest tune used in *The Lure* is based on a Northumbrian tune. The work may have been performed in Chicago; there are stage directions but no conductor marks on the manuscript score.[31] The work remained unpublished throughout Holst's lifetime and, despite recent publication by Faber, remains relatively unknown.

On September 8th *The Hymn of Jesus* was performed under Holst's direction in Hereford Cathedral as part of the Three Choirs Festival. The cathedral's magnificent acoustics heightened the performance. Following the festival, Holst joined his friends Ralph Vaughan Williams and William Gillies Whittaker for week-long walking tour of the Herefordshire countryside. Whittaker brought along his camera and took some well-distributed pictures of his two friends together.

Another activity that involved Holst during the autumn of 1921 was the Pageant of St. Martin-in-the-Fields, held November 7th through the 12th at the Church House, Westiminster. Dick Sheppard, the church's priest had opened up the church's crypt for the homeless to spend the night. Money was needed not only for the church's continued mission but also for maintenance and improvements to the infrastructure, so it was decided to have a week-long pageant. Holst had an enormous amount of repect for Sheppard and was more than happy to supply the *Incidental Music for the Pageant of St. Martin-in-the-Fields* [App. III, 22]. The mixed chorus (satb) and orchestra consisting of Holst's students and friends performed under Holst's direction every evening of the pageant. The music arranged for the pageant was a compilation of the works of several composers. *St. Patrick's Breastplate* by Holst's late student Charles Burke served as the Prelude to the Pageant. Additional music consisted of works by Allegri (*Adoremus Te*), Tallis (*Third Mode Melody*), Bach (*Air in D*), Vittoria (*Sanctus*) and Holst (*Personent hodie* and *Turn back O man*) as well as Latin and English melodies.[32] The pageant itself was repeated in March of the following year, with Holst and his students involved just as much as ever. At the close of the pageant, Holst was presented with a silver cigarette box--just the gift for a non-smoker![33]

On December 11th, at a Royal Philharmonic Society concert in Queen's Hall, Albert Coates conducted the first concert performance of the "Ballet Music" from *The Perfect Fool*. It was another "hit" for Holst. He was lauded *The Musical Times* by a reviewer who could not help but take a good-natured swipe at the composer's modesty:

> Mr. Gustav Holst lives and works hard in the heart of London, and yet manages to be a recluse. Outside his special haunts--Hammersmith, the Royal College of Music, and Waterloo Road--he is personally unknown, and he is the last man in the world to court notoriety. It speaks then remarkably for his music, that--even when quite new, like his ballet music *The Perfect Fool* (Philharmonic Society, December 11)--it 'goes home' not only with the knowing few, but also with the bulk of an audience who mostly need some personal clue to the bearings of a new composer. Anyhow *The Perfect Fool* brought Mr. Holst pretty well as much recognition as it came to the hero of the evening's concert (the hero, the

> admirable Pablo Casals; the Concerto, Schumann's Op. 129). The ballet comes from an opera, we hear, a comic opera,--but we are left interested guessing. But with a number in it like this--quite on the bravest, soaring Russian scale--it must be a sort of its own. The brass first utters an unaccompanied Invocation, an utterance that runs through the three dances of Spirits of Earth, Water, and Fire. These are Holst in his full maturity of power, vitality, and invention....[34]

Holst's fame continued its meteoric ascent in 1922. On February 11th he once again conducted movements from *The Planets*, this time at Colston Hall in Bristol. During the previous month Albert Coates had continued his own quest of introducing complete performances of *The Planets* to the English-speaking world by guest-conducting the New York Symphony Society in a performance of the work on January 11th in Massey Hall, Toronto. It was the first time that the work had been performed in Canada. The conductorship of the New York Symphony actually belonged to esteenmed conductor and music educator Walter Damrosch, who was also the orchestra's founder. Possibly after hearing Coates extol the virtues of *The Planets*, Damrosch decided it was time to meet the work's composer and went to London for that purpose. At 5:00 p.m. on Monday, February 13th, Damrosch and Holst met.[35] Their meeting bore fruit five years later, when Holst was commissioned by the New York Symphony Society to write the work that would become *Egdon Heath*. The seeds of the work may have actually been sown only two months after the meeting. On April 22nd, Holst conducted Dan Godfrey's Bouremouth Municipal Orchestra in selected movements from *The Planets*.[36] While in that region of the country he did a two-day walking tour of the Dorset area, wandering along Egdon Heath itself and visiting novellist Thomas Hardy. Florence Hardy, always protective of her husband, almost didn't let Holst into Max Gate (the Hardy home), thinking that Holst was a photographer.[37]

Holst continued to lecture. On April 8th Holst addressed The Incorporated Society of Musicians in the Botanical Theatre at University College in London.[38] The topic of the lecture was Henry Purcell and Holst was assisted by his students from Morley College who provided choral and orchestral illustrations. Selections from Purcell's *Dioclesian* were included.

The 1922 Whitsun Festival was held at All Saints Church at Blackheath, in southeast London. In addition to the festival proper, the Morley College Dramatic Society performed Euripides' *Alcestis* on a nearby private tennis court. Holst could not help but include his *Seven Choruses from the Alcestis of Euripides* in their production.

At about the same time, Holst received inquiries from two different sources in the military band world. James Causley Windram, who had earlier assembled a military band suite consisting of transcriptions of three of Holst's *Choral Hymns from the Rig Veda*, had asked Holst if he could transcribe the "Ballet Music" from *The Perfect Fool*. Holst agreed and sent him the score on June 17th.[39] Holst also heard from John A. C. Somerville, Commandant of the Royal Military School of Music at Kneller Hall, about a special concert that was to take place on June 30th at Royal Albert Hall. *The Sunday Times* carried a review of the concert that explains its purposes:

> In connection with the British Music Society's annual conference, a concert was given in the Albert Hall on Friday night by the band of the Royal Military School of Music.
>
> They had three aims in view: To demonstrate the influence of the military band as a factor in the musical life of the nation; to encourage composers to write for it; and to secure public appreciation for military music and all concerned in its performance. Of these, perhaps, the most important was the second.[40]

Holst was asked to submit a piece for the concert. He actually submitted four: the *Second Suite in F for Military Band* and three of his *Festival Choruses* ("Turn Back O Man," Op. 36 A, No. 2 [H134]; "A Festival Chime," Op. 36A, No. 3 [H134], and "All People that on Earth do Dwell" [App. III, 17]) with their accompaniments arranged for military band. The *Second Suite in F* was problemmatical in that its scoring no longer fit the instrumentation requirements of the British military band. Holst originally composed the work for the British regimental band of 1911, but ten years later, on December 7, 1921, there had been a conference at Kneller Hall which had standardized and "modernized" the instrumentation. Gone was the B flat baritone horn; it was essentially replaced by the B flat tenor saxophone. Holst's notebook entries indicate that he changed the instrumentation of the suite at this time, not only replacing his baritone horn line with one for the tenor saxophone, but--since the entire 168-piece Kneller Hall band was involved in the concert--also expanding the number of horn parts from two to four:

> Booseys
> no piano part yet
> B flat Sax not Bar
> line dodges

horns on 1 line
note where doubled
(3 and 4 at bottom once)
(in F in finale

have copy of both agree
prefer to keep mechan
rights.[41]

By "mechan rights" Holst probably meant recording rights; the *Second Suite in F* was recorded shortly thereafter by R. G. Evans and the Coldstream Guards Band.

The concert itself was a huge success. Hector E. Adkins, Director of the Royal Military School of Music, conducted the *Second Suite in F* while C. Thornton Lofthouse conducted the *Festival Choruses*. In addition to Holst's works there were original band works by B. Walton O'Donnell and Cuthberth Harris as well as transcriptions of works by Ethyl Smyth, J. S. Bach, and Wagner. Holst was in attendence.[42]

Holst continued to be busy as a lecturer for the remainder of the year, and he spoke on various topics. On July 3rd Holst addressed the Marylebone Branch of the British Music Society on "The Education of a Composer,"[43] on October 18th, he spoke on "Music in England" at the meeting of the Newport Music Club held at the High School for Girls,[44] and, back "home" at St. Paul's Girls' School on December 1st, he gave a talk on "Stunted Choirs" to the Girls' Secondary School Branch of the British Music Society.[45]

As a composer, Holst's fame continued to soar on an international level. Eugene Goosens introduced *The Planets* to Berlin, Adrian Boult introduced them to Vienna, and Ernest Ansermet and the Orchestre de la Suisse Romande introduced his *Oriental Suite: Beni Mora* to Paris and Lodz, Poland. The press never did stop talking about him in the early 1920's. Reporters often found themselves grabbing at straws, sometimes resulting in hysterically incorrect accounts, such as this one of Holst's attendence at one of the summer, 1922 Proms concerts, covered in *The Evening News*:

> What was an exceptional audience even for the Promenade Concerts gathered in the Queen's Hall last night for a programme that included, besides Stravinsky the irrepressible, several other novelties.
>
> Dr. Vaughan Williams and Mr. Gustav Holst, those two bright stars of modern creative firmament in musical London, were standing together....

> Gustav Holst, as a member of the Queen's Hall orchestra afterwards remarked to me, was wearing a Panama hat of astonishing shape that looked as if it had been sat on by several stout 'cellists on several stools!

Holst, who almost never wore a hat, wrote to Isobel, "It's a Libel. It was Vaughan Williams who wore the hat, not I!"[46]

---

[1]Richard Greene, *Holst: The Planets* (Cambridge: Cambridge University Press, 1995), 37.
[2]*The Boston Herald*, January 27, 1923.
[3]*The Musical Times*, June 1, 1923.
[4]*Shields Daily News*, November 14, 1928.
[5]Richard Greene, *op. cit.*, 37.
[6]Imogen Holst, *Gustav Holst: A Biography* (Oxford: Oxford University Press, 1938), 83-84.
[7]Personal correspondence, Ralph Vaughan Williams to William Rothenstein, August 22, 1919, by permission of Houghton Library, Harvard University, bMS Eng 1148 (1552).
[8]Personal correspondence, Ralph Vaughan Williams to William Rothenstein, October 21, 1923, by permission of Houghton Library, Harvard University, bMS Eng 1148 (1552).
[9]Personal correspondence, Gustav Holst to William Rothenstein, October 5th, 1922, by permission of Houghton Library, Harvard University, bMS Eng 1148 (727).
[10]Personal correspondence, Gustav Holst to William Rothenstein, Sep[tember] 26[, early 1920's], by permission of Houghton Library, Harvard University, bMS Eng 1148 (727).
[11]Personal correspondence, Gustav Holst to William Rothenstein, November 13[, early 1920's], by permission of Houghton Library, Harvard University, bMS Eng 1148 (727).
[12]Herbert Howells.
[13]Personal correspondence, Gustav Holst to William Rothenstein, May 4[, early 1920's], by permission of Houghton Library, Harvard University, bMS Eng 1148 (727).
[14]Personal correspondence, Gustav Holst to William Rothenstein, n.d., by permission of Houghton Library, Harvard University, bMS Eng 1148 (727).
[15]*Hecuba's Lament* was premiered on December 2, 1922 by Arnold Barter and the Bristol Philharmonic Society chorus and orchestra. Edith Clegg was the contralto soloist.
[16]Gustav Holst, *Diary*, Wednesday, April 20, 1921, The Holst Foundation.
[17]Michael Short, *Gustav Holst: The Man and His Music* (Oxford: Oxford University Press, 1990), 192.
[18]Personal correspondence, Gustav Holst to William Gillies Whittaker, July 28[, 1921], quoted in Michael Short (ed.), *Gustav Holst: Letters to W. G. Whittaker* (Glasgow: University of Glasgow Press, 1974), 68.
[19]*Yorkshire Morning Post*, October 15, 1921.
[20]*The Daily Mail*, May 17, 1921.
[21]Arthur Bliss, *As I Remember* (London: Faber & Faber, 1970), 66.
[22]*The Musical Times*, August 1, 1921.
[23]Personal correspondence, Dorothy Silk to Jane Joseph, n.d. [1921], courtesy of Alan Gibbs.
[24]Gustav Holst, *Diary*, Sunday, June 5 and Tuesday, June 14, 1921, The Holst Foundation.
[25]Gustav Holst, *Diary*, Wednesday, August 17 and Saturday, October 8, 1921, The Holst Foundation.
[26]*The Musical Times*, August 1, 1921.

[27]Adrian Boult, *My Own Trumpet* (London: Hamish Hamilton, 1972), 51.
[28]Ralph Vaughan Williams supplied two military band transcriptions of Holst's *I Vow to Thee, My Country*, in E flat and D flat, respectively for the pageant *England's Pleasant Land* in 1938.
[29]Imogen Holst (ed.), *A Thematic Catalogue of Gustav Holst's Music* (London: Faber Music Ltd., 1974), 145.
[30]Personal correspondence, Gustav Holst to W. G. Whittaker, quoted in Michael Short (ed.), *op. cit.*, 69.
[31]British Library Add. MS 47829.
[32]Imogen Holst (ed.), *op.cit.*, 248.
[33]Michael Short, *op.cit.*, 198.
[34]*The Musical Times*, January 1, 1922.
[35]Gustav Holst, *Diary*, Monday, February 13, 1922, The Holst Foundation.
[36]Gustav Holst, *Diary*, Saturday, April 22, 1922, The Holst Foundation.
[37]Michael Short, *op. cit.*, 201.
[38]*The Times*, April 10, 1922.
[39]Gustav Holst, *Diary*, Saturday, June 17, 1922, The Holst Foundation.
[40]*The Sunday Times*, July 2, 1922.
[41]Gustav Holst, Notebook, starting January 1, 1922, The Holst Foundation.
[42]Gustav Holst, *Diary*, Friday, June 30, 1922.
[43]*Music News & Herald*, July 8, 1922.
[44]*South Wales Argus*, October 18, 1922.
[45]*Halifax (Yorkshire) Courier*, December 2, 1922.
[46]This entire account, including the excerpt from *The Evening News*, is quoted in a piece of personal correspondence from Imogen Holst to Helen Asquith, September 2, 1922, The Holst Foundation.

CHAPTER XIII

INVITATION FROM AMERICA

1922 had been thus far been one of Holst's busiest. *The Planets* had made his name a household word and activity had increased on all fronts. He was severely overworked, yet still found time for his myriad teaching duties, guest conducting appearances, and lecturing. During the second half of the year, he worked on a new lecture, on the tercentenary of Byrd and Weelkes. He affectionately referred to it as his "B and W lecture" (or simply as "BW") and presented it no fewer than seven times in various places throughout the United Kingdom during the first two months of 1923.[1]

In spite of all of his job-related activity, Holst still found time to compose. During the summer of 1922 he composed *A Fugal Overture*, Op. 40, No. 1 [H151], a personal favorite, and put the finishing touches on his comic opera *The Perfect Fool*, Op. 39 [H150], which had been occupying his thought processes for the past four years. A private run-through of the opera with vocalists and pianists was held in his music room at St. Paul's late that summer.

It was in the autumn of 1922 that Holst received two offers from the University of Michigan School of Music in Ann Arbor: (1) guest conducting at their Annual May Festival in 1923 and (2) a professorship. The first offer probably was instigated by Frederick Stock, conductor of the Chicago Symphony Orchestra and the second probably through Albert A. Stanley, an American organist and music educator who had recently acquired professor emeritus status at the university.

Following studies at the Leipzig Conservatory and positions at Ohio Wesleyan College and Grace Church in Providence, Rhode Island, Stanley became a professor at the University of Michigan in 1888 and eventually director of the Ann

Arbor School of Music (from 1892 the University School of Music was under the auspices of the University Musical Society). Stanley was also manager of the University Musical Society and conductor of its chorus. In addition to these duties, he was curator of the Stearns Collection of musical instruments.[2]

Stanley founded the first May Festival in 1894; a festival of the same name had already existed in Cincinnati since 1873. The University of Michigan festival, which became an annual event, featured the University Musical Society chorus in performances of major works, often oratorios and concert versions of operas. To insure the quality of performance, Stanley brought in professional instrumental ensembles. The Boston Festival Orchestra (not to be confused with the Boston Symphony) was brought in through 1905, after which time the Chicago Symphony Orchestra, following the death of its founder-conductor Theodore Thomas and the naming of Stock as his successor, was the featured ensemble.

Stanley retired from the University of Michigan in 1921 and immediately set out for Europe for a three-year stay during which he would visit various major instrument collections. It was during this trip that he met Holst and filled him in about the May Festivals and the possibility of a professorship at the university. For unknown reasons, written notification from the university was delayed and the composer first heard about the offers in writing from Stock. After waiting weeks for the university's mail to catch up to Stock's correspondence, Holst wrote the following letter to the conductor:

Dec. 7th, 1922

Dear Stock, (do let us drop the Mr!)

Thanks for your letter which arrived three weeks ago. I have been waiting to hear from Mr. Sink[3] before answering but apparently his letter has gone astray--in any case it has not reached me. On the other hand I have met Dr. Stanley who was able to tell me a good deal about Ann Arbor but could not tell me much about the performance of the *Hymn of Jesus*. The two suggestions are of course quite separate. I should be delighted to come and conduct the *Hymn of Jesus* next May if it could be arranged that I and my wife got a good holiday. We have both been overworking for some years and I have been looking for a chance to get a term off. Dr.Stanley has told me that he thinks it would be quite possible. On the other hand I fear I could not come out just to conduct and go away at once as I do not think I could stand the strain and also I should be upsetting my work in England almost as much as if I were away for two or three months. You mention the possibility of my conducting an orchestral work besides the *Hymn of Jesus*. It might be possible for me to finish an orchestral work that I am writing--a fugal overture.

With regard to the professorship I find that it is impossible to form any opinion until I have been there and I feel certain that the University authorities will feel the same. I am tempted by Dr. Stanley's telling me that the work is not very heavy as I should greatly appreciate having less teaching to do but on the other hand I have my roots very firmly fixed in London.

Would you kindly tell Mr. Sink that his letter has not arrived. Perhaps he would kindly write again and let me have details. Thank you very much for doing *Beni Mora* and for sending me the programme.

Yours sincerely,

Gustav Holst[4]

Holst finally received Sink's letter of invitation and responded via cablegram on the morning of December 26, "Yes Conditionally."[5] So, what were Holst's conditions? The May Festivals were gala affairs, featuring many of the nation's finest professional musicians. An invitation to have one's music performed there, not to mention conduct there, was indeed an honor for any composer. Holst's hesitation had nothing to do with the caliber of the Festival itself. In fact it had nothing to do in any way with music. Simply stated, Holst was a pragmatist. Figures in his personal notebooks tell us that, while not being a cheapskate, he was always concerned about money management. Then there was the human side of things. Holst was always thinking about his family as well as those who assisted him in his work. He undoubtedly expressed these concerns to Stanley when the two of them had dinner on January 9th and included these concerns in his next written correspondence to Sink:

St. Paul's Girls' School
Brook Green, Hammersmith. W.
Jan. 11th, 1923

Dear Mr. Sink,

I thank you for your letter of December 22nd. I have seen Dr. Maclean and he is kindly cabling to President Burton. I have much pleasure in accepting the fee of 1,000 dollars for conducting the "Hymn of Jesus" and, if you wish, another orchestral work on May 17th. I agree with you that the fee pays the fare and a little over. Unfortunately it does not suffice to pay the deputies for all the work in England that I am losing. Therefore I should be glad of a little more work--either conducting or lecturing--while I am in the States.

I have been told unofficially that when I reach Ann Arbor I may be offered the Professorship to which I have replied that I cannot even consider the offer unless my wife is present with me in Ann Arbor and of course I cannot afford to bring her for the fee you offer. Therefore Dr. Maclean is cabling to suggest that if she is to go I should have another 600 dollars for her expenses. Please excuse me mentioning this matter. You do not refer to it in your letter and it may be that no such offer is now contemplated, but as time is so short I think it essential that I explain my position fully so that we both understand the situation completely. Perhaps I should go further and tell you that I am very happy in my work in England and am not at all anxious to change. Moreover I could not make the change quickly but should have to give due notice to those kind people who have treated me so well for so many years and whom I am proud to serve.

In my letter to Mr. Stock I told him I had a new orchestral work--a fugal overture--lasting about five minutes and suggested that if you cared to you might have the first performance which I would conduct. Since then I have learned that owing to the copyright laws it would be a serious matter for me if the work was not first performed in England. I have just been asked whether I would consent to have it performed next month at the Royal Philharmonic Society in London. If that performance comes off I should be delighted to conduct it at your Festival.

I am sorry I have no spare photos of myself. I will try and send you some later. With regard to a biographical sketch I have not one by me but Mr. Stock has printed all necessary details in his programme already and would let you have anything you want of that sort.

I shall do my best to arrive on May 1st and am trusting to the kindness and experience of Dr. Maclean in the matter of booking a passage.

Yours sincerely,

Gustav Holst[6]

Maclean dined at the Holst's home the evening of January 19th and afterward cabled to the University of Michigan about matters concerning Holst's acceptance. Upon receipt of the cable Sink was quick to respond to Holst not once, but twice, providing the composer with detailed information about the university and the May Festival:

January 23, 1923

Mr. Gustav Holst
St. Pauls Girls School
London, Engalnd

Dear Mr. Holst:

We were delighted to receive Dr. MacLean's cablegram stating in substance that you and Mrs. Holst had accepted our invitation for the May Festival. We are especially delighted that Mrs. Holst can accompany you. We are sure that you will both enjoy a trip to America and that you will find the University life at Ann Arbor very interesting. This letter will confirm our arrangement to pay $1600.

The writer has had several conversations with Mr. Frederick Stock relative to the program for Thursday evening, May 17, at which your "Hymn of Jesus" is to be given. We desire to include on this program another of your works for orchestra. Will you be so good as to communicate regarding this with Mr. Stock so that we may know about the program as far in advance as possible. I am also asking Professor Earl V. Moore, our acting conductor of the Choral Union and May Festival, to write you more in detail about the Festival program. You will of course make sure that the necessary conductor's score and parts reach us in advance.

We hope you and Mrs. Holst may reach Ann Arbor not later than the latter part of April or the first of May so that we will have ample time to do things in a great big way.

You will be interested to know that the auditorium which seat about five thousand is practically sold out for the Festival. During your visit at Ann Arbor we will plan to have you and Mrs. Holst entertained at the Michigan Union Club about which Dr. Stanley has doubtless told you.

Under another cover we are sending you a package of pamphlets, etc., regarding the school and musical interests which you will be interested looking through.

President Burton, Professor Moore and others of our staff desire me to convey to you and Mrs. Holst their cordial greetings. We all anticipate a happy time at the Festival and know that we are going to enjoy getting acquainted with you both.

Very cordially

[CAS] Secretary[7]

January 23, 1923

Mr. Gustav Holst
St. Paul's Girls' School
London, England

Dear Mr. Holst,

We were delighted to receive your good letter of January 11. In order to avoid misunderstanding I immediately cabled you a second time that Mrs. Holst was included in our invitation and that an appropriation of $1600 had been made for your account. We are very glad that Mrs. Holst can accompany you.

In reference to your musical situation I deem it advisable to state that for the sake of avoiding any possible embarrassment we have refrained from saying much about the professorship in music until you and Mrs. Holst reach Ann Arbor and can see first-hand what the situation here is. We believe that you will be favorably impressed with conditions in Ann Arbor and we also believe from the splendid reports which have reached us that we are going to be similarly impressed with the Holsts.

The University of Michigan maintains a music department wherein courses in history and the theory of music are offered. On the other hand the University Musical Society, closely affiliated with the University, with a faculty of about 30 splendid musicians, offers courses in all branches of practical music as well as in theoretical subjects. Dr. Stanley held the chair of music in the University and also the directorship in the

University School of Music. It is this vacancy caused by his resignation which is to be filled.

Mr. Earl V. Moore, assistant professor of music in the University, is serving temporaily as acting head of the University department of music and also acting conductor of the Choral Union and May Festival concerts, while Albert Lockwood, head of the piano department of the University School of Music is serving as conductor. Both of these men desire, as soon as a permanent director is secured to gravitate to their regular positions. They, as well as other members of our faculty and music lovers who are on the "inside" are delighted at your coming and the possibility that you may become a permanent fixture here.

You will also be interested to know that the attitude of the University administrative authorities is very cordial with reference to developing the work in both institutions and I believe that the new director will find splendid and ample tools available for carrying out a broad and constructive policy.

Will you be so good as to convey the writer's most cordial greetings to Dr. and Mrs. Stanley and also, if you desire, show him our entire correspondence. He will be interested and I know will be able to give you much information first-hand which is difficult to write in a letter.

Very sincerely

[CAS] Secretary[8]

Holst next heard from Earl Vincent Moore. As attested to in Sink's letter, Moore was Acting Conductor of the Choral Union as well as Acting Head of the University Department of Music. At the time of these negotiations Moore's duties were in a state of transition, from that of professor of organ and theory to that of administrator. In fact he would become Director of the University of Michigan School of Music later in1923 would remain so until 1946, at which time he assumed the title of Dean (through 1960). Moore became a well-known and respected figure in college music education and was often at the center of the movement, having been a founding member of the National Association of Schools of Music (1924), president of the Music Teachers National Association (1936-1938) and president of Pi Kappa Lambda (1946-1950).[9] These were future things for 1923, of course, and it was in the capacity of choir director that the thirty-two year old Moore wrote to Holst:

February 3, 1923

Mr. Gustav Holst
St. Paul's Girls' School
London, England

My dear Mr. Holst:

It may be presumption on my part to presume that a writer's name is already known to you, but I feel reasonably certain that in any discussion you may have had with Dr. Stanley concerning the details of the situation here at Michigan, my name must have have come into consideration. The purpose of this letter is two-fold, first to assure you of my own personal pleasure occasioned by your acceptance of the invitation of the University Musical Society to be present at the forth-coming Festival and to conduct your own composition, "The Hymn of Jesus" and other works if same may be arranged.

Secondly, to inquire for any suggestions which you may have for the preparation of your work and which are in published score. If there are any special effects or particular details upon which you wish the Chorus to place special emphasis, I will be pleased to work the same out for you.

The chorus parts to the "Hymn" have just arrived, having been sent to Chicago by mistake, and I expect to begin work on them after the beginning of the second semester, February 12.

I expect Mr. Stock will come down from Chicago on the 18th at which time we will have further conferences upon detailed programs for the various concerts. Your suggestions about the "Fugal Overture" have been forwarded from Chicago and I assure you we are anxious to do everything possible to give your works an impressive performance. I would like very much to have "The Planets," but the difficulties incidental to the bringing of an orchestra larger than the regular Festival tour orchestra seem to be insurmountable at the present time. Incidentally we have unions to deal with in this country and Art suffers therby.

Have you received your copy of the official program book for the Festivals? A bundle of these and catalogues were sent to you some time ago. You will notice that there is considerable descriptive material in connection with each work. Will you be so good as to send me at your earliest convenience as much data concerning the composition of the "Hymn" and "Beni Mora" and the "Fugal Overture" as you can recollect or feel would be of interest to our public.

For biographical details I shall draw upon the Chicago Symphony Program book published in connection with the performance of your "Planets" unless you wish otherwise. Please forward us as soon as possible several photographs in order that we may have one for use in our program book. Do not hesitate to give us as much of the "human interest" detail concerning your works as possible. I will take the blame for the appearance in print and the publicity will in no ways indicate that you have pushed this information forwarded. This program book must go to press about the middle of April.

May I again reiterate my pleasure in knowing that you are coming to Ann Arbor at such an auspicious occasion and I trust that you may feel free to call upon any of us to work out any details which will make your trip more pleasant.

Mrs. Moore joins me in hoping that we may have the pleasure of entertaining you and Mrs. Holst in our home some time during your visit here.

With cordial greetings, I am

Sincerely
[EVM][10]

This letter was followed one week later with some very good news from Sink:

February 10, 1923

Mr. Gustav Holst
St. Paul's Girls' School
London, England

My dear Mr. Holst:

I am sure that you will not mind hearing from me again. I want to make certain that everything is well understood so that you and Mrs. Holst will have the happiest sort of trip to America. We have come to the conclusion that the allowance of $1600 which was mentioned to you will hardly suffice for your purposes. Accordingly I cabled Dr. MacLean today that we had increased it to $2000. I think that this will more adequately take care of your trip.

It may be possible also to do a little something in the way of lectures for you while you are here, but we cannot count on much in this direction.

You will be interested to learn that our Festival program now stands substantially as follows:

Wednesday evening, May 16--Orchestral program
Beniamino Gigli, tenor soloist (Metropolitan Opera Company)
Thursday evening, May 17--Holst concert
Erna Rubinstein, violinist, soloist
Friday afternoon, May 18--Childrens' concert
Suzanne Keener, soloist (Metropolitan Opera Company)
Friday evening, May 18--Artist night
Florence MacBeth, soloist (Chicago Opera Association)
Guiseppe Danise, soloist (Metropolitan Opera Company)
Saturday afternoon, May 19--Samson and Delilah
Jeanne Gordon, Clarence Whitehill, Henri Scott (Metropolitan Opera Company)
Charles Marshall (Chicago Opera Association), soloists.

Our Choral Union of 350 voices is getting on nicely and at the next rehearsal will probably tackle your Hymn of Jesus.

The writer assumes that you are communicating with Mr. Stock relative to some of your orchestral compositions for the Holst program to supplement your Hymn to Jesus. I expect to go to Chicago next week and will talk with Mr. Stock about the matter.

I want you to know how happy I am personally and how delighted music lovers connected with the School of Music and the University as well as the public generally are at your coming to America. We all are anticipating the event with much pleasure.

With cordial greetings to you and Mrs. Holst, Dr. Stanley and Dr. Maclean

[CAS]
Secretary[11]

This good news did not reach Holst, however, until after the composer had suffered a cataclysmic fall. On the 11th of February (the day following Sink's correspondence), while conducting a rehearsal at University College in Reading,

Holst fell from the rostrum and landed on his head.[12] At first the 48-year-old composer seemed to have suffered only a mild concussion and it appeared that repercussions, however obvious, would be minor. However, an additional February 13th Reading concert, or at least Holst's part in it, had to be postponed and the composer was ordered by his physician to stay in bed for a week. Physically he may have been a wreck, but Holst was not mentally prepared for a cessation of activity. When he received Sink's letter he immediately responded to it from his bed with the following uncharacteristically typed--and undoubtedly dictated--note:

St. Paul's Girls' School
Brook Green, Hammersmith, W.
February 15, 1923.

Dear Mr Sink,

I thank you most heartily for our two letters and cable to Dr Maclean re the two thousand dollars for which I am most grateful. I am writing to Mr Stock to arrange to arrive in New York on April 30th but so far we have not been able to book a passage and it may be that we shall be a few days late. I presume that you have the orchestral material of the Hymn of Jesus and that I am only to arrange with Mr Stock about the orchestral piece. The score and parts of the latter are, I believe, in the hands of Messrs Gray of New York and I am asking Mr Stock to write to them direct. On behalf of my wife and myself I thank you most warmly for the kind messages and can only say in return that we are looking forward to a very great treat.

Yours sincerely,

Gustav Holst

SS
I hope the photos have reached you.[13]

This was Holst's last piece of personal correspondence for nearly a month. Within a week's time he felt better and returned to his work, but such a resumption of activity was too quick and too intense. The resultant nervous breakdown kept Holst down for another month. He had to cancel all engagements during this time and his friends were more than happy to help him out in his work. Philip Collis and Ralph Vaughan Williams substituted for him at Morley College while his work at Reading was taken on by Balfour Gardiner.[14] Neither the fall nor the ensuing breakdown are mentioned in the composer's diaries; in fact there are no diary entries whatsoever for the entire second half of the year. Holst had been ordered to the country for a complete rest. He could do nothing; he wasn't even supposed to write letters. Isobel had to deputize for her husband in supplying information to the University of Michigan during this time period:

32, Gunterstone Road,
Barons Court, W. 14
Feb 26 1923

Dear Mr Moore

Unfortunately my husband is ill & so I have to attend to his correspondence. About a fortnight ago he fell backwards off the concert platform at Reading University where he was conducting, & got slight concussion of the brain. He was in bed about a week & then his doctor allowed him to go back to work but said he must look upon himself as an invalid. This, I am afraid he did not do & now he has had a nervous breakdown & the doctor has sent him away into the country for a complete rest cure of at least three weeks! He is not to have any letters or attend to any business. He is just to vegitate, as it is the only chance of his recovery. Before he went away he gave me brief instructions about his business matters. He says he does not wish to say anything about the music. It must speak for itself!

I sent you 6 photos about 2 weeks ago & am surprised you have not received them. I will send you some more as soon as possible. Also I am sending some books with articles about my husband, which you may like to take extracts from.

We are looking forward to our visit to America with much pleasure & I am doing everything in my power to get my husband well for it.

Yours sincerely

Isobel Holst.[15]

Her next letter, written three days later to Charles Sink, provides a little more detail:

32, Gunterstone Road,
Barons Court, W. 14
March 1st 1923

Dear Mr Sink,

I am attending to my husband's correspondence because he is ill. About a fortnight ago he fell backwards off the concert platform at Reading University, where he was conducting[,] on the back of his head.

He was in bed for a week with slight concussion & then he went back to work too soon & now he has had to see a specialist who says there is no permanent injury but he <u>must</u> have complete rest, away from here for at least three weeks. He is not to have any letters or think of any business arrangement at all, & so I shall not be able to send your letter on to him for another week.

Will this do?

It is most kind of you to allow us such a generous amount for expenses & we appreciate it greatly, & look forward with much pleasure to meeting you in America.

I will ascertain about the orchestral works as soon as possible & let you know.

I have just written to Dr MacLean telling him I sent 6 photos of my husband nearly four weeks ago & cannot understand how it is they have not arrived. Anyhow I am sending some more & hope they will arrive safely.

Very sincerely yours

Isobel Holst

We sail on the "Aquitania" on April 21st.[16]

Holst's condition did not entirely prevent him from correspondence. He had enough strength the following day to write the following in his own hand:

32 Gunterstone Rd.
London W 14

Mr R Appel
15 Hilliard Str
Cambridge
Mass
USA

March 2 [1923]

Dear Sir

Please excuse short note.
I am not supposed to write letters or do any work for three weeks!
I regret I cannot accept your invitation as my wife and I will probably sail for home before June 25.

Yours Sincerely,

Gustav Holst[17]

Cambridge, Massachusetts would be visited by Holst during his second American visit (1929) and would figure prominently in his third (1932).

News about Holst's condition was met with great concern by the organizers of the May Festival. It was, however, more of a humanistic concern for Holst rather than a concern for the festival itself. After all, they had started rehearsing Holst's music and it would be performed with or without his presence. The first to respond to Isobel was Earl V. Moore:

March 12, 1923

Mrs. Gustav Holst
32 Gunterstone Road
Baron's Court, W 14
London, England

Dear Mrs. Holst,

Your letter of February 26 at hand and needless to say I am shocked at the news. I trust that already Mr. Holst is feeling like himself again and

> that his recovery will be rapid and complete. I do not wish to put any extra burden on you in the details incident to the performance of his works here, but I do wish you to know that we have received the photographs (they probably crossed my letter on the ocean) and that the books you spoke of and the articles will appear in due time.
>
> Will you please communicate to Mr. Holst my sympathy and tell him Mr. Stock was here yesterday and heard the rehearsal of the Hymn of Jesus and seemed very much pleased with with the progress we were making although they had it in rehearsal only two or three times. You probably heard through Mr. Wessels[18] that we are planning to use "A Dirge for Two Veterans" in addition to the Hymn on the Thursday evening concert which will enlist the services of the male section of the University of Michigan Glee Club and the Choral Union. I trust that this will meet with Mr. Holst's approval. Mr. Stock and I believe the work deserves a place on our program.
>
> We are borrowing the parts from the Winnepeg Choir through the kindness of Mr. Ross and Mr. Wessels has either written or cabled Curwen to forward immediately 70 additional copies.
>
> Mr. Stock informed me yesterday that he was taking up with the H. W. Gray & Co., New York, details for the suite from "A Perfect Fool." As yet the orchestration for the Hymn has not arrived, but no doubt is on its way.
>
> In a few days I will be able to forward to you a draft of the two programs in which Mr. Holst's compositions will be heard so that he mat definitely know what we are planning on here. Again may I say that we are all looking forward with a great deal of interest to this particular Festival and assure Mr. Holst that the Chorus is eager and enthusiastic in the participation of his work....[19]

This was followed by an optimistic letter from Sink who wrote, "I sincerely believe that a few week's rest will bring about a complete recovery. His rest and the ocean voyage, if he is a good sailor, should put him in excellent condition."[20] After reviewing the same musical matters mentioned in the March 12th letter of Moore, Sink made some travel recommendations:

> We note that you are sailing on the Aquitania leaving April 21st. We presume that you will reach Ann Arbor about the first of May. You had better plan to leave New York over the Michigan Central Railroad. There is an excellent train which leaves the Grand Central Station, New York, at 5:00 o'clock and reaches Ann Arbor the next morning at about 8:00

o'clock. If you will telegraph me I will arrange to meet you at the station upon your arrival here...[21]

The following week, Sink forwarded a copy of the tentative Festival program. The program listed Holst conducting his "Suite for Orchestra from the opera 'A Perfect Fool'" [Ballet Music from *The Perfect Fool*, Op. 39] on the Wednesday evening concert as well as *The Hymn of Jesus*, Op. 37 and *A Dirge for Two Veterans* on the Thursday evening concert.[22]

Later that same week, Holst, feeling much better, wrote an idiosyncratic handwritten reply to Sink's earlier letter:

32 Gunterstone Road,
Barons Court, W. 14
March 16 [1923]

Dear Mr Sink

Thanks for your letter to my wife read today [and] please thank Mr Moore.

Both you and he say that Mr. Wessells wants 70 copies of my Dirge.

Mr Wessels only asked me to send 30--which have gone.

I have seen Curwen's today and they have promised to send you an extra 40 copies in case they are needed. This, I think, very kind of them.

Orchestral material of the Hymn is on its way--apparently your Jan order of it never arrived.

You or Mr Stock are arranging with Gray about the Perfect Fool ballet so all seems well.

I have done no work for a month and have another six weeks so I ought to be fit but it is slow work.

Just in case I am not up to much by May would you allow me to conduct one thing only? May we have this open until we arrive?

We may prefer to travel from New York to Anne Arbor by day--I presume this is possible.

(We want to see as much of America as we can!)

Needless to say, we are looking forward eagerly to our visit.

Yr Sincerely

Gustav Holst[23]

Holst followed this about two weeks later with another letter in response to Sink's latest piece of correspondence. His strength and humor had returned:

32, Gunterstone Road,
Barons Court, W. 14
April 6 [1923]

Dear Mr Sink

Thanks for your letter and program. I am writing as my wife is away.

Could you manage to separate the Bach choruses from the H of J partly because the mixture would be such a strain on the singers and partly because the 'B minor' is the greatest choral work ever written and no other choral work is fit to come after it!

If you cannot have an instrumental work between could you not have an interval?

I have never heard my dirge and should much like to. Could someone else conduct it so that I listen?

We are looking forward eagerly to May and Ann Arbor.

Yr faithfully

Gustav Holst

I am getting stronger every day--thanks for kind enquiries.[24]

By 1923 Holst was a seasoned traveller. Berlin (1903), Algeria (1908), Switzerland (1911), Spain (1913), and particularly his stint with the British YMCA (1918-1919) in Salonica and Constantinople had taught him to plan ahead. Entries into his notebooks are filled with detailed reminders such as this one regarding passports:

My passport will do for both
2 unmounted photos
for USA Canada
bring letter announcing coming
" " " return
go early to consulate

9-1 or 1-2[25]

No other entries, however, are as extensive as the list of compositions that Holst planned to take on this trip.[26] Most of his major works written up to that time are included:

Taking
[Planets][27] I 3
[Planets] II 3
[Planets] III 3
[Planets] IV 3
CM[29] 3
Alcestis[31] 3
H of J[33] 3
2 Psalms[35] 3
O to D[37] 3
TBOM[39] 3
Fest Ch[41] 3
Let All[43] 3
All People[45] 3
Te Deum[47] 3
Folk Songs[48] 3 each

Solo [Planets] I
II
III
V songs[28]
EP[30] 3
Past[32] 3
Hecuba[34] 3
Dionysus[36] 3
DD[38] 3
Carols[40]
OAG[42] 3 each
I vow[44] 3
SB[46] 3 each

He continued this entry onto another page:

H of J 3
Beni[49] 1
SPS[50] 1
both mil band Suites?[51]
Songs without Words[52]
Planets?

Then on another page of the same notebook, in a moment of almost reckless abandon, Holst included the following entry: a large number of copies of works to be shipped to W. H. Gray (Novello's agent) in New York:

Send Gray
250 CM
" all [Planets]

" all SB
" all H of J

---

[1]Gustav Holst, Diary for 1923, The Holst Foundation. The Byrd and Weelkes lectures were given January 9 (The Musical Association, London Academy of Music), January 13 (probably at Morley College), January 28, February 2 (St. Paul's Girls' School), February 10 (Burnley), February 16 (Glasgow) and February 17 (York).

[2]*New Grove Dictionary of American Music* (London: Macmillan, 1986) IV, 295.

[3]Charles A. Sink, Secretary and Business Manager of the University of Michigan School of Music.

[4]Personal correspondence, Gustav Holst to F.A. Stock Esq. December 7, 1922, Bentley Historical Library, The University of Michigan.

[5]Telegram, Gustav Holst to Charles A. Sink, December 26, 1922, Bentley Historical Library, The University of Michigan.

[6]Personal correspondence, Gustav Holst to Charles A. Sink, January 11, 1923, Bentley Historical Library, The University of Michigan.

[7]Personal correspondence, Charles A. Sink to Gustav Holst, January 23, 1923, Bentley Historial Library, The University of Michigan.

[8]Personal correspondence, Charles A. Sink to Gustav Holst, January 23, 1923, Bentley Historial Library, The University of Michigan.

[9]*New Grove Dictionary of American Music*, III, 267-268.

[10]Personal correspondence, Earl V. Moore to Gustav Holst, February 3, 1923, Bentley Historical Library, The University of Michigan.

[11]Personnal correspondence, Charles A. Sink to Gustav Holst, February 10, 1923, Bentley Historical Library, The University of Michigan.

[12]Imogen Holst (ed.), *A Thematic Catalogue of Gustav Holst's Music* (London: Faber Music Ltd., 1974), xv.

[13]Personal correspondence, Gustav Holst to Charles A. Sink, February 15, 1923, Bentley Historical Library, The University of Michigan.

[14]Michael Short, *Gustav Holst: The Man and His Music* (Oxford: Oxford University Press, 1990), 208.

[15]Personal correspondence, Isobel Holst to Earl V. Moore, February 26, 1923, Bentley Historical Library, The University of Michigan.

[16]Personal correspondence, Isobel Holst to Charles A. Sink, March 1, 1923, Bentley Historical Library, The University of Michigan.

[17]Personal correspondence, Gustav Holst to R. Appel, March 2 [, 1923], Boston Public Library Ms.Mus. 194 (1).

[18]F. J. Wessels, Manager of the Chicago Symphony Orchestra.

[19]Personal correspondence, [Earl V. Moore] to Isobel Holst, March 12, 1923, Bentley Historical Library, The University of Michigan. Ending clipped.

[20]Personal correspondence, Charles A. Sink to Isobel Holst, March 13, 1923, Bentley Historical Library, The University of Michigan.

[21]*Ibid.*

[22]Personal correspondence, Charles A. Sink to Isobel Holst, March 22, 1923, Bentley Historical Library, The University of Michigan.

[23]Personal correspondence, Gustav Holst to Charles A. Sink, March 26 [1923], Bentley Historical Library, The University of Michigan.

[24]Personal correspondence, Gustav Holst to Charles A. Sink, April 6 [1923], Bentley Historical Library, The University of Michigan.

[25]Gustav Holst, Notebook October 1922-Spring? 1923, The Holst Foundation.

[26]*Ibid.*

[27]Holst used the Sanskrit symbol rather than write the English word for *The Planets*, Op. 32 [H125]. "I," of course, meant Mars, "II" Venus, "III" Mercury, and "IV" Jupiter.

[28]Probably *Hymns from the Rig Veda,* Op. 24 [H90].

[29]*The Cloud Messenger,* Op. 30 [H111].

[30]*Two Eastern Pictures* [H112].

[31]*Seven Choruses from the Alcestis of Euripedes* [H146].

[32]*Pastoral* [H92].

[33]*The Hymn of Jesus,* Op. 37 [H140].

[34]*Hecuba's Lament,* Op. 31, No. 1 [H115].

[35]*Two Psalms* [H117].

[36]*Hymn to Dionysus,* Op. 31, No. 2 [H116].

[37]*Ode to Death,* Op. 38 [H144].

[38]Possibly Holst's editing of *Two Duets from King Arthur by Henry Purcell* [App. III, 11] or the early *Duet in D* for two pianos [H6].

[39]"Turn Back, O Man," No. 2 from *Festival Choruses,* Op. 36 [H134].

[40]*Three Carols* [H133].

[41]"A Festival Chime," No. 3 from *Festival Choruses,* Op. 36 [H134].

[42]*Old Airs and Glees* [App. III, 16].

[43]"Let All Mortal Flesh Keep Silence," No. 1 from *Festival Choruses,* Op. 36 [H134].

[44]*I Vow to Thee, My Country* [H148].

[45]"All People that on Earth Do Dwell," [App. III, 17] from *Festival Choruses,* Op. 36 [H134].

[46]Probably either the *Sanctus Byrd* [App. III, 21] or *Suite de Ballet*, Op. 10 [H43].

[47]*Short Festival Te Deum* [H145].

[48]This could refer to any of the following collections: [H83], [H84], [H85], [H136].

[49]*Beni Mora,* Op. 29, No. 1 [H107].

[50]*St. Paul's Suite,* Op. 29, No. 2 [H118].

[51]*First Suite in E Flat for Military Band,* Op. 28, No. 1 [H105] and *Second Suite in F for Military Band,* Op. 28, No. 2 [H106].

[52]*Two Songs without Words, Op. 22* [H88].

CHAPTER XIV

THE FIRST AMERICAN VISIT

On April 21, 1923 Holst and his wife set sail from England bound for America on board the *Aquitania*. The seven day journey was not a bad voyage by anyone's standards. The Holsts were not alone. On board was Arthur Bliss, who had conducted the first professional performance of *Savitri* some sixteen months earlier and whose recently commissioned work, *A Colour Symphony*, had been well-received at the 1922 Three Choirs Festival in Gloucester. Bliss was on his way to a two-year stay in the United States. He comments:

> When in 1923 I went to America with my father [Francis Edward Bliss] and his family, Holst was on board the same boat. One evening we were looking over the stern at the vanishing wake of the waves and Holst said, "How heroic the men with Columbus must have been!" He paused here and I thought he was thinking of the tiny boats, compared with ours, that made the dangerous crossing: but he then added, "for in their minds the earth was flat, and the night horizon that they saw [was] perhaps the final edge."[1]

Bliss' welcomed company bolstered Holst's spirits and conditions on board were sufficiently favorable to the degree that Holst was able to continue work on a composition then in its early stages. The work in question was *A Fugal Concerto*, Op. 40, No. 2 [H152], perhaps the most overtly neoclassical work of his entire compositional output. It was also the first work written by him since his fall at the University of Reading. The composer joked about the concerto in a letter written to Vally Lasker shortly before the Holsts' departure:

April 1923
Tuesday

Dear V

Thank you for everything. Of course there will be time to have a good talk.

No hurry about the Fugal Overture--I quite agree it would be better to wait until you've heard it....

Tell RVW[2] I want a composition lesson before I go. I've sketched two movements of the World's Shortest Concerto and have enjoyed doing so hugely. In fact I feel another being this week. I don't know that I shall enjoy listening to it as much. I'm afraid it won't do really.

Good luck to Holmwood at the Comp.

Love to Hedweg.

Y

G[3]

A Fugal Concerto has suffered somewhat of an identity crisis. Op. 40, No.1 was *A Fugal Overture* [H151] (mentioned early in the letter quoted above), but, aside from the shared opus number and implied contrapuntal similarity, the two works do not form a pair. *A Fugal Overture* is scored for full orchestra and was intended to serve as an overture to *The Perfect Fool*. *A Fugal Concerto*, on the other hand, is altogether more compact. It is a three-movement work, lasting only about eight minutes and thinly scored, for two soloists--flute and oboe--with string accompaniment. Though not particularly intended for amateurs, the work does exhibit the characteristic elasticity in instrumentation indicated so often by Holst. On this occasion, however, the optional instrumentation lies not in the accompaniment, but in the choice of soloists. The two woodwinds can be replaced by two violins. This very fact contributes further to the work's identity crisis, for *A Fugal Concerto* is sometimes confused with *A Double Concerto*, Op. 49 [H175], composed in 1929-1930 specifically for two violin soloists and small orchestra.

The Holsts arrived in New York on April 27th and took up lodgings in the Hotel Netherland, which Holst described as "a good hotel,"[4] located in Midtown Manhattan. The following morning the composer wrote to Earl V. Moore:

Hotel Netherland
Fifth Avenue and
Fifty Ninth Street
New York
April 28[,1923]

Dear Mr Moore

We arrived on the Aquitania last night and intend leaving by the 5pm next Monday so as to arrive in Ann Arbor on May 1st at about 8AM I hope this will suit you.

I have your letter to Mr Gray re note about my 'Perfect Fool' and have much pleasure in enclosing some information about the work. If it is not suitable I will try and do better when we meet!

Needless to say we are looking forward to seeing you all with the greatest pleasure.

Y faithfully

Gustav Holst

[P.S.]
'ThePerfect Fool' is a one act opera which is to be produced at Covent Garden London on May 14. The work begins with a ballet which has been arranged for concert performance by the composer and which has been performed in London, Munich, Barcelona and other cities with great success.
The music of the ballet is continuous and consists of

Invocation
Dance of the Spirits of the Earth
Dance of the Spirits of Water
Dance of the Spirits of Fire

The opening Invocation is heard before each of the dances. The dances themselves are so clearly contrasted that no explanation or description is necessary.[5]

The Holsts soon arrived in Ann Arbor and, after being greeted by their hosts, were put up for the length of their stay there at the Michigan Union. Located about forty miles east of Detroit, the university town of Ann Arbor could have reminded Holst of Reading, which was of similar size, type, and location with respect to London. The composer was obviously pleased with his surroundings and wrote about them in a letter to his friend W. G. Whittaker:

> ...A week or so in Ann Arbor is worth a month rushing about. The people are not only kind but intelligently kind and without fussing you in the least they will give you one of the happiest times of your life.
> I could write reams about Ann Arbor....[6]

Indeed Ann Arbor was characterized as the "Bayreuth of America" by the local press.[7]

Holst was very pleased not to be "rushing about," as he put it. He had nearly two weeks at the University of Michigan to relax, rehearse, and compose before the May Festival started. Still, much was on the composer's mind, if his notebook entries are any indication:

> Moore Music arrived?
> lost baton
> orch practice
> What do you conduct
> do I conduct Beni & PF
>
> Moore Wheeler sing in Prelude
> Chemist for arm
> try over with piano for conducting
> Bulletins
> hear orch
> see more of work
> see comps
> lecture if wanted
> mil band[8]

The first entry was a reminder to see Earl Moore about the soloist in the Prelude of *The Hymn of Jesus*. The next referred to Holst's bad right arm, occasionally crippled with neuritis. At St. Paul's Girls' School and other places that he taught, Holst would occasionally conduct left handed in order to relieve the tension in his right arm. He preferred not to do this with professional groups and wanted to have his right arm checked out. The other listings are self-explanatory, although it should be mentioned that Holst had at least contemplated bringing his military band suites with on this trip. By the 1920's the University of Michigan Concert Band had already an established reputation for fine performance under their conductor Captain Wilfred Wilson and Holst would have wanted to at least hear the ensemble. It is not known whether either of his military band suites were rehearsed or performed by the band during this visit.

Additional notebook entries indicate plans for *A Fugal Concerto* as well as lodging concerns:

> Moore
> finish concerto at library
> do it privately
> (copy parts?)
> (" score?)
> present original to
> University
> We stay over Fest?
> (make that clear)[9]

During this time, Holst was able to go into seclusion at the university's library and complete *A Fugal Concerto*.

Meanwhile, on the other side of the Atlantic, *The Perfect Fool* was given its world premiere on May 14th at the Royal Opera House, Covent Garden. The British National Opera Company was conducted by Eugene Goosens. The company was then quite new, having been in existence a mere three months. Holst had meant the opera to be funny, but the capricious story line and musical parodies thrust the audience into a state of confusion as to what it was all supposed to mean.

The event was covered extensively by the press. Edwin Evans wrote a four-page article about the work itself, including incipits, for *The Musical Times*. After commenting largely on Holst's using his non-theatrical background to his advantage, Evans remarked:

> The final impression left by this work is of energy in the domain of rhythm and of simplicity in that of tune. But for the experience that lies behind it one might describe it as boyish music. Perhaps it is this aspect of it that makes it peculiarly English, for most foreigners have remarked that an Englishman remains a boy for the greater part of his life.[10]

Evans also had a review of the performance in the same issue of *The Musical Times*:

> The production of Holst's opera, the Perfect Fool, made the opening night of the British National Opera Company's season an event of outstanding importance. It was very evident that great care had been taken to ensure a good performance as well as an adequate presentation. ....A major share of the credit must go to Mr. Eugene Goosens. It is all very well to be a virtuoso as a conductor, but Holst's rhythmic problems allow no respite. The slightest hesitation would be fatal. Goosens is a helpful conductor. He is more liberal than most in the giving of cues, and he must have been a comfort to those whose nerves were affected by the occasion. The result he obtained was almost without blemish....
>
> As for the reception of the opera, and what it denotes for the future, it is difficult to express an opinion. The audience was a highly specialized one, and not really representative of opera goers as a body....It remains to be seen whether a truly popular audience will swallow it whole. But of the general appreciation of the first night audience there cannot be much doubt. All the comment heard on leaving the theatre was of the same colour.[11]

Not all of the reviews were as positive as Evans'. It mattered little, for Holst didn't get to see any of the reviews for about two weeks. He had missed the premiere of *The Perfect Fool*, but made certain that he and Isobel would get back to London in time to see a later performance. For now he was safely isolated in America and had more immediate concerns.

Columnists were still trying to determine the significance of the work a year later, as attested to by the following commentary in *The Musical Times*:

> When The Perfect Fool was produced there was a good deal of speculation as to what the composer meant by it. The probability that he meant nothing at all, but was merely providing us with a rich and unusual type of entertainment, seemed to occur to few people. Even to-day dark and abstruse speculations are afoot, if we may judge from a communication received by the directors of the B.N.O.C. The writer thereof considers that 'this delicious piece is the composer's Koheleth or Ecclesiates on all theories about art,' and he proceeds at considerable length to give an analysis which, much condensed, is as follows:
>
> The Wizard is the Professional Musician; he deals in love and hate,

and from these he distils his Potion.

The Perfect Fool is the Public; it cares for nothing, but just exists, vegetable-like.

His Mother is the British Press; she tries to make him a force in art, but he ignores her efforts.

The Wizard--the Professional Musician, remember--doesn't exactly woo the Press, but he practices his art on her. She, however, gets between the Musician and the Public for her own ends. She, too wants the Public to be full of music. She steals the Musician's Potion--the art he has distilled from love and hate--and forces it upon the Public. To the Musician she gives cold water by way of hinting that he should be more simple, more natural--anything but Professional, in short.

Enter Music herself--the Princess--and, disdaining the Musician, apparently on the ground of his Professionalism, falls in love with the Public. She is wooed by Italian and German opera, but in vain.

Meanwhile the Professional makes a big blaze with his Technique and 'art for art's sake,' but Music ignores the display and sticks to the Public. However, as something has to be done about the incendiary Professional, the Public wakes up just enough to put out the fire of technique by sheer obtuseness, and the Professional disappears hurriedly, leaving behind no more than his hat--that is a monument, a name , or a few 'Ops.,' which is all the Public will ever know or care about him.

A good deal of grey matter seems to have been used in the evolution of this 'analysis.' Unfortunately the composer himself was unconscious of creating a 'Koheleth or Ecclesiates' on Art. We understand that, on being shown the above 'Explanation,' Mr. Holst remarked, with feeling, 'Why didn't I think of that myself?' We are glad he didn't.[12]

The Musical Times did not get it right, however, since Holst was isolated in Thaxted during the early spring of 1924 and Isobel would have been the only person who could have known his opinion of the analysis. He response to the situation: "This is a holy scream!"[13]

The Thirtieth Annual May Festival at the University of Michigan opened on Wednesday, May 16, 1923 at eight o'clock in the evening. The site for the festival was Hill Auditorium, one of the finest music halls in the entire country. The First May Festval Concert, listed as the seventh concert of the Choral Union's forty-fourth season, featured Holst conducting his *Oriental Suite: Beni Mora* on the second half of the program, sandwiched between an aria from Lalo's *L'Roi d'Ys* that was sung by Benjamin Gigli and selections from Wagner's *Die*

Meistersinger.[14]

The following day, a private performance of *A Fugal Concerto* took place at the home of university president Marion Le Roy Burton:

> At a reception given by president Marion Le Roy Burton and Mrs. Burton , in their home on the afternoon of May 17, Mr. Holst gave evidence of his appreciation of the university by presenting his most recent composition, a fugal concerto for flute and oboe or two violins with string orchestra. It was begun on the Aquitania while approaching this country and finished in the University Library on May 5. Members of the Chicago Orchestra played it on this occasion. It is a short composition, of rather light texture and with a gay last movement written around an old English tune that the composer's daughter had been singing:
>
> If all the world were paper
> And all the ocean ink,
> And all the trees were bread and cheese--
> What would we do for drink?
>
> The original manuscript was presented by Mr. Holst to the University Library.[15]

The title page of Holst's manuscript score tells the story:

To MRJ and ICH[16]

A Fugal Concerto for Flute and Oboe
(or two violins)
with accompaniment for string orchestra

Gustav Holst
Op 40 no 2

This Score was written in the Library of the University of Michigan (excepting the first page which was written on board the 'Aquitania') and is presented to the University as a token of gratitude for all the kindness shown to my wife and myself during our visit to Ann Arbor

Gustav Holst

May 1923
First performed May 17 at President Burton's house
Members of the Chicago Symphony Orchestra

A. Quensel--Flute
A. Barthel--Oboe
Stephen Gordon Violin
Walter Hauerstein
George Dasch
Fritz Itte
Franz Esser Viola
Otto B. Rucherbiem
Alfred Wallenstein Cello
Carl Bruskner
Vaclav Jistera Contrabass

Frederick A. Stock
Conductor[17]

The twelve listed members of the Chicago Symphony Orchestra who took part in the first performance, including Stock, signed the title page. Holst made a copy of the score and took it with him to London, where he himself conducted the European premiere of the work on the following October 11th. That Queen's Hall performance featured Robert Murchie (flute), Leon Goosens (oboe) and the strings of the New Queen's Hall Orchestra.[18] The work was published later in the year. It was generally well-received and remained in the repertoire of a number of conductors. Harvey Grace commented in 1939, "...it is good news that [Adrian] Boult is including in his Monte Carlo programme the Fugal Concerto--one of the best and most attractive of his [Holst's] shorter works."[19]

The world premiere performance at President Burton's house was by all accounts a very pleasant affair, but it was not the only thing on the composer's mind, for earlier that day Holst had received two eye-opening telegrams:

NX NEW YORK NY 911 A MAY 17 1923
GUSTAV HOLST
MUSICAL COMPOSER ANN ARBOR MICH
NEWS IS ANNOUNCED IN LONDON YOU HAVE BEEN OFFERED DIRECTORSHIP EASTMAN SCHOOL OF MUSIC WILL APPRECIATE YOUR COURTESY IF YOU PLEASE TELEGRAPH ME ABOUT HUNDRED WORDS WHETHER YOU WILL ACCEPT

WHEN YOU EXPECT ARRIVE LONDON AND WHAT YOUR PLANS
WILL BE AT EASTMAN SCHOOL PLEASE ADDRESS
WARREN MASON CORRESPONDENT LONDON DAILY EXPRESS
313 WORLD BLDG NY

835A[20]

SX NEWYORK NY 1220P MAY 17 1923
GUSTAV HOLST
ANN ARBOR MICH
REPORTED IN LONDON YOU CONSIDERING DIRECTORSHIP
EASTMAN SCHOOL MUSIC ROCHESTER WILL YOU KINDLY
TELEGRAPH ME WHETHER REPORT TRUE
W F BULLOCK LONDON DAILY MAIL
280 BROADWAY NEWYORK

1139A[21]

Was Holst offered the directorship of the then fledgling yet prestigious Eastman School of Music? Probably not. There does exist the following manuscript response, undoubtedly meant for a telegram:

> Have had no offer or negotiation whatsoever concerning Eastman School directorship
>
> Gustav Holst[22]

Holst's terse reply would normally have shut the door on any further Eastman speculation, yet the scrap of paper is not dated and it is not in Holst's hand. Holst indeed may have been offered the directorship but he had not yet been officially contacted. More than likely, however, a rumor may have developed in England that had its origins in the misconstruing of facts regarding the professorship that the University of Michigan had offered Holst. There was also a similar rumor that Jean Sibelius had been offered the Eastman School of Music directorship. This was also false, although in fact Sibelius had been offered a professorship there. According to the Eastman School of Music historian, Ruth Watanabe, there was only one person offered the directorship of the school and that was Howard Hanson who was offered it the following year, at the youthful age of twenty-eight![23]

Still, between May 16 and May 19, 1923, there were no fewer than four periodicals--*Public Opinion, The Daily Express, The Manchester Guardian,* and

The Daily Graphic--reporting that Holst had been offered the post. A fifth, *The Daily Telegraph*, reported something slightly different:

> I hear that Gustav Holst, composer of *The Perfect Fool*, which created a furor at Covent Garden on Monday, has been offered Arthur Alexander's post as director of the orchestra and orchestral classes at the Eastman Conservatory, Rochester, New York. If this be true, I can only say I congratulate Rochester and Eastman, and all concerned. To me it seems essential that the composers who are making history today should live more and have their being in the greater world. We here can lose nothing thereby; the world is too small for that. But we can gain for the greater growth of these history-makers, and precious little history of any value is made in these days round and round the parish pump. The parish pump laed to chauvinism that any other would seem like a farthing dip by comparison--"farthing rush light" was how Davison described Wagner about sixty years ago! Holst and Bliss--and others--will suffer nothing by a sojourn in the U.S.A., and we ourselves undoubtedly will be the gainers.[24]

Even if either offer had existed, Holst probably would not have considered them. The essence of the wording in his telegram to Mason was printed by the *Sunday Express* on May 20th, 1923; the brief article was of such a definitive nature that it derailed further media speculation.

The Second May Festival Concert was held that same evening (May 17, 1923). The featured work on the concert was Holst's *The Hymn of Jesus*, which rounded out the first half. As per Holst's request of April 6th,[25] an instrumental piece, Wagner's "Good Friday Spell" from *Parsifal*, was placed between the Bach *B Minor Mass* selections and *The Hymn of Jesus*. An early composition of Holst would not have been served well by this, but Holst had been writing works that were non-Wagnerian in nature for more than a decade previous to *The Hymn of Jesus* and the Wagner work turned out to be a perfect foil to Holst's choral masterpiece.

The first half of the concert went off without a hitch, but the second half was another story. It opened with an exhausted Holst conducting his own *A Dirge for Two Veterans*. Holst previously had asked that someone else conduct this work[26] so that he could listen to it, but obviously changed his mind sometime after his arrival in Ann Arbor. This decision may not have been the best thing, for half-way through the performance--in front of a packed house--he stopped! This was noted in the press:

> The Hymn of Jesus was followed by the more unique Dirge for Two Veterans and Holst gave us a touch of the eccentricities of genius. Half way through the work was stopped to rectify an error. While he pondered over the score, the audience buzzed. What was it all about? Who knew? The music finally altered, the piece was started over and successfully concluded.
>
> This sort of thing is not uncommon in musical history. The bigger the musician, the more attention paid to the minutist detail is the rule. Many concerts have likewise been stopped without a break in the musical atmosphere. Beethoven presenting a long program of his works in Vienna one cold day, stopped the orchestra when they erred late in the Fifth Symphony. The house was poorly heated, but in spite of this, the work had to be started all over again. Sokoloff, conductor of the Cleveland Orchestra, often stops concerts to chide offensive members of his audience who cough unseemly or even talk. Indeed, Mrs. William Wheller of the University School of Music stops performances most charming, effecting no break in her work whenever the whims of her caprice so dictate.[27]

> When it comes to modern music, nothing so well conveys its trend as the Chicago Symphony. Everyone must be thoroughly alive in the performance of Holst's music, for the ideas come tumbling over each other. No one is permitted to: orchestra and chorus alternate, and if one misses a cue, the whole thing goes to pieces. There was a time during the concert when Mr. Holst had heed of all his British nerve, for through some misdirection of the people supplying the score, the MS was found to be incorrect. Nothing daunted the composer stopped the performance and proceeded to correct the music after which all went well. It was a typical example of the old country poise.[28]

A Dirge for Two Veterans is scored for male chorus, three cornets and either two tubas or, as an option, trombone and tuba. A trombone was used on this performance, for another source identified the "error" to have been in the that part:

> ....[Holst] made his way to the third trombone desk , had a *sotte voce* but evidently warm argument with the player, produced a telescoping gold pencil, and made some alterations. The work started again and ended in tumultous applause.[29]

Nine long years had passed since Holst had composed the work and this was the first time heard it performed in concert. Perhaps he hadn't anticipated the power of the dissonant effects created by the clash of the vocal parts and the basso ostinato. Following the concert Eric DeLamarter, the Associate Conductor of the Chicago Symphony (who had played organ on the concert) stopped by Holst's dressing room to congratulate him. During their subsequent post-concert walk, Holst confided to DeLamarter that, upon conducting the "corrected" passage for the second time, he had realized that it had been right in the first place![30]

The Fourth May Festival Concert, held the next day was billed as a "Miscellaneous Concert." The Friday evening program featured no fewer than five vocal selections scattered among the orchestral works. During the second half of the concert Holst guest-conducted his *Suite* ["Ballet"] *from the Opera, "The Perfect Fool,"* apparently without incident. The closing of the festival the following day did not feature Holst in a conductor's role, although he was recognized:

> At the end of the final concert Mr. Holst was called to the stage and presented with a music case, the gift of the Choral Union. L. D. Wines made the presentation speech. Mr. Holst, in his reply, declared himself entirely satified with the result of his visit to Ann Arbor, saying that this performance of the "Hymn of Jesus" was, with one exception, the finest of a considerable number which he has heard. Mr. and Mrs. Holst accepted the invitation of friends to remain in Ann Arbor until the first of June.[31]

The festival itself had been deemed an unqualified success. An extensive summary of the event was printed in *The Musical Leader*. Praise was given where praise was due:

> Hill Auditorium housed its customary "five thousand" audience at each of the six concerts and Charles A. Sink, the business manager who is reponsible for the present era of prosperity, has the satisfaction of knowing that notwithstanding a somewhat new regime, the program was perhaps the most successful given.
>
> Since Dean Albert A. Stanley departed for Europe, the management of the festival chorus has been in the hands of Earl V. Moore, whose gifts for attaining effects were well shown in everything the Choral Union offered. It is no easy matter to follow in the steps of a man who had wielded control for twenty-seven years, but Mr. Moore justified the confidence reposed in him by the directors and prepared his forces so that Mr. Stock,

> who conducted the big works, had only to concern himself with final rehearsals.
> ....One of the main features of interest was the appearance of Gustav Holst, the English composer, who came to America on the invitation of the Michigan University School of Music and who has been here some four weeks. He made a definitely agreeable impression both as composer and leader on the several occasions he conducted....[32]

The May Festival having coming to an end, the Holsts were now free to do some sight-seeing, visit family, and to renew some old aquaintences. One old friend who came to Ann Arbor for a visit was William Vowles, who had served with Holst at Salonica and Constantinople in 1918-1919.[33] Vowles was now employed in Chicago at the Church of St. Thomas the Apostle, located near the University of Chicago, in the city's Hyde Park Area. Among other duties there, Vowles was music director and conductor of The Cecilian Opera Club, made up of members from St. Thomas' Church.[34] He responded to an invitation extended to him by Holst:

> Church of St. Thomas the Apostle
> 5472 Kimbark Avenue
> Chicago, Ill.
> May 17, 1923
>
> Dear Friend
>
> I find I can get away Sunday afternoon so I propose to arrive at Ann Arbor at 9:38. I shall put up at the Whitney & you must not change any plans to meet me, but give me some of your time the next morning. I wonder if you could reserve a berth for me on the "Wolverine" for Monday. It might be a little late if I leave it until I come. It is a pity I could not get up for the Festival, but this has been a very full week, & there was no loophole of escape.
>
> Yours ever
> William Vowles
>
> I am sailing on the 'Homeric' May 26th. The 'Zeeland' has been cancelled.[35]

Holst was more than pleased about Vowles' visit and replied:

Dayletter.

William Vowles
5478 Kimbark Ave.
Chicago, Ill.

Will meet you at station Sunday night. Have arranged lower on Wolverine Monday. You will stay at Michigan Union with us.

Gustav Holst[36]

Before departing the University of Michigan, Holst wanted to arrive at some conclusion regarding the proposed professorship. It was an offer to which Holst gave much serious thought. He jotted down some considerations either intended for President Burton or taken from him during a meeting:

Burton
4 points
1) relations to the university
school separate
University professor
2) conductor (chorus)
3) recognized composer (not merely teaching comp)
4) administration[37]

Ultimately Holst decided against accepting the professorship. Ann Arbor was not London. Holst had been settled into a rather cozy working life in the British capitol for the previous two decades, with many close friends and wonderful colleagues at the schools where he taught. He felt comfortable and was satisfied with his working conditions, whether composing in his room at St. Paul's Girls' School, mentoring private students at the Royal College of Music, or facing the arduous task of constantly rebuilding the musical ensembles at Morley College. He also had an established domestic life, with an apartment in London and a country house in Thaxted. His pattern of recreation--London walks, country walks, and times spent at the George--would have had to have been modified. The main factor in Holst's decision, however, was Imogen, who was sixteen at the time and enrolled as a student at St. Paul's Girls' School. Holst did not want to uproot her. When all things were taken into account the decision to reject Michigan's offer was not a difficult one for him to reach.

Upon departing Ann Arbor, the Holsts first set out for Chicago, to visit Holst's younger half-brother Thorley and his family. The two brothers had never been close--there were born fifteen years apart--but that did not prevent them from having a good time. The Holsts then returned to Ann Arbor for two nights before heading back east.[38] They journeyed to the east coast via Detroit, where they visited their friend Eric (Beryl) Clark. In an extensive letter to Vally Lasker, Isobel discussed the May Festival, travel plans, and Detroit:

University of Michigan Union
Ann Arbor
May 21st 1923

Dear Vally

At last I have a moment to write & tell you about the Festival. I have enclosed the press cuttings to Mabel[39] & she will pass them on to you. The critics don't write so well as ours but they were all very much impressed & talked a lot after the concerts about it being "grand stuff" & what America wants & has been waiting for, etc.--"It's been just dandy having you right here with us Mr. Holst--" The extraordinary thing about Americans is that their taste in music is appalling & yet when they get anything like the H of J[40], they go right over at once & just worship it.

Poor Gustav nearly gave up in despair over the Amen Chorus but in the end they sang it beautifully & the performance was the finest I have heard. Stock's orchestra is splendid--with the exception of the double basses who play with the old "grunt" bow & are consequently rather rough & a bit heavy--but the woodwind & brass are perfect. Gustav finished his concerto here--the Librarian gave him a private room in the library to work in and he presented the original score to the University Library. They are fearfully proud of it & have put it in a glass case in the entrance hall with the outside cover with its dedication open & the first pages open also. Several players of Stock's orchestra played it <u>twice</u> beautifully at a Reception at President Burton's house last Thursday.

May 27th

at Beryl Clark's house 760 Webb Avenue Detroit.

You wouldn't believe how difficult it is to get letters written here! The telephone goes all day and someone you to go out or they want to come & see you & there you are--just in the middle of this letter someone rang up & offered to take me on a 40 mile drive & of course I went which was bad for the letter.

We are spending the weekend with the Clark's & then at 5 p.m. on Sunday we take the boat from Detroit to Buffalo & thence on to Niagara Falls--we are 14 hours on the boat & it ought to be a very jolly journey. We shall be two or three days at Niagara Falls. The conductor there gave a Holst Concert there not long ago & he came over to Ann Arbor for the Hymn & asked us to come to Niagara. Then we go on to Toronto in Ontario State & then through Washington to Asheville, North Carolina. After that Gustav wants to get home as soon as possible for the P.F.[41] so we shall try for the first boat from Montreal.

We have a lovely invitation to go to Keene Valley in the Adirondacks for the whole summer, or as long or as short a time as we like, but alas the P.F. will prevent it! Why do things always happen that way? Gustav wants me to stay behind and accept it & they are most pressing but I feel it is my duty to come back even if we are too late for a performance of the P.F. Of course if it should happen that we can't get a boat we shall go to the Adirondacks for a short time while we wait. These people own 4000 acres there, all forest land & a lake & two motor cars & of course we should have a lovely time. The letters & notices of the P.F. have just arrived--it's good that it went so well & I'm hoping to see it.

....Detroit is the great place for making cars & the streets are full of them. The deaths from reckless driving are about 20 per day & endless accidents & there are notices all over the place--They just had "Safety Week"--"Make <u>every</u> week safe," "Save the Babies," etc. Henry Ford has built a special hospital for the people knocked down by his own cars & it is always full. It is getting very hot now & towns are rather trying.

We are trying to get home by the first week in July & I expect we shall soon fix on a boat & then we will let you know. More news later.

Much love

Isobel[42]

The Holsts then traveled on to Niagara Falls, where they visited Frank Austin Lidbury, who made a tremendous positive impression. Lidbury, a native of

Middlesex, England, had lived in the United States since 1903 and had been an American citizen since 1913. During the time of the Holsts' visit he was president and general manager at the Oldbury Electrochemical Company in Niagara Falls, New York and had a high professional profile, having been president of the American Electrochemical Society in 1914.[43] More important to Holst, however, was the fact that Lidbury was an amateur musician, one of the best he had met. Even more important than this, however, was the fact that Lidbury happened to own a pre-Prohibition wine cellar. The country had been dry since 1920 and would still be dry during Holst's 1929 and 1932 American visits. Though never a heavy drinker, Holst did occasionally imbibe and after six weeks in Prohibition Era America, he graciously accepted Lidbury's hospitality. Holst wrote to his friend W. G. Whittaker:

> Lidbury is head of some chemical works at Niagara. His family come from Lancashire and he has kept the real feeling for music. However busy he may be at times he makes time to see musicians and to entertain them. He's the greatest thing in Niagara--the Rapids are second, the power stations third, Lidbury's cellar fourth, the country around fifth and the falls twentieth....
>
> My advice is, don't go out of your way to see [Frederick] Stock or [Cecil] Forsyth unless you've got plenty of time but if you go to Niagara or near it don't miss Lidbury....[44]

Holst later wrote to Lidbury about the fine hospitality he and Isobel had received: "You gave us what we call a 'Royal time.' (I suppose you'd call it a Republican one!)."[45]

Lidbury was also a columnist for the *Niagara Falls Gazette*. He felt sufficiently comfortable with Holst's music to write the following:

> Mendelssohn Choir Festival at Toronto
> Four of Holst's Choral Hymns from the Rig Veda
>
> ....I am acquainted with nearly all he [Holst] has produced for chorus and have no hesitation in saying that he seems to me the most original and interesting writer for chorus of today.[46]

From Niagara Falls, the Holsts continued east. The rather extensive sight-seeing itinerary hinted at in Isobel's letter was entered into one of Holst's notebooks:

from Niagara
first go to Toronto   Trickier?
    1000 islands
    Montreal
from Niagara
Philadelphia
Washington
Asheville
return
Washington
New York[47]

It is unknown to this author whether or not the Holsts were able to do all of this. One determining factor was expense. Holst did receive a $100 loan from the University of Michigan before leaving there; he repaid it immediately upon his return to England.[48] There were also concerns about time and physical stamina. Holst did want to return to London in time to see *The Perfect Fool.* From notebook entries, it appears that the Holsts were in the Niagara area at least from June 8th through the 10th and Holst did write the following characteristic letter to Austin Lidbury only nine days later, while on the return voyage:

On board S. S. Belgenland
June 19, 1923

Dear Lidbury,

Anything that is unnecessary is bad art.

This letter is unnecessary. For it is to introduce Whittaker[49] to you. But you know him already in his music.

Therefore:

a) What could be more unnecessary?
b) What could be worse art?
c) This letter shall be short so as to lessen the amount of bad art in the world.

Nuf ced!
I Mean check!!!

Yours ever,
Gustav Holst[50]

The following relative account appeared in print in 1939, five years after Holst's death. It was a third-hand account, but when one takes into account who the three hands were--Austin Lidbury to Duncan McKenzie (Holst's agent for his 1932 America visit) to Harvey "Feste" Grace (an organist friend of Holst and columnist for *The Musical Times*)--it appears to be quite creditable. McKenzie quoted from Lidbury:

> One wishes that there could have been preserved more of Holst's conversational dicta; his thinking and his expression were as forthright and terse in conversation as in music; and you never knew what he was going to produce, in that mock-solemn quizzical way of his. For example: "When I come across a piece of music for the first time, I ask myself--was it necessary?"
>
> As Lidbury says this is a perfect essay of criticism in three words.[51]

Holst's first visit to America may have concluded, but many new lasting friendships had been established. Among these was that of Earl V. Moore, who wrote to Holst:

> October 19, 1923
>
> Mr. Gustav Holst
> 32 Gunderstone Rd.
> Barons Ct., W14
> London, England
>
> Dear Mr. Holst:
>
> The package of music which you were good enough to forward to me came to hand recently and I want you to know that I appreciate sincerely your efforts to secure the "Sea Drifts" for me. More than that I am glad to have the score of your "Planets Symphony" arranged for four hands.
>
> The season has opened most auspiciously here, the concert series having been completely sold out more than a week before the first concert and the school having a comfortable increase in enrollment. We have not made definite plans for the Festival yet, but I intend to do something more of the B Minor Mass and something of Delius. What do you know of the reception "A Mass of Life" received if it has been performed in London?

We hope you had a pleasant voyage home and that you arrived in time for the final performance of "A Perfect Fool" at Covent Garden.

At this time I cannot say definitely where we will be for the summer or next fall, but we are hoping to be able to pay you a visit during that time if affairs can be arranged here.

Mrs. Moore joins me in greetings to Mrs. Holst and yourself.

Cordially
[Earl V. Moore]
Director

P.S.
Did you get the kodak pictures that Mrs. Moore sent you from Omena?[52]

Two years later Earl Moore went to England to study with Holst.

---

[1]Arthur Bliss, *As I Remember* (London: Faber & Faber, 1970), 65.

[2]Ralph Vaughan Williams.

[3]Personal correspondence, Gustav Holst to Vally Lasker, April, 1923, The Holst Foundation.

[4]Personal correspondence, Gustav Holst to William Gillies Whittaker, June 19 [1923], quoted in Michael Short (ed.), *Gustav Holst: Letters to W. G. Whittaker* (Glasgow: University of Glasgow Press, 1974), 80.

[5]Personal correspondence, Gustav Holst to Earl V. Moore, April 28 [1923], Bentley Historical Library, The University of Michigan.

[6]Personal correspondence, Gustav Holst to William Gillies Whittaker, June 19 [1923], quoted in Michael Short (ed.), *op. cit.*, 79.

[7]*Michigan Daily News*, May 17, 1923.

[8]Gustav Holst, Notebook from 1923, The Holst Foundation.

[3]Telegram, Gustav Holst to Charles A. Sink, June 6, 1923, Bentley Historical Library, The University of Michigan.

[10]*The Musical Times*, LXIV, No. 964 (June 1, 1923), 389-393.

[11]*Ibid.*, 423.

[12]*The Musical Times*, LXV, No. 974 (April 1, 1924), 334.

[13]Personal correspondence, Imogen Holst to Helen Asquith, March 29, 1924, The Holst Foundation.

[14]Program, Thirtieth Annual May Festival of the University of Michigan: First Concert, Wednesday Evening May 16, 1923.

[15]*The Christian Science Monitor*, May 26, 1923.

[16]Mabel Rodwell Jones and Imogen Claire Holst.

[17]Gustav Holst, *A Fugal Concerto*, Op. 40 No. 2, autograph score, University of Michigan.

[18]Imogen Holst (ed.) and Colin Matthews (ed.): *Gustav Holst: Collected Facsimile Edition of Autograph Manuscripts of the Published Works: Volume II: Works for Small Orchestra* (London:Faber Music Ltd., 1977), 89. Robert Murchie and Leon Goosens also performed *A Fugal*

Concerto on December 19, 1929 as the opening selection on an otherwise all-choral concert given by The Harold Brooke Choir.

[19]'Feste' [Harvey Grace], "Ad Libitum" in *The Musical Times*, LXXX, No. 3 (March, 1939), 182.

[20]Telegram, Warren Mason to Gustav Holst, May 17, 1923, Bentley Historical Library, The University of Michigan.

[21]Telegram, W. F. Bullock to Gustav Holst, May 17, 1923, Bentley Historical Library, The University of Michigan.

[22]Undated non-manuscript piece of written correspondence from Gustav Holst, for response telegrams to Warren Mason and W. F. Bullock, Bentley Historical Library, The University of Michigan.

[23]Personal correspondence, Sion M. Honea, Special Collections Librarian and Archivist, Sibley Music Library, Eastman School of Music to the author, October 29, 1996.

[24]*The Daily Telegraph,* May 19 [1923].

[25]Personal correspondence, Gustav Holst to Charles A. Sink, April 6, 1923, Bentley Historical Library, The University of Michigan.

[26]*Ibid.*

[27]*Michigan Daily* (Ann Arbor), "Festival Upholds Renown in Music," May 27, 1923.

[28]*The Musical Leader (Chicago)*, May 24, 1923.

[29]Michael Short, *Gustav Holst: The Man and His Music* (Oxford: Oxford University Press,1990), 209.

[30]'Feste' [Harvey Grace], *op. cit.*.

[31]*Musical America*, June 2, 1923.

[32]*The Musical Leader (Chicago)*, May 24, 1923.

[33]For a rather humorous account of Vowles' YMCA work with Holst see William Vowles, "Gustav Holst with the Army: Salonica and Constantinople, 1919," *The Musical Times*, LXXV, No. 1 (September, 1934), 795.

[34]Personal correspondence, Theresa McDermott, of St. Thomas the Apostle Catholic Church, to the author, July 29, 1999.

[35]Personal correspondence, William Vowles to Gustav Holst, May 17, 1923, Bentley Historical Library, The University of Michigan.

[36]Personal correspondence, Gustav Holst to William Vowles, undated, Bentley Historical Library, The University of Michigan.

[37]Gustav Holst, Notebook from 1923, The Holst Foundation.

[38]Telegram, Gustav Holst to Charles A. Sink, June 6, 1923, Bentley Historical Library, The University of Michigan.

[39]Mabel Rodwell Jones.

[40]*The Hymn of Jesus,* Op. 37 [H140].

[41]*The Perfect Fool*, Op. 39 [H150].

[42]Personel correspondence, Isobel Holst to Vally Lasker, May 21 and May 27, 1923, The Holst Foundation.

[43]*Who Was Who in America, 1974-1974* (Kingsport, TN: Kingsport Press, 1976), 247.

[44]Personal correspondence, Gustav Holst to William Gillies Whittaker, June 19 [1923], quoted in Michael Short (ed.) *op. cit.*, 79.

[45]Gustav Holst quoted in Imogen Holst, *Gustav Holst: A Biography, 2nd ed.* (Oxford: Oxford University Press, 1969), 87.

[46]"Musical Comment" by F. Austin Lidbury in *Niagara Falls (NY) Gazette*, n.d. [1923].

[47]Gustav Holst, Notebook from 1923, The Holst Foundation.

[48]Business correspondence, Manager, London County Westminster & Paris Bank Limited to

Charles Sink, 25th June 1923, Bentley Historical Library, the University of Michigan.
[49]William Gillies Whittaker.
[50]Personal correspondence, Gustav Holst to Austin Lidbury, June 19, 1923 quoted in Imogen Holst, *Gustav Holst: A Biography*, p. 88.
[51]'Feste' [Harvey Grace], *op. cit.*.
[52]Personal correspondence, Earl V. Moore to Gustav Holst, October 19, 1923, Bentley Historical Society, The University of Michigan.

CHAPTER XV

RECORDINGS, FIRST CHORAL SYMPHONY, AT THE BOAR'S HEAD, MUSIC FOR AMATEURS

Holst and his wife had returned home from their first American visit by June 28, 1923, in time to see Percy Pitt conduct a double billing of two of his operas at the Royal Opera House, Covent Garden. *The Perfect Fool* was served reasonably well by the theatre's size and acoustics though *Savitri*, conceived on a much smaller scale, was not. In spite of the inherent problems in the production of these two operas back-to-back, they continued to be double billed by the British National Opera Company throughout the1923 autumn touring season. Regardless of the awkward coupling, Holst was appreciative of the fact that his operas were being performed and expressed his thanks to all concerned.

Holst also found that in his absence another one of his works, the *First Suite in E Flat for Military Band*, had been recorded, released, and subequently reviewed in *The Musical Times*:

> ....His [*First*] *Suite in E Flat,* for military band, played by the Grenadier Guards under Lieut. G. Miller, has been recorded by the Columbia Company on two 10-inch double-sided disks--the *Chaconne* and *Intermezzo* on one, the *March* on the other, the remaining side of the latter being filled by Schubert's *March Militaire*. I always felt the Schubert piece was poor; heard after the Holst March it seems tamer than ever. There is a fine, broad folk-songy tune for the second subject in Holst's march, and we get a real thrill when it is used as a bass to the jolly opening theme. The Suite is a most stimulating affair. We need more works of this kind. They will soon deal a lusty smack at the desolating

> operatic fantasias with which our military bands have hitherto defrauded the musical public.[1]

Holst had his own recording project to finish--*The Planets*--but that would have to wait until after he and his family took some time for themselves.

The Holsts spent much of the summer of 1923 at Paycocke's, a sizeable two-story half-timbered house of five bays built in the late fifteenth century. Located on West Street in Coggeshall, Essex, the house was built by John Paycocke and passed through descendency to the Buxton family sometime in the seventeenth century. From 1904 to 1910 Noel Buxton, a cousin to Thaxted's vicar Conrad Noel, restored the house. In 1924, the year in which Buxton became Minister of Agriculture and the year following the Holsts' stay, the house was presented to the National Trust. Imogen Holst, an impressionable sixteen year-old in 1923, drew some watercolors of the house and commented about it in a letter to her school friend Helen Asquith:

> ....This house is absolutely too wonderful for words. I believe I told you something about it, didn't I, during a drawing lesson one day? Well, it is a dream. And it is great fun living in a dream....
>
> Apart from the historic interest of the house, it really is most extraordinarily beautiful. Gussie and I have been having long arguments as to whether it is more beautiful than the Manor House at Mells [Somerset]. Gussie is in favor of Mells, but I have my doubts..though of course the styles are so utterly different that one cannot possibly compare them. The house is supposed to be the best example of the period in the whole of England, and artists and architects make pilgrimages from all over the country to see it. We are tremendously proud of it, and as it isn't our own we can swank about it to our hearts' content.[2]

Later that summer Holst completed recording *The Planets* in its entirety for Columbia records. *The Daily Mail* called it "a capital stroke of enterprise by the Columbia Company."[3] The orchestra involved was the London Symphony and Holst conducted the work himself. He had already recorded "Jupiter" with them the previous September; it was released in March, 1923 as a prelude to the entire set.[4] Holst had a number of legal concerns and entered them into him notebook:

> Columbia X
> exclusive service as conductor
> of my works [crossed out] for mechanical reprod.

exclusive rights of reproductions
of MS works

notify publishers not to loan MS parts for mech reproduction or give anyone except Columbia the right to orchestrate part and score for mechan reproduction.
contract for 5 years
they guarantee minimum 3 sessions a year at £30 each (extras at same rate)
give me £100 for signing

X Col: is to have exclusive right of making orchestrations or right of using orchestrations exclusively for mechan reprod of all works not pub or if pub, no orch are printed[5]

If his notes are any indication, then the contract that Holst had with Columbia was quite beneficial. Over the next two years he also recorded the *Beni Mora Suite*, *St. Paul's Suite*, and *Two Songs without Words* for them These were acoustical recordings, generally made with reduced and/or modified orchestral forces. Due to the severe limitations inherent in the process some of the orchestrations were changed (for example tubas added to or even replacing string basses) in order to strengthen the recording.

Holst's 1923 recording of *The Planets*, at forty-three and one-half minutes is faster than what one might expect.[6] There are both aesthetic and technical reasons for this. Firstly, Holst himself had a light yet direct approach to conducting. His recordings of both "Mars" (6'05")[7] and "Jupiter" (7') are very fast. Secondly, the twelve-inch 78 r.p.m. record (the only disk available until about 1947) has a maximum of about four minutes of recording time per side. Columbia wanted get the most efficiency out of the number of disks used, hence seven disks were allotted for the set; a total of thirteen sides were used for *The Planets*; the fourteenth side was filled by "Country Song" from *Two Songs without Words.* This meant that six of the seven movements had to fit onto two sides and one movement onto one. Thus "Venus" (8'10") had to be hurried slightly in order to fit onto two sides and "Mercury" (3'35") had to be hurried to fit onto one.

By 1926 electronic recording had become a reality and Holst jumped at the chance to rerecord *The Planets*. The "Marching Song" from *Two Songs without Words* filled the fourteenth side this time. Conditions for recording had greatly improved and both works were recorded with the original instrumentation intact. While there is better definition in sound, this recording of *The Planets* still cannot be considered an "urtext" recording. The timing limitations of the 78 r.p.m. record were still there in addition to the fact that there now was generally more distortion in the grooves toward the center of the record than at the outside. This may account for Holst taking an even faster tempo for "Venus" (7'20") than in 1923. In a letter to Adrian Boult, who conducted the premiere of *The Planets* in 1918, Imogen Holst comments about this recording:

9 Church Walk
Aldeburgh, Suffolk
IP 15 5DU
February 1, 1973

Dear Adrian,

Do PLEASE forgive me for my long delay in replying to your letter. And thank you for having written

I think the chief 'revelation' in the tempi of G's recording of the Planets was the flow and continuity, most of the way through most of the movements, without any of the 'holding back' to make a point before big moments which some other conductor (NOT you!) have indulged in during the last thirty years, and which have made unwanted 'joins' in the music.

The speed of the opening of Venus was a reminder that his written 'Adagio' could often be an 'Adagio quasi Andante' in his own mind.

I find the speed of Mars as I can remember him doing it in the Queen's Hall--BUT This is only my memory of it! I remember watching him practise conducting this when I looked through the glass door of his sound-proof room at St. Paul's, & I remember thinking 'If he does it any quicker, the crotchet will be too quick to walk to! But here again is only my memory of it.

I think there is no doubt whatsoever that the extreme discomfort of the recording conditions and the agony of having to go on (because they weren't allowed to stop) must have distracted him on many occasions. My chief disappointments are Mercury and Neptune. I think Uranus is superb. And the legato continuity of the low lying flutes in the slow march in Saturn is very impressive.

I think it would be quite wrong for anyone to think of this recording as 'authentic.': he himself learnt a lot about conducting it as the years went by, and the way he did it for instance at the Cheltenham 'Holst' festival in the late 20's was already different in several ways from this recording. And I think had he lived as long as Ralph lived,[8] he probably would have made further changes in the way he conducted it. And I think it would have be a great mistake for conductors to imitate what he does in this 1926 recording. But I still find the recording a revelation--as it gives such a clear impression of what the composer was doing with the work at that particular moment in history.

Once more, my very real regrets for having kept you waiting for a reply to your letter.

With love to you both and every possible fond wish, from

Imogen[9]

Another event involving *The Planets* during the summer of 1923 was the military band concert held on July 4th on the grounds of the Royal Military School of Music at Kneller Hall. The military band concert held at Royal Albert Hall during the previous year had been an unqualified success and within four months a project was in the works to have some of *The Planets* movements transcribed for military band. Holst's notebook entries from this period read "Atkins' scoring of Planets" and, a few lines later, "Cadet Smith."[10] Whether the transcriptons were instigated by Hector E. Adkins, Director of Music at Kneller Hall, by Holst himself, or by someone else is unknown. What is known is that no fewer than four movements were transcribed at this time. Three of them, "Mars," "Venus" and "Jupiter," were transcribed by George Smith and the other, "Mercury," was done by Louis Pay. "Jupiter" was not performed at the July 4th concert, possibly due to time limitations, but turned up in Kneller Hall programming that autumn. All four of the military band manuscript full scores bear no markings or corrections in Holst's hand and it is unknown whether or not the composer had any input into the process beyond the initial discussions.[11]

The programming for this concert is of considerable interest. In addition to the movements from *The Planets*, it featured some guest conducting by Royal College of Music director Hugh Allen as well as the premiere of Ralph Vaughan Williams' *Folk Song Suite*, his first work for military band:

Wednesday, July 4th, 1923

1. Quick March — Pendower — Student G. Perdue
conducted by the composer

2. Three movements from "The Planets" Holst
(a) Mars (b) Venus (c) Mercury
First performance by Military Band
conductor--Student L. Pay L.R.A.M., A.R.C.M.

3. Toccata and Fugue in C Major Bach
conductor Sir H. P. Allen M.A., Mus. Doc.
Director, Royal College of Music

4. Prelude Beatrice Harrison
Conductor--Student J. R. Bell A.R.C.M.

5. Suite[12] R. Vaughan Williams
I. Seventeen Come Sunday II. Sea Songs
III. My Bonnie Boy IV. Folk Songs from Somerset

First Performance
Conductor--Student B. Gubbings

6. Overture Othello Harrison
First Performance
Condcutor--Student A. Stringer A.R.C.M.

"Rule Britannia"
"God Save the King"[13]

The concert was favorably covered in the press:

> To sit under the spreading chestnuts in perfect July weather and to listen to a military band some 150 strong, playing Bach, Holst, and Vaughan Williams--that was the pleasant experience of those who attended the usual Wednesday concert at Kneller Hall yesterday afternoon. The word "Usual" sounds rather out of place in such a connection and, though the Royal Military School of Music is very much alive, the programme yesterday was certainly of exceptional interest. Five of the six works performed were given for the first time. These included arrangements of Holst's "Planets"--the Mars, Venus, and Mercury movements--of Bach's Toccata and Fugue in C major, and a new Vaughan Williams suite, specially written for a military band. The last is a

> beautifully scored work in four movements, written round folk and other song tunes, equally pleasing the connoisseur and the elderly lady, who does not allow music to interfere with her knitting. So, too, the Bach, though the Fugue hardly transcribes as well as the Toccata, where all sections of the wood-wind charmed and delighted us--altogether it was a very skillful piece of playing. "The Planets" is a tougher proposition. One felt here in the "Mars" movement that without the strings the sharp angular rhythms tended to become blurred, and in the "Mercury" the clarinets and flutes had almost too much to do. But it was interesting for all that, and the courage of the Kneller Hall band is an example for all others.[14]

The "Planets" movements and Vaughan Williams' *Folk Song Suite* were performed several times that summer and autumn. Boosey and Hawkes, seizing upon the opportunity, published Smith's transcriptions of "Mars" and "Jupiter" immediately. The transcriptions of "Venus" and "Mercury," however, remain in manuscript.

It wasn't long before Holst started to think about the autumn terms at St. Paul's Girls' School and Morley College. Reinvigorated by recent events, he planned some ambitious programming:

Autumn term
SPGS orch Elgar Pomp no II
Bach Wachet auf[15]
Br Haydn Var?[16] Symph Haydn
sing Sleepers Wake

Morley
Xmas Orat[17]
Beethoven PF con C minor[18]
Haydn Oxford Sym [crossed out]
or Mozart Don Giovanni[19]
Borodin Pr Igor

Xmas Orat
Weelkes Gloria [crossed out]
Palestr?

Xmas Or	60
Concerto	30

Mozart	5
Borodin	15
Palestr	10
	120[20]

Indeed a Bach Cantata was performed at St. Paul's Girls' School at the end of the fall semester. The December 17th concert was covered in *The Morning Post*:

> ....When the enlightened teacher has a free hand seeming miracle are performed. A boy's school does Bach's B minor Mass. Now it is a girl's school--St. Paul's at Hammersmith, where Mr. Gustav Holst is in charge--that had challenged choral societies on their own ground, and given a Bach Cantata without any assistance from outside except for a few fathers, willing conscripts, no doubt, who sang bass. Apart from this family help, it was the whole school and nothing but the school that performed Bach's "Sleepers, wake" yesterday afternoon. The very orchestra was home-grown, even to the horn players,[21] with their specially-written part, and the girl oboist, who played an obbligato. Girls, being much the same everywhere, there is no reason why St. Paul's should take an isolated lead in such matters as this. It only needs a few more Mr. Holsts.[22]

The Daily Telegraph had much the same to say for the cantata, but offered more information:

> Before the cantata an old Latin carol was sung; this had been arranged for voices and orchestra by one of the girls; it revealed a knowledge of both theory and practice far beyond reasonable expectations.
>
> After being in the presence of so much fair promise there could be grounds for nothing but high hope. One hardly knows whether to write "Happy St. Paul's" or "Happy Mr. Holst!"[23]

Earlier in the fall Jane Joseph composed a short unaccompanied non-metrical choral piece for Holst's forty-ninth birthday. It bears the following inscription:

Ad Festa Natalicia
Gustavi Holstii
A.D. 1923

The words indicate that it also served as a homecoming gift:

Slogan No. 2 J.M.J.

> Sing ye all!
> Your voices raised in greeting to him, who ruleth our song,
> With wise and kindly sceptre.
> He travelled far into the West,
> (Raise your voices)
> Bringing the blessing of joyous song to a waiting nation
> And, on this day of days,
> We bless his return. Hail![24]

The autumn of 1923 was the busiest time of Holst's career. In addition to St. Paul's Girls' School and Morley College, he retained his positions at the Royal College of Music and University College, Reading and still had some lecturing duties at the James Allen's Girls' School. His fame continued to grow as his own works were being performed not only all over England, but throughout the world. Yet it was not just Holst's works that represented England on the international level. Maurice Ravel commented to the press:

> ....in England you are developing a school of your own in a way that has not been done since Purcell. Elgar is international. Bax, Holst, Lord Berners, Arthurs Bliss and Vaughan Williams--particularly Williams--are all doing individual and different work, but they are helping to create a definite English style, assisted, no doubt, by the French, Russian, and Italian influences.[25]

Unlike Ravel, Holst tried to stay away from the press. His evasive tactics soon became well-known, as detailed in "A short, sharp 'interview,'" which appeared in *Era*:

> Mr. Gustav Holst is among the most retiring of musicians. He evades advertisement. When he has cause to suspect that a representative of the press is waiting on the front steps of the Royal College of Music--where he teaches--he escapes out of the back.[26]

The reporter continued about his frustrations in trying to find out information with regard to the British National Opera Company's production of *The Perfect Fool.*

He finally reached Holst on the telephone:

"I am going away."
"To Bournemouth, for the Festival?"
"Oh, dear no! I can't conduct!"

That was it.

Holst himself was involved in a number of guest-conducting engagements that autumn, including the British premieres of *A Fugal Overture* and *A Fugal Concerto* on October 11th. In addition to these performances, he conducted the New Queens Hall Orchestra in a complete performance of *The Planets* on a Promenade Concert October 13th. It was the first time that Holst had conducted *The Planets* in its entirety.

Holst sought what little respite he could. While preparing the *Oriental Suite: Beni Mora* and the "Ballet Music" from *The Perfect Fool* for the Margate Festival in mid-September, he spent some relaxing moments on the seashore at Deal. One of the people he came into contact with was ballerina Lydia Lopokova, who a few years later would be instrumental in the founding of the Camargo Society. She wrote to her husband economist John Maynard Keynes:

41 Gordon Square
Sunday,16th September
1923

....Deal, that is the spot in Kent....Another guest Holst (famous English composer) charming man gave me suggestions how I should diminish the expenses with a small orchestra. I promised (I do it so often) to hear his Planets at Queen's Hall 13th Oct. With Mrs. Johnston we discussed sex. She is studying psychologie [sic], she is much more serious than I, and it is intellect don't you think?[27]

She continues in another letter:

41 Gordon Square
Saturday, 13th October, 1923

I have had so many occupations. I remembered Holst's Planets, telephone to Mrs. Johnstone, take off my dancing pyjamas, fly into a taxi to the Savoy Grill, lunch with oysters, 1 hour later I behold that great

> Victorian veneration Sir Henry Wood. As for Planets I may use the same words of Segonzac, when he looked at some pictures, "Tres puissent."[28] Now many peoples love music, curious, it is better than eating bananas, probably they do both. Holst was sorry as he could not undertake, and I did not ask about Purcell; it was not the moment. I met his wife, a handsome woman with a good country complexion; she is usually chosen as a Madonna in spiritual plays....
>
> With a sad kiss.
> L.[29]

The following, also from the pen of Lydia Lopokova, probably refers to some projected ballet setting to Holst's music:

> ....another incident is that Vera[30] knows very well. Mr. Bernard and he told about Holst (also he is her supposed conductor) and me, so she is in the course of affairs. How curious, indeed....[31]

Creativity begat more creativity. In this midst of this flurry of activities Holst continued the work that he had begun earlier on his *First Choral Symphony*, Op. 41[H155],[32] a massive work for soprano soloist, mixed chorus, and orchestra. Holst chose his text from various unrelated poems by John Keats. Holst often referred to this symphony as his "Keats Symphony," or by the abbreviation "KS." The symphony contains four movements plus an introduction:

Prelude: Invocation to Pan
I. Song and Bacchanal
II. Ode on a Grecian Urn
III. Scherzo: Fancy and Folly's Song
IV. Finale: "Spirit here that reignest"

Holst had begun work on the symphony at Paycocke's in August. Imogen Holst commented:

> ....Life is very pleasing just at present, we are having a heavenly time doing absolutely nothing. I say "we," but that is not exactly true: as a matter of fact, Gussie is awfully busy writing a Choral Symphony. And, what do you think? he is setting it to Keats![33]

By September 1st Holst had determined the overall layout of the movements. He sent some preliminary materials and the accompanying letter to Vally Lasker:

Sep[tember] 1[, 1923]

Dear Vally

These are just sketches for some of the choral writing in 'Fancy'--the scherzo of the Keats Symphony.

I is hard but possible

II and IV form the problem. As far as I can see they are quite unsingable so probably the orchestra will do most of the work--glockenspiel, piccolo, etc.--while the voices do something like II.

I had thought of making some picked Morleyites and Paulinas sing parts of 'Fancy' to me. Possibly we will do so later. But meanwhile I cannot resist 'trying it on the dog.'

So when you've nothing better to do start at the beginning and see how far you can get. II and III should sound alike to a listener. III is impossible so don't worry about him.

Have a good time. I think you will because you've got such a sensible (absence of) program.

I am open to receive picture postcards, snapshots and even letters.

Nuf Ced

Gustav[34]

He had sketched the entire work by early winter but, being dissatisfied with his efforts, rewrote much of it the following spring. In spite of these difficulties, Holst was still able to have some fun with some of the materials and the following February gave Vally Lasker an interesting birthday present:

For Vally Lasker
and the School Organ
(when the girls have gone home!)

A Fugal Song without Words, Melody, Voice part, End,
Concord or Appropriate Expression
of Birthday Feeling

The appropriate Expression of Birthday Feeling to be supplied by the kind imagination of the player
The voice part to be supplied by the collaboration of John Keats and the High Mistress of a 'girl's school at St. Paul's'!

The End to be supplied by the composer if he does not tear up the thing first.[35]

Holst's attempts at humor didn't stop there. He had always respected the works of composers such as Stravinsky or Schoenberg who were on the cutting edge, yet this didn't mean that he couldn't poke fun at the "Modern Idiom." In the same collection of manuscripts he provided the following title page:

Unvocal Duets
in the
Modern Idiom

Dedicated to Nora Day, Vally Lasker, and the New Forest

Motto Modern Music is neither
a) Modern
nor
b) Music

This copy is that of Vally Lasker.

On the accompanying envelope Holst wrote:

The Contents of the Package must not be
exposed to the Proximity of Human Beings,
Dogs, Cows, Cathedrals, Pleasant Sunday
Afternoons or Persons or Institutions
likely to suffer from contact with the
Modern Idiom[36]

On December 19th, Ralph Vaughan Williams conducted the London Bach Choir in Holst's *Short Festival Te Deum* and the London premiere of *Ode to Death* at Queen's Hall. Vaughan Williams had been a member of the choir since

1903 and had succeeded Hugh Allen as conductor of the ensemble in 1920. Holst was ecstatic:

Dear R

I've nothing more to say so I will merely give you the recapitulation section in close stretto.

1) It's what I've been waiting for in 47 1/2 years

2) The performance was so full of you--even apart from the places I cribbed from you years ago.

3) Are you willing to sign a contract to conduct every first performance I get during the next ten years or so?

4) You are teaching those people to sing!

5) Please accept my Blessing

Y

G[37]

By the Christmas holidays, Holst was physically and mentally exhausted from all of the activity. He wrote to William Gillies Whittaker from St. Paul's Girls' School on December 23rd, "What a term it's been! I've had 5 shows at QH,[38] a lot of teaching at the RCM and huge classes here, Dulwich,[39] and Morley."[40] Just when there appeared to be no way out of his predicament, help came in the form of a £1500 gift from Claude Johnson, a director at Rolls Royce. Johnson originally intended to cover the expenses of a Holst festival, but since the composer's works were then being programmed with great frequency, the money was given directly to Holst. The composer could now take life easy. By January Holst was spending the bulk of his time at home in Thaxted, having reduced his teaching load so as to go into London only one day per week. He had previously reduced his teaching duties at Morley College and H. Balfour Gardiner took over for him (initially for a period of fourteen days) at University College, Reading and at the Royal Conservatory of Music.[41] Holst still was able to do some guest conducting and lecturing until late February, when further deterioration of his health forced him to cancel all such activities, including an engagement to conduct *The Cloud Messenger* in Newcastle. He wrote to Whittaker:

32 Gunterstone Road

Barons Court, W. 14
Thursday [February, 1924]

Dear Will,

This is a horrible blow. My head got queer on Monday and worse on Tuesday. In order to get fit for tomorrow I sent a deputy to the RCM yesterday and spent most of the day dozing by the fire and lying in bed. But it was of no use and I realise now that my presence in Newcastle would be a greater disappointment than my absence. Also I should be fit for nothing for the following week at least. Not that it matters for it may happen anyhow. But I daren't run any more risks over this silly business.

What I feel most is not hearing the CM.[42] I had looked forward to it so much and you have done so much for the work that I look on it as your property.

And I do hate letting you down like this after all you've done and been to me. I'm going to indulge in Silence, Solitude and Heat (not mere warmth) and in my waking intervals I shall think of my three dear good people Will, Vally, and Nora having a good time together.

Yrs ever,

Gustav[43]

Holst was ordered by his doctor to cease all activity for the remainder of the calendar year. This meant giving up all of his teaching, at least for the time being. Holst retained his post (and his sound-proof music room) at St. Paul's Girls' School; teaching there had become a part of him and he and everybody else knew that he would return. His college positions, however, had to be sacrificed. Benjamin Dale succeeded Holst at permanently at Reading and Balfour Gardiner stayed on at the Royal College of Music. Coincidentally, at about this same time and much to his disapproval, Holst was elected to the Fellowship of the Royal College of Music. These two positions--Reading and RCM--were not difficult to abdicate; Holst had been on the faculty at each of these institutions for less than five years. The really difficult position for him to relinquish was Morley College. Holst loved Morley; over the past seventeen years he had nurtured and developed that program. It had been the evening counterpart to St. Paul's Girls' School. Holst was succeeded at Morley at the end of the 1924 summer session by Arnold Goldsborough, organist at St. Martin-in-the-Fields, who was in turn succeeded by

Arnold Foster in 1928.

Without the income provided from these teaching positions, 1924 would have been financially disastrous had it not been for Claude Johnson's gift as well as a weekly supplement in the amount of £8 that was placed into Holst's accounts by Balfour Gardiner.[44] It was neither the first time nor the last that Holst had benefitted from Gardiner's generosity. In addition to these sources of income, Holst was collecting royalties from some of his published works as well as from his recent recording of *The Planets*.

For the next six months Holst led the life of a recluse, venturing out of Thaxted only on rare occasions. He was assisted back to health by Isobel, of course, and by Hubert Adams, a valet who served Holst for four and a half years. Afterwards, Adams worked for Balfour Gardiner.[45] Sixteen year-old Imogen Holst commented about her father's illness to her friend Helen Asquith:

> ....Gussie's illness is really a very great trial to his family; we get hundreds of letters every day from adoring females (strangers, fo course) asking how he is and sympathizing and hoping it won't affect his genius in any way. Poor Gussie, if he saw half his correspondence it would affect his genius in a great many ways!
> ....Gussie won't let us come anywhere <u>near</u> him at Thaxted, so I expect we shall spend the hols in London....[46]

The cessation of teaching and concertizing activities during this period of convalescence were not without benefits; in addition to some smaller pieces Holst wrote two major works. He completed the initial full score draft to the *First Choral Symphony* and sent it to Jane Joseph in time for her birthday on May 31. He was also able to sketch most of his new opera, *At the Boar's Head*, Op. 42 [H156]. For this sixty-minute "musical interlude in one act," Holst had a librettist with a definite command of the English language: William Shakespeare. The opera itself was based upon a number of scenes from *Henry IV* set at The Boar's Head tavern and centering around the character Falstaff. Holst assumed the role of compiler as well as that of composer; with the exception of three of his own tunes, Holst borrowed "Old English Melodies" from a variety of sources and set Shakespeare's words to them.

By August Holst had regained enough of his strength that he was able to record *St. Paul's Suite* and "Country Song" from *Two Songs without Words* for Columbia, although he did not feel strong enough to resume his duties at St. Paul's until January. In the meantime Jane Joseph had been secretly soliciting subscribers to a fiftieth birthday present for Holst. The gift would be in the form of a check accompanied by the signatures of the subscribers and was intended to allow the composer to take a holiday abroad. Everybody wanted to be a part of this, from professional conductors to students. Before she was finished, Jane had collected a total of £350 from 160 subscribers[47]; the listing of signatures reads like a "Who's Who" of Holst's life to that point. The money, which provided Holst with more than enough funding to take a trip to Switzerland and Germany during the following summer, was not nearly as important to Holst as the support of his friends. One month after receiving this gift Holst benefitted from another entirely unexpected source. For his achievement in the arts Yale University awarded him the Henry Elias Howland Memorial Prize and sent him a check for $1350. Holst appeared to be set financially for the remainder of the year.

Upon his return to public life, Holst's appearance had changed slightly; his hair had turned white (which was at least partially attestable to the Thaxted garden sun) and he had gained weight. Nonetheless, he was healthy and able to become involved in various projects. True, his teaching load had been reduced to only St. Paul's, but he was still in demand as a speaker. Holst was in Liverpool in October, 1925 to deliver the first of his seven James W. Alsop lectures at the university there. He spoke on a variety of topics, from "England and her music" to his own experiences as a trombonist. "England and Her Music" was a very important lecture to Holst; he repeated it on numerous occasions on both sides of the Atlantic. He spoke about this topic from the defensive:

> He [Holst] said that about seven years ago a Frenchman said, "Englishmen, being clear-headed and practical, have at last discovered that they have no music in them." That was a slight to English music, and he (Mr. Holst) had not got over it yet. A statement by a French artist, however, that "the English like music but they can do without it" was about the best thing that had been said about English music....it was true to say that 50 years after the death of nearly every great English composer English music was just as if it had never existed....From 1700 until a few years ago was a dark period in English music, and it was possible to be an English gentleman without being musical....[48]

From this point Holst's speech incorporated several highlights in the history of English music, including "Sumer is i cumen in," contributions of Dunstable, the Tudor period, the Puritans, "worship of foreign names" during Victorian times, through topics of the present [1926]. From an early 21st century viewpoint, some of this speech appears to be somewhat chauvinistic, yet Holst's sincerity in calling attention to the contributions of English composers cannot be denied.

The Alsop lectures were very well received and after the series had concluded, the following letter appeared in the Liverpool Daily Courier:

> Sir,
>
> During the past few weeks we have had Mr. Gustav Holst in Liverpool. We realise that with him we are in the forefront of a great onward movement that in the future lie undreamt of possibilities of English music.
>
> Would it not be fitting that the council of the University, with the help of the citizens of Liverpool, and the inhabitants of the surrounding districts should consider the desirability of founding a chair of music in the university to be occupied by Mr. Holst (if he could be prevailed upon to take it), and, subsequently, establishing a Faculty of Music in the University?[49]

This did not happen in Liverpool at that time, but Holst was invited to Glasgow to give the Cramb lecture series immediately thereafter. For this concentrated group of lectures (ten in four weeks) Holst's focus was on the orchestra. It had been over twenty years since he had played second trombone in the Scottish Orchestra, yet Holst was more than happy to serve as a cheerleader for the organization. The aim of his January 15, 1926 lecture was "to try to foster and increase the enjoyment which the audience might have in listening to an orchestra."[50] For the remaining lectures Holst spoke primarily about specific orchestral works. In addition to garnering support for the Scottish Orchestra, Holst's lectures served another purpose: within three years a Music Department was established at the University of Glasgow, with William Gillies Whittaker appointed its first Gardiner Professor of Music.[51]

With regard to his own compositions, Holst was able to attend the touring British National Opera Company's series of rehearsals for *At the Boar's Head* in the early spring of 1925.. Malcolm Sargent conducted the premiere of the work on April 3, 1925 in Manchester. Coupled with *At the Boar's Head* was Puccini's forty-five minute comedy *Gianni Schicchi*, an exemplar of tension and release. Unfortunately this pairing did nothing to endear Holst's opera to either the listeners or the critics. Audiences found Holst's melding of Shakespeare's words with folk tunes to be ingenious but difficult to follow, and the general absence of dramatic continuity contributed to its lack of success. Although published by Novello in 1925, *At the Boars' Head*, according to Michael Short, has rarely been performed since the 1925-26 season.

The *First Choral Symphony* hardly fared better, although its publication was highly anticipated. Novello's ran an advertisement in the November, 1925 issue of *The Musical Times*, calling for subscriptions for folio-sized copies of the full score; it was subsequently published in that format the following year. The work was premiered on October 7, 1925 at the Leeds Triennial Festival. Albert Coates conducted the Leeds Festival Chorus and the London Symphony Orchestra in that performance; Dorothy Silk was the featured soprano soloist. Reaction to the Leeds performance was favorable but at the second performance, given in tandem with Beethoven's *Ninth Symphony* on October 29th at Queen's Hall in London by the same personnel, the work fared poorly both in the performance and in the reaction accorded it by the press. Sometime after the initial press reaction Harvey Grace had the following to say about the chorus in *The Musical Times*:

> ....it is only fair to Holst that those who were disappointed with his 'Choral Symphony' at Queen's Hall should realise that the performance did the work a great deal less than justice....I have so often groused at certain defects in Yorkshire choralism that I am glad to bring forward some support for views that may have regarded as prejudiced or faddish. My conscience is clear on both points. After reading the glowing reports of the choral work at the Leeds Festival I went to Queen's Hall prepared to be enthusiastic. Instead I was disappointed. I heard a magnificent lot of voices, but a choir with curious limitations and lacking in vision and subtlety. I don't know any choir that could so brilliantly meet the demands of the Ninth Symphony; but I know several in various parts of the country that could show more musicianship, alertness, and appeal. The fact is, either choir or the conductor, or both, took the task too lightly. The singers left Leeds before eight in the morning, and most of them must have risen before any but the most foolish and restless of larks (The Huddersfield contingent, I understand, left before 5 a.m.!). They reached London at 1:30, rehearsed the Ninth Symphony, but not Holst--at all events, only a bit of it, and that without orchestra; went straight off and spent the interval till tea-time making gramophone records ; took tea, and went to Queen's Hall to dress for the concert. This is not the way to ensure a first-rate performance of a new and exacting work. The Holst Symphony ought to have been rehearsed thoroughly. A performance, however good at Leeds some weeks earlier, was no guarantee of similar success at Queen's Hall, especially after the fatigues of the journey, and in a hall that was unfamiliar to many of the singers. Despite eulogies in the press, no one who heard the subsequent discussions of the performance

can avoid the conclusion that the prestige of Yorkshire singing had suffered a nasty jar. However good the choir may have been at the Leeds festival (and with such splendid material it might have been superlative), it was nothing to write home about at Queen's Hall....[52]

Imogen Holst identified this Queen's Hall performance as the turning point when Holst's popularity started to wane.[53] Expecting a more universally appealing work like *The Planets* or even *The Hymn of Jesus* and then not getting it, most of London's critics had a field day tearing the *First Choral Symphony* apart. As usual, this did not bother Holst, but the initial reaction from Ralph Vaughan Williams, who was in the London audience, did:

Dear Gustav,

I feel I want to write & put down (chiefly for my own benefit) why I felt vaguely disappointed after the Phil (so you need not read this.) Not perhaps disappointed--I felt cold admiration--but did not want to get up & embrace everyone & then get drunk like I did after the H of J.[54] I think it is only only because it is a new work & I am more slowly moving than I used to be & it's got to soak in.

But first I want to set down the bits where I was all there, viz. the opening (a great surprise to me)
Dorothy's first solo,
the orchestral end of the scherzo,
the two lovely tunes in the Finale.
then again I've come to the conclusion that the Leeds Chorus CANNOT SING--the Bacchus Chorus sounded like an oratorio.
As to the Grecian Urn it was pattered not sung--No phrasing & no legato--If only the B.C.[55] cd sing in tune or Morley had any tenors we cd show them how to do it.

In the scherzo they made the words so common.

I couldn't bear to think that I was going to 'drift apart' from you musically speaking. (If I do, who shall I have to crib from?)--I don't believe it is so--so I shall live in faith till I have heard it again several times & then I shall find out what a bloody fool I was not to see it all the first time.

Forgive me this rigmarole--but I wanted to get it off my chest.

Yrs

RVW[56]

Holst replied:

St. Paul's Girls' School
Brook Green, Hammersmith,
W. 6
Nov[ember] 11[, 1925]

Dear R

It was good to read and re-read your letter today. One of the reasons for its goodness being that it contains much that I felt but failed to get into words about 'Flos.'[57]

The only point in which I differ from you is about the fear of drifting apart musically or in any other way. I expect it is the result of my old flair for Hindu philosophy and it is difficult to put simply.

It concerns the difference between life and death which means that occasional drifting is necessary to keep our stock fresh and sweet. It also means a lot more but that's enough for one go.

Of course there's another side and about this I'm absolutely in the dark. I mean the real value of either Flos or KS,[58] Beethoven's 9th or anything else--barring things like the B minor.[59] During the last two years I have learnt that I don't know good music from bad, or rather, good from less good.

And I'm not at all sure that the KS is good at all. Just at present I believe I like it which is more than I can say about most of my things. I'm quite sure that I like the Mass and P.S.[60] best of all your things. I couldn't get hold of Flos a bit and was therefore disappointed with it and me. But I'm not disappointed in Flos's composer, because he has not repeated himself. Therefore it is probably either an improvement or something that will lead to one. Which seems identical with your feelings about the KS.

I am now longing to apologize for all this rigmarole but I see you call your letter one and if getting all this off my chest gives you a quarter of the pleasure that your letter gave me it will have been well worth writing.

I was very sorry to miss the violin concerto.[61] So far I've only heard Vally's account which was glowing. She also surprised herself by liking van Dieren.

Yr

G

P.S. I am seriously contemplating giving up all lecturing and conducting after this season. I've spouted and waggled quite enough![62]

In addition to the premieres of *At the Boar's Head* and the *First Choral Symphony*, 1925 was chacterized by the completion of some smaller works. Among the latter was the two-movement *Terzetto* [H158], written for three instruments (flute, oboe, and viola) with each in a different key. Holst also composed two motets for unaccompanied mixed chorus, *The Evening Watch*, Op. 43, No. 1 [H159] set to words by Henry Vaughan and *Sing Me the Men*, Op. 43, No. 2 [H160] set to words by Digby Mackworth Dolben. Holst wrote to Robert Bridges, Poet Laureate of Great Britain, about copyright information for the latter. Bridges replied:

Chilswell
nr Oxford
May 26[, 1925]

My dear Holst,

It interests and delights me to hear that you have set Dolben's poem. The copyrights of his poems is with his kinsman Herbert Paul. You can get him best through M.S. Milford Esq (Oxford University Press, Amen Court EC4) who will no doubt willingly accord you the necessary permission to print. I conveyed the copyright to the family after publication. I think your title 'Sing me the men' is all right: and should advise you that you should use it without asking leave, lest an objection might be raised.--I wish that some day you would look at a poem of mine which I wrote deliberately for a cello obligato: for if it should appear to you to possess the peculiar cello suggestion which I intended, it is possible that you might like to supply it: The poem is 'Awake my heart to be loved'--I wrote it after hearing Piatti lavishing his wonderful passion on some quite paltry words. But I write this only on the oft chance of your sympathy with my intention--and should be quite as sorry to burden your free inclination as I should be pleased if you thought the poem satisfactory in its purpose.

If you ever want to get a few days quiet, I wish you would come and spend them here. Your muse would be quite undisturbed, and there is no knowing what you might compose. Just now everything is very beautiful. Nothing to be heard of Oxford but its distant bells--which this morning were loyally pealing for Queen Mary's birthday (as I learned by reference to the Almanack.) But the city with all its towers and spires lying sunlit in the valley beneath us makes a wonder of our long landscape. I really wish very much that you should come--at any time--and hope you will. Just now is the best of times.

yours sincerely

Robert Bridges[63]

Holst had already set Bridges' "Awake, my heart" to music more than two decades earlier. It was published as the fourth of *Four Songs*, Op. 4 [H14] (1898) for voice and piano. Holst did not employ cello, but may have thought about it after reading the above letter. In a 1926 sketch book he began to set another melody to these words, but stopped writing after the fourth measure.[64] Holst sent a copy of *Sing Me the Men* to Bridges, to which Bridges responded:

Chilswell
nr Oxford
June 9[, 1925]

My dear Holst,

Many thanks for sending me your setting of Dolben's poem. I am glad that the copyright operation did not impede you.

I am altogether delighted by you dealing with the mood--the music was full of surprises to me--and when I came to the page which carries your interpretive "Ah" it seemed to me that Dolben's spirit must have been with you. But it was with the eye only that I could follow you there. I was not able to imagine what the actual sounds would be like.

I feel sure that you must have had pleasure in writing the thing, and I long to hear it; I wish Dolben could--Perhaps he can! I hope the public will like it.

I was interested to hear that you once tried my cello piece: but ashamed of myself in having failed you. It was definitely the cello that I had in mind, and I imagined its obligato passion to be quite free of the singer's particular preoccupation.

Do come here some day when you can.

yours sincerely

Robert Bridges[65]

Inspired by this correspondence, Holst decided to set more of Bridges' words to music in a number of unrelated projects. The *Seven Part Songs*, Op. 44 [H162], for soprano solo, women's chorus and strings, date from 1925-26. The anthems *Man Born to Toil* [H168] and *Eternal Father* [H169] (with words from Bridges' *The Growth of Love*), both scored for mixed chorus, organ and bells ad. lib., date from 1927. *Eternal Father* also features a solo soprano. Bridges' free adaptation of Isaac Watt's words provided the basis for *Christ Hath a Garden* [H167] (1928?), set for mixed chorus (satb) and chamber orchestra (strings, flute, oboe, and clarinet).

The *Seven Part Songs* include "Say who is this?," "O Love, I complain," "Angel spirits of sleep," "When first we met," "Sorrow and joy," "Love on my heart from heaven fell," and "Assemble all ye maidens." Publication by Novello & Co., Ltd, which had published most of Holst's larger works in the 1920's, was settled before the first complete performance! On December 2, 1926 Harold Brooke's Choir sang numbers 2 through 5 from manuscript; Brooke, a part owner of Novello, thought highly of the work. Holst was very pleased with things and, as a token of appreciation, gave the full score manuscripts to Brooke:

St. Paul's Girls' School
Brook Green Hammersmith,
W. 6
Feb[ruary] 13[, 1927]

Dear Brooke

I would like to give all the seven full scores to you and all the seven piano versions to Mabel Rodwell Jones.[66] I gave her one at Xmas and have borrowed it without giving an adequate reason--here it is. I hope all the others are in my writing otherwise I must do some wrangling. Would you put enclosed letter in Miss Jones' set. I would like to have hers by

April 1.

I much regret I cannot spring a surprise on you!

Y ever

GH

If you've got a nice green for your binding I'd like hers to be the same instead of the one I chose.
If there is another piano version of 'Love on my heart' in my writing use that and return this.[67]

The first complete performance of the *Seven Part Songs* was at an informal occasion at Robert Bridges' house on July 2, 1927, when Holst and several of his students made the journey to the Oxford area. Bridges wrote to Holst:

Boar's Hill
July 4[, 1927]

My dear Holst

I hope you were as well satisfied as we with the general success of your venture. It was a blessing that there was no rain, but if only we had had the weather on Saturday which came to us a day late yesterday, all would have been perfect. You asked me once or twice about the music, whether I liked it: if I did not say much it was because I felt it impertinent in me to pretend to judge of our work and I thought that the pleasure, which I could tell you the professionals were feeling was a better compliment than mine would be, because they are accustomed to modern writing, whereas I am old fashioned. I was relieved to find that they were somewhat in my predicament: which was that I did not understand any piece well on the first hearing, but I liked it at second hearing and came in the end to full pleasure. I liked the 'Songs' especially, When first we met and Sorrow and Joy. The only piece that I did not take to was 'Assemble all ye maidens' and that could be accounted for by the great dislike I have for the poem. Its history is queer. I will tell you of it someday.

Our gratitude is enormous. We had a most delightful time: all our guests were enthusiatic. We hope you will do it again someday.

My wife will be writing about some objects which the girls left behind them. I hope they got home safely and comfortably.

yours very sincerely

Robert Bridges

Your way of treating the words is so novel, and so unlike anything I could have imagined, that I think I got on astonishingly well in appreciating your inventions so far as I did. For I really liked them very much: and want to hear them again.[68]

Seven Part Songs was not the largest work that Holst composed in 1926, but it may have been the most musically satisfying. Two choral ballets, *The Golden Goose*, Op. 45, No. 1 [H163] (with a libretto by Jane Joseph) and *The Morning of the Year*, Op. 45 No.2 [H164] (words by Steuart Wilson) supercede it in length. *The Golden Goose* was composed early in the year for the students of Morley College and St. Paul's Girls' School to sing at a Whitsun Festival held at Bute House. *The Morning of the Year*, begun that fall, was the first work commissioned by the music department of the British Broadcasting Corporation. Holst himself conducted the first broadcast performance on March 17, 1927, although strangely enough he dedicated this "radio" work to the English Folk Dance Society, which was involved in the first staged performance on June 1st of that year.

Just a few days after the radio broadcast of *The Morning of the Year* Holst was honored by his home town. The original intent of those involved was to present Holst with a portrait of himself, but he preferred that the money be used to fund a concert of his own works instead. It turned out that there were sufficient funds to provide for back-to-back (afternoon and evening) performances of the same program. The Cheltenham Festival was held on Tuesday, March 22, 1927, with The City of Birmingham Symphony Orchestra engaged for the event. The orchestra's regular conductor Adrian Boult, who conducted two of the pieces in performance, acted as "set-up" man for Holst, rehearsing the ensemble before Holst was able to go to Birmingham himself. Featured works on the program included *A Somerset Rhapsody*, *Two Songs without Words*, "Ballet Music" from *The Perfect Fool*, and *The Planets*. The event was covered in *The Times*:

Cheltenham has to-day honoured its distinguished son, Gustav Holst, in the way which a musician most appreciates: by performing his works on an adequate scale. Two concerts (with the same program) have been

> given by the City of Birmingham Orchestra. At the first, this afternoon, the Mayor and the Corporation were present to offer to Mr. Holst a civic welcome and as a memento of the happy occasion, presented to the composer a picture painted by a local artist, Mr. Harold Cox, of the Cotswold Hills by night.
>
> In making his acknowledgements, Mr. Holst said that, speaking impersonally, Cheltenham was to be congratulated on doing the most important thing for music in England by organizing a festival which combatted in its very nature the prevalent fallacies that music was a foreign language and that composers were all dead: and had further shown understanding of the practical difficulties by arranging for adequate rehearsals.
>
> ....There is something to be said against one-composer programmes, but it could not be said to-day.[69]

During the intermission of the evening performance, congratulatory messages were read; it was truly a tribute. After the festival had taken place, the committee found that it had the surplus funds available to fulfill its original intent and commissioned a portrait of Holst by Bernard Munn of Birmingham.[70] It is now displayed in the Holst Birthplace Museum.

Musically, 1927 was off to a great start for Holst and greater works loomed on the horizon. Financially, however, Holst was still suffering the effects from his reduced teaching load. There was enough money to live on, but not much that was disposable. Since 1925 he and Isobel had been living at Brook End, a Tudor farm house in Easton Park, Dunmow, Essex that they had rented from Lady Warwick. Located about four miles from Thaxted, it was very peaceful place but had no "den" there for Holst to retreat to in order to compose. Once again it was Balfour Gardiner who came to the rescue. From September, 1926 through May, 1927 he provided bi-monthly payments of 200 pounds to the Holsts which allowed Isobel to have essential improvements made and to have a barn converted into a suitable music room. Percy Grainger commented in a 1950 letter to Henry Rolf Gardiner, "Balfour's deeds in connection with Gustav Holst will go down in history as the great acts of a great man."[71]

In April, 1927 Holst took advantage of the break between terms at St. Paul's Girls' School and set out on a walking trip, this time through Yorkshire. When he returned to London, he found a cable from Walter Damrosch, conductor of the New York Symphony Society, commissioning an orchestral work. This resulted in his great symphonic poem *Egdon Heath*, Op. 47 [H172], which occupied his compositional thought throughout the remainder of the spring and summer.

That autumn, Holst was once again in demand as a lecturer. On November 12th, he returned to Morley College to reprise his lecture on "England and Her Music" and later that month gave a series of three lectures on the works of Samuel Wesley and Robert Pearsall. It was at the second of these lectures, one concentrating on Wesley, that Holst announced the important results of research efforts done by two of his former students (now colleagues):

> Mr. Holst mentioned that during the week an interesting discovery about Wesley had been made. On Wednesday Mr. Walter Gandy, a member of Morley College, who had been struck by the similarity of the work of Willam Byrd and Samuel Wesley, found a motet by Byrd with the same words and note for note the same as one attributed to Wesley. Later in the week Miss J. M. Joseph went to the British museum and found other motets in Wesley's handwriting which had been copied from previous works by Byrd. We now know for the first time that far from being Wesley's composition they merely proved his interest in 16th century composition.
>
> Miss Joseph stated later that as the result of a hurried search on Friday she had found about nine works by Byrd copied in Wesley's handwriting.[72]

On December 4th Holst received another commission. This time the soliciting organization was the British Broadcasting Corporation and the ensemble was BBC Military Band:

> May we ask you how you would view a request from us to compose for Military Band a piece in one movement, lasting from twelve to fifteen minutes in performance, in the form of a Concert Overture, or Fantasy, or Symphonic Poem?[73]

Holst had just completed a work in this form--*Egdon Heath*--and responded:

> I should be delighted to write a piece for military band . I suggest that, if it suits you equally well, we will leave the form of the piece until later as I might wish to write something in more than one movement. Of course, if you have any particular reason for asking for a one-movement piece, I should be delighted to fall in with your wishes. If there is no immediate hurry, I would like to postpone writing this piece and first arrange one of Bach's Organ Fugues for military band. I have had this at the back of my mind for many years....[74]

Holst eventually wrote a one-movement work that fulfilled the commission. *Hammersmith*, Op. 52 [H178] (1930-31), is an unqualified masterpiece. In accordance with his wishes, the BBC allowed him to do a "warm-up" first--a military band transcription of the Fugue, BWV 577 (1706) by Johann Sebastian Bach. It is uncertain whether Bach composed it for organ or for a harpsichord with some sort of pedal mechanism. Whatever the case, when Holst completed his military band transcription in the spring of 1928 he gave it the title *Bach's Fugue a la Gigue* [App. III, 25]. Before he could start work on either of these projects, however, there were a number of previous commitments that required Holst's attention, including a holiday abroad. The month-long trip to central Europe was to feature more concert-going and less walking than was customary for Holst.

On December 19, 1927, which marked the end of the St. Paul's Girls' School term, Holst left London by train for the Harwich docks, from whence he sailed for Germany, Austria, and Czechoslovakia. The first stop for was at Karlsruhe, in southwestern Germany, where he stayed for two days.[75] On the 22nd he took the train to Munich, where he stayed another two days. There he visited the Alte Pinokatheke art museum, lunched with Clemens Freiherr von Franckenstein (1875-1942), composer and Intendant of the Munich Opera, and saw Strauss' *Salome*. From there Holst boarded a train for Vienna, arriving there at 6:00 p.m. on Christmas Eve.[76]

Holst was in Vienna for the next two weeks and took full advantage of what the city had to offer. He saw the sights, including Schoenbrunn Palace, the Belvedere Palace, the Art History Museum, Schubert's birthplace and the Haydn monument and museum. He attended performances of numerous operas, including Wagner's *Die Meistersinger*, Beethoven's *Fidelio*, Johann Strauss Jr.'s *Gypsy Baron*, Richard Strauss' *Ariadne* and *Der Rosenkavalier*, Puccini's *Turandot*, an unspecified opera by Korngold, and a dress rehearsal of Krenek's *Johnny Spielt Auf.* Other performances included a Bruckner Mass and concerts by the Vienna Choir Boys and ex-Paulina Joan Elwes. He also met with many people integral to Vienna's music life, including musicologist Egon Wellesz and Universal Editions editor Alfred Kalmus. This flurry of activity was more or less capped off by an anticlimactic "dull cinema" two days before his departure.[77]

On Friday, January 6, 1928 Holst arrived in Prague and took lodgings at the Hotel de Paris. The following day he went to the Czech Music Society, Hudebni Beseda. There he met Edmund Cykler, a young American musicologist doing doctoral studies at Charles University. Cykler eventually settled in to a professorship at the University of Oregon and also became Associate Dean for the

School of Music there. He commented about meeting Holst in a letter to the composer's daughter:

> ....One of the most memorable events was in 1928 winter when I was called by the Hudebni Beseda--the Czech Music Society--and asked if I would act as interpreter and guide to your father, Gustav Holst. I believe we spent three or four days together visitng a number of musical events at the opera house--The Bartered Bride, for example--and some of them specially arranged for him such as a visit to the quarter tone studio of Alois Haba[78] where Irwin Schulhoff performed some examples on the specially built quarter tone piano. Most memorable is the evening when your father, Leos Janacek and Alois Haba met at supper in the restaurant of the City Concert Hall and I had the great experience of acting as interpreter between them and keeping the conversation flowing mostly via German and English. Your father confessed to a knowledge of Wagnerian German!![79]

The supper meeting of Holst, Haba, and Janacek to which Cykler referred happened on the first evening, January 7, 1928. The timing was propitious. According to Holst's diaries, this was the only time Holst that met Janacek; the Bohemian composer passed away later that year.

As in Vienna, Holst took full advantage of what Prague had to offer. Cykler took him for a sightseeing walk over the Karlov Most (Charles Bridge) and up the steep streets to the castle and St. Vitus Cathedral. On another occasion Holst saw the Mozart house, old town and the Jewish ghetto. On Wednesday, December 11th, Joan Elwes arrived from Vienna and assisted Cykler in keeping Holst company. This was most welcome, although Holst would not have been deprived of musical camaraderie. In addition to composers Leos Janacek, Alois Haba, Erwin Schulhoff, and Josef Suk, Holst met Jaroslav Kricka, a professor of composition at Prague Conservatory, and many others. Bruno Walter was also in town to guest conduct and Holst caught Walter's dress rehearsal and concert. He also saw two operas: Smetana's *Bartered Bride* (with Cykler), *Two Widows* (with Kricka) and Offenbach's *Tales of Hoffman*. Other concerts attended included those given by the Prague Philharmonic, the Prague Teachers Choir, and (with Schulhoff) the Andricek String Quartet.[80]

On Saturday, January 14th Holst boarded the overnight train for Leipzig and arrived there at 6:30 the next morning. He continued the same touring pattern, seeing as much of Leipzig and as many musicians as time allowed. This time he included visits to the publishers Breitkopf & Haertel and Edition Peters. He heard performances given by the Ross String Quartet, the Philharmonic, and saw Johann Strauss Jr.'s *Die Fledermaus*. He also heard a concert of madrigals at the Conservatorium and attended rehearsals of the choirs from the Gewandhaus and Thomaskirche. Among the many people he met was Carl Straube, organist at the Thomaskirche (Johann Sebastian Bach's Church), with whom he had two teas. He also attended a party at Straube's house following a Schubert recital given by pianist Ernst Pauer, director of the Leipzig Conservatory.[81]

Weary, but musically refreshed, Holst arrived back in London on the 20th, two days after the St. Paul's Girls' School winter semester had begun. In addition to his teaching and composing, Holst was slated to take over the directorship of the London Bach Choir. In the autumn of 1927, Ralph Vaughan Williams, who had been conductor of the organization since 1920, announced his intentions of leaving the post and, in keeping with a well-established pattern that had now existed for three decades, recommended Holst for the position. Holst was hired and his succession was announced in the press in January and February. One such entry featured a cartoon of Holst with the following caption:

> "Music Hath Charms." Her beauties up-to-date
> Low brows annoy: High-brow but titillate.
> Holst's art austere aims not the mob to please.
> There is no kitten on our Gustav's keys.[82]

The succession, however, did not take place as Holst, after consulting with his physician, decided that it was not in his best interests to accept a position with an ensemble that had such a wide public exposure. There were plenty of other things to do.

During the early months of 1928 Holst was commissioned by Herbert Whiteley, editor of *The British Bandsman*, to write the contest piece for that year's National Brass Band Championships, to be held in September at London's Crystal Palace. The work had to be composed fairly expeditiously in order for it to be distributed to the bands in order to insure adequate rehearsal time. For Holst this meant having to put his other commission, *Hammersmith*, on the back burner for a while, since the BBC had given him no particular sense of urgency. The three-movement work that he composed for the National Brass Band Championships was *A Moorside Suite* [H173], as such the first work written for the brass band medium by a major composer. Initially condemned by some unenlightened souls in the brass band world for not having any sixteenth notes, it soon became a brass band classic. *A Moorside Suite* is in three movements ("Scherzo," "Nocturne," and "March"). The work looks to both the past and future. Although more contrapuntal, the "Scherzo" proper is somewhat reminiscent of the "Jig" from *St. Paul's Suite* while the "March" is a later musical commentary on the closing movement of the *First Suite in E Flat for Military Band.* It is the uncompromising austerity of the "Nocturne," however, that reveals the work to be one of Holst's later compositions. Holst also began setting the work for military band, but left it unfinished after the thirty-eighth measure of the "Nocturne." Reasons for this remain unknown, although Holst had at least one other work on his compositional palette at this time.

In October, 1927 he had been approached by George Bell, then Dean of Canterbury, about writing incidental music for John Masefield's play, *The Coming of Christ*. The drama was to be performed in Canterbury Cathedral on Whitsun, 1928. Political obstructions--both musical and non-musical--had to be overcome. First of all, Bell had to receive permission from the Archbishop to perform the play, which was no easy task, since no church drama had been performed in an Anglican cathedral in modern times. The permission was secured with the understanding that the figure of Christ would not actually be portrayed before the audience. Secondly, the cathedral's organist, C. Charlton Palmer, threw a fit since he perceived that Bell had gone over his head. Two meetings in Canterbury with Bell, Holst, and Palmer in attendence quieted things down.[83] Holst's *Incidental Music for the Coming of Christ* [H170] (1927) was performed on the 28th of May as scheduled. Holst's students from St. Paul's Girls' School and a group from Morley College made up the performing ensemble. The work is scored for solo soprano, alto, baritone and bass, four-part mixed chorus, trumpet, organ and piano, and optional strings.

One person who was impressed with the music was John Masefield. Masefield, then two years away from becoming Great Britain's Poet Laureate, wrote to Holst:

Hill Crest
Boar's Hill
Oxford

Dear Holst,

Glad you liked doing some of the rhymes. Your music stays in my head continually.

Your baton should go to you in a day or two; it is nearly ready.

Greetings to your wife and to Imogen.

Yours sincerely,
John Masefield[84]

---

[1]Gramophone Notes by 'Discus' in *The Musical Times*, LXIV, No. 964 (June 1, 1923), 409.
[2]Personal correspondence, Imogen Holst to Helen Asquith, Thursday, July 26 [, 1923].
[3]*The Daily Mail* (London), February 5, 1923.
[4]Michael Short, *Gustav Holst: The Man and His Music* (Oxford: Oxford University Press, 1990), 204-205.
[5]Gustav Holst, Notebook, June, 1923, The Holst Foundation.
[6]Most recordings average about fifty minutes and one Pro-Arte compact disk produced in 1987 featuring the late Eduardo Mata conducting the Dallas Symphony clocks in at a lethargic 55:29--about 25% slower than Holst's timings.
[7]For an interesting commentary on Adrian Boult's treatment of "Mars" see John Knight, "Exploring Holst's Planets with Adrian Boult" in *The Instrumentalist*, XLIV, No. 4 (November, 1994), 24-28.
[8]Ralph Vaughan Williams died in 1958, at the age of eighty-five.
[9]Personal correspondence, Imogen Holst to Adrian Boult, February 1, 1973, British Library Add. MS 60498.
[10]Gustav Holst, Notebook, October, 1922, The Holst Foundation.
[11]Royal Military School of Music Student Archives Collection.
[12]Ralph Vaughan Williams' *Folk Song Suite* originally had four movements, as indicated in the program. "Sea Songs" was later removed (probably by Boosey & Hawkes) and published as an independent composition in march-size format. According to Gordon Turner, reason for this was spatial: all four movements wouldn't fit neatly onto the allotted pages.
[13]Programme Book, Royal Military School of Music Archives.
[14]*The Morning Post*, July 5, 1923.
[15]Johann Sebastian Bach, *Cantata No. 140 "Wachet auf" ("Sleepers Awake")*.
[16]Johannes Brahms, *Variations on a Theme by Haydn*, Op. 56a.
[17]This probably meant excerpts from J. S. Bach's Christmas Oratorio, BWV 248. The entire work is nearly three hours in length. Holst's note could also have meant Camille Saint-Saens' *Christmas Oratorio*, which lasts about forty minutes.
[18]Ludwig van Beethoven's *Piano Concerto No. 3 in C minor*, Op. 37.
[19]Holst's timings indicate that he was thinking of programming only the Overture to Mozart's *Don Giovanni* and the "Polovetsian Dances" from Borodin's *Prince Igor*.
[20]Gustav Holst, Notebook, June, 1923, The Holst Foundation.
[21]One of the horn players was Imogen Holst.
[22]*The Morning Post*, December 18, 1923.
[23]*The Daily Telegraph*, December 18, 1923.
[24]Royal College of Music MS 4555.
[25]Maurice Ravel, quoted in *The Daily News (London)*, October 7, 1923. Vaughan Williams had studied with Ravel in 1908, hence Ravel's "especially Williams" aside.
[26]"A short, sharp 'interview'" in *Era*, April 4, 1923.
[27]Personal correspondence, Lydia Lopokova to John Maynard Keynes, September 16, 1923, quoted in Polly Hill (ed.) and Richard Keynes (ed.), *Lydia and Maynard: The Letters of John Maynard Keynes and Lydia Lopokova* (New York: Charles Scribner's Sons, 1989), 103.
[28]Very powerful.

[29]Personal correspondence, Lydia Lopokova to John Maynard Keynes, October 13, 1923, quoted in Hill (ed.) and Keynes (ed.), *op. cit.*, 110.

[30]Vera Bowen, Lydia Lopokova's friend and confidant.

[31]Personal correspondence, Lydia Lopokova to John Maynard Keynes, October 27, 1923, quoted in Hill (ed.) and Keynes (ed.), *op. cit.*, 117. Readers are warned not to read too much into this quote; Lydia Lopokova, while very literate, did not have a real command of the English language.

[32]This was Holst's only completed choral symphony. Sketches from 1926 to 1931 exist for a *Second Choral Symphony*, but they were not brought to fruition.

[33]Personal correspondence, Imogen Holst to Helen Asquith, Sunday, "August the something" [1923], The Holst Foundation.

[34]Personal correspondence, Gustav Holst to Vally Lasker, Sep[tember] 1[, 1923], The Holst Foundation.

[35]Royal College of Music MS 4568.

[36]*Ibid.*.

[37]Personal correspondence, Gustav Holst to Ralph Vaughan Williams [n.d.], quoted in Ursula Vaughan Williams (ed.) and Imogen Holst (ed.), *Heirs and Rebels: Letters to Each Other and Occasional Writings by Gustav Holst and Ralph Vaughan Williams* (Oxford: Oxford University Press, 1959), 59-60. The contents of this letter fit this performance, although Holst would have been 49 years old, not 47 1/2.

[38]Queen's Hall.

[39]James Allen's Girls' School.

[40]Personal correspondence, Gustav Holst to William Gillies Whittaker, Dec[ember] 23[, 1923], quoted in Michael Short (ed.), *Gustav Holst: Letters to W. G. Whittaker* (Glasgow: University of Glasgow Press, 1974), 80.

[41]Stephen Lloyd, *H. Balfour Gardiner* (Cambridge, England: Cambridge University Press, 1984), 156.

[42]*The Cloud Messenger*.

[43]Personal correspondence, Gustav Holst to William Gillies Whittaker, Thursday [February, 1924], quoted in Michael Short (ed.), *op. cit.*, 82.

[44]Stephen Lloyd, *op.cit.*, 156.

[45]*Ibid.*, 177. It would have been entirely in Gardiner's character to pay for Adams' services to Holst.

[46]Personal correspondence, Imogen Holst to Helen Asquith, Tuesday, March 25, 1924 and Sunday, April 6, 1924, The Holst Foundation.

[47]Subscribers--Holst's 50th Birthday Gift, Holst Foundation Microfilm, Holst Birthplace Museum.

[48]*The Times*, November 14, 1927.

[49]*Liverpool Daily Courier*, January 5, 1926.

[50]*Glasgow Herald*, January 16, 1926.

[51]Michael Short, *op. cit.*, 244.

[52]"Ad Libitum by 'Feste' [Harvey Grace]," in *The Musical Times*, December 1, 1925.

[53]Imogen Holst, *Holst* (Borough Green, Seven Oaks, Kent: Novello, 1972), 13.

[54]*The Hymn of Jesus*.

[55]The London Bach Choir.

[56]Personal correspondence, Ralph Vaughan Williams to Gustav Holst, n.d. [1925], quoted in Ursula Vaughan Williams (ed.) and Imogen Holst (ed.), *op. cit.*, 60-61.

[57]Vaughan Williams' *Flos Campi*, suite for viola, wordless chorus, and small orchestra.

[58]Holst's *First Choral Symphony* ("Keats Symphony," or, simply, "KS").

[59]J. S. Bach's *B Minor Mass*.

[60]Vaughan Williams' *Symphony No. 3*, "Pastoral."

[61]Vaughan Williams' *Concerto Accademico* was premiered at Queen's Hall on October 10, 1925.

[62]Personal correspondence, Gustav Holst to Ralph Vaughan Williams, Nov[ember] 11[, 1925], quoted in Ursula Vaughan Williams (ed.) and Imogen Holst (ed.), *op. cit.*, 61-62.

[63]Personal correspondence, Robert Bridges to Gustav Holst, May 26 [, 1925], quoted in Donald E. Stanford (ed.), *The Selected Letters of Robert Bridges* (Newark, Delaware: University of Delaware Press, 1984), 843-844.

[64]British Library Add. MS 57910B [App. IV, 3].

[65]Personal correspondence, Robert Bridges to Gustav Holst, June 9[, 1925], quoted in Stanford (ed.), *op. cit.*, 844.

[66]A former student of Holst and co-dedicatee of *A Fugal Concerto*, Op. 40, No. 2 [H152].

[67]Personal correspondence, Gustav Holst to Harold Brooke, Feb[ruary] 13[, 1927], British Library Add. MS 57895.

[68]Personal correspondence, Robert Bridges to Gustav Holst, July 4[, 1927], quoted in Stanford (ed.), *op. cit.*, 880.

[69]*The Times*, March 23, 1927.

[70]Michael Short, *op. cit.*, 253.

[71]Personal correspondence, Percy Grainger to Henry Rolf Gardiner, July 10, 1950, quoted in Stephen Lloyd, *op. cit.*, 156.

[72]*The Times*, November 28, 1927.

[73]Business correspondence, D. Millar Craig to Gustav Holst, December 3, 1927, BBC Written Archives Centre.

[74]Business correspondence, Gustav Holst to D. Millar Craig, Dec[ember] 5, 1927, BBC Written Archives Centre.

[75]Gustav Holst, *Diary*, Monday, December 19, 1927, The Holst Foundation.

[76]Gustav Holst, *Diary*, Thursday, December 22, through Saturday, December 24, 1927, The Holst Foundation.

[77]Gustav Holst, *Diary*, Sunday, December 25, 1927 through Thursday, January 5, 1928, The Holst Foundation.

[78]It is not known what Holst thought of Haba's quarter tone experiments. It is very likely that Holst shared some musical ideas with both Haba and Schulhoff. It is most interesting to compare the openings of Holst's *Double Concerto*, Op. 49 [H175] (1929) with Schulhoff's *Concerto for String Quartet and Wind Orchestra* (1930).

[79]Personal correspondence, Edmund A. Cykler to Imogen Holst, October 13, 1982.

[80]Gustav Holst, *Diary*, Friday, January 6 through Saturday, January 14, 1928, The Holst Foundation.

[81]Gustav Holst, *Diary*, Sunday, January 15 through Wednesday, January 18, 1928, The Holst Foundation.

[82]*The Passing Show*, February 18, 1928.

[83]Michael Short, *op. cit.*, 259-260.

[84]Personal correspondence, John Masefield to Gustav Holst, n.d. [1928]. Permissioned obtained from The Society of Authors, Literary Representative of the Estate of John Masefield.

CHAPTER XVI

THE DAMROSCH COMMISSION

Gustav Holst considered *Egdon Heath*, Op. 47 [H172] (1927) to be his finest musical composition. Opinions vary on this, of course, but most musicians would agree that the work is an unqualified masterpiece. With its austere linear writing and an ambience full of musical feeling yet devoid of sentimentality, this symphonic poem launched a fourth and final period of musical creativity for the composer.[1]

Made famous by the English novelist Thomas Hardy (1840-1928) in *The Return of the Native* (1878), Egdon Heath is a factual place, located in southern England in Dorset County near Dorchester. At the time of the novel's composition Hardy and his first wife Emma were living at Riverside Villa, in Sturminster Newton, a small town located some twenty miles north of the heath country. Within a decade, however, they had moved to Max Gate, a house Hardy had built specially for them. It was located a couple of miles east of Dorchester, right in the middle of Hardy's fictional "Wessex" and not far from Egdon Heath itself. For all practical purposes the Hardys spent the remainder of their lives there and, fifteen years following Emma's death in 1912, it was there that Holst would visit Hardy and his second wife, Florence.

Holst had always been quite a hiker; he had a passion for the countryside. For him, walking was not as much a leisure activity as it was an inseparable part of life, much as the writing of letters to family and friends or the extracting of parts for performance at St. Paul's Girls' School or Morley College. His treks in the Cotswolds with such notable personalities as his brother Ernest Cossart, Ralph Vaughan Williams, and William Gillies Whittaker are well-documented as are his walks down the old Roman *vias* and other backroads of south central England.

Just as Beethoven had done a century earlier by walking in the Viennese suburbs of Grinzing and Heiligenstadt, Holst fervently sought inspiration through treading through rural areas or even on what countryside he could find within greater London. During the particularly fruitful five-year period (1908-1913) in which he composed *Savitri*, the two *Suites for Military Band*, four sets of *Choral Hymns from the Rig Veda*, *The Cloud Messenger*, and the *St. Paul's Suite*, Holst and his family had even lived on the banks of the Thames, at 10, The Terrace, Barnes. After that time, the Holsts vascillated between the country town of Thaxted and several apartments in London, never living far from some type of park. Adrian Boult comments on his first meeting with Holst:

> We first met when I came to London in 1916 and he took me on his famous "country walk in London"! I wish I could give it in more detail, but I seem to remember a clever amalgam of Kew Gardens, Sheen Common, Richmond Park, and other beauty spots, linked by the Thames towpath.[2]

Such walks often provided Holst with musical inspiration. One of the earliest manifestations of his love for the natural environment was *The Cotswolds: Symphony in F*, Op. 8 of 1899-1900. It is not surprising then that Egdon Heath made quite an impression on the composer, serving as the inspiration for a major orchestral work. Yet, rather than place his own descriptive program note onto the title page of the full score, he decided to let Hardy's imagery of Egdon Heath, given in the first chapter of *The Return of the Native*, suffice:

> A place perfectly accordant with man's nature--neither ghastly, hateful, nor ugly: neither commonplace, unmeaning, nor tame; but like man, slighted and enduring; and withal singularly colossal and mysterious in its swarthy monotony.[3]

It is not so strange that Holst would let Hardy speak for him here. Though far from being a literary connoisseur, Holst was nevertheless a Hardy enthusiast. He did own a number of Hardy's novels and he had set Hardy's words to music at least four times previously. These include the final three of his *Six Songs*, Op. 15 [H68] (1903) for baritone voice and piano ("The Sergeant's Song," "In a Wood," and "Between Us Now"), as well as *The Homecoming* [H120] (1913), a male chorus setting of "Gruffly Growled the Wind." Though of different generations--Hardy was writing novels before Holst was born--their mind-sets, at least in regard to nature, were compatible. Spearing comments:

> It was inevitable that Holst should feel at home with Hardy, to whose bleak landscape in *The Return of the Native*, *Egdon Heath* owes its origin. Both men shared a similar philosophy of life. They both felt the power of natural forces, and they both saw man in close relationship with them. Sentimentality has no place in such philosophy, and neither would own it.[4]

Holst spoke of the genesis of his own *Egdon Heath* to his American friend Austin Lidbury in a letter that he wrote on August 11, 1927 from the Phoenix Hotel in Dorchester:

> Your gift of *The Return of the Native*, combined with a walk over Egdon Heath at Easter, 1926, started my mind working, and I felt that according to my usual slow method I might write something in 1930 or thereabouts. However, a cable came last Easter from the New York Symphony Orchestra asking me to write some thing for them! With the result that my *Egdon Heath* was half done by the end of July.[5]

At the time of *Egdon Heath*'s conception, New York City was blessed with two professional symphony orchestras--the New York Philharmonic and the New York Symphony Society. The Philharmonic, of course, remains to this day a vital musical entity not only to the City of New York, but to the entire nation. The New York Symphony Society, on the other hand, no longer exists *per se*, although during much of its existence it was at least on a musical par with the Philharmonic. The Symphony was founded in 1878 by Leopold Damrosch (1835-85), the eminent German-American violinist and patriarch of a New York-centered American musical dynasty that included his two sons, choral conductor Frank Heino Damrosch (1859-1937) and the highly respected opera and symphony conductor Walter Johannes Damrosch (1862-1950). Each of the brothers had an enormous impact on music education in America.

Frank Damrosch was Superintendent of Music for New York's public school for many years. He was best-known as the conductor of the Musical Art Society (an ensemble of professional singers) and succeeeded his younger brother as conductor of the Oratorio Society.[6] He also conducted many amateur groups.

Walter Damrosch attained the conductorship of the New York Symphony Society upon the death of his father in 1885. Although only twenty-three, he was already an experienced conductor, having conducted a season of the New York Metropolitan Opera. In many ways opera would remain his first love; he had two conducting stints with the Met (1884-91 and 1900-02) and during the interim, from 1894 to 1899, founded and directed his own Damrosch Opera Company. He also composed five operas. Still, the New York Symphony Society was his base; in one thirteen-year period with them (1907-20) he conducted a remarkable string of 366 consecutive concerts.[7]

The players in the New York Symphony had a considerable amount of respect for Damrosch. He was a strong leader and a competent, not flambouyant, conductor whose trademark was a clear and steady beat. Still, out of order, there was chaos. Richard Schikel comments:

> The orchestra was known in music circles as "the Foreign Legion" and it included among its personnel a former Bessarian sheep stealer, a reformed Istanbul white slaver and a man who had once been a cook on a Latvian tramp steamer. It contained a man who carried no money on him but was never without his cello. Needing subway fare, he would simply unpack his instrument and start playing. Several dollars worth of change always found their way into the innards of the instrument, apparently not affecting its tone in the slightest. Another man dreamed of being a conductor. Otherwise an admirable violist, it was his habit to retire to his hotel room to conduct an invisible orchestra for hours. He had signs on each chair indicating the various sections....Then there was the great flautist George Barrere, who, bearded, wearing a broad hat, a Prince Albert coat and pink trousers would stalk into rehearsal, pull an atomizer from his pocket, and proceed to disinfect his colleagues who included members of the French Legion of Honor, Algerian longshoremen, ex-wrestlers, Gipsy fiddle players, Ukranian professors and failed composers.[8]

It was with this orchestra that Damrosch began to make his mark on music education in America, instituting a series of Children's and Young People's Concerts that were broadcast nationally on radio from 1923 to 1928. The idea of offering youth concerts was not new, although it was familial. Frank had actually originated the concept with his Young People's Symphony Concerts at Carnegie Hall a quarter of a century earlier, in 1898. Walter's Children's and Young People's Concerts, however, reached an infinitely larger audience and laid the ground work for his revered Music Appreciation Hour. Broadcast nationally on NBC from 1928 to 1942, the Music Appreciation Hour featured the National Orchestra, an ensemble organized specifically for this purpose. Over the airwaves twenty-four Fridays each year, this remarkable 4-tiered series[9] reached an estimated five million listeners in 70,000 schools throughout the country.[10] The Music Appreciation Hour also set the stage for Leonard Bernstein, whose nationally televised Young People's Concerts would educate the budding musicians of the next generation. Damrosch, one of the first conductors to recognize the power of the radio, commented:

> I had always dreamt of a time when I could reach music through a wide and limitless audience....
> Radio magically offered me the means. I realized that with one performance I could reach more people through the radio than I could previously in five years of concert work.[11]

Damrosch retained the position of Musical Director with the New York Symphony Society until 1927, when he retired into the unfortunately short-lived role of Guest Conductor. That same year he accepted an appointment to the Advisory Counsel of the National Broadcasting Company and later accepted the post of musical counsel to NBC, a position he would hold until 1942. Always one to use available media for the musical education for the masses, he accepted featured roles in at least two motion pictures. The first was a 1939 Paramount motion picture, *The Star Maker*.[12] Essentially a vehicle for Bing Crosby, the picture was well-received. The second was Boris Morros' *Carnegie Hall* (Federal Films,1947), featuring an assortment of classical and popular artists. It was not nearly as successful and was described by one critic as "the thickest and sourest mess of musical mulligatawny I have yet to sit down to."[13]

Thus it was that Damrosch and Holst shared a common unselfish mission: the musical education of ordinary citizenry. Holst accomplished this largely through lecture tours and the notoriety of his work at Morley College for Working Men and Women. Damrosch achieved this through his Children's and Young People's Concerts, Music Appreciation Hour, and Evening Concert Hour broadcasts. Yet it wasn't music education that drew the two men together; it was Holst's music. Damrosch's interest in it is documented in a letter written to Adrian Boult:

Hotel de France & Choiseule
239-241 Rue St. Honore

Adresse telegraphique:
Francheul Paris
Tel. Central 41-92

May 23, 1923

My dear Mr. Boult

I remember with so much pleasure your friendliness during my visit to London in January 1922 that I venture to impose on it the [this] following extract. I am anxious to see some of the scores of Arnold Bax but do not know who the publishers are.

Could you and would you ask them to send me two or three of his best and latest works to Paris in that I could examine them here as I am afraid I shall not get to London this summer.

I should also like to get the Ballet Music from Holst's comic opera [*The Perfect Fool*] of which I hear charming things.

In fact--any more works by Britishers that seem to you fine, and--if you have the time to write us about your own doings and Sir Hugh Allen. Please give him my best greetings and, if you and he feel you need a rest from the Royal College of Music, [ring] and we'll fly [you] across the Channel some day next week. I'll give you the best dinner Paris can offer.

("I know a place where the wild thyme grows.")

Cordially yours,

Walter Damrosch[14]

As a conductor (and composer) Walter Damrosch was firmly rooted in the romantic realm of tonal music. He recognized the need for conducting new works, however, in order to increase the size of the repertoire and to encourage the efforts of living composers. When he first entered the profession, composers were writing works that were musically accessible to a great number of listeners. The act of advocating newly-composed works by a Brahms or a Tschaikowsky in the 1880's was not nearly as difficult as introducing the works of a Schoenberg or a Stravinsky in the 1920's. By that time a deepening chasm between the composer and audience had begun to develop, and the conductor of new works was now assigned the onerous task of being a musical architect--building bridges in order to rekindle the mutual respect between composer and audience that had rather quickly deteriorated. When *The Planets* took the world by storm in the early 1920's, Damrosch undoubtedly saw in Holst a contemporary composer who, while using twentieth-century techniques, was capable of having his music accepted and understood by a large audience.

In December of 1926, Damrosch announced his impending retirement as conductor of the New York Symphony Society effective with the end of the

1926-27 season. What was not announced at this time was a secret agreement, essentially ironed out during the previous summer, of a merger between the New York Symphony and the New York Philharmonic. The Philharmonic had already profitted from two other so-called "mergers" earlier in the decade. In 1921-1922 it had absorbed the National Symphony as well as its conductor, Willem Mengelberg, and in 1923 it had assimilated the Musical Society of the City of New York. When the merger with the New York Symphony Society was officially announced on March 16, 1928,[15] it came as a great shock to many people. The majority of the musicians associated with the Symphony, including Damrosch, were not served well by it. The two boards became one, with Clarence H. Mackay, the extremely successful Chairman of the Board of the old Philharmonic becoming Chairman of the new board and Harry Harkness Flagler, Chairman of the Board of the New York Symphony, becoming President. The new Philharmonic-Symphony was united under the baton of Arturo Toscanini, and both Damrosch and Mengelberg would soon be cast adrift.

In April, 1927 Damrosch commissioned Holst to write a work for the orchestra. The work was to be programmed on a concert projected for the following February, during Damrosch's second guest conducting series. Holst was offered the sum of $500 (half in advance); the New York Symphony Society was in turn offered the premiere of the work and the next two performances.[16] The work in question, already well underway by this time, was *Egdon Heath.* This commission provided the composer with the right amount of incentive needed to complete the piece. It is doubtful that Holst knew anything about the impending merger; his knowledge of it probably would not have affected his acceptance of Damrosch's offer.

Holst's chief correspondent in matters dealing with the New York Symphony Society was Harry Harkness Flagler, Chairman of the Board. Erskine comments about Flagler's well-known philanthropy:

> In 1903 the Symphony Society, after some financial vicissitudes, was subsidized by Harry Harkness Flagler, whose name is not likely to be forgotten by the city to whose education and delight he has devoted his fortune and his enthusiasm. Through his aid the Symphony increased the number of its rehearsals and concerts. In 1914 he began to underwrite all deficits, and in 1920 he provided for a European tour, the first made by an American orchestra.[17]

In the first of nine extant letters to Flagler, Holst discusses not only the progress of the work, but also his own embarrassing absentmindedness:

St. Paul's Girls' School
Brook Green Hammersmith
London W. 6
July 30 [1927]

Dear Mr. Flagler

Would you please give my humble apologies to Miss Viborg.

She kindly invited me to dinner in London but I was unable to do more than drop in for a few minutes later in the evening. I arrived very tired and extremely stupid and quite forgot all the matters I wished to mention to her.

I had hoped to show her a sketch of the work later but I only got half of it sketched by the beginning of the month and when I wrote to her at her London address I received no answer so I presume that she has left England. It was silly of me to delay writing so long and I trust that you will both forgive me.

The piece I am writing for New York is half sketched and I am badly stuck in the middle so that I cannot be sure at this moment that I shall be able to finish it as it shouldbe finished in time for your next season (I warned Mr. Damrosch that I am a slow writer). It may be that I shall have to put it on the shelf to mature and therefore I do not wish any details to be made public. But I feel hopeful of finishing the sketch next month and the full score by Sep 30 and therefore I send you the following details for yourself, Mr. Damrosch and other good friends but not for the public press until I write later to tell you that the work is finished.

It is to be called 'Egdon Heath' and is the result of reading and re-reading the first chapter of Thomas Hardy's novel *The Return of the Native* and also of walking through the country he describes there and calls 'Egdon Heath.' I first thought of writing it early in 1926 and put the idea away to fructify according to my usual custom. But Mr. Damrosch's delightful cable made me decide to try and finish it for you.

The score would be marked 'To Thomas Hardy and The New York Symphony Orchestra' although that is the real expression of my feelings on the matter.

Later on I shall want to know if I am to send complete orchestral parts as well as score. Unless I hear from you I shall conclude that Oct 1 would suit you for receiving the MS. It will be of a quiet nature and will not require any special instruments.[18] I think it will last about 18 minutes. It was kind of Mr. Engles[19] to send the cheque for $250.

Please remember me cordially to Mr. Damrosch.

Y Sincerely

Gustav Holst[20]

As the work began to take shape, Holst wrote toThomas Hardy of his compositional activity and of his intent to dedicate the work to the novelist. Hardy responded with the following invitation:

Max Gate
Dorcester

6 Aug. 1927

Dear Mr. Holst:

We shall be delighted to see you on Tuesday next, and my wife says will you come to lunch at one o'clock.

I will not go into the news you give me of the musical creation you have contrived on Egdon Heath. I am sure it will be very striking. I accept the dedication with pleasure.

Sincerely yours

Thomas Hardy[21]

And what a pleasure the visit was! Holst hiked all the way from Bristol to Dorchester, traveling south through the Mendip Hills, Wells, Sherbourne[22] and Cerne Abbas. Florence Hardy comments about Holst's day out with Hardy:

> ...on August 9 Hardy drove with Gustav Holst to "Egdon Heath", just then purple with heather. They went on to Puddletown and entered the fine old church, and both climbed up into the gallery, where probably some of Hardy's ancestors had sat in the choir, more than a century earlier.[23]

One can only imagine what the pair of them looked like: the near-sighted Holst, then age 52, and the frail Hardy, then 87, who probably drove--each of them enthusiatically gazing upon the heath country that had meant so much to both of them. Egdon Heath in its summer adornment obviously served as an impetus to Holst, who was readily able to finish the work, including two full scores, over the next seven weeks. For Hardy, it was a time to reminisce. Ascending the stairs to the gallery of the old Puddletown church might have required a substantial effort on the part of Hardy, although for the walker Holst, this would have been no problem.

Holst commented about the day's events and of the hazards of walking in a letter written that same evening to Vally Lasker:

Phoenix Hotel
Dorchester
August 9th, [']27 Tuesday

Dear Vally

Thanks for your card which I found at the post office this morning. I also had another from Adrian[24], letters from Mabel[25] and Jane[26], my shirt from Bristol and an invitation to lunch from Thomas Hardy! It's been a marvellous day--after lunch we had a motor drive Egdon Heath, Tolpuddle etc. He was in great form and told me that

a) what are now call folk dances were once ball-room dances

b) he became acquainted with my *Planets* owing to Col. Lawrence[27] ('Lawrence of Arabia'!) owning a set of records and a gramophone when he was in camp near here.

I've also met Mrs. Methuen the widow of my old rector of Wyck Rissington.

Yesterday I had a real stiff day's walking and now know what it is to be a 'tenderfoot.' (But not a 'pale face'--I'd make a fine understudy to a beet root.) After four day's walking I ought to be in good physical condition although I don't think that my weight can have altered much for 'what I have lost on the swings I have made up on the roundabouts.'

(swings=perspiration)
(roundabouts=blisters)

I shan't be going near Beaminster as I wish to keep on Egdon Heath when I leave here on Thursday morning.

Probably I shall take train to London on Sunday arriving at 103 at 7:30 p.m. (In that case I shall come straight from Waterloo and not go to school until Monday). But if my Left Big Toe (who annoyed me considerably last Saturday) misbehaves I may arrive 24 hours earlier. This is not likely neither is it likely that I shall feel so fresh and vigorous that I shall stay on Egdon Heath until Monday.

So 7:30 Sat unless I write again.

Y

G[28]

Holst also wrote a humorous letter to his daughter Imogen, giving more details of his day and including one of his axioms:

> ....It's been an unbelievable day--lunch, a long motor ride and tea with them both [the Hardys] during which time he [Hardy] showed me Tolpuddle, Rainbarrow, Egdon Heath, 'Melstock' and told me that what are now called folk dances were once ball-room dances that had to be taught to the rustics; also that he made the acquaintence of the 'Planets' from a gramophone belonging to Col. Lawrence--'Lawrence of Arabia'!
>
> The Great Virtue of Life is that it is Improbable.
>
> Both Mr. and Mrs. Hardy hope you will call and see them some day--they thank you for your birthday greetings a little time ago....
>
> I had more Improbable Bits of Life at Cerne Abbas yesterday which I will tell you verbally....[29]

The meeting with Hardy had left a deep impression on Holst's mind. The memories of that day make a rather unexpected appearance in the midst of a lecture on Haydn given by Holst at Harvard University in 1932:

> A few years ago I had a non-musical experience, the memory of which is, to me, an embodiment of the essence of Haydn at his best. It was an afternoon with Thomas Hardy shortly before his death. There was a wealth of experience of town and country, deep and controlled emotion, wisdom and humour, all clothed in perfect courtesy and kindliness.[30]

Holst spent the remainder of August putting the finishing touches on *Egdon Heath* in his sound-proof room at St. Paul's Girls' School. A letter from Flagler at the end of the month prompted the following response from the composer:

St. Paul's Girls' School

Brook Green Hammersmith W6

Sep[tember] 9[, 1927]

Dear Mr. Flagler,

Thank you for your delightful letter of Aug. 31. You shall certainly have the score of 'Egdon Heath' early in October but I fear I cannot send the parts quite so soon.

The score that I send will be a special copy for you and the orchestral society--in my handwriting of course.

I don't know whether I ought to bother you or Mr. Damrosch or Mr. Engles about the details but I shall want to know soon how many string parts you will want, when must you have them, how many performances do you wish to give before the work is 'released' to other orchestras, and when would be the date of the last one.

I am so glad you like the idea. I trust you will not be disappointed in the way I have carried it out.

Yr sincerely

Gustav Holst[31]

P.S. I hope you got my cable and letter announcing the completion of the score and telling you to publish the name.

Holst remained true to his word, finishing his score before October 1:

St. Paul's Girls' School
Brook Green Hammersmith
W6
Sep[tember] 30[, 1927]

Dear Mr. Flagler

Will you please accept this MS score of 'Egdon Heath' with my cordial greetings and thanks.

By next mail I hope to send you details of the orchestral material.

Y sincerely

Gustav Holst[32]

Holst had also made arrangements for the London firm Novello & Co. Ltd. to publish the work. This decision helped facilitate the handling of materials. He wrote to Flagler:

St. Paul's Girls' School
Brook Green Hammersmith W6
Oct[ober] 6 [, 1927]

Dear Mr. Flagler

I write to tell you that 'Egdon Heath' is to be published by Messrs Novello whose agent is Mr. H. W. Gray 159 E. 48th St., NY.

He will arrange all details with your society. I have merely stipulated that you are to have a score and parts presented to you and also, of course, the first performance.

I hope that all will be decided for your satisfaction.

Y Sincerely

Gustav Holst[33]

But this was not to the society's satisfaction. Holst had forgotten about the terms of Damrosch's original written communication, which called for the New York Symphony to have the first three performances. This led to an embarrassing situation for Holst, who had since secured additional performances for the work in England. He wrote to Flagler:

St. Paul's Girls' School
Brook Green Hammersmith W6
Nov[ember] 8[, 1927]

Dear Mr. Flagler

I was delighted to hear that 'Egdon Heath' has reached you.

I am sending an arrangement for 2 pianos for your private use and trust that it will give you some pleasure. (It will not be ready for another fortnight).

I have found the original cablegram that Mr. Damrosch sent me in April and see that he stipulated for the first <u>three</u> performances. As this point was not mentioned in any subsequent letter I--to my deep regret--forgot all about it. I told Novello's that you were to have <u>the</u> first performance and I understand from them that it is to be on Feb. 10.

Novello's have therefore arranged that the first London performance should be on February 23rd by the Philharmonic[34]. The latter body are kindly allowing my native town Cheltenham (which is struggling to maintain orchestral music and which I am anxious to help) to have the first English performance on Feb. 13.

I fear that it is beyond my power to cancel the Philharmonic performance on Feb. 23rd. I gave Novello's a free hand and approved their decision when asked. Of course I can cancel or postpone the Cheltenham one if you wish but that is relatively unimportant. It was most careless of me not to have reread the cable before. But what grieves me most is that I have let the New York Symphony, the London Philharmonic, and Novello's down badly. For the sake of the two latter would you and your society be willing to be content with the first performance only?

Y Sincerely

Gustav Holst

PS
If you want anything else of mine as a contrast on Feb 10 I suggest my 'Fugal Overture' (<u>not</u> Fugal Concerto) which has never been done in the USA I believe. It is short and exciting and is published by Novello. I want it revived because I spoilt its first performance in London[35]. I was feeling ill and took it too slowly. It should have <u>romped</u>!

(The Fugal Concerto is very different and has been often done--I wrote it at Ann Arbor in 1923).[36]

Flagler and his board acquiesced and *Egdon Heath* entered the repertoire via an awkward three orchestra quasi-consortium spearheaded by the New York Symphony's premiere performance.

[1]In his book, *From Kneller Hall to Hammersmith: The Band Works of Gustav Holst* (Tutzing, Germany: Haus Hans Schneider, 1990), p. 121, the author has identified and defined four creative periods in Holst's musical output: 1887-1905 (romantic, under Wagnerian influence), 1906-1913 (influenced by English folk music and Indian Sanskrit elements), 1914-1926 (harmonic expansion), and 1927 through 1934 (linear and contrapuntal mastery). All dates are approximate and none of the three latter periods are vǒid of stylistic tendencies displayed in any previous period.
[2]Adrian C. Boult, "Gustav Holst" in *The Royal College of Music Magazine*, LXX, No. 2 (Summer, 1974), p. 52.
[3]Gustav Holst, *Egdon Heath*, Op. 47, manuscript score, Columbia University Library, New York, New York. There are actually two manuscript scores to this work; the second is at the British Library. Both are authentic.
[4]Robert Spearing, "Holst--The Mystic" in *The Royal College of Music Magazine*, LXX, No. 2 (Summer, 1974), p. 59.
[5]Personal correspondence, Gustav Holst to Austin Lidbury August 11, 1927 quoted in Imogen Holst (ed.), *A Thematic Catalogue of Gustav holst's Music (London: Faber & Faber Ltd., 1974)*, p. 170.
[1]John Erskine, *The Philharmonic Society of New York: Its First 100 Years* (New York: The MacMillan Co., 1943), pp. 27-28.
[7]George Martin, *The Damrosch Dynasty: America's First Family of Music* (Boston: Houghton Mifflin, 1983), p. 306.
[8]Richard Schikel, *The World of Carnegie Hall* (New York: Julius Messner, 1960) pp. 255-256.
[9]Martin, op. cit., pp. 368-369. The four levels, each aimed at a different audience, were A (grades 3 and 4), B (grades 5 and 6), C (junior high), and D (high school and college). Each year twelve one-half hour programs were offered, broadcast sequentially, every other Friday. After the first year, A and B were broadcast back-to-back one week, with C and D offered the next week. Thus Damrosch (and, often the orchestra as well) broadcast for an hour on twenty-four consecutive Fridays.
[10]David Ewen, "The Growth of Radio Music" in Elie Siegmeister (ed.) *The Music Lover's Handbook* (New York: Morrow & Co., 1943), p. 639.
[11]Walter Damrosch, quoted by David Ewen, op. cit., p. 639.
[12]John Walker (ed.), *Halliwell's Film Guide*, 8th ed. (London: Harper Collins, 1992), p. 1053.
[13]James Agee quoted in JohnWalker (ed.) op. cit., p. 189. Among the featured personalities were Artur Rodzinski, Leopold Stokowski, Bruno Walter, Artur Rubenstein, Jasha Heifetz, Lily Pons, Riise Stevens, Jan Peerce, Ezio Pinza, Harry James, Vaughan Monroe, and the New York Philharmonic-Symphony.
[14]Personal correspondence, Walter Damrosch to Adrian Boult, British Library Add Ms. 60998.
[15]Martin, op. cit., pp. 308-309. Only twenty-three of the Symphony players received contracts with the new Philharmonic-Symphony.
[16]Personal correspondence, Gustav Holst to Harry Harkness Flagler, November 8, 1927 and July 19, 1928, The Pierpont Morgan Library, Mary Flagler Carey Music Collection.
[17]John Erskine, *The Philharmonic Society of New York: Its First 100 Years* (New York: The MacMillan Co., 1943), pp. 27-28.
[18]Holst's final instrumentation consists of two flutes, two oboes, cor anglais, two clarinets in B flat, two bassoons, contrabassoon, four horns, two trumpets, two tenor trombones, bass trombone, tuba, and strings. Piccolo and bass clarinet were also indicated on the original score in the British Library (Add MS 57899), but the composer changed his mind and crossed them out. These instruments do not appear on the (second) manuscript score that Holst prepared for the New York

Symphony Society. Also, on the British Library score Holst, continuing his policy of flexible instrumentation (even for works demanding professional-level ensembles), included the following note: "The following instruments are cued and may be dispensed with: 2nd oboe, Double Bassoon, 3rd and 4th Horns, 3rd Trumpet, Tuba."

[19]George Engles, business manager of the New York Symphony Society.

[20]Personal correspondence, Gustav Holst to Harry Harkness Flagler, July 30, 1927, The Pierpont Morgan Library, The Mary Flagler Carey Music Collection.

[21]Personal correspondence, Thomas Hardy to Gustav Holst, August 6, 1927, The Holst Foundation.

[22]Personal correspondence, Gustav Holst to Frank Austin Lidbury, August 11, 1927, quoted in Imogen Holst, *Gustav Holst: A Biography* (Oxford, Oxford university Press, 1938), 126-127.

[23]Florence Hardy, *The Life of Thomas Hardy, Vol II: The Later Years of Thomas Hardy, 1892-1928* (London: Macmillan, 1930; new edition published by London: Studio Editions Ltd., 1994), p. 256.

[24]Adrian Boult.

[25]Mabel Rodwell Jones.

[26]Jane Joseph.

[27]Thomas Edward [T. E.] Lawrence (1888-1935). In a letter to Austin Lidbury dated August 11, 1927, Holst wrote of the same story, ending with "I wish I could invent tales like that!".

[28]Personal correspondence, Gustav Holst to Vally Lasker Tuesday, August 9th, [19]27, The Holst Foundation.

[29]Personal correspondence, Gustav Holst to Imogen Holst, Tuesday [9 August, 1927], The Holst Foundation.

[30]Gustav Holst, quoted in Ursula Vaughan Williams (ed.) and Imogen Holst (ed.), *Heirs and Rebels: Letter to Each Other and Occasional Writings by Gustav Holst and Ralph Vaughan Williams* (Oxford, England: Oxford University Press, 1959), p. 89.

[31]Personal correspondence, Gustav Holst to Harry Harkness Flagler, Sep[tember] 9[,1927], The Pierpont Morgan Library, Mary Flagler Carey Music Collection.

[32]Personal correspondence, Gustav Holst to Harry Harkness Flagler, Sep[tember] 30[,1927], The Pierpont Morgan Library, Mary Flagler Carey Music Collection.

[33]Personal correspondence, Gustav Holst to Harry Harkness Flagler, Oct[ober] 6[,1927], The Pierpont Morgan Library, Mary Flagler Carey Music Collection.

[34]The London Phiharmonic.

[35]Ths first performance of *A Fugal Overture*, Op. 40 No. 1 (1922) [H151] was given on October 11, 1923 by the New Queen's Hall Orchestra at Queen's Hall, London, Holst conducting.

[36]Personal correspondence, Gustav Holst to Harry Harkness Flagler, Nov[ember] 8[,1927], The Pierpont Morgan Library, Mary Flagler Carey Music Collection.

CHAPTER XVII

THE PREMIERES OF EGDON HEATH

The person to whom *Egdon Heath* was dedicated would never hear it performed. After a month-long illness, Thomas Hardy died of a heart attack on January 11, 1928. Holst immediately amended the dedication of his composition to read:

Homage to Thomas Hardy
Egdon Heath

Florence Hardy in turn wrote to the composer:

Max Gate
Dorchester
Dorset

7th February '28

Dear Mr. Holst:

I thank you so much for your kind sympathy. I am sure you realize what a shattering blow the loss of my husband is to my whole life.

Your postcard came at the beginning of his illness but he was well enough to be interested and pleased in what you told him. February 11th--the day that was suggested for the first performance--would have been the 14th anniversary of our marriage.

I thank you for the music that arrived today. It is a noble tribute to my husband. How much I wish he could have lived to know, and to thank you.

I fear I shall not be able to go to Cheltenham, but I should much like to go to London to hear it on February 23rd if you would kindly let me have particulars later.

He was so pleased with your visit to us last August.

Again Thanking You.

Yours sincerely,

Florence Hardy[1]

The performances went on as scheduled, with Walter Damrosch and the New York Symphony Society giving the world premiere of *Egdon Heath* at Mecca Auditorium in New York on February 12, 1928. The work was not judged to be an immediate success. Olin Downes, powerful music critic of the *New York Times*, gave the following account of the performance:

New York Symphony Orchestra

It was a curious coincidence that a few days after the death of Thomas Hardy there should be played for the first time the orchestral rhapsody "Egdon Heath," which Gustav Holst composed last Summer, after spending some days in Wessex with the novelist. This took place at the concert given by the New York Symphony Orchestra, Walter Damrosch, conductor, yesterday afternoon in Mecca Temple. The event was observed with all due ceremony, and a part of the opening chapter of Hardy's "Return of the Native," that chapter which contains the noble and sombre beauty of the description of the Wessex moor was read, prior to the orchestral performance, by Paul Leyssac.

Unfortunately for many in the audience, Mr. Leyssac misjudged the acoustics in the auditorium, so that his words were not audible to everyone there. But the program contained fragmentary quotations from Hardy, among them this description of the plain: "A place pefectly accordant with man's nature, neither ghastly, hateful nor ugly; neither commonplace, unmeaning nor tame, but like man, alighted and enduring and withal singularly colossal and mysterious in its swarthy monotony." Much more could be quoted from the matchless page of Hardy, but these words will

> serve, perhaps, as a keynote to the mood of the music, which only momentarily refers to the Heath awakening at nightfall, or swept away by the tempest unleashed. The prevailing mood of the music, appropriately enough, is melancholy, mysterious, with the final measures which return to the music of the opening. A large orchestra is employed. The form is naturally free rather than classic, except in general outlines.
>
> Repeated hearings of this music might reveal to the attentive ear certain distinctions of harmonic color or mood that were not apparent yesterday. Is Holst the composer of whom a temperamental sympathy with Hardy could be expected? There are pages in Vaughan Williams' "London Symphony" which have for us a nearer affinity to the spirit of Egdon Heath. But that is somewhat beside the point. A composer, inspired by a literary subject, has often produced music quite inappropriate to the subject, but good music. It must be admitted that the hearing of yesterday afternoon did not give the impression of a significant composition. To attempt to embody in tones the thoughts so eloquently revealed by Hardy's prose is a risky proceeding under most circumstances, and it might have been better for the composer if Mr. Leyssac had not reminded the audience of the music of the original text. Under the circumstances the new score seemed long and rather undistinguished....[2]

Downes' review, though certainly not positive, did not outwardly condemn the work. The critic acknowledged that the work might be better received with another hearing. Had Downes been out to doom the work or Holst, he would have done so. During the previous two years, Downes' columns alone almost singlehandedly destroyed Wilhelm Furtwängler's chances for the conductorship of the New York Philharmonic by his strong support of Arturo Toscanini.

Two factors mentioned in Downes' review worked against *Egdon Heath* at its premiere. Paul Leyssac's inaudible readings of selections from *Return of the Native* not only made the audience restless, but also tied Holst's music too firmly to Hardy's text. After all, Holst knew Egdon Heath intimately; he had hiked all over it. While Hardy's words provided Holst with the incentive to begin the work, it was personal contact with the heath itself that had given Holst the impetus to bring the composition to completion. The other factor, revealed later in the review, was the programming itself. The concert opened with *Festival Overture*, composed by the conductor's father. Then followed *Egdon Heath*. Two favorites, Rachmaninoff's *Piano Concerto No. 3 in D minor*, Op. 30, with Vladimir Horowitz as soloist and Beethoven's *Symphony No. 5 in C minor, Op. 67*, made up the remainder of the program. Undoubtedly, the majority of the audience was already craving Horowitz, Rachmaninoff, and Beethoven before Damrosch had even picked up the baton to conduct the then-modernistic *Egdon Heath*.

There were additional factors as well that contributed to the non-success of *Egdon Heath*'s world premiere. For one thing, times were tough artistically for the New York Symphony Society. In 1920, the Symphony was the most prestigious of the New York orchestras; it had been the first to go on a world tour. Since that time, however, the Philharmonic had become the more powerful of the two, having secured greater financial and artistic support through its recent "mergers". By 1927, the Symphony was seen by many as an also-ran--the second-best orchestra in the city. On the very same afternoon that Damrosch was premiering *Egdon Heath*, Toscanini was conducting the New York Philharmonic in Elgar's *Enigma Variations* and Brahms' *Second Symphony* at Carnegie Hall. Even the standing-room for the Philharmonic concert was sold out.[3] Damrosch was a highly-respected and competent conductor, but neither he nor the Symphony could keep pace with the excitement wielded by the impassioned Italian maestro.

Finally, Holst's compositional style had undergone a significant change since the writing of *The Planets* and *The Perfect Fool*. Instead of receiving a crowd pleaser, the New York Symphony Society received a work from a composer who now realized musical strength through his own brand of antisentimentality. Even Damrosch was unprepared for the austerity of the new Holst.

The poor reception afforded *Egdon Heath* hit Holst hard. He commented to Flagler:

St. Paul's Girls' School
Brook Green Hammersmith
W6

April 20[,] 1928

Dear Mr. Flagler

Messrs Novello have just sent me the program and two newspaper cuttings of the New York performance of 'Egdon Heath.' I had been waiting for some time and now that it has arrived I am most disappointed both for your sake and for mine.

It only remains for me to thank you both for the honour you have done me and for the delightful letters you have sent me and to assure you that I should not have sent you the work if I had not felt so deeply and definitely about it when I finished it--a feeling which has since been intensified by hearing it in public three times.

Yours sincerely,

Gustav Holst[4]

Egdon Heath did not fare much better at its other "premieres." It met with mild success in the British premiere performance given on February 13th at Town Hall in Cheltenham. There, however, the composer was fully in control of the situation. He could do no wrong at the Cheltenham performance. Holst had become a hero in his home town and had been made a Freeman of the city. He himself conducted the City of Birmingham Symphony and was able to modify the programming according to his own wishes, which he mentioned in the following correspondence to Flagler:

St. Paul's Girls' School
Brook Green Hammersmith
W6
May 8[,] 1928

Dear Mr. Flagler,

Thank you for your nice long letter. I am sorry that you have been so ill and that you were unable to hear 'Egdon Heath.' I am naturally disappointed that the work was not a success. So far its greatest success was at Cheltenham. After the performance it was received with mild applause and some expressions of dissent. It was followed by a more popular work of mine, 'A Fugal Overture,' which the audience insisted on encoring. To their dismay I insisted on repeating 'Egdon Heath' instead, and this time the work really got home and made a deep impression indeed. I am hoping to have an autumn performance in London. If it is ever done again in New York, I suggest that it should be done without the quotation from Thomas Hardy.

I trust you are well again. If you ever come to England I hope I shall have the pleasure of meeting you.

Yours sincerely,

Gustav Holst[5]

The London premiere of *Egdon Heath* was given February 23, 1928 at Queen's Hall by the orchestra of the Royal Philhramonic Society. Vaclav Talich (1883-1961), the gifted Bohemian conductor of the Czech Philharmonic, was the featured guest conductor. The occasion, however, was less than auspicious, as was confirmed by the following concert review appearing in *The Times*:

Royal Philharmonic Society
Brahms and Holst

Neither M. Vaclav Talich who conducted the Royal Philharmonic Society's orchestra for the first time last night at Queen's Hall nor Mr. Gustav Holst, whose new work, "Egdon Heath," was performed in London for the first time, was entirely fortunate in being cast for this particular night. The London Symphony Orchestra is away on tour and that means that the Royal Philharmonic Orchestra is not for the moment quite itself, since London orchestras are made up of interchangeable parts. A good many of the leading members were away, and their places were taken by deputies. Nevertheless, M. Talich was, on the whole, well able to get the results he wanted, and no doubt his experience as conductor of the Scottish Orchestra through last season has [muted?] him to the rough-and-ready conditions of orchestra concert-giving in this country.

The uncompromising style of Holst's "Egdon Heath" was emphasized by its place between Berlioz' hilarious "Carneval Roman" overture and Brahms' gracious violin concerto. It was difficult to feel it to be "perfectly accordant with man's nature" or indeed to attach to it any of the qualities named in the quotation from Thomas Hardy on the title-page of the score. It is clearly accordant with the composer's nature, but that, we feel is not the same thing. There seems to be something left out, something which is essential in order that the music may be a communication from man to man. At the end the audience applauded persistently to show their appreciation of Mr. Holst, but not with that spontaneity which shows that a piece of music has come home to the hearers. There is nothing bewildering about a first hearing of it. The whole has that simplicity of plan and crystalline clearness of instrumentation which belongs to Holst's deliberate technical style. It leaves no room for doubt that he has said precisely what he meant to say. Each listener may decide for himself whether it is what he wants to hear.

> Brahms used to be called uncompromising. His concerto, played by M. Szigeti, sounded almost too ingratiating after the Holst work....[6]

The rather lengthy concert also included a performance of Dvorak's *Symphony No. 4 [8] in G.*

The review from *The Times*, however, tells only part of the story. Imogen Holst spared few words in her description of the London premiere, labelling it "disastrous:"

> The concert organizers had put *Egdon Heath* as the second item on the concert, after the overture, and the foreign conductor [Talich] was not used to Queen's Hall audiences. He made the fatal mistake of starting the orchestra before some of the late arrivals in the stalls had got into their places. The quiet start, mysterious opening for muted double basses was inaudible; one could see the players' arms moving to and fro, but nothing could be heard through the buzz of conversation and the shuffle of feet. Those members of the audience who were already in their places glared at the late-comers and said 'ssshhh,' which added to the confusion. the guilty late-comers glared back, furious with the conductor for having started so soon, and even more furious with the composer for having written such a quiet opening. After this, the music had little chance of making an impression on those who had not yet seen the score.[7]

Still, two of the people who mattered the most to Holst had a great deal of praise for the work. On February 28th Jane Joseph wrote:

> ....This being the Eve of the Day when ladies may say what they like, may I take the opportunity (be Calm!) of saying how much I love Egdon Heath! In the excitement of everything I forgot to. Which was dreadful. And I know I shall love it more and more--like "Sleepers Wake" and other good things. This is a most "impressing" work (impressive gives the wrong meaning--at least I think it does: I mean the impression it leaves is very vivid and haunting and lasting one [ ).]
>
> It is difficult to say more--the music does it for one. Thank you so much.
>
> Love from Jane[8]

Ralph Vaughan Williams, who was often Holst's greatest critic, was only slightly less exuberant, writing to the composer:

> I've come to the conclusion that E.H. is beautiful--bless you therefore[9]

Perhaps it was a combination of receiving such personal accolades, involvement in his teaching, plus his continued contact with nature that kept Holst from entering a state of depression. Whatever the case, there is no sense of despair and in fact a great deal of Holstian humor contained in a remarkable letter that he wrote to cheer up Adeline Vaughan Williams, who had been ill. He had been walking in Shropshire and, finding no writing paper available, wrote the following on the backs of twelve miniature picture post cards!:

> Buchnell
> April 4 9PM [1928]
>
> Dear Adeline
>
> I have not managed to get to Clun today partly because I spent so long in Cooking round Ludlow that I did not leave it until one and partly because when I did leave it I took a wrong turn and went some miles out of my way and partly because I felt lazy and took life easily.
>
> Shropshire remains an ideal walking county and the weather has been better today for I have actually had two hours' sun!
>
> Looking at the map of Shropshire has made me wonder where one would go if when [one] chose to go places because one was attracted by their names. For instance, one would avoid Llanfihangel Rhydithon especially if one had to ask the way. It would be far better to go to Evenjobb in spite of its extra 'b.' And although I had an excellent tea at Leintwardine today yet if one had the choice one would possibly be more attracted by Albright Hussey especially as Fiddler's Arm, which I passed today, is not a pub but a gorge. And by that I mean a narrow valley between two hills and not the meal that I've just finished.
>
> Although it is, strictly speaking, off the point, I think it worth mentioning that the rate collector at Ludlow is Mr. Tantrums. Which--like most other details of life--is improbable.
>
> Last night's inn was a real hotel with a hot bath containing water that was hot as well as writing paper and electric bells and other luxuries. This place is a real country inn and as they don't seem to have any writing paper I am using the backs of these photos.

I shall post it in Clun if I ever get there, which, like everything else on a walk, is uncertain. The great rule in walking tours is to plan to go somewhere and then drift somewhere else by mistake.

Which I am doing.

Y
Gustav[10]

Holst usually went solo on such walking trips, but did not discourage others from joining him. Two months later Holst's American friend Austin Lidbury visited England. Holst entertained him at the George on June 7th and three weeks later the two of them went walking in the Cotswold Hills.[11] Always eager to "spread the wealth" of Lidbury's merry company to his own countrymen, Holst dropped a postcard to Edwin Evans:

E Evans Esq
31 Colherne Rd.
Earl's Court
London SW7

An American friend of mine Mr. Austin Lidbury wants to meet you. He will probably ring you up on Thursday night or Friday afternoon to invite you to dinner on Friday evening. In case you get this in time would you drop him a line at Howard Hotel Norfolk The Strand telling him if you are free and suggesting time and place. (I suggest Pagani). Will you please consider this as an informal introduction. He is having a 2 day walk with me in the Cotswolds and sails for home on Saturday and friday is his only free evening.

Y
Gustav Holst
Sherbourne
July 6[12]

Another factor which kept Holst's spirits from collapsing was the fact that he continued to be in demand as a composer. In terms of compositional output, the spring and summer of 1928 was a productive period for Holst. His *Incidental Music for The Coming of Christ* [H170], mostly completed the preceding year, was performed at Canterbury Cathedral on Whitsuntide. A major band composition, *A Moorside Suite* [H173], commissioned for the National Brass Band Championships was well underway and, after a May 8th meeting with B. Walton O'Donnell[13], conductor of the BBC Wireless Military Band, two transcriptions of *Bach's Fugue a la Gigue* [App. III, 25], for military band and--at the wishes of Boosey & Hawkes--for orchestra, were completed at this time.

Holst's works continued to be performed with great regularity. Stanford Robinson, the youthful Master of Choral Music at the BBC, conducted the Wireless Chorus in the Third Group of the *Choral Hymns from the Rig Veda* on a June 14th broadcast. Holst himself conducted the BBC Wireless Military Band in a broadcast of both of his military band suites on July 22nd[14] and conducted these same works again plus the second movement ("Nocturne") of *A Moorside Suite* and *Bach's Fugue a la Gigue* at a concert at the West End Cinema in Birmingham featuring the Birmingham Police Band on October 14th.[15] During the previous week, *Savitri* was performed for the first time in Melbourne, Australia.[16] In the midst of this flurry of activity, however, Holst could not forget about *Egdon Heath*. Musically, its stark linear clarity continued to be felt in the "Nocturne" of *A Moorside Suite* as it could in its more obvious reincarnation in the "Prelude" of *Hammersmith*. Personally the failure of *Egdon Heath* continued to gnaw away at his soul. He wrote again to Flagler, this time about financial and monetary matters:

St. Paul's Girls' School
Brook Green Hammersmith
W6
July 19[, 1928]

Dear Mr. Flagler

I am sorry to trouble you further about 'Egdon Heath' but two points have arisen.

a) The original offer from the New York Symphony Orchestra was for 500 dollars, 200 to be paid immediately and 300 on rect. of score. I received the first installment over a year ago but the second has never reached me although I had a delightful letter from you on Oct 19th acknowledging rect. of the score.

b) You stipulated for the first three performances. You kindly altered this later for the first three in America. (I was most grateful for this). Owing to the non-success of the work it seems doubtful if the 2nd and 3rd performances will ever be given by your orchestra.

Meanwhile Mr. Stock[17] writes from Chicago telling me that he hopes to do it very often next autumn! I should be sorry to disappoint him but of course must abide by any conditions you make.

Perhaps you would kindly advise me.

Y very sincerely

Gustav Holst[18]

Flagler responded quickly and sent Holst the remainder of his commission. The composer in turn sent a receipt, enclosed with his final letter to Flagler:

St. Paul's Girls' School
Brook Green Hammersmith
W6
Aug[ust] 17[, 1928]

Dear Mr. Flagler

It was well worth waiting in order to get another delightful letter from you for which I thank you heartily.

I enclose formal rects. There is just one thing more I beg of you. Please don't suggest lending parts to another orchestra! It is so rough on the publishers and they need every encouragement to print parts of serious orchestral music.

I am sure you are right about a 2nd and 3rd perf of 'Egdon Heath.' I am conducting it at Queen's Hall next month and wish you could be there.

Y Sincerely

Gustav Holst[19]

Holst never gave up on *Egdon Heath*. He later autographed a copy of the printed score and gave it to Serge Koussevitzky, the Boston Symphony Orchestra conductor who would help make the composer's third and final American visit an artistic as well as an academic success. Holst's inscription is simple:

Serge Koussevitzky

from
Gustav Holst
with greetings
Sep 1932[20]

As in the case of many other works by Holst, *Egdon Heath* fell into a semi-oblivion in the decades immediately following his death. Still, the work was known and appreciated by some, as this 1956 letter from Percy Grainger to Imogen Holst indicates:

[Grainger Museum
University of Melbourne
Melbourne, Australia]
Feb 22, 1954

Dear Miss Holst,

Shorthly before his death Balfour Gardiner sent me your deeply touching and unforgettable book about your father and his genius. I would have written long ere this to thank you for this anguish and reverence this glorious record arouses had I not been ill all these last years. I have been in and out of hospitals all the time & have undergone10 operations--some major, some minor. However I seem now to have recovered well & my wife & I are very busy (working from 6.00 am to 7 pm) arranging the exhibits in this museum, which is given over to processes of composition. But that I mean that we try to show things throwing light on what makes composers compose (influence of parents, fellow-composers, friends, wives, etc.) & how they do it (their letters to each other, etc., their sketches, etc.)....

I had unforgettable impressions of your father & his cosmic music at the Balfour Gardiner Concerts of 1912, 1913. I not only enjoyed *Beni Mora* more than any other composition I had ever heard based on oriental themes (such as Saint Saen's *Algerian Suite* or *Scheherazade*) but I thought it was the BEST DONE of such works. The curator of this museum (Richard Fenlay) gives programmes of grammophone records & the other day he did *The Planets* & Balfour's *Philgheia* for me--both glorious works, both so perfect & so strangely different. *The Planets* have for me the beauty of facts. The music is so strangely lovely always & so utterly personal & original. Apart from that it seems to me the best kind of program-music.

The main purpose of this letter is to ask you if you would feel inclined to ask the publishers to donate to this museum 2 copies of such scores as you would like to see shown in this museum--one copy for display on the slanting desks, the second copy for study in the library (presuming you would like any shown, of course). I cannot afford to buy much music just now, as I have not been earning (concertising) for so long & have had heavy doctor's and hospital expenses. In the future I could buy the scores of course, it would speed up matters greatly if the publishers would donate some now. If you & they approved of this (to make a beginning) I would like you to decide which ones we should begin with. My own choice would be to begin with these I already know & love:

The Planets
Beni Mora
Rig Veda hymns
The Hymn of Jesus
Egdon Heath
Both Band Suites
6 Choral Folksongs, opus 36

....Of course I have the desired 2 copies of your book on your father here already.

If any music is to be sent please kindly mark it "Gift to Grainger Museum," to avoid duty at this end.

When my wife & I come to England next I hope we may have the joy of meeting you. Perhaps we could discuss our making photostat copies of some of your father's [25?] works. I feel it is so all-important that the works of genius of our races & our era are preserved for the future.

Again thanking you for the soul-satisfying book on your great father,

Yours admiringly

Percy Grainger[21]

Imogen Holst enthusiastically answered Grainger's letter, but had to comment on the sad realities regarding the availability of her father's music in the 1950's:

> ....I wish I could be more helpful about sending you scores of my father's works. The sad thing is that so many of his works are out of print.
> *Egdon Heath* is unobtainable.[22]

Fortunately, for those living several decades later, this is no longer the case.

---

[1]Personal correspondence, Florence Hardy to Gustav Holst, 7 February[,19]28, The Holst Foundation.
[2]*The New York Times*, February 13, 1928.
[3]*Ibid.*
[4]Personal correspondence, Gustav Holst to Harry Harkness Flagler, April 20[,1928], The Pierpont Morgan Library, Mary Flagler Carey Music Collection.
[5]Personal correspondence, Gustav Holst to Harry Harkness Flagler, May 8, 1928, The Pierpont Morgan Library, Mary Flagler Carey Music Collection.
[6]*The Times* (London), February 24, 1928.
[7]Imogen Holst, *Holst*, 2nd ed. (London: Faber & Faber, 1981), pp. 72-73.
[8]Personal correspondence, Jane Joseph to Gustav Holst, February 28, 1928.
[9]Personal correspondence, Ralph Vaughan Williams to Gustav Holst, Feb[ruary] 25[,1928], quoted in Ursula Vaughan Williams (ed.) and Imogen Holst (ed.): *Heirs and Rebels: Letters to Each Others and Occasional Writings by Gustav Holst and Ralph Vaughan Williams* (Oxford: Oxford University Press, 1959), 64.
[10]Personal correspondence, Gustav Holst to Adeline Vaughan Williams, April 4 [,1928], British Library Add. MS 57853.
[11]Gustav Holst, *Diary*, Thursday, June 7 and Thursday, June 28, 1928, The Holst Foundation.
[12]Personal correspondence, Gustav Holst to Edwin Evans, July 6[, 1928], Central Public Library, Westminster.
[13]Gustav Holst, *Diary*, Tuesday, May 8, 1928, The Holst Foundation.
[14]Gustav Holst, *Diary*, Sunday, July 22, 1928, The Holst Foundation. On this same broadcast Stanford Robinson conducted three selections ("There was a tree," "I sowed the seeds of love," and "Swansea Town") from the *Six Hampshire Folk Songs*, Op. 36b [H136] (1916).
[15]*Birmingham Post*, October 15, 1928.
[16]Personal correspondence, Clive Carey to Gustav Holst, October 13, 1928, The Holst Foundation.
[17]Frederick Stock, conductor of the Chicago Symphony Orchestra.
[18]Personal correspondence, Gustav Holst to Harry Harkness Flagler, July 19[, 1928], The Pierpont Morgan Library, Mary Flagler Carey Music Collection.
[19]Personal correspondence, Gustav Holst to Harry Harkness Flagler, Aug[ust] 17[,1928], The Pierpont Morgan Library, Mary Flagler Carey Music Collection..
[20]Gustav Holst, *Egdon Heath*, Op. 47 (London: Novello, 1928), autographed published score with corrections card, Boston Public Library.
[21]Personal correspondence, Percy Grainger to Imogen Holst, Feb[ruary] 22, 1956, The Grainger Museum, University of Melbourne, Melbourne, Australia.
[22]Personal correspondence, Imogen Holst to Percy Grainger, 6th March, 1956, The Grainger Museum, University of Melbourne, Melbourne, Australia.

CHAPTER XVIII

A SECOND AMERICAN INVITATION

The genesis of Holst's second visit to America occurred during the autumn of 1924, when he received word that he had been awarded Yale University's Henry Elias Howland Memorial Prize. Holst normally shunned such offers, but perhaps it was the wording of the correspondence that helped the composer recognize the sincerity behind the international honor that was being bestowed upon him:

> ....We hope you will accept these [medal and check] as a testimonial of the high esteem in which your work as a composer is held by the University and an earnest [expression] of our hope that you may secure the conditions necessary for uninterrupted creative work...[1]

The check amounted to $1350, a hefty sum in those days. While the money was nice, it would not have been the decisive factor in Holst's acceptance of the award. True, Holst had been seriously ill earlier in the year, still suffering the after-effects of his University of Reading accident as well as overwork. He therefore had to to relinquish a significant portion of his teaching responsibilities, including his beloved post at Morley College. This resignation resulted in a significant loss of income, but the reception of a substantial monetary gift made possible through the generosity of Claude Johnson[2], a director of Rolls Royce Ltd., had helped Holst to overcome his financial shortcomings and enjoy a life of active artistic creativity without sacrificing his family's needs. While leaving his other teaching positions, Holst stayed on at St. Paul's Girls' School, and the income from this plus Johnson's gift was bolstered by moneys received from other sources, primarily royalties and recording contracts. Two major works, the massive *First Choral Symphony*, Op. 41 [H155] and the Shakespearean opera *At the Boar's Head*, Op. 42 [H156] are products of this period of relative leisure.

Two weeks after Holst received the award, it was made public in the *New York Times*:

> The award of the Howland Memorial Prize to Gustav Holst, noted composer of the modern English school, is announced by Yale University today. This is the third award of the prize, which, in the fields of fine arts and government, might be compared in purpose with the Nobel Prize for Scientific achievement. It was first awarded in 1916 to the late Rupert Brooke, poet, and in 1918 to Jean Jullien Lemordant, the French artist who lost his eyesight in the war....
>
> The Henry Elias Howland Memorial Prize, consisting of a medal and the income from a fund, was established at Yale university on June 3, 1915, by a gift of Charles P. Howland, B.A., Yale, 1891, of NewYork, and Dr. John Howland, B.A., Yale, 1894, of Baltimore, in memory of their father, Henry Elias Howland, B.A., Yale, 1854, who died in New York on Nov. 7, 1913.[3]

This was indeed a great honor for Holst, who must have recognized it for what it was. He felt a personal debt of gratitude to Yale University. The opportunity to repay this imagined debt, however, would not present itself until more than four years had passed.

The fall of 1928 was one of Holst's busiest. He was now in his mid-fifties and in good health, having long since regained his strength. During the first week of September he took a quick trip to France and Luxembourg. There he visited Fontainebleu and visited the Louvre twice.[4] Back home he found himself with band music on his mind. The commission from the British Broadcasting Corporation to write the work that would eventually become *Hammersmith*, Op. 52 [H178] was just the beginning.[5] There were guest conducting engagments before both live and broadcast audiences. He also served as an adjudicator at the National Brass Band Championships, held during late September at the Crystal Palace in Southeast London. The test piece that year was his own *A Moorside Suite*, specially commissioned for that event. He heard it played over and over again.

While all of this was going on, Holst continued with his usual busy schedule of teaching and lecturing. The composer was once again in need of a sabbatical. He wanted to clear his mind of everyday problems in order to compose, so he decided not to teach during the winter term at St. Paul's Girls' School. Instead. he sought a replenishing of his musical thought in sunny Italy. On December 17th, he sent the following postcard to Frances Gray, former High Mistress of St. Paul's[6], who was also planning on spending some time in Italy, with her sister:

St. Paul's Girls' School
Brook Green, Hammersmith W6

Dear Miss Gray,

Just a line to say

a) I am running away from school from Dec 20th until Easter 1929.

b) I shall be in Rome on the evening of the 24th and shall stay until the 27th or later before going on to Naples.

c) I want to see you--lots of you!

d) I don't know where I shall be staying but letters sent to me @ Mrs. Dyer[7], Excelsior Hotel, Rome will reach me on arrival.

e) Thank you for being in Rome.

Yr ever

Gustav Holst[8]

On December 20, Holst left England for Italy, arriving in Rome on Christmas Eve, and meeting Louise Dyer and her husband, James, as he had planned. Rome was just the beginning. He also visited Pompeii, Naples and at least a dozen other locations in Italy before returning home. He happened to be in Florence when the following invitation from the American Academy of Arts and Letters caught up with him:

February 20, 1929

Gustav Holst,
Care of Stainer and Bell Ltd.,
58 Berners St., W.1. London

The American Academy of Arts and Letters earnestly invites your presence as guest of the Academy celebration twenty-fifth anniversary New York April twenty third and twenty fourth. Academy has voted allowance of 200 pounds for ocean travel and incidental expenses. Kindly cable reply, Interpax, New York.

Butler, President

Johnson, Secretary[9]

This cable came as a complete surprise to Holst, who was obviously pleased. He wired his acceptance immediately[10] and commented about it in the following letter to Isobel:

Perugia
Feb 26 [1929]

Dear Iso

I wrote to you from Pisa on Saturday and the next day on returning to Florence I got the American Cable that Nora had forwarded to me. It invites me as guest to the 25th anniversary of the Academy of Arts New York on April 23 and 24. It may be that they have sent a full letter and that Nora made up the cable. In that case I shall hear from her on my return to Florence on Friday. The cable mentions the offer of £200 for expenses. It is a great lesson in humility to realise that the world offers one five times as much for doing nothing as it does for doing one's job! I suppose the idea is that I go just to look pretty. In that case I'd better grow a beard.

The matter is complicated by the fact that if I go to the U.S.A. I must offer to give that lecture in Yale University which I should have given four years ago when they gave me that prize. That involves being in the U.S.A. a week or more before and that involves probably leaving England on Sat Ap. 6.

I've written to Douglas Kennedy[11] asking him whether he could get anyone else to do the singing at Keswick and if not, whether he will let me off the last day so that I can leave Keswick at midday on April 5. If there were a boat on the 6th from Liverpool I could catch it easily.

Another complication is that I ought to leave NY by the first boat after April 24 so as to be back in town for the beginning of term and for the rehearsals for Canterbury. I have cabled to New York accepting the invitation. On my return to Florence on Friday next I shall write to Yale offering to lecture and to New York explaining that I can only come on condition that I can get a boat home directly [after] the function is over. I suppose it will be a super convention and I shall hate it on the whole but I ought to save over £100 and therefore it will be worth it.

Vally told me that you would be staying with her so I am sending this to 103[12]. Please thank her for her letter. I'll answer it on my return to Florence[13] as I wrote to Nora yesterday and I believe they share letters. Also I shall have more news then. I had thought of shortening my holiday because of this New York business but the Italian agents have bought my railway tickets and engaged my rooms at hotels right up to March 22 and it would be the devil's own job to alter the tour. Moreover I don't see that I could do much by returning earlier. The chief object would be to find out about boats especially those returning from New York. I believe they all get filled up months beforehand at that time. If you know anyone who could do this for me set them to work.

I wish I could be at the RCM[14] tomorrow. I shall revenge myself by writing a long letter to her.[15]

BL

G

PS My only address after March 1 and before returning to London will be

Hotel Boston
Calle Specchieri
Venezia

from March 9 to 15.[16]

Indeed, Holst did "revenge" himself by writing a very lengthy letter to Imogen, who was then a student at the Royal College of Music. Some of her compositions were being played in a competition at the school. Holst commented:

Perugia Feb 27 [1929]

Dear Imogen

How I wish I were with you today! Perugia is a fine place but just now it's not a patch on Kensington Gore even apart from the weather (it is a drizzling cold thaw and there is mist instead of scenery). You ought to get a first rate performance as a result of that competition. Why, oh why wasn't I that outside examiner? The only thing left for me to do now is to look forward to a well planned and lengthy Revenge next term--an Imogen Festival lasting a week during which I hear at least one thing of yours every day. Even then I suppose it's no use hoping to hear the quartet. You'll have to arrange it for piano and violin and bring in Vicky. Or can't you get it replicated at a concert next term 'by desire'? Tell the Director that I'll do the desiring. In fact, I'm doing it ferociously now....

I have the rest of my tour planned out but am thinking that perhaps I had better cut it short by a day or so as to catch the American mail on the evening of March 22. Could you get the times and fares of the Tillbury-Dunkirk line from Cook (they have them on a pamphlet I think) and let me have them at the Hotel Boston?...Don't go out of your way as perhaps I can find out for myself in Venice. It is queer that the line seems unknown in Florence. I am booked to return via Bale and Brussels and had looked forward to spending a day at the latter and had intended asking what to see and leave out.

I suppose youv'e heard of the American invitation. Isn't it rum?[17] And doesn't it make one feel umble[;] instead of being paid £5, £10 or £15 pounds for doing a job, one is offered £200 for keeping quiet. At least I <u>hope</u> I'm not expected to make an after-dinner speech!

I look forward to hearing of your great success. And many more. <u>No</u>--I don't want to
hear of any more of your successes. I want to be there on the spot and to gloat as only a Proud Parent gloats.

BL

G[18]

Two days later, upon his return to Florence, Holst wrote an official yet tentative letter of acceptance to Nicholas Murray Butler, president of the American Academy of Arts and Letters:

Florence
March 1 [1929]

Dear Sir

Your delightful invitation was sent to me here and I take this opportunity of thanking you very heartily.

I cabled my acceptance the other day but now I regret that I must qualify it as it depends on whether I can get a boat back directly [when] the celebration is over and I cannot find out about this until my return to London on March 23rd.

You shall have a definite answer as soon as possible and I must regret having to keep you waiting but I have some important work in London early in May. I feel fairly confident that I can arrange everything but feel that it is only fair to you to explain the situation fully.

Excepting for a few days in Venice I shall be travelling about until March 23 so if you wish to write to me would you address the letter to my business address:

St. Paul's Girls' School
Brook Green
London W. 6

If I come I shall probably arrive in time to pay a short visit to Yale before the celebration. If Mr. Henry Flagler is a member of the Academy of Arts and you happen to meet him would you kindly give him my greetings and tell him how much I hope to be able to see him if only for a short time. I have not his address with me otherwise I would not trouble you.

Once more, I beg you to accept my warmest thanks for the honour you do me.

Yr Sincerely

Gustav Holst[19]

Naturally, the above letter crossed Johnson's response to Holst's earlier cable in the mail. In addition to merely acknowledging Holst's acceptance, Johnson's letter explained the purpose of the celebration.

Mr. Gustav Holst
Care Stainer and Bell Ltd.,
58 Berners St. W.1.
London, England

March 8, 1929

My dear Mr. Holst:

It is with great pleasure that we have received your cablegram accepting the invitation of the American Academy of Arts and Letters to be its guest on the occasion of the Twenty-fifth Anniversary of its founding, which celeberation will take place in the city of New York on April twenty-third and twenty-fourth next.

It is our purpose at that time to emphasize the significance of the Academy in advancing the ideals of letters and the arts in the United States, as well as its close relations of association and interdependence with representatives of letters and the fine arts in lands other than our own. In particular we wish to emphasize this association and interdependence in the case of Great Britain.

For your further information I take pleasure in sending you by this post, under separate cover, marked Personal, the latest copy of our official publication which gives the membership of the academy, its organization and its method of work, on the list of its membership, past and present, you will find many names of those who are or have been familiar to you.

We deem it a great honor to have you as a guest on this important occasion which will, we trust, be recognized as important throughout the English Speaking world. It will give us pleasure to offer you the service of the Academy in booking accommodations across the Atlantic voyage in either direction, and in securing suitable hotel accommodations in the city of New York.

Confirming our cablegram the Academy desires and expects to meet your necessary personal expenses in connection with the trip across the Atlantic and with your stay in the City of New York for the period of the celebration and for the few days preceding and following. The Academy desires the privilage of placing at your service the sum of One Thousand Dollars, approximately Two Hundred Pounds Sterling, to meet those necessary expenses to which you will be put through your acceptance of our invitation.

With heartiest personal greeting, I am, my dear sir,

Faithfully yours,

[Robert Underwood Johnson]
Secretary of the Academy[20]

In the meantime, Isobel had assigned the task of seeking out available ships for Holst's passages across the Atlantic to Imogen, who took the job quite seriously, as testified by this letter:

42a Craven Road
March 6th 1929

Dear Gussie,

Very many thanks for your letter from Perugia.

This American stunt is certainly very rum; but it ought to be a terrific lark. I've been finding out about boats for you.

The "Scythia" (Cunard line) leaves Liverpool for New York on April 6th. There isn't a 2nd class single cabin left, but they could let you have a double cabin all to yourself for 32.10/- I'm enclosing a plan of the boat--you are B7. If you think this is a good example, would you cable to the High St. Cook's and they will book it for you. Also would you send them a deposit of £6?

About the return journey:--the first boat to leave NY after April 24th is the "Samaria," which sails on the 27th. The Cook's man says it is bound to be pretty full, and you'd have to cable to N.Y. immediately if you wanted to try for a place on it. So when you cable to Cook's about the outward journey, would you mention whether you want them to cable to N.Y. about the "Samaria"?....[21]

Crossing the Atlantic in 1929 was generally not a difficult task, but it did take a lot of figuring and a certain amount of guesswork to determine what was the best course of action to follow. The only way for Holst to keep track of things was to write them down. He entered the following into his notebook:

boats to NY
April
6 Scythia
13 Cedric Liverpool
9 days
6 Scythia via Boston X

8 or 9 days
6 New York Southampton 8 days

and, on another page:

reserve KOC[22] a cabin
on Scythia
or Aquitania?
get berth single cabin
Samaria 27th April NY
or 1st boat after 25th[23]

On Saturday, March 9th, upon arrival at the Hotel Boston in Venice, Holst found himself deluged by no fewer than nineteen new letters--a tremendous amount of correspondence even for the avid letter-writing circle of friends and relatives with whom Holst associated![24] Two days later he cabled to Yale University about the possibility of lecturing there sometime between April 16th and the 20th[25], and on the following day, amidst sight-seeing at San Marco and the Piazza, he began to tackle the job of responding to most of the aforementioned letters. He started with a letter to his wife:

Venice
March 12

Dear Iso

Thanks for your letter of the 6th. It was the first one I opened out of a bundle of eleven, the last one being from Nora containing eight more. Imogen has been splendid about boats and I've cabled to Yale to ask if I may lecture there. I'll keep this letter open until I get their answer....[26]

Holst kept the letter open for another two days. During this time news arrived of one of the most severe tragedies to hit Holst and his circle of friends: the death of Jane Joseph at age thirty-four. Holst had known Jane since she had been a student during his early years at St. Paul's Girl's School. Later, she had substituted for him on various occasions, helped organize some of his festivals, and served as an amanuensis to him. She was also an ardent supporter of his music, but, most of all, she had been a great friend. Holst knew that Jane had been ill, but news of her death really stunned him. He continued his letter to Isobel:

March 14

Vally and Nora have told me of Jane's death. It is a great blow and I am trying not to feel too selfish about it.
The cable has come from Yale. I am to lecture on April 19....[27]

Holst followed this up with a quick letter to Robert Underwood Johnson at the American Academy of Arts and Letters:

Venice
March 14

Dear Sir

When I wrote to Pres. Butler from Florence I did not realise that I could book a passage from London to New York and back while still in Italy. I have been to the agents today and hope to reach New York between April 12 and 17, to lecture at Yale on the 19th and to accept your most delightful invitation on the 23d and 24th, returning to England directly after.

I will write again on my arrival in London on March 23.

Y Sincerely

Gustav Holst[28]

Meanwhile, Holst's presence was being anticipated by Carl Albert Lohmann, Yale University secretary:

Miss Helen McAfee
Yale Review

March 14, 1929

Dear Helen:--

In 1924 the Howland Prize was given to Gustav Holst, the English composer, who was then quite ill. He was unable to come to this country to conduct a concert of his works, or to do anything in return for the University. He has now been invited by the American Academy of Arts to come to this country for their celebration late in April and this gives him an opportunity to repay what he considerd an obbligation to the University. He has offered to lecture at Yale and I have fortunately been able to give him the date of April 19th. He suggests as his subject "The Teaching of Art." There may be an article in this for the Review if you want it.

Very truly yours,

Carl Lohmann[29]

Holst remained in Italy for another week. He continued his sight-seeing in Venice, the pleasantries of which were interrupted by a "loud loudspeaker on canal and row in cafe at night."[30] Short visits to Verona, Milan and Bale followed. On the morning of Friday, March 22nd, he started his return journey to England via Strassbourg and Dunquerque. The diary entry for Saturday, March 23rd contains only one word from the exhausted sojourner: Home.[31]

By the following Monday, Holst was back to his usual frenetic pace, with scheduled appointments. On the following day, in addition to seeing Herbert Howells at St. Paul's Girls' School in the morning and lunching with Wallingford Davies at The George, Holst wrote the following letter to Robert Underwood Johnson:

St. Paul's Girls' School
Brook Green, Hammersmith,
W. 6.
March 26

Dear Mr. Johnson

Thank you for your kind letter of the 8th and your cablegram re the Berengaria and the Samaria. Please thank President Butler for the second cable asking me to wire. I am doing so today to tell him that I am certainly accepting your delightful invitation. I leave Liverpool on April 6 on the Scythia' which should arrive in New York on the 16th. I shall then go direct to Yale and give my lecture there on the 19th and return immediately after to New York for the Celebrations leaving for England on the 27th on the 'Samaria'.

In consequence of your kind offer of the services of the Academy I am asking some American friends to write to me at your address.

Yr Sincerely

Gustav Holst[32]

The composer also wrote a similar letter to Mrs. Vanamee at the Academy, characteristically asking her to "Please thank Dr. Hadley[33] whom I look forward to meeting. In fact, I am looking forward to meeting and making many friends."[34]

Holst stayed in the London area for less than a week before heading north with Imogen to Keswick, Cumbria, where the English Folk Dance Society was having its Easter session. This short trip acted as a springboard for the composer's Liverpool departure for his second American visit. On the way to Keswick, the two of them stopped in Carlisle for two days,[35] possibly to visit members of the Lediard branch of their family. Four years later father and daughter would return together to Carlisle to conduct the St. Stephen's Brass Band in a concert given in memory of Dr. Lediard, Holst's uncle.

In Keswick, Holst was able to get in some country walking and also take part in some of the English Folk Dance Society festivites. He judged a competition and also had the opportunity to try out his Yale University lecture, "The Teaching of Art,"[36] mentioned in Lohmann's letter.

At 7:00 a.m. on April 4th, Holst left Keswick by car for Windermere, where he caught a train for Liverpool. At "about 4:00"[37] the *Scythia* departed for America with Holst safely on board.

---

[1]Written correspondence, Yale University to Gustav Holst, October 24, 1924, The Holst Foundation.

[2]Michael Short, *Gustav Holst: The Man and His Music* (Oxford: Oxford University Press, 1990), 217.

[3]*New York Times*, November 9, 1924. The award has been given out a number of times since Holst received it. Ralph Vaughan Williams was the 1954 recipient.

[4]Gustav Holst, *Diary*, Sunday, September 2 through Friday, September 7, 1928, The Holst Foundation.

[5]For a detailed account of events surrounding *Hammersmith* as well as Holst's other band works see Jon C. Mitchell, *From Kneller Hall to Hammersmith: The Band Music of Gustav Holst* (Tutzing, Germany: Haus Hans Schneider, 1990).

[6]Frances Gray had retired from St. Paul's Girls' School in 1927.

[7]Louise Dyer, founder of the Lyre-Bird Press.

[8]Personal correspondence, Gustav Holst to Frances Ralph Gray, December 17 [1928], The Holst

Foundation.
[9]Telegram, Amercan Academy of Arts and Letters to Gustav Holst, February 20, 1929, printed with the permission of the American Academy of Arts and Letters, New York City.
[10]Telegram, Gustav Holst to Nicholas Murray Butler, February 26, 1929, printed with the permission of the American Academy of Arts and Letters, New York City.
[11]Douglas Kennedy had become director of the English Folk Dance Society upon Cecil Sharp's death in 1924.
[12]103 Talgarth Road was the address of Vally Lasker's apartment.
[13]In a rather lengthy letter written to Vally Lasker dated March 2 1929 10a.m., Holst reiterated these thoughts: "I hope you approve of my going to the U.S.A. It ought not to interfere with things and I ought to clear at least £100." The Holst Foundation.
[14]Royal College of Music.
[15]Imogen Holst.
[16]Personal correspondence, Gustav Holst to Isobel Holst, February 26 [1929], The Holst Foundation.
[17]British slang meaning strange or peculiar.
[18]Personal correspondence, Gustav Holst to Imogen Holst, February 27 [1929], The Holst Foundation.
[19]Personal correspondence, Gustav Holst to Robert Underwood Johnson, March1 [1929], printed with the permission of the American Academy of Arts and Letters, New York City.
[20]Personal correspondence, Robert Underwood Johnson to Gustav Holst, March 8, 1929, printed with the permission of the American Academy of Arts and Letters, New York City.
[21]Personal correspondence, Imogen Holst to Gustav Holst, March 6th, 1929, The Holst Foundation.
[22]"King of the Castle" meaning, in this case, Holst himself.
[23]Gustav Holst, *Notebook* starting Jan. 1929, The Holst Foundation.
[24]Gustav Holst, *Diary,* Saturday, March 9, 1929, The Holst Foundation.
[25]Gustav Holst, *Notebook* starting Jan. 1929, The Holst Foundation.
[26]Personal correspondence, Gustav Holst to Isobel Holst, March12 and March 14 [1929], The Holst Foundation.
[27]*Ibid.*
[28]Personal correspondence, Gustav Holst to Robert Underwood Johnson, March 14 [1929], printed with the permission of the American Academy of Arts and Letters, New York City.
[29]Personal correspondence, Carl Albert Lohmann to Helen McAfee, March 14, 1929, Yale Collection of American Literature, Beinecke Rare Book and Manuscript Library.
[30]Gustav Holst, *Diary,* Friday, March 15, 1929, The Holst Foundation.
[31]*Ibid.*, Saturday, March 23, 1929.
[32]Personal correspondence, Gustav Holst to Robert Underwood Johnson, March 26 [1929], printed with the permission of the American Academy of Arts and Letters, New York City.
[33]Henry Hadley.
[34]Personal Correspondence, Gustav Holst to Mrs. Vanamee, March 26 [1929], printed with the permission of the American Academy of Arts and Letters, New York City.
[35]Gustav Holst, *Diary,* Thursday, March 28, 1929, The Holst Foundation.
[36]*Ibid.,* Tuesday, April 2, 1929.
[37]*Ibid.,* Thursday, April 4, 1929.

CHAPTER XIX

THE SECOND AMERICAN VISIT

The trans-Atlantic voyage on board the *Scythia* was much rougher than anything that Holst had experienced on the *Aquitania* in 1923. The first part of the voyage was apparently without incident, but after the ship had made a scheduled early morning stop at Belfast and journeyed into the North Atlantic, the weather turned stormy. An early morning squall on the fourth day out was enough to convince Holst to leave the ship at the first opportunity. He wrote about this in a letter to his wife on her birthday:

On Board the Cunard
R.M.S. "Scythia"
April 12 [1929]

Dear Iso

Many Happy Returns of the Day and Many Congratulations on it. I don't see why you shouldn't have some of the honour and glory. And now is the time to have some when she is having one success after another.

You once said you'd like a long voyage in a one-class boat. My advice is Don't.

If I ever cross the Atlantic again I want a most exclusive cabin in a very fast boat and my Missus to keep undesirable people away.

But what I really want is to keep off the sea altogether. I've not been sea sick but I'm very sick of the sea, the ship (which is a very good one) and the passengers (who are, on the whole, harmless) and above all, the noise--engines, waves, wind, gramophones, chattering.

Also sudden squall[s] at 3AM are not fair.

The bad weather has delayed us so I'm going to get off at our first stopping place Halifax (in Canada) and take the train to Yale.

There is just a chance that we may get to Halifax tomorrow evening in which case I shall catch an early train on Sunday morning and get to Yale midday Monday. I'm expecting great things of Yale--nice men, a quiet room, one or two walks; also my lecture is the least bad I've written[,] not that that is saying much.

I hope all the SW gales we've had have brought you lots of rain in Essex. This has been the one cheering thought about the weather. And presumably you are not as cold as we are--we are near Newfoundland and its icebergs which are excellent things in books.

There is too much grousing about this letter. But the truth is that I've had too much gadding about--four months on end. And when I get home I want to live a humdrum monotonous existence with lots of routine work, lots of new 'things' that don't disappoint me too much, and occasional conducting jobs and 3 day walks--I want this for the next three or four years!

It doesn't seem an unreasonable desire!

B L

G[1]

Holst wrote immediately to the American Academy of Arts and Letters about his change of plan:

On Board the Cunard
R.M.S. "Scythia"
April 12 [1929]

Dear Mrs. Vanamee

As the "Scythia" has been delayed by bad weather I have decided to land at Halifax NS and go by train to Yale University where I am to lecture on the 19th. I hope to get there by Monday afternoon. I am most sorry to trouble you at a time when you must be very busy but would you kindly forward any letters that come for me to Yale? I shall be there until the 20th or 21st....

Yours Sincerely

Gustav Holst[2]

The difficult voyage had been made even worse by the grief brought on by Jane Joseph's death. Holst had more than enough time to ponder this and to write an article about Jane for *Morley College Magazine*. He comments about this in a letter to Vally Lasker:

On Board the Cunard
R.M.S. "Scythia"
April 13 [1929]

Dear Vally

....Here is the article on Jane. It has been a labour of love but more of a labour than I had expected--life on board ship is boring and demoralising....

If there is no immediate hurry about the article would you show it to people who knew Jane and loved her so that on my return I can have the benefit of criticism before starting to rewrite.

If it is wanted at once--

a) Shall we leave out 'Marian' in her name? I fancy she didn't like it

b) Was "Whitsunday' really dedicated to Morley College?

c) If it is too long cut out the part between

[left blank]

and

[also left blank]

d) get someone to overhaul the spelling and general lay out.

It ought to be better but I have worked hard at it and am quite certain that I cannot improve it until I get home....

And I Hate the Sea.

Y ever

Gustav[3]

Holst's article was full of respect and admiration. He wrote:

> Jane Joseph, more than anyone else I have ever known, had that infinite capacity for taking pains which amounts to genius. It was some thing instinctive in her and it was combined with great sensitiveness and a passion for accuracy. In all her sayings and doings there was a complete absence of anything superficial or casual. No detail in a scheme was too small for her and no scheme, however big, was allowed to be obscured by too much concentration on detail, whether the scheme was a charitable one for helping someone in trouble, organising accommodation for someone during a Whitsuntide Festival, or arranging a ballet....
> Jane gave the minimum of worry to each person concerned by giving herself the maximum of hard work and forethought.
>
> Working with her was made a constant delight by her courtesy--a recognition of what was due to other people and a real consideration for their feelings. Nothing gave her greater joy than the discovery of this sensitive courtesy in others.
>
> It was my good fortune to be her teacher in composition, and she was the best girl pupil I ever had. From the very first she showed an individual attitude of mind combined with eagerness to absorb all that was beautiful....In the death of Jane Joseph we have lost an artist before her powers were fully developed. In having known her we are rich in possessing the memory of one whose genius for friendship will remain a living inspiration.[4]

Holst's voyage woes continued. To add insult to injury, the *Scythia*'s entry into the harbor at Halifax was postponed due to the inclement weather. Finally on April 14th, two days after he had to decided to leave the ship, Holst was able to disembark and spent the night at Halifax's Lord Nelson Hotel. There he had plenty of time to think about the next few days and to revise his lecture:

> lecture note
> some Stress natural
> laudable benefits
> stress may be good or bad
> bring in counterpoint?

and

Yale
hotel? letters?
lecture only 25 min
overhaul "

and

lecture
confirm
GBS Angry Men
you only amateur
2) Man Super those who can
3) Nicholas Nickelby
window
4) Ian Hay [?] school stories
Write Introduction[5]

The next day he continued his journey by rail, leaving Halifax at 8:00 a.m. and transferring trains at St. John and at Boston on the way. He arrived at New Haven at 12:20 p.m. on April16th and was met at the station by Carl Lohmann, Yale University secretary, and David Stanley Smith, Dean of the Yale University School of Music and Conductor of the New Haven Symphony Orchestra.[6]

Holst was wined and dined at Yale and stayed at the Graduates' Club. On the afternoon of the17th he attended a lecture given by Smith. Holst's diary entry for the following day is a rather confusing jumble: "11 Sprague Hall Bruce Simond dinner Borchards 8:15 Myra Hess supper". The first portion seems to indicates that Holst had an appointment with pianist and Yale music history professor Bruce Simonds at Albert Arnold Sprague Memorial Hall at 11:00 a.m.. The dinner that is mentioned was probably at the home of law professor Edwin Borchard. That same evening the well-known English pianist Myra Hess gave a recital at 8:15 in Sprague. She was championed by Simonds, who had met her in London, probably during the time of his studies with Tobias Matthay. Although not a Yale University School of Music faculty member, Myra Hess gave frequent performances on campus during the 1920's and 1930's.[7]

On the morning of Friday the 19th, Holst toured Yale's picture gallery and met Bruce Simonds again for lunch and an afternoon drive.[8] At 8:15 that same evening, Holst gave his Henry Elias Howland lecture, "The Teaching of Art,"[9] which was capstoned with a post-lecture walk with one of Howland's sons.

The lecture was quite a success and Carl Lohmann wanted to print it in its entirety in the *Yale Review*. Soon after Holst's departure from Yale, Lohmann asked him for a revised version of his lecture notes and Holst wanted to comply. Holst's notebook entries indicate that he was considering many possibilities:

Lohmann
prospectus
notes of lecture for press?
" " " " pub[lishers]
paragraphs, punctuation, etc.
printer omit pencil note?
who corrects proofs? I?
send copies
OK?
see Myra Hess
tips?
years sub for review[10]

and

Lohmann
lecture
I 'considered' last page[11]

He wrote to Lohmann the day of his departure from the country:

On Board the Cunard
R.M.S. "Samaria"
May 1 [1929]

Dear Mr. Lohmann

By the time you receive this I hope you have also received my lecture notes. If not would you write to my brother

Mr Ernest Cossart
186 Riverside Drive
New York City

and ask him to send them.

There is just one alteration I would like to make. In the middle of the last page, in the sentence beginning 'It is fairly safe to say that when such articles are considered great' would you take out the word 'considered.'

Please accept my warmest thanks for your kindness to me in Yale and please convey the same to the authorities of the Graduates' Club for their hospitality.

Yr Sincerely

Gustav Holst

P.S. If my lecture is not to be printed please return it to me at

St. Paul's Girls' School
Brook Green
London W6
England

If it is published in Yale Review I take it for granted that the copyright belongs to the latter to whom I shall refer anyone wishing to publish it in England.[12]

Wilbur Lucius Cross, Dean of the Graduate School at Yale University and editor of *The Yale Review*, took a special interest in this project. The future Governor of Connecticut (1931-1939) asked Holst for some revisions and wrote to the composer, who had been staying at the University Club in New York. This did not work, for Holst had already departed the country. According to the composer's brother, actor Ernest Cossart [Emil von Holst], the materials were rerouted.

186 Riverside Drive
New York

21st May [1929]

Dear Mr. Cross

You are quite right in assuming that the manuscript & your letter have been forwarded to my brother at his "English" address.--They were redirected to me from the University Club & I forwarded them on to him.

With much regard,

Yr sincerely

Ernest Cossart[13]

When his lecture notes and Cross' letter finally caught up with him at his office at St. Paul's Girls' School, Holst could not have been too pleased. Holst saw himself as a composer and teacher, not an editor. Still, Holst did write some articles, or at least supplied the material for them. By 1929 no fewer than ten articles had been published under his name and in at least one case, in a letter to his friend Edwin Evans, he had actively pursued publication:

32 Gunterstone Road
Barons Court, W. 14.
July 20 [1923]

Dear Evans

Good luck to Comus. Would you like a short article on my favourite composer Thomas Weelkes? As his tercentenary is in Nov., it might be appropriate. But have the interview if you prefer--it will be far less bother to me.

Y Sincerely

Gustav Holst[14]

He followed up on it nine months later, during the long convalescence from his University of Reading accident.

Thaxted
Dunmow
Essex
April 28, 1924

Dear Evans,

Has your musical journal appeared yet? And if so, is my article in it? I am out of things here & have lost touch with so much but I am feeling much better than I was and am half thinking of going to the Salzburg Festival in August if I can stand so much new music.

I hope things are going well for you!

Yours sincerely

Gustav Holst[15]

Excuse dictated letter.
--hand rather bad.[16]

The Weelkes article finally appeared nearly two years later--in the January 4, 1926 issue of *Midland Musician*. Holst probably had little trouble writing it. That publication was intended to be an article from the very beginning; "The Teaching of Art" was not. Holst wrote the following reply to Cross:

July 31 [1929]
St. Paul's Girls' School
Brook Green, Hammersmith
London W6

Dear Prof Cross

I have taken a good deal of trouble over my lecture notes which you kindly returned to me and regret that I cannot see my way to expanding them into an essay. I have had no experience in such work and these notes are so obviously a foundation for a lecture.

Would you care to publish them as "Notes for a lecture" or would you prefer to allow me to keep them in MS? I should prefer the latter as I think they are quite unworthy of the Yale Review, but I want to meet your wish in the matter.

Yrs Sincerely

Gustav Holst

P.S. Please don't spoil your holidays by answering by return. There is no hurry about the matter.[17]

Cross reluctantly closed the book on the matter with the following response:

September 10, 1929

Gustav Holst, Esq.
St. Paul's Girls' School
Brook Green, Hammersmith W6
London, England

Dear Mr. Holst,

I am sorry that you do not see your way to expanding the notes of the delightful lecture into an essay. But I understand perfectly your hesitation in undertaking the work with all the other things you have to do. And I am also sorry that on my part I feel unable to publish the lecture notes just as they stand. We do often print, as I have written you, an address given at Yale in the magazine, but in order to make a good article for a group of magazine readers I have always found it necessary to ask that the material be recast or readjusted especially for them. Thank you very much, however, for letting me hear from you again. I have the pleasantest memories of our meeting in this country, and I send you all good wishes for your work in your special art, which I like to think lies next door to mine.

Very sincerely yours,

G*[18]

On the morning of Saturday, April 20th, Holst sent the following telegram to Robert Underwood Johnson:

1929 APR 20 AM 10 51

N45 13=NEW HAVEN CONN 20 1039A
SECY ACADEMY OF ART AND LETTER=
633 WEST 155 ST

ARRIVING TONIGHT ADDRESS UNIVERSITY CLUB ONE WEST FIFTY SIXTH STREET PLEASE TELL HADLEY[19]=

GUSTAVE HOLST[20]

The composer then viewed the newly restored Steinert Collection of Musical Instruments after which he bade New Haven farewell, leaving on the 3:15 train with David Stanley Smith. Upon arriving in New York, Holst checked into the University Club, where he was met by his niece Valerie Cossart.

In April of 1929, New York City was the undisputed heart of the American entertainment industry. The opulence of the 1920's would be present for another six months and billboards around the Times Square area, 46th Street and Broadway, were lit up with the names of countless plays, musicals, and concerts. Vaudeville was still present although on its last legs, for the motion picture industry, now revolutionized by sound, was rapidly putting it out of business. Advertisements for "All Talking" and "Singing and Talking" movies such as *Broadway Melody*, *Madame X* and *The Letter* were everywhere. The death knell had been tolled for silent movies.

New York's offerings may have been somewhat overwhelming for Holst, were it not for the fact that his brother Emil [Ernest Cossart] and niece Valerie were on hand to show him the town. The 21st of April was spent with the two of them plus Austin Lidbury, Holst's ebulient friend from Niagara Falls. The four of them saw a string quartet perform that evening. On the following day, the 22nd, Holst spent the morning with Emil and the two brothers had lunch at the Players Club.[21] Holst's diary entry for later events of that day mentions "evening 'Strange Interlude' with Valerie." This does not mean that Holst and his niece had any unusual experience that evening. They simply attended "Strange Interlude," a Theatre Guild Production being performed at the John Golden Theatre on 58th Street, just east of Broadway. Valerie, then a young actress following in her father's footsteps, was probably not featured in the play; she would make her official New York debut a year later in "Lost Sheep."[22]

On Tuesday, April 23rd and Wednesday, April 24th the event which precipitated Holst's second trip to America took place. The American Academy of Arts and Letters' twenty-fifth anniversary was a gala affair with the majority of the festivities occurring at the Academy's 155th Street headquarters. Activities for this veritable "Who's Who" were scheduled over a two-day period:

April 23

Spring Meeting and Election of Members and Corresponding Members

11:00 a.m.
Installation of the President, Nicholas Murray Butler, Address by the President
12:00 p.m.
Award of the Gold Medal of the Academy, the Gold Medal for Good Diction on the Stage and the Gold Medal for Good Diction in Radio Announcing
Presentation by Robert Underwood Johnson, Secretary of the Academy, of an Historic Eagle Pen
Luncheon in the Academy Library
1:30 p.m.
Dinner at the Ritz-Carlton Hotel in Commemoration of the Twenty-Fifth Anniversary of the Founding of the Academy
7:30 p.m.

April 24
Address in the Academy Library by George Pierce Baker, Member of the Academy, (Evangeline Wilbour Blashfield Foundation)
2:45 p.m.
Reception of Guests and Exhibition of Memorabilia of Academy Members
4:15 p.m.
Concert of American Music at Carnegie Hall
8:30 p.m.[23]

According to his diary, Holst attended all of the first day's activities.[24] The formal session held on the 23rd at 11:00 a.m. was headed by Cass Gilbert, since American Academy of Arts and Letters President Nicholas Murray Butler was in the hospital recovering from surgery and unable to attend. New members as well as members from a new category, "Corresponding Members," were elected. The latter category included James M. Barrie, Reginald Blomfield, Edward Elgar, and William Orpen--all knighted citizens of the British Empire.[25] Recipients of Gold Medals included Edith Wharton (Gold Medal of the Academy--for distinction in literature), Julia Marlowe (Good Diction on the Stage), and Milton J. Cross (Good Diction over the Radio). Two years later Milton Cross would become the announcer for New York's Metropolitan opera broadcasts, a position he would hold for forty-three years. Wilbur L. Cross, editor of *The Yale Review*, presented Edith Wharton her award.[26]

Wilbur Cross also presided at the dinner held at the Ritz-Carlton that evening.

The Guests of Honor were listed in the program for that evening:

GUESTS OF THE AMERICAN ACADEMY
OF ARTS AND LETTERS

from Great Britain
Gilbert Bayes, Esq., R.S.B.S.
Sir Reginald Blomfield, R.A.
Gustav Holst, Esq.
J.C. Squire, Esq.
Chairman of the English Association
William J. Locke, Esq.

from France
M. Andre Chevrillon
Member of the Academie Francais
M. Funck Brentano
President of the Academie des Sciences Morales et Politiques

from South America
Dr. Alfredo Colmo

Their Excellencies
Don Orestes Ferrara, Ambassador from Cuba
Vincent Massey, Minister from Canada
Michael MacWhite, Minister from the Irish Free State
Dr. Chao-Chu Wu, Minister from China
and representatives of Academies and Other
Learned Societies[27]

Indeed, Holst was in good company. Better still, as he had anticipated, he didn't have to do a thing!

Holst had indicated to the Academy that he would be in attendence at George Pierce Baker's mid-afternoon address the next day[28] (the 24th) although this is not mentioned in his diary. He did have luncheon on that day at the University Club at 1:00 and a 6:15 rendevous with Valerie before heading over to Carnegie Hall to attend the Academy's closing concert of works by American composers. The program, featuring works by Frank Van der Stucken, Edward MacDowell, John Powell, Henry Hadley, Deems Taylor, and George Whitefield Chadwick, was conducted by Hadley. Members of the Academy were assisted by the New York

Philharmonic-Symphony Orchestra.[29]

For Holst, the concert-going did not stop there. The following evening, after visiting with Emil and Valerie for the entire day, Holst met up with Tertius Noble, the British-born organist then employed at St. Thomas Episcopal Church in New York, and from there probably attended portions of two performances, each receiving excellent reviews in the *New York Times*.[30] The Composers League presented two ballets at the Metropolitan Opera House: Monteverdi's *Combat of Tancredi and Clorister*, conducted by Walter Josten, and Stravinsky's *Les Noces*, conducted by Leopold Stokowski. Not far from there, at Town Hall, H. Alexander Matthews was conducting the Choral Art Society of Philadelphia in a concert featuring an opening segment of works by British composers. Parry, Stanford, Weelkes, and Coleridge-Taylor were represented in the first third of the concert. The second third featured Holst's *Three Rig Veda Songs for Women's Voices*, Warlock's arrangement of an old Corpus Christi, and the "Agnus Dei" and "Sanctus" from Pizzetti's *Missa di Requiem*. The final third of the concert consisted of works by Beasly, Bax, Taveryof, Rimsky-Korsakov, Dargomyshaky, Palmgren, Sanchez Marraco, and Koshetz.

Holst's *Diary* includes an optimistic 9:15 entry for *Rig Veda* following an 8:30 one for *Les Noces*.[31] His *Notebook* entry for this day, however, tells a different story. Here it can be seen that Holst was at least considering attending a third concert--one in which his *Dirge for Two Veterans* was being presented:

> Thursday
> Choral Art Soc
> Philadelphia
> Town Hall 8(15?):30
> (Matthews)
> meet Noble 8:15
> Veda come 5th in prog
> University Glee Club
> Carnegie Hall
> Channing Lefebre, conductor
> D. Woodruff emeritus conductor
> Dirge last but one
> concert begin?
> Metropolitan Opera
> Monteverdi 8:45
> Les Noces 9:15?[32]

The concert in question was the thirty-fifth anniversary concert of the University Glee Club given at Carnegie Hall. The University Glee Club, described by the *New York Times* as "a graduate organization in which are united the musical traditions of many colleges,"[33] was conducted by Channing Lefebvre, who had just succeded Arthur Woodruff as music director of the organization. This rather elaborate concert featured an opening portion of college songs and works by Bach, Brahms, Gretchaninoff and Morley, followed by Holst's *Dirge for Two Veterans* and Stanford's *Songs of the Sea*, which featured vocal soloist Reinald Werrenrath. The remainder of the concert was comprised of works by Schubert, Halliday, Specks, Spier, Gaul, Forsyth, and Foote.

After attending whichever of these concerts he did, Holst headed to Grand Central Station in order to catch the 12:30 a.m. train for a rather brutal one-day excursion to Boston.

After a very short night the train pulled into Boston's South Station at about 6:30 a.m. on April 26th and Holst proceeded from there to nearby Cambridge. He had lunch with Edward Burlingame Hill, Chairman of the Harvard University Division of Music, at 144 Brattle Street, before succumbing to fatigue. His diary entry says it all: "2:30 bed." At 8:15 that evening, Holst, obviously refreshed, reprised his lecture "On the Teaching of Art" for a Harvard University audience. This turned out to be an unofficial audition for a visiting lecturer position there. After a late dinner, he boarded the midnight train for New York.[34]

The following morning Holst had breakfast with Emil, Valerie and Claude Bragdon before boarding the *Samaria* for the long trip home. The return voyage, described by the composer as "fine and warm on the whole" was made more pleasant by the company of Reginald Blomfield, whom Holst had met at the Academy of Arts & Letters festivities. Holst made a writing list, as had become the custom whenever he paused on a long journey. The names of fourteen people appear on this one, including such notables as conductors Henry Hadley and Leopold Stokowski. American Academy of Arts and Letters Secretary Robert Underwood Johnson, also listed, was the recipient of the following thank you letter:

On Board the
Cunard RMS Samaria
May 1 1929

Dear Mr. Johnson

I write to thank you very heartily for inviting me to the Twenty fifth

> Anniversary of the American Academy. I also want to congratulate you on the success of the Celebration Activities. It must have been a great joy to you who have watched the growth of the Academy from the first and I am sure that many others felt this as deeply as I did. I trust that you are now enjoying a well deserved holiday after all your labour and anxiety.
>
> Yr Sincerely
>
> Gustav Holst[35]

Johnson's exact response is unknown, but one can get a sense of his modesty from the note that he scrawled on the top of Holst's letter:

> Dear Mrs. Vanamee--If you will kindly give me his address I'll write to him and tell him how comparatively little credit is due me for *your* celebration.
>
> R.U.J.[36]

---

[1]Personal correspondence, Gustav Holst to Isobel Holst, April 12 [1929], The Holst Foundation.

[2]Personal correspondence, Gustav Holst to Mrs. Vanamee, April 12 [1929], printed with the permission of the American Academy of Arts and Letters, New York City.

[3]Personal corrsepondence, Gustav Holst to Vally Lasker, April 13 [1929], The Holst Foundation.

[4]Gustav Holst, "Jane Joseph," in *Morley College Magazine,* XXXIV, 9 (June 1929), 104-105.

[5]Gustav Holst, *Notebook* [April 14, 1929], The Holst Foundation.

[6]Gustav Holst, *Diary*, April 13-16, 1929, The Holst Foundation.

[7]Personal correspondence to the author from Suzanne Eggleston, August 22, 1997.

[8]Gustav Holst, *Diary*, April 17-19, 1929, The Holst Foundation.

[9]A reconstructed version of this lecture appears in Ursula Vaughan Williams (ed.) and Holst, Imogen (ed.), *Heirs and Rebels: Letters to Each Other and Occasional Writings on Music by Ralph Vaughan Williams and Gustav Holst* (London: Oxford University Press, 1959), 66-73.

[10]Gustav Holst, *Notebook* [1929], The Holst Foundation.

[11]*Ibid.*

[12]Personal correspondence, Gustav Holst to Carl Lohmann, May 1 [1929], Yale Collection of American Literature, Beinecke Rare Book and Manuscript Library.

[13]Personal correspondence, Ernest Cossart to Wilbur Cross, 21st May [1929], Yale Collection of American Literature, Beinecke Rare Book and Manuscript Library.

[14]Personal correspondence, Gustav Holst to Edwin Evans, July 20 [1923], Central Public Library, Westminster.

[15]Personal correspondence, Gustav Holst to Edwin Evans, April 28, 1924, Central Public library, Westminster.

[16]This letter is in Isobel Holst's handwriting.

[17]Personal correspondence, Gustav Holst to Wilbur Cross, July 31 [1929], Yale Collection of American Literature, Beinecke Rare Book and Manuscript Library.
[18]Personal correspondence, Wilbur Cross to Gustav Holst, September 10, 1929, Yale Collection of American Literature, Beinecke Rare Book and Manuscript Library.
[19]American conductor and composer Henry Kimball Hadley.
[20]Telegram, Gustav[e] Holst to Secretary, American Academy of Arts and Letters, April 20, 1929, printed with the permission of the American Academy of Arts and Letters, New York City.
[21]Gustav Holst, *Diary,* April 20-22, 1929, The Holst Foundation.
[22]*The New York Times,* January 12, 1995.
[23]The American Academy of Arts and Letters, "Order of Events: April 23 and 24, 1929."
[24]Gustav Holst, *Diary,* April 23, 1929, The Holst Foundation.
[25]*Proceedings in Commemoration of the Twenty-fifth Anniversary of the Founding of the American Academy of Arts and Letters* (New York: American Academy of Arts and Letters Publication No. 72, 1930), 2-3.
[26]*Ibid.,* 3-5.
[27]*Program: Dinner of the American Academy of Arts and Letters at the Ritz-Carlton Hotel, New York in Commemoration of the Twenty-fifth Anniversary of the Founding of the Academy and in Honor of Visiting Representatives of Letters and Arts,* Tuesday, April 23, 1929.
[28]Gustav Holst, response card to the Assistant to the President of the American Academy of Arts and Letters [April, 1929], printed with the permission of the American Academy of Arts and Letters, New York City..
[29]*Proceedings,* 214-215.
[30]*New York Times,* April 26, 1929.
[31]Gustav Holst, *Diary,* April 25, 1929, The Holst Foundation.
[32]Gustav Holst, *Notebook,* Thursday [April 25, 1929], The Holst Foundation.
[33]*New York Times,* April 26, 1929.
[34]Gustav Holst, *Diary,* April 26, 1929, The Holst Foundation.
[35]Personal correspondence, Gustav Holst to Robert Underwood Johnson, May 1, 1929, printed with the permission of the American Academy of Arts and Letters, New York City.
[36]*Ibid.*

CHAPTER XX

1929-1931

The *Samaria* pulled into the Liverpool docks at 8:00 p.m. on Sunday, May 5th. Holst spent the evening in the Liverpool area with his friend Frederick "Wilkie" Wilkinson and his wife. Wilkinson was the headmaster of a grammar school in Wallasey. He and his wife often stayed at Vally Lasker's apartment when visiting London. Though not a musician, Wilkinson assisted Holst in producing a number of his works in the Liverpool area. Yet it was friendship, not business, that prevailed and Wilkinson was happy to help out. He commented, "One advantage of my living in Wallasey was that we could be of assistance to Gustav whenever he was going to or returning from America."[1] The following morning, Holst caught the 8:45 train to London, arriving at St. Paul's Girls' School at 2:00 p.m.[2]

After four and one-half months of travel Holst was more than eager to settle back into a more normal existence. Yet the desire for a "humdrum monotonous existence with lots of routine work," expressed in his April 12th letter to Isobel, was not to happen for, at least in terms of musical composition, the second half of 1929 was to be one of the most fruitful periods he had known. After two weeks of catching up with close friends and reorienting himself to the London musical scene, Holst began work on the *Twelve Songs*, Op. 48 [H174], for solo voice and piano, set to the words of English poet Humbert Wolfe.[3] Not intended as a song cycle, these songs represent Holst's first major work for this combination since his group of nine *Hymns from the Rig Veda*, Op. 24 [H90] of 1907-1908. Later that summer he would write his *Double Concerto*, Op. 49 [H175] for two violins and chamber orchestra. The work was specifically written for the Hungarian-born sister violinists Jelly D'Aranyi and Adila Fachiri, grandnieces of violin virtuoso

Joseph Joachim. That same autumn Holst began work on what would be his last opera, *The Tale of the Wandering Scholar*, Op. 50 [H176]. The libretto of this *opera di camera* was written by Clifford Bax and is based upon a vignette from Helen Waddell's book, *The Wandering Scholars.* The work is dedicated to Helen Waddell. Bax comments:

> Our last collaboration produced a one-act opera....the story came from 'The Wandering Scholars', a more than delightful book by Miss Helen Waddell. It was, too, a book of which Gustav became immeasurably fond, not without cause. Every now and again he would summon me to sup with him at The George Hotel in Hammersmith Broadway, and here he had a corner-table which was regarded as his property and even a special waiter who became his portly Ganymede. Perhaps an epicure would not consider that Burgundy was a suitable accompaniment to a plate of fried onions, but these were usually our drink and our main fare: and I would give much if I could meet Gustav over the same dish. He never wore a hat; his thin white hair accepted the rain and the wind; he always carried an ancient music-case: and he always peered doubtfully, through his magnifying glasses, at the approaching guest. By grace of fortune I had become acquainted with Miss Waddell and was therefore able to bring her to one of our reunions at the George. She talked so brilliantly that Gustav was in an enchanted state, nor shall I ever forget his complete happiness when she told us the long story of Saint Pelagia, who had once been a courtesan.[4]

The plot of *The Tale of the Wandering Scholar* is quite Chauceresque. There is only one scene: a kitchen of a farmhouse in thirteenth century France. The are only four characters: Alison, a "buxom and comely young woman;" Louis, her husband; Father Philippe, a lecherous priest; and the wandering scholar, Pierre. Louis, "a cheerful farmer of about thirty, takes an armful of straw from the heap. On his way to the door he stops to tease his wife."[5] While Louis is out, Father Philippe keeps a rendezvous with Alison, who has prepared food and drink. More is suggested, but they are interrupted by a call from Pierre, who notices what is about to take place. Father Philippe sends Pierre away, without giving him food or drink. Father Philippe suggests to Alison that they go to the attic and as he tests the ladder. Pierre returns with Louis and the priest quickly hides under the straw. Alison feigns innocence, pretending that she has no food, but Pierre tells a tale in which he points out where the food and drink are hidden, and discloses the priest's hiding place. Louis angrily chases the priest from the house and then chases his wife up the ladder to the attic.

At twenty-five minutes, this is Holst's shortest opera. It is also his smallest in regard to forces: four characters, no chorus, and an instrumental ensemble consisting of one piccolo, one flute, one oboe, one English Horn, two clarinets, two bassoons, two horns, and strings that by eliminating optional instruments, can be reduced to as few as ten players: a woodwind quintet, a string quartet, and a bass. Holst's underperformed opera is a gem. A. E. F. Dickinson, who could be somewhat trenchant in his opinions about Holst's works, comments:

> On every account the opera is maintained as a light comedy, less artificial than the sophisticated encounters of *At the Boar's Head*, free from the mixed trickery of *The Perfect Fool*, and making no claim to match the visionary experience of *Savitri*, it remains Holst's most successful on its own slight scale.[6]

In the meantime Holst's services were in demand. He played organ at a Golders Green funeral, attended rehearsals and an open air performance of *The Golden Goose* by the Bute House orchestra in Warwick, and hosted his friend William Gillies Whittaker on numerous occasions at the "Jolly Talgarth." Although no longer the subject of popular attention, Holst's works were still being performed with great regularity--and on both sides of the Atlantic. G. Wallace Woodworth, Conductor of the Radcliffe Choral Society in Cambridge, Massachusetts wrote to the composer:

> 16 Holden Green
> Cambridge, Massachusetts
> July 4, 1929
>
> Dear Mr. Holst,
>
> It was good of you to write me about our performance of the Hymn of Jesus on May 31. All gratitude, however, should go from us to you, for giving us such an experience as came to everyone who part in the performance. We shall be singing the Hymn again next December. Would that your path might chance to lead this way at that time!
>
> I am now helping Mr. Surrette at his summer school[7], and we are enjoying "Man Born to Toil" and the three hymns from the first group of the Rig Veda collections.
>
> With warmest greetings, and deep appreciation of your thoughtfulness

in writing me.

Sincerely yours,

G. Wallace Woodworth[8]

Holst may have met Woodworth for the first time during his one-day stay in Boston on April 26th.

Later that summer Holst was engaged by the BBC Symphony Orchestra to conduct *The Planets* at a festival to be held in Canterbury Cathedral. On August 16th, after rehearsing the orchestra in London from 10:00 a.m.to 1:00 p.m., Holst caught the 2:00 p.m. train bound for Rochester. From there he characteristically walked in the rain to Maidstone. The next two days he walked "chiefly on Pilgrim's Way"[9] to Canterbury. There, on Wednesday, August 21st Holst rehearsed the BBC Symphony at 2:00 p.m., and conducted them in a 5:00 p.m. performance of *The Planets.* The remainder of the concert was conducted by Adrian Boult. Holst reprised a portion of this concert when he conducted the same orchestra in three of the movements from *The Planets* at a British Composers' concert held in Queen's Hall on October 3rd.

On October 15th, Holst embarked via Boulogne on the first of two trips that he would make to Paris that autumn. Imogen, the recipient of a Royal College of Music Octavia Scholarship for Composition which allowed for study abroad, was able to be with him. The reason for this trip was the French premiere of *Egdon Heath.* James and Louise Dyer, who had relocated from Rome since Holst had visited them earlier in the year, served as gracious hosts at the Hotel Peiffer, treating Holst to dinner on a number of occasions and driving him out to Sevres and Versailles. On Sunday, October 20th, after seeing the Louvre in the morning, Holst attended the 4:00 p.m. performance of *Egdon Heath* given by Pierre Monteux and l'Orchestre Symphonique de Paris.[10] Monteux was no stranger to Holst's music, having introduced *The Planets* to Boston during his brief tenure as music conductor there. Sandwiched between Wagner's *Flying Dutchman Overture* and Saint-Saens' *Piano Concerto No. 2* on the first half of the program,[11] *Egdon Heath* was poorly received and even hissed. Paris was never known for its tolerance of slow thought-provoking music; even Mozart had to write a new second movement for his *Symphony No. 31 in D* "Paris," K. 297, although that had occurred some150 years earlier. To Monteux, who had conducted the scandalous premiere of Stravinsky's *Le Sacre du Printemps* in 1913, the failure of *Egdon Heath* to win its Paris audience was merely something to take in stride; to Holst, judging from his thoughts expressed earlier to Henry Harkness Flagler, it may have hurt just a bit. Three premieres of *Egdon Heath*--New York, London, and Paris--had been poorly received and a fourth--Cheltenham--succeeded only because Holst himself had "educated" his audience by conducting it twice.

Holst's second trip to Paris that autumn also involved the premiere of one of his compositions, although this time is was not just the French premiere, but the world premiere of the Humbert Wolfe songs. On Thursday, November 7th Holst left London, boarding the 4:00 p.m. train bound for Paris. He was accompanied by Nora Day, Vally Lasker, and Dorothy Silk. The train arrived in Paris at 3:30 a.m. the following morning, some four hours late. Holst stayed at the Hotel de l'Universet du Portugal this time. Later that day, he had lunch with Louise Dyer at the Inter Allies Club and supervised a rehearsal of the songs at the Dyers' apartment. The following evening, the Dyers threw a party which lasted from 9:30 p.m. until 1:00 a.m..[12] It was at this party, before an invited audience, that ten of the twelve Humbert Wolfe songs (omitting "Rhyme" and "Betelgeuse") were performed. Dorothy Silk sang and was accompanied by Vally Lasker. Listed under the umbrella title *The Dream City*, the songs were well-received.

Dorothy Silk had to leave at noon the following day, but the others made a holiday of it, remaining in Paris for the next three days. There were meals at Medici and St. Cecile and an automobile excursion to Chartres, but the highlight of these days occurred on the evening of Monday, the 11th, when Holst met Nadia Boulanger and her mother. Nadia Boulanger wrote to Holst:

36, Rue Ballu.9:
Les Maisonnettes
Gargenville (S.O.)
[November, 1929]

My dear Mr. Holst,

I have read with the great joy the pure, exquisite & moving songs Mrs. Dyer had the charming idea of giving us--I explained her what my disappointment had been not to join the friends welcoming you--But quite by myself, I have been somewhat consoled with these pages I did not know, I am ashamed to confess.

And I beg you to find here all what I am unable to express--awkward in French, paralised in English I am, knowing so poorly your language--but, you will understand, is it not, Dear Mr. Holst, in which deep feeling of sincerity, I thank you.

Nadia Boulanger[13]

She continued in another note:

> I am afraid, Dear Mr. Holst, in receiving your exquisite little note! Have I written badly your address, or what else--but your letter & music sent before leaving Paris reached me perfectly well--I answered immediately, delighted with thought, music & everything. That you took trouble again for me, touches me deeply & more than ever, I thank you very much.
>
> Could I only make you feel how often mother & I are speaking of the wonderful evening we owe you & your dear friends. It was so cordial, so sincere & so nice. Such hours make you understand a word at fraternity so often without meaning. Indeed what we feel toward your music helped a great deal however, at the phone unknown the one to the others, before midnight to hear! It meant so much & it is so wonderful.
>
> Thanking you again & again--hoping in a new meeting, we send, Mother & I, wishes, greetings, remembrances & hopes
>
> Nadia Boulanger
>
> Be indulgent for my poor English!
> Who does whatever he can, must be forgiven![14]

Holst returned to England on Wednesday, December 13th. When the end of the term at St. Paul's Girls' School came in December, he celebrated it in characteristic fashion--by walking. This time it was in the Norwich area.[15]

1930 arrived and Holst continued to compose at a what was for him a torrid pace. He finished his sketch for *The Tale of the Wandering Scholar* on January 13th and soon started work on *A Choral Fantasia*, Op. 51 [H177]. He was also at work on the military band version of the "Marching Song" from *Two Songs without Words*. His symphonic poem *Hammersmith*, Op. 52 [H178], commissioned by the BBC Military Band, would begin to take shape in the latter part of the year.

Kathleen Long, Imogen's piano instructor at the Royal College of Music gave two concerts during the early months of 1930: the first on January 25th at Grotian and the second on March 25th at the Wigmore Theatre. From Holst's diary entries, it appears that he planned on attending both. Her playing may have prompted Holst to write his "Nocturne" [H179, No. 1], a short piano piece intended as a late twenty-first birthday present for Imogen. Late it was; Imogen was twenty-three by the time she played it under the title of "An Un-named piece" at a recital at the Royal College of Music. It may have been as a token of thanks for her work with Imogen that Holst invited Kathleen Long to dinner:

St. Paul's Girls' School
Brook Green, Hammersmith,
W6
Oct[ober] 8[, 1928?]

Dear Miss Long,

Imogen tells me that you will give me the pleasure of spending an evening with me at my pub--the 'George' Hammersmith Broadway (upstairs room).

Would Thursday suit you?

And since you dislike late hours (as I do) would 6:30 do?

And have you any special diet?

The George is best in rather heavy things--beef, beer, and Burgundy. If this won't do for you let me know and I would call you and we would wander towards Soho.

Y Sincerely

Gustav Holst[16]

Holst's absentmindedness, however, got in the way but he still was able to save the situation through his sense of humor:

Tuesday
St. Paul's Girls' School
Brook Green, Hammersmith,
W6

I	carefully	wrote enclosed	yesterday.
"	"	stamped "	"
"	"	put it in my pocket	"
"	"	found it there	today.

whereupon
" " said---------------- (never mind)

Anyhow I shall expect you at the George at 7 unless you write.

Y

GH[17]

Dorothy Silk performed the Humbert Wolfe songs again at Wigmore Hall on February 5, 1930. Newspaper accounts in at least two newspapers were quite favorable:

> Mr. Holst's new style has become very spare--more than ever sinewy and direct; a bleak style, some may now say of it, but one of the admirable technical craft, serving exactly the composer's intentions.[18]

> These [songs] represent presumably the latest development of Mr. Holst's art, a development that holds out features of peculiar interest for the musician, but also increases the distance from the style of the "Planets," which won Mr. Holst the greater part of his admirers.[19]

The songs were also received favorably in Holland, according to the following letter:

The Studio
42 Balcombe Street
Dorset Square
N.W. 1

Dec[ember] 18th[, 1930]

Dear Mr. Holst,

At last I have leisure to write and tell you how your songs were received in Holland last November. All critics were very interested and only one--the "Avordpost"--had anything to say that was uncomplimentary.

The best papers say as follows:

Vaanland: "Some remarkable Gustav Holst songs (interesting art; of which I shall make a study some time) (kind of him!! (N.S.T.)) was interpreted with clear understanding of the poetical atmosphere."

De Telegraaf: "She[20] brought us....magnificent songs of Wolf[e] and Holst: the latter more interesting than usual. All this she sang with great control and care, each song convinced us that her art is fully developed."

England on the 7th?

Yrs sincerely
Norah Scott Turner[21]

On Monday, February 24, 1930 Holst returned to his hometown of Cheltenham to conduct the first concert performance of *The Golden Goose*. The program also featured the orchestral version of *Bach's Fugue a la Gigue*.

The next orchestral progam that involved Holst was given by the Royal Philharmonic Society in Queen's Hall on April 3rd. On that occasion, Jelly D'Aranyi and her sister Adila Fachiri premiered Holst's *Double Concerto*; Oskar Fried conducted. The three-movement fourteen-minute piece had actually been in the soloist's hands since the previous October. Other works on the same program were Strauss' *Til Eulenspiegel*, Hindemith's *Scene from Cardillac* and Brahms' *Symphony No. 1 in C Minor*. Reviews of the *Double Concerto* were mixed:

> ....one of the best things Holst has ever done.[22]

> A rambling, uneven work with the violins like two plaintiff spirits wandering in a wood filled with trombone-like noises and disjointed rhythms. It is certainly original in thought, but it seems rather muddled-headed thought.[23]

> It is a sober, lucid, and beautifully expressive composition, and revives my almost abandoned hope in Mr. Holst as a composer. He has eschewed the pretentious and grandiose in this direct and yet ingenious composition, so that we may expect him now to follow his own bent and write critically to please himself without considering fashion or public taste. If he does this he may do good work.[24]

Holst heard from his friend and Royal College of Music colleague R. O. Morris:

30 Glebe Place
London S.W.3

Sat [April, 1930]

Dear Gustav

I enjoyed the Concerto very much, & think it is probably the best thing you have done. I didn't get hold of the Ground as well as the other 2 movements, but think that was partly because I wasn't very well placed for hearing.

You made your two keys sound like one key & how otherwise should it be? Any fool can write in Xn keys & make it sound like Xn keys.

Yours

R.O.M.
[Reginald Owen Morris][25]

After the performance of the concerto, Frederick Austin presented Holst with the Royal Philharmonic Society's Gold Medal. Holst was the thirty-eighth recipient of the medal in the society's 118-year history; Ralph Vaughan Williams had received his a month earlier and both Elgar and Delius had been bestowed with the same honor in 1925. *The Daily Telegraph* commented about Holst and Vaughan Williams:

> ...Arcadians both, together upholding the highest ideals of their art. Mr. Holst, replying with characteristic modesty, remarked that when he read the list of other British composers upon whom the Philharmonic medal had been bestowed he felt he was receiving 'the greatest honour this world could give, the fellowship of honourable men.'"[26]

Holst normally shunned such ceremonial honors and felt embarrassed by them. Vaughan Williams acknowledged this in the following letter. He had become familiar with Holst's concerto through a "field day" or two, and ultimately favored a different pair of movements from those preferred by Morris:

The White Gates
Westcott Road,

Dorking
[April 4, 1930]

Dear Gustav,

I was distressed not to see you last night. I know you hate it all--but we had to tell you in public that we know you are a great man.

The Lament & Ground are splendid--I'm not quite so sure about the scherzo--and even that boils down to not being quite sure about the 6/8 tune.

Yrs

RVW[27]

As if to get away from it all, Holst left the country during St. Paul's Girls' School's Easter break. He arrived in Rotterdam, The Netherlands on Thursday, April 10th, beginning a walking tour of the low countries that would last for sixteen days.[28] When he returned to England, Holst spent most of his free time working on *A Choral Fantasia*, although he was able to attend Vaughan Williams' Leith Hill Festival later that month and to organize the musical part of a Whitsunday Festival in Chichester for early June. The Chicester festival, organized under the auspices of Bishop George Bell, involved enormous musical forces: 120 singers from St. Paul's Girls' School and Morley College plus another120 local singers, including students from Bishop Otter College.[29]

The week following the festival had its moments, too. On June 10th Holst and his American friend Austin Lidbury, who happening to be in England on a visit, rode by car to Cocking. From there the two of them spent the next day in the South Downs walking to the Norfolk Arms in Arundel.[30] This venture served as sort of a reprise of the two-day walk that they had taken together two years earlier in the Cotswolds. When the mood struck him, Holst walked. He took two additional solo walks in the next two weeks before rejoining Lidbury in London on June 28th. Later that summer he walked from Southwell to Lincoln--a week's worth--and from there to Alford.

All of this walking had a positive effect on whetting the composer's creativity--it usually did--and Holst was finally able to get started on *Hammersmith*. After writing a plethora of melodic and developmental sketches[31] (blissfully "spoiling paper," as Holst might say), he was able to assemble a two-piano version by late October. At St. Paul's Girls' School on November 4th,

Nora Day and Helen Bidder played this version for B. Walton O'Donnell, who, as conductor of the BBC Military Band, was the intended conductor of the work. Holst had other things going on that autumn as well, including conducting the *Double Concerto* and "Ballet Music" from *The Perfect Fool* at Queen's Hall on September 18th. An entry in his diary indicates that he may also have met Swiss composer Artur Honegger on September 9th.[32] All of this indicates that Holst was having a great year, yet his greatest personal achievement during such productive times may have been an utterly selfless act on behalf of another composer.

Holst was heavily involved with Ralph Vaughan Williams' ballet *Job*: *A Masque for Dancing* during the years 1929 to 1931. The work was first performed as a suite for large orchestra at the 1930 Norwich Festival. Through Holst's advocacy, *Job* was eventually produced by the Camargo Society. Founded in 1930 in the wake of the death of Sergei Diaghilev (1872-1929), the society took its name from the Parisian ballerina Marie-Anne de Cupis (1710-70), known as La Camargo. It was spearheaded by ballet dancer Lydia Lopokova and her husband John Maynard Keynes. Edwin Evans served as its chairman and Constant Lambert was its music director. The society played a vital role in establishing English Ballet, but ceased operations after only two years due to the increase of activities at Sadler's Wells.[33]

Job's first rehearsals took place in Norwich, with Holst and Arthur Bliss in attendence. Bliss commented on Holst's role:

> ...in 1930, I was sitting next to him [Holst] at a first run-through of Vaughan Williams' *Job*. Suddenly Holst, and when he was listening to music he listened at a frightening intensity, said to himself "This doesn't come off and I must go and tell him." He stepped on to the platform, looked at the score with Vaughan Williams, discussed and suggested, and then came back to his place, while the composer spoke to the players. The section was then tried over again, but with what a difference in sound!--clarity instead of thick obscurity. Holst always probed like a fine surgeon to the root of the difficulty. I wish I had grasped the chance to know his unique personality better....[34]

The Norwich performance of *Job* went very well--so well in fact that Holst was able to convince the Camargo Society to put on a full production of it in London's Cambridge Theatre the following July. There was one problem, however; surprisingly, the Camargo society would have a smaller orchestra available for its performances than what had been available in Norwich. Holst wrote to Edwin Evans:

St. Paul's Girls' School
Brook Green Hammersmith,
W6
Dec[ember] 3rd, 1930

Dear Evans,

I have looked through the score of Vaughan Williams' Job and in my opinion it would have to be entirely re-scored for performance by small orchestra. I have told him so, and at present I do not know whether he would cue in or follow my suggestion. He begs me to tell you that, if he is told in time, he would supply the fresh score if he thought it necessary, but he must be told as soon as possible if the work is wanted at all. He is only part owner as the inventor of the Ballet has to be consulted also. If the Camargo produced Job, Vaughan Williams would prefer them to do it in London first.

On December 12th we are trying over some things of mine. The performance will be very rough and the performers are all enthusiatic amateurs. I do not like definitely to invite you, but if you care to come would you be here at half-past seven (entrance 48, Rowan Road[)].

Yours sincerely,

Gustav Holst[35]

The "trying over some things of mine on December 12th" that Holst referred to inthis letter was the infamous field day that Holst and Vaughan Williams had with Holst's major 1930 works--*The Tale of the Wandering Scholar*, *A Choral Fantasia* and *Hammersmith*--which together last an hour. Vaughan Williams later referred to that evening as "the great night at SPGS."[36]

Nearly two decades after Holst's death, Vaughan Williams wrote the following:

> I should like to place on record all that he [Holst]did for me when I wrote *Job*. I should be alarmed to say how many 'Field Days' we spent over it. Then he came to all the orchestral rehearsals, including a special journey to Norwich, and finally he insisted on the Camargo Society's performing it. Thus I owe the life of *Job* to Holst....I remember after the

first rehearsal his almost going on his knees to to beg me to cut out some of the percussion which my inferiority complex had led me to overload the score.[37]

On December 21st Holst sent Nora Day an early Christmas gift. She had apparently requested a setting of something by the composer for the holidays:

Dec[ember] 21[, 1930]
St. Paul's Girls' School
Brook Green, Hammersmith

Dear Nora

Here is another Unsuitable Present. I fear that apart from its un-Xmas-like spirit it isn't at all what you wanted. But I sent it to you because I've looked forward for so long to setting these words for you: also because I wrote it quite unexpectedly last night and find that I don't dislike it sufficiently to tear it up today. With greetings and best wishes.

Y

G[38]

The "Unsuitable Present" turned out to be a short one-page setting of "God Be in My Head" [H180A] for soprano and organ.

After such a prolific year, the promise of an equally productive1931 was dashed by a number of major disappointments: the cancellation of a proposed radio performance of *Savitri*, the failures of both *A Choral Fantasia* and *Hammersmith* to find their audiences, and the miniscule release and quality of the soundtrack to *The Bells*, Holst's only film score.

Early in the year Holst heard from Adrian Boult, then director of music for the British Broadcasting Corporation and conductor of the BBC Symphony Orchestra, about broadcasting a week of his music. *Savitri* and *The Planets* were to be included:

British Broadcasting
Corporation
Savoy Hill, London W.C.2
13th January, 1931

Dear Gustav,

We are doing Savitri soon, I believe at a studio performance, and I was wondering whether you would like to have fuller Strings at any time or whether we shall stick to the double quartet.

I have discovered that in my score to Mercury on page 55, the bar before figure IV, the E flat entry of the First horn has been changed to E natural. Is this right, please?

Yours ever,

Adrian[39]

Holst sent the following response:

St. Paul's Girls' School
Brook Green, Hammersmith
Jan[uary] 18[, 1931]

Dear Adrian

Welcome home! I hope Sicily meant as much to you as it did to me.

The horn note in Mercury should be E natural[,] not flat[,] and the fault was the composer's who was a bigger ass than usual when he let the flat slip in.

Will you decide about the strings in Savitri. I don't know what is best for broadcasting but I am all in favor of leaving the score as it is because I've found that solo instruments come through so well.

Thank you very much for doing it. May I come and bring 3 or 4 friends?

I've heard a rumor that the BBC tried to get Dorothy Silk to sing Savitri on Feb 13 but found she was engaged. If it is not a) too late b) too interfering would you consider altering the date? DS does it so beautifully.

But don't consider it if you've approached anyone else.

I wish we could meet more in 1931. Barring Mondays a 1.30 lunch is nearly always as possible as it would be jolly for me. If the same ever applies to you let me know. But you speak first as your'e the busier. And

I suggest 'no treating'.

Yr coming performance of Savitri has awakened my old dream of writing a real radio opera. But it remains a dream.

Y ever

Gustav[40]

In the end, *Savitri* was dropped from the BBC program for technical reasons and Holst's dream of composing a radio opera remained just that--a dream. Michael Short comments:

> It is tantalizing to to speculate as to what such a work might have been like; Holst's recurrent problems with stagecraft in the theatre would be minimized in a radio production, allowing full reign to his creative imagination.[41]

A consolation prize for the non-broadcast of *Savitri* was in the works, however, as Boult approached Holst about *Hammersmith*, then awaiting a performance by the BBC Military Band:

British Broadcasting
Corporation
Savoy Hill, London, W.C.2
11th March, 1931

Dear Gustav,

First of all I have got to say how sorry I am that I have made a terrible mistake and agreed to the postponement of the day on which I am to talk about you over the wireless to March 27th, completely ignoring the fact that I have to do a Studio Orchestral Concert at the same moment. I cannot think how I can have been so idiotic, but there it is, and I am am going to ask Victor Hely-Hutchinson to do the talk for me, if you don't mind. We will go through things together beforehand, and I think there will be gramophone illustrations, which I have no doubt he will be able to play as well as I can--there is every possibility of his doing the Talk considerably better.

You know that it is necessary that we should keep our eyes open for new work here, as well as old things. If 'Emma'[42] would be suitable or there is any chance of your giving us some other new work as well I hardly need say how delighted we should be, and personally how delighted I should be if we were allowed to take charge of it.

Yours ever

Adrian[43]

Holst replied:

St. Paul's Girls' School
Brook Green, Hammersmith,
W6
March 13[, 1931]

Dear Adrian

Bless you but you forgot the One Important Matter--how are you?

Get Mrs. Beckett[44] to send me her private opinion on this point. I'm hoping to have a week's middle-aged walking in Normandy from the 27th so shall miss the talk.

I shall send Emma to you first. I'd rather you and the BBC orchestra introduced her than anyone else.

If you'd like my two pianists[45] to come and play her to you as they did to O'Donnell they'd be proudanappy to do so. Or would you like to hear the military version?

No need to reply.

Y Ever

G[46]

In the weeks that followed Holst not only rescored *Hammersmith* for orchestra, he also revised the original military band version. Notebook entries confirm this:

Emma
entire list of corrections

opening bars [bass?] in tromb
Euph and bass (until I)
--parts to be done (except E Flat Sax)
and after XVI
in orch wind against str?
I do bass pp. 31, 72

and

Emma
end
tromb louder
tr softer[47]

Additional notes indicate that Holst had considerable help from Amy Kemp and Helen Bidder in copying out score and parts:

Emma rehearse from
" ABACA Frid 12
cond to AK
" " Bid
AK tromb tuba[48]

Holst also changed the full title of the work, from *Hammersmith: Prelude and Fugue* to *Hammersmith: Prelude and Scherzo*.

There are many differences between the military band and orchestral versions of *Hammersmith*, the most obvious being that the orchestra version is pitched one-half step higher than the band version. The trombone *glissandi* are also different: ascending in the band version, descending in the orchestral. The Hawkes pocket score of the orchestral version contains the following note:

> Hammersmith was originally written for military band. The composer then wrote this orchestral score, which differs from the military band version in several essentials: even the number of bars is not the same.[49]

Adrian Boult and the BBC Symphony Orchestra gave the orchestral premiere of *Hammersmith* at Queen's Hall on November 25, 1931. Placed on a concert which also featured the London premiere of William Walton's *Belshazzar's Feast,* it did not create a sensation with the public. Imogen Holst commented:

> Most of the listeners at the first performance of the orchestral version of *Hammersmith* found the river Prelude too slow, too quiet, too montonous, and--like *Egdon Heath*--too uncomfortable.[50]

While Holst did not consider public acclaim of his works to be very important, it still bothered him on occasion. He entered the following into his notebook:

> Emma Imogen
> Gussie disconsolate
> and want our revenge[51]

If this is what Holst meant by this entry--recognition of *Hammersmith* for being the great work that it is--then revenge would come, but it would not arrive until two decades following its composer's death.

---

[1]Frederick Wilkinson, "Gustav Holst as Friend" in *The R.C.M. Magazine*, LXX, No. 2 (Summer, 1974), 55.

[2]Gustav Holst, *Diary*, Monday, May 6, 1929, The Holst Foundation.

[3]Ten of the twelve songs have been arranged and orchestrated for voice and chamber orchestra by Colin Matthews under the title *The Dream City*, which was used for the work's 1929 premiere. This version was published by Novello in 1983.

[4]Clifford Bax, "Recollections of Gustav Holst" in *Music and Letters*, XX, No.1 (January, 1939), 4.

[5]Imogen Holst (ed.), *Gustav Holst: Collected Facsimile Edition of Autograph Manuscripts of the Published Works, Vol. I: Chamber Operas* (London: Faber Music, Ltd., 1974), p. 81.

[6]A. E. F. Dickinson, ed. Alan Gibbs, *Holst's Music: A Guide* (London: Thames, 1995), 78.

[7]Thomas Whitney Surrette's Concord Summer School in Massachusetts.

[8]Personal correspondence, G. Wallace Woodworth to Gustav Holst, July 4, 1929, The Holst Foundation.

[9]Gustav Holst, *Diary*, Friday, August 16 through Sunday, August 18, 1929, The Holst Foundation.

[10]Gustav Holst, *Diary*, Tuesday, October 15 through Sunday, October 20, 1929, The Holst Foundation.

[11]*Orchestra Symphonique de Paris, Programme Officiel, Nouvelle Salle Pleyel*, 20 Oct. 4:00 [1929].

[12]Gustav Holst, *Diary*, Thursday, November 7 through Saturday, November 9, 1929, The Holst Foundation.

[13]Personal correspondence, Nadia Boulanger to Gustav Holst (1) [November, 1929], The Holst Foundation.

[14]Personal correspondence, Nadia Boulanger to Gustav Holst (2) [November, 1929], The Holst Foundation.

[15]Gustav Holst, *Diary*, Sunday, December 22 through Sunday, December 29, 1929, The Holst Foundation.

[16]Personal correspondence. Gustav Holst to Kathleen Long, Oct[ober] 8[, 1930?], The Holst Foundation.

[17]Personal correspondence, Gustav Holst to Kathleen Long, "Tuesday" [October, 1930?], The Holst Foundation.
[18]*The Evening News* (London), February 6, 1930.
[19]*The Daily Telegraph*, February 6, 1930.
[20]This probably referred to Dorothy Silk.
[21]Personal correspondence, Norah Scott Turner to Gustav Holst, Dec[ember] 18th[, 1930], The Holst Birthplace Museum.
[22]*The Sunday Times*, April 6, 1930.
[23]*The Daily Express*, April 4, 1930.
[24]*Truth*, April 9, 1930.
[25]Personal correspondence, R. O. Morris to Gustav Holst, Sat[urday, April, 1930], The Holst Foundation.
[26]Gustav Holst, quoted in *The Daily Telegraph*, April 4, 1930. Compare this with what Holst had to say about the teaching profession, quoted in the Folk Songs and Girls' Schools chapter.
[27]Personal correspondence, Ralph Vaughan Williams to Gustav Holst [April 4, 1930], quoted in Ursual Vaughan Williams (ed.) and Imogen Holst (ed.), *Heirs and Rebels, Letters to EAch Other and Occasional Writings by Gustav Holst and Ralph Vaughan Williams* (Oxford: Oxford University Press, 1959), 74.
[28]Gustav Holst, *Diary*, Thursday, April 10 through Sunday, April 26, 1930, The Holst Foundation.
[29]Michael Short, *Gustav Holst: The Man and His Music* (Oxford: Oxford University Press, 1990), 290.
[30]Gustav Holst, *Diary*, Tuesday, June 10, 1930, The Holst Foundation.
[31]For a detailed description of these, see the author's "The Hammersmith Sketches" in *College Band Directors National Association Journal*, III, No. 1 (Spring, 1986), 8-17.
[32]Gustav Holst, *Diary*, Tuesday, September 9, 1930, The Holst Foundation.
[33]Milo Keynes, ed., *Lydia Lopokova* (London: Weidenfeld and Nicolson, 1983), 109.
[34]Arthur Bliss, *As I Remember* (London: Faber & Faber, 1970), 65-66.
[35]Personal correspondence, Gustav Holst to Edwin Evans, Dec[ember] 3rd, 1930, Central Public Library, Westminster.
[36]Personal correspondence, Ralph Vaughan Williams to Gustav Holst [December, 1930], quoted in Ursula Vaughan Williams (ed.) and Imogen Holst (ed.), *op. cit.*, 74-75.
[37]Ralph Vaughan Williams, "A Musical Biography," in *Some Thoughts on Beethoven's Choral Symphony with Writings on Other Musical Subjects* (Oxford: Oxford University Press, 1953).
[38]Personal correspondence, Gustav Holst to Nora Day, Dec[ember] 21[, 1930]. British Library Add. MS 60381.
[39]Personal correspondence, Adrian Boult to Gustav Holst, January 13, 1931, British Lbrary Add. MS 60498.
[40]Personal correspondence, Gustav Holst to Adrian Boult, Jan[uary] 18[, 1931], British Library Add. MS 60498.
[41]Michael Short, *op. cit.*, 296.
[42]*Hammersmith.*
[43]Personal correspondence, Adrian Boult to Gustav Holst, March 11, 1931, BBC Written Archives Centre.
[44]Adrian Boult's personal secretary. In a letter dated February 6 [1931] and in other instances Holst jokingly referred to belonging to a "Bother Mrs. Beckett" Club.
[45]Nora Day and Helen Bidder.
[46]Personal correspondence, Gustav Holst to Adrian Boult, March 13[, 1931], BBC Written Archives Centre.

[47]Gustav Holst, Notebook, 1931, The Holst Foundation.
[48]*Ibid.*.
[49]Gustav Holst: *Hammersmith: A Prelude and Scherzo for Orchestra, Op. 52* (London: Hawkes & Son, Ltd., 1963.
[50]Imogen Holst, *Holst,* 2nd ed. (London: Faber & Faber, 1981), 76.
[51]Gustav Holst, Notebook, [after November 25] 1931, The Holst Foundation.

CHAPTER XXI

THE BELLS

It is fortunate indeed that so little of what Gustav Holst composed has been lost. A great deal of credit must be given to Imogen Holst, who kept her father's music alive in the two or three decades immediately following his death. In *A Thematic Catalogue of Gustav Holst's Music* (London: Faber & Faber, 1974), Imogen Holst included 192 main catalogue ("H") works composed from 1895 onwards and another forty-two pieces composed before 1895 ("App. I") for a total of 234 completed original works. When one adds to this the seventeen incomplete original works ("App. II"), and twenty-five transcriptions done by Holst of other people's music ("App. III"), the total swells to 276 known catalogued works. The vast majority of Holst's works are extant in both manuscript and published forms; some exist in only one of these forms. Amazingly, fewer than a dozen of Holst's known works are missing altogether.

Of paricular interest among the missing (or"lost") works are a *Suite in G Minor* for string orchestra [H41] (1898), incidental music to John Masefield's play *Philip the King* [H122] (1914), the military band version of two sets of *Morris Dance Tunes* [App. III, 12] (1911), incidental music to the motion picture *The Bells* [H184] (1931) and incidental music to the Hollywood pageant *The Song of Solomon* [App II, 17] (1933-34). The impact of the loss of three of these, while not insignificant, may not be that great. The *Suite in G Minor*, while interesting, was a relatively early work and the incidental music for *Philip the King*, according to Imogen Holst's catalogue entry, may not have amounted to much. While one may mourn the disappearance of the military band version of the sets of *Morris Dance Tunes*, the parts for Holst's chamber orchestra version are published and available. This trims the "heavy casualty" losses to two late works: *The Song of*

Solomon, covered in a later chapter, and *The Bells*.

Sound came to the British cinema two years after it had arrived in Hollywood. In 1929 a young Alfred Hitchcock directed his last silent movie, *Blackmail*. Hitchcock wanted to experiment with sound and received permission to film the last reel of his movie--and only the last reel--with synchronized sound. When his bosses left for a week, Hitchcock took advantage of the situation and reshot not only the last reel but also enough of the rest of the picture to pass it off as a "talkie." This sound version of *Blackmail* was such a success that not only did a number of companies make the switch to sound, but additional motion picture companies came into existence for the sole purpose of making sound pictures. Among these was Associated Sound Film Industries, which started up in November, 1929. ASFI, as it was known, at first specialized in "super productions" aimed at European distribution. Their first product was *City of Song* (1930) featuring Italian location shots and starring tenor Jan Kiepura. It was a huge critical success.[1] Their next major undertaking was *The Bells* (1931).

The Bells had its origins in the French play, *Le Juif Polonais (The Polish Jew)* by Erchmann and Chartrian. It was translated into English by Leopold Lewis and first produced in England in 1871. Actor and theatrical manager Sir Henry Irving [John Henry Brodribb] (1838-1905) played the lead. The play was revived several times. A silent movie version of the play, starring Lionel Barrymore and Boris Karloff, was made in 1926.[2] The screenplay for ASFI's 1931 75-minute production, the only sound movie version of the play to date, was written by C. H. Dand. The photography was handled by Gunther Krampf and Eric Cross.

The plot of *The Bells* is melodramatic:

> "The Bells" is described as a drama of conscience. The story tells of the Burgomaster of a small town who had murdered a man seven years before. An agent is sent to investigate the almost forgotten murder, and as the past is recalled, the old man's crime wells up in his brain until at last he is forced to still his gnawing conscience forever in a way that supplies the drama with a grimly impressive climax.[3]

The film was produced in three languages: English, French, and German. Oscar Werndorff and Harcourt Templeman were listed as the directors. It is not known how much the three versions overlapped or whether a different cast was used for each. The principals in the English language version were:

The Burgomaster..Donald Calthrop
His Daughter..Jane Welsh

The Sergeant..Edward Sinclair
The Night Watchman..O. P. Clarence
The Drunken Philosopher...Wilfred Shine
The Blacksmith..Ralph Truman[4]

Just exactly how Holst felt about films is not known. A lack of Diary entries about seeing movies seems to indicate that he did not attend them regularly. He may have accompanied the silent movies for the troops on occasion during his 1918-19 stint with the British YMCA, but, since his chosen art involved sound media, would have found concerts and plays more to his liking. By 1931 the sound film had proven itself, but it was still a new medium. Holst undoubtedly saw tremendous potential in the sound film[5], or he would not have accepted the commission to write the music for *The Bells.* Announcement of Holst's association with the film was made in *Musical Mirror and Fanfare*:

> I hear that Gustav Holst has been commissioned to compose the incidental music for the sound-film version of The Bells, now in the course of production in the ASFI studios at Wembly. This is the first time that a composer of Holst's standing has accepted such a contract and, judging by the rubbish that is usually associated with sound-films, it is indeed a welcome sign. Among the numbers which Holst will write are a Storm Prelude, Wedding Music, and several drinking songs. He is being allowed a perfectly free hand, but is working in the closest cooperation with the directors of the film to achieve results which should provide something more original and refreshing in the musical treatment of sound films than has yet been accomplished.[6]

On March 9th, Holst wrote to his daughter Imogen, "....I've finished some sketches for my Talkie...,"[7] and on the twentieth he attended a meeting at the ASFI studios at Wembley. Philip Braham, the musical director at ASFI as well as coordinator of the movie directors, wanted to move things along and asked Holst to have his music ready in a month. Holst complied, although in the midst of things his wanderlust prevailed and he took off on March 27th[8] for a previously planned week-long walking tour in Normandy.

Some of Holst's notenook entries reveal his concern for timings as well as the instrumentation of the musical ensemble available to him:

> Ass. Sound Film Wembley 3041 Mr. C. H. Dand
> Sketches for dances in 3 weeks finished Ap 20

film 90 ft=1 min
ft multiply by 2 divide by 3=seconds
orch 5 1st 4 vlas div 2 VC 1 bass 1 sousaphone
fl (poor) ob 2 cl fag 2 tr 2 horns 1 tromb
2 or 3 drummers extras harp celesta
extend march
delete dance
sleigh bells in orch?
Annette's song tune must Annette sing it or my singer?[9]

In doing her research on the film, Imogen Holst wrote to C. H. Dand, and received some information. She commented:

> Mr. Dand's most vivid recollection of the music was of a two-track sequence in which a brass band and a pipe band, playing their own tunes, marched from different directions and came together.[10]

Dand's description of this Ives-like scenario is uncanny; it corresponds directly with additional notes that Holst had written to himself:

Bells
March
Br [cresc.] last 3/4 f
    end [decresc.] p
    I pipes cresc.
        pp
    II pipe f
        br cres
    III all ff[11]

From the above notes it is, of course, impossible to reconstruct anything. Of the actual music that Holst composed for the film, the only thing that has survived is an eight-bar fragment of a 'film valse' that he notated in one of his sketchbooks.[12]

The filming itself was done quickly and Holst went to the ASFI studios at Wembley on a number of occasions to conduct the music and act as a consultant. There were the usual delays--some technical, others attributed to Donald Calthrop's heavy drinking[13]--that caused lulls in the filming. During one such lull, Holst was asked to be an extra. He wrote about this to Adeline Vaughan

Williams:

Sunday SPGS
[April, 1931]

Dear Adeline,

I feel sure that you agree with me that you are the right person to break the news to him[14], which is that I have appeared in a film! At least I think I have. Or rather, I probably shall when it is developed. Unless I am killed in the 'cutting room.' They wanted some people in the crowd last Thursday so I volunteered and acted with Eric's ma who is a dear. He first appeared in a film five years ago. He is now eight years old. Her last job was in a shipwreck and owing to an accident she will never be able to move her big toe again. I wish I could remember the rest--there was a lot of it at each break.

And that reminds me that O B Clarence, who is acting the part of the burgomaster[15] in the film as well as appearing in St. Joan each night (and who is also a dear) told me that once they were a whole day filming a hole in the heel of his sock.

Y ever

Gustav[16]

Holst commented further:

> Perhaps the gem in our film is when the two lovers, after a motortrip, go shopping on old London Bridge. I haven't asked why--it isn't done. But I imagine that the reason is that a replica of old London Bridge was made for the Wembley exhibition[17], and my film's studio is at Wembley.[18]

Adeline Vaughan Williams responded, "Every good wish for the Talkie.--please see that it gets to Dorking."[19]

A preview was held upon completion of the film in April, 1931 and both Holst and Imogen attended. She commented, "The only thing I can remember clearly is my father's white-faced look of dismay when he heard the distortion of the sound-track."[20] At least three factors may have contributed to Holst's dissappointment: (1) the electronic sound recording process itself had been around for only about a half dozen years, (2) sound movies were still in their infancy in 1931 and the recording engineers were still inexperienced in regard to recording techniques, and (3) the sound-on-film technique[21] (fortunately utilized by ASFI) which replaced Vitaphone (a system of huge discs) was brand new. Yet for its time *The Bells* must have been a real technical achievement; the artistic quality of the film--in terms of both sight and sound--was praised by the critics. Announcements of the release of *The Bells* were made at least twice: in October, 1931 and again in March, 1932 (while Holst was at Harvard). Notices and reviews appeared in both trade journals and in the general presses, although no release date had yet been fixed. The following extensive review appeared in *The Cinema*; it begins with a synopsis and leaves one with a good overall idea of what the movie was about:

> Psychological melodrama. Sombre story of guilty Burgomaster hounded into confession of crime through cumulative effect of sleigh bells ringing in his ear. Enthralling pictorial beauty of natural landscapes dominates every other aspect, superb camera work combining to provide unforgettable vistas of Nature in harshest mood. Imaginative and at times brilliant direction makes most of narrative material, but this later proves vague and meandering, while attempted symbolism is above heads of average patrons. Development has moment of stark drama, touches of calculated romance and interludes of amusing alcoholic comedy, but actual climax, following on brilliant scene of Burgomaster's confession, is tame and abrupt. Sympathetic leading portrayal, uneven support, good types among smaller roles, effective village atmosphere, clear recording in main. Distinctive offering for students of screen art.
>
> ---
>
> Few British pictures have even remotely approached, in beauty of camera work and in imaginative direction, the superb technical qualities of this latest ASFI production. The work of Gunther Krampf [the lead cameraman], in particular, is enthralling in its poetic imagery, and to see his pictures of leafless trees threshed into wildest tersichorean abandon against the backgrounds of snowcapped crag and tempestuous torrent, is to envisage Nature herself in all the vivid beauty of a winter landscape.
>
> This stark pictorial realism is often duplicated in other portions of the production, and had the narrative element been on anything like a corresponding plane, then "The Bells" would have been a great picture.

> Truth to tell, however, the telling of this tale of a stricken conscience, of the gradual unnerving of a guilty Burgomaster by legal suspicion and inquiry, of the final collapse of his shattered nerves at his daughter's wedding, and of the paying of his last dread penalty on the very spot where his victim had met his doom--this telling, we say, will strike many as being vague and meandering, and not even the haunting beauty of the natural exterior settings or the occasional bursts of directorial brilliance will compensate as accepted film entertainment.
>
> The picture has its dramatic moments, notably in the sombre scene when the ultra-romantic young policeman first suspects the Burgomaster, of again in the more animated sequence where the now nerveless Burgomaster, playing "Blind Man's Bluff" at his daughter's wedding and hearing the tinkling bells which the players advertise their nearness, collapses utterly and turns roystering comedy into dreadful tragedy by confessing himself the murderer. The latter scene is probably the best in the picture in its animated surge, although its attempted symbolism may miss its mark except with the most discerning patron.
>
> The portrayal features some excellent types among the local peasantry. O. H. Clarence being prominent as a doddering night watchman and Wilfred Shine making a personal hit with his cameo of an alcoholic philosopher. Of course, Donald Calthrop has most of the limelight with his study of the Burgomaster, and the characterisation is at least sensitive and dignified. As we have suggested, Edward Sinclair savours somewhat of a musical comedy lead in the role of the inquisitive sergeant, nor does Jane Welsh seem an ideal choice as a Continental village maiden.
>
> For the most part, the recording is good--one may detect a little unevenness here and there--particularly of the blizzard effects in the opening and middle scenes. These latter definitely enhance the prevailing atmosphere, and indeed achieve an awe-inspiring realism.[22]

What of Holst's contribution? G. A. Atkinson, film critic of *The Daily Telegraph*, mentioned Holst in his review:

> There is no pot-boiler flavour in "The Bells," the Associated Sound Film Industries production, which gives his first feature role to Donald Calthrop....
>
> The direction is by Oscar Werndorff and Harcourt Templeman, and the musical setting, stamped with genius throughout, comes from Gustav

Holst.

> This English film is a great work of art, and is as near flawless as makes no matter.[23]

This was echoed in *The Christian Science Monitor*, which said, "Gustav Holst, a British composer, despite his name, has given the film an excellent musical atmosphere."[24]

Not all of the reviews were as positive:

> Even Donald Calthrop's brilliant performance is unable to put life into this screen version of the melodrama made famous by Sir Henry Irving.
>
> Besides the fact that Calthrop is hopelessly miscast, there is no real vitality about the picture; it is entirely artificial and very slow in action.
>
> To some extent, this is counteracted by very clever camera work, which includes various kaleidoscopic effects, rapid "blackouts," and a general tendency to follow the lines of German technique.[25]

> From the technical point of view the film is something of an achievement. But as entertainment it is tedious and unreal.[26]

The film, if released at all, was a box office failure; it certainly didn't make it to Dorking, as Adeline Vaughan Williams had wished. In fact *The Bells* had only seven bookings in the United Kingdom before being sold to an unnamed American company[27] for distribution in the United States. If released in America, it is probable that the film would have been given a different title, as was often the case in the 1930's.

Any combination of factors could have accounted for the film's lack of success at the box office:

> 1. The subject matter. Effects of the worldwide great depression had just begun to be felt. The Bells was a heavy psychological melodrama. Much of the general populous attended movies to get away from the drudgery of life, not to be reminded of it.
> 2. Some negative reviews. ASFI may have sensed that their film needed more positive reviews to convince the public to see it and decided even before the film to cut losses by selling it.
> 3. Unknown inside factors. Perhaps there was someone in the studio--an administrator or producer--who, for personal reasons, did not want the

film released. There also may have been some absolute perfectionists working on the film who killed its release for artistic reasons, although this appears to be highly unlikely.

4. Unknown outside factors. There may have been lawsuits or other red tape that could have tied up the film in Europe. There may have been international difficulties. The fact that there were three different language versions of the film intended for release in three different countries, or that the original may have had a French copyright, could have placed the film at the heart of some legal battles.

The film itself deserves to be found, if for no other reason than for its artistic merit. As time passes, however, the odds of finding anything at all continue to diminish. Even if found, would the movie be watchable? In the early 1930's movies were made on a nitrate stock, which disintegrates if not properly stored. The majority of all films made before 1930 have been lost, and the odds of locating one made just one year later are not good.

Another factor working against locating the film is the fate of the ASFI Studios. Apparently *The Bells* was the studio's last quality effort and the company had great difficulty remaining solvent. In 1934 ASFI itself was sold to Fox-British.[28]

Still more tragic than the fortunes of either the movie or the studio is the fate of Holst's music. The score may be irretrievably lost--motion picture studios appear to have been in the habit of jettisoning musical manuscripts just as much as publishers were--and the film may be also be irretrievably lost, yet if even the film's soundtrack were located,[29] at least Holst's music could be reconstructed. The aesthetic reward of finding Holst's incidental music for *The Bells*--a late work and quite possibly his most significant from 1931--would be substantial.

---

[1]Personal correspondence, David McGhie to Colin Matthews, June 7, [1984].

[2]Leslie Halliwell, rev. and ed. John Walker, *Halliwell's Film Guide, 8th ed.* (New York: Harper Collins, 1991), 98.

[3]*Film Weekly*, March 12, 1932.

[4]*Ibid.*.

[5]Holst's 1933 letter to his daughter Imogen, disclosing a hint of his attitude on "talkies" is included in *The Song of Solomon* chapter.

[6]"Gustav Holst and Talkie Music," in *Musical Mirror and Fanfare* [1931].

[7]Personal correspondence, Gustav Holst to Imogen Holst, March 9[, 1931], The Holst Foundation.

[8]Gustav Holst, *Diary*, March 27, 1931, The Holst Foundation.

[9]Gustav Holst, Notebook, April, 1931, The Holst Foundation.

[10]Imogen Holst, *A Thematic Catalogue of Gustav Holst's Music* (London: Faber Music Ltd., 1974), 189.

[11]Gustav Holst, Notebook, April, 1931, The Holst Foundation.
[12]Gustav Holst, Sketchbook [App. IV, 6], British Library Add MS 47837.
[13]Personal corrspondence, David McGhie to Colin Matthews, August 7th [1984].
[14]Ralph Vaughan Williams.
[15]Holst was mistaken here. O. B. Clarence played the part of the Night Watchman. Donald Calthrop played the part of the Burgomaster.
[16]Personal correspondence, Gustav Holst to Adeline Vaughan Williams, Sunday [April, 1931], British Library Add. MS 57853.
[17]This exhibition was held in 1924 and featured, among other things, the premiere of Ralph Vaughan Williams' *Toccata Marziale.*
[18]Gustav Holst quoted in Imogen Holst, *Holst*, 2nd ed. (London: Faber & Faber, 1981), 77.
[19]Personal correspondence, Adeline Vaughan Williams to Gustav Holst, April 9, 1931, British Library Add. MS 57853.
[20]Imogen Holst, *The Music of Gustav Holst, 3rd ed. rev. and Holst's Music Reconsidered* (Oxford: Oxford University Press, 1985), 158.
[21]The system was called Movietone in the USA.
[22]*The Cinema*, October 14, 1931.
[23]*The Daily Telegraph*, October 14, 1931.
[24]*The Christian Science Monitor*, n.d..
[25]*Picturegoer*, March 12, 1932.
[26]*Film Weekly*, March 12, 1932.
[27]C. H. Dand, quoted in Imogen Holst, *A Thematic Catalogue...*, 188-189.
[28]Personal correspondence, David McGhie to Colin Matthews, June 7th[, 1984].
[29]This is exactly what happened to parts of *Lost Horizon* (1937). For the missings links of the full-length "restored version" stills were used to supplement the soundtrack.

CHAPTER XXII

HARVARD BECKONS

A brief entry made by Holst into a notebook dated April, 1931 may present the first evidence that he was considering another visit--his third--to the United States. It is very simple:

> Harvard
> Wallace Woodworth[1]

This was a reminder for Holst to write to George Wallace Woodworth at Harvard University. Holst's speech on "England and Her Music" given at Harvard two years earlier had been very well received and paved the way toward some sort of standing invitation for the composer to make a reappearance.

The thought of returning to America was a positive spot in what otherwise had been a rather depressing spring season for the composer. In 1930 three substantial--even great--works had flowed from his pen--*Tale of the Wandering Scholar*, *A Choral Fantasia*, and *Hammersmith*--yet none of these had made their mark with the public. *Tale of the Wandering Scholar* would have to wait another four years for its premiere, the *AChoral Fantasia* had been performed at the Three Choirs Festival in Gloucester but was poorly received, and although *Hammersmith*'s two premieres (band and orchestral) would take place within the next year, the work faced two vacuous decades before ascending to masterpiece status. Holst's only substantial work in the first half of 1931, if indeed it was substantial, was the incidental music (now lost) written for the motion picture *The Bells*. It is no wonder then that Holst, feeling frustrated and unappreciated as a composer, went through a dry spell and feared that his creative powers were on the wane. He equated these feelings with what he had experienced two and a half years earlier, just before his second American visit. Entries into the same notebook say it all.

> mental
> no comp Aug
> income end of July extra work thin
> good rest begin Aug--poor result
> fall asleep instead of work
> loss of memory much worse
> like this in 1928
> began term off end in 29
> Sicily, Italy 3 months
> Then invitation USA fortnight
> wrote steadily and well
> May 29 to Dec 30
> then got weary (not continuously)
> no good Xmas holiday[2]

It is not surprising that Holst would seek an infusion of anything different, perhaps exotic, in his quest to escape the doldrums. Another notebook entry, made following some August, 1931 choral lists, contains a letter-writing list that suggests Holst may have been envisioning some sort of substantial visit that would involve the East Coast, the Midwest and beyond:

> USA
> write Spalding chance
> of Harvard after Xmas
> Warner
> Basil Cameron
> Earl Moore   Anne Arbor
> Bulley   Victoria
> Goosens
> Lidbury
> Edw Yeomans
> Westport Point
> Mass--USA[3]

By the end of October, 1931 Holst already knew that he was being offered a visiting lecturer position at Harvard University for the following spring semester[4].

His impending arrival was heralded in the Boston press:

> The Divison of Music at Harvard is again profiting by the Lamb Bequest, which the generosity of Mrs. Horatio A. Lamb, makes possible the occasional visits of distinguished composers to give instruction in the higher branches of composition. For the 2nd half of the present Academic Year (February to May) Gustav Holst, the Englishman, will come as guest and teacher.
>
> So much of Boston and Cambridge as follows/remembers music will recall his "Hymn of Jesus" in concerts of the Harvard Glee Club and Radcliffe Choral Society; his lesser pieces for men's voices in concerts of the Glee Club by itself. In Mr. Monteux's time, the Symphony Orchestra played his "Planets." Possibly in the course of the winter or in the spring, Dr. Koussevitzky will find opportunity to pay some compliment to an eminent visitor.[5]

As sometimes happens, the press leaked the story. Official action wasn't taken by the university until the middle of the following month, when Kenneth Ballard Murdock, who had just taken over as Dean of the Faculty of Arts and Sciences following the death of Clifford H. Moore, wrote his letter of recommendation:

Faculty of Arts and Sciences
Office of the Dean
20 University Hall

President A. Lawrence Lowell
5 University Hall
Harvard University
Cambridge

November 17, 1931

Dear Mr. Lowell,

At the request of Professor Hill[6], Chairman of the Division of Music, I recommend that Mr. Gustav Holst be appointed Lecturer on Music on the Horatio Appleton Lamb Foundation for the second half of the present academic year, at a salary of $3000, to be paid from the accumulated interest of the Horatio A. Lamb Bequest.

Mr. Holst received his education at the Royal College of Music, London. He is a composer and a teacher of Music at St. Paul's School for Girls, Brook Green, Hammersmith, London, W. 6. Among his compositions are the following: Hymn of Jesus, The Planets, Ode to Death, Hymns from the Rig Veda, Cloud Messenger, Beni Mora, and many short choral works.

Very truly yours,

Kenneth B. Murdock[7]

The letter is stamped "Of Record Nov 30 1931."[8]

The original Horatio Appleton Lamb bequest was $25,000. It was established in 1927 by Annie L. Lamb in memory of her late husband in order to bring visiting faculty members to the Division of Music at Harvard. Elliot Forbes comments:

> From its inception, this generous gift was welcomed by the department because it would broaden and invigorate the offerings and attitudes of an essentially ingrown faculty, all of whom had been students of either [John Knowles] Paine or [Walter Raymond] Spalding.[9]

Holst was in good company. The first Lamb lecturer had been the Romanian composer and violinist Georges Enesco, who was on the Harvard University campus in 1929-1930. Others would follow, including Hugo Leichtentritt in 1933-34, Bela Bartok in 1943, and Aaron Copland in 1944.

The $3000 that Holst was to receive for one semester's work was quite a large sum in the early 1930's. At that time it exceeded the average annual American family income. In fact at the rate of $6000 per year, it more than doubled Woodworth's initial $2200 salary offer for the 1931-32 academic year and quadrupled that of fellow faculty member Frank Wells Ramseyer Jr.[10] From his notes, it is apparent that, although $3000 was a lot of money, Holst still had his concerns. Most of these centered around estimates and exchange rates. At that time the British pound was worth about four U.S. dollars:

3000 $ £750
28
20

journey £1100
13 weeks at £5
loss of work England £200

and

USA
at $4=£

journey £50 =	$200
16 week at $20 =	320
return journey	200
	$720
loss of SP £100	$400
extra £50	200
	1320
should clear $1500 =	£375

2 inc taxes[11]

The $1500 that Holst expected to clear on this trip would have been more than enough for him to have brought his wife along for the entire duration. Unlike the preparations that the composer made prior to his 1923 visit to the United States, there is nothing here to suggest that Holst had even the faintest notion of taking his wife Isobel on this trip. From all available accounts, the two of them had had a very enjoyable 1923 trip. Yet they may have already begun to drift apart from each other. Isobel did not enjoy Holst's wanderlust; she preferred to stay home, either decorating or doing some other aspect of homemaking. The seeds leading to separate existences may have been sown as early as 1914, when the family moved to the small country town of Thaxted. With his heavy workload of balancing at least three teaching jobs combined with the usual rehearsals and performances, Holst by necessity and design stayed in London for much of the time. Fours years later, however, Holst's dutiful stint with the British Y.M.C.A. at Salonika and Constantinople in 1918-19, while physically separating husband and wife, made the hearts grow fonder. After his return, from1922 to 1925, partially through the charity of friends, the Holsts were able to rent two places: their London apartment at 32 Gunterstone Road, located not far from St. Paul's Girls' School, and their Thaxted residence. Toward the end of the normal three-year lease period, Imogen graduated from St. Paul's and apparently neither Holst nor his wife saw the necessity in maintaining two places. They not only gave up their London apartment but also moved their principal residence from Thaxted to

Dunmow. Imogen Holst comments:

> He was still 'oriental' enough to have no desire for a fixed home. In Macedonia, when he had been moving about from one camp to the next, he had longed for a home where he could put his boots 'on the best droring-room sofa and so on'. But now, when he had the most beautiful home he was ever to live in, he preferred to be on the move the whole time. The home was Brook End, a Tudor farm-house in Easton Park, four miles from Thaxted. It was full of old oak beams that had never been stained but had worn to a soft grey. There were large open fires, and the glow from the logs was reflected in the shining pewter and the rich colour of the hangings. There was a barn that his wife had converted into a perfect music-room, with golden thatch on the roof and lead-lights in the windows, and electricity and central heating and all that one could desire.
>
> But Holst only came down for occasional week-ends. He had no use for property of any sort. His room need only be warm and silent, with a large enough writing-table in it. His luggage could always be packed between the full scores in his music bag....
>
> This homeless existence may have seemed ideal to him, but the great disadvantage was that he had nowhere to lose his temper when the occasion rose....there was no respite from the courtesy and the kindliness and the over-anxious consideration that he always showed for other people. It was an aspect that never occurred to him. He did not realize that he was tying his brain into knots with a network of tiny, unimportant details.[12]

So where did Holst stay in London? Although Imogen Holst referred to her father's "homeless existence" in the above paragraph, he did have what many would consider to be a second home. He usually spent the night on the couch or in a spare room at Vally Lasker's townhouse at 103 Talgarth Road. Located about a half-mile east of St. Paul's Girl's School--and very near the Holst's former apartment on Gunterstone Rd.-- it was the ideal place for Holst to spend the night. Holst had a nickname for this place, the "Jolly Talgarth" and often referred to it as the "J.T."

While this sleeping arrangement may appear to have been unorthodox and could raise some eyebrows, available evidence points to there having been no improper relationship between Holst and Vally Lasker. In addition to being a teacher, accompanist and amanuensis, Vally was also a hostess for St. Paul's Girls' School, often giving food and lodging to the school's visitors. Still, Holst and

Vally had developed a very close relationship and, possibly by his second trip to America in 1929 and certainly by his third in 1932, Vally had displaced Isobel (and later, Imogen) as the person to whom he had the most written correspondence. This may have been due in part to professional concerns, but the fact remains that sometimes Holst's most personal and wittiest commentary was reserved for her. Yet, even if their marriage was not what it once had been, Holst and Isobel remained devoted to each other. There is nothing to prove otherwise. As late as the autumn of 1933 Holst wrote to Imogen "....I hope Iso is coming to London for a week from next Friday and that we shall paint the town a middle-aged red."[13]

Holst's 1929 American visit had been a solo voyage. This in itself meant nothing, for Holst was dealing with time and budget constraints. Yet, when he first received the invitation from the American Academy of Arts and Letters, he was in the midst of an extended solo visit to Italy--and this trip was on the heels of a solo visit to Germany, Austria, and Czechoslovakia the previous year. On a subsequent trip to the European Continent in November, 1929 following the second American visit, he was also alone. Thus by 1931, Holst appears to have been well past the point of inviting his wife to share in his travels--even if the itinerary called for him to spend five months on the opposite side of the Atlantic.

Notebook entries indicate that Harvard University was not the only institution of higher learning that was interested in Holst. He may have been offered a position at Boston's Berklee School of Music as well:

Harvard Feb-May
Berkeley Jan or June
(may be cancelled before 20th)
1 term or 11/2 or 2[14]

With Berklee under consideration, Holst was considering various departure dates. With trans-Atlantic air travel still in its infancy (Lindbergh's historic flight had taken place only four and one half years earlier), the only viable means of passage was by ship. Holst made several notebook entries:

Aquitania Jan 27
Bremen Jan 28
Berengaria Jan 6
Majestic Jan 20 X
Europa Jan 8[15]

Any plans for a late departure or for teaching at Berklee, however, were scuttled when Holst received an invitation to conduct the Boston Symphony Orchestra in three concerts set for mid-January.

In late 1931, Holst heard from Duncan McKenzie, who offered to serve as Holst's agent. McKenzie was well-qualified and, certainly to Holst's liking, a real musician. After achieving the equivalency of a Master of Arts degree from Edinburgh University, McKenzie emigrated from Scotland to Montreal during the war. There he held several positions: Director of Music in the High School for Girls, Director of Music in the Commercial and Technical High School, and a theory/organ position at McGill University Conservatorium of Music. After a stint with the Canadian Army, he relocated in Toronto, where he was Director of Music for the Toronto Public Schools and Lecturer in Public School Music at Toronto Conservatory. Having immigrated to the United States, McKenzie became the first editor and manager of the New York office of Oxford University Press and in addition to this took on the role of Educational Director for Carl Fischer Inc. of New York. He also organized the Bach Cantata Club of New York, itself sponsored by Oxford University Press.[16]

It is no wonder then, that Holst sent McKenzie the following response:

St. Paul's Girls' School
Brook Green, Hammersmith,
W. 6
Dec[ember] 4 [, 1931]

Dear Mr. McKenzie,

I thank you for your most helpful letter and should be delighted if you would be my agent and accept 20% commission for every engagement you get me.

I have never had an agent before and am quite ignorant as to details but take it for granted that I may make final arrangements about two or three offers of conducting engagements, that have been offered me by friends, without consulting you. I am sending you an article in 'La Revue Musicale' with the best photo I ever had--(I will send another copy of this photo) also three articles of the Musical Times by Edwin Evans (I regret these are so untidy), one by Dunston Green in 'The Chesterian', one on my new songs in the 'Record' and a list of my compositions. I will see that scores and parts of my things are available in the USA and will bring over score and parts of my latest orchestral work 'Hammersmith', which was produced last week. I hope to come over on the 'Bremen' which sails on

Jan 8 and shall go direct to Harvard as I believe I am to conduct in Boston about the 22nd. I hope to have at least a week in New York before I begin work at Harvard on Feb 8 and shall probably stay at the University Club.

As far as I know I am free to do anything (or nothing!) between Jan 24 and Feb 8. I understand that I shall be free at weekends during my stay at Harvard but Mr. Hill of the Division of Music there would tell you definitely about my duties.

My lecture subjects are:

'England and her music'
(either one or two on this subject)
'The Teaching of Art'
'Joseph Haydn'

I will conduct any work of mine with the proviso that if 'The Planets' are wanted I must have all seven done or none. Although I am sincerely grateful to you for your offer yet I am also a little anxious. In fact I rather hope that you won't get me too many engagements! I am not as strong as I was and public engagements are best for me if they come singly.

Normally I lead a very quiet life and have to forego much that would otherwise give me great pleasure. One great favor I would ask and that is to be quiet and alone before any public appearance.

Yr Sincerely

Gustav Holst[17]

McKenzie's skills and connections would help Holst secure supplementary work and keep the composer more than solvent during his stay in the United States. Yet there were additional problems with which McKenzie could not assist. One involved St. Paul's Girls' School. Holst needed to line up reliable substitutes and they had to be people whom he could trust. He drew up a list of possible replacements that included Jay Smith, Irene Bonnett, Elsie Finch, and his daughter Imogen. He also had Vally Lasker in mind to take charge of the junior orchestra, but "only with helpers"[18] so that the strain on her would not be too great.

It was now time to commit to the Boston Symphony Orchestra. According to his notebook, money matters were constantly on Holst's mind:

come to Bank Dec 15

letter of intent to Boston[19]
remit money home
in dollars
don't keep big balance
accepting their rects.
bring home $
open acct at
Boston[20]

Edward Burlingame Hill sent Holst a cash advance of $1000, enabling the composer to pay for his ocean liner passage up front. Holst then set up the voyage and penned an uncharacteristically brief laundry list of personal items to bring onto the ship:

bank get $1000 to me or you [McKenzie?]
sailing Jan 6 or 8--have it cabled?
Cooks Berengarice or Europa
3d tourist (sep cabin)
USA office
Barkers wh instead?
fount pen pyjamas
boots
purse
Bremen not Europa[21]

The last days before departure were marked by a flurry of activity. On New Years Day 1932, Holst went to Dorking to visit Ralph and Adeline Vaughan Williams. A few days later, on January 6th, the two composers had one of their "field days" at St. Paul's Girls' School. As was customary, Vally Lasker and Helen Bidder played through the piano drafts of one or more of the compositions in progress. This time it was Vaughan Williams' *Symphony No. 4 in F minor*, a work which would not see completion for another two years. The following day, Holst had a farewell dinner with Isobel and Imogen at the George before attending a Queen's Hall concert conducted by fellow music educator and former Royal College of Music colleague George Dyson. Holst and Isobel then spent the remainder of the evening at the "Jolly Talgarth."

The following morning, Friday, January 8th, Holst caught the 8:18 train from Waterloo Station which took him to Southampton, where he boarded the *Bremen*, a ship of German registry. After leaving Southampton, the vessel made an intermediary stop at Cherbourg before crossing the Atlantic.[22] According to the following letter, the trans-Atlantic voyage was apparently uneventful and boring:

Norddeutscher Lloyd Bremen
D. "Bremen" Jan 13 [1932]

Dear Imogen

I hope the interview with HM[23] will have results and that you'll be rushed off your feet and torn from pillar to post and be pitchforked into all sorts of unexpected little jobs and that by Easter things will settle down into one or two Real Jobs.

As you are a Sensible Modern Female I take it for granted that youv'e lost that silly cold long ago.

Owing to the vibration the only things I can read with ease are my own scores which I have been trying to memorize while walking up and down the deck 3 1/4 hours per day. In short, Life has been Dull. [coda sign]

But we've just passed Nantucket Light boat!

B L G

[coda sign] One afternoon I began to realise why people don't like my music![24]

---

[1]Gustav Holst, Notebook [April, 1931], The Holst Foundation.
[2]Gustav Holst, Notebook [August, 1931], The Holst Foundation.
[3]*Ibid.*.
[4]Personal correspondence, Gustav Holst to Earl V. Moore, October 30, 1931, Bentley Historical Library, The University of Michigan.
[5]*Boston Evening Transcript*, November 10, 1931.
[6]Edward Burlingame Hill.
[7]Business correspondence, Kenneth B. Murdock to A. Lawrence Lowell, November 17, 1931, Harvard University Archives.
[8]*Ibid.*
[9]*Elliot Forbes, A History of Music at Harvard to 1972* (Cambridge, MA: Harvard University Department of Music, 1988), p. 57.
[10]Business correspondence, Clifford H. Moore to F[rank] W. Hunniwell, May 4, 1931, Harvard University Archives. This was during the heart of depression, yet some $100,000 came into the Harvard University Department of Music. In a letter to President Lowell dated July 13, 1931, Moore advocated that this additional money be used first for increasing salaries.

[11]Gustav Holst, Notebook [August, 1931], The Holst Foundation.
[12]Imogen Holst: *Gustav Holst: A Biography,* 2nd Ed. (Oxford: Oxford University Press, 1969) 118-119.
[13]Personal correspondence, Gustav Holst to Imogen Holst, September 4, 1933, The Holst Foundation.
[14]Gustav Holst, Notebook [August, 1931], The Holst Foundation. It is possible, although unlikely, that Holst's "Berkeley" entry may also have meant the University of California.
[15]*Ibid.*
[16]"Official News Release," New Jersey College for Women, August 20, 1943.
[17]Personal correspondence, Gustav Holst to Duncan McKenzie, Dec[ember] 4[, 1931], The Holst Foundation.
[18]Gustav Holst, Notebook [August, 1931], The Holst Foundation.
[19]Boston Symphony Orchestra.
[20]Gustav Holst, Notebook [August, 1931], The Holst Foundation.
[21]*Ibid.*
[22]Gustav Holst, Diary, January 1, 6, 7 and 8, 1932, The Holst Foundation.
[23]Possibly the High Mistress of St. Paul's Girl's School.
[24]Personal correspondence, Gustav Holst to Imogen Holst, Jan[uary] 13 [, 1932], The Holst Foundation.

CHAPTER XXIII

THE STAR CONDUCTOR

The *Bremen* arrived in New York at about 9:00 p.m. on January 13, 1932. Holst was met by his personal agent Duncan McKenzie and American publishing agent H. W. Gray. There was scarcely enough time for them to visit, however, for Holst had to be on board the 12:45 a.m. overnight train bound for Boston.

Holst was met the following morning at Boston's South Station by Archibald and Dorothy Davison, who immediately took him in under their wing. Their home at 22 Francis Avenue, practically on the Harvard University campus in Cambridge, became Holst's place of residence for the next two weeks.

Boston bred Archibald Thompson Davison was a real fixture around Harvard. All three of his degrees were from that institution and he had served as organist and choirmaster there since 1910. At the time of Holst's visit, Davison was still conductor of the organization to which his name will forever be connected--The Harvard Glee Club. Davison's work is brought to light in the Harvard Class Album:

> It is hardly necessary to speak of the quality of the work done by a chorus trained by Dr. Davison. The Club would not be asked repeatedly to work with the Boston Symphony Orchestra unless its standards were of the highest. As a whole, the Club may thank him for its prestige and its standards; individually its members owe him the practical cultivation of an instinct for fine choral music. The debt is paid in part by the deep admiration and respect in which the Club holds a hard taskmaster of the ability and character of Dr. Davison.[1]

Howe comments from a 1931 perspective about the important relationship between the Harvard Glee Club and Boston Symphony Orchestra:

> That part of an orchestra's repertory which choral music should occupy has been made possible by Archibald T. Davison and his unexampled creation, the 'Harvard Glee Club.' To this rare men's chorus, which first appeared with the orchestra under Pierre Monteux, Dr. Davison has added the Radcliffe Choral Society, now left to the skilled handling of G. Wallace Woodworth. The mixed chorus has been one of this orchestra's most priceless windfalls. Without them, certain difficult scores could scarcely have been achieved...[2]

In addition to being a conductor and organist, Davison was an outstanding scholar; he authored or co-authored no fewer than thirteen books. His thought-provoking *Music Education in America: What Is Wrong with It? What Shall We Do about It?*, released in 1926, had secured his place as a writer, but his best-known work, the *Historical Anthology of Music*, lie fourteen years in the future. Grout comments:

> That Dr. Davison was commonly referred to as "Doc" is doubly symbotical; he was a learned man but not an arrogant one....Doc's music centered about the music itself; the experience of music as beauty and the total experience, neglecting neither the intellect not the emotions.[3]

Davison was also a religious man. Some of his publications dealt either directly or indirectly with church music. Woodworth comments:

> Dr. Davison was an idealist and a reformer; he was a realistic idealist and a practical reformer....His fundamental purpose was educational and, I dare say it, spiritual.[4]

Both Davison and Holst had an unquenchable thirst for practicing music education. This coupled with their respective scholarly pursuits (Davison's in writing and compiling, Holst's in composing, and both in education) would have been more than enough to forge a solid friendship. Yet religion may have played a role as well. Certainly Davison's resolute Protestantism and Holst's liberal Anglicanism peppered with teachings from multifarious spiritual bases (Theosophist, Hindu, mystical, and astrological) would have provided fodder for many stimulating conversations.

The Davisons treated Holst like a king, treating him to day trips, taking him to concerts, and introducing him to fellow composers. On his second full day in Cambridge Holst met composer Walter Piston, a former student of Edward Burlingame Hill, who had been a member of the Harvard University music faculty since 1926 and would remain so in various capacities until his retirement in 1960. The two composers had at least two things in common: (1) an acquaintence with Nadia Boulanger (Piston had actually studied with her) and (2) experience with military bands (Piston had played saxophone in the Navy Band during World War I). They hit it off quite well.

The next day, January 16th, was a Saturday and the Davisons invited Holst and G. Wallace Woodworth to do some sight-seeing and to visit their second home at Brant Rock. Many Bostonians owned get-away property either on the Southeast Coast or on Cape Cod; the Davisons were no exception. After spending some time at Brant Rock, the four of them went further down the coast to see Plymouth Rock. The trip left a lasting impression on Holst. Later, when asked in an interview about what had impressed him the most about America, he commented:

> Your colonial architecture. Europeans--Englishmen--come by and speak about America in terms of the skyscrapers of New York. But this is not America. On an automobile trip to Plymouth I was tremendously struck by a sense of continuity as I looked, as an Englishman, on your charming Colonial houses.
>
> I have heard it said that Americans have no traditions, but here I found you have traditions and you have kept them better than we have in England.
>
> I can't think of anything more charming than to live in one of your Colonial houses.[5]

Indeed the greater Boston area was full of colonial architecture; it still is. Yet the Boston that Holst knew in 1932 was quite different from the center of technology that it had developed into in the later twentieth century. More people lived in the core cities of Boston and Cambridge; with 1930 populations of 781,188 and 118,075 respectively[6]; each had about 20% more people than today. Boston had always been referred to as "The Hub of the Universe," by rather myopic New Englanders, but in 1932 the boundaries of its metropolitan area were quite confined. There was still significant rural landscape between Boston and Worcester, Boston and Providence, Boston and Lowell. And the center of Boston bore more likeness to a European city than an American one. It is not surprising that Holst referred to the "skyscrapers of New York," without mentioning those of Boston. A couple of twelve or thirteen story buildings located downtown notwithstanding, Boston had only one true skyscraper in 1932 and that edifice was the result of a very strange modification to an earlier structure:

> The United States Custom House (1847) designed by Ammi B. Young and Isaiah Rogers, was among the last monuments of the Greek Revival. A dome with which it was originally crowned is concealed within the tall shaft of floors which in 1915 transformed the building into a 500-foot skyscarper and a fitting mausoleum to the era of Greek affection.[7]

Holst's indoctrination to Harvard and the greater Boston area was quickly coming to a close, however, for he had to think about his concerts with the Boston Symphony. However, his diary entry for Sunday, January 17th, the day before rehearsals began, indicates a very busy day. Rather than being able to spend the day in quiet score study, he had a morning rehearsal "with Robinson," attended an afternoon flute recital, met composer Arthur Foote, and dined at Eliot House[8], which would be Holst's place of residence during Harvard's spring semester.

Holst had his first rehearsal with the Boston Symphony Orchestra at 10:00 the next morning. The orchestra was in its fifty-first season, having been founded by Major Henry Lee Higginson in 1881. As such it was and remains the third-oldest orchestra in continuous existence in the United States. The orchestra's home is Symphony Hall, located on Huntington Avenue about one mile west of downtown Boston. That particular stretch of Huntington Avenue and the surrounding area is known as Boston's artistic center and, in addition to Symphony Hall, features the Museum of Fine Arts, Isabella Stewart Gardner Museum, Christian Science Mother Church, the New England Conservatory of Music,and a number of other colleges and universities. Symphony Hall was built in 1900 and features a performance hall with fine acoustics that seats 2500 persons. It is also home to the Casadesus Collection of Musical Instruments.

Serge Alexandrovitch Koussevitzky, originally a string bass virtuoso, was conductor of the Boston Symphony at the time of Holst's guest appearance. The Russian ex-patriot had succeeded Pierre Monteux as conductor in 1924 and would remain with the orchestra for the next quarter of a century. Koussevitzky was a fireball. Although never fluent in English and wrongfully accused of musical illiteracy, he skillfully developed the orchestra into a vehicle of astonishingly deep musical sensitivy. During his tenure the Boston Symphony enjoyed a period of remarkable artistic growth, as evidenced by the recordings made at the time as well as an expansion of the repertoire that included the commissioning of such works as Roussel's *Symphony No. 3* and Stravinsky's *Symphony of Psalms* (1930). Another of Koussevitzky's major contributions--some would say his most important--was the establishment of the Berkshire Music Center at Tanglewood in 1940, where such esteemed conductors as Leonard Bernstein and Seiji Osawa would study the art of conducting.

From the beginning of his tenure Koussevitzky was in the habit of taking a two-week midwinter break in order to refresh himself and regain his energies. During this time each year the services of two guest conductors (who were often composers as well) were obtained in order to give the orchestra and the concert-going public an exposure to different creative artists. Thus Holst's week-long guest conducting stint with the Boston Symphony was one of an established tradition. Through 1931 this roster of very distinguished guest conductors included the following:

Henry Hadley	1925
Michael Press and Eugene Goosens	1926
Alfredo Casella and Ottorino Respighi	1927
Sir Thomas Beecham and Maurice Ravel	1928
E. Fernandez Arbos and Artur Honegger	1929
Eugene Goosens and Alexander Glazounov	1930
Henry Hadley and E. Fernandez Arbos	1931[9]

The reputations of nearly all of these composers survived through the remaining years of the twentieth century, although in his notorious tome *The Maestro Myth: Great Conductors in Pursuit of Power*, Norman Lebrecht takes issue with the conducting skills of four of them:

> His [Kousseivitzky's] competence as a conductor was open to question and he engaged as guest conductors eminent composers who were unlikely to show his deficiencies--Ravel (whom he had previously paid to orchestrate Mussorgsky's Pictures at an Exhibition), Glazunov, Respighi, and Stravinsky. Monteux was never asked back to Boston while Koussevitzky was in command and the dazzling Dmitri Mitropoulos was banished after a brilliant triumph.[10]

Even if Lebrecht's point of view can be interpreted as the absolute truth, it would probably be incorrect to assume that Holst's guest conducting appearance resulted from Koussevitzky's own insecurities. The fact that Holst's Harvard appointment had already been arranged made it convenient for Koussevitzky to invite him. Here was an established composer arriving in Boston at the exact time that Koussevitzky was to take his mid-winter break. Archibald Davison's position as conductor of the Harvard Glee Club, which frequently sang with the Boston Symphony, may also have had something to do with the securing of Holst's services.

R.D. Darrell of the *Phonograph Monthly Review* was on hand for Holst's first rehearsal. He comments about Holst's podium technique:

> ...One had to watch Mr. Holst on the conductor's stand no more than a few minutes to get a vivid impression of the man and musician. He is no sensationalist, no showman. To him the orchestra men are flesh and blood, not merely mechanical instruments. Informally, good-humoredly, without condescension or affectation, he painstakingly goes over the ground to be covered, much as an alert and sensitive tutor would go over a difficult but engrossing problem with a group of talented students.
> ....without sacrificing anything to correctness, he refused to be enslaved by it, getting a natural fire and spontaneity to his performance that are all too often missing from the overly studied "interpretations" of many virtuoso conductors.[11]

Darrell was of course waiting for an interview with Holst. At 1:00 p.m., following the rehearsal, he got what he had wanted. A tired Holst spoke to Darrell with a cutting frankness that he often reserved for the press:

> I don't go in for this sort of thing at all at home, but I have been received so kindly in America that I feel I must make an exception to my rule about not giving interviews. But please don't ask me the conventional reporters' questions. I've been here only twice before and for a very short time. All I know about America, all most people in England can know is that it is very big, bigger and richer in variety than we can conceive. And I'm heartily sick and tired of visiting Europeans who rush into print with their personal opinions and prejudices on anything and everything American!
> ....I'm not going to give personal views on controversial topics. Who am I to lay down the law? There are too many questions, too many tastes. The only place I state my mind, and I don't stand for any nonsense either, is in teaching. And that's my business![12]

Holst saw the press as a necessary evil. He was still wincing from the sudden and unwanted thrust into fame that *The Planets* had brought him more than a decade earlier. Interviews made him nervous. Sometimes he would freeze. Laning Humphrey, for example, was able to get Holst to comment about only one thing--colonial architecture (quoted above)--for his entire article. It is fortunate for Holst that reporters such as Darrell and Humphrey could tell that the composer simply felt uncomfortable speaking to the press and that he was not trying to be subversive.

Following the interview with Darrell, Holst received a cable from Imogen. Its contents are unknown, but it is probably reasonable to conjecture that it was one wishing him luck in his upcoming series of concerts. That evening Holst attended a Bach cantata concert. His friend Steuart Wilson sang *Cantata No. 53, "Schlage doch., gewuenschte Stunde."*[13]

The next day, January 19th, was very eventful. Holst conducted another Boston Symphony rehearsal in the morning at Symphony Hall, after which the entire orchestra made the forty-seven mile trip to Providence, Rhode Island. It was there, in the E. F. Albee Theatre, that Holst conducted the first of his three Boston Symphony Orchestra concerts. The concert began with Haydn's *Symphony in E-flat Major (B. & H. No. 3)*, the "Drumroll," now known as No. 103. The remaining works on the program were all by Holst: *St. Paul's Suite*, *Somerset Rhapsody*, *Ballet Music from the "The Perfect Fool," Prelude and Scherzo, "Hammersmith"* (American premiere) and Holst's orchestral arrangement of *Bach's Fugue a la Gigue.*[14] Prior to the Providence concert, the Boston Symphony had performed only two works by Holst. *The Planets* had been performed under Monteux on January 26, 1923 and the *Ode to Death* appeared during the Koussevitzky era on February 10, 1928.[15]

Among the performers listed on the program was a relatively young violist and celesta player named Arthur Fiedler. Fiedler was, of course, the conductor of the Boston Pops, although he performed other duties as well. One of them was to prepare the women's chorus for *The Planets*, which would be performed on Holst's second and third Boston Symphony concerts.

Two contrary reviews of Holst's Albee Theatre concert appeared in the Providence newspapers. The highly philosophical one by Dr. Louis Chapman which appeared in two papers--*Providence Journal* and the *Providence Bulletin*--was laudatory:

> Gustav Holst, Noted English Composer, Conducting Boston Symphony Orchestra, Warmly Greeted in Praiseworthy Concert at Albee Theatre
>
> The Boston Symphony Orchestra last evening gave the third of its

concert series in the Albee Theatre. The concert was directed by Gustav Holst, distinguished English composer.

Only occasionally is the Boston Symphony Orchestra presided over by a guest conductor during Dr. Koussevitzsky's mid-season siesta, whereas the New York Philharmonic Orchestra has three or four guests during the season. It is not to be expected that any visiting conductor will make any particular impression upon his men in a brief season. The claims of personality and the many features that combine to make genius require time to make themselves felt, and it is impossible to throw off the habits of many months in a few days.

It is probably no easier for the conductor than it is for the men. He, too, is accustomed to another team; he, too, must become adjusted to other tonal qualities, notwithstanding the cordiality of his reception by the band, he must feel strange and somewhat ill at ease.

Holst comes to a magnificent instrument: he handles it ably; he accomplishes highy artistic results. Haydn, Bach, and Holst receive their meed of performance and praise. Consciously and unconsciously we compare their merits and graces and to most persons the concert is over. But there is much more to be said; there are many features to contemplate. There are diverse values to be appreciated and, after all is done and said, we realize that the music we have heard is very interesting, that our visitor is carrying on the torch of musical learning worthily and that his compositions are of a very high order of esthetic and musical thought....

Comes now a composer from across the seas whose musical and literary preparation has been most thorough, thus thus assuring a capable medium for his talents. These are unusual; his gifts are varied and of a high order, his thematic material is often rich and highly original and his harmony is tinctured with by a modernism that is so much his own that it may be said to be his idiom.

There is nothing commonplace about Holst's orchestration. This, too, has personality and originality and if it is reminiscent of anyone it recalls Edward Elgar. He is appreciative of the keyed glockenspiel with its suggestion of musical galsses, the xylophone now coming into its own in orchestral music, of the matchless baritone of the bass clarinet and the resonant reinforcement of the double bassoon. In these facilities he has the advantage over the older composers who were limited as to orchestral possibilities. Frequently one notes trumpet figures which are suggestive of jazz, but we must remember these are not the only episodes in music that are debased by unworthy exposition and that because jazz has borrowed of the best in music there is no reason for belittling the value of the musical timbre or for failing to distinguish between the splendid and the cheap. In his orchestration Holst brings to us much that is apparently in the jazz idiom , but it clothes fine thematic material and is well worthy of sympathetic attention....

In the exquisite old time Symphony of Haydn, Holst conducted with a light hand and with only a few directions. His adagio is more rapid and his allegretto more slow than to which we are accustomed. In his own compositions, however, he was much more alert, more exacting in his beat and more vivacious in his manner. The orchestra gave its very best efforts and undivided attention and assisted his artistic efforts to the fullest, which is a quality of the highest type of musicianship and of personality.

This brief hearing of Holst shows him to be an able conductor of the classics, an original thinker in orchestration, a highly individual and personal composer of significant music in characteristic, but not entirely exclusive idiom, and one capable and vital in his apperciation of bach in his lighter vein.

Mr Holst was received with the warmest cordiality by the capacity house. He was recalled after each offering and more than once called upon the orchestra to share the acknowledgement of his success.[16]

Chapman's opinions were not echoed by the unknown critic from the *Providence News Tribune*; that critic's remarks were caustic and trenchant:

....Last night came Gustav Holst of England, who is better known as a composer than he is a conductor--so we are informed. We grant readily that Mr. Holst is an accomplished musician, even if we are not prepared to concede that his distinction is such as to justify a program made up of four of his original compositions, one arrangement which he has made of a Bach fugue and one not-very-important Haydn symphony. Not is it to be ignored that the Haydn came first, that it was played listlessly and that Mr. Holst seemed much less interested in it than in what followed.

We do not see any need to go in detail into the merits of Mr. Holst as a composer. He is an accomplished technician with a fine sense of melody, but when he gets hold of a theme or a tune he never seems to know when to let go. He never challenges anything deep within us, never dazzles us with brilliancy; he is precise, lustreless, and reminiscent.

Of course we are aware in saying all this, we are trying to remember that Mr. Holst was trying to pinch-hit for Serge Koussevitzky, one of the

> most brilliant, glamorous and adventurous of present-day conductors. But in saying what we do say, we are, perhaps, pointing out what other people will regard as meritorious in Mr. Holst. Certainly there was plenty of applause for him last night and, in other circumstances, we might have enjoyed the unexciting fare he offered us. But this was a Boston Symphony concert, we repeat, one of only four we get in a season, and what is the use of asking any lover of great music to take anything less than music worthy of it attention from that splendid organization which has thrilled us for so many years.[17]

The *Musical Courier* put things in a simpler light:

> ....one of the most interesting concerts of the season;....his [Holst's] first appearance with the Boston Symphony Orchestra. He made a fine impression especially in his own compositions, which he lead with verve and authority.[18]

Holst's Providence concert was very successful, but more lie just ahead. The following day, the first of two morning rehearsals was held at Symphony Hall for the Friday afternoon-Saturday evening pair of concerts. The program was different; this time it was all Holst. Three works, *St. Paul's Suite*, *Ballet Music from "The Perfect Fool,"* and *Hammersmith*, constituted the first half of the program while the second half was devoted entirely to *The Planets*. Still, in the midst of preparations for these concerts Holst was able to enjoy life. He attended a tea during which Jelly d'Aranyi (one of the dedicatees of his *Double Concerto*) performed one of Bach's Chaconnes on the violin. He also watched a performance of Kreuzberg dancing at Symphony Hall that Thursday night.[19]

On Friday, January 22nd at 2:30 p.m. in Boston's Symphony Hall, Holst conducted the first of the two remaining concerts. The Boston critics, not a very docile group as a whole, gave him rave reviews. Moses Smith, a producer for Columbia Records who would later write a biography of Koussevitzky, had the following to say in *The Boston Evening American*:

> ....Holst is rightfully placed among the leaders of the current English musical renaissance. Here is that rarity among modern composers--a man who writes because he likes to and must.[20]

Philip Hale was one of the most feared musical critics in America, yet he had a high opinion of Holst. In addition to providing Holst with some of the best programme notes he had ever had (Hale wrote notes for every single Boston Symphony Orchestra program from 1901 to 1933), Hale wrote the following in *The Boston Herald*:

> [regarding the *St. Paul's Suite*] It was written for the orchestra of the St. Paul School for Girls. For Practice or Performance? If for performance, these girls must be singularly accomplished in the use of stringed instruments.
> *Hammersmith*...gives Mr. Holst a high position in the rank of contemporaneous composers....This is not program music in the anecdotal of pictoral sense. There are two moods, eloquent in tonal expression. The searcher after symbolism in all art might say, "Nature healers of mortal's joys or sorrows"...but Mr. Holst, a thinker even outside of music, and this cannot be said of every composer: a man fascinated by the poetry and the philosophy of India, when he girds up his loins to write music is first of all a musician. In Hammersmith there is no waste of notes, no undue elaboration of musical ideas, no infuriating elegencies; no incongruous orchestration.
>
> Warming greeted, he was warmly applauded throughout the concert.[21]

Other reviews followed suit:

> Holst scored a decided artistic and popular success....his music resembles his conducting in that it is straightforward and businesslike....Mr. Holst's "Orientalism" has probably been exaggerated. *The Planets* is, we believe, Mr. Holst's greatest work. [*Christian Science Monitor*][22]

> ...[*St. Paul's Suite*] audience was especially delighted with the finale....*Hammersmith*, at first hearing is a bit labored, a bit crabbed. It failed to capture the audience's attention....*The Planets* is the finest music written by a living Englishman. [*Boston Globe*][23]

> ...[*St. Paul's Suite*]--essentially British in its bluff heartiness. On the whole a grateful piece of music, a welcome addition to the repertoire for string orchestra....[*Hammersmith*] River Thames, though it might as well be the Charles. [*Boston Post*][24]

> [*St. Paul's Suite*] He must have taught apt pupils well, if they played what is set down for them. [*Boston Massachusetts Transcript*][25]

Holst continued with his socializing. After the concert Holst met Mrs. Arthur Foote and Cecilia Payne, a St. Paul's Girls' School alumna, who was studying astronomy. The next morning Holst set out on a brisk walk and was greeted with the first delivery of English mail since his arrival in Boston. That evening Holst conducted his final Boston Symphony concert (a repeat of the previous day's) and met Serge Koussevitzky, who in all likelihood, attended the concert. The maestro must have been impressed, for later that week he wrote the following letter of invitation to Holst, who had since departed for a two-week stay in New York:

University Club
1 West 54th St.
N.Y.C.

January 28, 1932

My dear Mr. Holst,

The Boston Symphony Orchestra is giving a concert in Cambridge on February 11. Would you like to conduct one of your works at this concert,--perhaps the charming Ballet "The Perfect Fool"? I thought it would be most appropriate in view of your present position at Harvard and because I know that it would meet with the desire of your many friends and admirers. Naturally, it will still have to be a contribution to Harvard University, and an acceptance on your part will be greatly appreciated.

May I hear from as soon as possible?
With best greetings, I am
Most sincerely yours,

[Serge Koussevitzky][26]

Holst responded immediately:

The University Club
1 West 54th Street
[New York, New York]

Jan 31 [1932]

Dear Mr. Koussevitzky

Thank you for your letter which has only just reached me. I should be delighted to conduct the PF ballet on Feb 11 and presume that the concert is in the evening.

I return to Cambridge next Sunday.

Thanks for the honour you do me.

Y Sincerely

Gustav Holst

P.S. If the concert is in the afternoon I should first have to get leave of absence from Prof. Hill.[27][28]

---

[1]*Harvard Class Album (1932)* (Boston, MA: The Washington Press, 1932), 173.

[2]Mark Antony DeWolfe Howe, *The Boston Symphony Orchestra 1881-1931* (Boston and New York: Houghton Mifflin Co., 1931), 163.

[3]Donald Jay Grout, "The Scholar and Teacher," in *College Music Symposium,* I (Fall, 1961), 18-19.

[4]G. Wallace Woodworth, "The Conductor and Reformer," in *College Music Symposium,* I (Fall, 1961), 15-16.

[5]Gustav Holst quoted in Laning Humphrey, "Noted Composer Unknown at Harvard Dormitory," in *The Musical Courier*, February 13, 1932.

[6]Federal Writer's Project of the Works Progress Administration, *Massachusetts: A Guide to Its Places and People* (Boston: Hougton Mifflin Co., 1937), 135 and 183.

[7]*Ibid.*, 160-161.

[8]Gustav Holst, *Diary,* Sunday, January 17, 1932, The Holst Foundation.

[9]Howe, *op.cit.*, 159.

[10]Norman Lebrecht, *The Maestro Myth: Great Conductors in Pursuit of Power* (New York: Carlo Publishing Group, 1991), 135-136.

[11]R. D. Darrell, "Holst in America: An Interview with One of the First Contemporary Composers to Conduct His Own Works for Recording" in *Phonograph Monthly Review*, VI, No. 5 (February, 1932), 82-83.

[12]Gustav Holst quoted in R. D. Darrell, *op. cit.*, 82 and 110.

[13]Gustav Holst, *Diary*, Monday, January 18, 1932, The Holst Foundation.

[14]*Programme, Boston Symphony Orchestra,* Tuesday Evening, January 19 [1932] at 8:15.

[15]Howe, *op. cit.*, 203.

[16]*Providence Journal and Providence Bulletin*, January 20, 1932.

[17]*Providence News Tribune*, January 20, 1932.

[18]*Musical Courier*, review by BMD [n.d.].

[19]Gustav Holst, *Diary,* Wednesday, January 20 and Thursday, January 21, 1932, The Holst Foundation.

[20]Moses Smith, "Holst Presents Programs of His Own Works at Symphony," in *Boston Evening American,* January 23, 1932.
[21]Philip Hale, "Symphony Concert," in *The Boston Herald,* January 23, 1932.
[22]*Christian Science Monitor*, January 23, 1932.
[23]*The Boston Globe*, January 23, 1932.
[24]*The Boston Post*, January 23, 1932.
[25]*Boston Massachusetts Transcript*, January 23, 1932.
[26]Personal correspondence, Serge Koussevitzky to Gustav Holst, January 28, 1932, The Holst Foundation.
[27]Edward Burlingame Hill, Chair of the Harvard Division of Music.
[28]Personal correspondence, Gustav Holst to Serge Koussevitzky, Jan[uary] 31[, 1932], Library of Congress.

CHAPTER XXIV

NEW YORK

Following his exhausting guest conducting stint with the Boston Symphony, Holst was able to take it easy for a couple of days in Cambridge. There was some folk singing at the Davisons' home on Sunday, but, aside from one appointment with a physician, Holst spent Monday " resting all day."[1] On the next day Holst boarded the 10:00 a.m. train for New York, arriving there in time to have dinner with his brother Emil and niece Valerie. He stayed at The University Club in Midtown Manhattan. It was there that Holst wrote one of the longest and most characteristic pieces of correspondence he would ever write--a letter to Imogen, describing in great detail the events of the past week:

The University Club
1 West 54th Street NY

Jan[uary] 26 [,1932]

Dear Imogen,

I

Before leaving the Bremen I wrote to Iso, you, Miss Strudwick, Mabel, Vally and Nora. I finally got away from the boat and the customs, just before midnight of the 13th and traveled that night to Boston. Dr and Mrs Davison met me in the morning and I have been their guest until today. They have been quite perfect hosts and I want to try and show my gratitude when they come to Europe in Sep 1933. So far the only definite idea I have is that he must meet Straube![2]

On the Saturday they motored me to Cape Cod and Plymouth Rock and I met a real old New England woman who talked most beautiful English. But I just missed a retired stage coach driver who holds the NE Coast Record for Bad Language.

Then came Last Week--the most exciting one of my life. I, who previously had never conducted an entire symphony concert, had to conduct three in one week also four rehearsals.

I filled up my spare time in going to

1) a chamber concert where a man sang my violin songs,

2) a Bach performance where Steuart[3] sang 'Schlage doch' beautifully

3) an At Home at the house of the son of Henry James[4] where Jelly[5] played the Chaconne beautifully,

4) (and chiefly) Bed.

Jelly is getting as affectionate as her older sister[6]. She came round to see me with several others during the interval of Friday's concert and when she had finished embracing me Mrs Davison set to work to wipe the powder off my *crepe de chine*.

Which reminds me that I have fallen in love with Amanda. She is a Swede who had triplets and three other children and whose husband committed suicide a few months ago so she decided to go into service. All the sensible people in Harvard tried to get her but, being a wise woman, she chose the Davisons. Her capacity for hard work is unbounded and when they are at their Cape Cod house she spends her spare time in collecting fallen trees and disused telegraph poles and dragging them home where she converts them into firewood with the aid of what she calls a 'hamsledge'. I fear she despises me as I let out the fact that I don't love the Atlantic.

I had only met one of the Boston orchestra before--Stanislas[7] an oboe player who played for me in Bach cantatas at the Passmore Edward Settlement many years ago. He sends his cordial greetings to Iso who he remembers as a violinist.

The band treated me royally. At two of the rehearsals they insisted on staying half an hour extra and at every possible occasion they cheered me. Just as they had finished doing so after the first rehearsal I got your delightful cablegram. And yet you and Uncle Ralph[8] won't allow moments to be psychological! It may be that when you are older and wiser you will learn not to waste money on such frivolities. If so please keep the fact to yourself.

The only fault of the orchestra was that they were over anxious. On Friday's concert there were half a dozen extraordinary slips in the Planets: in the PF[9] the harpist missed a line and the water music sounded quite modern; while in St. Paul's Suite I broke a collar stud.

But Saturday's concert was really good and I seem to be in for more stick-wagging than I bargained for. Nothing settled yet but I may go to Chicago, Ann Arbor, Minneapolis and Canada. And--please forgive me--I've had to employ an agent!

II

I came from Boston today and have had a meal with Emil and Valerie who send love. I go to see her in 'Hay Fever' tomorrow and him in 'The Devil Passes' on Thursday. Otherwise I want to be fairly quiet this week after last week's orgy.

While on the boat I had a cablegram from Lidbury[10] who was on his way to Europe. Have you seen him? He returns soon. I had another from the Beethoven Association of New York asking me to be their guest on Jan 31. I radio'd back 'not arf' or something of the sort. But now I find that they want me to speak on modern music. I hope my answer is polite as it is ambiguous.

I've promised to jaw some organists next Tuesday otherwise I've nothing to do in NY except to avoid seeing too many people. I go back to Harvard on Feb 7 and will then write some more letters. I want to avoid doing so just now so as to give my hand a good rest. So if you think this letter is fit for your elders to read you might pass it round.

Dr Davison is anxious to know when Uncle Ralph is coming here and where he will be. Could you find out and let me know?

Would you thank the Twin and Vally for forwarding letters and tell them I shall be writing after Feb 7. I'll send some junk[11] to Iso when that agent is done with it. I suggest she sends it to Nora for people at St Paul's to see and that after that it all goes to the Twin.

I met one ex Paulina at Harvard--Cecilia Payne who is doing research in astronomy.

At the Tuesday concert at Providence, Rhode Island, I met a chap with whom I used to play in Cheltenham somewhere about 1882. And after Saturday's concert I met a man of 92 who married the daughter of John

Francis Barnett in Cheltenham many years before I was born.
I think that is all up to now.

B L
G

P.S. It isn't quite all--if I go into Canada it will probably mean that I shan't be home much (if any) before July 1. This is all in the air at present.

Wed morn
P.S.2 My rest cure in NY is degenerating into a business man's working day. It is now 10 AM and I've been spending most of the time phoning and making appointments. If it goes on much longer I shall hire a stenographer, a nasal voice, golf clubs and a weak liver.

P.S. 3 Unless I decide on being a star conductor. In that case I really must cultivate a more picturesque back view. How is it done?[12]

Imogen responded with her own story about agents:

Hill Cottage
Great Easton
Dunmow, Essex
Sunday, Feb. 7th.

Dear G,

I've just read your letter of Jan. 26. How exciting it all sounds. I'd forgotten how very bad American journalese can be, but I gather from the extraordinary collection of "dope" that you sent Iso, that Boston approves of you. I hope you've been fortunate in your choice of agents. When we were out there we had three:--terrible creatures;--who followed us from Boston to Cleveland, puffing cigar smoke down our necks and luring us with promises of free tickets for Toscannini--though when it came to the point they forgot all about Toscannini and rushed us miles away from New York to be shot by the Fox Film Co. We used to run in the opposite direction.

....Iso is much better. She sends love and says she is writing in a day or two....[13]

Fortunately for Holst, Duncan McKenzie was not the type of agent described by Imogen in her letter.

The morning after writing his lengthy letter to Imogen, Holst set out for a constitutional in New York's Central Park, located five blocks north of the University Club. His diary indicates that there was a "gale blowing."[14] Weather like that never stopped him from walking before; likewise it did not stop him this time. He returned to the club in time to have lunch with Duncan McKenzie and then called on Carl Engel, editor of the *Musical Quarterly*, president of G. Schirmer, Inc., and Head of the Music Division at the Library of Congress in Washington, D. C.. Engel eventually arranged for Holst to speak at the Haydn Bicentennial celebrations held at the Library of Congress that March.

All of this activity was wearing on Holst, but he had his brother and niece around to prop up his spirits--and he was able to see them display their considerable acting talents. That same evening Holst had dinner with Emil and Valerie at Longchamps before continuing on to the Avon Theatre. There Holst saw Valerie perform in Patterson McNutt's revival of Noel Coward's 1926 play, "Hay Fever." She played the part of Jackie Coryton--a supporting role that happened to be one of her favorites.[15]

The next day, Thursday, January 28th, paralleled much of the same activity. In the morning Holst again met Duncan McKenzie, and the two of them called on Arthur Judson, concert manager of the New York Philharmonic and Philadelphia Orchestras. Judson also owned Columbia Concerts Corporation, setting up conductors and performing artists with professional orchestras throughout the country. Judson's double-dipping was well-known in the music industry and he incurred the wrath of certain New York critics, particularly Virgil Thomson. Holst, McKenzie, and Judson could have met with regard to fitting Holst into any one or more of Judson's handlings. In the afternoon Holst had lunch with Richard Aldrich, former music critic of *The New York Times*, and met composer Daniel Gregory Mason. That evening, after another walk in Central Park, Holst sat down to dinner with Emil at The University Club. Following dinner, Holst was once again treated to watching a relative perform on stage. This time it was Emil, who played the role of Louis Kisch in "The Devil Passes," at the Selwyn Theatre. The *New York Times* described it as "a religious comedy in which the devil appears as the patient servant of the Lord."[16] Basil Rathbone was among those featured in the "all star cast."

In the three years since Holst had last visited them, Emil and Valerie had moved from their Riverside Drive apartment. On the following day they drove Holst up to their new place located on Palisades Drive in Spuyten Duyvil[17], a neighborhood on the shores of the Hudson in northwest Bronx. There would be many return visits there and elsewhere, as the three of them tried to make up for years of lost time. They also did some sight-seeing. Some of the items on the docket were the Metropolitan Art Museum, a nighttime visit to the then-new Empire State Building, meals at the Players Club, and of course the requisite plays and concerts.

Holst wrote to Vally Lasker:

NY
Jan[uary] 29[, 1932]

Dear Vally

Thanks for your second letter enclosing Grace's. You will probably have got all the news from my letter to Imogen as I won't repeat it.
....I've managed to see a fair amount of Emil and Valerie. I've been to their new place at Spuyten Duyvil today. Last night I saw him in 'The Devil Passes' and the night before I saw Val in Hay Fever. They both had small parts and they both acted very well indeed. Altogether I feel proud of my family.
....My time in New York seems to consist largely in telephoning....New York fascinates and sometimes terrifies me. One can compare Cambridge[,] Massachusetts with Cambridge[,] England but New York is like nothing I know. Perhaps Ninevah and Constantinople were like it when they were young. But the telephone habit must be unique. New Yorkers rush to the telephone as a drunkard to whiskey--or rather, as an inveterate smoker does to to cigarettes. And I'm convinced that it does not help one to get things done a bit. It's an amazing place to visit but give me Emma[18] for living in....

Yr ever

G[19]

Holst indeed had every right to be proud of his niece and brother. In 1932 Valerie was at the start of a very productive and continuous stage career, appearing in many Broadway and Off Broadway productions. Among her credits would be several productions of Noel Coward's "Blythe Spirit," three movies (*The Verdict*, *Edward, My Son*, and *Fail Safe*), and television's first long-running soap opera, "The First Hundred Years." She would marry a non-actor, Graham Livingston.[20]

Emil, on the other hand, had been an established stage actor in New York for nearly a quarter of a century before Holst's 1932 visit. One might say that he was a real character. His story is a very interesting one and certainly worth telling. The only surviving full sibling of Gustav Holst, Emil Gottfried von Holst (stage name Ernest Cossart) was two years his junior. As a child, Emil had tried to run away from home several times and finally succeeded. While still in his teens, Emil became a clerk for a wine merchant. Discharged when a depression hit the wine business, he became an actor and made his debut in "Robert Macaire" at the old Novelty Theatre in London in 1896. It was a job that lasted only two weeks; he was discharged when his on-stage laugher at a fellow actor's antics ruined a scene. Due to a shortage of acting opportunities brought on by a depression at home, he hooked up with a stock company that toured the South African provinces for five years.[21] Emil would later refer to these formative years as his "if it" days--"If it" pleased the audience, the actors would get payed.[22]

By 1903 Emil was back on the London stage and for a while things looked more promising. During this period he married Maude Davies. Stage work in England, however, turned out to be more sporadic than he had hoped for and in late 1906 Emil decided to try his luck on the other side of the Atlantic. During his early months here, in June, 1907, Maude--still in London-- gave birth to the couple's only child, Valerie. She and Valerie soon crossed the Atlantic and joined Emil.

Emil's New York stage debut was at the Knickerbocker Theatre on September 2, 1908 in the role of Colonel Finkhausen in "The Girls of Gottenberg." He then settled in the States and continued acting on Broadway and in various touring companies, including the Marlowe Players and Granville Barker's company. When America entered World War I in 1917, Emil, by that time an American citizen, served his country. Maude and Valerie returned to England. Shortly after the war ended Valerie, at about age 12, returned to the States to live with her father and took his stage last name as her own. On the other hand Maude decided to stay in England with her very domineering mother, who had been dead set against Maude's ever having married an actor. As a result, Valerie would not see Maude for fifteen years.[23]

The post-war years were a boon for Emil's acting career. He was one of the original members of the Theatre Guild when that organization was formed in 1922. Emil was so successful that by the time Holst caught up with him in 1929, he had been featured in no fewer than twenty-seven productions; by Holst's 1932 trip, he had been in thirty-four.[24] Yet the most fabulous phase of his career was yet to come.

In 1933-34 Emil played the part of Lord Throgmorton in the Guild production of "Mary of Scotland" and from his impressive acting in that play he was tapped by Ben Hecht and Charles MacArthur for their film *The Scoundrel*. Shot at Paramount's Astoria Studios on Long Island, the movie starred Noel Coward. Emil was featured in the role of Jimmy Clay--seventh billing. *The Scoundrel* was released in 1935 and was an artistic, if not a commercial success.[25]

Few actors begin movie careers at the age of fifty-nine, but Emil was up to the task. Over the next fourteen years he would have featured roles in thirty-eight more films. He never had an actual starring role; he was a character actor in films, just as he had been on stage. His specialty role was that of a butler; his corpulence and buffoonery made him well-suited to the part. Still, Emil avoided type-casting and appeared in a wide variety of roles. Among his better-known parts were Tom Clink, the chimney sweep in *The Tower of London* (1939), Ginger Roger's father in *Kitty Foil* (1940) (opposite her Academy Award-winning performance), Ronald Reagan's father-in-law in *King's Row* (1942), and a Roman Catholic priest in *The Jolson Story* (1946). The tragedy of all of this is, of course, that Holst did not live to see any of it.

Emil continued with his stage career while making movies; his last role on stage was that of Mr. Underwood in "People Like Us," produced in October, 1949, some fifteen months before his death. Emil and Valerie appeared on stage together twice. The first time was in a 1915 production at Wallack's Theatre of "A Midsummer Night's Dream." Emil played Bottom and Valerie, at the age of eight, was Peasblossom. Both also appeared in the New York's Broadhurst Theatre production of "Madame Bovary" in 1938. Emil played Homais and Valerie, Felicite.[26]

The next professional event that involved Holst was a reception given in honor of Richard Aldrich held at the Beethoven Association on January 31st. The *New York Times* reported the event:

> Honored at Reception:
> Beethoven Group to Mr. and Mrs. Aldrich and Gustav Holst
>
> The Beethoven Association gave a reception that was attended by many musicians at its clubrooms yesterday afternoon in honor of Mr. and Mrs. Richard Aldrich and Gustav Holst. Mr. Aldrich was greeted in speeches by Carl Engel, William J. Henderson[27] and Olin Downs recalling his "wisdom and tolerance" during his many years as writer and music critic for the New York Times. Mr. Holst also spoke as a representative

> of modern music overseas, who will be associated with the music department of Harvard University.
>
> The composer was introduced by Olga Samaroff-Stokowski, who presided in the absence of Harold Bauer, pianist, for many years the head of the association, now on tour.
>
> Among those present were: Mrs. Walter Damrosch, Rubin Goldmark, Bruno Walter, Sigismond Stojowski, Kurt Schindler, Oscar Thompson, Victor Harris.[28]

In all likelihood, Holst gave at least a part of his "England and Her Music" lecture; a *Musical America* article states that he "discussed the progress of modern music in England."[29]

The Beethoven Association was founded in 1918. During its twenty-two year existence the association promoted concerts, gave grants to libraries and charities, and arranged for the first English-language edition of Thayer's *Life of Beethoven*. Many of the world's greatest musicians appeared there in chamber music performances. The confines of the Beethoven Association soon became a favorite watering hole for Holst. There he "held court," having no fewer than eight meetings and/or meals with people (including Valerie and Emil). Harold Bauer, the Anglo-American virtuoso pianist who had founded the the association and served as its president, had actually been one of Holst's acquaintances when both were growing up in Cheltenham. A week following the reception, Holst had a meeting at the Beethoven Association with another Bauer--American composer Marion Bauer. Perhaps the name association prompted him to write a quick letter to Harold Bauer:

> The Beethoven Association
> 55 West 44th Street
> New York
> Feb[ruary] 6[, 1932]
>
> Dear Bauer
>
> I leave for Harvard tonight and before doing so I am writing to
>
> 1) suggest that we have taken so long in meeting, we make up for lost time by dropping the 'Mr':
>
> 2) thank you very heartily for giving me the privilege of making myself at home in this delightful place:
>
> 3) hope that our next meeting may be soon and long.

Y Sincerely

Gustav Holst[30]

Bauer responded almost immediately:

190 Riverside Drive
New York, Feb[ruary] 15,
1932

Dear Holst

Many thanks for your extremely friendly note. I hope indeed that we may meet before long and that you will find me the opportunity of trying to efface any lingering traces of your boyhood resentment against me in Cheltenham! It is said that the impressions of childhood last a lifetime, but please give me a chance!

The Beethoven Association is honored by your acceptance of its guest privileges and if you communicate with Carl Engel or me when you return to New York it will be a pleasure to send you a card enabling you to make use of the club rooms for as long as you desire.

Yours sincerely,

Harold Bauer[31]

Holst had already started taking advantage of the Beethoven Association's generosity in the two weeks preceding Bauer's letter. On Monday, February 1st (the day after the reception) he met ex-Paulina Una Lucas, Valerie, and Emil there for lunch, and then met Quaintence Eaton of *Musical America* there for a three o'clock interview. As always, Holst was uncomfortable with speaking to any reporter, but Miss Eaton was able to get Holst to open up; she gleened enough information from him to write a very telling article. After recounting his early days, Holst was asked about his teaching. He responded:

Have I got any theories you mean? No, no theories. No fixed ones. It all depends upon the students. How can I set a formula and abide by it, when every individual is different? Oh, you Americans, how you love to analyse eveything!

Holst continued:

> I really came over also to see my brother, Ernest Cossart. He's an actor, playing in "The Devil Passes" on Broadway. He has a daughter, [Valerie] who is in the New York production of "Hay Fever." He has been here more than twenty years.
> ....If you really want passionately to do some things, you will find time. I used to study Sanskrit on the train--I learned the alphabet at least. Much good it did me, but I learned it. Now, however, my attitude is much better than yours. I frankly admit I'm lazy when I don't want to do anything very much. It save so much wear and tear.[32]

Holst had dinner that evening with Edwin Franko Goldman, founder and conductor of New York's Goldman Band and president of the fledgling American Bandmasters Association. Goldman was at the forefront of American band activity; since the First World War and well beyond the second, he commissioned and conducted more world and American premieres of original band works than any other band director in the country. Goldman's connection with Holst and *Hammersmith* was triggered by an inquiry made by Capt. R. B. Hayward, Bandmaster of the Toronto Concert Band, and Boosey & Hawkes:

> In a communication to Messrs. Boosey & Hawkes Ltd., he [Hayward] asked if they could recommend new numbers specially written for the military band and as a result of correspondence Mr. Edwin Franko Goldman, that famous American conductor, was successful in arranging matters with Mr. Gustav Holst.[33]

Goldman lined up Holst to conduct the world premiere of the original military band version of *Hammersmith* at the upcoming American Bandmasters Association Convention on April 17th in Washington D. C.. Holst agreed and made the following notebook entries:

> send list
> find out if Hawkes
> have mil parts
> Emma[34]
> Band concert

April 17 (Sunday)
no fee[35]

Part of Holst's assignment was to flesh out the orchestration of *Hammersmith* to meet the instrumentation needs of the American concert band. He made the following notes to himself:

Add Sop Sax B flat doubles cl
baritone E flat
alto cl doubles E flat sax alto
bass cl[36]

Upon receipt of the full score, which Boosey & Hawkes may have been lent to Goldman, Holst wrote the following letter regarding instrumentation and what appeared to be *Hammersmith*'s imminent publication:

Harvard University
Division of Music
Feb[ruary] 12[, 1932]
Cambridge Massachusetts

Dear Mr Goldman

Thank you for sending the score and for your kind letter. I have written a bass clarinet part and hope to do the others in a few days. Am I right in thinking that the Sop Saxophone is in B flat, the baritone in E flat and the alto clarinet in E flat in unison with the alto saxophone? If I am wrong would you kindly let me know.

With regard to the alto clar would it not be simpler for the copyist to make a second copy of the alto saxophone part merely leaving out the parts marked solo?

I have a great desire to have the military band full score of 'Hammersmith' published. Do you think anyone would buy it?

My idea is that Hawkes should first ascertain the cost and fix the price and then issue an announcement of publication by subscription--the score would be only published if a sufficient number applied by a certain date. If this is done it ought to be announced by April 17. Would you discuss it with Mr. Winkler and ask him to send your views and his to Mr R Hawkes to whom I am writing. I don't want to press this but only to ask opinions.

Yr Sincerely

Gustav Holst

In your list of instrumentation the bass clarinet is marked in E flat. Surely this should be B flat?
Another point has just struck me. If the score is published we must decide whether it shall be British or American list. At present I rather favour the latter.
This need not be discussed yet.[37]

A number of points are discussed in the letter. It appears that Holst may have had help in copying out the extra parts for *Hammersmith*, for he refers to "the copyist." He also talks about wanting the work to be published in full score. This seems to have been obvious, but in 1932 very few band works were available in full score. Neither of Holst's military band suites, by then performed with regularity on both sides of the Atlantic, would appear in full score until 1948. Thirdly, he refers to British and American "list." If he was referring to instrumentation , then Holst would have been dissappointed when, in 1956, the work was published without the extra American concert band parts.

The day following the Goldman meeting was also eventful. After meeting Harold Samuel at the Beethoven Association for lunch, Holst reprised his lecture "England and Her Music" at a dinner party of the National Association of Organists at New York's Pythian Temple. Tertius Noble, a Royal College of Music graduate and organist at St. Thomas Episcopal Church in New York, chaired the meeting.[38]

Two days later, Holst had breakfast at the University Club with Nathaniel Skilkret, Director of Light Music for the R.C.A. Victor Company since 1916. Shilkret was one of the most successful musicians in the business. When Holst made his acquaintence in 1932, Shilkret was only thirty-seven, yet he had a wealth of performance experience, having played clarinet in the bands of John Philip Sousa, Arthur Pryor, and Edwin Franko Goldman as well as in the New York Symphony, New York Philharmonic, and the Metropolitan Opera Orchestras. In 1924 he created the Victor Salon Orchestra, a jazz orchestra modeled after that of Paul Whiteman. Shilkret made numerous compositions, arrangements, and recordings with his ensemble, including "Dancing with Tears in My Eyes" and "It's a Million to One You're in Love." He later went to Hollywood to write music for movies.

Shilkret commisioned Holst to write a short work for his Victor Salon Orchestra. It was to be one part of a composers' series of works based on American themes. This was not the last time that Shilkret would organize such a project. Fifteen years later he was able to commission Schoenberg, Stravinsky, Toch, Milhaud, Castelnuovo-Tedesco and Tansman to contribute one movement each for a biblical cantata, *Genesis*.[39] Holst, as always, took commissioned work seriously. Notes that he wrote to himself indicate concerns about instrumentation, performance rights, and notation for an instrument which he hadn't yet composed for--the banjo:

> Shilkret
> piece for orchestra
> on American air or airs
> to last 4 or 5 min
> 6.3.3.3.2 str
> fl ob cl fag
> Sax E flat alto or B flat sop (cl)
> 2nd " or (cl)
> 3rd B flat tenor or bass cl or --
> 4th E flat baritone alto cl
> 3 cornets
> 2 trbn tenor
> tuba
> 2 horns banjo or guitar
> 2 trap
> 2 piano (or celeste, harp)
> sole rights for one year
> after that Shilkret has
> free per rights for self
> for $200
> would like score by Xmas
> yes or no Oct.1
> banjo C,G,D,A
> viola pitch
> written 8-- higher[40]

After lunch at the Beethoven Association with Valerie and Duncan McKenzie, Holst again met with Carl Engel about his Haydn lecture. That evening he had dinner at the home of American composer Randall Thompson, after which he went to the Columbia Broadcasting System radio studios to hear Shilket's band rehearse. Holst wrote of these incredible last few days in an extensive letter to Vally Lasker:

The University Club
1 West 54th Street
New York
Feb[ruary] 4[,] 1932

Dear Vally

There seems no way of making sure that this will arrive on *Der* (or *Den*?) *Tag*[41] so I'm starting it today as I feel I'd rather be early than late. And if it doesn't come on the 13th
I hope you'll find it waiting when you arrive, tired and happy, from Overstone on Thursday.

In any case it brings best birthday greetings and voluminous best wishes for a moderately overpoweringly pleasing twelve months. And the question arises as to whether the wording of the last sentence is due to intercourse with American newspaper headlines.

I fear my last letter was very dull--I was tired and sleepy. I forget whether I told you that while stopping with the Davisons at Cambridge I had an inward struggle to keep my promise not to invite people--in this case, <u>them</u>--to the J T[42]. On the last evening when I was feeling weary I just managed to keep my verbal promise and did not invite them. But when we started discussing their visit to England in Sep 1933 I fear I casually mentioned that the J T existed. I tried to dwell on its drawbacks but all in vain. They 'fell' for it. Nothing definite was said but I fear it will be later on.

Life continues to be fantastic. This morning I had breakfast with The Man Who Makes More Money In Music Than Anyone Else In The World[43]. As I expected, he turned out to be quite nice and simple and straight. He wants me to write a piece for his band which consist of 17 str 1 fl 1 ob 1 cl 1 bassoon, 4 saxophones, 2 horns, 3 cornets, 2 trombones, tuba, 2 pianos, harp, 2 trap drummers and a banjo.

I also had an invitation to see a rehearsal of a Dalcroze ballet founded on my Mars, directed by the daughter of my superior officer in Salonica and played (on the piano) by two ex-Paulinas Una Lucas and Fiona McLeary. I may or may not go to it on Sat. (she has telephoned--nothing doing!)

Last Tuesday Harold Samuel played Bach to me alone all afternoon.

And last night I went to Eugene O'Neill's masterpiece 'Mourning Becomes Electra.' It is a trilogy lasting from 5:30 till 11:15 with an hour's interval. It moved me more than any other play since I first saw Ibsen over 30 years ago.

A young American composer[44] called here last week and invited me to dinner tonight. I now find that I haven't got his address and it is not in the telephone book. Otherwise life is fairly simple.

I lectured in NY last Tuesday, I am to conduct the PF ballet next Thursday in Cambridge and to lecture in Washington on March 26. Other engagements are in the air, some of them very much so. And on Saturday I leave NY and settle down in Harvard for the term, anyhow theoretically. Practically, I expect to be jumping around from time to time. I may conduct the military version of Emma[45] at a State concert at Washington in April.

Feb 5

The young composer rang up just as I had finished the above last night so I got his address and went to the party but left at 10 PM to go to a radio station to hear the Richest Musician in the World conduct his band.
Oh Vally, Wot a Country!

They played with a religious intensity and during a short bit of soft treacle an announcer fervently proclaimed the virtues of somebody's cigarettes[46]; and when it was over they played some special bits of tripe for my benefit and showed me all their latest collection of marimbas and Chinese gongs etc. I got home at midnight. They rehearsed until 1 AM after which the composer went home and--so I understand--composed.

This morning has brought mail from London--a lovely long letter from Irene Brockman, with splendid news of her health), one from Mabel[47] and yours of Jan 2nd, telling me about Mrs. Windle's cat and your brother!....

Don't bother to send press cuttings--they can wait until I return.

My birthday present must wait until my return to Boston.

Today I merely send my warmest greetings and best wishes. May your shadow never grow less and may your aura expand and may all sorts of nice things come to you so they will certainly flow from you to others.

Y

G[48]

Friday, February 5th was a day taken up by concert-going. After a lunch at the Beethoven Association, Holst and Valerie attended a New York Philharmonic matinee performance conducted by Bruno Walter. That same evening Holst had dinner with Emil at the Players club and then went with Duncan McKenzie to see Deems Taylor's *Peter Ibbetson*.at the Metropolitan Opera House.[49]

The next day was Holst's last day in New York. After a lunch at the Beethoven Association with Valerie, Duncan McKenzie and a Harvard contingent that included the Davisons and G. Wallace Woodworth, Holst boarded a boat, not a train, bound for Boston. New York had been exceptional; he was in no hurry to leave. On the peaceful moonlit journey he saw the coast of New England blanketed in snow.

---

[1]Gustav Holst, *Diary*, Monday, January 25, 1932, The Holst Foundation.
[2]Karl Straube, organist at St. Thomas Cathedral, Leipzig, Germany.
[3]English tenor Steuart Wilson.
[4]American ex-patriot novelist Henry James.
[5]Violinist Jelly D'Aranyi.
[6]Violinist Adila Fachiri. She and Jelly D'Aranyi were the dedicatees of Holst's *Double Concerto*, Op. 49 [H175](1929).
[7]H. Stanislaus (according to the listing on *Boston Symphony Orchestra Programme*, January 22-23, 1932).
[8]Ralph Vaughan Williams.
[9]Ballet Music from *The Perfect Fool*, Op. 39 [H150](1920).
[10]Holst's friend, American industrialist Frank Austin Lidbury.
[11]Press clippings and other public relations material.
[12]Personal correspondence, Gustav Holst to Imogen Holst, Jan[uary] 26 [and 27, 1932], The Holst Foundation.
[13]Personal correspondence, Imogen Holst to Gustav Holst, Feb[ruary] 7[, 1932], The Holst Foundation.
[14]Gustav Holst, *Diary*, Wednesday, January 27, 1932, The Holst Foundation.
[15]*Who Was Who in the Theatre*, 535.
[16]*New York Times*, January 10, 1932.
[17]According to New York City Parks and Recreation sources on the Internet, there are three theories regarding this Dutch name: (1) a trumpeter dispatched to the bronx during the British invasion of New Amsterdam moved to cross a creek "en spijt dem Duyvil" (in spite of the devil), (2) a 1647 reference to a flowing fountain that emptied into the creek, "Spuit den Duyvil" ("Spout of the Devil") or (3) the creek itself ("Devil's Spate").
[18]The London Borough of Hammersmith.
[19]Personal correspondence, Gustav Holst to Vally Lasker, Jan[uary] 29[, 1932], The Holst Foundation.

[20]*New York Times*, January 12, 1995.
[21]*New York Herald Tribune*, April 16, 1944.
[22]*Ibid.*.
[23]Patricia Roger's taped interview with Valerie Cossart, late 1993.
[24]*Who Was Who in the Theatre*, 534-535.
[25]*Magill's Survey of Cinema: English Language Films, Second Series, Vol. 5* (Englewood Cliffs, NJ: Salem Press, 1981), 2113.
[26]*Who Was Who in the Theatre*, 534-535.
[27]Critic of *The Sun.*
[28]*New York Times*, February 2, 1932.
[29]*Musical America* [n.d., from February, 1932].
[30]Personal correspondence, Gustav Holst to Harold Bauer, Feb[ruary] 6[, 1932], Library of Congress.
[31]Personal correspondence, Harold Bauer to Gustav Holst, Feb[ruary] 15, 1932, The Holst Foundation.
[32]Gustav Holst quoted in Quaintence Eaton, "Gustav Holst, on American Visit, Approves Our Ways," in *Musical America*, LII, No. 3 (February 6, 1932), 6.
[33]*Musical Progress and Mail*, April, 1932.
[34]Holst's pet name for *Hammersmith*; when said with a Cockney accent, the name of the composition comes out "Emma Smith."
[35]Gustav Holst, *Notebook*, January to July, 1932, The Holst Foundation.
[36]*Ibid.*.
[37]Personal correspondence, Gustav Holst to Edwin Franko Goldman, Feb[ruary] 12[, 1932], Library of Congress.
[38]Gustav Holst, *Diary*, Tuesday, February 2, 1932, The Holst Foundation.
[39]Nicholas Slonimsky (ed.) *The Concise Baker's Biographical Dictionary of Composers, Eighth Edition* (New York: Schirmer Books, 1994), 934.
[40]Gustav Holst, *Notebook*, January to July, 1932, The Holst Foundation.
[41]*Der Tag*, or The Day, a reference to Vally Lasker's birthday.
[42]J.T., abbreviation for "Jolly Talgarth," Vally Lasker's townhouse at 103 Talgarth Road.
[43]Nathaniel Shilkret.
[44]Randall Thompson.
[45]*Hammersmith*, Op. 52 [H178].
[46]Shilkret's group was sometimes referred to as The Chesterfield Orchestra, reflective of their cigarette sponsor.
[47]Mabel Rodwell Jones.
[48]Personal correspondence, Gustav Holst to Vally Lasker, Feb[ruary] 4 and 5, 1932, The Holst Foundation.
[49]Gustav Holst, *Diary*, Saturday, February 6, 1932, The Holst Foundation.

CHAPTER XXV

THE HARVARD PROFESSOR

On Sunday, February 7, 1932 at 8:30 a.m. Holst's boat pulled into Boston Harbor. From there the composer went to Cambridge and moved into the suite in the new dormitory where he would be staying for the length of the Harvard spring term. Eliot House, facing the Charles River on Memorial Drive, was one of a group of seven "New Houses" located southwest of Harvard Yard:

> Something more than dormitories for the three upper classes, they serve as units for special types of study concentration, with resident masters and tutors, and their own libraries and dining-halls. Some of them were built originally as Freshman dormitories, but their amalgamation into the Houses has done a good deal to shift the center of the University toward the river, and has created a little university town of great charm.
> Of the completely new Houses--Lowell (1930), Dunster (1930), and Eliot (1931), all designed by Coolidge, Shepley, Bulfinch, and Abbott--perhaps Lowell, which is the largest, is also the handsomest. In all of them may be seen the following-out of the Georgian colonial motif, with now and then a heavy leaning on Holden Chapel (as in the frequent use of arms and mantling on the gables) and University Hall (as in the dining roon of Lowell, which bears a close resemblance to the Faculty Room). The rapidity with which they were built has made them possibly a shade too uniform, despite the deliberate attempts of the architects to vary them.[1]

There was still some socializing to do; Holst was then treated to lunch with the Davisons, after which he heard his friend Steuart Wilson sing at Eliot House.

The following day marked the beginning of Harvard's spring term. Holst's duties were as of yet undetermined and he met with Edward Burlingame Hill and Walter Piston regarding the pupils he was to teach. It was difficult for him to settle down, for his head was still reeling from New York. He wrote that evening to Vally Lasker:

Eliot House
Harvard University
Cambridge
Feb[ruary] 8[,] 1932

Dear Vally

I am back at Harvard and either Eliot House or Division of Music will find me. I had a lovely journey by boat--my ideal sea voyage because there was so much dry land in it.

We left NY at 5PM and skirted the city in the twilight just as the city lit up. At 7 the next morning my first thought was that the white cliffs of Old England were not nearly as white as those of New. And then I discovered that all of New England was and is under snow--it was dazzling under the rising sun but now we are having a messy thaw.

There is rather more work for me here than I had expected so I must hurry up. Yrs of Jan 19th written in train has only just arrived--the one containing L Dyer's[2] prospectus etc. Send all press cuttings to Iso in future....

Thank you for allowing me to send dollars as a birthday present. They are the only sendable things. Other splendid things don't travel--such as the glorious exciting air of New York and the view from the Empire State Building (well over 1000 ft high).

I also send you the first copy of the first photo of these two brothers ever taken as far as we can remember. Valerie took it and is sending some enlargements.

Yr Ever

Gustav

P.S. It may be that I shall not return until July 1 in order that I may go to Vancouver Island to see Bulley[3] and the Rockies and do a little

> promiscuous jawing and stick-wagging. Of course if H, M, ND, VL[4] or Ruthven were to cable forbidding it I should have to obey. Otherwise please forgive me if it comes off.[5]

On the next day, Tuesday the 9th, a piano arrived at Holst's Eliot House apartment, aiding him in his compositional pursuits. He also taught his first two composition classes that day, one at 11 and the other at 3; these would continue throughout the term on a Tuesday-Thursday schedule.[6] Holst took his teaching seriously from the start; he knew no other way. He listed his course rosters and what music educators would call individual "entry level behaviors" in his notebook:

> Pupils course
> Benjamin organist
> Intermezzo
> Contemp[?] rather than harmony
>
> Haggerty
> violinist good orchestrator
> slow working
>
> Rogers piano violin
> not so much harm count
> as others
>
> Miss Wheaton
> pianist
>
> Carter piano oboe
> more experienced
> sensitive musically
>
> Bixby
> good counterpoint
> "   all round student
> musical
>
> Orr
> piano

Nichols piano
not much experience

undergraduate
Rogers require grading
Nichols "

and

special class in advanced composition
Music 20
Tuttle (absent)[7]
Valente
Prophette
?
come singly when they have work[8]

He followed through, keeping tabs not only with the progress of the individuals, but also with the progress of the classes as a whole. Diary entries confirm this, from "small class and little work" to "good class with lots of work."[9] Holst's concerns for and frustrations incurred from his students affected him more and more as the term progressed. His diary entry for Wednesday, March 2 confirms this: "evening concert of my pupils' music with subsequent bad night."[10]

At least two of his students would have successful careers in musical composition: Elliott Carter, to whom Holst referred as "more experienced" and "sensitive musically," and Henry Leland Clarke, whose name, while not appearing in the above notebook listings, does appear in later *Diary* entries.

Holst spent the entirety of the next day at Eliot house writing music. During his stay at Harvard, he was working on *Six Choruses*, Op. 53 [H186] for male voices. These were settings of Helen Waddell's translations of Latin texts by the medieval French philosopher and theologian Peter Abelard. Holst also began to write out the additional parts for *Hammersmith.*[11]

The following day was Thursday, February 11th and for Holst that meant fulfilling his commitment to Serge Koussevitzky by reprising his performance of the "Ballet Music" from *The Perfect Fool*. There was a rehearsal at Symphony Hall in the morning and a concert that night at Sanders Theatre on the Harvard University campus. Sandwiched between them were Holst's classes and an unavoidable afternoon tea with Mrs. Annie L. Lamb, the benefactor of the Horatio

Appleton Lamb bequest. In addition to the Boston Symphony performance, Holst had been thinking about *The Perfect Fool* in a different light and for another purpose, as notebook entries disclose:

> PF
> a chain of fine theatres throughout USA need filmed operas for children.
> E Br is collecting operas and singers
> Must not last more than 1/2 hr.[12]

From these notes, it is difficult to know exactly what Holst was thinking. *The Perfect Fool* lasts at least an hour; Holst would have had to cut it in half for this project. It is interesting to note that the length of Holst's more recently composed *Tale of the Wandering Scholar*, may have fit the bill better than *The Perfect Fool*. Still the subject matter of *Tale of the Wandering Scholar* and the fact that it had not yet been performed may have quickly eliminated it from consideration for this project. Holst's earlier masterpiece *Savitri* is of similar length, although its deliberate pace disqualifies it from being any type of children's opera.

Holst wrote of the events of these days to Vally Lasker:

> Harvard University
> Division of Music
> 8:30 PM
> Feb[ruary] 13[,] 1932
>
> Dear Vally
>
> I thought I had posted my birthday letter to you in plenty of time but was startled in finding that letters from London sometimes take a fortnight. So just in case mine was too late I sent a 'night letter' to you yesterday which, I was assured, would reach you this morning. (A night letter is the cheapest sort of cable).
>
> Everything considered, I think I have celebrated this day rather well--that is if I have done it. For instance we've had hot sun, blue sky and snow on the ground. Next, I began using your MS book. Also I have spent nearly the whole day trying to set another of Helen Waddell's Medieval Latin Lyrics. It isn't exactly a birthday ode[,] but it's a cheerful poem--'How Mighty are the Sabbaths' from Peter Abelard.
>
> After breakfast tomorrow I shall have to decide whether today's work makes me feel sick--I'm not going to look at it tonight. I went out to buy

music paper and get letters from the Music Building and found the first copies of the first of my male voice choruses 'Intercession'. I'm asking Hawkes to send Nora a dozen copies. As I wrote to her yesterday would you tell her about them. You two had better begin by presenting copies to each other and then to SPGS, RVW, WGW, CKS, MRJ[,][13] Imogen and Helen Waddell, 3 Ormonde Terrace NW8. Nora knows where the rest are to go.

I also celebrated *Der/Den Tag* by giving tea to myself for the first time in my apartment. And a new pupil turned up so I gave him some also--he's a nice chap.

But the really important thing that has happened--or nearly happened today is that I have found-or nearly found--that I can spoil music paper here. (Tomorrow I will define'spoil'!) I have five rooms all to myself. At the back, looking onto a jolly courtyard, are my bedroom and bathroom. The front looks onto the river, on the other side of which is Boston. There is a large sitting room which I don't use much because my neighbor that side is addicted to jazz. Then a large spare which I hope my brother will use when he comes to act in the new GBS[14] play next month. Lastly my study--it is small and crowded up with large writing desk, piano, shelves, and chairs. But my neighbour this side is a real dear. A professor of comparative religion from Cambridge England, who quotes almost in one breath from Plato, St. Augustin and P G Wodehouse, and who has decided views on and a delicate taste in alcohol.

I've not been able to finish the string arrangement of my brass band suite[15] because other things are pressing. I am to conduct the Military band version of Emma[16] at Washington in April and have to add four extra parts pdq. Then I want to dedicate two male choruses to Davison and he wants to do them at a concert they are giving in my honour in April. (The 2nd isn't written yet!) Then I'm down to lecture on Haydn in Washington next month. Why oh Why?--Because Vally and Nora were not at hand to prevent me promising such a rash thing I suppose.

Later on I'm to lecture about my work at Morley in Cleveland and would like a few details and programs of present times. Would you ask Foster to let me have some? Also give him and them my warm congratulations on this last concert (These are some--but only some--of the 'warmest other things' mentioned in my birthday cable.) The others are--but no! This is no time for such details. Also I've no more writing paper. So goodbye till next time.

Yr

G[17]

The next few weeks were spent in relative bliss. On Tuesdays and Thursdays Holst was able to compose during the mornings and teach in the afternoons. On the other days he often composed all day. Evenings were generally spent dining and socializing at the homes of colleagues or patrons of the arts. He often attended Boston Symphony Orchestra concerts and on the 19th heard one that featured Jelly D'Aranyi performing works by Mozart and Ravel.

The same day he wrote to Imogen; her letter of February 7th had just caught up with him:

Harvard University
Division of Music
Cambridge
Feb[ruary] 19[, 1932]

Dear I

Thanks for your nice long letter of Feb 7. You say Iso is better--has she been ill? You also mention a previous letter you wrote in the Dumps--I never got it! That's why I wrote a frantic letter to Iso three days ago.

What a lovely time you must be having with Vicky and Ivor James[18]--congratulations all around.

I saw Una Lucas in NY and she thinks you could get quite a good school job in New England or NY state. Will you think it over? She is returning in July and you might like to talk it over. But if you'd really like something of the sort it ought to be decided before then and I know the three or four most important people in the eastern states and could probably fix up something. So if you decide you'd like the idea will you write to me very fully--perhaps the ideal thing would be two letters, one for private consumption only. Iso and I would miss you damnably but, as Rochefeller the first[19] said, there ain't no damn sentiment about business. If you decide <u>against</u> trying for a USA job send me a short letter.

My agent--McKenzie of the OUP[20] is a dear. He's having endless work over me and very poor results as people either can't have me or want me for expenses only and he works on a commission.

As you say, I'm settling down to a university life. But I've one tremendous and unexpected event. My apartment at Eliot House is the only place I've struck in the last 20 years barring my room in SPGS[21] where I can spoil music paper easily. It looks as if I shall write steadily while I'm here. Then--if luck holds--I go to Ann Arbor and then Vancouver and across Canada to Montreal then home.

But I must save my arm and am going to cut down letter writing--perhaps even send typed ones. You might warn people.

BL

G[22]

One of the "three or four most important people in the eastern states" to whom Holst was referring was undoubtedly Thomas Whitney Surrette, an eminent music educator who, in collaboration with Archibald Davison, produced the influential *Concord Series of Music* and *Books on the Teaching of Music.* Surrette and Holst were no strangers, Surrette having visited the composer in England on a number of occasions prior to Holst's visit. In his later years--he was already seventy at the time of Holst's stay at Harvard--Surrette served as a consultant for many school music programs throughout the country. He was also founder of the Concord Summer School of Music in 1914. The school served Concord well until its closing in 1938. Among other things, it gave a series of three public chamber music concerts each summer and offered free public classes in folk dancing.[23]

On the afternoon of Saturday, February 20th, Dorothy Davison drove Holst to Concord. He had lunch at the Surrettes and stayed overnight. Located about twenty miles northwest of Boston, Concord was and is an arts center. In many ways it served as the literary capitol of nineteenth century America, counting novelist Louisa May Alcott, transcendentalist Ralph Waldo Emerson, and naturalist Henry David Thoreau among its residents. Holst spent the following day here with the Surrettes, before attending a Harvard Glee Club concert at St. Mark's School and heading back to Eliot House.[24] He returned to Concord three days later to hear the Radcliffe Choir perform his cantata *Hecuba's Lament*.

Sandwiched between the two trips to Concord was the Ninth International Choirs Festival at Symphony Hall, sponsored by Community Service of Boston and the Women's Municipal League. In the first part of the festival individual choirs sang and competed for prizes that were presented by Thomas Whitney Surrette. This was followed by a short program of massed forces under the baton of Russell Ames Cook. "Turn Back O Man," the second of Holst's three *Festival*

Choruses, Op. 36, closed this portion of the festivities.[25]

After a disheartening class at Harvard the next day he finished a letter to Vally Lasker:

Harvard University
Division of Music
Cambridge Massachusetts
Feb[ruary] 23[, 19]32

Dear Vally

Thanks for your Cambridge letter of Feb. 7. I'm sorry you've had to wait so long for letters but hope all is well now.

After writing those letters on board the Bremen I had no chance of doing more for a fortnight. The first 10 days at Boston were hectic and probably the most successful 10 days of my life. At New York I thought the best plan was to write one long letter to Imogen and get her to pass it around as my arm was still weak.

I made enquiries about mailboats and thought I had planned your birthday letter beautifully. But afterwards I found that one cannot depend on anything as it depends on which boat the mail goes by. So to make sure I sent a birthday cable.

I had another disappointment--I sent my birthday present in such a way that you didn't get the full value of the dollar. However you won't mind that bless you.

The final blow was a nice long letter from Imogen in which she mentioned a previous letter which I never got! I wonder how many others are lost.

I think I told you that I celebrated your birthday by composing all day. I've kept it up since and feel tremendously happy in consequence. But my arm is distinctly weak so I shall have to cut down letters. (I've done one and a half more male voice choruses from Helen Waddell's words in 8 days--Davison's singers are going to try them over.)

———

Since writing above I've had a most disappointing class--half of them away and half of the other half bringing no work. These people have learnt almost as much about music as I have forgotten. It feels impertinent to tell them anything because they know everything (in theory) much better than I. They are all humble and diffident and full of inhibitions and I've only one thing to say to them and that is 'Write, and then write more--and More'!

In some ways I feel that I am just the man for them. But I hope there will be something to show for it all. So far it is I who have done the composing.

I hope you enjoyed your birthday as much as I did, that Charlie is happy at SPGS and that Nora is spoiling your sofa.

Yr Ever

G

Nora tells me that the Paulinas are giving her a splendid time--bless them![26]

Holst was always thinking of his students; as in the case of any teacher, it really bothered him when they had little or no work to show him. It concerned him too that he would be gone a good part of the time and he did not want to let them down. His random thoughts on teaching composition appear in notebook entries:

Hill
idea reading [orchestra?] OK
leave then May 9
but I teach that week
warn them <u>now</u> to get good themes
If they do work now it won't be so good--It will have missed five weeks' teaching
marks for clear technique
themes beautiful and varied
unity of style
advanced pupils entire
1st movement
lower grade to double bar[27]

From these entries, it appears that Holst wanted his students to spend time on getting a hold of good melodic themes. His comments about doing work too early, "missing five weeks' teaching," may have referred to some future project he had planned for them to do in regard to a concert scheduled for April 14th:

> pupils score 'I vow' for strs?[28]

At the end of the month Emil was able to come to Boston. He was in the Theatre Guild production of George Bernard Shaw's play "Too True to be Good." Billed as the world premiere, the play was directed by Leslie Banks and presented at Boston's Colonial Theatre.[29] Emil played the part of Colonel Tallboys. Beatrice Lilly, Hope Williams, and Hugh Sinclair were also in the cast. J. Brooks Atkinson reviewed it for the *New York Times*:

> [George Bernard Shaw] writes some of his most ingratiating, cynical dialogue for an army Colonel and a superhuman private.
> ....Ernest Cossart is admirably comic as the bumptious colonel....[30]

Holst mentions this in a letter written to Vally Lasker the following day:

> Harvard University
> Division of Music
> Cambridge Massachusetts
> March 1 [1932]
>
> D V
>
> Thanks for yrs of Feb 13. I hope you've had mine of the same date also the one that ought to have reached you that day and the one that contained the birthday present besides a short one I wrote 10 days ago.
>
> Enclosed is rather late for a birthday present but I want you to consider as such because its the tune I wrote on Feb 13.[31] Also I like it. And I think I shall like the whole work when I've done it. And I hope you'll do the same. Will you tell Nora to get Amy to make two copies[,] one for the school and one for Nora. You'll find the original words in Late Latin Lyrics (Waddell). None of the other verses suit this tune. Of course that doesn't matter in the complete work.
>
> But I have a desire to issue a unison setting of the poem and tune and am going to ask Helen Waddell if she would care to consider altering certain lines for the sake of making a popular hymn--(if it <u>is</u> popular!). If she does I'll ask her to get in touch with you and Nora and either or both can explain the trouble which is usually very slight. (The best plan would

be for you to invite them both to dinner at 103 and make ND promise lots of wine. HW is strong on sherry.) If such a version were made in time it would be a great lark to do it on Speech Day.

The complete setting of the poem is dedicated to Dr Davison and the Harvard Glee Club. I'm trying to get it done in time for them to produce it at a concert they are giving in my honour with a women's chorus on April14. Besides it and another new one (also Helen Waddell) I am to conduct Hecuba[32], the Whitman Dirge for 2 Vets[33], the 2nd Psalm[34], I love my love and Swansea[35]. Which reminds me that I must break it gently to you and other SP friends--on Tuesday next I am conducting a

Pierian Sodality!![36]

Forgive me--I'll try and not do it again.

Last night I saw Emil in GBS's new play. The latter is a weak imitation of bad Shaw. All the actors were good and Emil was splendid. He will be in Boston for a fortnight and I hope he'll sleep here part of the time.

Yr

G

I'm dedicating another male voice thing 'Good Friday' to Ernest Bullock of Westminster[37] and have asked him to let Nora know if he does it.[38]

The Pierian Sodality to which Holst referred was a tradition dating back to 1808. The *Harvard Class Album (1932)* offers commentary:

> The orchestra's programs during the last three years have been of a singularly high order; appearances of soloists of Prof. Edward Ballantine, Malcolm H. Holmes '28, Miss Dorothy Brewster Comstock, Ralph Kirkpatrick '31, and others, together with Mr. Gustav Holst as guest conductor in the first concert in Paine Hall this spring, have been among the unusual events of the past seasons.[39]

Holst's friend G. Wallace Woodworth, had conducted the ensemble since 1928. Woodworth would give it up in 1933, when he succeeded Archibald Davison as conductor of the Harvard Glee Club. Walter Piston had also been a conductor of the Pierian Sodality--during his undergraduate days in the early 1920's. Time being short, Holst had only one rehearsal with the Pierian Sodality before conducting his *St. Paul's Suite* on their concert of Tuesday, March 8th.[40]

The previous Sunday Emil had come to stay with Holst at Eliot House. The two brothers celebrated by inviting the Davisons over to the apartment for tea and supper;[41] this was the first time in forty years that the two had slept under the same roof. Just as Emil and Valerie had done for him, Holst decided to take his brother for a tour of some of his favorite spots. On Thursday, the two of them went to Concord in the morning and had lunch with the Surrettes before heading back to Harvard. After such a splendid time with his brother, Holst felt a bit of a let down. His diary entry for the latter part of the day is characteristically succinct: "Classes fair[,] weather cold, throat weak."[42]

Still, there was a lot to look forward to; the next morning Holst was bound for Montreal.

---

[1]Federal Writers Project of the Works Progress Administration, *Massachusetts: A Guide to Its Places and People* (Boston: Houghton Mifflin, 1937), 200.

[2]Louise Dyer.

[3]Possibly a reference to Mt. Rushmore in South Dakota, which features Theodore Roosevelt as one of the four presidents carved into the mountain.

[4]Holst's helpers at St. Paul's Girls School: Helen Bidders, Mabel Rodwell Jones, Nora Day, and Vally Lasker. Ruthven was the school's porter.

[5]Personal correspondence, Gustav Holst to Vally Lasker, Feb[ruary] 8[,] 1932, The Holst Foundation.

[6]Gustav Holst, *Diary*, February through May, Tuesday and Thursday entries, The Holst Foundation.

[7]Probably Elizabethan specialist Stephen Tuttle, who shared a room with Elliott Carter.

[8]Gustav Holst, Notebook, January to July, 1932, The Holst Foundation.

[9]Gustav Holst, *Diary*, Tuesday, February 23, and Thursday, February 25, 1932, The Holst Foundation.

[10]Gustav Holst, *Diary*, Wednesday, March 2, 1932, The Holst Foundation.

[11]Gustav Holst, *Diary*, Wednesday, February 10, 1932, The Holst Foundation.

[12]Gustav Holst, Notebook, January to July, 1932, The Holst Foundation.

[13]St. Paul's Girls' School, Ralph Vaughan Williams, William Gillies Whittaker, Charles Kennedy Scott, Mabel Rodwell Jones.

[14]George Bernard Shaw.

[15]*A Moorside Suite* [H173].

[16]*Hammersmith* [H178].

[17]Personal correspondence, Gustav Holst to Vally Lasker, Feb[ruary] 13[,] 1932, The Holst Foundation.

[18]English cellist Ivor James, who taught at the Royal College of Music.

[19]American industrialist John D. Rockefeller (1839-1937).

[20]Oxford University Press.

[21]St. Paul's Girls' School.
[22]Personal correspondence, Gustav Holst to Imogen Holst, Feb[ruary] 19[, 1932], The Holst Foundation.
[23]Federal Writers Project of the Works Progress Administration, *op.cit.*, 215.
[24]Gustav Holst, *Diary*, Saturday, February 21 and Sunday, February 22, 1932, The Holst Foundation.
[25]*Boston Herald*, February 23, 1932.
[26]Personal correspondence, Gustav Holst to Vally Lasker, Feb[ruary] 23, [19]32, The Holst Foundation.
[27]Gustav Holst, Notebook, January to July, 1932, The Holst Foundation.
[28]*Ibid.*.
[29]*Boston Globe*, February 23, 1932.
[30]*New York Times*, March 1, 1932.
[31]"How Mighty Are the Sabbaths," No. 5 of *Six Choruses*, Op. 53 [H186].
[32]*Hecuba's Lament*, Op. 31, No. 1 [H115] (1911).
[33]*Dirge for Two Veterans* [H121](1914).
[34]"Lord, who hast made us for thine own," (Psalm 148), the second of *Two Psalms* [H117] (1912).
[35]"I love my love" and "Swansea Town" are two folk songs used by Holst in various settings, most notably in the *Second Suite in F for Military Band*, Op. 28, No. 2 [H106]. Here, however they were two of the *Six Choral Folk Songs*, Op. 36 [B] [H136] (1916).
[36]A Harvard University student orchestra.
[37]Westminster Abbey.
[38]Personal correspondence, Gustav Holst to Vally Lasker, March 1[, 1932], The Holst Foundation.
[39]*Harvard Class Album (1932)* (Boston: The Washington Press, 1932), 173.
[40]GustavHolst, *Diary*, Tuesday, March 8, 1932, The Holst Foundation.
[41]Gustav Holst, *Diary*, Sunday, March 6, 1932, The Holst Foundation.
[42]Gustav Holst, *Diary*, Thursday, March 10, 1932, The Holst Foundation.

CHAPTER XXVI

MONTREAL AND RETURN TO NEW YORK

At 9:00 a.m. on March 11, 1932 Holst set out from Boston on a whirlwind four-day trip that included Montreal and New York. This was intended to be a preliminary trip to Canada; Holst was testing the waters for a projected grand tour of that country in June; he mentioned this in his February 19 letter to Imogen. At the heart of the March trip was an invitation to guest conduct the Montreal Orchestra.

Surprisingly, the Montreal Orchestra was in its infancy.[1] Odd though it may seem, its formation came about more from the necessity of keeping professional musicians employed than from the aesthetic needs of Canada's largest city. During the late 1920's motion pictures had entered the "talkie" era. This development sent shock waves throughout the music industry. The orchestras in large cities that had been suppling musical accompaniment for silent movies quickly became defunct. Movie theatres throughout the world were disbanding their orchestras and those on St. Catherine Street in Montreal were no exception. Thus it was that a number of theatre orchestra musicians spearheaded by clarinettist Giulio Romano founded an orchestra, originally called the Montreal Concert Orchestra and then simply the Montreal Orchestra. There had been at least three previous attempts to establish a permanent orchestra in Montreal; the latest reincarnation was an ensemble founded in 1927 by conductor J. J. Gagnier that met in the Princess Theatre. The fate of this orchestra was sealed by the October, 1929 stock market crash.[2]

Shortly thereafter Romano and his group approached Douglas Clarke, Dean of the Faculty of Music at McGill University, about establishing a more permamanent professional symphony orchestra in Montreal. Clarke readily took up the challenge and, with Canada in the early stages of a world-wide depression, agreed to conduct the orchestra without charging for his services. It was truly an entrepreneurial affair for Clarke as he also supplied much of the repertoire himself.[3] Concerts were held on Sunday afternoons, first at the Orpheum Theatre, and later at His Majesty's Theatre on Guy Street. In 1930-31, its first season, the orchestra played twenty-six programs; in 1931-32, twenty-one. The concert that featured Holst was the twentieth of the 1931-32 season.[4]

Clarke certainly had the credentials to serve as the orchestra's conductor. He had studied with Holst and Vaughan Williams at University College in Reading and had been elected a Fellow of the Royal College of Organists. He then served as conductor of the Cambridge Musical Society from 1923 to 1927 and, after emigrating to Canada, conducted the Winnipeg Male Voice Choir and Philharmonic Society from 1927 to 1929. In the latter year he became Director of the McGill Conservatorium of Music in Montreal and in 1930 was named Dean of the Music Faculty there, a position he would hold for a quarter of a century.[5] Clarke's connection as a former student of Holst would have been enough by itself to entice the composer to come to Montreal. There was, however, a second connection. Holst's agent Duncan McKenzie himself had been at one time a "lecturer on theoretical subjects and teacher of organ at McGill University Conservatorium."[6] Whatever the case, Holst had instant ties to Montreal. His appearance was trumpeted in advertisements such as this:

Montreal Orchestra
Conductor: DOUGLAS CLARKE
70--Musicians--70
Second Season--Forty-Sixth Concert
His Majesty's Theatre
March 13--3 p.m.
GUSTAV HOLST will conduct his
"Mars the Bringer of War"
...From the Planets
Prices: \$.35 to \$1.50. Tickets now selling.[7]

Holst arrived in Montreal at 6:15 p.m. "at wrong station."[8] Nevertheless Clarke found him and took him to the Drinkwater residence on Peet Street, his lodgings for the evening. The following morning (Saturday, March 12) Holst had a rehearsal with the orchestra at a hotel. It had already decided beforehand to rehearse and perform "Jupiter" instead of the advertised "Mars;"[9] The latter may have already been performed earlier in the season. Following the rehearsal Holst was given a tour of the city by car and that evening was taken to dinner at the Pen Club.

The next day, on Sunday, the 13th, Holst had a morning rehearsal and a three o'clock concert with the orchestra at their usual venue, His Majesty's Theatre. The concert was no ordinary affair; in addition to Holst, His Excellency, the Governor-General was on hand for the festivities. As expected, the *Montreal Daily Star* was also on hand:

> Composer Conducted Montreal Orchestra in Sunday Concert
>
> With the Governor-General [Lord Bessborough] to listen to them, Mr. Gustav Holst to conduct them, and an audience larger than the average, the members of the Montreal Orchestra had every reason for doing some of their best playing on Sunday afternoon and they did. The most important part of the program was, of course, that in which Mr. Holst appeared; a change had been made here, and instead of "Mars," which was originally on the program, the planet chosen was "Jupiter, the bringer of jollity," much more appropriate to a festive occasion. Composers are very often not good conductors, even of their own music; Mr. Holst is not a composer of this kind; he knew so exactly what he wanted and had such complete control of the orchestra that it has never played better and gave a very fine performance which had to be repeated and went perhaps better still the second time.
>
> For the rest of the concert the orchestra was repeating music that it has already played this season. The music was all British or French, with Bax's "Garden of Fand," Elgar's "Prelude and Angel's Farewell" and Ravel's "Pavane pour une enfante defunte" as its principal numbers. This was all rather serious music, and some lightness was given to the beginning and end of the program with Vaughan Williams' overture to Aristophanes' "Wasps" and Dukas' "[L']Apprenti Sorcier." And no one could find much ground for complaint in the way in which the orchestra, under Mr. Clarke, played everything in this program.[10]

The *Montreal Daily Star's* coverage continued in a separate article that touted the occasion:

> Vice-Regal Party Hears Orchestra
>
> Yesterday was English Day for the Montreal Orchestra at His

Majesty's Theatre. It was also one of the most auspicious concerts in the career of the institution so far....[11]

La Patrie gave a slightly different account:

Gustav Holst est applaudi avec
enthusiasme hier, avec
l"Orchestra de Montréal

L'Orchestra de Montréal a reçu hier après-midi, au théâtre His Majesty's outre Leurs Excellencies lord et lady Bessborough, le grand compositor anglais Gustav Holst. C'est M. Holst qui dirigea l'exécution d'un extrait de son oeuvre: "Les Planèts". M. Douglas Clarke remonta au pupitre pour le reste du programme. A l'exception de la "Pavane pour une infante défunte" de Ravel et de l'"Apprenti Sorcier", l'oeuvre humoristique et populaire de Dukas, le programme se composait de compositions anglaises.

M. Holst prit la baguette du chef d'orchestra pour diriger l'exécution de "Jupiter". A la fin, orchestre et auditoire se leverent ensemble. Des applaudissements si enthousiastes saluerent M. Holst que son oeuvre dut être bissec.[12]

[The Montreal Orchestra, received yesterday afternoon, at His Majesty's Theatre in addition to Their Excellencies Lord and Lady Bessborough, the great English composer Gustav Holst. It was Mr. Holst who directed an extract from his work "The Planets." Mr. Douglas Clarke returned to the podium for the rest of the program. With the exception of Ravel's "Pavane pour une infante defunte" ("Pavane for a Dead Princess") and Dukas' humorous and popular "l'Apprenti Sorcier," ("The Sorcerer's Apprentice") the program was composed of English compositions.

Mr. Holst took the baton to conduct the performance of "Jupiter." At the end, the orchestra and audience stood up together. Mr. Holst was greeted so enthusiatically that his work had to be encored.]

For any composer, this concert would have rounded out a perfect day--for any composer but Holst. That same evening, at the Church of the Messiah, Holst addressed the People's Forum in his well-worn but well-received lecture on "England and Her Music."[13] After that the exhausted composer hopped on an overnight train bound for New York.

This was not the last time in the 1931-32 season that Holst's music would be performed in Montreal. There was one remaining concert for the orchestra, a request program to be given the following week. *The Montreal Daily Star* reported the following information:

> A request programme will be featured by the Montreal Orchestra at its final concert of the season, which will be held tomorrow afternoon [March 20] at His Majesty's Theatre at the usual hour, three o'clock.
>
> Two weeks ago leaflets were distributed among the audience listing the more important works played by the orchestra since the opening of the present season. The audience was asked to vote from these items the programme they would like to hear at the final concert. From among the compositions chosen by the largest number of votes the following programme was selected and will be played tomorrow:
>
> 1. Introduction to Act III, "Dance of the Apprentices" and "Procession of the Masters" from Wagner's "Mastersingers of Nuremberg."
> 2. Beethoven's Symphony No. 5 in C minor.
> 3. "Mars, the Bringer of War," from Holst's "Planets."
> 4. Brahm's Variations on a Theme of Haydn.
> 5. Grieg's "Peer Gynt" Suite No. 1[14]

This may not have been entirely accurate, for *The Montreal Gazette* went into greater detail and cited different results for the top two positions. After mentioning that for the voting "the sixty-five most significant compositions played this season were listed on a leaflet," it pointed out that Beethoven was the top composer. His name topped the list with forty-eight votes and his *Symphony No. 5 in c minor*, the most-requested composition, received twenty-eight votes. Cesar Franck and his *Symphony in d minor* ranked second in both categories with twenty-seven votes. The article continues:

> ....The composer ranking third was a surprise. He was Gustav Holst, the only modern to break into the sacred circle of classics. Holst received 25 votes on three compositions, 19 of which were awarded to "The Planets" suite. Incidentally "The Planets" was the third most popular work of the season...[15]

Holst's appearance was a shot in the arm for the Montreal Orchestra. Throughout the depression, the orchestra was riddled by financial and--unfortunately--political difficulties. Although billed as a bilingual city at the time of Holst's visit, the reality of the situation was that Montreal was two cities in one: English speakers (who, while constituting about forty percent of the population, controlled the economy) and the French-speaking majority. Douglas Clarke was Dean of the Music Faculty at McGill University, the most influential English-speaking university in the province of Quebec. This in itself did not endear him to certain factors of Montreal's Francophile community. Clarke's orchestra was supported very well in *The Montreal Daily Star* and in *The Gazette*, but there were at least two other dailies. In the otherwise positive concert review of the March 13 program carried by *La Patrie* (above), works by English composers other than Holst were not detailed--composer's names were not even listed--and *Le Devoir*, another French language Montreal daily, carried no news at all about the orchestra in its weekly music columns for the month of March, although it did carry news about the death of the American March King John Philip Sousa. Thus Clarke, either through his own volition or through the perceptions of Montreal's Francophile community, found himself catering primarily to the Montreal's Anglophiles. If the *Montreal Daily Star* article is accurate, then none of the five works selected by the Montreal Orchestra's audience for inclusion on the 1931-32 request concert were by French composers.

At least two of Holst's works were programmed by the Montreal Orchestra during the following season. "Jupiter" was performed again on the forty-ninth concert on October 30, 1932 and *Bach's Fugue a la Gigue* was performed on the fiftieth, on November 6th of that year.[16]

At the end of the 1933-34 season, two years after Holst's visit, the orchestra's board of directors split in a dispute with Clarke regarding his refusal to provide more openings for conductors and soloists from Quebec. One largely French-speaking faction, headed by Madame Athnase David and journalist Henri Letondal, walked out and formed their own organization, the Société des Concerts Symphonique de Montréal[17] which, according to the *New Grove Dictionary,* had uneven offerings and lacked overall musical direction. Montreal native and New York Metropolitan Opera conductor Wilfred Pelletier was brought in to serve as principal conductor of this orchestra.[18] Many of its performers still played in the Montreal Orchestra. Although there were now two orchestras, Clarke's continued to dominate musically until the early days of Second World War, when it disbanded. After the war, the Société des Concerts Symphonique resumed and, perhaps having learned a lesson, their board hired Belgian conductor Desiré Defauw, offered bilingual programs and adopted a new bilingual name: Orchestre Symphonique de Montréal-Montreal Symphony Orchestra.[19]

Holst arrived in New York at 7:30 in the morning on Monday, March 14, 1932. He had all three meals that day at the Beethoven Association: breakfast with Emil, who had just returned from Boston, lunch with Valerie and his publishing agent H. W. Gray, and dinner with Valerie and Duncan McKenzie. In the afternoon he was taken to Spuyten Duyvil, where he was able to take a nap[20]

That evening, Holst went to Carnegie Hall to hear a concert by the New York Oratorio Society. Its program for the evening had been altered:

> The recent arrival in New York of the English composer, Gustav Holst, is the occasion of a change in the Oratorio Society's program for its concert on March 14 at Carnegie Hall. With Mr. Holst's presence expected at the coming recital, the performance of Bruckner's Te Deum, previously scheduled for March 14, is postponed until a later date by Conductor Albert Stoessel; and two Psalms for chorus, string orchestra, and organ, by Mr. Holst will be offered instead. These Psalms, first given by the Oratorio Society in 1929, are to be followed the same evening by Elgar's Dream of Gerontius.[21]

After the concert--and a mere seventeen hours in New York--Holst boarded the 12:30 a.m. train bound for Boston. By the time he arrived there the next morning, Holst had spent more than twenty-five of the past ninety-four hours on three different trains.

---

[1]In fact, Canadian symphonic music was in its infancy. According to the *International Cyclopaedia of Music and Musicians*, Canada's other leading orchestra, The Toronto Symphony, was unable to give its first regular serious evening concerts until 1932.

[2]Personal correspondence, Christine St-Gelais, Communications Department of the Orchestra Symphonique de Montreal to the author, July 10, 1996.

[3]Stanley Sadie (ed.), *The New Grove Dictionary of Music and Musicians* (London: Macmillan & Co., 1980), XII, 540.

[4]*The Montreal Daily Star*, March 12, 1932.

[5]*The International Cyclopaedia of Music and Musicians*, 11 th ed. (New York: Dodd, Mead, & Co., 1985), 427.

[6]"Official News Release," New Jersey College for Women, August 20, 1943.

[7]*The Montreal Daily Star*, March 11, 1932.

[8]GustavHolst, *Diary*, Friday, March 11, 1932, The Holst Foundation.

[9]Gustav Holst, *Diary*, Saturday, March 12, 1932, The Holst Foundation.

[10]*The Montreal Daily Star*, March 14, 1932.

[11]*Ibid.*.

[12]*La Patrie* [Montreal], Mars 14, 1932.

[13]*The Montreal Daily Star*, March 14, 1932.

[14]*The Montreal Daily Star*, March 19, 1932.

[15]*The Montreal Gazette*, March 14, 1932.

[16]*Programme,* The Montreal Orchestra, 49th and 50th Concerts.

[17]Personal correspondence, Christine St-Gelais to the author, July 10, 1996.
[18]Nicholas Slonimsky (ed.), *The Concise Baker's Biographical Dictionary of Musicians. 8th ed.* (New York: Schirmer Books, 1994), 755.
[19]*The New Grove Dictionary, loc. cit.*. This name was retained until the passage of Quebec's language laws.
[20]Gustav Holst, *Diary*, Monday, March 14, 1932, The Holst Foundation.
[21]*Musical Courier*, February 13, 1932.

CHAPTER XXVII

BOSTON AND WASHINGTON, D.C.

Holst needed one day to recover from his taxing Montreal-New York trip, but Tuesday, March 15th, the first day back, was not to be it. A brisk morning of "20 degrees of frost," helped him to be sufficiently alert in order to teach his Harvard classes, which he described as "fair," before he collapsed into bed at eight o'clock that evening.[1]

The next week and a half were spent in scoring "Before Sleep," the last of the *Six Choruses* Op. 53, No. 6 [H186] and the second dedicated to Archibald Davison and the Harvard Glee Club. He also revised the string parts to *Hecuba's Lament* and sketched some themes for the piece promised to Nathaniel Skilket and his Victor Salon Orchestra Holst also spent considerable time writing his Haydn lecture (to be given at the Library of Congress on Saturday, the 25th) and made up for lost time in written correspondence.

In addition to all of this, Holst took time for some socializing. On one evening he met Walter Piston for dinner, attended a lecture on Goethe at Memorial Hall, and rounded out the evening at the Davisons.[2] He also spent some time with ex-Paulina Cecilia Payne, meeting her for lunch one day and for dinner at her place on another. This was followed by her lecture on a subject of great interest to him, the Zodiac. He also found time to attend a Boston Symphony Orchestra concert which featured Liszt's *Symphony on Dante's Divine Comedy*. Holst wrote in his diary that he had to "walk home to get over it."[3] He wrote of the past week's events to Vally Lasker that evening:

Harvard University
Division of Music

Cambridge Massachusetts
March 18[, 19]32

D V

Thanks for the 2 letters the 2nd of which (March 6) came yesterday.

I hope I shall be able to write more letters in April although it is looking doubtful. There are heaps of rehearsals for 'my' concert of April 14. And I've got to go again to Montreal. I was there last Sunday--rehearsal in morn, concert, in afternoon, lecture in evening, 9:30 PM train to New York, where I had breakfast with Emil who was going to Washington, lunch with Valerie who let me have a nap at their house, and a concert of Gerontius and my 2 Psalms in the evening; midnight train back to Boston, classes etc the next day and bed at 8 PM for 11 3/4 hours.

The Montreal concert was good--the Governor General came in state.--I only conducted Jupiter but they brought me on 7 times after and after the 4th the band decided to do it again so I obeyed....

To answer questions--

I've got over the last attack of homesickness about 10 days ago when my pupils mildly reformed.

Valerie is in Hay Fever which is coming here on the 28th--she will arrive in the afternoon of the 27th just in time for the B minor Mass!

Emil was the major in GBS.[4] Last week he stayed with me here--we were under one roof for the first time for over forty years and it was more than rather good.

Eliot House food is not more than fair but the Faculty Club meals are really good. And I had a delightful host in Montreal of the quite inappropriate name of Drinkwater.[5]

I'm thinking of taking the 'Empress of France' from Quebec on June 23, arriving Southampton June 30.

I must write to Helen Waddell now--I ought to have done so a month ago.

Y

G[6]

In addition to his teaching Holst had at least eight pressing concerns for the not-too-distant future: (1) his Haydn lecture at the Library of Congress for March

26th, (2) a concert of his own works at Harvard, set for April 14th, (3) the premiere of the original military band version of *Hammersmith*, set for April 17th, (4) a return to Montreal sometime in April, (5) the piece for Shilkret, (6) a Music Educators National Conference address in Cleveland, (7) a return engagement at the University of Michigan's May Festival and, ultimately, (8) a grand tour of Canada The totality of these things consumed him and eventually proved to be overwhelming.

Of the above concerns, the Haydn lecture was perhaps the one that was most under his control. It was also the most imminent. According to his diary enries, Holst worked on his lecture steadily; speaking at the Library of Congress in connection with the Haydn Bicentennial was a major event and he knew it.. Three days before departing for Washington D.C., he tried out his lecture on Davison and then revised it. Plans were being made at the Library of Congress as well. Among those invited to attend were a number of congressmen and Lou Henry Hoover, the First Lady.[7] Invitations, such as this one, were sent to ten selected schools:

Library of Congress
Washington D. C.
Division of Music

Hendley-Kaspar School
1858 Kalorama Road
Washington, D.C.

February 24, 1932

Dear Sir:

Mr. Gustav Holst, the eminent English composer, at present giving a course of lectures and classes in composition at Harvard, will give a lecture in the auditorium of the Library of Congress, in honor of the Bicentenary of Joseph Haydn, on Saturday March 26th, at 3:00 o'clock.

The Roth String Quartet will play Haydn's String Quartet in D minor, Opus 76, No. 5.

Will you please bring this to the attention of your students and notify me of the number of tickets you may wish to have reserved for them. As the demand for tickets is likely to be large and the seating capacity of the hall is limited, please return as soon as possible any tickets which you find yourself unable to make use of.

Sincerely yours,
[Eleanor A. Fay]
Secretary, Division of Music[8]

Time was not so much a factor as sense of place in determing Holst's Harvard concert, projected. for April 14th. This concert was still more than three weeks away, yet Holst had already begun rehearsing the strings as early as March 21th.[9] Sanders Theatre, a beautiful auditorium built in the Tudor style and adorned with Latin sayings, was to be the venue and, if the following letter is any indication, Sanders was just as much in demand in 1932 as it is today; it had to be booked well in advance:

F. W. Hunnewell, Esq.
Harvard University
Cambridge

March 2, 1932

My dear Mr. Hunnewell:--

The Harvard Glee Club in conjunction with the Radcliffe Choral Society, wishes to give a concert on Thursday, April14 next in honor of Gustav Holst. This concert will not be public and there will be no charge for admission. We should like to hold it in Sanders Theatre. There will be the necessary rehearsals prior to the concert and we should like to have the use of Sanders Theatre for them, as well as for the concert. The dates and hours during which we wish to use the hall are as follows:
Rehearsals--
Monday, April 11, at 4 p.m.
Monday, April 11, at 7 p.m.
Wednesday, April 13, at 7 p.m.
Concert--
Thursday evening, April 14

I hope it will be possible for the Corporation to grant the Harvard Glee Club the use of Sanders Theatre.

Sincerely yours,

Keith Martin
Manager[10]

The use of the theatre was granted.

Early in the planning stages for this concert, Holst received a rather extensive piece of written correspondence from the west coast:

Henry C. Huntington Library
and Art Gallery
San Marino, California

My dear Mr. Holst,

In Boston about a fortnight ago you may remember that at Mrs. Lamb's house, I spoke to you about the possibility of setting Harvard words to the melody in the "Jupiter" section of your "Planets," which impressed me as a song. One season I had heard the Symphony Orchestra play that composition. You then told me that you had used the melody previously for Cecil Spring Rice's "I vow to thee, my country," but if I did not misunderstand you, that you would not object to my attempting some verses in the same measure that might prove suitable for Harvard choruses. In a journey across the continent I have just made such an attempt, and enclose the result--with the hope that you may not too unwillingly have your stirring song joined, at Harvard, with these words. If you are not, I shall be happy to call the matter to the attention of Dr. Davison, for the Glee club and Mr. Malcolm [,] for the Harvard Alumni Chorus. Is what I have done at all worthy of your music?

....You may notice that instead of following in the model of repeating two complete frames, the stanza and Spring Rice's which you set, I have written four new lines--fitting the same musical space, I hope in an appropriate verse.

Whether the words of mine are worthy to be sung or not, I have to thank you for the impulse towards creating them--one of the consequential attributions from a long journey.

If you are not unwilling, a word if what I have done is at all worthy to your music, I cannot help thinking that Dr. Davison with the Glee Club and Mr. S. Malcolm with the Harvard Alumni Chorus--or both of them--will want to undertake the quest.

DeWolfe Howe[11]

At the time of the above letter, Mark Antony DeWolfe Howe was a visiting scholar at Huntington Library in San Marino, California. He was a well-known and respected author, generally dealing with non-fiction and musical happenings. In 1931, the year before Holst's lectureship, the revised and extended second edition of his book *The Boston Symphony Orchestra* was published in coordination with the orchestra's golden anniversary. Howe was also an editor, having edited *The Atlantic Monthly* (as well serving as its vice president from 1911 to 1929), *Harvard Alumni Bulletin*, and *Harvard Graduate Magazine*. Having been an Overseer of Harvard University, he carried a lot of weight.

This was not the first time that Holst had been approached about such a thing. Nine years earlier he had received a similar request from English poet and playwright John Drinkwater. Holst gave the following response:

St. Paul's Girls' School
Brook Green, Hammersmith
W6
Dec. 11, 1923

Dear Mr. Drinkwater,

Thank you for your kind letter. I am very glad that you realize the difficulty of occasional work. I am bad at this sort of thing and get worse every year. In fact the last time I was asked to do anything of the sort I failed completely until a lucky day when I discovered that the poem that had been sent me fitted a tune in one of the Planets. I am going to keep your poem by me for some time and earnestly hope that I shall be able to rise to the occasion. I have known your work and enjoyed it for many years and it is both a privilege and a pleasure to feel that we are working together.

Yours sincerely,

Gustav Holst

Let us try and meet soon![12]

This was not the first time that the Boston Symphony Orchestra and Harvard University Glee Club had been approached about singing words written to somebody else's music. In fact in 1920, Howe had written "The Answer of the Stars" with the two groups in mind. Pierre Monteux, then conductor of the Boston Symphony, started working on it but did not want to take the chance in performance with only one full rehearsal.[13]

This time, for whatever reason, Howe received a positive response:

Harvard University
Division of Music
Cambridge Massachusetts
March 16 [1932]

Dear Mr. Howe

Please excuse delay. We are going to try to sing your words at the concert of April 14.

Thank you for them!

Yrs in haste

Gustav Holst[14]

Being the professional that he was, it was probably not Holst's intent to let his response to Howe slide. Holst was extremely busy. There is a possibility, however, that Holst's response could have been prompted by another request from Howe, a request sent to Archibald Davison:

March 11, 1932

Dear Dr. Davison,

I have been of several minds about writing you this letter and enclosing the verses which accompany it. Some ten days ago I sent a copy of them to Mr. Holst in pursuance of a talk I had had with him before leaving Boston about the possibility of setting Harvard words to a melody in the Jupiter section of his suite "The Planets" which greatly impressed me when I heard him conduct it in Symphony Hall. He confirmed my belief that it would lend itself to the singing of a male chorus by telling me that he had himself so emplyed it in connection with some words of Cecil Spring Rice--"I Vow to Thee, My Country." Mr. Holst had no objection to a Harvard setting to it and my words, written on my journey to the West, represent an attempt in this direction.

I should not be writing to you but should be patiently to hear from him, if I had not seen in a recent Bulletin that you were preparing a Holst concert for Sanders Theatre in April. It occurs to me that he may himself hesitate to suggest the singing of these words to his stirring melody. Perhaps I should feel the same hesitation, but if they are ever to be used, this would certainly seem to be the time and place for them. I am therefore throwing modesty to the winds and calling the matter to your attention. If there does not seem to you to be a Harvard song in the joining together of Mr. Holst's music and my words, please say so quite candidly and be assured that I shall understand.

Very sincerely yours,

Mark Antony deWolfe Howe[15]

A rejection, however, was not in the works:

Harvard University
Division of Music
Cambridge, Massachusetts
March 19, 1932

Dear Mr. Howe,

Some time ago Mr. Holst showed me your Harvard words. We both liked them very much, but thought that in some particulars they could be improved for singing. I understand that he has not yet gotten around to writing you. We are going to sing your words as they stand to the Jupiter tune at the concert in April.

When you return to Boston, we might talk over the text and I can show you what his suggestions are.

With very best wishes,

Sincerely yours,

Archibald T. Davison[16]

Howe was thrilled:

March 26, 1932

Dear Dr. Davison:

I am delighted to learn from your letter of 3/19 that you are going to try my "Shores of Harvard" at the Holst concert in April and hope I may be back in time to hear it. Of course I shall be only too glad to add anything in my power to make the words more satisfactory for singing if they prove difficult to manage.

I appreciate very much your cordial response to my bold-faced offer and am

Very sincerely yours,

Mark Antony DeWolfe
Howe[17]

Hammersmith was another matter. The issue here was one of diplomacy, not process, for Holst had long finished writing out the extra parts that Goldman had requested for the April 17th concert at the American Bandmasters Association convention in Washington D.C..[18] The work had been commissioned in late 1927 by the British Broadcasting Corporation, who had requested an original one-movement work of twelve to fifteen minutes duration for its military band, a musical ensemble that performed only over the airwaves. Holst met with B. Walton O'Donnell, the band's conductor on May 8, 1928[19], but another two years would pass before Holst was able to compose the piece. As it was, Holst was paid for the work in December, 1930, even before he had orchestrated it. Once finished, *Hammersmith* was tried out in the B.B.C. Studios at Savoy Hill in rehearsal on May 19, 1931, with the composer in attendence.[20] O'Donnell instantly recognized the greatness of the work and held up its performance in the hopes that a special public concert could be arranged. In the meantime Holst, not wanting the work to remained unperformed, rescored it for orchestra. It was fortunate indeed that his friend Adrian Boult had just succeeded Percy Pitt as

Music Director for the B.B.C., for Boult was able to sanction and conduct the orchestral premiere of *Hammersmith* himself in October of 1931. In spite of this fact, Holst still felt morally obligated to ask the B.B.C.'s permission to conduct the world premiere of the military band version on the A.B.A. concert. He wrote to Boult and received the following reply:

Gustav Holst
Eliot House,
Cambridge
Massachusetts.

3rd March, 1932

I was very glad to have your letter of February 10th. Alas the double concerto with Jelly and Adila[21] is not mine to conduct. Leslie Heward is doing it that night and I am passing on to him the notes you gave me.

About "Hammersmith" and Washington on April 17th, please include it if you want to. O'Donnell tells me that he held it up because he wanted to put it into an important Military Band programme when he gets a public concert, but this is not likely to be yet I am afraid, and you must go ahead with it in Washington if you wish.

I am glad you are having such a good time. We are all well here and tremendously busy.

A.C.B.
[Adrian Cedric Boult][22]

Holst sent the following reply:

Harvard University
Division of Music
Cambridge Massachusetts
March 17, 1932

Dear Adrian:

I think it is very generous of you and O'Donnell to let me have the first military band performance of 'Hammersmith' in America, and I thank you most heartily.

Thanks for your letter. I shall not be back until July 1 and fear you will then be on your holidays. I hope the B.B.C. orchestra is enjoying life and giving enjoyment as much as ever.

My greetings to all.

Yours ever,

Gustav

P.S. I hear Stanford Robinson's performance of my two Motets[23] was even better than the one last year. Please thank him for me.[24]

With the Haydn lecture taking shape, the April 14th concert set, and the premiere of the military band version of *Hammersmith* approved, Holst was able to envision things having to do with travel. In his March 18th letter to Vally Lasker he mentioned the necessity of returning to Montreal in April. This probably did not indicate a return engagement with the Montreal Orchestra, since its last concert (a request concert) was set for March 30th. More than likely it had to do with the orchestra at McGill University, where Douglas Clarke was Dean of the Music Faculty. Entries in his notebook contain repertoire considerations:

Do Montreal concert in April no fee.

Montreal
SP Suite
Egdon
PF[25]
Emma[26]
Double Concerto
or Fugal Overture
2 Songs WW[27]

Holst's thoughts about travel did not stop with Montreal. Additional entries in his notebook indicate that he was thinking of traveling coast-to-coast. The first appears to contain thoughts on the contents of letters to Duncan McKenzie and Douglas Clarke:

letters
McKenzie D Clarke

I know Evanston prof[28]
Would Evanston make
me late for Vancouver
Don't want to give you
bother without recompense
Don't want to lose
" " " profit on Canada
leave it to you

and

Me studying Canada
best bets [illegible][29] and [illegible] Quebec
could Winnepeg be later than 9th
2) Seattle NY?
1) Robt Nelson of Pullman Wash[30] if both
NY go after Ann Arbor into Canada Banff-Vic.
Then leave by Can Nat[31] for Jasper?

and

Go direct Winnepeg to Quebec or Mont
if W NY go direct from Jasper or Banff
May have to return one day from Montreal for
final exam about June 19[32]

Cleveland, Ann Arbor, and Canada lie in the not-too-distant future, but Holst's first visit to Washington D.C. lie on the immediate horizon. Holst was extremely busy and therefore concerned about making this trip as expeditious as possible. He wrote to Carl Engel:

Harvard University
Division of Music
Cambridge Massachusetts
March 22[, 1932]

Dear Mr Engel,

If it would be possible and convenient to you and everybody else concerned for me to catch the 5 PM train from Washington to New York on Saturday directly after my lecture would you kindly send me a telegram tomorrow at Eliot House, Cambridge. In normal times I would not dream of bothering you like this but just now every moment of my time is taken up and I feel bound to ask this favour of you. If I do not hear from you by 4 PM tomorrow I will conclude that it will not suit you that I leave so early and will arrange to leave by the midnight train. So please do not trouble to answer this if you wish me to stay later.

When I come to conduct in Washington on April 17 I hope to see something of the beauties of that famous place. But this time I can only arrive on Friday at about 8:30 PM and shall only have Saturday morning free. I shall be stopping at the Continental.

Y Sincerely

Gustav Holst[33]

Engel responded with the following telegram:

Gustav Holst
Eliot House
Cambridge, Mass

LECTURE BEGINS THREE O'CLOCK SHARP. PERFECTLY FEASIBLE CATCHING FIVE O'CLOCK.

ENGEL

Library of Congress
Elisabeth Sprague Coolidge Foundation[34]

On Friday, March 25th, Holst took the 8:30 a.m. train from Boston's South Station. He arrived at New York at 2:10 p.m. and was met by Duncan McKenzie, who drove him over to New Jersey in order to catch the 3:50 p.m. express train for Washington D.C.. He arrived at Union Station at 8:30 p.m. and checked into the Hotel Continental, located just a couple of hundred feet away.[35] Holst was right; he would not see much of Washington D.C.. Union Station and the hotel were located only a few blocks due north of the Library of Congress. He wrote Engel from his hotel room:

Hotel Continental
Washington, D.C.

Dear Mr. Engel

Thank you for your kind letter of welcome.
I shall be breakfasting at about 8:30 tomorrow and would be delighted if you would join me then or later.

Yr Sincerely

Gustav Holst[36]

The following morning Carl Engel met Holst and took him to the Library of Congress. At three o'clock the composer gave his forty-minute lecture on Haydn in the Chamber Music Auditorium, followed by the Roth String Quartet's performance of Haydn's *String Quartet in D minor*, Op. 76, No. 5. The whole presentation was sponsored by the Elizabeth Sprague Coolidge Foundation. Holst wrote in his diary that he "felt faint after it."[37] The pressures of the past few weeks had taken their toll; the stress had manifested itself physically.

In an extremely weak state, Holst took the 5:00 p.m. train from Washington, retracing his route via New Jersey to Boston. It was a very difficult ride. He finally arrived at Eliot House at 8:00 a.m. the next morning. Shortly thereafter Dr. Townsend, who had tended him earlier, took Holst to New England Deaconess Hospital in Boston.[38]

---

[1]Gustav Holst, *Diary*, Tuesday, March 15, 1932, The Holst Foundation.
[2]Gustav Holst, *Diary*, Tuesday, March 22, 1932, The Holst Foundation.
[3]Gustav Holst, *Diary*, Friday, March 18, 1932, The Holst Foundation.
[4]George Bernard Shaw's play "Too True to be Good."
[5]While his Montreal host was indeed named Drinkwater, Holst may have been taking an indirect swipe at America's policy of Prohibition; Canada was not dry.
[6]Personal correspondence, Gustav Holst to Vally Lasker, March 18[, 19]32, THe Holst Foundation.
[7]Business correspondence, Eleanor Fay, Secretary, Division of Music, Library of Congress to Doris Goss, Secretary to Mrs. Hoover, March 15, 1932, Library of Congress.
[8]Business correspondence, Eleanor Fay, Secretary, Division of Music, Library of Congress to Hendley-Kaspar School, February 24, 1932, Library of Congress.

[10]Business correspondence, Keith Martin to F. W. Hunnewell, March 2, 1932, Houghton Library, Harvard University.
[11]Personal correspondence, Mark Antony DeWolfe Howe to Gustav Holst, 26 February 1932, by permission of the Houghton Library, Harvard University, bMS Am 1524 (670)..
[12]Personal correspondence, Gustav Holst to John Drinkwater, Dec[ember] 11, 1923, The Holst Foundation.
[13]Personal correspondence, Mark Antony DeWolfe Howe to Archibald Davison, April 10, 1920, by permission of the Houghton Library, Harvard University, bMS Am 1524 (344).
[14]Personal correspondence, Gustav Holst to Mark Antony DeWolfe Howe, March 16[, 1932], by permission of the Houghton University, Harvard University, bMS Am 1524 (670).
[15]Personal correspondence, Mark Antony DeWolfe Howe to Archibald Davison, March 11, 1932, by permission of the Houghton Library, Harvard University, bMS Am 1524 (344).
[16]Personal correspondence, Archibald T. Davison to Mark Antony DeWolfe Howe, March 19, 1932, by permission of the Houghton Library, Harvard University, bMS Am 1524 (344).
[17]Personal correspondence, Mark Antony DeWolfe Howe to Archibald Davison, March 26, 1932, by permission of the Houghton Library, Harvard University, bMS 1524 (344)..
[18]Gustav Holst, *Diary*, Saturday, February 13, 1932, The Holst Foundation. This is the last entry that mentions the writing of extra parts for "Emma" (*Hammersmith*).
[19]Gustav Holst, *Diary*, May 8, 1928, The Holst Foundation.
[20]Personal correspondence, Gustav Holst to B. Walton O'Donnell, May 4[, 1931], BBC Written Archives Centre.
[21]Sister violinists Jelly d'Aranyi and Adila Fachiri were the dedicatees of Holst's *Double Concerto,* Op. 49 [H175]; they premiered the work on April 3, 1930 accompanied by the Royal Philharmonic Society Orchestra under Oskar Fried. They reprised the performance two years later with Leslie Heward.
[22]Personal correspondence, A[drian] C[edric] B[oult] to Gustav Holst, 3rd March, 1932, British Library Add. MS 60498.
[23]"The Evening Watch," Op. 43, No. 1 [H159] (1924) and "Sing me the men," Op. 43, No. 2 [H160] (1925).
[24]Personal correspondence, Gustav Holst to Adrian Boult, March 17, 1932, British Library Add. MS 60498.
[25]*The Perfect Fool*, Op. 39 [H150].
[26]*Hammersmith*, op. 52 [H178].
[27]*Two Songs Without Words*, Op. 22 [H88].
[28]Probably a professor friend at Northwestern University, Evanston, IL.
[29]Brackets indicate illegible words.
[30]Home of Washington State University.
[31]Canadian National Railway.
[32]Gustav Holst, Notebook, January to July, 1932, The Holst Foundation.
[33]Personal correspondence, Gustav Holst to Carl Engel, March 22[, 1932], Library of Congress.
[34]Telegram, Carl Engel to Gustav Holst, n.d. [March 23 or 24, 1932], Library of Congress.
[35]Gustav Holst, *Diary*, Friday, March 25, 1932, The Holst Foundation.
[36]Personal correspondence, Gustav Holst to Carl Engel, 9 PM[, March 25, 1932], Library of Congress.
[37]Gustav Holst, *Diary*, Saturday, March 26, 1932, The Holst Foundation.
[38]Gustav Holst, *Diary*, Sunday, March 27, 1932, The Holst Foundation.

CHAPTER XXVIII

RECOVERY

Holst was diagnosed with hemorrhagic gastritis brought on by a duodenal ulcer. He remained in New England Deaconess Hospital for sixteen days. During this time he was cheered up by a letter from Imogen:

Hill Cottage
Gt. Easton,
Dunmow,
Essex
March 14th [1932]

Dear G,

Thank you for your letter. Eliot House is proving a serious rival to Brook Green.[1]

Your last batch of press-cuttings are quite as annoying as Spider Boy:--and I notice that your technique is somewhat similar to the famous chapter where the victim signs the contract....[2]

She continued, rejecting Holst's proposal about her seeking a teaching position in the United States. Holst responded from his hospital bed:

New England Deaconess
Hospital
Deaconess Road

Boston, Massachusetts
March 31[, 1932]

Dear Imo

Thanks for your nice long letter. I agree with every word of it. I only asked you because if you wanted a job over here I could wrangle you a far better one than you would have got any other way except sheer chance.

I hope you'll receive this but fear you won't because it ought to have gone 2 days ago.

Please spend enclosed in Riotous Living.

B L

G

You can cash it at a
bank or ask Woody.
Val is a darling.[3]

Indeed Val was a darling. A touring company of "Hay Fever" came to Boston on Easter Sunday, March 27th, the very day that Holst was taken to the hospital. Valerie was in the cast and took time for daily visits.

For Holst, professional activity had ground to a halt. All commitments made up to April 14th were cancelled; this suspension would eventually be extended to include his conducting of *Hammersmith* in Washington, D.C. and lecturing on his work at Morley College at the Cleveland Music Educators National Conference. He was forced to rest--and to ponder. He wrote about his hospital experiences, both outer and inner, in a lengthy letter to Ralph Vaughan Williams:

Harvard University
Division of Music
Cambridge, Massachusetts
April 15[, 1932]

Dear R

I'm sorry--

a) that I didn't stop to see you at the Dyson concert the night before

I sailed; but I was tired and rather bored:

b) that my boat got in to NY six hours late so that I could not send a cable to you and Biddy[4] during the Dorking concert as I had meant to:

c) that all the time I have merely thought of all the tings I wanted to write to you instead of doing the job.

And now comes your lovely long letter--many many thanks.

And its grand news about the Magnificat and I hope to see it soon. Steuart's theology sounds a little unorthodox but his common sense is unquestionable.

I've had a lovely suite of rooms at Eliot house with a good quiet study. So far I've written two more male voice choruses for Davison's choir.

How's the New Sym? When I get home in July I want a 2 piano field day of both old and new versions. When do you arrive in the USA? How long will you stay? And will you be able to visit Harvard? In that case I'll lend you Davison's front door key. Please tell HPA I'll do the same to him. It's a useful thing to have in this country.

I'm very glad I've made use of Duncan McKenzie (OUP) as an agent. He has been really helpful and I hope you'll at least consider using him. The alternative would be to print 1000 forms--

> 'Dear Sir or Madame
>
> I'll be damned before I'll conduct, lecture, dine, be interviewed, be photographed'--

I forget the others but there are a few left. You'd probably have to accept all the Mus Docs[5]--I've just refused the 2nd in a month.

I've had three new experiences this year:

I. Pretending to be a star conductor. You know all about that now. It was wildly exciting and I had a lovely time with the orchestra.

II. Pretending to be a University Professor. Which is Rum. My idea of composition is to spoil as much MS paper as possible. But my pupils here would rather write a thesis on Schoenberg's use of the bass clarinet compared with von Webern's: or, better still, talk vaguely about the best method of introducing the second subject in the recapitulation. And some of these boys have studied hard--if not music, anyhow books on music. Is it this University or is it America? I got square with one ultra-modernist, wrong-note merchant by pointing out that I was an old fogey who was here only two months more and that when

I'd gone he could make up for lost time but that until then he'd better humour me and even, occasionally, write a tune. And he answered cordially, 'Sure'!

III. On Easter Day, after lecturing on Haydn in Washington the previous day and having a horrid 14 hour journey back at night, they took me to hospital with a duodenal ulcer. And I learnt the real meaning of the phrase 'A Bloody Nuisance'. They reckoned that I lost two quarts. They gave me

a) blood transfusion which was invigorating at first but which gave me a high fever the next day:

b) morphia which is altogether delightful:

c) five days diet of 'creamed milk' every hour which was infernal.

I had one beautiful experience which was repeated two nights later. I felt I was sinking so low that I couldn't go much further and remain on earth. As I have always expected, it was a lovely feeling although the second time, as it began, I had a vague feeling that I ought to be thinking of my sins. But a much stronger feeling was that there was something more important on hand and that I mustn't waste time. Both times, as soon as I reached bottom I had one clear, intense and calm feeling--that of overwhelming Gratitude. And the four chief reasons for gratitude were Music, the Cotswolds, RVW and having known the impersonality of orchestral playing.

I was in hospital 16 days and since then have been staying at the Davisons who are dears. Every day I've been getting stronger and walking more....

My movements are uncertain. If the doctor allows I go to conduct at Ann Arbor about May 17 and then on to Vancouver Island after which a holiday in the Rockies and then home.

But I'm running many risks and if all these nights and meals on trains won't do I'll come back in the middle of June.

Love to Adeline.

Get on with the Symphony.[6]

Yrs Ever

Gustav[7]

Two days before he left the hospital he wrote to Vally Lasker:

New England Deaconess
Hospital
Deaconess Road
Boston, Massachusetts
April 9. [19]32

D V

Thank you for yrs of Good Friday.

I wrote the night before[,] giving you all my plans which are now so much waste paper. Youv'e heard of my illness before now. If you'd like details I'll tell you them later on. At present I'm too lazy.

This is a fine hospital with a first rate doctor who is a good amateur Bach singer and he took no end of trouble for me. One of the first things that happened when he brought me here[8] was that they gave me blood tranfusion. I found out after that he'd given his own--he said he'd love to feel that his blood helped to make beautiful music.

The Davisons have just called to tell me that I'm to go there when I leave here early next week, and that Amanda is sharpening her biceps in case I ever need carrying up to bed!

Valerie has been playing in Boston and has spent every spare moment here. She is a dear and I love her wildly.

This is a hurried bed written scrawl for you to get before the mail goes.

Later on I'll write you a real Letter!

Y

G[9]

By Monday, April 11th, Holst had recovered sufficiently to leave the hospital. He spent the next week with the Davisons at their home on Francis Avenue, where he stayed in an upstairs bedroom.[10] He wrote a high-spirited letter to Imogen:

April 12[, 1932]
Music Dep:
Harvard

Dear Imo

Many many birthday greetings with much happiness and hard grind for the next 12 months. I'm celebrating your birthday by leaving hospital. I am staying at the Davisons and giving them lots of bother therefore Amanda is in perfect bliss.

Valerie has been a darling. She and Emil are coming to England for June and have to return by July 1 just when I hope to get home (It is just possible that I may come earlier but not likely).

Emil is a superb character actor and is one of those lucky artists who is known and admired by everyone with brains and ignored by everyone who hasn't. But he badly needs a holiday and Val and I want June to do wonders for him. I'm just telling you this although I don't see what you can do. Probably he and Val will have a walk in the Cotswolds and I know they'd love to have you. (How I'd love to be with you all!)

I've suggested

Burford--Bourton on Water
Bourton--Chipping Campden
Campden via Winchcome, Stanway
Stanton and perhaps Broadway
(2 days or a bit of motorbus) to Cheltenham.

I hope Gerald Forty will meet him and that they will visit all the spots where they behaved badly when young and will generally wallow in sentamentalism! After that there's Cireter[11]!

But the important duty for you towards your uncle is to see that the material for his reminiscences gets written either by him, Val or you. Take him to the George[12] and make him talk! Few living people know the stage as he has known it and his stories are priceless.

Time's up and I meant to have written about you and it's too late! Set your Pa a good example by doing so yourself.

I hope that life continues Good!

B L G[13]

Valerie visited Holst at the Davisons on Wednesday, the 13th. The following day she bade him farewell, apparently with her company, before departing for New York.[14] That evening, which originally had been set aside for the Holst concert at Sanders Theatre, was now used for a Glee Club rehearsal. The concert itself had been postponed to the 27th, with rehearsals scheduled for the 21st and

25th.[15]

Holst continued to recuperate. He spent much of his week at the Davisons writing letters, although he was able to do some arranging as well. On April 17th, safeguarded at the Davisons from a freak spring snow, Holst finished his string arrangement of *A Moorside Suite* [H173] (1928), originally composed for brass band, and now intended for the St. Paul's Girls' School Junior Orchestra, the training orchestra that Vally Lasker conducted. He was thinking about adding some optional woodwind parts (as per the *St. Paul's Suite*) and of making a cut:

> Moorside
> March
>   cut F?
> ob cl in scherzo[16]

Holst decided against the cut, although he did simplify the end of the march. He wrote to Vally Lasker:

> Harvard University
> Division of Music
> Cambridge, Massachusetts
> April 17. [19]32
>
> Dear Vally
>
> At last I have finished and more or less corrected the string arrangement of the Moorside Suite[17] and am sending it to you with this letter. (It may arrive a bit later.)
>
> This arrangement is written for your orchestra (I mean the SPGS Junior not any of your others[18]!). But I shall not write any dedication until I know that it is satisfactory. At present I feel that it just <u>won't</u> <u>do</u>!
>
> I only like the music in places. But apart from that I've not been able to make it easy enough. The obvious truth being that it is not real string music.
>
> Still, if you like to have a shot at it get Amy or someone to copy the parts and ask Nora to pay the bill and to add it to all the other bills she will present to me on my return.
>
> You and others are at liberty to edit it freely. As you know, it has been done at odd moments when I've usually been too tired to do anything else and I've finished it during convalescence when I've felt a bigger ass than

usual. The chief stupidity is the scratching out of the last bar of line 3 of page 1 which--as far as I can see in my present addled condition--is OK. So see that it is copied into the parts.

The USA is a wonderful country and apparently it manages to exist without gum![19] I hope the patches will stick on until the score gets to the J.T.[20].

Well, here it is with my greetings and love to the SPGS Junior Orchestra and its conductor.

Y Ever

Gustav

When you have been through it I think you'll agree that it is my duty to write a Real string suite for the SP Jun Orch.[21]

Re my brother Emil. If Valerie wants to go walking in the Cotswolds with him and you still have the macintosh would you lend it [to] her? Also there is a second rucksack for her in my dressing room at school. I'm afraid I've suggested to him that he ask you to put him up if he needs a room in town for a night.

Re Emil's brother. I'm getting stronger every day and am getting in a fair amount of walking.[22]

April 17th was also the day that Holst was to have conducted the world premiere of the original military band version of *Hammersmith*, Op. 52 [H178] at the American Bandmasters Association convention in Washington D.C.. According to the *Marine Band Leader's Log* Captain Taylor Branson, Conductor of the United States Marine Band, conducted the work on the concert.[23] The printed program contains the following brief note from the composer to Victor Grabel, ABA Secretary, thanking the association for conferring an honorary membership[24] upon him:

Dear sir:

Thank you for your letter and for the honour you do me, which I have much pleasure in accepting.

It was a deep disappointment to me that I was unable to come to the

Washington concert.

Yours sincerely,

Gustav Holst[25]

On the following day, Monday, April 18th, Holst returned to his lodgings at Eliot House. Though not fully recovered--if fact, he would never be fully recovered--he felt strong enough to resume independent living. The next day was a Tuesday, which would have meant teaching his composition classes, had it not been for the fact that this particular Tuesday was April 19th, Patriot's Day, a holiday in Massachusetts that features the running of the Boston Marathon. Holst was undoubtedly thankful for the extra time off. He was able to do some more sketches for the Shilkret piece and attended a string quartet concert the next evening.[26] He resumed teaching the next day and at least attended, if not assuming an active role in, some choral rehearsals for the upcoming Sanders Theatre concert.

The next few days were spent in preparing a second version of "How Mighty Are the Sabbaths." Holst had had some difficulty with the original male-voice version of this chorus, particularly at the end, where he realized the necessity of adding a treble chorus. To get around this, he did an alternative unison version. Notebook entries reveal his difficulty:

X How Mighty are X
needs women's chorus at end or transposition
would you prefer another one dedicated to you[27]--
take score.
how much do I pay Schmidt for correcting?

Another entry states:

How mighty
alter opening
2 scores, 1 pf score[28]

Holst, as always, wanted to have his music performed and was not opposed to reorchestrating his work as needed The title page of the full score reveals this:

To Archibald Davison and the Harvard Glee Club

Full Score
How Mighty are the Sabbaths

Words by Helen Waddell from the Latin of Peter Abelard — Music by Gustav Holst

Chorus for male voices
and _ad lib_ chorus forof treble voices

with accompaniment for full orchestra or string orchestra or organ

Note: When a chorus of trebles is not available and the work is accompanied by strings only or by organ the melody for the treble voices is to be played by a trumpet.

When accompanied by strings or organ the effect will be heightened by the addition of a piano playing the melody in octaves.

Eliot House
Harvard
Feb-March 1932[29]

Holst finished the unison version on Sunday, April 24th. In spite of the time put into its creation and its dedication, neither version of "How Mighty Are the Sabbaths" would be performed during Holst's stay.

The next day, Monday, April 25th, Holst, feeling significantly better, decided that Davison could use a break (as well as a partial repayment for his kindness) and took over his morning class in choral composition. That evening a full rehearsal, choirs plus orchestra, was held for the concert. Duncan McKenzie arrived the following morning presumably for the next day's concert, but almost certainly he also came to discuss Holst's recent cancellations and to see what plans, however modified, could be made for professional appearances during composer's remaining time in the United States. The reminders of broken engagements and a teaching day summed up by the simple diary designation of "class poor"[30] could not have left Holst in high spirits. He rested most of the next day.

That evening, at 8:30 p.m., the once-postponed concert honoring Holst was given by the Harvard Glee Club and the Radcliffe Choral Society at Sanders Theatre. The substantial program, made possible by the friends of the Harvard

Glee Club and the Radcliffe Choral Society[31], featured the following:

St. Paul's Suite	Gustav Holst
On the Plains, Fairy Trains	Thomas Weelkes
Five Love Songs	Johannes Brahms
Adoramus Te	Giovanni Pierluigi Palestrina
Fire, Fire, My Heart	Thomas Morley
I Will not Leave You Comfortless	William Byrd

Intermission

The Shores of Harvard	Gustav Holst
A Dirge for Two Veterans	Gustav Holst
I Love My Love	Gustav Holst
Hecuba's Lament	Gustav Holst
Swansea Town	Hampshire Folk Song (Holst)
Before Sleep	Gustav Holst
Psalm CXLVIII	Gustav Holst[32]

Holst was really moved by the concert; his spirits soared. He mentions the concert in a short unaddressed letter written to Vally Lasker, one in which he also clarifies his handwriting on a previous letter:

Harvard University
Division of Music
Cambridge, Massachusetts
April 28. [19]32

Of course it's Wildly. There ain't nothing Mild about me and my Valerie. Congratulate me!-- After wasting countless opportunities in my youth I have at last fallen in love with an actress! I'm also bursting with family pride when I think of my little (?) brother.

I only wish I could have them both here. It's still doubtful whether we can all travel back together.

I wish also that you--and they--and ND[33]--and RVW[34]--and the other people who matter--could have been here last Wednesday. It was a lovely experience.

Perhaps the climax was the Dirge[35]. Some of those boys sang it by heart!

Yrs in five weeks!

Gustav[36]

He later wrote to Imogen:

> That concert was the happiest night I've had in the USA. It was like Morley College on a large scale. Those youngsters sang some of my things by heart. One can't have a higher compliment than that! And the 1st trumpet of the Boston Symphony Orchestra *wanted to return his fee!*[37]

Mark Antony DeWolfe Howe arrived in time from California to hear the concert and the Harvard Glee Club to sing "The Shores of Harvard," which he set to the middle section of Holst's "Jupiter." He wrote to Archibald Davison:

> April 28, 1932
>
> Dear Dr. Davison:--
>
> I tried to see you after the concert last night, so say in person how greatly I appreciated the use of my words written for Mr. Holst's melody. The tune seemed to justify completely my first feeling that it was well adapted to choral singing. I only hope that the joining of the words and music bore some relation to Milton's definition, "Sphere born harmonious sisters voice and verse."
>
> If you and the others were as little disturbed as I was by the uses of the letter S, perhaps no revision will be called for. But I stand ready to make any experience which you may recommend. Before the lines are printed again, I should be able to see the word "those" in the fourth line from the end changed to "these" and "towards" to "toward"--which will eliminate one S. When we next meet, I should like also to make one small suggestion on a point of emphasis. Much as I enjoyed the rendering last night, I shall still be eager to hear the first singing of the song by men alone, under your leading.
>
> Very sincerely yours,
>
> Mark Antony DeWolfe Howe

Whether this was dilitantism, pedantry, or just a sincere quest for perfectionism is not clear. Whatever the case, Davison responded diplomatically:

Harvard University
Division of Music
Cambridge, Massachusetts
May 7, 1932

Mr. Mark Antony DeWolfe Howe
26 Brimmer Street
Boston, Massachusetts

Dear Mr. Howe,

I will see that the slight changes you made are entered in the text.

We are planning to do "The Shores of Harvard" Harvard Night at the Pops when we shall have the full body of Symphony strings and men's voices. It ought to sound well. For some curious reason the whole thing is quite ineffective when accompanied by piano only. I am of the opinion that we may be able to rectify this by arranging the accompaniment for four hands. I intend to talk to Mr. Holst about the possibility.[38]

I am delighted that you could be at the concert Wednesday, but I am sorry that you did not get some public recognition for the splendid text[39]. Incidentally, I am planning to do "The Shores of Harvard" at Commencement with brass band when perhaps it will be even more impressive than with strings. We shall see!

Very sincerely yours

Archie Davison

[P.S.] I have just learned that for reasons of economy our Commencement band is to be cut from 31 to 25 men. This will force us to make some changes in the program. If Holst thinks 25 men a sufficiently large group we shall do the "Shores of Harvard."[40]

Howe replied:

May 10, 1932

Dear Davison:--

Thank you very much for your letter of the 7th. I shall certainly try to be on hand when "The Shores of Harvard" is sung at the Pop[s] Concert, and I shall hope to hear that the reduction of the band on Commencement Day will not eliminate the "number."

When I last wrote, I mentioned a small point of which I wanted to speak to you some day. May I do so now--of course with the understanding that I am offering nothing but the merest suggestion. It is that at the end of the sixth line it might be well to make a slight hold and pause on the word "wise." This would mark the distinction between the young and the old which I tried to put into my verses, and missed in the singing of the song under Mr. Holst's leadership. You will know far better than I whether anything is to be gained by acting on this suggestion, and I hardly need add that I am sure to be satisfied, whatever you may do with it.

Very sincrely yours,

Mark Antony DeWolfe Howe[41]

It is quite natural that Howe would miss his own textual inflections in a performance under Holst's leadership. The composer did not originally conceive the piece to be sung! Such "popularizations" of his pieces bothered Holst, and having to conduct Howe's words to the middle section of "Jupiter" may have been internally upsetting. Nothing has survived in writing, however, that indicates any specific displeasure that Holst may have had with Howe's verse. Davison had to be diplomatic; it is not known whether he shared any information from Howe's letters with Holst. It is also possible that, being a triple alumnus of Harvard University, Davison may have felt differently from Holst. More than four years later, on the morning of September 18, 1936, at an alumni function held as part of the Harvard Tercenteniary Celebration, Howe's words set to "Jupiter" were sung once again.[42]

The day after the concert honoring him, Holst finished correcting proofs of "How Mighty Are the Sabbaths" and "Before Sleep." That evening he attended a Boston Symphony concert featuring works by Haydn and Hill. He may have been approached by Koussevitzky after the concert about additional recent works that he might have written, for he wrote the following three days later:

Harvard University
Division of Music
Cambridge, Massachusetts
May 1[, 1932]

Dear Dr Koussevitzky

In answer to your kind request I am sending you my double concerto[43] score. It has not been done in America yet as far as I know but of course it is not in my power to promise you the first performance here.

I take this opportunity of thanking you and your famous orchestra for all the delight I have had in your splendid concerts.

Yr Sincerely

Gustav Holst[44]

Holst also attended a concert of the Bach Cantata Club at the Fogg Art Museum the following evening, but did not want to overextend himself. He stayed overnight with the Davisons since there was a ball held at Eliot House.[45]

On the first of May, Holst began to work in earnest on the commissioned piece for Nathaniel Shilkret. He finished the sketches in a mere three days and wrote out an amazing twenty pages of the full score on the next. Holst attended the Boston Pops concert on the fifth, when the orchestra performed George Gershwin's *Second Rhapsody*, but it is doubtful that his hearing Gershwin had much of an effect on the Shilkret piece since it was already so far along. He wrote of his work to Vally Lasker:

Harvard University
Division of Music
Cambridge, Massachusetts
May 6. [19]32

D V

Thanks for [your] nice long letter of April 26. I can't make out two or three words but gather that you've spring cleaned and are well and have a nephew who will protect you from an influx of my family. Since you wrote you've learnt that I am coming home early in June. Emil doesn't yet know when he'll be free but we ought to be in London around June 8.

I've only one piece of fresh news and I fear you won't approve of it. In fact you may dislike it very much indeed. But I feel sure you would rather know the truth without further prevarication and then try to get over the shock, however great it may be. The news I feel I ought to break to you gently but firmly is that at about 5 PM on May 1, I suddenly ceased to feel homesick. And I haven't managed to get back the feeling since.

Probably the reason is that at the above mentioned moment--or thereabouts--I started writing something for the super jazz band conductor in New York and I've thought of little else since--except, of course, writing strictly business letters like this one, paying income tax, giving lessons, seeing the doctor who approves of my condition. He--the jazz merchant not the doctor, wanted me to write something on American tunes but I find that I prefer my own. So probably he won't accept it. But it's good fun to be spoiling MS paper again.

All the same, the thought of being in Brook Green again is a pleasing one.

Will both orchestras play for the League Sale? And Together or separately? And shall we invite fathers like Joseph and Eliot to join in?

Y

G

And now for a piece of nice news--I find that the Boston Symphony Orchestra loves me as much as I love it![46]

Yet things were not quite as good as they seemed. Friday, May 6th, the day of his letter to Vally Lasker, Holst was very busy, with tutoring at nine o'clock in the morning followed by a trip to the Boston income tax office, lunch at The Harvard Club with Arthur Foote, a meeting with Dr. Townsend at 2, a visit to an art gallery, and a good walk.[47] All of this activity was too much and Holst had a mild relapse that night. Townsend came to see him the next day and apparently gave the composer a clean bill of health since, according to his diary, there was no cessation of activity. Holst was cautious, however, and did take it easy, not doing any work until that evening. On the following day, Sunday, May 8th, Holst finished the Shilkret full score. Two days later he accompanied Thomas Surette to Beaver School and on the following day completed the piano duet version of the Shilkret piece.

It appears that Holst had little trouble in writing the work. One item that did cause him difficulty, however, was finding an appropriate title. *Shilkret Piece*, *Mr. Shilkret's Dump* and *Mr. Shilkret's Folly* were tried out before he finally settled on *Mr. Shilkret's Maggot*.[48] By the term "maggot," Holst was not referring to insect larva, but to a fetish or fancy. It was not the first time this term had crossed his path. A 1926 diary entry reads "Memo Purcell etc. Mr. Isaac's Maggott."[49] In the long run, however, the title didn't. matter. Shilkret rejected the piece for the reason cited in Holst's letter--it wasn't based on a folk theme. Later in the year he wrote to Duncan McKenzie:

> I regard to your recent letter regarding Mr. Gustav Holst; I spoke to Holst about writing something for my composers' series on folk-music themes, for a short radio piece (not longer than 5 or 6 minutes). Instead Mr. Holst gave me a short modernistic composition called "Shilkret's Maggot." I am very enthusiastic about this little number and hate to give it up, but I cannot play it...because it is not based on a definite English or American folk theme. Will Mr. Holst write me another composition (I think I mentioned "Three Blind Mice" to him) for the stipulated $200.00?[50]

He did not. Even if Shilkret had accepted the work, it is doubtful that the piece would have won acceptance with the average 1932 jazz listener. For one thing, it begins with an extended viola solo; for another, there is no real jazz in it, only some syncopation. *Mr. Shilkret's Maggot* [H185] is still Holst, just as *The Ebony Concerto* that Stravinsky wrote for Woody Herman's band more than a decade later is still Stravinsky. In the late 1960's Imogen Holst edited *Mr. Shilkret's Maggot* for symphony orchestra and renamed it *Capriccio*, but it would be another two decades before the work would be performed in its original version.[51]

In the meantime, Holst had decided to follow through with his plans to go to Ann Arbor. He wrote of the past week's activity and future plans to Vally Lasker:

Harvard University
Division of Music
Cambridge, Massachusetts
May 12[, 1932]

D V

Yrs of the 3rd arrived and I'm duly shocked. If it had come in Feb I'd have taken you at your word and written about once in 6 weeks--(probably I should have kept it up for nearly a fortnight!)

As for questions I don't mind answering them when they are not silly--and asking if I mind if you add oboe and clar to Moorside Is![52]

After which I feel better.

Thanks for offers to put up the family but there's no need to. Everything is still vague. Probably Valerie won't be able to come until August. But I shall be deeply disappointed if Emil doesn't come with me because he wouldn't be able to come later and we're counting on being together again in Cheltenham and thereabouts.

All I can do is to hold myself ready to go the moment he finds he is free. I fear it looks as if I should arrive on Tuesday June 7 but I can't tell yet. I have all sorts of wild dreams about what we'll do when we do arrive. Probably we shall both need two days in London. Anyhow I want a Thursday at school if Charles allows so I'm certain to see both you and Nora. But I'm not going to settle down until Emil goes which will be about June 20 I expect.

I started my piece for the NY Jazz band on May 1 finished the sketch on the 3rd, began to score on 4th, finished it on the 8th when I began the 2 piano version which I finished yesterday (the 11th).

The score has gone to Shilkret the bandmaster in NY and I'm sending the pf duet to Amy to be copied. He wanted folktunes and I've used my own but he's going to try it just before I sail for home.

I suggest that you three ND, HB, VL[53] make it a trio by one playing the opening melody on the viola whenever it comes (always at the viola pitch as at first) bearing in mind that in bar 2 on p 10 the rhythm alters. Also the viola might sustain the long holding notes for violin in places. However you three can settle it for yourselves. I've not written anything so quickly for years and have no idea whether I shall be able to listen to it without feeling ill.

I go tomorrow to Ann Arbor and get back here on the 21st. Of course letters will be forwarded.

On the 26th I finish my last class at 4 PM and with luck, catch the 5 PM boat for NY. The rest depends on Emil but I hope to hear my piece at the radio on Shilkret's band before I leave, and to leave by the Mauretania on June 1 at the latest. I'm almost certain to arrive in time to get to Ealing on my first night but if it is very late I'll send a wire from Southampton to you unless it's a Tuesday or Wednesday in which case I'll go to Ealing no matter how late it is.

I did not a) conduct Emma[54] at Washington, b) lecture at Cleveland c) go again to Montreal: and I'm not going to Vancouver.

I've done most other things I meant to.

Y

G

Will[55] has invited me to jaw in Glasgow. I've invited him him to the J. T.[56] en route for his holiday in Eisenach. Anyhow I've given him a broad hint:

I hope Mrs. Eslemond is really well now also Miss Wix: and that Overstone flourishes.

The following day Holst began his journey to Ann Arbor by boarding the 4:15 p.m. train from South Station.

---

[1]St. Paul's Girls' School, where Holst did most of his composing, is located on Brook Green in Hammersmith.

[2]Personal correspondence, Imogen Holst to Gustav Holst, March 14 th[, 1932], The Holst Foundation.

[3]Personal correspondence, Gustav Holst to Imogen Holst, March 31[, 1932], The Holst Foundation.

[4]Helen Bidder.

[5]Honorary Doctor of Music degrees offered by various institutions of higher learning.

[6]Ralph Vaughan Williams' *Symphony no. 4.*

[7]Personal correspondence, Gustav Holst to Ralph Vaughan Williams, April 15[, 1932], quoted in Ursula Vaughan Williams (ed.) and Imogen Holst (ed.), *Heirs and Rebels: Letters to Each Other and Occasional Writings by Gustav Holst and Ralph Vaughan Williams* (Oxford: Oxford University Press, 1959), 79-81.

[8]This plus Holst's diary entry for March 27, 1932 would seem to indicate that this was Dr. Townsend.

[9]Personal correspondence, Gustav Holst to Vally Lasker, April 9, [19]32, The Holst Foundation.

[10]Gustav Holst, *Diary*, Monday, April 11 and Tuesday, April 12, 1932, The Holst Foundation.

[11]Possibly Cirencester.

[12]The George, on Hammersmith Broadway, Holst's favorite pub.

[13]Personal correspondence, Gustav Holst to Imogen Holst, April 12[, 1932], The Holst Foundation.

[14]Gustav Holst, *Diary*, Thursday, April 14, 1932, The Holst Foundation.

[15]Petition, Keith Martin, manager of the Harvard Glee Club to the Corporation of Harvard University, n. d. [April, 1932], Houghton Library, Harvard University.

[16]Gustav Holst, Notebook, January to July, 1932, The Holst Foundation.

[17]This version of *A Moorside Suite* [H173] received its world premiere November 21, 1994 by the University of Massachusetts Boston Chamber Orchestra, the author conducting.
[18]Borough Polytechnic and Overstone, North Anston.
[19]Glue.
[20]The "Jolly Talgarth," Holst's nickname for Vally Lasker's townhouse at 103 Talgarth Road.
[21]Holst's *Brook Green Suite* [H191], composed the following year.
[22]Personal correspondence, Gustav Holst to Vally Lasker, April17[, 19]32, The Holst Foundation.
[23]*Marine Band Leader's Log*, April 17, 1932, Marine Barracks, Washington, D.C..
[24]According to the *American Bandmasters Association Annual*, 1932, pp. 13-14, Carl Busch, Percy Grainger, Henry Hadley, Ottorino Respighi, and Leo Sowerby also received honorary memberships.
[25]Personal correspondence, Gustav Holst to Victor Grabel, quoted in *American Bandmasters Association Annual*, 1932, 12.
[26]Gustav Holst, *Diary*, Wednesday, April 20, 1932, The Holst Foundation. The diary mentions "LSQ concert."
[27]In reference to the dedication to Archibald Davison and the Harvard Glee Club, a dedication that was allowed to stand.
[28]Gustav Holst, Notebook, January to June, 1932, The Holst Foundation.
[29]Gustav Holst, "How Mighty Are the Sabbaths," No. 5 from *Six Choruses, Op. 53* [H186], manuscript full score, Houghton Library, Harvard University.
[30]Gustav Holst, *Diary*, Tuesday, April 26, 1932, The Holst Foundation.
[31]Program, *A Concert Given in Honor of Gustav Holst*, Sanders Theatre, April 27, 1932.
[32]*Ibid.*.
[33]Nora Day.
[34]Ralph Vaughan Williams.
[35]*A Dirge for Two Veterans* [H121] (1914).
[36]Personal correspondence, Gustav Holst [to Vally Lasker], April 28[, 19]32, The Holst Foundation.
[37]Personal correspondence, Gustav Holst to Imogen Holst, quoted in Imogen Holst, *Gustav Holst: A Biography, 2nd ed.*, (London: Oxford University Press, 1969), 158.
[38]Holst had already done a two-piano arrangement of *The Planets*, but probably did not take it with him on his 1932 trip. Nora Day and Vally Lasker had likewise arranged the entire work for piano duet, which was published by F & B Goodwin in 1923. Neither arrangement was done with the possibility of adding voices in mind.
[39]In fact, Howe's name is printed beneath his words to "The Shores of Harvard" in the program.
[40]Personal correspondence, Archibald Davison to Mark Antony DeWolfe Howe, May 7, 1932, by permission of the Houghton Library, Harvard University, bMS Am 1524 (344).
[41]Personal correspondence, Mark Antony DeWolfe Howe to Archibald Davison, May 10, 1932, by permission of Houghton Library, Harvard University, bMS Am 1524 (344)..
[42]Personal correspondence, Dorothy Davison to Imogen Holst, August 30, 1936, The Holst Foundation.
[43]*Double Concerto*, Op. 49 [H175] (1930).
[44]Personal correspondence, Gustav Holst to Serge Koussevitzky, May 1[, 1932], The Holst Foundation.
[45]Gustav Holst, *Diary*, Friday, April 29, 1932, The Holst Foundation
[46]Personal correspondence, Gustav Holst to Vally Lasker, May 6. [19]32, The Holst Foundation.
[47]Gustav Holst, *Diary*, Friday, May 6, 1932, The Holst Foundation.
[48]Gustav Holst, *Mr. Shilkret's Maggot*, British Library Manuscript Add MS 47833, title page, both

sides.
[49]Gustav Holst, *Diary*, Saturday, August 21, 1926, The Holst Foundation.
[50]Business correspondence, Nathaniel Shilkret to Duncan McKenzie, November 29, 1932, quoted in Imogen Holst, *A Thematic Catalogue of Gustav Holst's Music* (London: Faber Music Ltd., 1974), 191.
[51]The original version of the work was premiered October 12, 1990 at the Mellon Institute Auditorium, Pittsburgh, Pennsylvania by the Carnegie Mellon University Wind Ensemble, the author conducting.
[52]Holst's own earlier notebook entries indicate that he was thinking of adding these parts himself.
[53]Nora Day, Helen Bidder, and Vally Lasker.
[54]*Hammersmith.*
[55]William Gillies Whittaker.
[56]The "Jolly Talgarth," Vally Lasker's townhouse at 103 Talgarth Rd.

CHAPTER XXIX

RETURN TO ANN ARBOR

Holst's return visit to the University of Michigan's May Festival in Ann Arbor had been in the works ever since he knew of Harvard's lectureship offer. Holst remembered with fondness the visit that he and his wife had made in 1923. He himself initiated the correspondence about the possibility of a return engagement, writing to Earl V. Moore, who was now Musical Director of the Festival. This was the beginning of a steady stream of correspondence:

St. Paul's Girls' School
Brook Green, Hammersmith,
W. 6
Oct[ober] 30[, 1931]

Dear Mr. Moore

I have accepted an engagement to teach composition at Harvard from February to May 1932 and hope to arrive in New York on Jan. 1.

I may go west during January but whether I do or not I hope I shall have a chance of seeing you and other Anne Arbor friends.

I would love to conduct or lecture again in Anne Arbor but probably it is too late to arrange anything. Do let me know if there is a chance. If there is not let us try and meet in NY.

Yr Sincerely

Gustav Holst[1]

Moore responded:

November 20, 1931

Mr. Gustav Holst
St. Paul's Girls' School
Brook Green, Hammersmith, W.6
London

My dear Mr. Holst:

Your letter of recent date, bringing the welcome news of your impending visit to this country as exchange professor of composition at Harvard for the second semester, has made us very happy here in Ann Arbor at the thought of a visit from you.

We are making some tentative plans for the May Festival, and this letter is to secure as much information, as you can give us at this time, as to your plans for next spring. Would it be possible for you to come to Ann Arbor in May as a guest conductor of the Festival? I have received your copy of the "Choral Phantasy" on the text by Robert Bridges and it has occurred to the writer that perhaps it would be a happy combination to have you here to conduct that work in view of Mr. Bridges' connection with this institution under the regime of Dr. Burton. All we need to know at this time is whether we can count on you being in this country at that time and whether you would care to come to Ann Arbor on that occasion. The other details will be arranged by Mr. Sink as soon as we have an answer to this query.

Hastily, but cordially yours, and with best regards to Mrs. Holst and your daughter from all the Moores, I am

Very Sincerely yours,

Earl V. Moore
Musical Director[2]

Holst's *A Choral Fantasia*, Op. 51 [H177] (1930) had been composed for Herbert Sumsion, organist of Gloucester Cathedral. Its text is from *Ode for the*

Bicentenary Commemoration of Henry Purcell by Robert Seymour Bridges (1844-1930), poet laureate of England from 1913 to 1930. Bridges' *Ode* is in ten sections; Holst used the seventh and eighth for *A Choral Fantasia.* The connection between Bridges with the University of Michigan referred to in Moore's letter is that Bridges held the Fellowship in Creative Art there during the 1923-24 academic year. During the completion of *A Choral Fantasia* Bridges passed away and Holst dedicated the work "In Homage" to him. At the time of Moore's letter, *A Choral Fantasia* had probably been performed only once, under the composer's direction on September 8, 1931 at the Three Choirs Festival at Gloucester Cathedral. Dorothy Silk, Holst's preferred soprano soloist, sang at that occasion. Now recognized as a masterpiece, the work, with its coldly austere organ solo passages, was not received favorably by the press:

> Holst Work Did Not Impress [Headline]....seemed to lack points of interest.[3]
>
> Unfortunately, with every new work he becomes more and more vague. He experiments with first one thing and then another, and in this case he not only experiments with dissonances but uses them to cover up other queer noises.[4]

Ralph Vaughan Williams offered his own commentary about this in a letter to Holst:

The White Gates
Westcott Road
Dorking
[September, 1931]

Dear Gustav

I played through the fantasia again yesterday & it is most beautiful--I know you don't care, but I just wanted to tell the press...that they are misbegotten abortions.

Yrs

RVW[5]

Although he was not swayed by the press, Holst was eager to give *A Choral Fantasia* a new lease on life through a May Festival performance. He wrote to Moore:

St. Paul's Girls' School
Brook Green, Hammersmith,
W. 6
Dec[ember] 29[, 1931]

Dear Mr. Moore

If you decide to do my Choral Fantasia would you notify the publisher (Curwens) as soon as possible as a new score[6] and set of parts will have to be copied. I send you a copy of my Double Concerto in case you care to consider doing it as well.

I leave England on Jan 8 on the Bremen and hope to reach Harvard about the 15th or 16th.

With Greetings to all

Yr Sincerely

Gustav Holst[7]

Holst also wrote to Charles A. Sink, now President of the University of Michigan School of Music, who had officially invited the composer to the May Festival:

Harvard University
Division of Music
Cambridge, Massachusetts
January 16, 1932

Mr. Charles Sink
University School of Music,
Ann Arbor, Michigan

Dear Mr. Sink:

Thank you for your kind invitation. I do not feel able to fix a fee myself and, therefore, am putting the matter in the hands of my agent, Mr. Duncan McKenzie, who will write to you from New York.

With regard to the music, I am delighted to know you are doing the "Choral Fantasia." It will probably be the first performance in America. Would you also care to do some of the part-songs for women's voices with Robert Bridge's words[8], which are published by Novello? I sent Mr. Moore my double concerto for two violins, in case he would like to include that in the program. This would be a first performance in America.

With cordial greetings to Mrs. Sink and my other friends in Ann Arbor,

Yours sincerely,

Gustav Holst[9]

One month later Holst received the following detailed letter from Sink:

February 25, 1932

Mr. Gustav Holst,
Department of Music
Harvard University
Cambridge, Massachusetts.

My dear Mr. Holst--

It is a pleasure to have completed negotiations through Mr. Duncan McKenzie whereby you are to be with us in the capacity of guest conductor at one of our Festival concerts. We shall look forward with pleasure to the event. We trust that you will enjoy your visit to Ann Arbor as much as we know that we are going to enjoy your coming.

I have not learned whether Mrs. Holst is in this country with you or not but if she is, I trust that she may come to Ann Arbor with you.

Our program is going to be very full and we are not sure whether it will be possible to include one of your orchestral selections recommended by Mr. McKenzie or not. Mr. Moore has the matter under consideration and in working out the details of the Festival program, will decide the matter as soon as possible, letting you know.

You will be interested to know that we have engaged the services of the following distinguished musicians for the event:

Goeta Ljungberg, Soprano
Juliette Lippe, Soprano
Ruth Rodgers, Soprano
Gladys Swartout, Contralto
Beniamino Gigli, Tenor
Frederick Jagel, Tenor
Nelson Eddy, Baritone
John Charles Thomas, Baritone
Chase Baromeo, Bass
Gitta Gradova, Pianist
Palmer Christian, Organist
Mr. Stock and the Chicago Symphony Orchestra
with Eric DeLamarter, Assistant Conductor, and
well as yourself in the role of guest conductor.

In addition to your own choral number, Mr. Moore with the Choral Union will present the American premiere of Rimsky-Korsakov's "Legend of the Invisible City of Kitej," which is being translated into English, Strawinsky's "Psalms" and Haydn's "Creation."

We shall probably have you appear at the opening concert, May 18, the program in which Ljungberg will probably appear. We may find it necessary, however, to shift to the following day.

Mrs. Sink joins me in cordial personal greetings.

Very cordially yours,

[Charles A. Sink]
President.

P.S. Will you be so good as to communicate with Mr. Paul C. Buckley, Manager, Michigan Union Club, as to your entertainment requirements, stating that you are doing so at my suggestion. This should be done at your early convenience, since as you know the Club there is in great demand.[10]

Holst responded immediately:

Harvard University
Division of Music
Cambridge, Massachusetts
February 29, 1932

Dear Mr. Sink:

Thank you for your letter of the 25th. My wife is not with me this time and Mr. Lockwood[11] has kindly invited me to stay with him at Ann Arbor. Therefore, I need not trouble you about the matter. Would you let both Mr. Lockwood and me know when the date of my first rehearsal is? I might be able to leave here on the night of May 12. I do not want to bother Mr. Moore about orchestral works, but as my Choral Fantasia is rather a gloomy work, I thought it might be good if we could add my orchestral arrangement of Bach's Fugue a la Gigue, which only lasts 3 1/2 minutes.

Many congratulations on your wonderful program of choral works.

Yours sincerely,

Gustav Holst[12]

Sink responded:

March 4, 1932.

Mr. Gustav Holst,
Division of Music,
Harvard university,
Cambridge, Massachusetts

My dear Mr. Holst:--

Thank you for your letter of February 29. I am sorry that Mrs. Holst is not with you. I am sure, however, that you are going to enjoy spending a few days with Mr. Lockwood at his home here.

I have conferred with Dr. Moore, and as the result of this conference, we are going to ask you to do the Bach "Fugue" which you suggested. We assume that this number will be played before the "Fantasia."

By this same mail, or shortly, you will receive a communication from another office of the University, the confidential contents of which will please you, I trust, as much as it has pleased me.

Very cordially yours,

[Charles A. Sink]
President.

[Written postscript not included in carbon copy][13]

Holst responded upon his return from Montreal and New York:

Harvard University
Division of Music
Cambridge, Massachusetts
March 16[, 1932]

Dear Dr. Sink

Please excuse delay--I have been in Canada. I enclose a synopsis of the Fantasia.

There is one word in your postscript that I cannot read. It comes after 'Please send to us the orchestral'-- for the 'Fugue'.

Could the 'Fugue a la Gigue' be played <u>after</u> the Fantasia? It must not be played just before as it would spoil the mood of the latter. The fugue is published by Boosey and Hawkes USA agent Belwyn Inc 43 W 23d Str NY (president Mr Winkler).

The organist on the Fantasia is very important and his name should appear prominently in the program. Also he and I ought to practice together.

Let me know about rehearsals. I could leave here on the evening of May 13 at the earliest. (I might even manage late on the 12th if I know in good time.)

Yr Sincerely

Gustav Holst[14]

Sink responded immediately:

March 19, 1932

Mr. Gustav Holst
Harvard University,
Division of Music,
Cambridge, Massachusetts.

My dear Mr. Holst:--

Hastily acknowledging receipt of your letter of March 16, beg to say that the word which you were unable to decipher was undoubtedly material. What I desired was to make sure that there would be no mistake in the matter of orchestral score and parts for the Fugue and also for another number which I think Dr. Moore has written you about.

Palmer Christian, our organist, is a musician of distinction and you will enjoy your work with him.

We think that it will be ample if you leave there on the evening of May 13. You could then work with Mr. Christian on Sunday etc.

Hastily, but very cordially,

[Charles A. Sink]
President.[15]

Holst also heard from Earl V. Moore, who had news of the tentative program. A performance of the *Double Concerto* would not take place, but performance of another Holst piece would:

March 22, 1932

Mr. Gustave Holst
Department of Music
Harvard University
Cambridge, Mass.

My dear Mr. Holst:

Needless to say I am delighted that you are coming to Ann Arbor to conduct at the Festival. A little later I will give you an exact schedule of the rehearsals during Festival week.

This present letter is to get your answer to a tentative program which Mr. Stock and I made up last week in Chicago.

I am sending herewith a copy of the rough draft so that you may see how we planned to present your work. At the end of the first half of the program we contemplated having you conduct (a) "A la Gigue" and (b) the "Ballet" from your opera, "A Perfect Fool." The latter you conducted on your former appearance here.

Directly after the intermission we propose to have you perform the "Choral Fantasy." We feel that this is better than trying to mix chorus and orchestra numbers in the same half of the program. If you have other suggestions, please let me know promptly so that we can include them on the advance announcement which is going to press within a few days.

Did Mrs. Holst come to this country? We are anxious to hear what Imogene is doing, and we hope that you will come to Ann Arbor sufficiently early so that we can have a visit before the rush of Festival week starts.

Very cordially yours,

Earl V. Moore
Musical Director[16]

Holst then heard again from Sink:

March 31, 1932.

Mr. Gustav Holst,
Department of Music,
Harvard University,
Cambridge, Massachusetts.

My dear Mr. Holst:--

I wonder if it would be an imposition to ask you to send us some more photographs. We could use easily a dozen or fifteen. These are utilized by us, by newspapers, and also in the preparation of large group pictures which are put on display in various windows, etc.

Hastily, but cordially,

[Charles A. Sink]
President.[17]

By this time Holst was lying in bed at Boston Deaconess Hospital, recovering from hemorrhagic gastritis brought on by a duodenal ulcer. The first notebook entry that he made there was:

cable Lambert 63 Baker Street London W1
Please send 6 of my photos[18]

He next heard from Sink:

April 16, 1932.

Mr. Gustav Holst,
Department of Music
Harvard university,
Cambridge, Mass.

My dear Mr. Holst:

I am enclosing a copy of our May Festival announcement giving in full the program for Thursday evening, May 19. You will note that Dr. Moore has you down for the "Fugue a la Gigue" as well as the "Fantasia" but not for the other two numbers. We assume that you will either send this material to us in advance or that you will bring it with you. Will you be so good as to confirm this arrangement so as to avoid any possible misunderstanding.

For your further information I am taking the liberty of sending to you under another cover a small quantity of the announcements which I thought you might like to have. Through an inadvertence your name also appears on the list of those who participate on Friday. This of course should be disregarded.

Hastily, but cordially,

[Charles A. Sink]
President.[19]

Meanwhile, word had arrived in Michigan about Holst's illness. He heard from Moore:

April 28, 1932

Mr. Gustav Holst
Department of Music
Harvard University
Cambridge, Massachusetts

My dear Mr. Holst:

I am sorry to learn of your recent illness. I knew that you must either have been away from the university on a lecture tour or else my letter had gone astray. I sincerely hope that you have recovered your strength and that you can be with us next month.

The rehearsals are progressing satisfactorally. If you are here for a rehearsal on Sunday afternoon, May 15, we can give you some time to approximate concert conditions as we will be working in the auditorium where the organ is located, and will have the University Symphony orchestra go through the string and brass parts so that the chorus will become accustomed to the sound of the instruments. The rehearsal time with the Chicago Symphony will of necessity be limited on account of the large number of compositions which must be rehearsed on the spot. Therefore I am glad that you will be here for a day or two before the orchestra arrives in order that all these details may be smoothed out.

The parts for "the Perfect Fool" ballet are here and Mr. Sink has ordered the orchestral material for the Bach "Fugue."

With best wishes, I am

Sincerely yours,

Earl V. Moore
Musical Director[20]

Holst responded:

Harvard University
Division of Music
Cambridge, Massachusetts
May 2[, 1932]

Dear Dr Moore

Thank you for your kind letter. I am getting on finely and am looking forward to arriving at Ann Arbor on the morning of the 14th. Could I go through the Choral Fantasia with Dr Christian at the organ before the rehearsal on Sunday afternoon? This would save much time.

Does the University Orchestra know the work? If not it would be better to use a piano with the organ on Sunday. Please do as you think best in the matter.

I fear I may have to leave Ann Arbor on the 20th as, owing to my illness, all my work is behind time and I have much to do before I sail for home on June 1.

It will be a big disappointment if I have to miss your performance of 'Kitesh' but at present there seems to be no chance of being able to stay for it.

Yr Sincerely

Gustav Holst[21]

Moore filled Holst in on the rehearsal situation:

May 5, 1932

Mr. Gustav Holst
Division of Music
Harvard University
Cambridge, Massachusetts

My dear Mr. Holst:

Thank you for your letter of May 2. Mr. Christian has already prepared the organ portion of your "A Choral Fantasia", and the orchestra has had two rehearsals of its share to date. I am sure Mr. Christian will be glad to go over the organ part with you after your arrival.

I am sorry that you are going to have to leave on the 20th. Perhaps you can hear the rehearsal of "Kitesh" that morning.

Cordially yours,

Earl V. Moore
Music Director[22]

Holst arrived at Ann Arbor at 9:30 a.m. the morning of Saturday, May 14th. As planned, he stayed at Albert Lockwood's Hillside Court home. That evening he had dinner at The University Club which was "followed by dull lecture."[23]

The following day, Sunday, May 15th, was Whitsunday. The rehearsal of *A Choral Fantasia* took place at 2:30 p.m., allowing Holst the time he had sought for running through the piece beforehand with Palmer Christian. All of this was followed by a garden party. Holst's diary indicates that there was a heat wave that day.[24]

Aside from a single rehearsal the following evening and, of course, the concert which involved him, the time spent by Holst in Ann Arbor was relatively relaxing. He was chauffered around by Lockwood, reacqainting himself with the university, and renewing the many friendships acquired on his previous visit. He also heard a private performance of some of his songs sung by one Miss Field.[25]

Two of Holst's relatives were on hand for the festivities. Holst's half brother Thorley, with whom he had visited during the 1923 trip, traveled from Chicago to Ann Arbor, arriving on Wednesday, the eighteenth. On the next day, the day of the concert, Thorley went to Detroit to meet Valerie and brought her (and her dog) back in time for the evening's activities.[26]

This concert, the second of the Thirty-Ninth Annual May Festival, was given on Thursday, May 19, 1932 at Hill Auditorium. In addition to Holst's compositions, the program featured works by Glazounoff, Ponchielli, Stravinsky, Wagner, and Brahms. Holst conducted his arrangement of *Bach's Fugue a la Gigue* and the "Ballet Music" from *The Perfect Fool* at the end of the first half. He also conducted *A Choral Fantasia*, which opened the second half. The university's press naturally heralded the American premiere of *A Choral Fantasia*, but in the local press Holst was upstaged by Swedish soprano Goeta Ljungberg, who sang on the same concert:

> Miss Ljungberg, according to the glowing accounts that have preceded her to Ann Arbor, possesses, in addition to an exceedingly well-trained and thoroughly delightful voice, an appearance in which are combined rare beauty and a most effective dramatic appeal. A recent reviewer in a well-known eastern paper lauded her "ravishing, dynamic blonde beauty, her amber hair, and her blue eyes that sparkled like the fjords of her native land."[27]

Holst had no chance against this latter-day Swedish nightingale; the headline toted only her. At the end of the same article appears some hilariously erroneous information about the composer:

> Tonight's performance will be the American premiere for..."A Choral Fantasia." Gustav Holst, the author, will conduct the Chicago Symphony orchestra during the performance. Mr. Holst is one of the most distinguished of the contemporary conductor-composers, according to Dr. Sink. He came to Ann Arbor as a guest conductor in 1923. Because of the great demand for his services in Germany, he has not been able to come to this country again until this year....[28]

The printed concert program gives no clue as to whether Goeta Ljungberg sang the soprano solo part on *A Choral Fantasia*. Whatever the case Holst, always skeptical of the press, would not have bothered by the attention given her.

Owing to his delicate condition, Holst decided not to stay in Ann Arbor for the remainder of the Festival and left the next morning on the 10:40 bound for Detroit. Persumably, Valerie was with him, for the two of them were able to spend four hours together in Detroit before Holst caught his train for Boston.[29] Once there, he wrote to Earl V. Moore:

> Harvard University
> Division of Music
> Cambridge, Massachusetts
> May 22[, 1932]
>
> Dear Dr Moore
>
> Many congratulations of the success of the Festival and many many thanks for training your chorus to sing my Fantasia so well. I regret that I

was unable to say goodbye to you but you were hard at work rehearsing on Friday morning and I had to hurry away as I am sailing for home next Friday, almost a week before I had arranged to go.

My greetings to Mrs. Moore.

Yrs Sincerely

Gustav Holst[30]

Shortly thereafter Holst received two letters of thanks:

May 23, 1932.

Mr. Gustav Holst,
Music Division
Harvard University,
Cambridge, Massachusetts.

My dear Mr. Holst:--

It was a real pleasure to have you with us again at the Festival, both as a friend and as a guest conductor. May I thank you warmly for your splendid contribution and help.

Mrs. Sink joins me in cordial greetings to you and Mrs. Holst.

Very cordially yours,

[Charles A. Sink]
President[31]

and:

May 26, 1932

Mr. Gustav Holst
Division of Music
Harvard University
Cambridge, Massachusetts

My dear Mr. Holst:

I am so sorry that you went away from Ann Arbor without our having a chance to say goodbye to you. I saw you at the rehearsal Friday morning and expected that I would have a chance to see you after the rehearsal was over. Mrs. Moore and I regret that we were unable to find mutually convenient time to have you over to the house. We understand perfectly that you wanted what little time you had on Thursday night with your brother and regret that you could not stay to join us on Saturday night when we had the artists of the "Kitesh" performance up for something to eat.

I want you to know that we all appreciate your coming to Ann Arbor to participate in this Festival and that your works have achieved a distinct success. I have seen only a few of the press clippings and they were all most commendatory.

For the chorus I wish to say that they felt honored that you should conduct them in the "Choral Fantasia." Of course the whole series of concerts was influenced by the passing of Dr. Stanley[32] more than we realized and I hope you will not think us ungracious in not seeing more of you during your visit here.

Mrs. Moore joins me in greetings and we hope that you will give our best wishes to Mrs. Holst and to those of our friends who may happen to inquire when you get back to England. Again may I say that it was a distinct pleasure and an honor to have you participate in this Festival and we hope that you visit us again when you come to this country.

Cordially yours,

Earl V. Moore[33]
Musical Director

A *Musical America* article that appeared after Holst's Ann Arbor departure mentions *A Choral Fantasia* in a favorable light:

> Mr. Holst's fertile gift of large scale composition was immediately thrown into relief by the inventiveness displayed by the rhythmic variety and the perfect unity achieved between orchestra and voice. The melodic lines, modal in Character but without any fixed tonal centre, flow ceaselessly to the end.

> Due to the obvious limitations of the text, the work is not very dramatic, though Mr. Holst's setting is most sympathetic.[34]

This certainly wasn't negative yet, regardless of what the press had to say about it, Vaughan Williams had been correct--and that was what mattered more to Holst.

---

[1]Personal correspondence, Gustav Holst to Earl V. Moore, Oct[ober] 30[, 1931], Bentley Historical Library, The University of Michigan.

[2]Personal correspondence, Earl V. Moore to Gustav Holst, November 20, 1931, Bentley Historical Library, The University of Michigan.

[3]*Cheltenham Chronicle*, September 12, 1931.

[4]*News Chronicle*, September 10, 1931.

[5]Personal correspondence, Ralph Vaughan Williams to Gustav Holst, n.d. [September, 1931], quoted in Ursula Vaughan Williams (ed.) and Imogen Holst (ed.), *Heirs and Rebels: Letters to Each Other and Occasional Writings by Gustav Holst and Ralph Vaughan Williams* (Oxford: Oxford University Press, 1959), 77.

[6]The full score was not published until 1974.

[7]Personal correspondence, Gustav Holst to Earl V. Moore, Dec[ember] 29[, 1931], Bentley Historical Library, The University of Michigan.

[8]*Seven Part-Songs*, Op. 44 [H162] (1925-6).

[9]Personal correspondence, Gustav Holst to Charles A. Sink, January 16, 1932, Bentley Historical Library, The University of Michigan.

[10]Personal correspondence, Charles A. Sink to Gustav Holst, February 25, 1932, Bentley Historical Library, The University of Michigan.

[11]Albert Lockwood.

[12]Personal correspondence, Gustav Holst to Charles A. Sink, February 29, 1932, Bentley Historical Library, The University of Michigan.

[13]Personal correspondence, Charles A. Sink to Gustav Holst, March 4, 1932, Bentley Historical Library, The University of Michigan.

[14]Personal correspondence, Gustav Holst to Charles A. Sink, March 16[, 1932], Bentley Historical Library, The University of Michigan.

[15]Personal correspondence, Charles A. Sink to Gustav Holst, March 19, 1932, Bentley Historical Library, The University of Michigan..

[16]Personal correspondence, Earl V. Moore to Gustav Holst, March 22, 1932, Bentley Historical Library, The University of Michigan.

[17]Personal correspondence, Charles A. Sink to Gustav Holst, March 31, 1932,Bentley Historical Library, The University of Michigan.

[18]Gustav Holst, Notebook, January to June, 1932, The Holst Foundation.

[19]Personal correspondence, Charles A. Sink to Gustav Holst, April 16, 1932, Bentley Historical Library, The University of Michigan.

[20]Personal correspondence, Earl V. Moore to Gustav Holst, April 28, 1932, Bentley Historical Library, The University of Michigan.

[21]Personal correspondence, Gustav Holst to Earl V. Moore, May 2[, 1932], Bentley Historical Library, The University of Michigan.

[22]Personal correspondence, Earl V. Moore to Gustav Holst, May 5, 1932, Bentley Historical

Library, The University of Michigan.
[23]Gustav Holst, *Diary*, Saturday, May 14, 1932, The Holst Foundation.
[24]Gustav Holst, *Diary*, Sunday, May 15, 1932, The Holst Foundation.
[25]Gustav Holst, *Diary*, Monday, May 16, 1932, The Holst Foundation.
[26]Gustav Holst, *Diary*, Thursday, May 19, 1932, The Holst Foundation.
[27]*Michigan Daily*, May 19, 1932.
[28]*Ibid.*.
[29]Gustav Holst, *Diary*, Friday, May 20, 1932, The Holst Foundation.
[30]Personal correspondence, Gustav Holst to Earl V. Moore, May 22[, 1932], Bentley Historical Library, The University of Michigan.
[31]Personal correspondence, Charles A. Sink to Gustav Holst, May 23, 1932, Bentley Historical Library, The University of Michigan.
[32]Albert Stanley, who had been instrumental in securing Holst's 1923 visit to Ann Arbor, died earlier in 1932.
[33]Personal correspondence, Earl V. Moore to Gustav Holst, May 26, 1932, Bentley Historical Library, The University of Michigan.
[34]*Musical America*, May 25, 1932.

CHAPTER XXX

FAREWELL TO AMERICA

Holst's train from Ann Arbor arrived at Boston's South Station at 11:15 a.m. on Saturday, May 21st. The next two days were spent packing and writing letters. He met with the Davisons the following morning and had dinner with Cecilia Payne at the Faculty Club that same evening. Although disappointed that his physical health would not allow him to take his planned vacation to Canada and the West, Holst must have felt some relief knowing that his responsibilities at Harvard were coming to an end and that he could return home soon.

There were now only two remaining events in Boston that involved Holst directly: a Boston Pops concert and finishing up the semester. "Harvard Night at the Pops" was an annual affair taking place at Symphony Hall. The concert held in 1932, featuring the Boston Pops, Puerto Rican Pianist Jesús María Sanromá, and the Harvard Glee Club, was held on Monday, May 23rd. The conducting responsibilities were shared by Arthur Fiedler, Archibald Davidson, and Holst. There was only one rehearsal in Symphony Hall for this program and that was on the morning of the concert. Dorothy Davison drove Holst to this rehearsal and then took him to see his physician Dr. Townsend.[1] The visit to his physician was probably routine; there is no indication in Holst's diary that any occurrence at the rehearsal had prompted the visit.

After having dinner at the Davisons, Holst and the Davisons returned to Symphony Hall for the 8:30 concert. A column in that day's *Boston Herald* contained a listing for the entire program:

Harvard Glee Club Sings at Pops Tonight

Songs by the Harvard Glee Club, the "Rhapsody in Blue" with Sanroma as soloist, and the presence of Gustav Holst as guest conductor of his own music, will be features of the annual Harvard night tonight at the Pops concert in Symphony Hall. The program follows:

March "Cruiser Harvard"..Strube

Overture to "Oberon"..Weber

Soviet Iron Foundry..Mossolov

Songs by the Harvard Glee Club:

A Dirge for Two Veterans..Holst

(Poem by Walt Whitman)

Fire, Fire, My Heart..Morley

Before Sleep..Holst

The Shores of Harvard..Holst

St. Paul's Suite, for String Orchestra..Holst

Rhapsody in Blue..Gershwin

Soloist--J. M. Sanroma

Songs by the Harvard Glee Club:

Gently, Johnny, My Jingalo..English Folk Song

The Foggy Dew..English Folk Song

Choruses from "The Mikado"..Sullivan

Waltz "Du und Du" from "The Bat"..Strauss

Prayer of Thanksgiving (Old Dutch Hymn)................arranged by Kremser

"Lohengrin" Prelude to Act III..Wagner

"Fair Harvard"[2]

Holst conducted "Before Sleep" and the *St. Paul's Suite*; Davison wielded the baton for the *Dirge for Two Veterans*, and Fieldler conducted the remainder of the program.[3]

Harvard Night at the Pops was not the only concert of interest in Boston that evening. In nearby Waltham, "Nuttings on the Charles" featured Duke Ellington and his orchestra.[4]

A review of the Pops concert appearing in the *Boston Herald* the following day contained some misinformation about Holst:

> Sons of fair Harvard and their ladies last night helped to pack Symphony Hall , more than 200 attending the annual Harvard night of the Pops...
>
> Sanroma was recalled time after time , his own arrangement of Gershwin's piano parts pleasing the audience immensely. Dr. Holst, who will be guest conductor at the Symphony next winter, presented a suite for stringed orchestra and a song dedicated to Dr. Archibald T. Davison and the Harvard Glee Club. Two of his earlier songs were sung by the club.[5]

It is highly doubtful that Holst was planning at this time to make another appearance the following year with the Boston Symphony Orchestra. It is more than likely that the reporter was confused about Holst's conducting stint of the past January and inserted it into the next year.

The *Boston Evening Transcript* used the concert as a springboard to giving Holst a hero's departure:

> The Farewells of Gustav Holst
> Leave-taking at Harvard Pops
>
> All of which digressions are to wander from a concert designed to speed the departing Holst and to bear witness once more to the friendly tie, grown closer of late, between the University and Symphony Hall. At the end of the month Mr. Holst returns to London, bearing with him the good memory of work well done, the good will of all whom he encountered. A composer of rank has taught the higher arts of musical composition, and his students have been the gainers. In Symphony Hall and in Sanders Theatre he has reminded audiences out of his own many-sided achievement that English music in the present may not be waived aside. In less public relations the fine quality of the man has shone through the erudite and accomplished musician. His own modesty would deny his stay as an event in our musical vineyards. Others

are bound to speak or write for him.[6]

Indeed, teaching the "higher arts of musical composition" was still very much on Holst's mind. Notebook entries indicate that, probably before departing for Michigan, Holst approached Edward Burlingame Hill about having a small ensemble available to play through his students' works:

> Hill
> pay str quartet
> for last week Piston (both days)
> 2 pianists
> extra vln in Qtet tuttis?
> come and listen on the Thursday[7]

Holst was successful in his request. On Thursday, the day after the concert, there was a two and one-half hour rehearsal of students' works in the afternoon, followed by a tea with Walter Piston at which the two composers settled on students' grades for the term. With Holst departing before grades were due to be turned in, it was essential that they collaborated. Notebook and diary entires confirm this:

> Piston
> do grading on May 26
> marks for melody
> clear form textures
> unity of style
> cleaness accuracy of writing try things over?

Another entry reveals Holst's consistency of thought on the matter:

> class
> no exam
> graded according to term's work
> marks for
> good themes
> clear form and texture
> unity of style
> accuracy of writing
> reading period week

May 15-21
Make fair copies correct
no [partway] staves
bring fair copies here
Meeting 23rd or lesson on 22nd at latest
--try and finish but this is not so essential[8]

According to his diary, Holst had a number of takers on his offer of private lessons that week.

Later that same evening, Cecilia Payne drove Holst over to the observatory to view Jupiter and a star cluster. Holst enjoyed her company and visited with her again the day of his Boston departure.

On the afternoon of Wednesday the 25th, Holst went to Piston's house and heard--or at least looked at--Piston's 1930 *Flute Sonata*. The following day featured the final meeting of Holst's composition class and the performance of his students' works.[9] Already packed, with most of his luggage sent ahead two days earlier, Holst caught the five o'clock boat for New York. His trip was not smooth. That evening, between 8:00 and 8:45 p.m., the boat encountered a violent storm on the Cape Cod Canal.

Holst arrived in New York the following morning; it was to be the last day he would spend in North America. He walked through the Bowery to Cooper Square, where he stopped to see Duncan McKenzie. Following their visit, he continued on to one of his favorite New York haunts--the Beethoven Association--for a nap. This was followed by lunch there with McKenzie and Emil. In the afternoon Holst had the opportunity of watching Nathaniel Shilkret and the Victor Salon Orchestra in a prearranged rehearsal of *Mr. Shilkret's Maggot*. Holst's reaction to the run-through is not known; however, it is safe to assume that he never heard the work again.

After Shilkret's rehearsal Emil took the composer to Spuyten Duyvil for a chance to relax before having dinner at the Beethoven Association.[10] By 11:00 p.m. Holst was on board the *Europa*, bound for England. He would never again return to the United States; in fact, he would never again leave the United Kingdom. Increasing illness over the remaining two years of his life curtailed his travels.

An article appearing in *Musical Opinion* summed up Holst's third and final visit to the United States:

> ....America still holds on, giving honour to those who will teach or lead. The latest instance is the visit of Gustav Holst, at whose feet many have

sat. For three months he was installed as Horation Lamb lecturer of composition at Harvard University: and he has lectured before the Beethoven Association of New York, discourse on Haydn at Washington, and told the story of English music to the National Association of Organists in New York. He crossed the border to conduct the Montreal Symphony, directed the Boston Symphony Orchestra in three performances of his own works, and shared a program with Koussevitzky at Harvard University. Many composers have been honoured in America, but I know of no instance where one has been so well received as widespread newspapers' reports about Gustav Holst to have been at Harvard University. There the sweet [semester] about which I have spoken seems to have shown itself in all its fairness, with an added generosity....[11]

---

[1]Gustav Holst, *Diary*, Monday, May 23, 1932, The Holst Foundation.

[2]*Boston Herald*, May 23, 1932.

[3]Gustav Holst, *Diary*, Monday, May 23, 1932, The Holst Foundation.

[4]*Boston Globe*, May 23, 1932.

[5]*Boston Herald*, May 24, 1932.

[6]*Boston Evening Transcript*, May 24, 1932.

[7]Gustav Holst, Notebook, January to June, 1932, The Holst Foundation.

[8]*Ibid.*.

[9]Gustav Holst, *Diary*, Thursday, May 26, 1932, The Holst Foundation.

[10]Gustav Holst, *Diary*, Friday, May 27, 1932, The Holst Foundation.

[11]*Musical Opinion*, June 1, 1932.

CHAPTER XXXI

LATE 1932

Holst's week-long return journey to England was uneventful, and he was able to get some much needed rest. He made it back to London in the wee hours of the morning on Thursday, June 2, 1932, arriving at St. Paul's Girls' School at 5:00 a.m..[1] The next few months would be spent recovering from his semester-long "sabbatical" and reentering the productive state of semi-retirement he had been enjoying the past few years.

The first composition that Holst worked on upon his return was *Eight Canons for Equal Voices* [H187]. These were not meant to be as a cycle, for there are three dedications. Nos. 4 ("David's lament for Jonathan") and 8 ("If 'twere the time of lilies") are dedicated to St. Paul's Girls' School, Nos. 2 ("Lovely Venus"), 3 ("The field of sorrow"), 5 ("O strong of heart"), and 6 ("Truth of all truth") to Wallace Woodworth and Radcliffe College, and No. 7 ("Evening on the Moselle") to Overstone School, where Vally Lasker taught. No. 1 ("If you love songs") bears no dedication. The first six of these are *a cappella*; the seventh and eighth have piano accompaniment. Nos. 2, 3, 4, 6, 7, and 8 feature the polytonality that served Holst so well in *Terzetto* and in *Hammersmith*. He wrote to Imogen in mid-June, "I'm writing some canons for female voices in 3 keys and 3 voices and need 3 singers. Any offers?"[2] He continued in a letter to William Gillies Whittaker, "One of them is for two choirs and three keys. However the attack is nearly over and I don't think I shall repeat the offense."[3] Vaughan Williams had his own input:

The White Gates
Westcott Road,

Dorking
[n.d.]

Dear Gustav

For our sake you must keep well--but for the sake of music you must go on writing canons--so try and continue the two.

I like especially Fields of Sorrow & David's Lament--the two big ones I feel I am going to like--but can't visualize them yet. I liked the old Trio[4]--but always felt that its being in 3 keys was more seen by eye than felt by the ear. After all, 'Lovely Venus' depends a lot on the 'natural chord' doesn't it? I don't think I like your notation. After all, key signatures are simply a means of avoiding accidentals--isn't that so? And I believe that on the balance you wd get fewer accidentals by putting a Christian key signature--& not, incidentally, make unhappy people, like me, who try to play them on the pfte, permanently cross-eyed....

Yrs

RVW[5]

On Sunday, June 19th Emil arrived from America.[6] Holst had hoped that both Emil and Valerie would be able to visit him that summer. He got his wish, although the two of them would not see him at the same time; Emil had just a week in June and Valerie would arrive in August. Emil stayed his first night in London at Vally Lasker's townhouse at 103 Talgarth Rd.

The Cotswolds walking tour with Emil that Holst had proposed in his April 12th letter to Imogen became a reality--but not on foot. It had been only three months since Holst's bleeding ulcer attack and he was not in the best of health. He described his walking to W. G. Whittaker as "even more middle-aged than before."[7] On Tuesday, the 21st, Emil, Imogen, and Holst took the train to Oxford, arriving at 4:40 p.m.. There they stayed at the Golden Cross Hotel and met up with Douglas Clarke, himself on summer vacation from McGill University and The Montreal Orchestra. Clarke had a sizeable car at his disposal and the four of them rode around the Cotswolds, through Broadway, Cheltenham, and Cirencester. The following morning, after bidding Clarke good-bye, the three returned by train to London, where they met Isobel for lunch at The George.[8] That morning was not the last time Holst would see Clarke; the two of them had dinner at Pagani's the following week. Two days later, on Saturday, June 25th, Holst and

Isobel had a farewell lunch at The George for Emil, who was due back in the States by July 1st.[9] This get-together was the last time that the two brothers would ever see each other. Neither realized it as Holst was still months away from his inescapable decline.

In late July Holst kept himself busy by assisting with another Stepney Pageant and by attempting a walking tour in the Chicester area. On Wednesday, July 27th, he took the train to Arundel with Mabel Rodwell Jones. From there he walked to Winterton, where he stayed at the Winterton Arms. The following morning he walked around the village in the rain until 10:00 a.m., when he went back to bed. Realizing he had taken on too much, Holst took the bus to Chicester, where he wandered around for the next three days before watching Vally Lasker conduct the Byrd *Three-part Mass* and other works (including his own *This Have I Done for My True Love*) in Chicester Cathedral on August 1st. Following the Bank Holiday festivities, he took the bus to Downs. From there he stubbornly attempted to walk to Guildford, but was picked up in the woods by Irene Bonnett's family, who drove him the rest of the way. Holst then took the train from Guildford to London.[10] Walking had always been an integral part of Holst's life--it helped him clear his mind--and he was not going to allow a thing so trivial as a bleeding ulcer to get in his way, even if it meant cutting his walks short.

On August 12th Holst set off by train for a weekend in Durham, where he stayed at the Castle Hotel. If walking as much as he'd like was next to impossible, then at least he could search for another less strenuous type of relaxation. He found it in the city's cathedral, where he spent the next few days writing musical sketches.

By the time he had returned to London, his niece Valerie had arrived from New York. He had anticipated her arrival ever since his own return and joked about it in a letter to Whittaker:

> Don't come back between Aug 14 and 20 because I shall be in the Cotswolds part of that week with a New York actress with whom I fell in love. She will be accompanied by her aunt and cousin but they are old pals of mine and they won't get in the way seriously, so I am looking forward to having a good time.[11]

The Golden Cross in Oxford turned out to be one of Holst's favorite points of departure for the Cotswolds. On Friday, August 19th he entertained Valerie there, in the company of Isobel and Imogen.[12] They all stayed together for the next three days. thoroughly enjoying each other's company. Just as it had been with Emil two months earlier, this visit would be the last time that Holst and Valerie would ever see each other.

The following week was a busy one for Holst. On Tuesday the 23rd, he conducted three movements from *The Planets* in Queen's Hall. The concert was broadcast by the BBC. Later in the week he conducted some rehearsals for the 1932 Three Choirs Festival, to be held at Worcester. He set out for Worcester himself on Wednesday, the 31st, first taking the train to Oxford and then the bus to Burford. He then spent the next four days walking most of the way from Burford to Worcester. His route took him through Wyck Rissington, where coincidentally or not, he celebrated the fortieth anniversary of his first music position there with some of the people who had sung for him. He arrived in Worcester on Sunday, September 4th, in time for the start of the festival. On Wednesday the 6th, he conducted his Ballet music from *The Perfect Fool* and the next day he conducted *The Hymn of Jesus*. He left Worcester on the 9th and, with the exception of one short ride, continued to walk through the Cotswolds through the 14th.[13] He had done more walking in the two weeks enclosing the Three Choirs Festival than he had done in at least nine months. It was quite a recovery.

In mid-September Holst was back at his usual post at St. Paul's Girls' School. He taught because he wanted to, not because he needed the money so badly. For once he was in the position of being able to offer others, among them Helen Bidder, whose father had just passed away. He wrote to her, "For the first time in my life I have more money than I need--just at a time when everyone else is hard up. It is partly owing to living in Harvard being cheaper than I had expected and partly to having been paid in dollars with the pound off the gold standard."[14] Holst was fortunate to have been paid in dollars at that time; the dollar would likewise be off the gold standard within a year.

At the end of September, Thomas Whitney Surrette and his wife came from Boston for a visit and Holst and Isobel entertained them for lunch on the 30th. Holst had aother lunch appointment during the following week, with Ralph Hawkes, perhaps in hopes of hearing some news about the impending publication of *Hammersmith*. Publication had been announced as early as April, but there had been no movement on the part of Hawkes & Son. While Hawkes would provide Holst with some figures later, the ultimate decision not to publish the work--unless Holst paid for it--would not be made until the following year. This unfortunate decision caused the work to remain unpublished for the next twenty-four years.

Holst continued to teach, lecture, and conduct throughout the fall term, even though his health varied. Composing was another matter and his physical condition sometimes prevented him giving it his best effort. He had known dry spells before, but they were mental in nature and had nothing to do with his physical condition. He wrote to Whittaker:

> I find it impossible to sit up at night. Although I am quite well the doctor tells me that I have to go easy because my blood is not up to the mark either in quantity or quality as a result of my trouble in America. This should all come to an end next Easter, but until then I must live as quietly as possible....
>
> The worst of the business is that I cannot write. When I settle down to compose I usually fall asleep. However, it is only temporary.[15]

Holst may have found himself unable to compose at that time, but his compositional processes were being discussed by others. His former student Edmund Rubbra produced an article, "Holst: Some Technical Characteristics" that was published in the October issue of *Monthly Musical Record.* Holst's *Diary* entries of this period include many meetings with Rubbra, perhaps for the purposes of defining and discussing the article. Rubbra's essay, based upon Holst's *Choral Hymns from the Rig Veda*, is very analytical and to the point, although at the end he issues the following caveat:

> My technical analysis--necessarily rather dry--has not, I hope, discouraged any reader from a closer examination and understanding of the works themselves. No discussion of technical characteristics can yield up the essential secrets of any music. The play of the mind and spirit upon the stuff of sound defies a literary analysis: for a real understanding of Holst one must go to the actual music, There will be found one of the finest and clearest musical minds of this age....when most of the would-be music of this age has passed into oblivion his music will survive as an inspiration to all who endeavor to write from the core of their being.[16]

Indeed, Holst was not forgotten. He was the Guest of Honor at the Annual General Meeting of the Music Teachers' Association on Saturday, October 29th at the Langham Hotel in London.[17] A concert of his works featuring a number of participants, including soprano Rose Morse accompanied by Imogen on the piano, followed the meeting. There were many other performances of his works that fall, including the premiere of "Good Friday," the second of *Six Choruses*, Op. 53 [H186], which he had written during his time at Harvard. The piece was performed by its dedicatees, Ernest Bullock and the Westminster Abbey Choir, on December 13th. There were also two Scottish premieres on successive nights (*The Cloud Messenger* and *Egdon Heath* on December 16th and 17th, respectively) that were set up through Whittaker.

In the meantime, Ralph Vaughan Williams was having the time of his life on his second visit to America. He held the prestigious Mary Flexner Lectureship position at Bryn Mawr College, Bryn Mawr, Pennsylvania for the fall term. He was surprised to discover that Una Lucas, the former Head Girl at St. Paul's Girls' School whom Holst had seen on his last American visit, was also there. Vaughan Williams took some weekend trips as well; in the early autumn he travelled to the Boston area to spend some time with Archibald and Dorothy Davison. He wrote to Holst, "I had a splendid two days with the Davisons--they were both so nice--and while in Boston I went to a i) football match and ii) Boston Symph. Orch; both suffer from being too much organised...."[18] Following the Boston Symphony Orchestra concert, Davison introduced Vaughan Williams to Serge Koussevitzky, who later rehearsed and programmed the *Fantasia on a Theme by Thomas Tallis* at the composer's request. Later Vaughan Williams had a chance to see Emil act. Emil was then on tour, playing the part of Herr Krug in *Reunion in Vienna*. Vaughan Williams wrote to Holst:

> I've met Ernest Cossart at last--it was all perfect--he was playing in Phila. and asked Una and me to dine and come on to the show.
>
> We picked up again at once after 30 years and reminisced as hard as we could--then we went to the show--a very good amusing play--and he was absolutely perfect in it--funnily, *on the stage* he kept reminding me of you.[19]

On his way home in early December, Vaughan Williams returned to Boston to visit the Davisons. This time, however, Dorothy Davison was ill, having suffered appendicitis. All three of them made light of the situation and sent Holst the following three-person postcard:

> After your being good enough to send Mr. Vaughan Williams to me to be taken care of, what should I do but rush into the hospital and have my appendix out! That sounds more like you than me. All going well. Best wishes to you.
>
> Dorothy Davison
>
> Three of us fill up this hospital room to too full; but if you were here there would be room for you--as there always will be with us.

A. T. D.

I am now included in this.

R. Vaughan Williams[20]

Vaughan Williams returned to England in time to conduct at the annual Albert Hall festivities of the English Folk Dance and Song Society, which had just elected him president. He was also back in time to conduct his *Fantasia on Christmas Carols* (1912) at St. Paul's Girls' School. As a form of relaxation Holst had recently returned to the trombone and played in the orchestra for this occasion. This may not have been the only occasion that December for which he played trombone. Diary notes indicate that Holst at least considered playing for a December 3rd function of the English Folk Song and Dance Society at the Cecil Sharp House that involved Imogen.[21]

The fall term at St. Paul's Girls' School ended on December 20th, and Holst characteristically did some serious walking. He took three one-day walks--on the 21st (in Greater London, from Southwark to Barking), the 22nd (from Barking to Theydon Bois), and the 23rd (Bishop's Storford to his home at Great Easton). He planned to do some more extensive walking after Christmas, but suffered a relapse and was unable to do so. Though laid up physically, Holst's creative juices started to flow again and for the first time since August he was able to do some meaningful composing. Sketches for two significant works, the *Brook Green Suite* [H190] and the *Lyric Movement* [H191] were started during the winter holidays.

---

[1]Gustav Holst, *Diary*, Thursday, June 2, 1932, The Holst Foundation.

[2]Personal correspondence, Gustav Holst to Imogen Holst [, June 17, 1932], quoted in Imogen Holst (ed.), *A Catalogue of Gustav Holst's Music* (London: Faber Music Ltd., 1974), 197.

[3]Personal correspondence, Gustav Holst to William Gillies Whittaker, July 19[, 1932], quoted in Michael Short (ed.), *Gustav Holst: Letters to W. G. Whittaker* (Glasgow: University of Glasgow Press, 1974), 117.

[4]*Terzetto* [H158] (1925), for flute, oboe, and viola.

[5]Personal correspondence, Ralph Vaughan Williams to Gustav Holst, n.d. [late 1932 or early 1933], quoted in *Ursula Vaughan Williams (ed.) and Imogen Holst (ed.), Heirs and Rebels: Letters to Each Other and Occasional Writings by Gustav Holst and Ralph Vaughan Williams* (Oxford: Oxford University Press, 1959), 82-83.

[6]Gustav Holst, *Diary*, Sunday, June 19, 1932, The Holst Foundation.

[7]Personal correspondence, Gustav Holst to W. G. Whittaker, July 19[, 1932], quoted in Michael Short (ed.), *loc. cit.*.

[8]Gustav Holst, *Diary*, Tuesday, June 21 through Thursday, June 23, 1932, The Holst Foundation.

[9]Gustav Holst, *Diary*, Saturday, June 25, 1932, The Holst Foundation. Also in attendence at this luncheon was someone named Mary, probably Holst's cousin Mary Lediard.
[10]Gustav Holst, *Diary*, Wednesday, July 27th through Monday, August 1, 1932, The Holst Foundation.
[11]Personal correspondence, Gustav Holst to W. G. Whittaker, July 19[, 1932], quoted in Michael Short (ed.), *loc cit.*.
[12]Gustav Holst, *Diary*, Friday, August 19, 1932, The Holst Foundation.
[13]Gustav Holst, *Diary*, Wednesday, August 31st through Wednesday, September 14th, The Holst Foundation.
[14]Personal correspondence, Gustav Holst to Helen Bidder, August 9, 1932, quoted in Michael Short, *Gustav Holst: The Man and His Music* (Oxford: Oxford University Press, 1990), 316.
[15]Personal correspondence, Gustav Holst to W. G. Whittaker, Oct[ober] 17[, 1932], quoted in Michael Short (ed.), *op. cit.*, 118.
[16]Edmund Rubbra, "Holst: Some Technical Characteristics," in *The Monthly Musical Record,* LXII (October, 1932), 173.
[17]*The Music Teacher*, December, 1932.
[18]Personal correspondence, Ralph Vaughan Williams to Gustav Holst [Fall, 1932], quoted in Ursula Vaughan Williams, *R. V. W.: A Biography of Ralph Vaughan Williams* (London: Oxford university Press, 1964), 192.
[19]Personal correspondence, Ralph Vaughan Williams to Gustav Holst [late Fall, 1932], quoted in Ursula Vaughan Williams, *op.cit.*, 193.
[20]Personal correspondence, Dorothy Davison, Achibald Thompson Davison, and Ralph Vaughan Williams to Gustav Holst, December 9, 1932, The Holst Foundation. Vaughan Williams' handwriting is often difficult to decipher. It is possible that he wrote "I am not included in this."
[21]Gustav Holst, *Diary*, Saturday, December 3, 1932, The Holst Foundation.

CHAPTER XXXII

CARLISLE

It was during the autumn of 1932 that Holst received some written correspondence from Mary Lediard, a cousin from his mother's side of the family. Her father (Holst's uncle) H. A. Lediard, a physician active in Carlisle, had recently passed away and she wanted to organize a fitting memorial to him in the form of a concert. The program, to be given early in the following year, was to feature Holst, his daughter Imogen, and Mary Lediard herself, as active participants. Performing ensembles would include two well-known local groups: the Carlisle St. Stephens Band and the Goodwin Male Voice Choir. The St. Stephens Band was at that time under the direction of William Lowes. It was no ordinary band; indeed it was one of the best in the country, having won the National Brass Band Championships held at London's Crystal Palace in 1929 after a third place finish the previous year. The Goodwin Male Voice Choir, centered at the Bishop Goodwin School in Carlisle, was conducted by W. H. Reid. It too had received its share of accolades. The music to be performed would consist primarily of Holst's own compositions.

Holst's response to his cousin's proposal was swift and positive:

Nov 9 [1932]
St. Paul's Girls' School
Brook Green, Hammersmith,
W. 6.

Dear Mary,

What a delightful proposal! Of course Imogen and I would love to come as long as it is not too early in January. There are two more male choruses published and 'How Mighty'[1] has not yet been done in England as far as I know.

There are also two more to be written and I am wondering whether I could write one of them in time to be rehearsed for the Carlisle concert. (probably not!)

Could you come to London to discuss details? If you don't want to stay at the Langham, one of my two helpers here, Miss Lasker, has a spare room in her flat and always putting up people....

If you don't think you could come I'll write at length. But it would be far better if we could meet.

Thanks for that excellent photo.

With Love

Gustav

I also send a unison version of 'How Mighty' just for you to have.[2]

Things moved along very swiftly. Plans for the concert were already being reported five days later in the press:

> A musical event of outstanding interest in Carlisle and district is being arranged for a date towards the end of January, when Mr. Gustav Holst, the distinguished composer who is a nephew of the late Dr. Lediard has consented to visit the city and conduct a concert which will be regarded as In Memoriam to his late uncle. Dr. Lediard was keenly interested in the welfare of the unemployed in Carlisle, and the proceeds of the concert will be given to the Mayor's Fund for the relief of those out of work in the city. Compositions by Mr. Holst will be played under his conductorship by St. Stephen's Band and some of his works will be sung by the Goodwin Choir....
>
> Miss Mary Lediard is taking an active part in making the arrangements for the forthcoming concert, which will probably be given at the Lonsdale Cinema.[3]

Over the ensuing weeks, additional personnel were secured for the concert. Two outstanding soloists were lined up: Ena Mitchell, a soprano from Carlisle and Rose Morse, a young mezzo soprano from London. Holst already had heard Rose Morse sing at the concert in his honor following the Annual Meeting of the Music Teachers' Association on October 29th. Treble choristers were obtained through the addition of boys of the Upperby Church and Carlisle Cathedral Choirs as well as women of the Carliol Ladies' Choir.

The venue was established as Her Majesty's Theatre and the date was set for February 12th, 1933-- later than originally anticipated. The world was gripped by a devastating depression, one which deeply affected the Cumberland area. Therefore, it was decided early on, in keeping with the spirit of Dr. Lediard's work, that this should be a non-profit concert:

> The proceeds of the concert were in aid of the Mayor of Carlisle's Fund for Unemployment, and Mr. A. J. Stewart, the lessee of [Her Majesty's] Theatre, granted the use of the building absolutely free in every respect, lighting and service included....The late Dr. Lediard was an ardent lover of Fine Arts, especially Music. In his capacity as a co-opted member of the Corporations Public library and Museum Committee he did valued work at Tullie House to further interest in the study and practice of music, and it is safe to say that Sunday Night's concert was no less an inspiration which would have received his cordial support, for Dr. Lediard, while interested in music, was keenly sensitive on the subject of the plight of the unemployed and the need for helping them through a drab period of their life.[4]

Holst took this concert very seriously. He had written for both male chorus and brass band in the recent past. The choral selections were not difficult to find. The *Six Choruses*, Op. 53 [H184], were brand new and five of the *Six Choral Folk Songs*, Op. 36 [H136] (1916), had been arranged by the composer for four-part male chorus and published as such in 1925.

The brass band selections were slightly more difficult for Holst to determine. Obviously, the concert would feature *A Moorside Suite* [H173], the commissioned contest piece for the 1928 National Brass Band Championships, but what else was there? Over the next four weeks Holst gradually recalled the existence of other suitable works. On November 17, he wrote to Mary Lediard:

> ....Boosey published a Chaconne in E Flat of mine arranged for brass band. Do come as soon as you can so that we can discuss the whole matter.[5]

Holst was referring here to the first movement of his *First Suite in E Flat for Military Band*, Op. 28 No. 1 [H105] (1909), which had been arranged by Sidney Herbert for brass band. Boosey and Hawkes, eager to cash in on the composer's new found fame from *The Hymn of Jesus* and *The Planets*, saw no harm and greater profit in releasing two versions of the same work. It is not known whether or not Holst even saw Herbert's brass band version before its publication. Both settings of the suite--Holst's military band original and Herbert's brass band transcription--were published in 1921. In addition to these two versions of the complete suite, there was also Henry G. Ley's organ transcription of the "Chaconne" movement that would be published by Novello in 1933. Holst's memory may have been clouded by its impending publication.

Less than a week later he remembered another work:

> ....Can the male voice choir do my dirge? I've never heard it in England although it is popular in the USA.[6]

Holst himself had conducted *A Dirge for Two Veterans* [H121] at the University of Michigan in 1923.

Holst's own works were not the only ones being considered for the Lediard concert; it was not in his nature to seek all (or any) of the glory for a project such as this. According to his Diary, Holst and his cousin met at Pagani's for dinner on November 30th and obviously they would have discussed the concert then. At that meeting Holst may have shown Mary the following timing sheet that verified his intentions:

	Feb 12
Elgar Suite	15 min
Vaughan Williams Songs	10
Mozart Piano Duet	15
Interval	
Moorside Suite	15
Male Voice Folksongs	6
Vedas solo voice	10
Nocturne piano	4
Dirge male voice brass	5
Wolfe Songs	10

Piano folksongs	5
Male voice Intercession	
How Mighty	10
Folksong Suite	15
	120[7]

Much information can be gleaned from this timing sheet. It is not known when Holst made out this list; but it is obviously preliminary. His guesses at timings for individual selections are actually very good, although one wonders about the practicality of a first half (featuring works of other composers) being projected to last forty minutes and a second half (consisting of his own compositions) lasting eighty. None of the three selections slated for the first half were actually performed on the concert.

Brass band afficionados would immediately identify the "Elgar Suite" entry with the *Severn Suite*, composed by Elgar in 1930. However, the following is written immediately after the entry in parentheses in a hand other than Holst's: "White Rider."[8] Whatever the case, the entire entry and its timing are crossed out and no Elgar work appears on the final concert program.

The piano duet by Wolfgang Amadeus Mozart, possibly the *Sonata in D Major for Two Pianos*, K. 446, in which Imogen was to have played a part, was also crossed out. It had to be discarded due to physical problems she was then having with her left arm.

Of the works listed after the interval, all were performed except the *Folksong Suite*, if indeed Holst meant the *Folksong Suite* originally written by his friend Ralph Vaughan Williams in 1923 for military band. Neither it nor the "Vaughan Williams Songs" entry slated for the first half actually ended up on the concert.

Still, Holst may not have meant the Vaughan Williams *Folksong Suite*. Sometimes Holst's notes that he wrote to himself, as they occur in lists and diary entries, are diffiicult to decipher. By the simple "Folksong Suite" entry, Holst also could have been referring to his own *Second Suite in F for Military Band*, Op. 28, No. 2 [H106] (1911-1922)[9], which is based on folk songs and folk dances. That work, however, is not mentioned in any of the correspondence regarding this concert. It is also unlikely that Holst meant his *First Suite in E Flat*. Indeed it was to the "Chaconne" of that suite that Holst referred in his earlier letter, but the *First Suite in E Flat* suite is not based on folk songs. Another possbility is that the "Folksong Suite" entry did not refer to any Holst work, but rather to a brass band suite composed by Imogen. In his next letter Holst makes reference to this work:

St. Paul's Girls' School
Brook Green, Hammersmith,
W.6.
Dec. 12th, 1932.

Dear Mary,

Thanks for letter. Imogen's left arm has collapsed and she has had to abandon all piano playing for the present. As far as we know it is not my complaint and we are hopeful that she would be able to play my *Nocturne*, which I wrote for her, on February 12th, but the Mozart duet must be abandoned. Also she would not be able to accompany Rose Morse, the singer. Would you do this? If so, would you care to come to London to rehearse with her? This would not be really necessary, but it would be a splendid excuse for getting you south again, and if you decided to come Vally could put you up next week-end in her flat and you could hear Vaughan Williams conduct his *Christmas Fantasia* here on Monday afternoon. The only drawback is that I should not be able to have my aunt at the George, which is a real pity. I only remembered after you left that Imogen wrote a Suite for Brass Band some time ago. I have asked her to send it to you. Would you shew it to the bandmaster and ask him whether he would care to do the first performance of either one movement or the whole. In that case, would he get the parts copied and send the bill to me. If that is too much for the band, I suggest leaving out one of my things. I am writing to Boosey's about arranging 'How Mighty' and will let you know the answer.

Love to Auntie,
Yours,

Gustav

Vally could accompany Rose Morse if you would rather not. It would be easier for rehearsing.[10]

The "Suite for Brass Band" mentioned in the above letter is Imogen Holst's *The Unfortunate Traveller*,[11] based upon *The Unfortunate Traveller, or The Life of Jack Wilton (1594)*, a novel by Thomas Nashe (1567-1601). The novel, about an Englishman's adventures on the European continent, is Nashe's best-known work and was highly influential in its picturesque style. Originally composed between October, 1928 and February, 1929 as a Royal College of Music examination piece, Imogen Holst's *The Unfortunate Traveller* is in four movements:

I. Introduction: Allegro moderato 4/4 attacca
II. Scherzo: Vivace 6/8
III. Interlude: Quasi lento-poco piu mosso-meno mosso-Tempo Io.
IV. March: Allegro molto 4/4

The work itself contains no written reference to Nashe's novel.

Gustav Holst's influence is clearly present in this work. Of significance is the fact that Imogen Holst began the work in October, 1928, the month following the National Brass Band Championships at which her father's *A Moorside Suite* was the contest piece. Still, *The Unfortunate Traveller* is a well-written work and a substantial one as well (fifty-three pages). It deserves to be in the repertoire of all British brass bands. The work was featured on the Carlisle concert program, with the composer conducting.

Of the other works listed on the timing sheet, the "Moorside Suite" and "Dirge male voice brass" are self-explanatory. The "Male Voice Folksongs" refer to the *Six Choral Folk Songs*, Op. 36, mentioned earlier. The "Vedas solo voice" refers not to any of the four settings of *Choral Hymns from the Rig Veda*, Op. 26 [H97-100], but to an earlier work, the *Hymns from the Rig Veda*, Op. 24 [H90] (1907-08) for solo voice and piano. There are nine hymns total in the Op. 24 collection, divided by the composer into three groups. The first group, containing "Ushas" (Dawn), "Varuna" (Sky), and "Maruta" (Stormclouds) would be performed by Ena Mitchell on the Carlisle concert.

The "Nocturne piano" entry was the "Nocturne" referred to in Holst's December 12, 1932 letter. Composed in 1930, it was the first of Two Pieces for Piano [H179] (the second was a jig from 1932) that Holst had written for Imogen as a belated twenty-first birthday present. There are no folk tunes in it. The exact opposite is to be found in the "Piano folksongs," listed on the concert programmme as "Three pieces on North Country Tunes." These three pieces were never part of a single entity. Two of them, "Chrissemas Day in the Morning" [H165] (1926) and "O! I hae seen the roses blaw" [H166] (1927), are from the Op. 46 collection published by Oxford University Press in 1928. The third, "Toccata" [H153] (1924), founded on the Northumbrian Pipe-Tune "Newburn Lads," was published by Curwen.

The "Wolfe Songs" were part of the collection of *Twelve Songs*, Op. 48 [H174] (1929) for voice and piano that Holst set to the poetry of Humbert Wolfe.

Collectively, they have been presented under the title of "The Dream-City." Four of these songs, No. 4: "A Little Music," No. 3: "Now in these Fairylands," No. 1: "Persephone," and No. 5: "The Thought" would be sung by Rose Morse, accompanied by Imogen Holst, on the Carlisle concert.

The "Male voice Intercession and How Mighty" refer to Nos. 1 and 5 of the *Six Choruses*, Op. 53 [H186] (1931-32). The orchestral accompaniment to "How Mighty Are the Sabbaths" was transcribed for brass band for this concert. Holst also considered doing the same for "Intercession." In a letter dating from January, 1933, after insisting on a good thorough rehearsal with the choir, he stated "Intercession can be piano or band."[12] Whether or not "Intercession" was ever arranged for brass band is not known; whatever the case, it was sung on the concert with piano accompaniment.

There was also discussion about Holst's ode for chorus and orchestra, *The Cloud Messenger* [H111] (1909-1910), initiated by Mary Lediard, who had probably heard W. G. Whittaker's choir perform it in on December 16th in Glasgow. A forty-minute work, it would have been far too long and far too ambitious for this concert. Still, Holst was happy to hear that anybody had even remembered the work and commented:

> ....It gave me great a thrill to hear you speak of the old 'Cloud Messenger' the other day for I had looked on it as 'not only dead but damned' as Disraeli said once....[13]
>
> It was wonderful to get your letter about the old C.M. Including translation it took me seven years--seven happy years of course. I'm not grumbling at them--and the performance was frost. Dear old Whittaker is the only man who has done the work since as far as I can remember.[14]

Preparations for the concert ran fairly smoothly. About a month before the concert took place, Imogen had the opportunity to go to Carlisle to rehearse the St. Stephen's Band in her suite, "The Unfortunate Traveller." She mentions this in a letter to her father:

> ....Then came to Carlisle and yesterday morning we went to a brass band rehearsal. It was thrilling to walk down a deserted-on-Sunday-morning high street and hear bits of my fugue getting nearer and nearer.
>
> A great many of the "boys" were down with the flu, but the survivors read my suite magnificently and I rehearsed it most of the morning, and we all got very hot and very happy over it. I'm to take another rehearsal

tonight. They are dears.[15]

The cooperation displayed by the members of the St. Stephen's Band speaks well for the all-male membership of the organization and attests to Imogen Holst's often overlooked talents as a composer and conductor. There weren't many women involved in either field in 1933. She commented about both in a post-concert interview:

> This is the first time I have conducted a band of male performers and it is the first time, so far as I know, that a woman has conducted a brass band at a public concert. I have conducted at the Royal College of Music, and I have a folk-dance band in London.
>
> I love conducting and it has been a delight to rehearse the St. Stephen's Band. It was their first performance at the Crystal Palace festival that inspired me to write this suite, which I have dedicated to them.
>
> I do not think there is enough music for brass bands. These men are the most responsive amateurs I have met. One has only to mention a point once and they play
> it right immediately.
>
> I am told that one of the bandsmen, a railway fireman, came back from a night journey from Aberdeen to Carlisle and has rehearsed all day. To-night he will go on duty again. I think that is wonderful.[16]

Both Holsts arrived a few days early. On Saturday, February 11th, they attended with Mary Lediard a "country dance tea" in Carlisle's Queen's Hall. The event was held in connection with the Cumberland Branch of the English Folk Dance and Song Society. Imogen, always an active member of the society, gave a well-received lecture-demonstration and conducted the singing of some folk songs.[17]

The "Gustav Holst Concert in Memory of Dr. Lediard" took place on Sunday, February 12, 1933 at 8:30 p.m. in Her Majesty's Theatre in Carlisle. It was a highly publicized sold-out affair which, according to one columnist, attracted many people who didn't normally attend such events:

> I am doubtful about these Sunday night concerts. This was the fourth I have attended recently. They bring large audiences, but they include many non-musical people who would not be present if the performances were on a week-night, when alternative amusements exist. It said much for the standard of interpretation that these people sat through an evening entirely

> given over to modern music without chattering and fidgetting. It is said that modern music bewilders the lay mind, but here it gripped the audience. Mr. Holst, in his speech of thanks at the close, said that to refer to the predominence of amateur music in this country in a spirit of apology or a spirit of boasting was equally silly. One may similarly say that to speak of modern music in a sneering way or in an extravagant way is equally silly.[18]

From all accounts, the concert was a huge success. The press was generous in their praise for the performances of all the works on the concert, particularly for "How Mighty Are the Sabbaths" (heard in England for the first time), the world premiere of "The Unfortunate Traveller," and "A Moorside Suite":

> ....The most important works given during the evening included two choruses for male voices--"Intercession" and "How Mighty Are the Sabbaths"--which were performed "for the first time in Europe" under Mr. Holst's baton. "Intercession,"which has a pianoforte accompaniment, played in this instance by Mr. William Merrill, is a setting to music of some medieval Latin lyrics by Helen Waddell. The words of "How Mighty Are the Sabbaths" have been culled from the same source but the supporting accompaniment has been written on broad lines by Mr. Holst and it was played last night for this production by St. Stephen's Band....In both works Mr. Holst seeks to express deep religious sentiment.[19]

> A concert with a remarkable array of novel features was held at Her Majesty's Theatre, Carlisle, on Saturday [sic] night....
>
> ....Certainly it was the first occasion on which an original brass band work by a woman composer has been publicly performed. The only item in the programme not by Gustav Holst was a new suite written by his daughter, Miss Imogen Holst, entitled "The Unfortunate Traveller."
>
> The suite was given under the personal direction of Miss Holst, who is an accomplished conductor. The suite is admirably written. The music is evidently strongly influenced by that of Gustav Holst, and particularly by the "Moorside" suite for brass, an admirable performance of which concluded the concert.[20]

> I have never heard the St. Stephen's Band in such good form....The alert touch which has always distinguished the St. Stephen's Band was much in evidence in this concert. But what one most admired was the

> beautiful tone which the band produced, notably in the Nocturne of the Moorside Suite."[21]

Holst himself was more than generous in sharing the honors at the end of the concert:

> Mr. Holst, speaking to the audience at the close of the concert, expressed gratification that Miss Lediard had originated the idea of giving the concert in memory of her father. He (Mr. Holst) regretted that he did not know him as well as members of the audience would. He wished to thank the audience for helping the most necessary work of to-day--the helping of the unemployed. (Applause.)
>
> In thanking Miss Lediard for what she had done he also wished to thank two others who had done a lot of work behind the scenes--Mr. Reid and Mr. Lowes--(applause)--and in this connection, as before, he was speaking on behalf of his daughter as well as himself. He also thanked those amateurs on the stage who had taken part in the concert. Much good work was done by amateurs, and one knew that when help was needed, the amateurs of Carlisle were always ready to assist. (Applause.) "To the amateurs behind us," said Mr. Holst, "my daughter and myself wish to express our gratitude, our regard, and our admiration." (Applause.)[22]

This was quintessential Holst. Here was the modest composer who dodged personal fame yet sought to give credit where credit was due. Here too was the seasoned professional music educator who considered his greatest successes to be in recreating the joys of music with amateur musicians. Furthermore, the lessons that Holst had learned from William Morris and the Hammersmth Socialist Club some four decades earlier and had born fruit at Morley College two decades earlier were manifested in the non-musical circumstances surrounding this concert. If this were indeed the last public concert in which Holst took an active part, then this departure from the concert stage would have been to his liking. For composer, performer, and audience alike, it was truly a most extraordinary affair.

---

[1]"How Mighty Are the Sabbaths" is the fifth of *Six Choruses, Op. 53,* for male voices. It was written while Holst was at Harvard during the spring of 1932. The words were translated from the original Latin of Peter Abelard by Helen Waddell.

[2]Personal correspondence, Gustav Holst to Mary Lediard, Nov[ember] 9[, 1932].

[3]*Cumberland Evening News*, November 14, 1932.

[4]*Cumberland Evening News*, February 13, 1933.

[5]Personal correspondence, Gustav Holst to Mary Lediard, Nov[ember] 17[, 1932].
[6]Personal correspondence, Gustav Holst to Mary Lediard, Nov[emder] 22[, 1932].
[7]Gustav Holst, timing sheet for the February 12, 1933 concert.
[8]The author was unable to locate any suite by Elgar bearing this title. It may have been a misrepresentation of a brass band suite arranged from Elgar's 1893 cantata, *The Black Knight.*
[9]A brass band arrangement of *The Second Suite in F for Military Band, Op. 28, No. 2 [H106],* arranged for brass band by Sidney Herbert, was published by Boosey and Hawkes in 1923. Severely truncated and *pitched in the key of E flat,* it could not have met with Holst's liking.
[10]Personal correspondence, Gustav Holst to Mary Lediard, Dec. 12th, 1932.
[11]Imogen Holst's suite, missing for decades, recently turned up in the estate sale of John Galland in England.
[12]Personal correspondence, Gustav Holst to Mary Lediard, Friday [January, 1933].
[13]Personal correspondence, Gustav Holst to Mary Lediard, Dec[ember] 19[, 1932].
[14]Personal correspondence, Gustav Holst to Mary Lediard, Jan[uary] 1[, 1933]. William Gillies Whittaker had previously conducted a performance of the work in Newcastle in 1924.
[15]Personal correspondence, Imogen Holst to Gustav Holst, Jan[uary] 10[, 1933].
[16]Imogen Holst, quoted in *The Daily Mail* (Yorkshire Edition), February 13, 1933.
[17]*Cumberland News*, February 11, 1933. This article also mentions the next evening's concert.
[18]*Carlisle Journal*, February 14, 1933.
[19]*Cumberland Evening News*, February 13, 1933.
[20]*News Chronicle (Manchester Edition)*, February 13, 1933.
[21]*Carlisle Journal*, February 14, 1933.
[22]*Cumberland Evening News*, February 13, 1933.

CHAPTER XXXIII

LYRIC MOVEMENT AND BROOK GREEN SUITE

The Carlisle concert proved to be too much physically for Holst. He made it through the concert in fine form, but starting just two days later an increasing number of cancellations begin to appear in his diary entries. He was still suffering from the relapse that had set during the Christmas holidays and found it increasingly difficult to involve himself in anything physical. For the next month he was able to teach at St. Paul's Girls' School, but that was about all.

On March 15th the eminent violist Lionel Tertis visited Holst at his room St. Paul's Girls' School.[1] Tertis' name was practically synonymous with "viola." In addition to being an incredible violist, he was also an inventor, having designed the "Tertis Viola," which is some 16 3/4 inches in length. Tertis was also Professor of Viola at the Royal Academy of Music for many decades, but his greatest accomplishment was in getting composers to take the viola seriously as a solo instrument. He did this through commissioning various works from composers of stature.

It was for Tertis that Holst composed the *Lyric Movement* [H192] (1933) for viola and chamber orchestra. The work is scored sparingly for soloist, strings and single woodwind. Lasting about ten minutes, the work is cool and sleek, exhibiting the tender austerity that had marked most of Holst's works beginning with *Egdon Heath*. *Lyric Movement* begins with an unaccompanied solo in free time, originally marked "Ad lib" by the composer, but crossed out and replaced by the simple "*Senza mesura*." This passage later returns in a shortened form toward the end of the work and in many compositions this in itself would pass as a cadenza, but Holst provided the soloist with a true cadenza some twenty-four measures later. This cadenza is quite difficult. Holst knew that Tertis could play anything that was put in front of him, but he was also aware of the fact that not all viola solists would be able to, nor would they necessarily care to, perform the cadenza. So Holst offered an optional cut which removes four accompanied measures and the cadenza in its entirety.[2]

As in the case of most of Holst's serious compositions, he supplied a piano reduction of *Lyric Movement* in addition to the full score. At least two copies were made. As usual, there were many corrections to be made, yet Holst was able to keep his sense of humor, as demonstrated in the copy given to Vally Lasker:

Viola Piece

Note

This copy is illegible, inaccurate and the private property of Miss Vally Lasker.

Gustav Holst
St. Paul's Girls' School
Brook Green
W6[3]

Tertis himself wrote about the work:

> It is an invaluable addition to the library of viola solos with orchestra and viola players are indeed fortunate to have a work from this delightful composer, whose music is noted for its bold design, beauty of melody, superb coloring and virility. All these qualitites are embodied in this new work. It is short, and the orchestra consists of strings, one flute, one oboe, one clarinet, and one bassoon.
>
> Although the Lyric Movement was actually begun in 1932, Holst had it in mind for some years, and I take pride in the fact that this, and the many new works for viola which have been and are being produced are the direct outcome of my persistent invocation to our native geniuses of composition; and we are able to say, without a trace of bombast, that England has done more for the viola than any other country.[4]

For Holst *Lyric Movement* marked the culmination of a line of works for the members of the string quartet and small orchestra, beginning with *A Song of the Night*, Op. 19, No. 1 [H74] (1905), for violin, and continuing with *Invocation*, Op.

19, No. 2 [H75] (1911) for violoncello, and the *Double Concerto*, Op. 49 [H175] (1929), for two violins.

After meeting with Tertis, Holst felt ill and went to "bed at Elm Cresc." that same day.[5] He wrote to Whittaker the following day, "Just now I'm in bed for three weeks on a milk diet in order to get rid of the last vestige of that ulcer. I'm at Ealing but all letters are forwarded so I won't bother you with another address."[6] All of his engagements were then cancelled until mid-April, but it would be well beyond that before he could be active again. He had X-rays taken on Wednesday, April 12th and felt ill the next day. On the following day, which was Good Friday, he checked into Beaufort House nursing home in Ealing.[7] His presence was sorely missed at a number of functions, including one in the locality in which he was staying:

> Mr. Gustav Holst the eminent composer of 'King Estmere', which was performed by the Ealing Philharmonic Society in concert on Saturday, is lying ill in an Ealing nursing home. On Saturday he sent a special message to the chorus and orchestra...[8]

At one time in his carrer Holst had played trombone in the Ealing Philharmonic Society Orchestra.

Holst was still at Beaufort during Whitsuntide, a time of year which he had taken to heart ever since the first Whitsuntide Festival at Thaxted in 1916. This year the festival was held at Bosham, in Sussex, and was conducted by Vally Lasker. Holst wrote to her and the singers:

> Miss Lasker and her singers and players
> @ the Rev Street
> The Vicarage
> Bosham
> Sussex
>
> Ealing June 2. 33
>
> Blessings, Greetings, Good Wishes and Love to you all.
>
> May you give as much joy in music as you will get; and get as much as you give.
>
> Yours Ever
> Gustav Holst[9]

Holst also enclosed the following personal note to Vally Lasker:

> May you sing many top A's, learn several new instruments, enjoy lots of Whitsuntides, madrigal evenings and Morley concerts, also much billing and cooing and hedging and milking and all other nice things ending in (ing).

By mid-June Holst was well enough to go home and by the following week had recovered sufficiently so that he was given permission by his doctors to travel to Gregynog to hear Dora Herbert Jones sing Welsh folk songs. Among these was probably his own *O Spiritual Pilgrim* [H188], for soprano and mixed (satb) chorus.

For a time it appeared that Holst was on the mend; his spirits were up and he was able to return to St. Paul's Girls' School and teach on a restricted schedule--once a week. He was also able to do some travelling--he and Isobel visited H. Balfour Gardiner in Oxford--and to do some substantial composing. In June he received a commission from the United States. One Vadim Uraneff wanted him to write some incidental music for *The Song of Solomon* [App. II, 17], a Hollywood pageant planned for that fall.[10] Later in the month Holst composed one of his shortest pieces; it was also one that gave him great joy. *Come Live with Me and Be My Love* [H189], a two-part canon set to Christopher Marlowe's words was composed as a wedding present for Adrian and Ann Boult. Holst presented it to them in an envelope on their July 1st wedding day with specific instructions: "To be opened in Italy and not before." The title, written at the top of the work's only page reads "A Canon for A and A from GH for use in Italy, King's Langley, Gregynog and other nice places."[11] He wrote the following postcard upon their return, referring to the piece in the "P.S." section:

> St. Paul's Girls' School
> Brook Green, Hammersmith,
> W. 6
> July 31[, 1933]
>
> Dear Adrian,
>
> 1) Welcome Home
> 2) My love to your old Dutch

3) And tell her from me not to lead you astray so that you forget as many duties as possible.
4) If you honour me by doing my Choral Symphony I want you to have a free hand. But the more I think of it the more I want D. Silk.[12]

Yours

G.

P.S. 5) When are you two going to sing my latest op. to me?[13]

Another work that was on Holst's mind at during the summer of 1933 was of much larger scope. The classical symphonic cycle had always interested Holst, yet it had always befuddled him. To this point he had made four attempts at writing a symphony: the very early *Symphony in C minor* [App. I, 14] (1892), which he had disowned, the more substantial *The Cotswolds: Symphony in F*, Op. 8 [H47] (1899-1900), which had been performed but remained unpublished, the highly successful *First Choral Symphony*, Op. 41 [H155] (1923-24), and the abandoned *Second Choral Symphony* [App. II, 16] (1926-31), which was to have been based on the poems of George Meredith and for which he had sketchd only a few fragments. His fifth and final attempt was to have been an orchestral symphony. In late 1932, possibly at Durham Cathedral, he had written sketches for an *Allegro*, an *Adagio*, and a *Finale*. Preliminary sketches for the *Scherzo* [H192] came later, on March 22, 1933, when he was bedridden at Elm Crescent.[14] According to his Diary entries, Holst began actual work on the rough draft on Sunday, July 30th and finished the it on Friday, August 18th.[15] One month later, on September 16th, he finished the two-piano version of the *Scherzo*. One of the copies bears the title "Scherzo for two pianos and The Birthday of Nora Day."[16]

Holst had just enough time to complete the full score before his death in May, 1934. The work is scored for piccolo, two flutes, two oboes, cor anglais, two clarinets, two bassoons, four horns, three trumpets, three trombones, tuba, timpani, harp, and strings[17]. None of the other movements were even sketched out. In spite of a rather abrupt ending, the *Scherzo*, at just over five minutes, is long enough to stand on its own as an independent composition. As such, it is Holst's last completed work. The *Scherzo* is both a microcosm and a culmination of Holst's work. Shades of "Uranus," *Hammersmith*, and *A Fugal Concerto* appear throughout its length. Holst never heard the movement performed; it was premiered nearly nine months after his death, on a February 6, 1935 Queen's Hall concert featuring Adrian Boult and the BBC Symphony Orchestra.

While he was writing the two-piano version of the *Scherzo*, Holst was also working on the suite he had promised for the St. Paul's Girls' School Junior Orchestra. This orchestra, under the direction of Vally Lasker, was the training orchestra for the St. Paul's Girls' School Senior Orchestra, which Holst conducted. During the spring of 1932, while he was teaching at Harvard, Holst had transcribed his brass band work, *A Moorside Suite*, specially for the junior orchestra. It works very well but, in the composer's opinion, he couldn't make it sufficiently easy. So, he decided to write an original composition that would better fit the ensemble's needs. *Brook Green Suite* [H190] (1933) is Holst's *pastorale* suite. It is a model of clarity and is very direct, containing few octave doublings or any other unnecessary padding. The suite is only superficially easy; the last movement requires a certain amount of independence from the inner strings. It was into this movement that Holst inserted a tune that he heard at a puppet show in during his trip to Sicily in 1929.

Holst's diary entry for Friday, September 8th reads "finished sketch easy str suite."[18] He continued to refer to it in this manner when he entered the "easy string suite for SP junior orchestra" into his "List of Compositions."[19]

There are two extant manuscript full scores to *Brook Green Suite*; each reveals significant information. The older of these two manuscript scores (at least the one having the older of the two title pages) is the mostly non-autograph engravers' score in the British Library. It shows that Holst considered different titles; it also reveals that Holst had some input into the work's 1934 publication by Curwen, even though the actual publication occurred in the months following his death:

Dedicated to the SPGS Junior Orchestra

Suite for the SPGS Junior Orchestra [line drawn through this]
Brook Green Suite [in pencil]
Short Suite for Strings

Prelude
Gavotte [line drawn through this]
Air
Jig [line drawn through this]
Dance

This Suite is intended for performance by strings only, but optional parts for flute, oboe & clarinet are available [in pencil]

(Ad lib parts for flute, oboe, and clarinet have been added but these are not essential for performance) [ink, crossed out in pencil]

Gustav Holst
St. Paul's Girls' School
Brook Green
London W6

Engraver
Score to be the same
size and style as that
of St. Paul's Suite
herewith.[20]

Holst ultimately decided to call the work *Brook Green Suite*, after the street (and small park) on which St. Paul's Girls' School is located. Vaughan Williams thought that the title might mistakenly imply some programmatic connotation to the unenlightened (as was later the case of Aaron Copland's *Appalachian Spring*), but once Holst decided on the title he stayed firm.

The optional woodwind parts are marked on the score by red lines above and below the string staves. These are indicated with dotted lines in the published score. Unlike the publication of *St. Paul's Suite*, the published set of *Brook Green Suite* does include these optional parts.

At least two tempo markings were changed on this score, perhaps as a result of the first informal run-through of the suite in March, 1934. The tempo of the "Prelude" was marked in Holst's hand as *Andante*. It is the only marking on this page that is in Holst's hand. It was crossed out and replaced with *Allegretto*. Likewise, "Air" was first marked *Andantino* (non-manuscript), which was in turn replaced by *Andante*.

This suite, Holst's shortest, originally had four movements. The original second movement, "Gavotte," was removed after Holst heard the ensemble struggle with it in rehearsal. He said to Imogen, "I think we'll leave out the 'Gavotte,' don't you? It's not as good as the other movements."[21] Holst also altered the title of the final movement from "Jig" to "Dance."

The second manuscript full score is an autograph score at the Royal College of Music. This score is cleaner; the title page again indicates four movements. The 1934 forces of the St. Paul's Girls' School Junior Orchestra can be determined from Holst's own markings on the first page of the first movement:

wind 3fl, 2ob, 2cl
str 3.5.2.3.1[22]

The work was reviewed in *The Times* sometime after its publication:

> This Brook Green Suite (for strings with ad lib parts for flute, oboe, and clarinet) cannot rank amongst Holst's great things. It is far too modest in scope for that. Dedicated to the St. Paul's Girls' School Junior Orchestra, it leaves unexplored those avenues where only an expert technician may venture without fear. Yet it is just as characteristic, just as original in its way as a number from *The Planets*. No other modern composer could write 20 odd bars of an Air without a single "*p*" to describe its dynamic colour; no one else could have found so much variety in simplicity. The 1st movement (Prelude) and the last (Dance) are as devoid of artiface as a piece of Durante, and, as in Durante, every note has its purpose. There are no wheels within wheels; nothing else has been added to please the eye or cloak over mercifully a poor piece of workmanship. Everything is clean as daylight and as attractive. This is the kind of music a too well-known German composer would like to write--music for everybody, direct, unassuming, democratic.[23] Holst does it to perfection, because he is in direct line from Purcell, who wrote Dido and Aeneas or a Young Ladies' Seminary. Holst's foreign colleague, hampered by a tradition that conceives art as something larger and more elaborate than Nature, cannot get within miles of it.[24]

Throughout the year Holst continued to be in demand, although he could not accept any engagements. Fritz Hart, his friend from his Royal College of Music student days, had accepted the conductorship of the Honolulu Symphony Orchestra in Hawaii during the previous year, and invited Holst about doing some guest conducting there. Holst was amazed and amused; he in turn wrote to Imogen, "I've just been asked if I'd like to conduct in Honolulu for four months!"[25] He also heard from Archibald and Dorothy Davison, who were coming to London, probably as a result of a sabbatical from Harvard. The Davisons arrived in London on October 11th. Holst dinner with them on the 12th, but then became ill. The next several weeks were spent in and out of the Beaufort House in Ealing. Holst was given a printed leaflet "After Treatment of Gastric and Duodenal Ulcer" to keep handy at all times. His attending physician, Dr. A. N. Hobbs, of Woodville Rd., Ealing, wrote out several prescriptions for him; these were usually filled by J. W. Carter, MPS, Dispensing and Photographic Chemist.[26]

While under his doctor's supervision, Holst wrote to Whittaker about the Davisons:

St. Paul's Girls' School
Brook Green,
Hammersmith, W. 6

Oct[ober] 25[, 1933]

Dear Will,

Dr Archibald Davison conductor of the Harvard Glee Club and his wife are over here and are coming to Glasgow at the end of next week and he is most anxious to meet you so I have told him to write you at once in order to fix a meeting.

I expect you know of him and his work. He has had the Glee Club for 25 years and has transformed it from a social-function-free-and-easy-bright-and-brotherly-singsong affair into a first rate m v choir.

They were most kind to me last year and I want them to have a first rate time now. And therefore I send them to you!

Yrs Ever,

Gustav[27]

In his notebook, Holst wrote down some of the Davisons' itinerary:

Doc Davison
London Nov 9-20
Oxford a week
London till Xmas[28]

It also appears that Holst planned on having Davison conduct on the St. Paul's Girls' School concert at the end of the term. The name "Doc" appears above a proposed program.[29] Whatever the case, there were a number of occasions when Holst and/or Imogen met with the Davisons that fall. On Sunday, November 12th, Imogen was at St. Paul's Girls' School with the Davisons and two days later they celebrated Dorothy Davison's birthday. On Friday, December 1st, Archibald Davison and Holst met at St. Paul's Girls' School at 3 p.m..

There were other events happening as well that may or may not have involved the Davisons. Imogen was involved with another English Folk Dance and Song Society Concert at the Cecil Sharp House on the Saturday, the 2nd and a Holst-Vaughan Williams "field day," to which Whittaker was invited, was set up for Friday, the 16th.[30] Holst's *Hymn of Jesus* was performed by the Bach Chorale on the Tuesday, the19th. That day also marked the end of term at St. Paul's Girls' School, but Holst could not take his usual celebratory walking tour; he was far too ill.[31]

---

[1]Gustav Holst, *Diary*, Wednesday, March 15, 1933, The Holst Foundation.

[2]Gustav Holst, *Lyric Movement*, British Library Add. MS 47835.

[3]Royal College of Music MS 4567.

[4]Lionel Tertis, Notes for the *Radio Times Programs*, March 18, 1934.

[5]Gustav Holst, *Diary*, Wednesday, March 15, 1933, The Holst Foundation.

[6]Personal correspondence, Gustav Holst to William Gillies Whittaker, March 16[, 1933], quoted in Michael Short (ed.), *Gustav Holst: Letters to W. G. Whittaker* (Glasgow: University of Glasgow Press, 1974), 121.

[7]Gustav Holst, *Diary* entries Wednesday, March 15th through Friday, April 14th, 1933, The Holst Foundation.

[8]*Middlesex County Times*, May 6, 1933.

[9]Personal correspondence, Gustav Holst to "Miss [Vally] Lasker and her singers and players," June 2, 1933, Royal College of Music MS 4569.

[10]The next chapter is devoted to *The Song of Solomon.*

[11]Jerrold Northrop Moore (ed.), *Music and Friends* (London: Hamish Hamilton, 1979), 109-110.

[12]Dorothy Silk, Holst's preferred soprano soloist. Adrian Boult conducted the BBC Symphony Orchestra and Chorus in a broadcast performance of Holst's *First Choral Symphony* on April 11, 1934. Mirian Licette sang the soprano solo on that occasion.

[13]Personal correspondence, Gustav Holst to Adrian Boult, July 31[, 1933], quoted in Jerrold Northrop Moore (ed.), *op. cit.*, 111.

[14]British Library Add. MS 57910C.

[15]Gustav Holst, *Diary*, Sunday, July 30 and Friday, August18, 1933, The Holst Foundation.

[16]Gustav Holst, *Scherzo*, two-piano version, Royal College of Music MS 4545.

[17]Gustav Holst, *Scherzo*, British Library Add. MS 57908.

[18]Gustav Holst, *Diary*, Friday, September 8, 1933.

[19]Gustav Holst, "List of Compositions," British Library Add. MS 57863.

[20]Gustav Holst, *Brook Green Suite*, British Library Add. MS 57908.

[21]Gustav Holst quoted in Imogen Holst (ed.) and Colin Matthews (asst. ed.), *Gustav Holst: The Collected Facsimile Edition, Vol. II: Works for Small Orchestra* (London: Faber Music Ltd., 1977), 165. The "Gavotte" was later arranged for four recorders by Imogen Holst, who played in a recorder quartet with Benjamin Britten in Aldeburgh in the 1950's. It has always baffled this author why this version was published while publication of Holst's original "Gavotte," which displays Holst's artistry, his skillful orchestration, and original intent, was suppressed during

Imogen Holst's lifetime. Holst certainly did not conceive the movement in terms of a recorder quartet.

[22]Gustav Holst, *Suite for the SPGS Junior Orchestra*, Royal College of Music MS 4552.

[23]This appears to be a reference to Paul Hindemith (1895-1963) and his *Gebrauchmusik*.

[24]*The Times*, April 1945 (?); clipping in Vol. 20, on p. 45, of the scrapbooks at the Holst Birthplace Museum, Cheltenham.

[25]Personal correspondence, Gustav Holst to Imogen Holst, Thurs[day, 1933], The Holst Foundation.

[26]Gustav Holst, *Diary*, [1933], The Holst Foundation. Information from the pocket at the back of the binding.

[27]Personal correspondence, Gustav Holst to W. G. Whittaker, Oct[ober] 25[, 1933], quoted in Michael Short (ed.), *op. cit.*, 122.

[28]Gustav Holst, Notebook, starting September, 1933, The Holst Foundation.

[29]*Ibid.*. Davison was known as "Doc" to his friends and students around Harvard. Holst may also have called him by that name.

[30]Personal correspondence, Gustav Holst to W. G. Whittaker, Dec[ember] 7[, 1933], quoted in Michael Short (ed.), *op. cit.*, 123.

[31]Gustav Holst, *Diary*, Sunday, November 12th to Tuesday, December 19, 1933, The Holst Foundation.

CHAPTER XXXIV

THE SONG OF SOLOMON

Perhaps the most mysterious (if not the most obscure) of all of Holst's commissions came during the last year of the composer's life. Holst had been ill for some time; he had not been able to fully recover his health since the bleeding ulcer incident of his 1932 American visit. He had become an invalid and, during the remaining two years of his life, spent a great deal of time in hospitals and nursing homes. This cloud, however, had its silver lining as Holst now was able to write music with an ease that had eluded him for some time.

During the summer of 1933, Holst received the following lengthy letter from Hollywood. Its contents almost mimic the plot of a number of Mickey Rooney-Judy Garland "Let's put on a show!" depression-era film musicals. The letter's author was one Vadim Uraneff, a Russian immigrant who had acted on stage and in silent films. All of Uraneff's letters display fluency in English yet, for whatever reason (perhaps a Russian accent or a voice with little carrying power, etc.), his movie career seemed to be cut short by the advent of sound. Whatever the case, Uraneff was a man of high enthusiasm and, perhaps, even higher aspirations.

June 20, 1933

Gustav Holst, Esq.
c/o St. Paul's Girls' School
Hammersmith, London, England

Dear Sir:

Three weeks ago I sent you my play which is an adaptation of the Biblical Song of Solomon, and is arranged with your music of "The Planets." I hope you received it safely and were able to give it your kind consideration.

As I am not known to you, I have to begin by supplying a few facts in regard to myself. I came to America from Russia where I was born and received my first apprenticeship in the arts of the theater. While in New York I made several productions, associating with Arthur Hopkins, Robert Edmund Jones, Edna St. Vincent Millay and others. For two seasons I was with John Barrymore in "Hamlet" and was later called by Mr. Barrymore to London to participate once again in the production of the play. It was given in The Royal Haymarket Theater, and I wonder if you happened to witness one of the performances. The part of the production which I was particularly called for, was the play within the play (The Mousetrap) which I staged in a new and somewhat elaborate fashion. Very soon after my return to America I was called to Hollywood to play one of the principal parts in the picture "The Sea Beast," and I have remained here ever since. While playing in the motion pictures I continued to work on various theatrical plans, but especially on "The Song of Solomon."

During the work on the play I heard "The Planets" on records, and was overwhelmed by the beauty and the profound significance of the music. As I mention in the preface to the play, the music proved to be a revelation, fitting amazingly, if not miraculously, into its various scenes and my discovery of "The Zodiac Ritual" which was then assuming a definite form. I communicated with your representative in Philadelphia (Curwen, Inc.), and to my great delight received from them the permission to use it.

After a great deal of work envolving [sic] various sacrifices on my part, I completed the play, and I am very anxious to get your opinion about it; also your reaction to the way your music is used, for I would not want to do anything in regard to your music which might not meet with your approval. I am hoping, however, that my admiration for "The Planets" saved me from using your music unwisely and you will approve of the way in which it is arranged.

It is useless for me to say anything about the play itself, since the manuscript which I sent to you is sufficiently complete (with sketches and indications of the score) to give you a definite idea of what I am trying to do. Therefore, I will proceed with the outline of the plan by which the play is to be produced here in Los Angeles.

It is intended to give the play first for a limited engagement of two weeks in "The Shrine Auditorium." It is a very large theater with a seating capacity of over six thousand, a beautiful organ, and a stage with a hundred foot opening. The big seating capacity makes it possible to justify the cost of the production which, needless to say, will be quite considerable.

If the plans will materialize in time for the play to be produced in early October the Los Angeles Philharmonic Orchestra is to be engaged, making the production of the play an important musical event, as well as a dramatic one, and offering additional possibilities in its appeal to the public. As you most probably know, the Los Angeles Philharmonic Orchestra is one of the leading musical organizations in America, while the musical audiences here are quite large and intelligent, because of the Hollywood Bowl concerts, and various musical activities which in most cases are quite successful.

The singers of the Los Angeles Oratorio Society are to be used for the choruses in the play. This could be done without getting out of the budget since the Society would supply two or three hundred singers for a comparatively small contribution to the organization as a whole.

I do not want to conceal from you the fact that, because of conditions in America, the question of financial backing for such a large production is a very difficult one. The backing could only be obtained because of a strong personality of Mr. John Barrymore (the foremost actor of America) and Miss Katharine Hepburn (a new sensational rising star) appearing in the parts of King Solomon and Shulamite; apart from minor adjustments to be made as to their moving picture engagements, their appearance in the play can be arranged. Since I am contributing all my efforts on a percentage basis from the profits, and Mr. Barrymore and Miss Hepburn (two magnetic names with big drawing power) have agreed to do likewise, this practically eliminates the possibility of a loss of money, and large profits can be expected by all concerned.

A question of great imporatnce now is if you will be willing to undertake the writing or compiling of the additional music which is needed to complete the work. Needless to say, I cannot conceive of any other composer writing this additional music, and that the success of the plan would greatly depend on your decision in the matter. Though the portion of the additional music is not very large, since "The Planets" cover most of the music which is necessary, I realize, of course, that it will require a great deal of effort. Yet, judging by the miraculous experience with "The Planets," I would not be at all surprised if most of the additional music needed could be found in your other compositions which, unfortunately, I have had no opportunity to hear.

I am hoping that the play appeals to you sufficiently to justify your favorable decision in the matter, and that you would consider an offer of ten per cent of my own earnings, for my part of conceiving, designing, and staging of the play, as a suitable compensation for this work. It seems to me that this would be the only arrangement which will be practical, since by such an agreement our interests would be tied together, and which protect my rights, and securing the best possible arrangement for myself, I would be automatically protecting your interests as well. As soon as I hear from you that this arrangement would be satisfactory I will send you a signed contract confirming it.

Another question which I wish you would give your kind consideration is the posssibility of your coming to Los Angeles to conduct your music in the production of the play. While discussing this plan with Mr. Barrymore, who was very much impressed by "The Planets," we both thought that perhaps this possibility might be of interest to you.

In that case I propose that the compensation for the additional music would be limited to five percent from my earning for conceiving, designing and the staging of the play, and that you would suggest the sum of money you are to receive before leaving for America; the salary (per week) for the additional weeks of the performances and the salary (per week) for the additional weeks, if the play is to be continued after this limited engagement.

In deciding upon these questions I wish you would bear in mind that your presence would be necessary for at least two weeks before the opening night, in order to take charge of the musical end of the production and to bring it to a desired unity; also that since the earliest date for the play could be given would be the beginning of October, it would be desirable to have the score of the additional music not later than the end of August.

I would appreciate tremendously if you would inform me on the following questions by letter and also by cable (I enclose a money order for Two Pounds) since it is of utmost importance for me to know about your decision immediately.

1. Would you be willing to undertake the writing or compiling of the additional music on conditions stated in this letter?
2. How soon the score of the additional music could be sent?
3. Would you consider to come to conduct your music in the production of the play?
4. The amount, besides the salary, you would expect to receive before starting for America;
5. The salary (per week) for the guaranteed two weeks of the limited engagement;
6. The salary (per week) for the additional weeks.

I would suggest that because of the limitations of a cable you would put the numbers of the questions accompanied by your answers in a following manner: first, (yes or no); second, (the date); third, (yes or no); fourth, (the amount); fifth, (the amount); sixth (the amount).

Hoping to receive from you a favorable reply,

I remain,

Very truly yours

Vadim Uraneff

Vadim Uraneff
1007 1/2 North Alfred Street,
Hollywood, Calif., U. S. A.[1]

What sensational plans! The scope of this venture appears to have been too fantastic to bring to fruition unless, of course, Uraneff had an incredible network of connections. The nature and extent of Uraneff's friendship with John Barrymore is difficult to ascertain, although both appeared together in at least one movie, *The Sea Beast* (1926), the first and silent version of Herman Melville's classic novel *Moby Dick*. Barrymore starred as Captain Ahab. Four years later Barrymore reprised his role in the first sound version, which now carried the name of the novel. Uraneff's connections with Katharine Hepburn, if there were any, appear to have been through Barrymore, who starred with the young actress in *Bill of Divorcement* (1932), her motion picture debut. By 1933 both Hepburn and Barrymore were in high demand, both on and off the screen. She appeared in at least three major movies (*Christopher Strong*, *Little Women*, and *Morning*

Glory--her first Oscar-winning performance) that year; he in at least two (*Dinner at Eight* and *Topaze*). Finally, one must question any connections that Uraneff may have had with the leadership of the fledgling Los Angeles Philharmonic Orchestra. Although still in its infancy, the orchestra was lead by the great German conductor Otto Klemperer. Klemperer himself was brand new to the West Coast in 1933, having just emigrated from his homeland.

As if the length of the above letter were not enough to justify an international mailing, Uraneff included more. His set of instructions to Holst refer to the various scenes and page numbers of *The Song of Solomon* manuscript as well as rehearsal numbers found in *The Planets*::

> The Additional Music for the Play:
>
> I. The overture lasting from five to eight minutes, arranged from the music used later in the play. Manuscript, Page 8. Suggestions: Neptune (Parts V, VI and VII) and Uranus (Parts V, VI and VII) should not be used so as the striking effect of this music would be saved for scenes in the play. It is advisable to use Mars, so that the audience would get accustomed to its sound; also Jupiter and Venus. It might be effective to end the overture with the spectacular music of the finale of Mars.
>
> II. The scene between Shulamite and the Lover. Manuscript, Page 12, from "The lights are slowly dimmed around Shulamite...". The Lover sings the lines, Shulamite recites them to music. Suggestions: Perhaps it would be possible to arrange the song of the Lover to the music of Venus used later for the Dream Scene of the First Act.
>
> III. The Scene of Psalms. Manuscript, Pages 22, 23, and 24.
> Suggestions: Perhaps in several places the singing could be interrupted by orchestral interludes as on Page 23. Music, if desired, might play during the recitation of the lines by the Narrators on Page 23; also during Solomon's speech on Page 24.
>
> IV. The choruses returning after Shulamite's prayer. Manuscript, Page 85. (Two or Three minutes).
> Suggestions: It might be advisable to end the music with a passage from Neptune. (Part VII), while the curtains are opening and the tableau of the Adoration Scene is revealed, as this part of Neptune is used for the same purpose in the beginning of the Second Act.

V. Adoration of the Bride. Manuscript, Pages 27, 28. Female choruses only. Perhaps without orchestra.

VI. The Gold Choruses come down the steps in the scene of the Feast. Manuscript, Page 31. Music of Jupiter (Andante Maestoso of Part VIII and Part IX) to be arranged as a song without words for male voices.

VII. Egyptian number of the Feast scene. Manuscript, Page 32. (Three to five minutes.)

VIII. Bachanale of the Feast scene. Manuscript, Page 32 from: "As the Egyptian number ends..." (Three to five minutes.)

IX. Few bars of music for the end of the First Act.

X. The Revelation of the Bride's beauty. Manuscript, Pages 49, 50.

XI. Panic in the Palace. Manuscript, Page 52 from: "The sound of trumpets..."
Suggestions: Perhaps the effect of growing panic could be accentuated by music.

XII. Solomon's renounciation. Manuscript, Page 55. (Two minutes at the most.)

Uraneff's next letter, dated August 10, indicates that Holst had given him at least a tentative positve response. By this time, however, Uraneff was already having some difficulty with the *modus operandi* for his ambitious project and recognized the fact that an early October opening was not feasible. He now proposed a January or February opening. With his letter, Uraneff enclosed two copies of his own written statement of agreement for Holst to sign:

August 10, 1933

Gustav Holst, Esq.
@ St. Paul's Girls' School
Brook Green, Hammersmith W6

Dear Sir:

This is to confirm the agreement which was reached between us through our correspondence, stating:

1. That you approve of using the music of your orchestral suite, "The Planets," in the production of my adaptation of Solomon's Song of Songs;

2. That you agree to undertake the composing of the additional music necessary for this play which is listed in the manuscript and in the statement sent to you by me previously;

3. That you agree to start the composition of this music at your earliest convenience and forward me the manuscript of an orchestral arrangement of such not later than_______, 1933.

4. That I agree to pay you as a compensation for this work, ten percent (10%) of all the money earned by me for my services of conceiving, designing, and staging of the play.

Should a satisfactory agreement be reached in regard to your coming to America to conduct your music in the production of the play, the compensation will be limited to five percent (5%) of all the money earned by me for the above mentioned services.

Sincerely yours,

Vadim Uraneff [signature]
Vadim Uraneff [typed]
10071/2 N. Alfred St.
Hollywood, California

Approved and accepted
_________________, 1933

____
Gustav Holst [typed][2]

Uraneff had underestimated Holst. By 1933 the composer was certainly no novice when it came to signing contracts. In the past two years alone, he had learned much from contacts such as Duncan McKenzie and Arthur Judson. Holst countered with his own terms:

St. Paul's Girls' School
Hammersmith, London, W. 6
31st August 1933

Dear Mr. Uraneff,

Thanks for your letter of August 10th.
I will write the extra music for your play on the following conditions:--

(1) The score will reach you on or before Jan. 1st 1934.
(2) My fee for doing so will be 10 per cent of all the money earned by you, but I must have a guaranteed minimum of 60 (sixty) pounds; £30 to be paid before starting to write the music, and the other £30 to be paid whenever you receive the score.
(3) You are to have free use of this new music for this production. Apart from this, all rights of the music are my property.
(4) I cannot express approval or disapproval of your use of my "Planets" music, but I agree to your using it subject to satisfactory arrangements being made with my publishers Messrs Curwen or their agents in the U.S.A.
(5) I beg that no alterations are made in my "Planets". Whenever one of them is too long, would you pause and 'fade out' (*decresc.* to ppp) on a suitable chord. and not allow anyone to add a cadence or even a single chord.
(6) The full orchestra, as demanded in the score, to be used.
(7) For overture, any movement or movements fo the "Planets" may be used <u>entire</u> and not cut or altered in any way. I should suggest Uranus and Neptune, but I see you do not wish this. Perhaps Mars, Venus or Venus[,] Jupiter would do. I leave this to you, as long as the Planets you use as overture are played from beginning to end without alteration.
(8) If you insist on using the tune in "Jupiter" (Andante Maestoso) as a male chorus it must be sung in unison in the key of C. This has already been arranged and published to the words "I vow to thee my country." and the necessary orchestral parts can be hired from the publisher.

> (9) In writing the rest of the music I will bear in mind your suggestions, but of course I must decide whether or not to introduce melodies from "The Planets".
>
> I regret that it is impossible for me to undertake any conducting for some time to come. It would be splendid if you could get Mr Goosens[3] of Cincinnati, who knows all my music and always conducts it so well; but there is no lack of good conductors in the U.S.A..
>
> In order to save you the rush of copying so many orchestral parts all at once, it might be well for me to send each number as soon as it is finished.
>
> Yours sincerely,
>
> Gustav Holst
>
> P.S.:-- It is of course understood that all orchestral parts made by you of the new music become my property after your last performance, and are sent by you to my publishers Curwen Inc., 441 Abbotsford Road, Germantown, Philadelphia, U.S.A.[4]

While contemplating Uraneff's ideas, Holst received a second offer to write a film score. In ill health and with the problems of *The Bells* still fresh on his mind, the composer was not overly anxious to commit himself to such a project. Still, Holst respected the sound film as a viable medium for musical expression and was willing to give it another try. It appears, however, that Holst was not the only one to be experiencing a bout of reticence. He wrote about this to Imogen in a letter that reveals the Holstian wit to have been as strong as ever:

> ....The Film Producer has asked me to lunch on Wednesday! This after not answering my last six letters. If he is as angry with me as I am with him we should be worth listening to.
>
> I've sent my terms to the Song of Solomon 1007 1/2 etc. Hollywood and they ought to--judging by the terms he[5] offered me--upset him a bit. But if he accepts and the Film Chap tempts me to do his little job I shall be in a hole for [my] brain is addled and I've no ideas.
>
> On thinking it over I've decided that if I do let myself in for both[6] the simplest plan will be for you and me to change places. Of course I've forgotten all about the piano and I never learnt aural training but I could

> sit back in an easy chair and look wise and kindly and the people could do the rest. While you could make a fortune on the Talkies....[7]

Perhaps to Holst's surprise, his terms did not upset Uraneff, who responded, "...all the conditions stated in your letter are perfectly acceptable to me. One point only has to be modified..."[8] That point had to do with particulars concerning the orchestral parts. Uraneff also expressed a desire for an overture that "will have a spectacular finale."[9]

In the meantime, Holst's health had begun to deteriorate once again. He let Uraneff know about this and the problems that it would cause in meeting deadlines. Uraneff responded, offering to accommodate Holst's illness:

> November 1, 1933
>
> Dear Mr. Holst,
>
> I received your letter yesterday, and sent you immediately a cable, which I hope you have received safely. I was very sorry indeed to hear about your illness and I hope that this letter will find you in better health.
>
> Please do not worry about not being in time with the additional music. Needless to say, the sooner it is composed the more beneficial it will be for the play and to the plan in general. But this play of mine is of such a nature and the effort I already put into it is so great that I cannot afford to spoil it by the introduction of inferior music, by someone else, and as I said in my cable, I will wait until it is composed by you. It is the only way to bring about the desired unity, which to my mind is the most important thing about the work as a whole.
>
> Your plan to compose it suits me perfectly. If Psalms (III), the Song of the Zodiac Ritual (X) and the choruses of the Adoration Scene (V), are composed first it will help tremendously, for the reasons I mentioned in my last letter. The Egyptian number (VII) and the Bachanal (VIII), if composed next, would complete the important music that is necessary, as the other music is not as important.
>
> There are certain items on my list with which you now do not have to bother at all. One is the Overture (I); the other, "The Gold choruses" (VI) as it is already by you as a song. The third is the "Song of the Lover" (II). I wonder if I could use part of "Venus" for that, letting the lover recite the lines instead of singing. The unreality of the moment will be, I believe, sufficiently emphasized by the lighting and the presence of music. In case

this is agreeable to you, I would suggest that the "Song of the Zodiac Ritual" (X) would be written with a solo for a female voice (Contralto, perhaps) for it really would be more logical, since Shulamite at that moment is left with the Priestesses only.

It was planned originally for the tenor because of The Lover's Song, where the voice of the same singer was to be used. As you know, the good tenor is much rarer than a good contralto, and is therefore more expensive to have. In case of contralto we could get an excellent singer with a name, which would be an additional box office attraction, still remaining within the limits of the budget.

I am very thankful to you for your suggestion to use "Neptune" for "The choruses returning" (IV), as I think it will be very impressive; also for the last moment (XII) where it is inevitable, but I do think that there ought to be a moment of music to indicate the struggle of Solomon before the Neptune music is introduced. This, however, just as IX and XI[,] is very short and not so important. I believe this covers the ground as far as the music is concerned.

I am sending you the Money Order for Ninety-Six Dollars ($96.00) which is equal to £20, as there is a new rule in America, by which one cannot send to England more than $100.00 without a special permit which would take time. I will send you the remaining £10 shortly after, most probably from San Francisco, where I am going for a short visit. My usual address will reach me always, however.

Hoping once again that you are feeling better and will not be troubled by your illness again.

Sincerely yours

Vadim Uraneff
10071/2 N. Alfred Street
Hollywood, California

P.S.

1. I will be glad, of course, to take care of the copyright problem for you, if you authorize me to do so.

2. Your idea for the treatment of the Egyptian number is excellent.

3. If because of the rate of exchange, which is so uncertain at present, you would receive in pounds less than the mentioned amount, I will be glad, of course, to pay the difference as soon as I hear from you.[10]

Holst worked on *The Song of Solomon* as best he could. His final sketchbook, dating from mid-1933 until his death, contains rather extensive sketches for the work, some seven double-pages in all.[11] The composer was down for most of this time and two of his customary location entries "SOS (in bed 103)"[12] and "Ealing"[13] betray his state of being. Words on the sketches themselves-- "Chant," "dance rhythm," "tunes," "ostinato," "solo dance," "Scale for Psalm," "bass?," "S of S Bach (103)" and "Women's voices"--indicate that he was more or less following Uraneff's suggestions. He also wrote in a notebook "Song of Sol copy words of Psalm (pages 23, 24?),"[14] which may indicate that he was trying to have his music coincide with Uraneff's manuscript text. Holst's music for *The Song of Solomon*, as it exists in the form of sketches, is characteristic of the composer's late style, with occasional retrogressions (possibly intentional) to his harmonic writing from the time of *The Planets.*

According to a letter from Uraneff dated December 26, 1933, Holst had completed at least three of the sections by that date. Uraneff wrote, "I received the music for the Psalms, also for the "Adoration fo the Bride" and the "Zodiac Ritual"....[15] In the same letter Uraneff indicated that he cabled ten pounds to Holst, thus fulfilling the remainder of the first payment of the contract. Yet Holst, as far as can be determined, composed no more music for the project. The four remaining notebook sketches, beginning with "New Lodge Dec. 23 Sym I" and ending with "Jan 26," were for an unfinished symphony (of which only the "Scherzo" was completed), not for *The Song of Solomon*[16].

Holst's passing the following spring did not mean the end for *The Song of Solomon* project, however, since Imogen Holst offered to complete the music. In a letter written to her shortly after her father's death, Uraneff specified details of the monetary agreement, mentioning that the first 30 pounds had been sent. He also indicated that the ten additional musical numbers originally agreed upon[17] had been reduced to five, due to Holst's ill health. Four of them--"Psalms," "Adoration Scene," "Song of the Chief Priestess," and "Solo Dance at the Feast"--had been received, but a fifth, "The Bachanale," had not. He then asked Imogen to complete the "Bachanale," stipulating the length to be from five to six minutes and, since it was to end the first act of the play, to be "as wild and as sensuous as possble."[18]

To this point in the letter, Uraneff stayed within the terms specified in Gustav Holst's letter of August 31, 1933. Beyond this, however, he displayed the tendencies of a manipulator. Uraneff stated that for the overture he wanted to use Uranus (V-VI), Venus (I-IV) and Mars (VI-XII) and asked Imogen to write two connecting links, so that the overture would last six minutes. This was in direct violation of Gustav Holst's own wishes for his *Planets* movements. Holst had stipulated that the movements "be played from beginning to end without alteration"[19]. Uraneff also asked for a number of other items, including a short number for the "Panic in the Palace" (one of the original twelve pieces proposed), photographs of both composers, and a piano score in addition to the orchestral score. He also asked Imogen to supercede for him in regard to copyrights and publishers, and asked that two complete sets of the music be sold directly to him, instead of having to rent it from the publishers

What were Uraneff's true intentions? One can only speculate. At best, it appears that Uraneff was trying to take whatever shortcuts were available in order to save time. At that point (late June, 1934), Uraneff was expecting for the play to be produced in early October, less than four months in the future. At worse, it appears that Uraneff was taking advantage of Imogen Holst's grief-stricken state of mind in the months immediately following her father's death, in order to secure as much music from her for as little as possible.

In Uraneff's defense, however, it must be stated that he did relent in his demands for a *Planets* medley overture, suggesting the use of "Mars" (over Imogen Holst's suggestion of "Jupiter") in a letter dated August 30, 1934. He also promised to keep Imogen informed as to the progress of the project, although there is no extant documentation to support this. Of interest is Uraneff's postscript commentary on Imogen Holst's musical contribution to the project:

> P.S. I was ready to mail this letter when your music arrived. Though my opinion would be of little value to you as I am not a musician, I would like to say how much I admired the music you composed. Bachanal is most impressive and I am sure a marvellous Ballet can be staged to it because of its brilliancy and variety. Thank you once again for everything you have done.[20]

This marks the end of all extant correspondence from Uraneff. The music for *The Song of Solomon* remains enshrouded in mystery. The completed sections of the work--by either Gustav Holst or Imogen Holst--that were received and acknowledged by Uraneff are missing. What survives are the previously mentioned sketches, vocal score fragments (including a setting of "Camphire with spikenard, spikenard with saffron"), a dance, and the following Psalms :

1. "Behold, O God our shield" SATB and orchestra
2. "The King shall joy in thy strength" TBB unaccompanied
3. "Who covereth thyself with light" SSA and orchestra

4. "The floods have lifted up their voices" SATB and orchestra
5. "Praise ye the Lord from the heavens" SATB and orchestra[21]

On March 14, 1974, nearly forty years after Gustav Holst's death, the Linden Singers were featured in a BBC concert given in St. John's, Smith Square, London, during which a set of four choruses from *The Song of Solomon* received their premiere performance. Imogen Holst, who served as editor for these pieces, conducted. Timings for each are included:

Behold, O God, our shield	1'17"
The King shall joy in thy strength, O Lord	1'59"
Look from the top of Amana	24"
Camphire with spikenard	1'49"

This performance--consisting of only five and one-half minutes of music--may very well be all that has ever been performed of Uraneff's extremely ambitious project.

---

[1]Personal correspondence, Vadim Uraneff to Gustav Holst, June 30, 1933, The Holst Foundation.
[2]Proposed letter of agreement from Vadim Uraneff to Gustav Holst, August 10, 1933, The Holst Foundation.
[3]London-born Eugene Goosens (1893-1962) conducted the Cincinnati Symphony Orchestra from 1931 through 1947.
[4]Business correspondence, Gustav Holst to Vadim Uraneff, August 31, 1933, The Holst Foundation.
[5]Uraneff.
[6]*The Song of Solomon* and the film.
[7]Personal correspondence, Gustav Holst to Imogen Holst, September 4, 1933, The Holst Foundation.
[8]Personal correspondence, Vadim Uraneff to Gustav Holst, September 29, 1933, The Holst Foundation.
[9]*Ibid.*
[10]Personal correspondence, Vadim Uraneff to Gustav Holst, November 1, 1933, The Holst Foundation.
[11]British Library Add MS 47838.
[12]103 Talgarth Road, Vally Lasker's townhouse.
[13]Beaufort House, a nursing home at Ealing.
[14]Gustav Holst, Notebook, September, 1933, The Holst Foundation.
[15]Personal correspondence, Vadim Uraneff to Gustav Holst, December 26, 1933, The Holst Foundation.
[16]British Library Add MS 47838.
[17]According to "The Additional Music for the Play" sheet, there were actually twelve that

accompanied Uraneff's June 20, 1933 correspondence to Holst.

[18]Personal correspondence, Vadim Uraneff to Imogen Holst, June 28, 1934, The Holst Foundation.

[19]Business correspondence, Gustav Holst to Vadim Uraneff, August 31, 1933, The Holst Foundation. See point #7 in the main text.

[20]Personal correspondence, Vadim Uraneff to Imogen Holst, August 30, 1934, The Holst Foundation.

[21]Imogen Holst (ed.), *A Thematic Catalogue of Gustav Holst's Music* (London: Faber Music, Ltd., 1974), 238.

CHAPTER XXXV

THE FINAL MONTHS

On Friday, December 22, 1933 Holst checked into the New Lodge Clinic at Windsor Forest. There he would undergo a series of X-rays and tests. It was really the only thing to do since the treatments and medicines received thus far had had little or effect. New Lodge Clinic was expensive and Holst's friend, H. Balfour Gardiner, who had helped him so many times in the past, offered to pay for two months of the fees. After Holst's death Gardiner's generosity extended far beyond this; he paid for all of Holst's nursing and operation expenses.[1]

Holst's spirits started to improve in January, 1934. He was visited by his family, of course, and by many of his friends--Henry Walford Davies, E. H. Fellowes, Mabel Rodwell Jones, Vally Lasker, Archibald and Dorothy Davison, Frances Ralph Gray, and Balfour Gardiner, to name a few. He also had received a picture from former Morleyite Walter Gandy, who had been instrumental in the 1927 Samuel Wesley discovery. Holst wrote to him:

Jan[uary] 17[, 1934]
New Lodge Clinic
Windsor Forest
Berks

Dear Gandy

Thank you for your beautiful picture. Forgive delay in writing. I have been here during Xmas and hope to be let loose in a fortnight in the condition of a 100% He man instead of something on a fifty-fifty basis.

Which reminds me that Dr. Davison is both delighted and excited with your kind present. Your fame as an artist will spread in Cambridge Mass. We hope to have his birthday party by the end of March.

Y Sincerely,

Gustav Holst[2]

Holst was hoping to be released in time to attend the premiere of *The Tale of the Wandering Scholar* [H176] (1929-30) but that was not to be the case. The work was first performed on Wednesday, January 31, 1934 at the David Lewis Theatre in Liverpool. Dr. J. E. Wallace, a choir director who was also a broadcaster of music talks, conducted the University of Liverpool Music Society. The cast included Richard Pryce (Louis), Irene Eastwood--later known as Anne Ziegler (Alison), S. R. Maher (Father Philippe) and John Wood (Pierre). The opera was double-billed with Purcell's *Dido and Aeneas*. On the previous evening *Savitri* had been doubled-billed with Purcell's opera. *The Tale of the Wandering Scholar* was performed the next night (February 1st) as well and all three operas were broadcast on February 2nd.[3] The entire affair was produced by Frederick Wilkinson, who had hosted Holst on a number of occasions when the composer was in the Liverpool area. Wilkinson visited Holst at New Lodge Clinic shortly after the performances had taken place. Holst probably heard the broadcast--it is mentioned in his diary--but it may not have been to his liking. The performance was handicapped by an instrumental component of strings and piano, instead of the chamber orchestra instrumentation of strings, woodwinds, and horns indicated by the composer.

In the meantime Holst had little to do except to listen to the radio, write letters and read. He commented to Imogen, "Did I tell you I borrowed a Bible from Canon Fellows? I wanted to read the minor prophets but found they had too much Hitler in them for my taste."[4] He also commented about other sources:

> I expect you are right, and Shakespeare is the man for me. But I must wait till I can get him in larger print. At present I'm finishing Neale's 'Queen Elizabeth'.
>
> What a book!
> " " Woman!
> " an Age!
> Give me the 20th century[5].

An undated letter to Walter Piston probably dates from about this time. Holst's wit was as strong as ever:

St. Paul's Girls' School
Brook Green
London W

Dear Piston

After falling on the back of my head ten years ago I wrote a trio for fl, oboe and viola each in a different key.[6]

After getting a duodenal ulcer I wrote these things (see If t'were the time of lilies, Lovely Venus, Truth of all truth,)[7] in 1932 on my return home.

If your pupils at Harvard (to whom my warm greetings) still yearn to discover theories and to study musicology instead of writing notes on ms paper, you might set them to write a thesis on the relation of disease to multitonality.

Let me know how you are getting on and what you are writing.

Greetings to the Missus

Y Ever

Gustav Holst[8]

Holst never did accept the Harvard approach to teaching composition. Nearly two years earlier, shortly after his return from America, he wrote to Imogen, who had just began her teaching career, "Your school certainly sounds rum--almost as rum as Division of Music, Harvard, Mass."[9]

Holst may have also been able to do some orchestration, as is implied in the following letter to Adrian Boult:

New Lodge Clinic
Windsor Forest.
Berks.
Feb[ruary] 11[, 1934]

Dear Adrian,

I hope you and Anne had a terrific holiday, all sunshine and sea, with no letters or scores or other impediments.

The full score and parts of the Lyric Movement should reach you on Tuesday. Tertis[10] has the piano score if you want it.

If my ulcer has not healed by the 22nd the doctors suggest my leaving this nursing home and either having an operation or leading a 'restricted life.' I shall certainly do the latter in order to get further advice on the matter. But 'restricted life' will mean no going out at night (amongst other disablements) so that I shall not be able to come to the concert on March 18. So please invite me to all the rehearsals.

Don't bother to answer this now that you are so busy.

Y Ever

Gustav[11]

Holst left New Lodge Clinic during the last week of February unhealed. On February 23rd, Edward Elgar died at the age of seventy-six. Less than two weeks later, on March 5th, Norman O'Neill was killed in a car crash. The deaths of these two composers loomed large in the mind of Holst, who soon had to face the decision of either permanently leading a restricted life or having a life-or-death surgical operation. Nevertheless, in the next two weeks Holst was able to attempt to regain a sense of normalcy, returning to the Jolly Talgarth, meeting with Lionel Tertis about the forthcoming broadcast of *Lyric Movement*, attending a performance of madrigals by the St. Paul's Girls' School Music Society on Friday, March 2nd and travelling to Oxford for a concert featuring Imogen on Saturday, March 3rd.[12] Two days later he wrote to Adrian Boult via Boult's secretary Gwen Beckett:

St. Paul's Girls' School
Brook Green, Hammersmith,
W.6.
March 5[, 1934]

Dear Mrs. Beckett

I was going to write a long letter to Dr Boult when your kind one arrived so I'll live up to my principles and BMB.[13]

Would you thank the gentleman who sent me the three tickets for each of the rehearsals and the performance on March 18.[14] Could I have the same number again?

Would you tell Mr Lord that I regret I cannot write the program notes for my choral symphony. I'm not the man for that job because I hate all explanations of music unless I've heard the music beforehand (because they can't do any harm then). Mr. Tertis is writing the note for the viola piece[15] on March 18 and is leaving out the only imporatnt point which is that it is written for and dedicated to him!

Could I have the score and parts for the viola piece (Lyric Movement) for a few days in order to make a slight alteration. If this is not convenient I enclose a sketch of the bar to be changed. It is the second bar of the Poco Animato in E major (only the first three beats in the violins and violas are altered). If Dr Boult wants the score would you get this little alteration made in score and parts and let me have the bill?

I am so sorry that I never told him that I left the Clinic ten days ago unhealed. The doctors there wanted me to be operated on at once as they said I was in such good condition. I did not feel so at all and felt and still feel much disappointed and quite cross. I have gone back to my regular doctor[16] who is a sensible unpretentious GP. But he feels that as medicine has failed I ought to try surgery. A year ago I wanted to (he was against it then) because I though that surgery was a matter of kill or cure and I'm all for that. But now they tell me that at my age the only really useful operation would probably take a year to get over!!! So I've warned my GP that I'm thinking of trying quacks and he has promised not to be stuffy. But for the next week or so I want to try and lead a quiet normal life and to think things over and to lose my bad temper!

In answer to you two queries, I would love to be worried--which usually means 'interested'-- about work and am thinking most deliberately about consulting Sir John Weir. I've no brains for spoiling music paper yet and am not allowed to wag a stick so Misses Day and Lasker do the latter for me when I teach and the nearest I get to the former is to correct extremely badly copied parts.

Also I--as you may notice--have taken to writing very long letters.

Yr Sincerely

Gustav Holst[17]

It could have been during these days that Holst went to visit fellow composer Herbert Howells. Christopher Palmer comments:

> Herbert Howells recalled Holst turning up on the doorstep of his home in Barnes on a Saturday night in the 1930's. He looked sad and ill. He refused supper and went up instead to the 'den' to look at manuscripts and see the children, Ursula and Michael. A performance of *The Planets* was being broadcast that night, and with great difficulty, Herbert and Dorothy induced him to come down and listen. He seemed half dead and scarcely able to talk. He listened to *The Planets* in a far-off way and only came to life when the audience started joining in the great tune in 'Jupiter'. Then the tears rolled down his face. Afterwards Howells walked him to the bus-stop and Holst told him how pleased he was to have seen him that evening: 'Idon't think you'll be seeing much more of me'. And so it turned out.[18]

On Wednesday, March 7th Holst suffered a relapse at Elm Crescent.[19] It was not too serious and he was out and about in five days. He wanted to return to his teaching at St. Paul's Girls' School and, against his doctors' orders, sneak into the BBC studios for the March 17th rehearsal and March 18th broadcast of *Lyric Movement*. When the time came, however, Holst found that he was simply not up to the task of doing these things. He wrote to Boult:

> 2 Elm Cresc
> Saturday [March 17, 1934]
>
> Dear Adrian
>
> You and Tertis are to have absolutely free hand over my new thing. Just do what you like with it. And accept my thanks in advance, also my blessing. And do the same to L T[20] and the other players.
>
> Yr Ever
>
> Gustav
>
> I shall listen in tomorrow.[21]

Holst did indeed listen to the broadcast from his Elm Crescent room.

The exact date of the run-through of *Brook Green Suite* is difficult to determine from Holst's diary entries. His entry for Tuesday, March 20th reads "Junior Musical Comp" while his entry for two days later reads "SPGS rehearse 2:15 103."[22] A notebook entry reads "March 22 VL Invite Orchestra,"[23] perhaps indicating that this was indeed the day of the first rehearsal of the work and that both orchestras were involved in the reading. A likely scenario is that *Brook Green Suite* may have been tried out by the Junior Orchestra alone on the 20th, and that both orchestras were combined to run through it on the 22nd.[24]

Holst was ill again on Tuesday, the 27th and nine days later was again in bed at Beaufort House nursing home. It appears that Holst did not go out again. One week later, the *First Choral Symphony* was broadcast by the BBC Orchestra and Chorus, with Adrian Boult at the helm. Holst, who had listened to the performance on the radio, was very pleased and expressed his appreciation in mathematical terms to Boult:

April 12[, 1934]

A C Boult Esq
Broadcasting House
London W 1

nth 123 5678
(Thanks) X (Gratitude (blessings)

Gustav[25]

Holst tried hard to keep his spirits up and with some exceptions, such as his fatalistic comment to Howells, he was able to do just that. He thought about teaching, noting the start of summer term at St. Paul's Girls' School in his diary[26]. He continued to score the *Scherzo* and kept up with his correspondence. When he had heard that Imogen met up with Frank Winterbottom, tubist and instrumentation teacher at the Royal Military School of Music at Kneller Hall, Holst sent his greetings to his old friend:

> Give my warmest greetings to Winterbottom who is a fine artist and an old pal. We first played together in /99 at the Lyceum during the Carl Rosa London season and he was just behind me and what a splendid tone he had! (At Hull we were behind the basses but I think I've told you that tale).[27]

Holst was expecting to have his operation at the end of April, but it was postponed because of his weak condition. He wrote to Boult:

Beaufort House
Ealing W5
Wed eve
[May 2, 1934]

Good luck to the Festival. Just learnt definitely that my 'op' (not a musical one) is postponed for 2 1/2 or 3 weeks.

Y

Gustav[28]

He also wrote to Imogen, "Bloodily speaking, I'm in the middle sixties, and I've got to be over 80 before they carve me, so that's not likely to be before we meet on Sunday."[29]

Another Whitsuntide was approaching that would not involve him. Once again it was held at Bosham, near Chicester. Holst sent the following message, written on a St. Paul's Girls' School postcard, directly to the vicar, Rev. George Street, to be passed along to all of the particpants:

May 18[, 1934]
St. Paul's Girls' School
Brook Green, Hammersmith,
W. 6

I wish you all Good Luck, Good Weather, much playing and almost too much singing and many happy returns of the Day (I mean Days).

And I wish myself the joy of your Fellowship at Whitsuntide 1935.

Gustav Holst[30]

The positive tone of the last sentence is reflective of the optimism with which Holst as well as his friends and relatives approached his operation. He didn't want to worry about dying if he wasn't going to die. When his operation was finally scheduled, he was pleased. It meant that the whole affair would soon be over and that he could get back to his work.

At Beaufort House on Wednesday, May 23rd Holst underwent a major operation for the removal of the duodenal ulcer that had plagued him for more than two years. The operation itself was successful, but the doctors warned that Holst would not be out of danger for the next three days and that recovery would be slow. As it turned out, the strain to recover proved to be too great. Gustav Holst died of heart failure on Friday, May 25, 1934, with Isobel at his side. His passing was peaceful.

All those who knew him were shocked. Nobody was prepared for this worst case scenario. Holst had lived 59 1/2 years, about the average life expectancy for 1934, yet mentally and creatively he was not spent. There had been no tapering off in his compositional effort. In that regard, his death could be considered premature. Elgar's death had been taken in stride--he was seventy-six and had composed comparatively little in the past two decades--but Holst's was unexpected. He had his symphony to finish and other works loomed on the horizon. It is fitting that the final entry he made into his last sketch book is an imperfect half cadence. Holst's death was not the last composer death to come in 1934; on June 10th, less than three weeks later, Frederick Delius would pass away at the age of seventy-two. England lost three internationally acclaimed composers that year--four counting Norman O'Neill, whose music was not as well known.

Although always concerned about financials matters, Holst did not die a pauper. He left an estate of £9, 315 with a net personalty of £9, 064.[31] Some of this may have been in the form of life insurance payments or late collections of royalty payments. He had generally led a life of thrift, though not to the extreme.

Holst was cremated at Golders Green Crematorium on Monday, May 28, 1934.[32] Three weeks later, on June 19th a memorial service was held by St. Paul's Girls' School at St. John's Church, Smith Square. Bishop George Bell gave the eulogy, Rose Morse and Dorothea Walenn sang solos, and the school chorus sang some of Holst's favorite music.

At 9:20 p.m. on Friday, June 22nd The B.B.C. Orchestra and the Wireless Singers broadcast "Gustav Holst: A Memorial Concert." The program included works from various stages of the composer's career. Adrian Boult conducted three movements from the *Suite de Ballet*, Op. 10, three selections from the Second and Third groups of *Choral Hymns from the Rig Veda*, Op. 26, *A Dirge for Two Veterans*, *Egdon Heath*, Op. 47, *Ode to Death*, Op. 38, and "Turn Back O Man" from the *Festival Choruses*, Op. 36.[33] The concert was preceded by an extended talk given by Ralph Vaughan Williams.

On Sunday, June 24th, Holst's ashes were interred in the north transept of

Chicester Cathedral, just below the wall memorial to Thomas Weelkes, Holst's favorite Tudor composer. The Whitsuntide Singers had stood on that very spot to sing some of Weelkes' music during festivals. Bishop George Bell again presided over the service. Ralph Vaughan Williams conducted singers from St. Paul's Girls' School and Morley College. It was most fitting that the music should include Vaughan Williams' "Kyrie" from the *Mass in G Minor* that he had written with Morley College in mind. The service ended with Holst's joyous *This Have I Done for My True Love*.

There were many tributes given over the remainder of the year; most took the form of recitals or concert programs that featured Holst's music. Among them was a concert organized by Adine O'Neill in memory of Delius, Holst and her late husband Norman O'Neill. It was presented on October 20th and sponsored by the Society of Women Musicians. Two weeks later, on November 3rd, Malcolm Sargent conducted the Royal Philharmonic Society in a concert featuring works by Delius, Elgar, and Holst. The *Ode to Death* and *The Planets* were included.

Aside from performances and recordings, perhaps the most lasting tribute to Holst was engineered by his closest friend, Ralph Vaughan Williams. Vaughan Williams headed the establishment of the Gustav Holst Memorial Fund which led to the subsequent construction of the Holst Room at Morley College:

GUSTAV HOLST MEMORIAL FUND

Morley College
for Working Men and Women
61 Westminster Bridge Road
London, S.E. 1

[March, 1935]

It is proposed to raise a fund for the purpose of establishing a memorial to Gustav Holst. It seems particularly fitting that the memorial should take the form of helping to develop the study of music at Morley College for Working Men and Women, where, at present, adequate equipment is difficult to obtain.

It was at Morley College that Holst taught and inspired successive generations of students for so many years. It is therefore suggested to establish a music room, to be called the "Gustav Holst Music Room" as part of the new wing about to be erected there. The room will be equiped with a grand pianoforte, appropriate sound-proof devices, etc. Should the sum collected permit, additional rooms could be added for a music library and teaching room. A Committee for this purpose, of which I am Chairman, has been formed at Morley College.

We feel that such a memorial as this will be one of which Holst himself would have approved, and which will in some measure help to carry out his work. The proposal has the support of the following:

Sir Hugh Allen
Dr. Adrian Boult
The Bishop of Chicester
Dr. Davison (of Harvard, U.S.A.)
Mr. Gerald Forty
Dr. W. Gillies Whittaker
Miss Gray (ex High Mistress of St. Paul's Girls' School)
Mrs. Eva Hubback (Principal, Morley College)
Dr. Mackail, O.M.
Mr. John Masefield

Though naturally we should be very grateful for large donations, yet, we want everyone who loved and admired Holst and his work to participate, the smallest sum will be welcome. Subscriptions should be sent to the Honorable Treasurer, Mr. D. Marblacy Jones, Marclays Bank, 84, Roseberry Averua, E.C. 1, or may be given personally to the Secretary of Morley College. Cheques should be made payable to the Gustav Holst Memorial Fund.

Ralph Vaughan Williams[34]

The idea for the Holst Room didn't come out of thin air. According to one of his notebook entries, Holst himself was working on a proposal for Morley College's music rooms in early 1923, when plans were being made for the college's relocation:

New Morley music rooms
54 ft
72 ft
81 ft
mention hall holding 450
how high should it be
gallery?
Ask Adrian put case[35]

By early 1937, 1,100 pounds had been raised by the Gustav Holst Memorial Fund Committee, allowing for the construction for the Holst Room to begin. The fan-shaped room was designed by Edward Maufe. It features a Steinway grand piano selected by Myra Hess, the planets painted on the ceiling against a dark blue background, and carvings of the planets, designed by Edmund Burton, on the keystones on the outside windows.[36] Connected to the Holst Room are two smaller teaching rooms. The dedication was held on March 6, 1937. Queen Mary performed the ceremony. Much of Morley College was destroyed by Nazi air raids in 1940, but the Holst Room remained intact and survives today as a living, working memorial to one of England's finest composers and greatest music educator.

---

[1]Stephen Lloyd, *H. Balfour Gardiner* (Cambridge, England: Cambridge University Press, 1984), 188-189.

[2]Personal correspondence, Gustav Holst to Walter Gandy, Jan[uary] 17[, 1934], The Holst Foundation.

[3]Gustav Holst, *Diary*, Tuesday, January 30 through Friday, February 2, 1934, The Holst Foundation. The *Sunday Times* of January 28, 1934, had the 30th and 31st performances listed in reverse order.

[4]Personal correspondence, Gustav Holst to Imogen Holst, Jan[uary] 31, 1934, The Holst Foundation.

[5]Gustav Holst, quoted in Imogen Holst, *Gustav Holst: A Biography*, 2nd ed. (Oxford: Oxford University Press, 1969), 164.

[6]*Terzetto* [H158] (1925).

[7]Three selections from *Eight Canons* [H187] (1932).

[8]Personal correspondence, Gustav Holst to Walter Piston, n.d. [1934], Library of Congress.

[9]Personal correspondence, Gustav Holst to Imogen Holst, Aug[ust] 7[, 1932], The Holst Foundation.

[10]Violist Lionel Tertis.

[11]Personal correspondence, Gustav Holst to Adrian Boult, Feb[ruary] 11[, 1934], British Library Add. MS 58079.

[12]Gustav Holst, *Diary,* Friday, March 2nd and Saturday, March 3, 1934, The Holst Foundation.

[13]"Bother Mrs. Beckett," in reference to Mrs. Gwen Beckett, Adrian Boult's secreatary. Holst used to joke about belonging to the "Bother Mrs. Beckett" club.

[14]The *Lyric Movement* was to be premiered in a broadcast on March 18, 1934.

[15]Tertis' note is included in an earlier chapter.

[16]Either A. N. Hobbs or William Brown.

[17]Personal correspondence, Gustav Holst to Mrs. [Gwen] Beckett, March 5[, 1934], quoted in Jerrold Northrup Moore (ed.), *Music and Friends* (London: Hamish Hamilton, 1979), 114-115.

[18]Christopher Palmer, *Herbert Howells: A Centenary Celebration* (London: Thames Publishing, 1992), 275.

[19]Gustav Holst, *Diary*, Wednesday, March 7, 1934, The Holst Foundation.

[20]Lionel Tertis.

[21]Personal correspondence, Gustav Holst to Adrian Boult, Saturday [March 17, 1934], quoted in

Jerrold Northrup Moore, *op. cit.*, 115-116.

[22]Gustav Holst, *Diary*, Tuesday, March 20 and Thursday, March 22, 1934, The Holst Foundation. The "103" means either that the orchestra rehearsed in the largest room at Vally Lasker's townhouse at 103 Talgarth Rd., or that Holst, feeling better, stayed in a room there, as he often did during the week.

[23]Gustav Holst, Notebook [1934], The Holst Foundation.

[24]On p. 190 of *A Thematic Catalogue of Gustav Holst's Music* (London: Faber Music Ltd., 1974), Imogen Holst indicates that the first run-through was by the combined orchestras of St. Paul's Girls' School sometime during March, 1934, with the composer conducting.

[25]Personal correspondence, Gustav Holst to Adrian Boult, April 12[, 1934], British Library Add. MS 60498.

[26]Gustav Holst, *Diary*, Wednesday, April 25, 1934, The Holst Foundation.

[27]Personal correspondence, Gustav Holst to Imogen Holst, April 23, 1934, The Holst Foundation.

[28]Personal correspondence, Gustav Holst to Adrian Boult, Wed[nesday, May 2, 1934], British Library Add. MS 60498.

[29]Gustav Holst, quoted in Imogen Holst, *op. cit.*, 168.

[30]Personal correspondence, Gustav Holst via Rev. George Street to the Whitsuntide Singers, May 18[, 1934], Royal College of Music MS 4569.

[31]Royal College of Music MS 4555.

[32]Business correspondence, J. R. Horn to Helen Lilley, March 4, 1997, The Holst Foundation.

[33]*National Programme, Gustav Holst: A Memorial Concert* [June 22, 1934].

[34]Business correspondence, Ralph Vaughan Williams, Chairman, Gustav Holst Memorial Fund, to prospective donors [March, 1935], The Holst Foundation.

[35]Gustav Holst, Notebook, October, 1922-Spring? 1923. "Adrian" refers to Adrian Boult.

[36]Michael Short, *Gustav Holst: The Man and His Music* (Oxford: Oxford University Press, 1990), 331-332.

APPENDIX I

A CHRONOLOGICAL LISTING OF GUSTAV HOLST'S MUSIC

This comprehensive chronological listing is based primarily upon information from Imogen Holst (ed.), *A Thematic Catalogue of Gustav Holst's Music*, a catalog which takes into account all of Holst's works, from his earliest attempts (App. I) through his more mature works (H). Incomplete works (App. II) as well as his editions and arrangements of other peoples' music (App. III) are also included. While Imogen Holst's *Thematic Catalogue* lists numbers having the same opus number consecutively, the chronological listing presented here does not. Three works, *Penetential Fugue* [App. I, 28A], *Hymn Tune: Essex* [H142A] and *God Be in My Head* [H180A], not yet rediscovered at the time the *A Thematic Catalogue* was assembled, have been included here. No listing of this nature can be guaranteed to be 100% perfect. Many works overlap, some taking years to compose while others were conceived and finished during the interim.

Choral works are listed as s=soprano, ms=mezzo soprano, a=alto, t=tenor, bar=baritone, b=bass.

Orchestration is indicated by numbers of:
flutes (+1=piccolo), oboes (+1=*cor anglais*), clarinets (+1=bass clarinet), bassoons (+1= contrabassoon)/horns, trumpets (+2=cornets), trombones (+1=contrabass trombone), tuba, timp (timpani), sd (snare drum), bd (bass drum), tamb (tambourine), tri (triangle), cym (cymbals), glock (bells), xylo (xylophone), cel (celesta) pf (pianoforte), org (organ), hp (harp) str (strings).

ca. 1887	App. II, 1	*Horatius* 'Lars Posena of Clusium'; satb chorus and orch 1021/0221 sd, bd, cym, tri, str
1890 or 1891	App. I, 8	*March in C Major*; organ [First Voluntary for Organ]
1891	App. I, 1	*The Harper*; voice and piano; words: Thomas Campbell
?	App. I, 2	*The Exile of Erin*; bass and piano; words: Thomas Campbell
1891?	App. I, 3	*Die Spröde* (*The Coquette*); voice and piano; words: Goethe
1891	App. I, 5	*The Listening Angels*; anthem for solo conralto and hidden choir with organ accompaniment; words: Adelaide

Procter

?	App. I, 6	*Advent Litany*; unison voices and organ; no words in ms.
?	App. I, 7	*Christmas Carol*; satb and piano; words not attributed
1891	App. I, 9	*Allegretto Pastorale: Second Voluntary for Organ*
1891	App. I, 10	*Postlude in C; Third Voluntary for Organ*
1891	App. I, 11	*Funeral March in G Minor: Fourth Voluntary for Organ*
1891	App. I, 12	*Intermezzo*; orch 1010/0000 str
1891	App. I, 13	*Scherzo*; orch 1010/0, 0+1,00 str
1891 or 1892	App. II, 2	*Wedding March*; orch 0000/2000 timp, str
1891 or 1892	App. II, 3	*Funeral March*; orch 0000/2221 timp, bd, str
1891 or 1892	App. II, 4	*Sailor's Chorus*; tenor, bass and orch 0000/2000 timp str
1891 or 1892	App. II, 5	*Duet: Herald and Tom*; tenor, bass and orch of 0+1,001/0000 str
1892	App. I, 14	*Symphony in C minor*; orch 2222/2230 timp str
1892	App. I, 15	*Sanctus*; unison voices and organ; words: liturgical
1892	App. I, 16	*New Year Chorus*; satb and piano
1892	App. I, 17	*Arpeggio Study*; piano
1892	App. I, 18	*I Come from Haunts of Coot and Hern*; voice and piano; words: Tennyson
1892	App. I, 19	*Sing Heigh-Ho!* [first version]; voice and piano; words: Charles Kingsley
1892	App. I, 20	*Ode to the North East Wind*; male voices and orch 2222/4231 timp, str; words: Charles Kingsley
1892	App. I, 21	*Lansdown Castle, or The Sorcerer of Tewksbury*; operetta; s a tt bar bar b soloists and piano; libretto: A. C. Cunningham
1893	App. I, 22	*Song of the Valkyrs*; 2 sopranos and one alto; trumpet plus double string orch (harp *ad lib*)

1893	App. I, 23	*Introduction and Bolero*; piano 4 hands
1893	App. I, 24	*Bolero*; orch 1011/0,0+2,00 timp, str
1893	App. I, 25	*A Lake and a Fairy Boat* [first setting]; voice and piano; words: Thomas Hood
1893	App. I, 26	*There Sits a Bird on Yonder Tree*; voice and piano; words: Thomas Ingoldsby
1893	App. 1, 27	*Anna-Marie*; voice and piano; words: Walter Scott
1893	App. 1, 28	*The White Lady's Farewell*; voice and piano; words: Walter Scott
1893	App. 1, 28A	*Penetential Fugue*; satb
1893	App. 1, 29	*Theme and Variations*; str quartet
1893	App. II, 6	[Allegro fragment]; str quartet
1893	App. II, 7	[Scherzo fragment]; str quartet
1893	App. I, 30	*First String Quartet*
1894	App. I, 31	*Duet for Organ and Trombone*
1894	App. I, 32	*Air and Variations*; piano and str quartet
1894	App. I, 33	*Short Trio in E Major*; violin, violoncello, and piano
1894	App. I, 34	*String Trio in G Minor*; violin, viola, violoncello
1894	App. I, 35	*Ave Maria, Maiden Child*; sssa; words: Walter Scott
1894	App. I, 36	*Fathoms Deep Beneath the Wave*; sssa sssa; words: Walter Scott
1894	App. I, 37	*Now Winter's Winds Are Banished*; ssa; words: Meleager
1894	App. I, 38	*There Is Dew for the Flow'ret*; voice and piano; words: Thomas Hood
1894	App. I, 39	*Summer's Welcome*; ssaa; words: Fritz Hart
1894	App. I, 40	*Winter and the Birds* [first setting: ssaa; second setting: satb]; words: Fritz Hart

1894	App. I, 41	*Love Wakes and Weeps*; satb; words: Walter Scott
1894?	App. I, 42	*Ianthe*; operetta (missing)
1894	App. I, 42A	"Ländler" and "Storm Dance" from *Ianthe*; orch 2221/2, 0+2, 00 glock (or bells) str ("Ländler") and 2222/4200 timp str ("Storm Dance")
1895	App. II, 8	*Children's Suite*; 1010/02(cornets)10 str
1895	H1	*The Autumn Is Old*; satb; words: Thomas Hood
1895	H2	*The Stars Are with the Voyager* [first version: ssatb; second: satb]; words: Thomas Hood
1895	H3	*Spring It Is Cherry*; s ms a t bar b; words: Thomas Hood
1895, 1897	H4	*O Lady Leave that Silken Thread* [first setting: s ms a t bar b 1895][second setting: voice and piano 1897]; words: Thomas Hood
1895	H5	*[Two] Dances for Piano Duet* (4 hands)
1895	H6	*Duet in D*; two pianos (missing)
1895	H7	*The Revoke*, Op. 1; operetta; s a t bar b soloists; orch 2222/2200 timp str; Libretto: Fritz Hart
1896	H8	*Fantasiestücke*, Op. 2 [first version]; oboe and string quartet
1896	H9	*[Variations]*; oboe, clarinet, bassoon, violin, viola, violoncello
?	H10	*Sextet in E minor*; oboe, clarinet, bassoon, violin, viola, cello
1896	App. II, 9	*[Allegro]*; flute, oboe, 2 clarinets, 2 horns, bassoon
1896	H11	*Quintet in A Minor*, Op. 3; piano, oboe, clarinet, horn, bassoon
1896	App. II, 10	[Two Orchestral Pieces] *Andante con moto* and *Allegretto*; orch: 2(d2)121/22(cornets)20+euph timp perc hp str
1896	App. II, 11	*[Four Sketches for Unidentified Stage Works]* 1. *Adagio quasi andante*; orch as in App. II, 10 2. *Allegretto*; 1+1,21/22(cornets)21 timp tri str 3. *Tempo di Valse*; piano 4. [Ballet fragment]; piano

1896	H12	*All Night I Waited by the Spring*; ssa; words: unattributed
1896	H13	*[Three] Short Part-Songs*; ssa; words: Heine "In the forest moonbeamed-brightened," "All nests with song are ringing" "Soft and gently through my soul"
1896	H14	*Four Songs*, Op. 4; voice and piano No. 1: "Slumber-Song;" words: Charles Kingsley No. 2: "Margaret's Cradle Song;" words: Ibsen
1896	H15	*There's a Voice in the Wind*; s ms a t bar b; words: unattributed
1896	H16	*The Kiss*; satb; words: Ben Jonson
1896	App. II, 12	*The Magic Mirror*; piano sketches for the first scene of an opera; Libretto: probably Fritz Hart
1896	H20	*Light Leaves Whisper*; s ms a t b b; words: Fritz Hart
1896?	H21	*The Idea*; operetta for children; orch 1110/1000 str Libretto: Fritz Hart
1897	H14	*Four Songs*, Op. 4; voice and piano No. 3: "Soft and gently;" words: Heine
1897	H17	*Song to the Sleeping Lady*; voice and piano; words: George MacDonald
?	H18	*Ah Tyrant Love*; satb; words: Charles Kingsley
?	H19	*The Ballade of Prince Eric*; voice and piano; words: Fritz Hart
?	H22	*Not unto Us, Lord;* satb and organ; words: Psalm 115
1897	H23	*Scherzo for String Sextet*; 2 violins, 2 violas, 2 violoncelli
1897	H24	*O Spring's Little Children*; sssa; words: Francis Thompson
1897	H25	*A Lake and a Fairy Boat* [second setting]; voice and piano; words: Thomas Hood
1897	H26	*Sing Heigh-Ho!* [second version]; voice and piano; words: Charles Kingsley
1897	H27	*Airly Beacon*; voice and piano; words: Charles Kingsley

?	H28	*Twin Stars Aloft*; voice and piano; words: Charles Kingsley
?	H29	*The Day of the Lord*; voice and piano; words: Charles Kingsley
1897	H30	*Clear and Cool*, Op. 5; ssatb chorus; words: Charles Kingsley orch: 3222/4231 timp str
1897	H31	*A Winter Idyll*; orch: 2,2+1,22/4231 timp cym str
1897	H32	*Not a Sound but Echoing in Me*; voice and piano; words: George Macdonald
1897	H48	*Five Part-Songs*, Op. 9[A] No. 1: "Love is enough;" satb; words: William Morris
1898	H14	*Four Songs*, Op. 4; voice and piano No. 4: "Awake, my heart;" words: Robert Bridges
1898	H36	*My Joy*; voice and piano; words: Robert Bridges
?	H35	*Autumn Song*; voice and piano; words: Robert Bridges
1898	H33	*Whether We Die or We Live*; voice and piano; words: George Meredith
1898	H34	*Örnulf's Drapa*; bar and orch: 2,2+1,2+1,2/4331 timp cym hp str
?	H37	*Draw Not Away Thy Hands*; voice and piano; words: William Morris
?	H38	*I Scanned Her Picture*; voice and piano; words: unattributed
?	H39	*Two Brown Eyes*; voice and piano (missing)
?	H40	*Clouds O'er the Summer Sky*; ss and piano; words: Fritz Hart
1898	H41	*Suite in G Minor*; string orchestra (missing)
1898-99	H44	*Bhanavar's Lament*; voice and piano; words: George Meredith
1899	H48	*Five Part-Songs*, Op. 9[A]; No. 2: "To Sylvia;" satb; words: Francis Thompson No. 3: "Autumn Song;" [a] ssaa and [b] satb; words: William Morris
1899	H42	*Walt Whitman*, Op. 7; orch 2222/4331 timp cym str

1899	H43	*Suite de Ballet in E Flat*, Op. 10 (rev. 1912); orch: 3(d1)222/4,0+2,31 timp bd tamb cym tri glock hp str
?	H45	*Ah, Come Fair Mistress*; voice and piano; words: Walter Grogan
?	H46	*She Who Is Dear to Me*; voice and piano; words: Walter Grogan
1899-1900	H47	*The Cotswolds: Symphony in F*; orch: 2(d1)2(d1)22/4331 timp cym tri str
1900	H48	Five Part-Songs, Op. 9[A] No. 4: "Come away, death;" ssattb; words: William Shakespeare No. 5: "A Love Song;" satb; words: William Morris
1900	H49	*Ave Maria*, Op. 9[B]; ssaa ssaa; words: Latin Liturgy
1901?	H50	*Deux Pieces*; piano
?	H51	*Lieder ohne Worte*; violin and piano
?	H52	*A Spring Song*; violin or violoncello and piano
?	H53	*Ländler*; two violins and piano
?	H54	*Greeting*; violin and piano, or orch: 2121 2000 str
?	H55	*Maya*; violin and piano
?	H56	*Valse-Etude*; violin and piano
?	H57	*I Love Thee*; satb; words: Thomas Hood
?	H58	*Thou Didst Delight My Eyes*; satb; words: Robert Bridges
?	H59	*It Was a Lover and His Lass*; satb; words: Shakespeare
1902	H60	*The Youth's Choice*, Op. 11; sstb soloists; libretto: Holst orch: 3(d1),2+1,22/4231 timp perc hp str
1902-1903	H61	*Five Part-Songs*, Op. 12 No. 1: "Dream Tryst;" satb; words: Francis Thompson No. 2: "Ye little birds;" satb; words:

		Thomas Heywood No. 3: "Her eyes the glow-worm lend thee;" satb words: Herrick No. 4: "Now is the month of Maying;" ssaa [first setting] and satb [second]; words: anon 16th century No. 5: "Come to me;" satb; words: Christina Rossetti
1902-1903	H68	*Six Songs*, Op. 15; baritone and piano No. 1: "Invocation to the Dawn;" words: *Rig Veda* No. 2: "Fain would I change that note;" words: anon. No. 3: "The Sergeant's Song;" words: Thomas Hardy No. 4: "In a wood;" words: Thomas Hardy No. 5: "Between us now;" words: Thomas Hardy No. 6: "I will not let thee go," words: Robert Bridges
?	H62	*A Prayer for light*; voice and piano; words: Eric Mackay
?	H63	*Dewy Roses*; voice and piano; words: Alfred H. Hyatt
?	H64	*Song of the Woods*; voice and piano; words: Alfred H. Hyatt
?	H65	*To a Wild Rose*; voice and piano; words: Alfred H. Hyatt
1903	H66	*Indra*, Op. 13; orch 2+1,2+1,2+1,2+1/4,2+2,31 timp tamb cym tri gong glock hp str
1903	H67	*Quintet in A Flat*, Op. 14; flute, oboe, clarinet, horn, bassoon
1903	H70	*King Estmere*, Op. 17; satb and orch; 2222/4231 timp bd tamb cym tri hp str
1903-1904	H69	*Six Songs*, Op. 16; soprano and piano No. 1: "Calm is the morn;" words: Tennyson No. 2: "My true love hath my heart;" words: Sydney No. 3: "Weep you no more;" words: anon. 16th century No. 4: "Lovely kind and kindly loving;" words: Nicholas Breton No. 5: "Cradle Song;" words: Blake No. 6: "Peace;" words: Alfred H. Hyatt
1904	H71	*The Mystic Trumpeter*; soprano and orch 3(d1),2+1,2+1,2+1/4331 timp bd tamb cym hp str
1905?	H73	[Three Hymns for The English Hymnal] "In the bleak mid-winter;" words: Christina Rossetti "From glory to glory advancing;" words: St. James

"Holy Ghost, come down;" Words: F. W. Faber

1905?	H72	*Darest Thou Now, O Soul*; voice and piano; words: Walt Whitman
1905	H74	*A Song of the Night*; violin and orch: 2,1+1,22/2200 timp str
?	H76	*In Youth Is Pleasure*; satb; words: anon. [Robert Wever]
?	H77	*Now Sleep and Take Thy Rest*; voice and piano; words: James Mabbe, from Fernando de Rojas
?	H78	*Now Rest Thee from All Care*; satb; words: anon.
?	H79	*To Hope*; voice and piano; words: anon.
1905	App. III, 1	*Pan's Anniversary,* by Ralph Vaughan Williams; dances by Holst orch: 1121/2,0+2,00 timp perc str
1905	H80	*Songs from 'The Princess'*, Op. 20[A]; sopranos and altos; words: Alfred Lord Tennyson No. 1: "Sweet and low;" ssaa ssaa No. 2: "The splendour falls;" ssaa ssaa No. 3: "Tears, idle tears;" ssaa No. 4: "O swallow, swallow;" ssa No. 5: "Now sleeps the crimson petal;" sssaa
1905	H81	*Home they Brought Their Warrior Dead*; ssaa; words: Alfred Lloyd Tennyson
1899-1906	H89	*Sita*, Op. 23; opera in three acts, from the *Ramayana*; libretto: Holst s, ms, ms, t, bar, bar, b soloists; satb and tb choruses orch: 3+1,2+1,2=1,2+1, 4,2+2,3+1,0 tip perc hp str
1906?	App. III, 2	*Bouree* by W. C. Macfarren; arr. by Holst for piano quintet.
1906?	App. III, 3	*March* by B. Tours; arr. by Holst for piano quintet.
1906?	App. III, 4	*Dreaming* by B. Tours; arr. by Holst for small orchestra
1906?	App. III, 5	*Minuet d'Amour* by F. H. Cowen; arr. by Holst for violin and piano, also piano quintet, also small orchestra
1906	H88	*Two Songs without Words*, Op. 22; orch: 2122/2210 timp bd tamb str 1. "Country Song"

2. "Marching Song"

1906?	App. II, 14	*The Glory of the West*; piano sketch
1906	H86	*Songs of the West*, Op. 21 [No. 1] (rev. 1907); orch: 2222/4231 timp bd tamb cym tri str
1906	H87	*A Somerset Rhapsody*, Op. 21 [No. 2] (rev. 1907); orch: 22(or 1+ ob d'amour)22/4231 timp tamb bd cym str
1906-1908?	H83	*[Sixteen] Folk Songs from Hampshire*; voice and piano; "Abroad as I was walking," "Lord Dunwaters," "The Irish Girl,""Young Reilly," "The New-mown Hay;" "The Willow Tree," "Beautiful Nancy," "Sing Ivy," "John Barleycorn," "Bedlam City," "The Scolding Wife," "The Squire and the Thresher," "The Happy Stranger," "Young Edwin in the Lowlands low," "Yonder sits a fair young damsel," "Our ship lies in the harbour"
1906-1914?	H84	*[Nine] Folk Songs*; voice and piano "Sovay," "The Seeds of Love," "The Female Farmer," "Thorneyfield Woods," "Moorfields," "I'll love my love," "Claudy Banks," "On the Banks of the Nile," "Here's adieu"
1906?	H84A	*Stu Mo Run*; voice and piano (originally a part of H84)
1906-1914?	H85	*[Seven] Folk Songs*; unison voices and orch: 2222/2200 timp str "On the Banks of the Nile," "The Willow Tree," "Our ship lies in the harbour," "I'll love my love," "Claudy Banks," "John Barleycorn," "Spanish Ladies"
1907	H82	*Four Old English Carols*, Op. 20[B]; satb or ssaa and piano; words: anon. 15th century "A Babe is born," "Now let us sing," "Jesu, Thou the Virgin-born," "The Savior of the world is born"
1907	H93	*Seven Scottish Airs*; piano and strings
1907	H95	*The Heart Worships*; voice and piano
1907?	H94	*Nabou, or Kings of Babylon* (missing)
1907-1908	H90	*Hymns from the Rig Veda*, Op. 24; voice and piano;

		trans. by Holst First Group: Ushas, Varua I, Marits Second Group: Indra, Varuna II, Song of the Frogs Third Group: Vac, Creation, Faith
1907	H90A	*Ratri*; voice and piano (originally a part of Op. 24)
1907?	H91[A]	*A Welcome Song*; satb, oboe, and violoncello
1907?	H92	*Pastoral*; ssa
1908?	App. III, 6	*Andantino* by E. H. Lemare; arr. by Holst for piano quintet, also for small orchestra
1908?	App. III, 7	*How Merrily We Live* by Michael East; edited by Holst for ssa
1908? Byrd;	App. III, 8	"Benedictus" from the *Mass for Three Voices* by William ed. Holst for ssa
1908?	App. III, 9	*Help Me, O Lord* by Thomas Arne; ed. Holst for ssa
1908?	App. III, 10	*Adoramus Te Christe* by Orlando di Lasso; ed. Holst for ssa
1908-1909	H96	*Savitri*, Op. 25; chamber opera; libretto by Holst from the *Mahabharata*; s t b soloists; ssaa chorus; orch: 2, 0+1,00/0000 2 str quartets + bass
1908-1909?	H104	*A Song of Fairies*; ssa
1908-1910	H97	*Choral Hymns from the Rig Veda*, Op. 26: First Group; trans. by Holst; satb chorus; orch: 3,2+1, 2,2+1/4331 timp perc hp organ str No. 1: "Battle Hymn" No. 2: "To the Unknown God" No. 3: "Funeral Hymn"
1909	H98	*Choral Hymns from the Rig Veda*, Op. 26: Second Group; ssa divisi chorus; orch: 22,2+1,2/4330 timp perc hp str No. 1: "To Varuna" No. 2: "To Agni" No. 3: "Funeral Chant"
1909	H102	*Incidental Music to the Stepney Children's Pageant*, Op. 27B (missing)

1909	H102A	*A Song of London*; voices in unison and piano (from Op. 27B)
1909	H103	*O England My Country*; unison chorus, orch: 2221/2210 timp str; also for military band (non ms)
1909	H105	*First Suite in E Flat for Military Band*, Op. 28, No. 1
1909	H101	*Masque: The Vision of Dame Christian*, Op. 27A; ssaa; words: Frances Gray orch: 2222/2000 pf organ ad lib. str
1909?	App. III, 11	[*Two Duets from King Arthur*] by Henry Purcell, ed. Holst; ss and piano; words: Dryden, adapted by Rothery No. 1: "Shepherd, Shepherd, leave your labours" No. 2: "The Stream Daughters"
1909-1910	H107	*Beni Mora*, Op. 29 No. 1; orch: 3d1,2+1,22/4231 timp bd tamb cym tri gong 2hp str
1909-1910	H111	*The Cloud Messenger*, Op. 30; satb divisi; trans. by Holst from Kalidasa (rev 1912) orch: 3d1,2+1,2+1,2+1/43,3+1,0 timp perc 2hp organ str
1910	H99	*Choral Hymns from the Rig Veda*, Op. 26: Third Group; ssaa hp No. 1: "Hymn to the Dawn" No. 2: "Hymn to the Waters" No. 3: "Hymn to Vena" No. 4: "Hymn of the Travellers"
1910	H109	*Christmas Day*; satb; orch: [2222/2220 timp glock] str or organ
1910	H110	[Four Part Songs] for children's voices and piano; words: John Greenleaf Whittier No. 1: "Song of the Ship-builders;" ss No. 2: "Song of the Shoemakers;" ssa No. 3: "Song of the Fishermen;" ssa No. 4: "Song of the Drovers" ssa
1910	H114	*Incidental Music for The Pageant of London*; unison voices and military band
1910	App. III, 12A	*Morris Dance Tunes*, Sets I and II, harmonized by Cecil Sharp; set by Holst for chamber orchestra: 1010/0000 str

1911	H112	*Two Eastern Pictures*; ssaa and harp or piano
1911	H75	*Invocation*, Op. 19, No. 2; violoncello and orchestra; orch: 2222/2100 perc hp str
1911	H113	*In Loyal Bonds United*; unison voices with piano
1911	H115	*Hecuba's Lament*, Op. 31, No. 1; contralto solo, ssa, orchestra; words: Euripides, trans. Gilbert Murray orch: 2222/2231 timp bd cym hp str
1911?	App. II, 13	[*Four Folk Songs*]; piano sketches "On Monday Morning," "Pretty Nancy," "Jocky and Jenny," "Swansea [Town]"
1911	H106	*Second Suite in F for Military Band*, Op. 28, No. 2
1911	H118A	*Playground Song* [for SPGS]; unison voices and piano
1911	App. III, 12B	*Morris Dance Tunes*, Sets I and II, harmonized by Cecil Sharp; set by Holst for military band (missing)
1911?	App. III, 13A	*Sacred Round and Canons*: First Set; words: *The Bible*; set by Holst for ssa No. 1: "Glory be to God on high," by William Boyce No. 2: "Allelujah," by William Boyce No. 3: "As Pants the Heart," anon. No. 4: "Who can express...," Samuel Wesley
1912	H108	*Phantastes* (withdrawn--originally Op. 29, No. 2) orch: 3d1, bass fl, 2+1,2+1,2+1/4331 timp bd tamb cym cel str
1912	H117	*Two Psalms*; t solo, satb, str and organ or brass; words: Psalms 86 and 148
1912	H100	*Choral Hymns from the Rig Veda*, Op. 26: Fourth Group; ttbb; orch [0000/2230] timp perc hp str No. 1: "Hymn to Agni" No. 2: "Hymn to Soma" No. 3: "Hymn to Manas" No. 4: "Hymn to Indra"
1912?	App. III, 14	*News from Whydah* by H. Balfour Gardiner, arranged by Holst for small orchestra
1912-1913	H118	*St. Paul's Suite*, Op. 29, No. 2; [1120/1000 timp perc] str

1913	H116	*Hymn to Dionysus*, Op. 31, No. 2; ssaa; words: Euripides, trans. Gilbert Murray; orch: 3d1,2+1,3d1, 2/4331 timp bd tamb tri cym gong cel hp str
1913	H120	*The Homecoming*; ttbb; words: Thomas Hardy
1913?	H119	*The Swallow Leaves Her Nest*; ssa; words: Thomas Lovell Beddoes
1913?	App. III, 13B	*Sacred Rounds and Canons*: Second Set; words: *The Bible*; set by Holst for sopranos and altos No. 1: "I will magnify thee O God," by Samual Webbe No. 2: "From everlasting to everlasting thou art God," by Samuel Webbe No. 3: "Let the words of my mouth," by Richard Woodward No. 4: "Hallelujah, Amen," by Thomas Norris
1913?	App. III, 15	*Light's Glittering Morn*, by JohnWest; orch. by Holst
1913?	H106A	[*Three Folk Tunes*]; military band
1913-1916?	App. III, 16	*Old Airs and Glees*; ssa; words: Clfford Bax (except No. 3) No. 1: "Once in England's age of old," by Joseph Baildon No. 2: "Nothing fairer have I seen," anon. No. 3: "The Captive Lover," by Henry Lawes No. 4: "Beside a lake of lilies," by Thomas Augustine Arne No. 5: "Cherry-stones," George Spencer Churchill
1914	H121	*Dirge for Two Veterans*; ttbb and 3 cornets, 2 tubas, bd sd; words: Walt Whitman
1914	H122	*Incidental Music to John Masefield's Philip the King*; (missing)
1914	H123	*A Vigil of Pentecost*; voice and piano; words: Alice M. Buckton
1914	H125	*The Planets*, Op. 32; orch: 4 (3d 2 picc and alto fl), 3(1dHeckelphone)+1,3+1,3+1/643, tenor tuba,1 timp (2 players) bd sd tamb tri cym gong bells glock xylo cel 2hp organ str No. 1: "Mars, the Bringer of War" No. 2: "Venus, the Bringer of Peace"

		No. 4: " Jupiter, the Bringer of Jollity"
1915	H124	*Dirge and Hymneal*; ssa and piano
1915	H125	*The Planets*, Op. 32 No. 5: "Saturn, the Bringer of Old Age" No. 6: "Uranus, the Magician" No. 7: "Neptune, the Mystic"
1915	H126	*Japanese Suite*, Op. 33; orch: 2d1,1+1,22/4231 timp bd cym jingles gong xylo glock hp str
1915	H127	*Nunc Dimittus*; satb satb; words: Roman Catholic Liturgy
1916	H125	*The Planets*, Op. 32 No. 3: "Mercury, the Winged Messenger"
1916	H128	*This Have I Done for My True Love*, Op. 34 [No. 1]; satb; words: Cornish trad., edited by William Sandys
1916	H129	*Lullay My Liking*, Op. 34 [No. 2]; s or t solo and satb chorus; words: anon 15th century; edited by Mary Segar
1916?	H130	*Of One That Is So Fair and Bright*, Op. 34 [No. 3]; satb solos, satb chorus; words: anon.15th century, edited by Mary Segar
1916	H131	*Bring Us in Good Ale*, Op. 34 [No. 4]; satb; words anon.
1916	App. III, 21	*Short Communion Service* by William Byrd; ed. by Holst for ssa (also ssa and sat) from Byrd's *Mass for Three Voices*; Words: *Book of Common Prayer*
1916	H91[B]	*Terly Terlow*; satb, oboe and violoncello; words: anon
1916	H132	*Four Songs*, Op. 35; voice and violin; words: anon. edited by Mary Segar No. 1: "Jesu Sweet, now will I sing" No. 2: "My soul has nought but fire and ice" No. 4: "My Leman is so true"
1916	H134	*Three Festival Choruses*, Op. 36[A]; satb; orch 2222/2331 timp bells organ str No. 1: "Let all mortal flesh keep silence;" words: Liturgy of St. James, trans. G. Moultrie No. 2: "Turn back, O Man;" words: Clifford Bax No. 3: "A Festival Chime;" words: Clifford Bax

1916?	App. III, 17	*All People That on Earth Do Dwell*; satb; words: Day's Psalter; orch: 2222/2300 timp organ str
1916	H135	*Phantasy Quartet on British Folksongs* [originally Op. 36]; string quartet (withdrawn)
1916	H136	*Six Choral Folk Songs*, Op. 36[B]; satb, or ttbb Nos. 1 and 3-6; "I sowed the seeds of love," "There was a tree," "Matthew, Mark, Luke, and John," "The Song of the Blacksmith," "I love my love," "Swansea Town"
1916?	H133	*Three Carols*; unison chorus and orchestra orch: 2222/2200 timp tri bells organ(ad lib.) str No. 1: "I saw three ships;" traditional No. 2: "Christmas song" ("Persodent hodie"); Words:16th century; trans. Jane M. Joseph No. 3: "Masters in this Hall;" words: William Morris
1916?	App. III, 13C	*Sacred Round and Canons*: Third Set; words: *The Bible*; edited by Holst for sopranos and altos No. 1: "Young men and maidens," anon. No. 2: "I said, I will take heed...," by William Norris No. 3: "Glory be to the Father," by Samuel Webbe No. 4: "Alleluia," by William Hayes
1916-1918?	App. III, 18	*The Gordian Knot Untied* by Henry Purcell, edited into two suites for orchestra by Holst for (2221/2200 timp) str
1916-1918?	App. III, 19	*The Virtuous Wife* by Henry Purcell, edited for orchestra by Holst: (2221/2200 timp) str
1916-1918?	App. III, 20	*The Married Beau* by Henry Purcell, edited for orchestra by Holst: (2221/2200 timp) str
?	H137	*Diverus and Lazurus*; satb; words: traditional
1917	H132	*Four Songs*, Op. 35; voice and violin No. 3: "I sing of a maiden;" words: anon, ed. Mary Segar
1917	H138	*Two Part-songs for Children*; ss and piano; words: John Greenleaf Whittier No. 1: "The Corn Song" No. 2: "The Song of the Lumbermen"
1917	H139	*A Dream of Christmas*; ss and piano or strings; words: 15th century, edited by Mary Segar

1917	H140	*The Hymn of Jesus*, Op. 37; two choruses satb, semi chorus ssa; orch: 3d1,2+1,22/4230 timp bd sd cym tamb cel pf organ str
1917-1918	App. II, 15	*Opera as She Is Wrote*; voices and orchestra; libretto: Holst's Morley College students
?	H141	*May Day Carol*; voice and two violins; words: traditional
?	H142	*Here Is Joy for Every Age*; sa; words: trans. from Latin by J. M. Neale; melody from *Piae Cantiones*
?	H142A	*Hymn Tune: Essex*, appearing in *Public School Hymn Book, 1919.*
1918	H143	*The Sneezing Charm*; ms solo; words: Clifford Bax orch: 2+1,222/2200 timp tamb cym tri hp str
1919	H144	*Ode to Death*, Op. 38; satb; words: *Book of Common Prayer*; orch: 2, 2+1, 22/4230 timp cel hp organ str
1919	H145	*Short Festival Te Deum*; satb; words: *Book of Common Prayer*; orch: 2222/2230 timp bd cym str
1919-1920	H146	*Seven Choruses from the Alcestis of Euripides*; unison voices, harp and three flutes; words: Euripides, trans. Gilbert Murray No. 1: O paian wise! No. 2: Daughter of Pelias, fare thee well No. 3: On, a House that loves the stranger No. 4: Ah me! Farewell No. 5: Advance, advance No. 6: I have sojourned in the Muses' land No. 7: There be many shapes of mystery
?	H 147	*The Ballad of Hunting Knowe*; voice and piano
1921?	H148	*I Vow to Thee, My Country*; unison voices and orchestra orch: 2222/2231 timp organ pf str
1921	H149	*The Lure, or the Moth and the Flame*; orch: 2+1,2+1,2+1,2+1/4331 timp bd tamb cym gong xylo glock cel hp str
1921	App. III, 22	*Incidental Music for the Pageant of St. Martin-in-the-Fields*; satb chorus; orch: 2222/2200 timp bells str

1920-1922	H150	*The Perfect Fool*, Op. 39; opera with two speaking parts, s sss a t bar b soloists and b ens; chorus and dancers; libretto: Holst orch: 2+1,2+1,2+1,2+1/4431 timp bd tamb jingles gong xylo cel hp str
1922	H151	*A Fugal Overture*, Op. 40, No.1; 2+1,2+1,2+1,2+1/4331 timp bd jingles glock str
1923	H152	*A Fugal Concerto*, Op. 40, No. 2; flute and oboe soloists (or 2 violins) str
1916-23	App. III, 23	*Morley Rounds*; voices Set I: No. 1: "Hushabye Baby" by Joan Spink No. 2: "There was an old man who said 'How'" by Jane M. Joseph No. 3: "How many miles to Babylon?" by Jane M. Joseph No. 4: "As I rode this enderes night" by Mabel Rodwell Jones No. 6: "Alleluia" by A. W. Cox Set II: No. 7: "Agnus Day" by Jane M. Joseph No. 8: "Ave Maris stella" by Jane M. Joseph No. 9: "Fair Daffodils" by M. W. Harrison No. 10: "Kyrie eleison" by A. W. Cox No. 11: "Christ eleison" by A. W. Cox No. 12: "Let dogs delight to bark and bite" by Walter Gandy
1923-1924	H155	*First Choral Symphony*, Op. 41; soprano solo, satb chorus; words: John Keats; orch: 3d1, 2+1,2+1,2+1/4331 timp bd tamb cym tri jingles gong Xylo glock cel hp organ (*ad lib.*) str
1924	H153	*Toccata*; piano
1924	H154	*A Piece for Yvonne*; piano
1924	H156	*At the Boar's Head*, Op. 42; opera; libretto: William Shakespeare; s ms t t bar bar bar bb soloists, baritone chorus; orch: 1+1,1+1,22/2201 timp str
1924	H159	*The Evening-Watch*, Op. 43, No. 1; ssaattbb; words: Henry Vaughan

1925	H157	*Ode to the C.K.S. and the Oriana*; ssaattt bar bar bb; words: Jane M. Joseph
1925	H158	*Terzetto*; flute, oboe, and viola
1926	H160	*Sing Me the Men*, Op. 43, No. 2; sssaattbb; words: Digby Mackworth Dolben
1926	H161	[Four Hymns for *Songs of Praise*]; satb; No. 1: "O valiant hearts;" words: J. S. Arkwright No. 2: "In the world, the Isle of Dreams;" words: Herrick No. 3: "Onward, Christian Soldiers!" words: S. Baring-Gould; music: "Prince Rupert's March" No. 4: "I sought thee round about;" words: Thomas Heywood; adapted Percy Dearmer
1925-26	H162	*Seven Part-Songs*, Op. 44; s solo; ssa divisi; str; words: Robert Bridges No. 1: "Say who is this?" No. 2: "O Love, I complain" No. 3: "Angel spirits of sleep" No. 4: "When first we met" No. 5: "Sorrow and joy" No. 6: "Love on my heart from heaven fell" No. 7: "Assemble all ye maidens"
1926	H163	*The Golden Goose*; choral ballet; satb chorus and orchestra 2+1,2+1,22/2231 timp tamb tri glock cel str
1926	H165	*Christmas Day in the Morning*, Op,. 46, No. 1; piano
1926-1927	H164	*The Morning of the Year*, Op. 45, No. 2; choral ballet; satb 2+1,2+1,2, 2+1/4231 timp cym glock organ str
1927	H166	*Two Folk Song Fragments*, Op. 46, No. 2; piano; "Oh! I hae seen the roses blaw," "The Shoemakker"
1927	App. III, 24	*O Magnum Mysterium* by William Byrd; satb; ed. Holst from Samuel Wesley's ms copy
1927	H168	*Man Born to Toil*; satb and organ (bells *ad lib.*); words: Robert Bridges
1927	H169	*Eternal Father*; soprano solo, satb, organ (bells *ad lib.*); words: Robert Bridges

1927	H170	*The Coming of Christ*; solo satb, satb chorus; words: John Masefield; trumpet, organ, piano, optional strings
1927	H172	*Edgon Heath*, Op. 47; 2,2+1,2,2+1/4331 str
1927?	H167	*Christ Hath a Garden*; satb; words: Isaac Watts; orch 1110/0000 str
1928	App. III, 25	*Bach's Fugue a la Gigue*; first version: military band second version: orch: 2222/2221 str
1928	H171	[*Two Rounds*]; voices; words: Mabel Rodwell Jones No. 1: "Within this place all beauty dwells" No. 2: "To both Missis Bell"
1928	H173	*A Moorside Suite*; brass band
1929 Wolfe	H174	*Twelve Songs*, Op. 48; voice and piano; words: Humbert No. 1: "Persephone" No. 2: "Things Lovelier" No. 3: "Now in these Fairylands" No. 4: "A Little Music" No. 5: "The Thought" No. 6: "The Floral Bandit" No. 7: "Envoi" No. 8: "The Dream-City" No. 9: "Journey's End" No. 10: "In the Street of Lost Time" No. 11: "Rhyme" No. 12: "Betelgeuse"
1929	H174A	*Epilogue*; voice and piano; words: Humbert Wolfe
1929	H175	*Double Concerto*; 2 solo violins; orch:2222/2200 timp str
1929-1930	H88	"Marching Song" from *Two Songs without Words*, Op. 22; second version: military band
1929-1930	H176	*The Tale of the Wandering Scholar*, Op. 50; chamber opera; s t bar b soloists; orch: 1+1,1+1,22/2000 str
1926-1930?	App. II, 16	*Second Choral Symphony*; projected
1930	H177	*A Choral Fantasia*, Op. 51; solo soprao, satb chorus; words: Robert Bridges; orch: 0000/0331 org str

1930	H179A	[*Two Pieces for Piano*]; No. 1: "Nocturne"
1930	H180	[*Two Chants*]; unison male voices No. 1: "In the Lord I put my trust;" words: Psalm 11 No. 2: "All the powers of the Lord;" words: Canticle: *Benedicite omnia opera*
1930	H180A	*God Be in My Head*; unison voices and piano; words: *Sarum Primer*, 1558
1930-31	H178	*Hammersmith: Prelude and Scherzo*, Op. 52; first version: military band; second version: orch 2+1,2+1,2+1,2+1/4331 timp bd cym tri gong xylo str
1930-1931	H183	*Twelve Welsh Folk Songs*; satb (No. 6 sab); translated into English by Steuart Wilson "Lisa Lan," "Green Grass," "The Dove," "Awake, Awake," "The Nightingale and Linnet," "The mother-in-law," "The First Love," "O 'twas on a Monday morning," "My sweetheart's like Venus," "White Summer Rose," " The Lively Pair," "The lover's complaint"
1931?	H181	*Roadways*; unison voices and piano; words: John Masefield
1931?	H182	*Wassail Song*; satb; words: trad., collected by Jane M. Joseph
1931	H184	*The Bells*; motion picture score (missing)
1931-1932	H186	*Six Choruses*, Op. 53; male voices and organ or pf or str; words: Helen Waddell, from "Mediaeval Latin Lyrics" No. 1: "Intercession;" ttbb and str No. 2: "Good Friday;" ttbb and str No. 3: "Drinking Song;" ttbb and str No. 4: "A Love Song;" tb and str No. 5: "How mighty are the Sabbaths;" ttbb s (ad lib.); orch: 2222/4231 str or 2222/2200 pf org str No. 6: "Before Sleep;" tb str
1931	H 186A	*On the Battle Which Was Fought at Fontenoy*; ttbb str; words: Helen Waddell
1932	H185	*Mr. Shilkret's Maggot*; jazz orchestra: 1111,2as,ts,bs/2,0+3,21 timp bd sd cym tri glock marimba bells banjo cel hp pf str

1932	H179B	[*Two Pieces for Piano*]; No. 2: "Jig"
1932	H187	*Eight Canons*; equal voices; words: Helen Waddell No. 1: "If you love songs;" ssa or ttb No. 2: "Lovely venus;" ssa or ttb No. 3: "The fileds of sorrow;" s m-s a or t bar b No. 4: "David's Lament for Jonathan;" ssa or ttb No. 5: "O strong of heart;" ssa ssa ssa or ttb ttb ttb No. 6: "Truth of all truth;" s m-s a, s m-s a or t bar b, t bar b No. 7: "Evening on the Mosells;" sa piano No. 8: "If t'were the time of lillies;" s a piano
1933	H188	*O Spiritual Pilgrim*; soprano solo and satb; words: J. E. Flecker
1933	H189	*Come Live with Me*; two voices; words: Christopher Marlowe
1933	H190	*Brook Green Suite*; [1110/0000] str
1933	H190A	*Gavotte*; [1110/0000] str (originally a part of H190)
1933	H191	*Lyric Movement*; solo viola and orch: 1111/0000 str
1933-1934	App. II, 17	*The Song of Solomon*; soloists, chorus and orchestra (sketches extant, score missing; unfinished at the time of Holst's death; some movements composed later by Imogen Holst)
1933-1934	H192	*Scherzo*; 2+1,2+1,22/4331 timp hp str
1934	App. II, 18	*Symphony*; only H192 brought to fruition

APPENDIX II

PERSONALITIES

The following entries about people connected to Holst's life and/or career are meant to simply give the reader additional information. Length of entry does not indicate importance to Holst or to his legacy. Available information is sporatic; some people moved around a great deal while others stayed put. Locations cited are either obvious (such as Prague or Chicago) or British unless specified.

Adkins, Hector Ernest: b. 1885; Director of Music at the Royal Military School of Music at Kneller Hall, Twickenham, Middlesex, 1921-42; author/compiler of *Adkin's Treatise on the Military Band* (1931); d. 1945.

Aldrich, Richard: b. Providence, RI, July 31, 1863; music critic; ed. Harvard University, BA 1885, studied with Paine; music critis of *Providence Journal* 1885-1889, *Evening Star* 1889-1891, assistant critic at *New York Tribune* 1891-1901, music critic of *New York Times* 1902-23; *Guide to the Ring of the Nibelungen* (1905); d. Rome, Italy, June 2, 1937.

Allen, Hugh Percy: b. Reading, December 23, 1869; conductor and administrator; ed. Reading and Oxford; conductor of the London Bach Choir 1907-20; Professor of Music, Oxford University 1918-37; Director of Royal College of Music 1919-37; knighted 1920; d. Oxford, February 20, 1946.

Bainton, Edgar: b. 1880; conductor, administrator and writer about music; ed. Royal College of Music, FRCM, Mus. Doc. (Dunelm); cond. Newcastle-upon-Tyne Choral Society; Director, State Conservatorium of Music, Sydney; d. 1956.

Bauer, Harold: b. Kingston-on-Thames, April 28, 1873; pianist; studied with Paderewski; toured Europe, soloist with the Boston Symphony, 1900; founder and president, The Beethoven Association in New York, 1918-40; President of the Friends of Music in the Library of Congress; author *Harold Bauer, His Book* (1948); edited works of Schubert and Brahms; d. Miami, FL, March 12, 1951.

Bauer, Marion [nee Eugenie]: b. Walla Walla, WA, August 15, 1887; composer and writer; studied with Raoul Pugno, Nadia Boulanger, and Jean Paul Ertel; taught at New York University 1926-51 and Juilliard 1940-44 among other places; wrote mostly in small forms, including a significant amount of chamber music; d. South Hadley, MA, August 9, 1955.

Bax, Arnold Edward Trevor: b. London, November 8, 1883; prolific composer and writer; ed. Royal Academy of Music, studied with Frederick Corder; great interest in Celtic topics; 7 symphonies, 9 symphonic poems; knighted, 1937; Master of the King's Musick 1941-53; autobiography *Farewell, My Youth* (1943); d. Cork, Ireland, October 3, 1953.

Bax, Clifford: b. London, July 13, 1886; critic, playwright, author, and editor, brother of Arnold Bax; collaborated with Holst on numerous projects; founder Phoenix Society; d. November 18, 1962.

Bell, William Henry: b. St. Albans, August 20, 1873; composer and conductor; studied composition with Corder and Stanford; Professor of Harmony, Royal Academy of Music 1903-12; Director of Music, Pageant of London, 1911; director, South African College of Music 1912-35; Chair of Music at Cape Town University 1919-35; works include *The Purdover's Tale, Walt Whitman Symphony*, 2 other symphonies; d. Cape Town, April 13, 1946.

Bidder, Helen: b. 1891; pianist, teacher, and composer; ed. Royal Academy of Music ARAM, LRAM; piano teacher at St. Paul's Girls' School and Harrington, Ealing..

Bliss, Arthur Edward Drummond: b. London, August 2, 1891; composer and conductor; ed. Pembroke, Royal College of Music; studied with Stanford, Vaughan Williams, and Holst; in California 1923-25; Music Director of the BBC 1942-44; knighted 1950; Master of the Queen's Musick 1953- ; conducted first professional performance of *Savitri*; *Rout*, *A Colour Symphony*, *Things to Come*; d. London, March 27, 1975.

Boulanger, Nadia Juliette: b. Paris, September 16, 1887; French composition teacher extraordinaire; ed. Paris Conservatoire; studied with Guilmant and Faure; taught at Paris Conservatoire 1909-24, Ecole Normal de Musique 1920-39, and American Conservatory at Fontainebleu 1921- , Director there 1950- ; students included Aaron Copland, Roy Harris, Walter Piston, Harold Shapero, Virgil Thomson; d. Paris October 22, 1979.

Boult, Adrian Cedric: b. Chester, April 8, 1889; eminent English conductor; ed.Westminster School, London, Christ Church, Oxford, Leipzig Conservatory and Gewandhaus; DM from Oxford; Professor of Music at Royal College of Music 1919- ; conductor British Symphony Orchestra 1919-24, City of Birmingham Orchestra 1924-30, BBC Symphony 1930-50; London Philharmonic, 1950-57; premiered *The Planets* in 1918; d. London, February 22, 1983.

Bridge, (John) Frederick: b. Oldbury, December 5, 1844; organist, conductor, and composer; apprenticed to John Hopkins (Rochester Cathedral) and John Goss (Westminster Abbey); DM from Oxford 1874; taught harmony and organ at Royal College of Music 1883- ; conducted Royal Choral Society 1896-1922; knighted 1897; d. London, March 18, 1924.

Bridges, Robert: b. Walmer, October 23, 1844; poet; ed. Eton and Corpus Christi College, Oxford University; Poet Laureate of England 1913-30 ; *The Testament of Beauty* (1929); d. Boar's Hill, Oxford, April 21, 1930.

Butler, Nicholas Murray b. Elizabeth, NJ, April 2, 1862; philosopher; President, Columbia University, 1901-45, emeritus 1945-47; presdent, American Academy of Arts & Letters 1929; recipient of Republican electoral vote for US Vice President 1912; recipient of 1/2 of the Nobel Peace Prize 1931; President, Carnegie Endowment for International Peace 1925-45; d. NY, December 7,1947.

Butterworth, George Sainton Kaye: b. London, July 12, 1885; composer; ed. Eton and Trinity College, Oxford; studied with Thomas Dunhill; collector of folk songs; *Times* columnist; *A Shropshire Lad, The Banks of Green Willow*; d. Battle of Somme, France, August 5, 1916.

Capell, Richard: b. Northampton, March 23, 1885; writer and music critic, *The Daily Mail* 1911-, *The Daily Telegraph* 1933- ; ed. *Monthly Musical Record* 1928-33, *Proprietor* 1936- and *Music & Letters* 1950-54; specialist in Schubert lieder; d. London, June 21,1954.

Carey, Clive: b. 1883; baritone and producer; sung Satyavan in the first profreesional performance of *Savitri*; later active in Australia; d.1968.

Carter, Elliott: b. New York, January 11, 1908; composer; ed. Harvard University, MA 1932, and Longy School of Music; studied with Walter Piston, Edward Burlingame Hill, Nadia Boulanger, and Holst; taught at St. John's College, Annapolis 1939-41, Peabody Conservatory 1946-48, Columbia 1948-50, and Yale 1950-58. *Sonata for Flute, Oboe, Cello and Harpsichord, Syringa.*

Clarke, Douglas: b. Reading, April 4, 1893; organist, conductor, and musical administrator; ed. University College, Reading and Cambridge University; studied with Holst; conducted Cambridge Musical Society 1923-27, Winnipeg Male Voice Choir and Philharmonic Society 1927-29, Montreal Orchestra 1930-41; Director of McGill Conservatorium, Montreal 1929-30, Dean of Faculty of Music there 1930-1955; d. Warwick, 1962.

Clarke, Henry Leland: b. Dover, NH, March 9, 1907; musicologist and composer; ed. Harvard

University, MA 1929, PhD 1947, also Ecole Normal de Musique, Paris, and Bennington College; studied with Edward Burlingame Hill, Nadia Boulanger, Otto Luening, and Holst; taught at Westminster Choir College, PA 1938-42, University of California at Los Angeles 1947-58, University of Washington, 1958-77; *Monograph, The Sun Shines Also Today.*

Coates, Alfred: b. St. Petersburg, Russia, April 23, 1882; English conductor; ed. Liverpool University, Leipzig Conservatory, 1902-05; studied with Klengel (cello), Teichmuller (piano), and Nikisch (conducting); conducted opera at Elberfeld 1905-07, Dresden 1907-09, Mannheim 1909-10, St. Petersburg 1911- ; Johannesburg Symphony, 1946-53; taught at Eastman Conservatory 1923-25; gave first complete public performance of *The Planets*, *First Choral Symphony*; d. Cape Town, December 11, 1953.

Coleridge-Taylor, Samuel: b. London August 15, 1875; composer and violinist; ed. Royal College of Music 1890-97; studied with Stanford; taught at Royal Academy of Music 1898-1912 ; prof. of composition Trinity College, London 1903 and Guildhall School 1910; conductor of London Handel Society 1904-12 ; 3 concert tours of USA; *Four Novelletten*, *Hiawatha's Wedding Feast*; d. London September 1, 1912.

Colles, H(enry) C(ope): b. Bridgnorth, Shropshire, April 20, 1979; music scholar; ed. Royal College of Music, Worcester College, Oxford University; MB 1903, MA 1907; music critic of *The Times*, 1905-40; taught at Royal College of Music 1919-; music director, Cheltenham Ladies College; ed. 3rd, 4th eds. of *Groves' Dictionary of Music and Musicians*, vol. VII of *Oxford History of Music*; d. London, March 4, 1943.

Collins, Anthony: b. Hastings, September 3, 1893; conductor, violist, composer; studied with Holst at Royal College of Music from 1920; led viola sections of London Symphony and Covent Garden Orchestras 1926-36; d. Los Angeles, December 11, 1963.

Coolidge, Elizabeth [Penn] Sprague: b. Chicago, October 30, 1864; American music patron; established Berkshire Festivals of Chamber Music 1918, Elizabeth Sprague Coolidge Foundation in the Library of Congress 1925, Elizabeth Sprague Coolidge Medal for chamber music, 1932-49; d. Cambridge, MA, November 4, 1953.

Cossart, Ernest, see **Holst, Emil Gottfried von**

Cossart [Livingston], Valerie: b. London, June 27, 1907; daughter of Emil Gottfried von Holst (Ernest Cossart) and niece of Gustav Holst; actress of stage, screen and television; stage: *Hay Fever*, *Blythe Spirit*, over twenty others; films: *Edward My Son*, *Fail Safe*, *The Verdict*; television: *The First Hundred Years*, *Love of Life*, *Kraft Television Theatre*, *The Defenders*, *Naked City*; d. New York, December 31, 1994.

Cowen, Frederick: b. Kingston, Jamaica, January 29, 1852; conductor and composer; ed. Leipzig Conservatory, Edinburgh University, DM 1910; studied with Hauptmann, Moscheles, Reineke and Richter; conductor of Philharmonic Society of London 1888-92 and 1900-07, Liverpool Philharmonic 1896-1913, Scottish Orchestra 1900-10, Handel Triennial Festival 1903-12; knighted in 1911; six symphonies, four operas, over 250 songs; book, *Music as She Is Wrote*; d. London, October 6, 1935.

Cross, Milton: b.1897; announcer for the Metropolitan Opera Broadcasts, 1931-74; author of *The Milton Cross Encyclopedia of the Great Composers and Their Music* (1953); d. 1975.

Cross, Wilbur Lucius: b.1862; Dean, Graduate School, Yale University, 1916-1930 and Sterling Professor of English, 1921-30; Editor of *The Yale Review*; Served four terms as Governor of Connecticut, 1931-1939; d. 1948.

Damrosch, Walter Johannes: b. Breslau, Germany (now Wroclaw, Poland), January 30, 1862; American conductor, composer, and music educator; studied with Leopold Damrosch (his father) and von Bulow; conducted New York Oratorio Society 1885-98, NY Symphony Society 1885-98 and 1903-1927, Metropolitan Opera 1885-91, Damrosch Opera Company 1894-99, NY Philharmonic Society 1902-03; musical advisor to NBC 1927-47; conducted the NBC Symphony in weekly broadcasts of music appreciation hours 1928-42; d. New York, December 22, 1950.

D'Aranyi [de Hunyadvar], Jelly Eva: b. Budapest, May 30, 1893; Hungarian-born violinist, sister of Adila Fachiri and grandniece of Joseph Joachim; studied with Hubay; many joint appearances with pianist Myra Hess; an advocate of modern music, gave first performances of Bartok's *First Violin Sonata*, Ravel's *Tzigane*, Vaughan Williams' *Concerto Accademico* and, with her sister Adila Fachiri, Holst's *Double Concerto*; d. Florence, Italy, March 30, 1966.

Davison, Archibald Thompson: b. Boston, MA, October 11, 1883; eminent music educator, organist, and conductor; ed. Harvard University, BA 1906, MA 1907, Ph.D. 1908; studied with Widor in Paris 1909-10; organist and choirmaster at Harvard, 1910-40; conducted Harvard Glee Club 1912-33, Radcliffe Choral Society, 1913-28; many books, incl. *Music Education in America, Protestant Church Music in America, Choral Conducting*; ed. *Historical Anthology of Music*, assoc. ed. (with T. Surrette) *Concord Series of Educational Music*; d. Brant Rock, MA, February 6, 1961.

Day, Nora: b. September 26, 1891; pianist and music educator; ed. St. Paul's Girls' School 1907-10 and Royal Academy of Music; studied with Adine O'Neill; taught at St. Paul's Girls' School, amanuensis to Holst; d. 1983.

De la Mare, Walter [John]: b.1873; author, children's books, including *Peacock Pie*; d. 1956.

DeLamarter, Eric: b. Lansing, MI, February 18, 1880; organist, conductor, critic, teacher, and composer; ed. Albion College; studied with Widor and Guilmant in Paris 1900-02; music critic Chicago *Record-Herald, Tribune*, and *Inter Ocean*, 1901-14; on faculty of Olivet College 1904-05, Chicago Musical College 1909-10, University of Missouri, Ohio State University and University of Texas in the 1940's; Associate Conductor of the Chicago Symphony Orchestra, 1918-1936; composed four symphonies, etc.; d. Orlando, FL, May 17, 1953.

Downes, [Edwin] Olin: b. Evanston, IL, January 27, 1886; music critic for *The Boston Post* 1906-24, *New York Times*, 1924-1955; Music Director, Cincinnati Conservatory, 1939; lecturer at Chatauqua and the Bershire Music Festival; d. New York, August 22, 1955.

Duckworth, Frank: b. 1866; organist and conductor; conducted Blackburn Ladies' Choir 1906-24; organist, St. Mark's Church in Blackburn 1902-36; d. Blackburn, November 25, 1946.

Dyer, Louise: b. Melbourne, Australia, July 16,1890; patroness of music and publisher; founded L'Oiseau-Lyre (The Lyre-Bird Press) in 1932, financed entirely out of her own pocket; m. James Dyer; d. Monaco, Novemebr 9, 1962.

Eggar, Katharine E.: composer, pianist, and writer about music; ed. Royal Academy of Music, ARAM, LRAM and Royal College of Music, FRCM; vice president of the Society of Women Musicians 1935.

Engel, Carl: b. Paris, July 21, 1883; musicologist; ed. University of Strasbourg, University of Munich; studied with Thuille; ed. and musical advisor of the Boston Music Co. 1909-21; chief, Music Division, Library of Congress, 1922-34; president of G. Schirmer, Inc., 1929-32 and 1934-; ed. *The Musical Quarterly* 1929-42; president, American Musicological Society 1937-38; many honors; essay collection *Alla Breve, from Bach to Debussy*; d. New York, May 6, 1944.

Evans, Edwin: b. London, September 1,1871; Music critic for the *Pall Mall Gazette*, 1912-23 and the *Daily Mail*, 1933-45; ed. *The Dominant*, 1927-29; notable series of articles in the *Musical Times*, 1919-1920; Chair, British section of the International Society for Contemporary Music, President, 1938; author *Music and the Dance* (1948); d. London, March 3, 1945.

Fachiri, Adila: b. Budapest, February 26, 1886, sister of Jelly d'Aranyi, grandniece of Joseph Joachim; Hungarian-born violinist; studied with Joachim; with her sister premiered Holst's *Double*

Concerto; d. Florence, December 15, 1962.

Fiedler, Arthur: b. Brookline, MA, December 17, 1894; conductor; studied violin with Emmanuel Fiedler (father)and in Europe with Hess (violin) and Dohnanyi, Kleffel and Krasselt (conducting); played violin, viola, and celesta in Boston Symphony Orchestra 1915- ; Arthur Fiedler Sinfonietta 1924- ; conductor, Boston Pops 1930-1979; recipient of Presidential Medal of Freedom 1977; d. Brookline, MA, July 10, 1979.

Findlay, John Joseph: b. 1860; Professor of Education, University of Manchester 1903-25, Dean, 1914-18, Civilian Advisor on Education, British Salonica Forces, 1918-19; d. 1940.

Flagler, Harry Harkness b. Cleveland, OH December 2,1870; financial backer of the New York Symphony Society, 1914-28, President, New York Philharmonic-Symphony Society, 1928-1934; President Millbrook, NY Free Library.

Gardiner, H(enry) Balfour: b. London November 7, 1877; composer, conductor, and patron of music; ed. Hochschule Conservatory, Frankfort (1894-96) and New College, Oxford 1896-1900; taught at University College, Reading 1924- and Royal Conservatory of Music 1924- ; organized and funded the H. Balfour Gardiner Concerts at Queen's Hall to promote music by young British composers 1912-13; d. Salisbury, June 28, 1950.

Geehl, Henry: b. London, September 28, 1881; composer and conductor; ed. London and Vienna; Professor at Trinity College of Music 1918- ; arranged significant amount of music for brass band and school groups; d. Beaconsfield, January 14, 1961.

Godfrey, Dan(iel) II: b. London, June 20, 1858; conductor; son of military band conductor Dan Godfrey I; ed. King's College and Royal College of Music; conducted London Military Band (a civilian ensemble) 1889-91, conductor and founder of the Winter Gardens Orchestra (later the Bouremouth Municipal Orchestra), 1893- ; knighted 1927; *Memories and Music*; d. Bournemouth, July 20, 1939.

Goldman, Edwin Franko: b. Louisville, KY, January 1, 1878; conductor and composer; studied composition with Dvorak, cornet with Levy and Sohst; solo cornetist of the Metropolitan Opera Orchestra 1899-1909; founded and conducted The Goldman Band, 1911-56 ; president, American Bandmasters Association, 1929; composed over 100 marches; author *Band Betterment*; d. New York, February 21, 1956.

Goldsborough, Arnold: b. Gomersal, October 26, 1892; keyboard artist and conductor; ed. Royal College of Music; organist at St. Anne's, Soho 1920-23, St. Martin-in-the-Fields 1924-35, assistant organist at Westminster Abbey 1920-27; director of music Morley College, 1924-29; taught at Royal College of Music 1923- ; founder, The Goldsborough Orchestra 1948, renamed the English Chamber Orchestra in 1960; d. Tenbury Well, December 14, 1964.

Goosens, (Aynsley) Eugene: b. London, May 26, 1893; conductor and composer; ed. Bruges Conservatory 1903-04, Liverpool Collge of Music, Royal College of Music; studied with C. Wood and Stanford; violinist Queen's Hall Orchestra 1911; conducted at Covent Garden 1921-23, Rochester Philharmonic 1923-31, Cincinnati Symphony 1931-47, Sydney Symphony and State Conservatorium of Music 1947-55; knighted, 1955; d. London, June 13, 1962.

Grainger, (George) Percy Aldridge: b. Melbourne, Australia, July 8, 1882; celebrated pianist and composer; ed. Hockschule Conservatory, Frankfort; studied there with Kwast, additional studies with Pabst and Busoni; toured throughout Europe; settled in USA in 1914; taught at Chicago Musical College in summers 1919-31, also at National Summer Music Camp at Interlocken; chair of music department at New York University 1932-33; founded The Grainger Museum in Melbourne 1935; *Lincolnshire Posy*; d. White Plains, NY February 20, 1961.

Gray, Frances Ralph: educator and administrator; ed. Plymouth and Newnham College, Cambridge; Headmistress St. Katharine's School, St. Andrews 1894-1903; High Mistress, St.

Paul's Girls' School 1903-26; book, *And Gladly Wolde He Teche*; d. November 10, 1935.

Grunebaum, Herman: b. Giessen, January 8, 1872; conductor; Chorus Master at Covent Garden 1907-33; co-founder of London School of Opera, where he conducted the premiere of *Savitri*; taught at Royal College of Music 1922-46; d. Chipstead, Surrey, April 5, 1954.

Haba, Alois: b. Vizovice, Moravia, June 21, 1893; composer and teacher; ed. Prague Conservatory 1914-15, studied with Schreker in Berlin 1918-22; taught at Prague Conservatory 1924-51; experimented with quarter-tones, fifth-tones and sixth-tones; works include Matka, fifteen string quartets, eleven piano sonatas; d. Prague, November 18, 1973.

Hadley, Henry Kimball: b. Somerville, MA, December 20, 1871; composer and conductor; ed. New England Conservatory; studied with Chadwick; conducted Seattle Symphony 1909-11; founder and conductor of San Francisco Symphony Orchestra 1911-15; associate conductor of New York Philharmonic Orchestra 1920-27; founder and conductor of Manhattan Symphony Orchestra 1929-32, formed to present works of American composers; founded Berkshire Music Festival 1934; d. New York, September 6, 1937.

Hale, Philip: b. Norwich, VT, March 5, 1854; eminent music critic; ed. Yale University (law), admitted to the bar 1880; studied organ with Dudley Buck, then studied organ in Europe 1882-87 with Haupt, Rheinberger, and Guilmant; music critic *Boston Home Journal* 1889-91, *Boston Post* 1890-91, *Boston Journal* 1891-1903, *Boston Herald* 1904-33; ed. of *Boston Musical Record* 1897-1901; Boston Symphony program notes 1901-33; co-author *Famous Composers and Their Works* (1900); d. Boston, November 30, 1934.

Hardy, Thomas: b. Higher Brockampton, Dorset, June 2, 1840; novelist; ed. Dorchester, London (architecture with John Hicks); practiced architecture before turning to writing; *Return of the Native*, *Tess of the D'Urbervilles*, *The Dynasts*; d. Dorchester January 11, 1928.

Harrison, Emily Isobel: see Holst, (Emily) Isobel von:

Hart, Fritz Bennicke: b. Brockley, Kent February 11, 1874; composer, conductor and writer; ed. Royal College of Music, FRCM; Director of the Melbourne Conservatory of Music; Conductor, Honolulu Symphony Orchestra, 1932- ; d. Honolulu, July 2, 1949.

Hess, Myra: b. London, February 25, 1890; pianist; ed. Royal Academy of Music; studied with Tobias Matthay; London debut in 1907, American debut in 1922; organized the National Gallery Concerts 1939; created Dame Commander, OBE 1941; d. London, November 25, 1965.

Hill, Edward Burlingame: b. Cambridge, MA, September 9, 1872; composer; ed. Harvard; additional studies with Widor, Whiting, Lang, and Chadwick; taught at Harvard 1908-40; wrote articles for *Boston Evening Transcript*, book: *Modern French Music* (1924); works (impressionistic) include *Lilacs*, 3 symphonies; d. Francestown, NH, July 9, 1960.

HOLST:

Adolph von: b. London, February 5, 1846; keyboard artist, composer, and music educator; father of Gustav Holst; ed. Hamburg; taught music in Cheltenham, gave recitals and conducted concerts there at the Assembly Rooms and the Montpellier Rotunda; organist, All Saints' Church 1868-95; local examiner for the Royal College of Music; m. Clara Cox Lediard July 11, 1871; m. Mary Thorley Stone August 20, 1885; d. Cheltenham, August 17, 1901.

Benigna ("Nina") Honoria von: b. Marylebone, London, 1849; piano teacher; sister of Adolph, aunt of Gustav Holst; d. 1920's.

Clara Cox von [nee Lediard]: b. Cirencester, April 13, 1841; pianist; wife of Adolph von Holst and mother of Gustav Holst; fifth child of Samuel Lediard; d. Cheltenham, February 12, 1882.

Emil Gottfried Adolf von [Ernest Cossart]: b. Cheltenham, Sepetmber 24, 1876; actor; brother of Gustav Holst, father of Valerie Cossart; ed. Dean Close School, Cheltenham; acting debut Novelty Theatre, London 1896; toured throughout South Africa; m. Maude Davis; immigrated to USA in 1908; American debut that year at New York's Knickerbacher Theatre; original member of the Theatre Guild; screen debut in *The Scoundrel* (1935); appeared in character roles in forty motion pictures; hobbies included golf and bridge; d. NY, January 21, 1951.

Evelyn Thorley von: b. Cheltenham, June 25, 1889; lawyer; half brother of Gustav Holst; son of Adolph von Holst and his second wife Mary Thorley Stone; immigrated to USA as a child, ca. 1901; practiced law in Chicago; d. 1969.

Gustavus Matthias von: b. London, 1833; keyboard artist and composer; uncle of Gustav Holst and brother of Adolph von Holst; organist, St. John's Episcopal Church, Glasgow 1867-68; d. Keith, January 17, 1874.

Gustavus Valentin(e) Johann (von): b. Riga, Latvia, September, 1799; composer, harpist, and pianist; grandfather of Gustav Holst; emigrated to England ca. 1804, settled in Cheltenham ca. 1832; m. Honoria Goodrich (the first English member of the family, d. Glasgow, February 15, 1873); d. Cheltenham, June 8, 1870.

Imogen Clare: b. Richmond, Surrey, April 12, 1907; composer, conductor, editor, and author; daughter of Gustav Holst; ed. Eothen School 1917-21, St. Paul's Girls' School 1921-25, and Royal College of Music, 1925-29, studied composition with Gordon Jacob; music organizer for Central England Music Association 1941-44; Director of Music at Dartington Hall 1943-51; amanuensis to Benjamin Britten 1952-64; conductor of The Purcell Singers 1953-67; artistic director of the Aldeburgh Festival 1956-84; created Dame Commander OBE, 1975; author/editor of nine books concerning her father and his music; d. Aldeburgh, March 9, 1984.

(Emily) Isobel [nee Harrison]: b. March 26, 1877; cellist and soprano; wife of Gustav Holst; daughter of Ralph Augustus Harrison and Jessie Elizabeth Davies; d. Stowmarket, April 16, 1969.

Mary Thorley von [nee Stone]: pianist and theosophist; stepmother of Gustav Holst, second wife of Adolph von Holst; daughter of Rev. Edward Stone; immigrated to California with son Thorley, ca. 1901.

Matthias: b. Riga, Latvia, 1769; pianist, harpist, and composer; great-grandfather of Gustav Holst; harp teacher to the Imperial family at St. Petersburg; m. Katharina Rogge (d. England, 1838); emigrated to London; d. Hampstead, London, 1854. [Note: Matthias is the earliest easily-traceable relative of Gustav Holst. During World War I, Holst maintained that his family name was Swedish. This is backed up by history; Sweden took Riga in 1621 and hung on to it for the next 100 years, ceding it to Russia in 1721. Holst's ancestors probably immigrated from Sweden to Riga during that time.]

Matthias ["Max"] Ralph Bromley von: b. November 28, 1886; cellist; half-brother of Gustav Holst, son of Adolph von Holst and his second wife Mary Thorley Stone; m. Dorothy Louise Arden; d. 1956.

Theodore: b. London, September, 1810; painter; great-uncle of Gustav Holst; studied with Fuseli; d. London February 12, 1844.

Howe, Mark Antony DeWolfe: b. Bristol, RI, August 28, 1864; author and editor; ed. Lehigh University BA, DL, Harvard University BA, MA; Asst. Editor 1893-95, *Atlantic Monthly*, v.p. Atlantic Monthly Co. 1911-29; ed. Harvard Alumni Bulletin 1913-19; Trustee, Boston Sympnony Orchestra 1918- ; director Boston Athenaeum 1933-37; overseer Harvard University 1925-31 and

1933-39; *Yankee Ballads*, *Barrett Wendel and His Letters*; d. 1960.

Howells, Herbert (Norman): b. Lydney, Gloucestershire, October 17, 1892; composer and music educator; ed. Royal College of Music, studied with Stanford and Charles Wood; taught at Royal College of Music 1920-62, succeeded Holst at St. Paul's Girls' School 1936-62, also Professor of Music at University of London 1954-64; knighted in 1953; *Fantasia for Cello and Orchestra*, *Triptych for Brass Band*, *The Coventry Mass*; d. Oxford, February 12, 1983.

Jacob, Gordon Percival Septimus: b. London, July 5, 1895; composer; ed. Dulwich College and Royal College of Music, DM 1935; taught at Royal College of Music 1926-66, students included Imogen Holst and Malcolm Arnold; knighted 1968; books include *The Composer and His Art*; *The Elements of Orchestration*; works include *An Original Suite*, *Music for a Festival*, *Trombone Concerto*, 2 symphonies; d. Saffron Walden, June 8, 1984.

James, Ivor: b. London, October 12, 1882; cellist; taught at Royal College of Music 1919- ; founder-member of the English Quartet and the Menges Quartet; d. London February 28, 1963.

James, Philip: b. Jersey City, NJ, May 17, 1890; organist and conductor; ed. City University of New York; studied with Goldmark, Herbert, and others; fellow, American Guild of Organists 1910; music dept. chair at New York University 1923- , also taught at Columbia 1931-33; conductor Victor Herbert Opera Co. 1919-22, conductor and founder New Jersey Symphony Orchestra 1922-29, Brooklyn Orchestral Society 1927-30, Bamberger Little Symphony 1929-36; d. Southampton, NY, November 1, 1975.

Janacek, Leos: b. Hukvaldy, Moravia, July 3, 1854; composer; ed. German College, Brno 1869-72, Prague Organ School 1874-5, Leipzig Conservatory 1879-80, studied with Oskar Paul, Leo Grill; director, Brno Organ School 1881-1919, also taught at Brno Gymnasium 1886-1902; *Her Foster Daughter*, *Sinfonietta*; d. Moravska, Ostrava, August 12, 1928.

Johnson, Robert Underwood: b. Washington D.C., January 12,1853; editor,author, and poet; American Civil War historian; Ambassador to Italy 1920-21; Secretary of the American Academy of Arts and Letters, 1904-37 ; d. October 14,1937.

Joseph, Jane Marian: b. London May 31, 1894; composer, percussionist, writer, and teacher; ed. St. Paul's Girls' School 1909-13, Girton College, Cambridge; amanuensis, substitute and festival organizer for Holst; d. London, March 9, 1929.

Judson, Arthur: b. Dayton, OH February 17, 1881; concert manager; manager, Cincinnati Orchestra, Philadelphia Orchestra 1915-36, New York Philharmonic Orchestra 1922-56; founder and owner of Columbia Concerts Corporation 1932, later renamed Columbia Artists Management, Inc.; d. Rye, NY January 28, 1975.

Kemp [Hammond Davies], Amy: b. Cairo, Egypt, 1897; pianist; ed. St. Paul's Girls' School, 1911-16 and The Malthay School; taught at St. Paul's Girls' School 1917-37; amanuensis for Holst; d. Newbury, July, 1986.

Koussevitzky, Serge Alexandrovich: b. Vishny-Volochok, Russia, July 26, 1974; bassist and conductor; ed. Musico-Dramatic institute of the Moscow Philharmonic Society 1888-94, studied bass with Rambousek; bassist with Bolshoi Theatre Orchestra 1894-1905; established Editions Russes de Musique in 1909; founded his own symphony in Moscow 1909; conducted State Symphony Orchestra in St. Petersburg 1917-20, Concerts Koussevitzky in Paris, 1922-24, Boston Symphony Orchestra 1924-49; founded Berkshire Music Center in 1940; d. Boston June 4, 1951.

Lambert, (Leonard) Constant: b. London, August 23, 1905; conductor, composer, and writer; ed. Royal College of Music 1915-22, studied with R. O. Morris and Vaughan Williams; conductor of The Camargo Society 1930, Vic-Wells (later Sadler's Wells) Ballet 1931-47, many guest appearances thereafter; *The Rio Grande*, *Horoscope*; d. London, August 21, 1951.

Lasker, Vally: b. Berlin, February 13, 1885; pianist, conductor, and music educator; taught at St.

Paul's Girls' School, Morley College, and Borough Polytechnic 1914-30; musical director and conductor at Overstone School; ananuensis to Holst, helped prepare many of his scores and made piano arrangements of many of them; many performances with Nora Day; d. London, March 29, 1978.

Lediard, Clara Cox see Holst, Clara Cox von

Lediard, Mary Croft [nee Whatley]: b. January 2, 1806; maternal grandmother of Gustav Holst; wife of Samuel Lediard; d. January 24, 1895.

Lediard, Samuel: b. ca. 1805; solicitor of Cirencester, civil servant; maternal grandfather of Gustav Holst; d. November 1, 1852.

Lidbury, Frank Austin: b. Middlewich, England, March 14, 1879; chemist and writer; ed. Owens College of Victoria University, Manchester BS 1898 and MS 1899, also studied at University of London 1899-1900 and University of Leipzig 1900-01; immigrated to USA 1903, naturalized citizen 1913; chief chemist Oldbury Electrochemical Co., Niagara Falls, NY 1903-05, works manager 1905-22, president and general manager, 1922-47.

Livingstone, Valerie see Cossart, Valerie

Lohmann, Carl Albert: b. 1887; university executive; ed. Yale, BA, 1910; studied music in Berlin, 1910-11; Treasurer, Institute of Music and Music School Settlement, Cleveland, OH, 1921-25; Secretary, Yale University 1927-53 and curator of prints, 1926-1930; d. 1957.

Long, Kathleen: b. July 7, 1896; pianist; ed. Royal College of Music 1910-16, studied with Herbert Sharpe; taught at Royal College of Music 1920-64; many recordings; d. March 20, 1968.

Lopokova, Lydia: b. St. Petersburg, Russia, 1892; ballet dancer; ed. Mariinsky Theatre; danced with Diaghilev's Ballet Russes 1910- ; m. economist J. Maynard Keynes, 1925; co-founder The Camargo Society 1930 and Arts Theatre, Cambridge 1936.

McKenzie, Duncan: music educator, organist, editor, and agent; ed. Edinburgh University MA, studied with Friedrich Niecks; director of music at the High School for Girls and Commercial and Technical High School in Montreal, lecturer of theory and organ at McGill University, head of music department at New Jersey College for Women 1943- ; first manager and editor of music department at Oxford University Press, NY 1926- ; educational director of Carl Fischer, 1930- .

Masefield, John: b: Ledbury, June 1,1878; poet; ed. King's School, Warwick; trained as a seaman, then turned to literature; Poet Laureate 1930- ; knighted 1935; d. Abingdon, May 12, 1967.

Mason, Daniel Gregory: b: Brookline, MA, November 20, 1873; composer, writer on music, teacher; ed. Harvard 1891-95; also studied with Chadwick and Goetschius; taught at Columbia University 1905-42, Mac Dowell professor, serving as head there 1929-42; d. Greenwich, CT December 4, 1953.

Mason, Edward: b. Coventry, June 28, 1878; cellist, conductor, music educator; ed. Royal College of Music; assistant music master at Eton College for fifteen years; London debut Beckstein Hall 1900; principal cellist, New Symphony Orchestra; founder and conductor of Edward Mason Choir; d. France, May 9, 1915.

Monteux, Pierre: b. Paris, April 4, 1975; conductor; ed. Paris Conservatoire, 1st prize for violin 1896; conducted Concerts Berlioz 1911, Ballets Russes 1911-13 (premiered Stravinsky's *La Sacre du Printemps*) and 1916-17, Paris Opera 1913-14, NY Civic Orchestra Society 1917-1919, Boston Symphony 1919-24, associate conductor of Concertegebouw Orchestra 1924-34, conductor of Orchestre de Paris 1929-38, San Francisco Symphony 1936-1952, Metropolitan Opera 1953-56, London Symphony 1961-64 d. Hancock, ME, July 1, 1964.

Moore, Earl Vincent: b. Lansing, MI September 27, 1890; music educator and administrator; ed. University of MI, BA 1912, MA 1915; additional studies with Widor and Holst; taught University of Michigan 1914-23, director of School of Music 1923-46, dean 1946-60; chair, University of

Houston music dept. 1960-70; founding member of National Assn. of Schools of Music 1924; president of Music Teachers National Association 1936-38 and Pi Kappa Lambda 1946-50.

Morris, R[eginald] O[wen]: b. York, March 3, 1886; musicologist, teacher, composer; ed. Royal College of Music, taught there to 1948; head of theory at Curtis1926-28; regular contributor to crossword puzzles of *The Times*; d. London, December 14, 1948.

Morris, William: b: Wathamstow, March 24, 1834; poet, textile designer, printer, medievalist, and socialist reformer; ed. Marlborough and Exeter College, Oxford; founded Morris & Co.which produced wallpaper, fabrics, and furniture; established Hammersmith Socialist Society 1884, Kelmscott Press 1890; writings include *Sigurd the Volsung, A Dream of John Ball*, many verse translations; d. Kelmscott, Oxon. October 3, 1896.

Mukle, May Henrietta: b. London, May 14, 1880; cellist; ed. Royal Academy of Music; London debut 1907; introduced Holst's *Invocation* in 1911; d. 1963.

Murdoch, Kenneth Ballard: b. Boston, June 22,1895; college professor and administrator; ed. Harvard University, Associate Professor of English, 1930-32, Professor 1932-1964, Dean of the Faculty of Arts and Sciences 1931-36, Master of Leverett House, 1931-41; d. November 15,1975.

Newman, Ann[a] Emily [nee Lediard]: b. 1846; school administrator; aunt of Gustav Holst; m. Richard Newman, a riding master; ran the St. Mary's School in Barnes with her daughter; d. 1908.

Noble, Tertius: b: Bath, May 5, 1867; organist and conductor; ed. Royal College of Music; founded and conducted York Symphony Orchestra 1898-1912; organist St. Thomas Episopal Church in NY 1912-1947; d. Rockport, MA, May 4, 1953.

O'Donnell, Bertram Walton: b. 1887; conductor; ed. Royal Marines and Royal Academy of Music, MVO, ARAM, FRAM; commissioned in the Royal Marines 1921; conductor of the BBC Wireless Military Band, 1927-1937; d. 1939.

O'Neill, Adine [nee Ruckert]: b. 1875; pianist; ed. Paris Conservatoire, studied with Clara Schumann in Frankfurt; m. Norman O'Neill 1899; taught piano at St. Paul's Girls' School; played at Proms 1904-17; London critic of *Le Monde Musicale*; President of Society of Women Musicians 1921-23; d. February 17, 1947.

O'Neill, Norman: b. London, March 14, 1875; conductor and composer; ed. Hochschule Conservatory, Frankfort 1893-97; musical director of Haymarket Theatre, London 1908-19 and 1920-34, St. James Theatre, London 1919-20; treasurer of Royal Philharmonic Society 1919-34; taught harmony and composition, Royal Academy of Music 1924-; d. March 3, 1934.

Parry, Charles Hubert Hastings: b. Bournemouth February 27, 1848; composer, teacher, and administrator; ed. Eton and Exeter College, Oxford, BM 1867, BA 1870, studied with Elvey, Pierson, Bennett, and Macferren; taught at Royal College of Music 1883-1918, director 1894-1918; professor at Oxford University 1900-08; knighted in1898, made a baronet in 1913; writings include *The Art of Music* and *Style in Musical Art*; compositions include five symphonies, *Jerusalem*; d. Knight's Croft, Rustington, October 7, 1918.

Piston, Walter: b. Rockland, ME, January 20, 1894; composer; ed. Massachusetts Normal Art School, Harvard University 1919-1924, also studied piano with Harris Shaw, violin with Winternitz, and composition with Nadia Boulanger and Paul Dukas; taught at Harvard 1926-60; *The Incredible Flutist, Tunbridge Fair,* eight symphonies; d. Belmont, MA, November 12, 1976.

Pitt, Percy: b: London, January 4, 1870; conductor, keyboard artist, and administrator; ed. Paris, Leipzig, and Munich; organist at Queen's Hall 1896; director Covent Garden 1907-24, British National Opera Co. 1922-24, musical dirctor of BBC 1922-1930; d. London November 23, 1932.

Robinson, Stanford: b. 1904; conductor; member of the BBC musical staff 1924-66; d.1984.

Ronald [Russell], Landon: b. London, June 7, 1873; composer, conductor, writer on music; ed. Royal College of Music, FRCM 1924; studied with Parry, Stanford, and Parratt; conductor New

Symphony Orchestra 1909-14, Scottish Orchestra 1916-20; principal, Guildhall School of Music 1910-38; knighted 1922; 300 songs; writings include *Variations on a Personal Theme*; compiler of *Who's Who in Music* (1935); d. London, August 4, 1938.

Rothenstein, William: b. 1872; ed. Slade School, Paris; portrait artist and administrator; taught at University of Sheffield 1917-20; principal, Royal College of Art 1920-35; trustee, Tate Gallery 1927-33, member, Royal Fine Arts Commission 1931-38; *Twenty-four Portraits* (two sets, 1920 and 1923); writings include *Men and Memories*; d.1945

Rubbra, [Charles] Edmund [Duncan]: b. Northampton, May 23, 1901; composer and pianist; ed. Royal College of Music and University College, Reading, studied with Holst and Vaughan Williams; style is frequently polyphonic though lyrical; works include *Sinfonia Concertante* (1934), eleven symphonies, and many liturgical choir pieces; d. Gerrards Cross, February 14, 1986.

Sanromá, Jesús María: b. Carolina, Puerto Rico, November 7, 1902; pianist; ed. New England Conservatory, BA 1920, on faculty 1930-1940; orchestral debut with the Boston Symphony Orchestra, 1926; toured Europe, Mexico and South and Central America; became head of piano faculty, Conservatorio de Musica, Rio Piedras, Puerto Rico; d. San Juan, PR October 12, 1984.

Scholes, Percy Alfred: b. Leeds, July 24, 1877; organist and writer on music; ed. University of Oxford, BM 1908, and University of Lausanne, D L, 1934; ed. *The Music Student* (later *The Music Teacher*)1907-21; wrote for *Evening Standard* 1913-20, *Observer* 1920-27, *Radio Times* 1923-29; writings include The Oxford Companion to Music, The Concise Oxford Dictionary of Music; knighted 1957; d. Vevey, Switzerland, July 31, 1958.

Schulhoff, Ervin: b. Prague, June 8, 1894; pianist, teacher, and composer; ed. Prague and Vienna; studied piano with Teichmueller, composition with Max Reger 1908-10; concertized in Russia and France; works include eight symphonies, *Concerto for String Quartet and Wind Orchestra*; d. in a concentration camp, Wuelzburg, Bavaria, August 18, 1942.

Schwiller, Isidore: b. 1878; violinist; leader and assistant conductor Carl Rosa Opera Company orchestra, leader of Schwiller Quartet and Leith Hill Music Festival Orchestra; d. May 28, 1956.

Scott, Charles Kennedy: b. Romsey, Hants. November 16, 1876; organist and choral conductor; ed. Brussels Conservatoire; founded Oriana Madrigal Society 1904, Philharmonic Choir 1919, and Bach Cantata Club 1926; edited early music; d. London July 2, 1965.

Shilkret, Nathaniel: b. New York, January 1, 1895; conductor, arranger, and composer; clarinettist in Russian Symphony Orchestra in New York, Metropolitan Opera Orchestra, NY Symphony, and NY Philharmonic as well as in the Sousa, Pryor, and Goldman bands; Music Director of the Victor Talking Machine Co., 1916-1936; organized the Victor Salon Orchestra in 1924 for records and broadcasts; many film scores, 1935+; tone poem *Skyward* (1928), *Trombone Concerto* (1942); d. Franklin Square, Long Island, New York, February 18, 1982.

Silk, Dorothy Ellen: b. King's Norton, Worcestershire, May 4, 1883; soprano; ed. Vienna; taught at Royal College of Music; London debut at Queen's Hall; specialty as a Bach singer, light in style; sang *Savitri* in its first professional performance; d. Alvechurch, Worcs., July 30, 1942.

Simonds, Bruce: b. Bridgeport, CT July 5, 1895; pianist and music administrator; ed. Yale University, BA 1917 and BM 1918; studied with Vincent D'Indy at Schola Cantorum in Paris 1919-20 and with Tobias Matthay at Matthay School on London 1920-21; taught at Yale 1921-73, Dean of the School of Music 1941-54; d. Hamden, CT, July 2, 1989.

Sink, Charles Albert: b. Westernville, NY, July 4, 1879; music administrator and politician; Secretary, University School of Music, University of Michigan, 1904-07, Secretary and Business Manager, 1907-1927, President 1927-1940; Member, Michigan House of Representatives, 1919-20 and 1925-26, Senate 1921-22, 1927-28, 1929-30; Republican candidate for Lt. Governor,

1932; d. December 17, 1972.

Smith, David Stanley: b. Toledo, OH, July 6, 1877; conductor, composer, and music educator; ed. Yale University, studied with Parker, BM 1900, studied with Widor in Paris; taught at Yale 1903-46, Dean of School of Music 1920-1946; conductor New Haven Symphony Orchestra; elected to National Institute of Arts & Letters; d. New Haven, December 17, 1949.

Smith, George: b. Hayes, Middlesex, 1899; ed. Royal Military School of Music and Royal Academy of Music, ARAM, FRAM; conductor and arranger; bandmaster, 1st Btn The Sherwood Foresters, 1925-40; orchestrated "Mars," "Venus," "Jupiter," and "Country Song" for military band.

Somerville, J[ohn] A[rthur C[oghill]: b. 1872; Commandant of the Royal Military School of Music, 1920-1925. During his short remarkable tenure there, the first documented performances of the Holst military band suites took place. He was also responsible for securing original military band works from composers such as Ralph Vaughan Williams and Gordon Jacob. British army band instrumentation was also standardized during his tenure; d. 1955.

Stanford, Charles Villiers: b. Dublin, September 30, 1852; composer, conductor, and teacher; ed. Royal Irish Academy of Music, Queen's College, Cambridge BA 1874, additional studies with Reinecke in Leipzig and Kiel in Berlin; professor of composition Royal College of Music 1883-1924, also at Cambridge 1887-1924; conducted London Bach Choir 1885-1902; knighted in 1902; works include seven symphonies, three piano concertos; d. London, March 29, 1924.

Stanley, Albert Augustus: b. Manville, RI May 25, 1851; conductor and music administrator; ed. Leipzig Conservatory; organist at Grace Church, Providence; taught at Ohio Wesleyan College and University of Michigan 1888-1921, also manager of the University Musical Society and curator of the Stearns Collection of Musical Instruments; d. May 19, 1932

Stock, Frederick: b. Juelich, Germany, November 11, 1872; conductor; studied with Humperdinck at the Cologne Conservatory 1886-91; violinist with the Cologne Municipal Orchestra 1891-95; violist, Chicago Symphony Orchestra 1895-1905, assistant conductor 1901-05, conductor 1905-42; d. Chicago, October 20, 1942.

Straube, (Montgomery Rufus) Karl Siegfried: b. Berlin, January 6, 1873; organist, choral conductor, and teacher; studied with Dienel and Reimann in Berlin; organist, cathedral of Wesel 1897-1902; organist, Thomaskirche, Leipzig 1902-50, conducted Bachverein there 1903-32; numerous collections of organ works; d. Leipzig, April 27, 1950.

Strode [nee Gotch], Nancy: b. Oxford, April 12, 1899; ed. in Oxford and at St. Paul's Girls' School 1913-17; studied with Holst; m. Maurice Strode 1920; d. Aldeburgh, January 11, 1978.

Surrette, Thomas Whitney: b. Concord, MA, September 7, 1861; music educator and composer; ed. Harvard, studied with Paine and Foote; lecturer American Society for the Extension of University Teaching, 1895; extension lecturer for Oxford University, 1907-10; founder Concord Summer School of Music, 1914-38; co-editor (with A. Davison) *The Concord Series of Educational Music*; publ. (with D. Mason) *The Appreciation of Music*, 5 vols., *Course of Study on the Development of Symphonic Music* and *Music and Life*; light operas *Priscilla, or the Pilgram's Proxy* and *The Eve of St. Agnes*; d. Concord, MA, May 19, 1941.

Swann, Irene [nee Bonnett]: b. January 4,1897; violinist and conductor; ed. St. Paul's Girls' School 1909-16, organ scholar at Girton College, also Royal College of Music ARCM, LRCM; conductor, Spring Grove Polytechnic Orchestra, SW Middlesex Music Festival for Secondary Schools; assisted Holst with Whitsun Festivals.

Tagore, Rabindranath: b. Calcutta May 7, 1861; poet, writer, and song composer; over 2000 songs; poem collection Manasi; received 1913 Nobel Prize in literature for *Gitanjale, Song Offerings*; knighted in 1915, repudiated by him in 1919; d. Calcutta, August 7, 1941.

Talich, Vaclav: b. Kromeriz, Czechoslovakia, May 28, 1883; violinist and conductor; ed. Prague Conservatory 1897-1903, studied violin with Sevcik and chamber music with Kaan, and Leipzig Conservatory, studied conducting with Nikisch; concertmaster, Berlin Philharmonic 1903-04 and Odessa Opera 1904-05; conductor, Slovenian Philharmonic 1908-12, Pilsen Opera 1912-15, Czech Philharmonic 1919-31 and 1933-41, Slovak Philharmonic 1949-52; d. Beroun, March 16, 1961.

Terry, Richard: b. Ellington, Northumberland, January 3, 1865; organist and choirmaster; organist and music master Elstow School 1892-96 and St. John's Cathedral, Antigua, West Indies 1896-1901; organist and director of music at Westminster Cathedral,1901-24; knighted in 1922; editor and compliler of many texts on Catholic church music; d. London, April 18, 1938.

Toscanini, Arturo: b. Parma, Italy, March 25, 1867; conductor; conducting debut at Rio de Janeiro 1886; chief conductor at La Scala Opera 1898-1903 and 1906-08, NY Metropolitan Opera 1908-15, artistic director of La Scala 1921-29; guest conductor of NY Philharmonic 1926-26 and 1928-29, associate conductor with Mengelberg 1929-30, conductor 1930-36; conductor NBC Symphony 1937-54; many guest and operatic appearances not listed; d. New York City, January 16, 1957.

Vaughan Williams, Adeline [nee Fisher]: b. July 16, 1870; pianist and cellist; m. Ralph Vaughan Williams October 9, 1897; d. Dorking, May 10, 1951.

Vaughan Williams, Ralph: b. Down Ampney, Gloucestershire, October 12, 1872; composer; ed. Charterhouse School, London 1887-90, Royal College of Music 1890-93 and 1895-97, studied with Gladstone, Parry, Stanford, and Parratt; also at Trinity College, Cambridge, studied with Charles Wood; BM 1894, BA 1895; DM 1901; additional studies in Paris with Ravel, 1908; active in English Folk Song Society, collecting over 800 folk songs; music editor of *The English Hymnal* 1906; taught at Royal College of Music 1919- ; conductor of London Bach Choir 1920-27; nine symphonies, *Job*, *Hugh the Drover*; d. London, August 26, 1958.

Waddell, Helen: b. Tokyo, 1889; writer, playwright, and novelist; daughter of a Presbyterian minister; grew up in Ulster; writings include *Lyrics from the Chinese* 1915, *The Wandering Scholars* 1927, *Mediaevel Latin Lyrics* 1929, *Peter Abelard* 1933; d. March, 1965.

Walter [Schlessinger], Bruno: b. Berlin, September 15,1876; assistant conductor (to Mahler) at Vienna State Opera 1901, principal conductor 1911-13; Royal Bavarian Musikdirector in Munich 1913-22; conductor of Stadtsoper in Berlin-Charlottenburg 1925-29, Leipzig Gewandhaus 1929-33, Vienna State Opera 1936-38, 1947-49, NY Philharmonic 1947-49; also CBS Symphony; significant guest appearances; d. Beverly Hills, CA February 17, 1962.

Whittaker, William Gillies: b. Newcastle-upon-Tyne, July 23, 1876; conductor, composer and writer about music; ed. University of Durham, DM 1921; taught at Armstrong College of the University of Durham; first Gardiner Professor of Music at Glasgow University; principal, Scottish National Academy of Music 1930-44 ; conductor Newcastle and Gateshead Choral Union and Newcastle Bach Choir; d. Orkney Islands, July 5, 1944.

Wilson, (James) Steuart: b. Clifton, Bristol, July 21, 1889; tenor; ed. Winchester and King's College, Cambridge; original member of The English Singers; Professor of Singing at Royal College of Music; taught at Curtis 1939-42; Music Director of Arts Council1945-48; principal, Birmingham School of Music 1957-60; knighted 1948; director of music for the BBC 1948-57; general administrator at Covent Garden 1949-55; d. Peterfield, December 18, 1966.

Windram, James Causley: b. 1886; conductor; ed. Royal Military School of Music; Bandmaster, 5th Royal Northumberland Fusiliers 1914-30; Bandmaster, Coldstream Guards 1930-44; transcribed three of Holst's *Choral Hymns from the Rig Veda* for military band; dedicatee of Holst's *Second Suite in F*; d. London, 1944.

Wolfe, Humbert: b. 1885; poet and civil servant; Principal Assistant Secretary in Ministry of

Labour 1918-38, Deputy Secretary 1938-40; d. 1940.

Woodworth, George Wallace: b. Boston, MA, November 6, 1902; conductor, organist and music educator; ed. Harvard University BA 1924, MA 1926, also studied with Malcolm Sargent at Royal College of Music 1927-28; Instructor of Music at Harvard and conductor of Radcliffe Choral Society1924 and Pierian Sodality Orchestra 1928-30; conductor Harvard Glee Club 1933-58, succeeded Archibald Davison as Ditson Professor of Music 1954-69; 1st president of The College Music Society 1958-60; d. Cambridge, MA July 18, 1969.

APPENDIX III:

RALPH VAUGHAN WILLIAMS' BROADCAST TALK DURING THE BBC GUSTAV HOLST MEMORIAL CONCERT JUNE 22, 1934

I want to speak to you for a few minutes about the great composer Gustav Holst whose music you are about to hear tonight.

Holst was a visionary, but at the same time in all essentials a very practical man. He himself used to say that only second-rate artists are unbusinesslike. It is the blend of the visionary with the realist that gives Holst's music its distinctive character.

Besides being a composer he was a great teacher, a wonderful friend, a helper and counsellor to all those who needed it. His teaching and friendship we can no longer experience directly, but the works of art which are the connotations of a fine character are with us forever and will, I firmly believe, be loved more and more as time goes on.

Holst's life gave the lie to the notion that a composer must shut himself away from his fellows and live in a world of dreams. Holst was, it is true, a dreamer: his whole nature, and the music which exemplifies his nature seems to be hovering on the verge of an unseen world. But he never allowed his dreams to become incoherent or meandering. He loved life in the best sense of the word too much, and he loved his fellow beings too much, to allow his message to them to appear in vague or incomprehensible terms.

Partly from necessity, and partly from choice, he lived in the common world of men. While he was still young he was strongly attracted by the ideals of William Morris, and though in later years he discarded the mediaevalism of that teacher the ideal of comradeship remained with him throughout his life. He wanted to work with and teach, and to have the companionship of his fellow beings.

His music is sometimes described as mystical and rightly so., but we must not imagine from this something remote or vague. His texture, his form, his melody, is always clean cut and definite. Whenever he puts pen to paper the signature Gustav Holst is clear to read.

It is sometimes true of English composers that though they may have fine and poetical ideas yet they lack that final power of realisation which is a necessary part of a complete work of art: but it is emphatically not true of the two English composers we have lately lost; and I think for the same reason in both cases, namely, that Elgar and Holst learnt their craft not so much from books in the study, as from practical experience and from the nature of their material.

Already in his student days Holst had to eke out his meager scholarship money by remunerative work and he deliberately chose not to shut himself up in an organ loft or to give half-hearted pianoforte lessons to unwilling pupils, but to go out into the world armed with his trombone, earning his living where he could, playing now in a symphony orchestra, now in a dance band, now in a Christmas Pantomime at a suburban theatre.

In later years came other activities--teaching and conducting. It was these experiences that gave him that grip of the facts of music which helped to build up his wonderful technique. To many men this constant occupation with the practical side of music would have been a hindrance to inspiration, but to Holst it seemed to be an incentive. The fact that his creative work had often to be crowded into the short two months of a summer holiday gave him his greatest power of concentration, and the intense will to evoke at all costs those thoughts that lay in the depths of his being.

Holst has no use for half measures whether in life or in art. What he wanted to say he said forcibly and directly. He, like every other great composer, was not afraid of being obvious when the occasion demanded it; nor did he hesitate to be remote when remoteness expressed his purpose. But whether he gives us the familiar chords and straightforward tunes of 'Jupiter' or leads us to the farthest hints of harmony as in 'Neptune,' his meaning is never in doubt. He has something to tell us that only he can say and he has found the only way of saying it.

RVW

APPENDIX IV

FACSIMILES

A. *Penitential Fugue* [App. I, 28A] (1893), an assignment composed for Robert Bridge's theory class at the Royal College of Music (Royal College of Music MS).

B. Notes about the rescoring of the *Second Suite in F for Military Band*, Op. 28, No. 2 [H106] (1911; 1922) and from Notebook starting January 1, 1922 (The Holst Foundation).

C. Piano (condensed) score of "IV. Finale: 'The Dargason'" made for publication of the *Second Suite in F for Military Band*, Op. 28, No. 2 [H106] (1922) (The Holst Foundation).

D. Sketch for *A Fugal Overture*, Op. 40, No. 1 [H151] from Notebook starting May 1, 1922 (The Holst Foundation).

E. "Unvocal Duets" title page (Royal College of Music).

F. "Tender Bars" title page (Royal College of Music).

G. *Staff Register*, James Allen's Girls' School.

H. *Diary*, March, 1929 (The Holst Foundation).

I. Confirmation form, American Academy of Arts and Letters, 1929.

J. From *Mr. Shilkret's Maggot* [H185] (1932) (British Library Add. MS 47833).

K. Postcard from Archibald Davison, Dorothy Davison, and Ralph Vaughan Williams to Gustav Holst, December 9,1932 (The Holst Foundation).

Penitential Fugue
Oh Doctor Bridge I have lost the proper subject and
Oh Doctor Bridge I have lost
I am very sor - ry very sorry in-deed and I
Oh Doctor Bridge I have lost the proper subject and
I am very sor - ry very sorry in-deed and I
hope I hope that you will forgive me for

A.

Booseys
no piano part yet.
Bb Sax not Bar
line dodge.
horns on 1 line
note where doubled
(3 and 4 at bottom once)
in F in finale
~~perhaps~~
~~keep~~ have copy of both agree
prefer to keep mechan
rights.

B.

IV Fantasia on the 'Dargason'
Conductor's Score
Allegro Moderato

C.

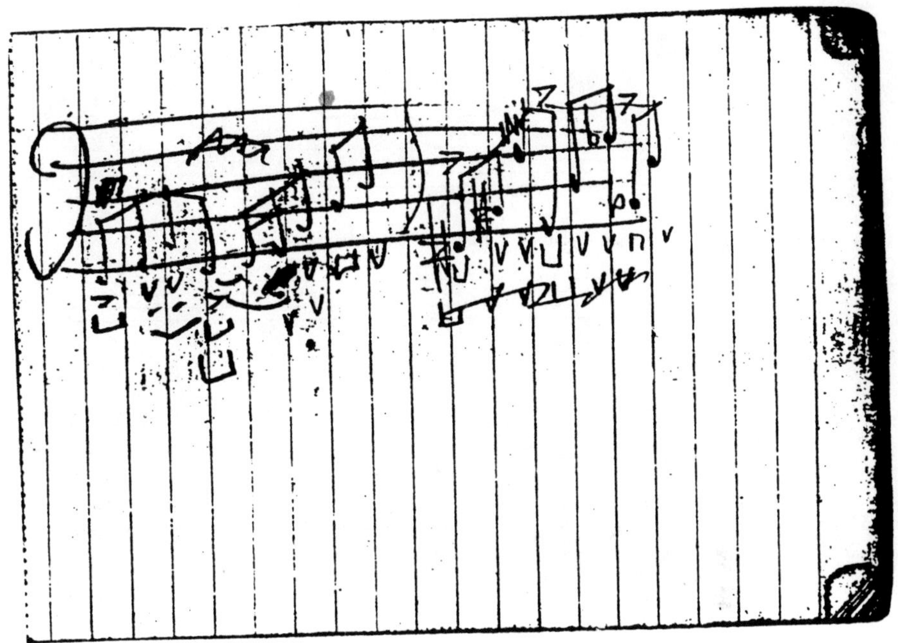

D.

Unvocal Duets in the Modern Idiom

Dedicated to Nora Day, Vally Lasker, and the New Forest.

Motto 'Modern Music is neither
a) Modern
or
b) Music!'

Sample only

No value

Tender Bars

Sent post free to all teachers of composition, Sir Richard Terry and the Nobility and Gentry

Great Reductions on taking a Quantity.

F.

1. Date of Birth.	2. Date of appointment on probation.	3. Date of definitive appointment.	4. Date of leaving.
Sep 21st 1874	April 20 1904	September 16 1904	July. 1920

5. Schools and Colleges at which educated, with dates. State names and types of institutions.	6. Particulars of Public and University Examinations taken, and certificates and degrees obtained, with dates.
Cheltenham Grammar School Royal College of Music Kensington May 1893 to July 1898	

7. List of teaching posts held, with dates.	8. Particulars of training in teaching, if any, and certificates or diplomas obtained, with dates.
Musical Director, Passmore Edwards Settlement WC September 1904 to June 1907 Musical Director Morley College SE April 1907– Singing master St Paul's Girls' School W Sep: 1905–	9. State external teaching or official work undertaken, if any, in addition to duties in the School. Musical Director Morley College SE Singing master St Paul's Girls' School W " " Wycombe Abbey School

10. Special subject or subjects.	11. State principal duties assigned, and subjects taken. (Any subsequent changes and their dates to be indicated in red ink.)
Music	Class Singing

12. Total annual emoluments.	13. Particulars of retiring allowance, if any.
Salary, with scale, if any. £50 Special War Grant of £8 a year from Sept 1916 Capitation ~~Fees,~~ & ~~if any.~~ Increase [illegible] retrospective from Nov. 1918 £78 Estimated value of board and lodging if given as part of emoluments.	14. Post, if any, taken up after leaving the School.

MARCH, 1929. Venice

Monday 11 ●

cabled to Yale
Sea mist all day
S M and P
Rialto

Tuesday 12

Bright sun all day
S M (and gallery) and P

Wednesday 13

news of J. M. J.'s death
S Maria [illegible] Frari (Titiano, Bellini, etc.)
S M (Baptistery) and P

Thursday 14

cable from Yale inviting me to lecture
Cook's, British and American consuls
walk through town
S M P and up the Campanile

MARCH, 1929. Venice

Friday 15

sea mist in morning
walk to S Giorgio and [illegible], S Luca
steamer to station and back
S M and P (sacristi)
loud loud speaker on canal and room café at night

Saturday 16 Sunshine

S M and P and gallery
all day until
4-38 train to Verona
Hotel Accademia

Passion Sunday. Sunday 17 St. Patrick's Day.

S. Zeno, Castelvecchio, P. Erbe [illegible]
Duomo, river side, S Giorgio
Porta del Pallio and walk on wall
S Fermo Mag.

Memo.

✓

THE AMERICAN ACADEMY OF ARTS AND LETTERS
ASSISTANT TO THE PRESIDENT
633 WEST 155TH STREET
NEW YORK

I ~~We~~ } shall be present at the Exercises at 12 o'clock and the Luncheon at 1.30 o'clock at 633 West 155th Street on Tuesday, April 23, 1929.

also at 3 PM on the 24th

Name Gustav Holst

Address University Club

Cresc e Accel
Piccolo
cresc e accel
à 2
arco staccato

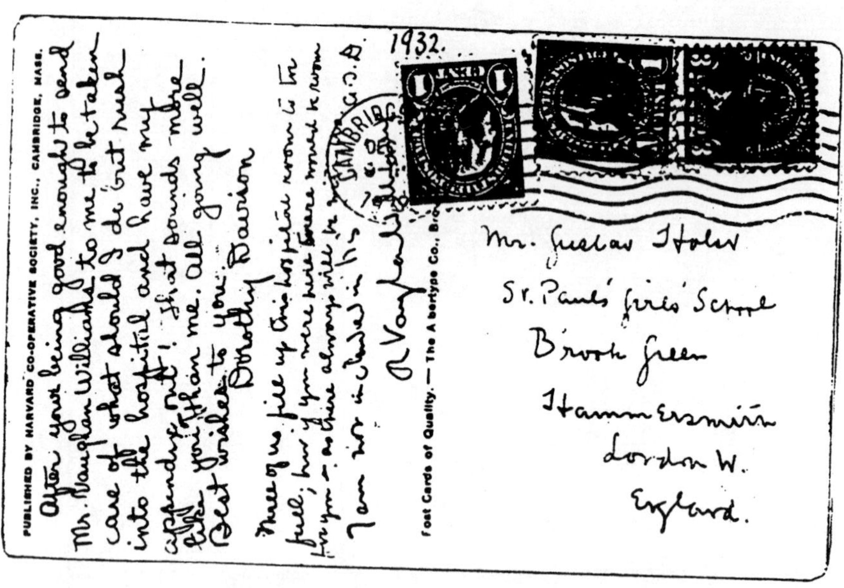

PUBLISHED BY HARVARD CO-OPERATIVE SOCIETY, INC., CAMBRIDGE, MASS.

After your being good enough to send Mr. Vaughan Williams to me to be taken care of what should I do but rush into the hospital and have my appendix out! That sounds more like you than me. All going well. Best wishes to you.

Dorothy Davison

Three of us fill up this hospital room to the full; but if you were here there would be room for you — as there always will be.

I am not included in U.S.

R. Vaughan Williams

Post Cards of Quality. — The Albertype Co., Bro

1932.

CAMBRIDGE

Mr. Gustav Holst
St. Paul's Girls' School
Brook Green
Hammersmith
London W.
England.

K.

APPENDIX V

SKETCHES AND CARTOONS

A. "Gustav Holst" in William Rothenstein, *Twenty-four Portraits*, Second Series, 1923.

B. "Gustav Holst [No. 4: Jupiter, The Bringer of Jollity]" by T. Sancha in *Fanfare* (1922).

C. "Gustav Holst" in *The Passing Show*, February 18, 1928.

D. "Scholar's Wisdom" in *Boston Evening Transcript*, November 10, 1931.

E. "Urge into Curve" in *Boston Evening Transcript*, January 22, 1932.

A.

"THE PLANETS."
(No. 4: JUPITER, the bringer of Jollity.)

B.

GUSTAV HOLST.

(Composer. The New Conductor of the Bach Choir.)

"Music Hath Charms." Her beauties up-to-date
Low-brows annoy; High-brows but titillate.
Holst's art austere aims not the mob [illegible]
There is no kitten on our Gustav's [illegible]

D.W.

C.

D,

Urge Into Curve

Gustav Holst

Conducting Today and Tomorrow in His Own Music at the Symphony Concerts

E.

APPENDIX VI

SELECTED PROGRAMS OF GUSTAV HOLST

A. "The Fairy Queen" (Morley College, June 10, 1911)

B. Morley College Students' Concert, June 9, 1917

C. University College, Reading, June 15, 1921

D. Boston Symphony Orchestra, January 22, 1932

E. Second May Festival Concert, May 19, 1932

ROYAL VICTORIA HALL,

WATERLOO ROAD, S.E.

PROGRAMME OF CONCERT PERFORMANCE

OF

"The Fairy Queen"

OF

Henry Purcell

BY

The Music Students of Morley College,

On SATURDAY, JUNE 10th, 1911, at 8 p.m.

Under the direction of GUSTAV VON HOLST.

The full score of this work was lost shortly after Henry Purcell's deat in 1695. It was recently discovered and the Purcell Society published it. B their permission, the Students of Morley College copied the entire Vocal an Orchestral Parts (1,500 pages).

COPYISTS

J. Buckingham } Principals.
C. Burke }

M. Arrigoni	J. Harrison	N. Ramsden
J. Boomer	E. Hoare	A. Zimmerman
L. Boomer	S. Keating	C. Renouf
F. Burrell	H. Wootton	M. Riedtmann
L. Daniels	J. Kerslake	E. M. C. Soame:
A. Elston	V. Lasker	R. Shapcott
A. Emberson	W. Lockett	C. Thompson
N. English	W. Newell	J. Westwood
R. Hamilton	W. Oldis	

PROGRAMME ... ... ONE PENNY.

All applications for Tickets should be made to Miss Sheepshanks, Vice-Princip Morley College for Working Men and Women, Waterloo Road, S.E.

Programme of *The Fairy Queen*, 1911

PRO[illegible]MME

STUDENTS' CONCERT, S[illegible]UNE 9th, 1917, 7.30 p.m.

THE "MACBETH" MUSIC - *Attributed to Matthew Locke* 1632—1677

For voices and string orchestra.

This music was written for a performance of Shakespeare's Tragedy in 1672. It consists of three scenes, the words by Davenant: (1) The witches rejoice at the murder of Duncan, (2) Hecate flies through the air surrounded by witches, (3) The witches brew their potion in the cauldron.

Hecate and First Witch - ERNEST HOARE.
Second Witch and Spirit Voice LILIAN TWISELTON.

SONG - "Flow not so fast" - *John Dowland*
DULCIE NUTTING 1562—1628

MOTET - "Sing aloud with gladness" *Samuel Wesley* 1766—1837

Originally intended to be sung with an organ accompaniment or unaccompanied. On June 9th it will be sung with an orchestral accompaniment written by Jane Joseph.

FIRST MOVEMENT FROM SYMPHONY IN B♭ *Joseph Haydn* 1732—1809

ODE FOR CHORUS AND ORCHESTRA *Charles Hubert Parry* 1848—

"THE GLORIES OF OUR BLOOD AND STATE"

Begins with a beautiful melody for orchestra alone. This is repeated later while the chorus sing "The garlands wither on your brow." Other points to be specially noticed are (1) The setting of the words "Some men with swords may reap the field;" and (2) the beautiful ending of the work

"Only the actions of the just
Smell sweet and blossom in the dust."

MINUET AND TRIO FROM SYMPHONY IN B♭ *Haydn* 1732—1809

CHORAL HYMNS FROM THE RIG VEDA - *Gustav von Holst* 1874—

Group II. For Female voices and Orchestra.
(Performed at the request of the Music Students.)

I. Hymn to Varuna (God of the sky)
II. Hymn to Agni (God of Fire)
III. Funeral Chant.

SONG - "Music when soft voices die" *Sydney Bressey*
LILIAN TWISELTON 1893—

This song was written last year in the firing line in France. Before the outbreak of war, the composer was a member of the Harmony Class. He has been badly wounded, and has won the Military Medal. The song, performed for the first time at the last Students' Concert, is to be repeated by general desire.

FANTASIA ON TWO IRISH HYMN TUNES *Charles Burke*
"St. Patrick's Prayer" 1849—1917

This work is to be performed in memory of the composer, our oldest music student, who died last February.

The first tune is played by the strings against repeated notes on the trumpets and drums. It is played again by the wind instruments, then by the full orchestra, and a third time, with a counter melody above it, by the bass instruments. The second tune is sung first by a solo voice, and later by the choir. The two tunes then alternate with one another in a series of variations ending in a powerful climax. From this point to the end the first tune is sung against repeated notes on the brass as at the beginning.

It is requested that there should be no applause owing to the special occasion of this performance.

God Save the King.

UNIVERSITY COLLEGE, READING.

The College Choral Society and Orchestra

will give a

CONCERT

On WEDNESDAY, JUNE 15,

1921,

at 8 p.m.,

IN THE COLLEGE HALL.

The Programme will include—

ODE: "The Glories of our Blood and State" (Parry).

SYMPHONY in D, No. 2 (Beethoven).

MOTET: "Sing Aloud with Gladness" (S. Wesley).

SUITE DE BALLET (Gluck).

TONE POEM: "Nature's Call" (Edmund Rubbra)
for Pianoforte and Orchestra (first performance).

MADRIGAL: "I love, and have my love regarded (Weelkes).

CAROL: "This have I done for my true love" (Holst).

Solo Pianoforte - - Mr. EDMUND RUBBRA.

Leader of Orchestra - - Miss MARY VENABLES.

Conductor - Mr. GUSTAV HOLST.

Doors open at 7.30 p.m *Carriages at 9.45 p.m*

Numbered and Reserved Seats, 3s. (including Tax). **Admission** (by tickets only, limited in number), **2s.** (including Tax)

[illegible] the Hall may be seen, and tickets may be obtained, at [illegible] Music Warehouse of Messrs. Barnes & Avis, Ltd., 5-7 Duke Street, Reading, and at the College Office, London Road, Reading.

FIFTY-FIRST SEASON, NINETEEN HUNDRED THIRTY-ONE AND THIRTY-TWO

Thirteenth Programme

FRIDAY AFTERNOON, JANUARY 22, at 2.30 o'clock

SATURDAY EVENING, JANUARY 23, at 8.15 o'clock

GUSTAV HOLST will conduct these concerts

Somerset Rhapsody

Ballet from the Opera, "The Perfect Fool"

Prelude and Scherzo, "Hammersmith"

. . . Holst

"The Planets"

I. MARS, the Bringer of War.
II. VENUS, the Bringer of Peace.
III. MERCURY, the Winged Messenger.
IV. JUPITER, the Bringer of Jollity.
V. SATURN, the Bringer of Old Age.
VI. URANUS, the Magician.
VII. NEPTUNE, the Mystic.

There will be an intermission before "The Planets"

A lecture on this programme will be given on Thursday, January 21, at 5.15 o'clock in the Lecture Hall, Boston Public Library

The works to be played at these concerts may be seen in the Allen A. Brown Music Collection of the Boston Public Library one week before the concert

CHORAL UNION SERIES—1931-1932

FIFTY-THIRD SEASON | TWELFTH CONCERT

COMPLETE SERIES 2025

Second May Festival Concert

THURSDAY EVENING, MAY 19, 8:15 O'CLOCK

SOLOISTS

GOETA LJUNGBERG, *Soprano*
MAUD OKKELBERG, *Piano*
MABEL RHEAD, *Piano*
PALMER CHRISTIAN, *Organ*
CHICAGO SYMPHONY ORCHESTRA
UNIVERSITY CHORAL UNION
FREDERICK STOCK, EARL V. MOORE, and GUSTAV HOLST (Guest), *Conductors*

PROGRAM

OVERTURE, "Carnaval" .... *Glazounoff*

ARIA, "Suicidio" from "La Gioconda" .... *Ponchielli*
GOETA LJUNGBERG

"SYMPHONIE DE PSAUMES" .... *Strawinsky*
UNIVERSITY CHORAL UNION

ARIA, "Du bist der Lenz" from "Die Walküre" .... *Wagner*
MISS LJUNGBERG

FUGUE À LA GIGUE .... *Bach-Holst*

BALLET from the opera, "The Perfect Fool" .... *Holst*
CONDUCTED BY GUSTAV HOLST

Intermission

"A CHORAL FANTASIA" (first performance in America) .... *Holst*
Incidental Solo by HELEN VAN LOON, *Soprano*
UNIVERSITY CHORAL UNION
CONDUCTED BY MR. HOLST

ARIA, "Liebestod" from "Tristan and Isolde" .... *Wagner*
MISS LJUNGBERG

HUNGARIAN DANCES .... *Brahms-Dvorak*

BIBLIOGRAPHY OF SELECTED PUBLISHED SOURCES

Bax, Clifford. *Inland Far*. London: William Heinemann Ltd., 1925.

______. "Recollections of Gustav Holst," *Music and Letters*, XX. No. 1 (January, 1939), 1-6.

Bliss, Arthur. *As I Remember*. London: Faber & Faber, 1970.

Boult, Adrian. *My Own Trumpet*. London: Hamish Hamilton, 1973.

Byrd, John. *Percy Grainger*. London: Elek Books Ltd., 1976.

Darrell, R. B.. "Holst in America," *The Phonograph Monthly Review*, VI, No. 5 (February, 1932), 82-83.

Eaton, Quaintence. "Gustav Holst, on American Visit, Approves Our Ways," *Musical America*, LII, No. 3 (February 10, 1932), 6.

Erskine, John: *The Philharmonic Society of New York: Its First 100 Years*. New York: The Macmillan Co., 1943.

Ford, Boris. *The Cambridge Guide to the Arts in Britain, Volume 8: The Edwardian Age and the Interwar Years*. Cambridge, UK: Cambridge University Press, 1989.

Godfrey, Dan. *Memories and Music: Thirty-five Years of Conducting*. London: Hutchinson & Co.,1924.

Greene, Richard. *Holst: The Planets*. Cambridge, UK: Cambridge University Press, 1995.

Hardy, Florence. *The Life of Thomas Hardy*. London: Studio Editions Ltd., 1994.

Hill, Polly (ed.) and Keynes, Richard (ed.). *Lydia and Maynard: The Letters of John Maynard Keynes and Lydia Lopokova*. New York: Charles Scribner's Sons, 1989.

Holmes, Paul. *Holst.* London: Omnibus Press, 1997.

Holst, Gustav. "Jane Joseph," *Morley College Magazine*, XXXIV, No. 9 (June, 1929) 104-105.

______. "Music in the British Salonica Force," *Musical Opinion*, XLIII, No. 505 (October, 1919).

Holst, Imogen. *Gustav Holst: A Biography*, 2nd ed. London: Oxford University Press, 1969.

______. *Holst*, 2nd ed.. London: Faber & Faber Ltd.,1981.

______. *Holst.* London: Novello, 1972.

______. *The Music of Gustav Holst and Holst's Music Reconsidered.* London: Oxford University Press, 1986.

______. *A Scrapbook for the Holst Birthplace Museum.* East Bergholt: Hugh Tempest Radford and The Holst Birthplace Museum Trust in association with G. & I. Holst Ltd., 1978.

______. (ed.) *A Thematic Catalogue of Gustav Holst's Music.* London: Faber Music Ltd., 1974.

Imogen Holst (ed.) and Colin Matthews (ed.). *Gustav Holst: Collected Facsimile Editions of Autograph Manuscripts of Published Works.* London: Faber Music Ltd. in association with G. & I. Holst Ltd:

Volume I: Chamber Operas, 1974.
Volume II: Works for Small Orchestra, 1977.
Volume III: The Planets, 1979
Volume IV: First Choral Symphony, 1983.

LeBrecht, Norman. *The Maestro Myth: Great Conductors in Pursuit of Power.* New York: Birch Lane Press, 1991.

Lloyd, Stephen. *H. Balfour Gardiner.* Cambridge, UK: Cambridge University Press, 1984.

Lumby, Sheila (ed.) and Hounsfield, Vera (ed.). *Catalogue of Holst's Programmes and Press Cuttings in the Central Library, Cheltenham.* Gloucester: Albert E. Smith Ltd., 1974.

Martin, George. *The Damrosch Dynasty: America's First Family of Music.* Boston: Houghton Mifflin, 1983.

Mitchell, Jon. *From Kneller Hall to Hammersmith: The Band Works of Gustav Holst.* Tutzing, Germany: Haus Hans Schneider, 1990.

Mueller, John H.. *The American Symphony Orchestra: A Social History of Musical Taste.* Bloomington, IN: Indiana University Press, 1951.

Northrop Moore, Jerrold. *Music and Friends: Seven Decades of Letters to Adrian Boult.* London: Hamish Hamilton, 1979.

Proceedings in Commemoration of the Twenty-fifth Anniversary of the Founding of the American Academy of Arts and Letters. New York: Academy of Arts and Letters Publication No. 72, 1930.

Rubbra, Edmund. *Gustav Holst.* Monaco: The Lyrebird Press, 1947.

Rubbra, Edmund (ed.) and Lloyd, Stephen (ed.) *Gustav Holst: Collected Essays.* London: Triad Press, 1974.

Short, Michael. *Gustav Holst: The Man and His Music.* Oxford: Oxford University Press, 1990.

______. (ed.). *Gustav Holst: Letters to W. G. Whittaker.* Glasgow: University of Glasgow Press, 1974.

Stanford, Donald E. (ed.). *The Selected Letters of Robert Bridges.* Newark, DE: University of Delaware Press, 1984.

Vaughan Williams, Ralph. "Gustav Holst," *Music and Letters* III (July, 1920), 186+ and IV (October, 1920), 312+.

______. Untitled broadcast talk during the BBC Gustav Holst Memorial Concert, June 22, 1934.

Vaughan Williams, Ursula. *R.V.W.: A Biography of Ralph Vaughan Williams*. London: Oxford University Press, 1964.

Vaughan Williams, Ursula (ed.) and Holst, Imogen (ed.). *Heirs and Rebels: Letters to Each Other and Occasional Writings on Music by Gustav Holst and Ralph Vaughan Williams*. London: Oxford University Press, 1959.

Vowles, William. "Gustav Holst with the Army: Salonica and Constantinople, 1919, " *The Musical Times*, LXXV, No. 1099 (September, 1934), 794-795.

INDEX

STUDIES IN THE HISTORY AND INTERPRETATION OF MUSIC

1. Hugo Meynell, **The Art of Handel's Operas**
2. Dale A. Jorgenson, **Moritz Hauptmann of Leipzig**
3. Nancy van Deusen (ed.), **The Harp and The Soul: Essays in Medieval Music**
4. James L. Taggart, **Franz Joseph Haydn's Keyboard Sonatas: An Untapped Gold Mine**
5. William E. Grim, **The Faust Legend in Music and Literature, Volume I**
6. Richard R. LaCroix, **Augustine on Music: An Interdisciplinary Collection of Essays**
7. Clifford Taylor, **Musical Idea and the Design Aesthetic in Contemporary Music: A Text for Discerning Appraisal of Musical Thought in Western Culture**
8. Thomas R. Erdmann, **An Annotated Bibliography and Guide to the Published Trumpet Music of Sigmund Hering**
9. Geary Larrick, **Musical References and Song Texts in the Bible**
10. Felix-Eberhard von Cube, **The Book of the Musical Artwork: An Interpretation of the Musical Theories of Heinrich Schenker**, David Neumeyer, George R. Boyd and Scott Harris (trans.)
11. Robert C. Luoma, **Music, Mode and Words in Orlando Di Lasso's Last Works**
12. John A. Kimmey, Jr., A **Critique of Musicology: Clarifying the Scope, Limits, and Purposes of Musicology**
13. Kent A. Holliday, **Reproducing Pianos Past and Present**
14. Gloria Shafer, **Origins of the Children's Song Cycle as a Musical Genre with Four Case Studies and an Original Cycle**
15. Bertil H. van Boer, Jr., **Dramatic Cohesion in the Music of Joseph Martin Kraus: From Sacred Music to Symphonic Form**
16. Willian O. Cord , **The Teutonic Mythology of Richard Wagner's *The Ring of The Nibelung*, Volume One: Nine Dramatic Properties**
17. Willian O. Cord, **The Teutonic Mythology of Richard Wagner's *The Ring of The Nibelung*, Volume Two: The Family of Gods**
18. Willian O. Cord, **The Teutonic Mythology of Richard *Wagner's The Ring of The Nibelung*, Volume Three: The Natural and Supernatural Worlds**
19. Victorien Sardou, ***La Tosca* (The Drama Behind the Opera)**, W. Laird Kleine-Ahlbrandt (trans.)
20. Herbert W. Richardson (ed.), **New Studies in Richard Wagner's *The Ring of The Nibelung***
21. Catherine Dower, **Yella Pessl, First Lady of the Harpsichord**
22. Margaret Scheppach, **Dramatic Parallels in Michael Tippett's Operas: Analytical Essays on the Musico-Dramatic Techniques**
23. William E. Grim, **Haydn's *Sturm Und Drang* Symphonies: Form and Meaning**
24. Klemens Diez, **Constanze, Formerly Widow of Mozart: Her Unwritten Memoir**, Joseph T. Malloy (trans.)
25. Harold E. Fiske, **Music and Mind: Philosophical Essays on the Cognition and Meaning of Music**

26. Anne Trenkamp and John G. Suess (eds.), **Studies in the Schoenbergian Movement in Vienna and the United States: Essays in Honor of Marcel Dick**
27. Harvey J. Stokes, **A Selected Annotated Bibliography on Italian Serial Composers**
28. Julia Muller, **Words and Music in Henry Purcell's First Semi-Opera, *Dioclesian*: An Approach to Early Music Through Early Theatre**
29. Ronald W. Holz, **Erik Leidzen: Band Arranger and Composer**
30. Enrique Moreno, **Expanded Tunings in Comtemporary Music: Theoretical Innovations and Practical Applications**
31. Charles H. Parsons (compiler), **A Benjamin Britten Discography**
32. Denis Wilde, **The Development of Melody in the Tone Poems of Richard Strauss: Motif, Figure, and Theme**
33. William Smialek, **Ignacy Feliks Dobrzynski and Musical Life in Nineteenth-Century Poland**
34. Judith A. Eckelmeyer, **The Cultural Context of Mozart's Magic Flute: Social, Aesthetic, Philosophical** (2 Volume Set)
35. Joseph Coroniti, **Poetry as Text in Twentieth Century Vocal Music: From Stravinsky to Reich**
36. William E. Grim, **The Faust Legend in Music and Literature, Volume II**
37. Harvey J. Stokes, **Compositional Language in the Oratorio *The Second Act*: The Composer as Analyst**
38. Richard M. Berrong, **The Politics of Opera in Turn-of-the-Century Italy: As Seen Through the Letters of Alfredo Catalani**
39. Hugo von Hofmannsthal, **The Woman Without a Shadow / *Die Frau Ohne Schatten***, Jean Hollander (trans.)
40. Bertil H. van Boer, Jr. (ed.), **Gustav III and the Swedish Stage: Opera, Theatre, and Other Foibles: Essays in Honor of Hans Åstrand**
41. Harold E. Fiske, **Music Cognition and Aesthetic Attitudes**
42. Elsa Respighi, **Fifty Years of a Life in Music, 1905-1955 / Cinquant'anni di vita nella musica**, Giovanni Fontecchio and Roger Johnson (trans.)
43. Virginia Raad, **The Piano Sonority of Claude Debussy**
44. Ury Eppstein, **The Beginnings of Western Music in Meiji Era Japan**
45. Amédée Daryl Williams, **Lillian Fuchs, First Lady of the Viola**
46. Jane Hawes, **An Examination of Verdi's *Otello* and Its Faithfulness to Shakespeare**
47. Robert Springer, **Authentic Blues–Its History and Its Themes**, André J.M. Prévos (trans.)
48. Paul F. Rice (ed.), **An Edited Collection of the Theatre Music of John Abraham Fisher: The Druids and Witches Scenes from *Macbeth***
49. Harold E. Fiske, **Selected Theories of Music Perception**
50. John-Paul Bracey, **A Biography of French Pianist Marcel Ciampi (1891-1980): Music to Last a Lifetime**
51. Cecil Kirk Hutson, **An Analysis of the Southern Rock and Roll Band, Black Oak Arkansas**
52. Richard Eflyn Jones, **The Early Operas of Michael Tippett: A Study of *The Midsummer Marriage*, *King Priam* and *The Knot Garden***

53. Larry Fisher, **Miles Davis and David Liebman - Jazz Connections**, with a foreword by Phil Woods
54. Karlton E. Hester, **The Melodic and Polyrhythmic Development of John Coltrane's Spontaneous Composition in a Racist Society**
55. Leonard Ott, **Orchestration and Orchestral Style of Major Symphonic Works: Analytical Perspectives**
56. Pierre-Augustin Caron de Beaumarchais, ***The Barber of Seville*** **or** ***The Futile Precaution*****: A New English Translation,** Gilbert Pestureau, Ann Wakefield, Gavin Witt (trans.)
57. Arthur Graham, **Shakespeare in Opera, Ballet, Orchestral Music, and Song: An Introduction to Music Inspired by the Bard**
58. Christopher J. Dennis, **Adorno's *Philosophy of Modern Music***
59. Hermine Weigel Williams, **Sibelius and His Masonic Music: Sounds in 'Silence'**
60. Michael J. Esselstrom, **A Conductor's Guide to Symphonies I, II, and III of Gustav Mahler**
61. Thomas L. Wilmeth, **The Music of the Louvin Brothers: Heaven's Own Harmony**
62. Geary Larrick, **Bibliography, History, Pedagogy and Philosophy in Music and Percussion**
63. Steven C. Raisor, **Twentieth-Century Techniques in Selected Works for Solo Guitar: Serialism**
64. Margaret Inwood, **The Influence of Shakespeare on Richard Wagner**
65. Marshall Tuttle, **Musical Structures in Wagnerian Opera**
66. Marilyn A. Rouse, **Jamaican Folk Music–A Synthesis of Many Cultures**
67. Johann Sebastian Bach, **Johann Sebastian Bach's *Die Kunst Der Fuge*, BWV 1080 for Organ or Keyboard with Commentary,** Jan Overduin (ed.)
68. Marie-Claude Canova-Green and Francesca Chiarelli (eds.), **The Influence of Italian Entertainments on Sixteenth and Seventeenth Century Music Theatre in France, Savoy and England**
69. Sylvia Olden Lee and Elizabeth Nash, **The Memoirs of Sylvia Olden Lee, Premier African-American Classical Vocal Coach: Who is Sylvia**, with assistance by Patricia Turner
70. Edward Brooks, **Influence and Assimilation in Louis Armstrong's Cornet and Trumpet Work (1923-1928)**
71. Gary Tucker, **Tonality and Atonality in Alban Berg's Four Songs, op. 2**
72. Hans Kagebeck and Johan Lagerfelt (eds.), **Liszt the Progressive**
73. Jon C. Mitchell, **A Comprehensive Biography of Composer Gustav Holst, With Correspondence and Diary Excerpts: Including His American Years**
74. Eric B. Kinsley (ed.), **Franz Joseph Haydn's *Divertimento* with Variations for Harpsichord Four Hands, Violin and Violone**

75a. Lawrence Casler, **Symphonic Program Music and Its Literary Sources: Book 1**

75b. Lawrence Casler, **Symphonic Program Music and Its Literary Sources: Book 2**

76. Philip Jones, **The Collected Writings of German Musicologist Max Chop on the Composer Frederick Delius**
77. John Palmer, **Jonathan Harvey's *Bhakti* for Chamber Ensemble and Electronics: Serialism, Electronics and Spirituality**
78. Ian Sharp, **Classical Music's Evocation of the Myth of Childhood**

79. Glenn G. Caldwell, **Harmonic Tonality in the Music Theories of Jérôme-Joseph Momigny, 1762-1842**
80. Wayne E. Goins, **Emotional Response to Music: Pat Metheny's *Secret Story***
81. Thomas R. Erdmann, **Problems and Solutions in Band Conducting**